ASH·MISTRY
AND THE
CITY OF DEATH

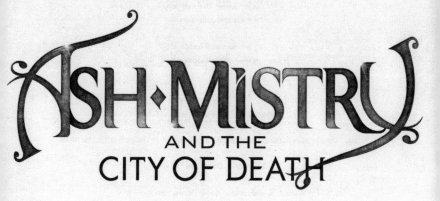

ASH·MISTRY
AND THE
CITY OF DEATH

Sarwat Chadda

HarperCollins *Children's Books*

First published in paperback in Great Britain by HarperCollins Children's Books 2013
HarperCollins *Children's Books* is a division of
HarperCollins*Publishers* Ltd
77-85 Fulham Palace Road, Hammersmith, London W6 8JB

Visit us on the web at
www.harpercollins.co.uk

Visit Sarwat Chadda at
www.sarwatchadda.com

I

ISBN 978-0-00-744737-4

Typeset by Palimpsest Book Production Limited,
Falkirk, Stirlingshire
Printed and bound in England by
Clays Ltd, St Ives plc

For my parents

When the stars threw down their spears,
And watered heaven with their tears,
Did he smile his work to see?
Did he who made the Lamb make thee?

"The Tyger" by William Blake

Chapter One

"*I can't do it,*" said Ash. *He'd beaten a demon king. He'd faced down an immortal sorcerer. He'd saved the world. He shouldn't be scared of anything.* But now fear grabbed at his chest with icy fingers. "It's suicide."

"C'mon, Ash," said Akbar. "It's now or never."

Josh murmured in agreement.

"Fine. I'll do it." That's if he didn't die of heart failure first. "How do I look?"

Akbar grimaced. "Honestly? A bit sick."

"Yeah," added Josh. "Sweaty."

"That's so helpful," Ash snapped back. His friends should be backing him up, not digging his grave. He swallowed and waited for his legs to stop shaking. "I'm going to do it. Now."

Akbar swept his long, straggly black hair away from his face and peered past Ash. "Whenever you're ready," he said.

❖

Josh did his tongue-wagging grin. Along with Sean, who was somewhere in the science block earning extra credit, the four of them were the Nerd Herd. The smartest, hardest-working, most socially inept and physically clumsy students to grace the hallowed halls of West Dulwich High.

Josh slapped Ash's shoulder. "Just go."

"Right. Now," said Ash. "I'm off."

He looked across the vast space of the crowded school canteen.

What's the longest distance in the world?

That between you and your heart's desire.

Gemma sat with her friends. She was laughing at something Anne was saying, and Ash watched as she brushed her golden hair from her face. Was it his imagination, or was it especially shiny today?

"Stop that, Ash," said Josh. "You're sighing again."

"I'm not actually asking her out. You know that, don't you?" Ash took another sip of water. How could his throat be so dry? "I'm just asking if she's got plans for tonight."

"Nope. Not asking her out *at all*," said Josh.

"Though I hear she and Jack are no longer together. Jamie's best friend, Debbie, heard it from her sister's boyfriend," added Akbar.

"Then it must be true. The golden couple have split." Josh leaned closer, eyes darting across the canteen. "So, if you were asking her out, which you are not, now would be the time. Or wouldn't, if you weren't."

"Whatever." Ash stood up. The chair's metal legs screeched as they scraped across the floor. It was strange how something

❖

as automatic as, like, walking, could suddenly become so difficult. Left, right, don't trip over anything or crash into a table. Why were there so many tables in here? And chairs? And people? He'd never make it over there!

Oh God, she's seen me.

Be cool. Remember who you are.

Ash Mistry. Eternal Warrior. The demons of hell wet their pants when they hear your name.

Gemma was still talking to Anne, but her head was half turned and her eyes were on him. She gave a little laugh. Why was she laughing? Was it something Anne had said, or because of him? Even from here Ash saw the light sparkle in her hazel eyes. She had amazing eyes, sometimes grey, sometimes green, sometimes brown. Amazing eyes.

But why is she looking at me like that?

Oh no, have I got snot hanging from my nostril? Is my fly open?

He should have checked. Surely one of his mates would have told him?

No, the scumbags. He bet they were laughing their heads off, watching him stroll over with a bogey dangling down his face. Or worse: with his Doctor Who boxers on full exposure. Maybe he could detour to the corridor and do a full body check.

"Hi, Ash," said Gemma.

"Er, hi, Gemma."

The table fell totally silent. All ten of Gemma's friends stopped eating, chatting and texting, and turned their attention to him.

Why oh why hadn't he waited 'til after school? Caught

❖

her on the way home or something? Or in maths? She sat next to him in maths. Maths would have been perfect.

"You OK?" she asked. "You're looking a bit pale."

Ash stared at her mouth. Her teeth were a row of perfect little pearls and her lips red and glossy. Two dimples appeared as her smile grew. He smelled the soft, flowery scent of her perfume, making him think of springtime and bright sunlight. Jeez, *she smelled of springtime and sunlight?* He needed to slap himself hard before he felt the overwhelming desire to write poetry. Again.

"I'm fine. Totally fine," he said. "How are you? Fine?"

Did I just say that? Beyond lame.

Gemma arched her eyebrows, waiting. "Was there something you wanted?"

Ask her out. Just ask her out.

"I was wondering," he began, pausing to lick his oh-so-dry lips. "Wondering about Bonfire Night. Y'know, it's Bonfire Night. Tonight."

Aaargh. So totally smooth.

"Yes?" She shifted around on her chair, her blonde curls bouncing as she looked up at him.

Oh my God. Was that a hair flick? It was some sort of code. Hair flicks meant something; he'd read about it in one of his sister's magazines. But what? He was deep in unknown territory: the world of girls.

"If you're going?" he said. "To the big bonfire in Dulwich Park. Tonight."

Like she couldn't work that out herself. That was so special needs.

"Why? Are you going?"

12

She's asking me? What does that mean?

"I was thinking—"

"Clear the way, loser."

Jack Owen dropped his bag on the floor and himself on an empty chair. He leaned the chair back on its two legs and flipped his mobile – the latest iPhone – from his Prada leather jacket. He glanced over his shoulder as he texted. "You still here?"

Jack Owen. Ash's arch-enemy. The arch-enemy of the entire Nerd Herd. Tanned, ridiculously handsome in that obvious 'big muscles, perfect features, straight nose and floppy hair' sort of way. Oh yeah, and captain of the football, rugby and cricket teams too. A company-director dad and all the toys money could buy.

I am Ash Mistry. I've done things that would melt Jack's brain. I've fought Ravana, the greatest evil the world has ever known. I've defeated the demon nations.

Then why do I want to puke?

Ash moved half a step back. That was the old Ash, who would back down and hide. Then the new Ash rose like a black snake up through his belly, driving a sharp, flint-hard anger into his throat. "I was talking to Gemma."

"And now you're not." Slowly, Jack got to his feet and faced Ash.

Gemma put her hand on Jack's wrist. "C'mon, Jack, this is stupid."

Jack looked Ash up and down.

"I see you've lost some weight. Turned some of that lard into muscle." Jack leaned so close that he was whispering in

Ash's ear. "Think you can take me? Is that it? You a tough guy now?"

Jack had no idea.

So many ways to kill you.

Two bright golden lights settled on Jack's neck – one just below his bulging Adam's apple, the other near the jaw.

Easy ways.

Ash closed his eyes. But he could see the bright points shining through his eyelids. He covered his face with his hands, but it did no good.

Jack laughed. "Look at him. He's going to cry." He prodded Ash in the chest. "Boo hoo."

"Leave him alone, Jack. It's not nice."

"Jesus, Gemma, I'm just trying to toughen the boy up." There was a laugh from one of the others round the table. "Everyone knows he's madly in *luurve* with you. Isn't that true, Ash?"

"Jack, I'm warning you."

Jack ignored her. "C'mon, Ash. We all know you fancy her. Be a man, just say it." He put his fingers on either side of Ash's chin, wiggling it up and down. "Say it. 'Gemma, I love you so much.'" He squeezed harder, burying his nails into Ash's skin. "Say it."

Ash opened his eyes and gazed at the brilliant lights that lay like a galaxy of stars over Jack. They glistened along his arteries. They shone upon his heart, his lungs. Joints sparkled. His eyes were golden bright.

The Chinese called it Dim Mak, the Death Touch. But to Ash it was *Marma Adi*, the 108 kill points. He knew them all – the points of weakness all living things possessed – and he could exploit these points to injure, disable, or kill. They moved and varied in intensity depending on the person. The old, infirm and very young had many more than the 108. Jack had fewer – he was young and strong and fit – but he had enough.

There was a spot glowing on the side of Jack's head. Ash just needed to touch it, not very hard. Enough to create a blood clot in the brain. Death would come in five seconds, maybe six.

It would look like an accident.

"I'd let go, Jack," said Ash. A warning. That was fair.

"Or what?"

Ash shivered. It wasn't fear that made his heart quicken; it was excitement. He slowly raised his right hand. He could just tap the spot with his finger…

"That's it." Gemma got up and grabbed her bag. "C'mon, Anne."

"Whatever," said Jack, letting go of Ash. He grinned at the audience and got a smattering of embarrassed giggles for his performance.

Gemma gave Jack a withering look as she slung her rucksack over her shoulder and strode off, almost knocking down some small kid. Jack turned to Ash and winked.

"Way out of your league." He picked up his own bag, making sure he tensed his biceps as he did so. "Leave the hot ones to guys like me. You stick to the farmyard animals." Then he left. The others round the table, the entertainment over, quickly gathered their own gear and began to break up. Anne gave Ash a half-shrug before scurrying off after Gemma.

Ash stood by the now-empty table. What was he thinking? He stared at his hand like it wasn't his. He'd almost killed Jack. Over what?

Josh joined Ash. "Well, that went down like the *Titanic*."

Ash looked at him. Lungs, heart... There were nodes of energy shining on Josh's throat, and on either side of his eyes too. So many... Ash retreated a step, afraid an accidental touch might kill his best friend.

"You all right?" Josh asked.

Ash braced himself against a table. "Just... catching my breath." The sensation passed. It felt like a cloud fading from his soul. The *Marma Adi* visions were happening more and more often. He needed to be careful.

"That was banging," said Josh.

"Banging?"

"Where were you over the summer, Ash? Oh yeah, out in India, bored out of your brain. Everyone's using it. 'Banging.' Impressive. Of an epic nature."

"What? Really? That was impressive?" Ash blinked, more than a little surprised by the assessment. "I thought I looked like a moron."

"You did," said Josh. "I was talking about Jack. That was a great line, don't you think? The one about the farmyard animals. Couldn't have thought it up himself, but he's got the delivery."

"I just wish I'd had something smart and devastating to say back," said Ash.

Josh nodded. "Like 'In your fat face, Jack'? That's pretty cool."

"If you're seven." Ash gazed towards the canteen doors, half hoping Gemma might turn round and come back. No such luck. "Why is it so hard to talk to girls?"

Josh slapped Ash's head. "Because we're nerds. Acting awkwardly around girls is our superpower. Anyway, forget about Gemma. You coming around next Tuesday?"

"Tuesday?" asked Ash.

"*Dungeons and Dragons*, old-school style. We're on the last level of the 'The Catacombs of Doom' and we need you, Ash."

Oh yeah, *Dungeons and Dragons*. Josh's dad had banned him from any sort of computer gaming – any sort of computer access at all. Josh hadn't explained why, but Akbar reckoned he'd been caught visiting a few sites *way* inappropriate for his age. So they'd dusted off their old role-playing games and miniature figures, and Tuesday nights were *D&D*.

Josh put his arm over Ash's shoulder. "It will bang to the utmost. You'll be fighting the demon lord of hell."

"Done that already."

"What?"

"Never mind." Ash wriggled out from under Josh's heavy arm. "Remind me again why I hang out with you?"

Josh gave a mocking sob. "What? After all I've done for you? If it hadn't been for me, remember, Gemma wouldn't know you even exist. That poem you wrote her was banging."

❖

"Uploading it on to the school blog wasn't what I had in mind."

"Then you should have a better password than 'TARDIS', shouldn't you?"

Chapter Two

Ash kicked a full rubbish bin on his way home. It must have weighed more than fifteen kilograms, but it lofted into the air and spun in a high arc over a long line of oak trees, a block of houses and the A205 road. He heard it splash down in a pond somewhere in Dulwich Park, half a mile away.

He could do that, but he couldn't ask a girl out. Anger surged within him, and Ash struggled to cool down.

But maybe he didn't want to cool down. Maybe he could show Jack and everyone what he was capable of. They'd look at him differently then.

Yeah, they'd look at him with horror.

Some days, it was as if nothing had ever happened, and Ash was just a normal fourteen-year-old boy trying to keep on the straight and narrow. Not exceptionally bright like

Akbar, nor as cool as Jack, just kind of in the middle, not making any ripples.

But then the dreams came. Dreams of blood and death.

Then Ash remembered exactly what he was.

The *Kali-aastra*, the living weapon of the death goddess Kali. He'd slain the demon king Ravana and absorbed his preternatural energies. He could leap tall buildings in a single bound and do five impossible things before breakfast. Six at the weekend.

Had it only been last summer? It felt like a lifetime ago. It *had* been a lifetime ago. Ash touched the scar on his abdomen that he'd got when his old life had, literally, ended. Three months had passed since his rebirth, and the powers had lessened somewhat, but that was like saying K2 was smaller than Mount Everest. It was still a huge mountain and Ash was still somewhere high above normal.

He remembered going running one night in September, just after coming back from India. Ravana's strength surged through every atom of his body, and it was threatening to explode out of him, so he'd needed to burn it off. He ran. And ran and ran. He'd stopped when he got to Edinburgh. He'd climbed the old castle, then run all the way back. He'd still been home before dawn.

But raw power wasn't everything. There was no point in having the strength to knock out an elephant if you didn't have the skill to hit it where it hurt most. So every morning before the sun came up, Ash crept out to the park or the nearby Sydenham Woods and trained. He'd been taught the basics of *Kalari-payit*, the ancient Indian martial art, and once

❖

he'd caught a glimpse of Kali herself and watched her fight. Somewhere in his DNA lay all the arts of combat. Kicks, high and low, sweeping arcs, punches, spear-strikes, blocks and grapples. He shifted from one move to another with instinctive grace. That rhythm, the dance of Kali, came to him more and more easily.

Would he ever be truly 'normal'? No. The death energies he'd absorbed from Ravana would fade away over time, but when? It could be decades. Centuries. There were no scales that could measure the strength of the demon king. And when – *if* – Ravana's energies did fade, Ash would for ever absorb more. Death was the one certainty, and death strengthened him.

Death was everywhere.

Now, in winter, the trees lining the road had lost their summer coats, and the gutters were filled with damp, golden leaves steadily rotting, steadily dying. A small trickle of power entered his fingertips as he passed along the decaying piles. At night Ash gazed at stars and wondered whether somewhere out in the universe there was a supernova happening, a star's life ending. A solar system becoming extinct, waves of energy radiating out across the cosmos. Were the heavens making him stronger too?

It felt too big sometimes, what he was and what it meant. So he liked to be normal at school. That was why he hid his powers. It was nice to pretend, to escape, even if it was just for a few hours a day.

He registered that it was cold, but it didn't bother him. He wore the sweater merely for show nowadays. It had just

❖

turned half past four, and the long, late autumn shadows led him home.

Ash stopped by his garden gate and looked up and down the road. For what? Gemma following him home? Not bloody likely, given his pathetic performance in the lunch hall.

You blew it.

So much about him had changed and not changed. He still didn't understand maths and he certainly couldn't get a date.

He turned into Croxted Road and saw a battered white van parked outside their drive. Must be to do with Number 43; they were having their house repainted. He'd ask them to move it before Dad got home. If they didn't, he could do it himself. It looked about three tons. No problem.

Lucky opened the door before Ash even knocked. His sister was still in her school uniform, green sweater and grey skirt, grey socks that came up to her knees. Her long black ponytail flicked across her face as she turned back and forth. "Ash—"

"Before you ask, the answer is no." Ash went in and threw his rucksack into the corner. "I did not ask Gemma out."

"Ash—"

"Just give it a rest, will you? Who says I'm interested in her anyway?" He passed through the hall to the kitchen. He really needed some comfort food right now, and that packet of doughnuts up on the sweets shelf would do nicely. Lucky grabbed his sleeve as he turned the door handle.

"Ash!"

"What?"

Lucky was the only one who knew what he'd been through in India, but she didn't treat him any differently, which was why, even though she was eleven and way too smart for her own good, he would die for her.

Had died for her.

You would think that would count for something, wouldn't you? But right now she was being a typical younger sister. Which was irritating.

Lucky stared hard at him, as if she was trying to project her thoughts directly into his head. Alas, while he could kill with a touch, Ash couldn't read minds. Maybe that would come later.

"What is it?" he said. Then he paused and sniffed the air. "Is Dad smoking again? Mum will go mental if he's doing it in the house."

"This is nothing to do with Dad." Lucky frowned and crossed her arms. Not good. "You've got visitors." Then she spun on her heels and stomped upstairs to her room. The whole house shook as she slammed the door.

Gemma? Had she come over to see him? She did live just down the road. It had to be. He checked that his fly was up and quickly wiped his nose. Then he opened the kitchen door.

So not Gemma. A gaunt old woman leaned against the sink, blowing cigarette smoke out of the half-open window. Her hair would have suited a witch: wild, thick as a bush and grey as slate. She dropped her stub into Ash's Yoda mug, where it died with a hiss.

❖

The old woman smiled at Ash, her thin lips parting to reveal a row of yellow teeth. It wasn't pretty. She searched her baggy woollen cardigan and took out a packet of Marlboro Lights. She flicked her Zippo and within two puffs the fresh cigarette was glowing.

"You're not allowed to smoke in here," Ash said. He'd been brought up to respect his elders – it was the Indian way – but there was something thoroughly disrespectful about this woman.

"So you're Ash Mistry," she said. "The Kali-aastra."

Ash tensed. "Do I know you?"

"I'm Elaine."

"I don't know any Elaines."

"She's a friend of mine."

Ash spun round at the new voice, one he recognised.

An Indian girl stepped out from behind the fridge. That was why he hadn't seen her, but then she was very good at being invisible. She played with a silver locket as she gazed at him through her big black sunglasses. She wore a pair of dark green trousers and a black cotton shirt, its collar and cuffs embroidered with entwined serpents. Looking at her, a stranger would guess she was about fifteen. They'd only be off by about four thousand years.

She took off her glasses, and her pupils, vertical slits, dilated with sly amusement. The green irises filled out the rest of her eyes, leaving no whites at all. Her lips parted into a smile, and Ash glimpsed a pair of half-extended venomous fangs where her canines should have been.

She looked like a vampire, cold and with a terrible beauty.

But no vampire could compare to her. She was the daughter of the demon king and born to end men's lives.

"*Namaste*," said Parvati.

Chapter Three

They looked at each other, neither moving. Then Ash came forward and somewhat awkwardly hugged Parvati. She stepped back and looked at him.

"You've changed," she said.

"For the better, right?"

"That remains to be seen."

Oh, nice to see you again too, Parvati.

"How have you been?" he asked. "It's been ages and I haven't heard anything."

"You missed me? How nice."

"I didn't say that. But I thought you might have dropped me an e-mail at least."

"I've been busy."

"Blimey, Parvati." He'd forgotten she didn't do sensitive. "I'm just saying, it's good to see you."

❖

"So who's this Gemma?" she asked. "Found true love, have we?"

"What?" How did she know about Gemma? Ah yes. Because he'd been shouting her name in the hallway. "Er, she's just a friend."

"Is she the one you wrote the poem about?"

Despite the cold air coming through the open window, Ash suddenly became very hot. And bothered. "You know about that?"

"I've been keeping up to date. Checking the blogs and boards. We do have the Internet in India, in case you didn't know."

"What did you think?" He had to ask. "Of the poem?"

Parvati tapped her chin, brow furrowed in contemplation. "Deeply disturbing. On many levels."

"Thanks, Parvati. A lot." She obviously knew nothing about poetry. "I assume you're not here to discuss my literary endeavours, so why *are* you here?"

Parvati didn't answer. Her attention was on a photo on the wall. Ash knew exactly which one.

An Indian couple, in black and white, sat stiffly looking at the camera. The man's hair was glossy ebony with oil. If he'd used any more, it would have been declared an environmental disaster. His black plastic-framed glasses sat firm on his thin nose.

The woman wore a traditional sari and had a puja mark on her forehead. She had a large gold nose ring, and thick kohl circled her deep black eyes.

Uncle Vik and Aunt Anita.

❖

The photo had been taken years and years ago, when they were newlyweds. Had they imagined how their lives would go? How their lives would end?

It had happened in Varanasi, the holiest city in India. Uncle Vik had been an archaeologist, teaching at the university. But there they'd met Lord Alexander Savage. The English aristocrat had asked Uncle Vik to translate some ancient Harappan scrolls, translations that were crucial to Savage's plans to resurrect Ravana. When Vik ultimately refused, Savage had killed Ash's uncle and aunt.

Savage was over three hundred years old, and when Ash had first met him, he'd looked it. A living skeleton with skin flaking off his withered flesh, the man was only kept going by his magic, and even that was beginning to fail. His plan had been to resurrect Ravana, the master of all ten sorceries, in the hope that the demon king would give him immortal youth in exchange for bringing him back from the dead. And it had all been going well for him until Ash had turned up and put his fist through Ravana's chest, ending him once and for ever.

Ash could still picture the young, rejuvenated Savage, fleeing through the chaos that had followed Ravana's destruction. He had wanted to go after the English sorcerer, but in the end, he knew where his priorities lay. He had a sister, parents and a home. This was where he belonged. It was Parvati's job to hunt down Savage — she had her own grudge against him. But Ash's anger was still there. He missed his aunt and uncle, and Savage needed to pay for what he'd done.

❖

"Have you found him?" asked Ash.

"No. But I'm still looking." Parvati put her hand on Ash's shoulder. "I will find him. I promise you." She looked him up and down. "How are you, Ash?"

"Great. Better than great." That was true. He was in perfect health. Beyond perfect.

"You certainly look good."

Ash nodded. "Don't need to sleep, eat, anything like that. I can run a hundred miles a day without feeling tired. Never get ill, not even a cold. There was a super-flu going around a month ago and half the school was off."

"I heard about that," said Parvati. "Made the news back in India."

Ash slapped his chest. "Not even a sniffle." He sat down and picked up an apple.

"It will fade, over time," said Parvati. "You'll return to being... more human. But never quite all the way."

"It's kinda cool being a superhero."

Parvati arched her eyebrow. "Just don't start wearing your underpants outside your trousers. It's not a good look for you."

"Thanks for the fashion tip."

"So you're managing?" She toyed with her sunglasses. "Restraining yourself? Not letting people see exactly who you are? What you are, I should say."

"Is that why you're here? To make sure I haven't fallen to the Dark Side of the Force?"

"Probably too late for that." Parvati laughed, and Ash's heart quickened. He'd forgotten how her laughter was like

❖

the chiming of silver bells. "But no, that's not why I'm here. I need your help." She looked towards Elaine. "My friend had best explain."

Elaine rummaged around in her pocket and put a postcard on the table. The card was a cheap one that you could get in any tourist shop in London. It showed two bejewelled crowns, a sceptre and a golden orb, each one sitting regally on a red cushion.

"The Crown Jewels?" said Ash. He'd visited the Tower of London loads of times on school trips. Every school kid in Britain recognised them.

"You've heard of the Koh-i-noor?" asked Parvati.

"Of course I have." He looked at the humongous diamond sparkling in the centre of one of the crowns. "The Mountain of Light."

"Stolen by the British in the mid-nineteenth century from the maharajah of Lahore," Parvati said. "It was given to Queen Victoria. The original stone was much bigger than what it is now. The British cut it in half and put the largest piece in here." She tapped the central image. "The Queen Mother's Crown."

"Not any more," said Elaine. "It was stolen five days ago."

"Impossible. It would have been in the news," said Ash.

Elaine shook her head. "No. This sort of news is kept very quiet. Why would the government want to admit a national heirloom has been stolen? You can count on the prime minister's office to cover this sort of thing up to avoid a scandal."

Ash sat down. "Why was it nicked? To sell it?"

"It is up for sale, that's for certain," said Elaine. "It's the buyer we're interested in."

"It is an *aastra*, Ash," Parvati replied.

"Ah," said Ash.

An aastra was anything made by a god – usually weapons. Ash had found one, a golden arrowhead, in an underground chamber in Varanasi, where a splinter of the aastra had entered his thumb. That minute piece of god-forged metal was the source of all his power and all the trouble that had followed: the death of his uncle and aunt, Lucky's kidnapping and his own demise and return.

"Will it work? The British cut it in half, didn't they?" he asked.

"You only have a fraction of the Kali-aastra, far less than a half, and it's served you well," replied Parvati.

She had a point. Ash peered at his thumb, at the scar marking where the splinter had entered. The sliver of metal was long gone, bound to every atom of his body.

"Whose aastra is it?" he asked. Each aastra was different, depending on which god had forged it. The aastra of Agni, the fire god, gained power from heat and fire. Could the Koh-i-noor be another Kali-aastra like his? That didn't bear thinking about.

Elaine looked down at her boots as she lit another cigarette and gave a slight shrug. "That we don't know."

Ash frowned. "Parvati? Any idea?"

"No," she declared. "The Koh-i-noor is exceedingly ancient, but I've never known anyone to successfully awaken it."

❖

"Awakened or not, we can't risk letting it fall into the wrong hands," said Elaine.

"And by the wrong hands, you mean Savage, don't you?"

Elaine nodded. "Savage has been a thorn in our side for a few hundred years."

"What do you mean, 'our side'?"

Elaine smiled. "I represent certain... interested parties. It's our job to know what's going on."

Ash leaned back in his chair. The Koh-i-noor was perhaps the most famous diamond in the world, and the most cursed. Every Indian knew the story of how it had been passed down through the ages, how many of its owners had come to hideous deaths.

"How did it get nicked?" asked Ash. The security around the Crown Jewels would be intense.

"Swapped, somehow, while the jewels were being given their monthly polish." Parvati inspected the fruit bowl and picked out an apple. Ash couldn't help but notice how her canines, slightly longer than normal, sank into the flesh and two thin beads of juice ran off the punctures. "The jeweller turned round for a moment, and when he turned back, the Koh-i-noor was gone and a piece of glass was there instead."

"No one else came in, was hiding behind the cupboard? Under the sink?"

"No."

"So we're not talking about a normal thief, are we?" said Ash. The stakes were getting higher every passing second.

"No, we're not."

"Any ideas who?"

"Name of Monty. He specialises in stealing such esoteric items. Word has got around that he's putting it on the market."

"We going to make him an offer?" said Ash.

Parvati smiled. It wasn't nice. "One he can't refuse."

Elaine picked up the card and tucked it away. "I've got feelers out and should have his address any time now."

Parvati spoke. "Such artefacts don't turn up every day. Savage will be after it."

"You think he might know how to use it?" asked Ash. Aastras were the Englishman's speciality. He'd spent years searching for the Kali-aastra before Ash found it accidentally, so it made sense that he'd be looking for others too.

"I really don't want to give him the opportunity. This is our chance to end this once and for all."

A tremor of excitement ran through him. "How?"

"With your help. If you're not too busy?"

"Can it wait until after *Doctor Who*?"

"Ash—"

"Joke."

Elaine buttoned up her cardigan. "We'd offer our services, but we've got some of our own business to take care of."

"What sort of business?" asked Ash.

"None of yours," interrupted Parvati. She put on her sunglasses. "Elaine will text us the address. We'll meet up later and visit this Monty."

Ash showed them to the door, where Elaine suddenly checked her pockets. "My cigarettes. I think I left them in

❖

the kitchen. You go and wait in the van, Parvati, I'll only be a minute."

Parvati nodded, then, with a small bow and smile for Ash, left.

Elaine and Ash returned to the kitchen. She made a show of searching the table, the worktop.

"Try your left pocket," said Ash. He'd seen her put them away and knew she knew that too. This was a ruse to have a quiet moment without Parvati listening.

"Ah." Out came the packet. Elaine tapped it idly, her attention on Ash. "Rishi told me a lot about you."

"You knew him?" Rishi had been the first person to realise that Ash was the Eternal Warrior, the latest reincarnation of some of the greatest heroes the world had ever known. The old holy man had started Ash on his training, but had been killed by Savage's henchman before he could teach Ash more about his new nature, what he had become.

"Getting any urges? Beyond those normal for a hormonal teen boy?"

"What do you mean?"

"Rishi suspected you'd found the Kali-aastra and asked me to keep an eye on you if anything happened to him. He wanted you to continue your training."

"Don't take this the wrong way," Ash said, "but you really don't look like the sort of teacher I need." She was breathing heavily just unwrapping the cigarette packet.

Elaine drew out a business card and pushed it across the table. "Rishi gave me a list of contacts. Most are out in India. You call me if you need any help."

"I've got Parvati."

"There are things Parvati can't teach you. And her agenda may not be the same as yours."

"Meaning?" Ash didn't like what she was implying.

Elaine glanced towards the door, checking that Parvati was out of hearing. "As much as I respect Parvati, I don't trust her, and neither should you. While Rishi was around, he was able to keep her in check, but she's a demon princess, and Ravana was her father."

"She hated Ravana. She helped me kill him."

"And now the throne of the demon nations sits empty." Elaine shrugged. "Parvati is ambitious. It's in her nature."

Ash reluctantly picked up the card. "'Elaine's Bazaar'?"

"It's a junk shop near Finsbury Park. Open all hours."

He looked at her a moment longer. He didn't need *Marma Adi* to see Elaine's weaknesses; her smoking habit was enough for anyone to have a guess at what was killing her. The lungs glowed brightest, but her veins and arteries were clogged and thin, the blood circulation poor. Death covered her, a ready shroud. She didn't have long.

She went pale. "What do you see, lad?"

He shook his head. "Nothing. I see nothing."

She looked at the half-empty packet. "I suppose I should cut down. Maybe quit."

"It wouldn't make any difference."

Elaine cleared her throat and put the packet back in her pocket. "Just watch yourself. You read these stories about kids who get hold of their parents' guns and... bang, someone ends up very sorry and someone ends up very dead."

❖

"Are you saying I'm a kid with my dad's revolver?"

"No, I'm saying you're a kid with a thermonuclear device, with a big red button saying PRESS ME." She tapped Ash's hand. "Keep out of trouble, lad."

Chapter Four

*A*nd just like that, Parvati was back in his life. Ash stood in the hallway, bewildered, well after the van had disappeared.

What should he do now?

He'd spent months wondering if he'd ever see her again, waiting every day for some message, getting none. First he'd been angry, then he'd tried to have a 'quiet' life. And just when he thought it was all back to normal, there she was, having tea in his kitchen! His guts felt like they were on spin in a washing machine.

A pair of bright headlights lit up the driveway. His parents were home. Ash opened the door just as his mum was unbuttoning her coat.

"Hi, Ash," she said, ruffling his hair as she entered. Briefcase went alongside the small table beside the door as her raincoat

❖

went over the banister, and she brushed imaginary dust from her smart navy-blue suit jacket. She gave a weary sigh and took off her shoes, wiggling her toes for a moment. She tucked her glasses in their case as she glanced at the answering machine for any messages. Then she turned slowly. "Anything wrong?" she asked. Ash was still by the door.

"Girl trouble, I bet," said Sanjay, Ash's father, as he followed his wife inside, his gaze on his BlackBerry. "That right, son?"

"Like you wouldn't believe," said Ash.

Ash's mum lifted the BlackBerry from her husband's hands. "That's enough, Sanjay."

"See what I mean?" Dad shrugged. "Girl trouble." Ash's mum was about to protest, but Sanjay took her hand and twirled her, clomping about in his boots. His own suit wasn't quite as neat or as smart as his wife's, but Sanjay worked as an engineer and spent half the week on building sites, making sure the walls stayed up and the roofs stayed on. He was at least half a metre taller and quite a bit wider than his wife, so when he pulled her towards him, Ash's mum was pressed against the globe of his belly.

"Is it Gemma?" asked Mum.

"The girl in the poem?" said Dad, and there was an irritating smirk across his face, the sort of smirk all parents get when they are about to mortally embarrass their children.

"Hold on. You know about that?" Ash said.

"I think it's very romantic," said Mum. "I would have been flattered if some boy had written me a poem."

Ash wanted to die, right there and then. Was there anyone in the Greater London area who didn't know about his stupid

❖

poem? It was meant to be private, and it had gone viral on the Internet. One day Josh was going to pay.

"How did it go, Bina?" Ash's dad dropped to one knee while still holding his wife's hand, cleared his throat, and began to recite. "'If I may be so bold, to say your hair is like fallen gold, and that when I see you smile, my heart flutters for a while...'"

"Dad, just shut up. It's got nothing to do with Gemma."

Both looked at him with more than mild surprise. Dad lightly punched Ash's arm. "Another girl? That's my boy. Come on, do it." He held up his fist. Ash groaned as he gave his father a fist bump. Parents trying to be cool. Seriously, had he been swapped at birth or what? "Just make sure it doesn't affect your school work."

Ash left his dad in the hallway undoing his boots and went back into the kitchen with his mum. The tap went on and soon the kettle was bubbling. She paused by the open window and sniffed suspiciously. "Someone been smoking?"

"Smoking? Of course not." Ash grabbed the Yoda mug with the cigarette stubs. He really didn't want to explain what had just happened. Frankly, it would sound quite mental. "Let me help wash up."

"This girl, she's someone important, isn't she?"

Weird, wasn't it? Normal girls like Gemma left him sweating and tongue-tied, but Parvati, a half-demon assassin? No problem.

There had been a moment when, well, if not exactly a girlfriend and boyfriend sort of set-up — there *was* a significant age gap between them — they had been something a bit

39

more than just 'friends'. She had kissed him, twice. Didn't that count for something? But once he'd left India there hadn't been a word. She'd completely forgotten him. And now, just when Ash himself was moving on, here she was, and it felt like not a minute had passed since they'd last seen one another.

"Mum, I just don't know."

The doorbell rang. Must be Josh. He'd planned to come over early so the two of them could head out to Dulwich Park together for Bonfire Night. Ash would have to tell him his plans had changed and he couldn't come. Not that he'd want to go to the park anyway if it meant bumping into Gemma and having to relive the humiliation of what had happened in the canteen.

"Ash," his dad called from the hallway. "It's your friend."

Ash went to the hall, and his dad winked at him as he passed. What was that about? Jeez, maybe it was Elaine again. What had she forgotten now – her walker?

Ash opened the door. "Look—"

"Hi, Ash."

Oh my God. Gemma.

"Er, hi. Er, Gemma." He looked around, wondering if she'd got lost or something. "Er, yes?"

He so wanted to punch his own face. Why oh why couldn't he just talk to her like a normal person rather than a cretin?

"Can I come in?"

"Here?" Yes, he should punch his own face repeatedly. "Of course."

Gemma stood in the hall. "Hi, Lucks."

Lucky sat at the top of the stairs, chin on her knees, watching. She waved back. "Hey, Gemma, my brother was—"

"Go away, Lucks," Ash said.

Lucky didn't move. She was totally immune to his threats.

"Please, Lucks?"

Lucky blinked. She didn't know how to respond to politeness. She blinked again, then left.

So. Gemma. Him. Standing in the hall. Well.

She'd tied back her hair, but a few curls had slipped free, framing her face. She looked uneasy. "Listen, Ash. I just came to say I'm sorry about Jack. He's not usually—"

"Such a git?"

She smiled. Ash felt another poem coming on. "Git. Just the word I was going to use."

"Is that why you're here? To apologise for him?"

"No. I never answered your question."

"Question?"

"About Bonfire Night." She smiled at him. "I am going. What about you?"

"No. Plans have changed."

"Oh. All right then." She gave a shrug. "Well, I'll see you later. At school." She adjusted her rucksack in an 'I'm about to leave now and you've totally blown it' sort of motion.

Hold on. He rewound the last few seconds, trying to understand the complex subtext of that last conversation. Somewhere he'd gone wrong.

"What I meant to say was I... yes, I am going. Totally. I am."

41

❖

"Great. What time?"

She was asking him. She was asking him. That hair flick in the canteen *had* meant something!

Time to play it cool. For once in your life.

Ash glanced at his watch. "I dunno, about eight?"

"Shall I pop over?" Then she laughed. "D'you remember when we were at primary school? I was here almost every day. Playing that board game." Gemma frowned. "What was it called?"

"The Orpheus Quest."

She snapped her fingers. "Down into the underworld to rescue the princess, right? You still have it?"

Ash shrugged. "Went to the charity shop years ago, sorry."

"What happened? We used to hang all the time. I only live round the corner."

"I stayed in the Nerd Herd and you didn't, I suppose." Ash put his hands in his pockets. "We ended up in different crowds. High school's a big place."

"Do you think I've changed that much?" she asked.

"We all change, Gemma."

"That doesn't have to be a bad thing."

Ash's mobile phone buzzed. It was Parvati, with an address. She wanted to meet at six-thirty.

Typical. Of all the days since time began, why today?

Gemma glanced down at the glowing screen. "Problem?"

"No. There's just something I need to do, but it shouldn't take long. I'll meet you there. In case I'm late or something."

"Oh, OK." Gemma paused by the door. "Bye, Ash."

"Bye, Gemma." He closed the front door behind her.

❖

Ash's parents both fell silent as he entered the kitchen. They were each staring intently at their mugs.

Ash's mum turned to his dad. "That Gemma, I know her family well. Very respectable."

"Yes, her father is a dentist. Perfect teeth, both Gemma and her sister. Have you ever seen more beautiful smiles?" said his dad. "There is the dowry, him having two daughters. But no rush. We will wait until Ash has finished university, then the wedding."

"But can she cook curries?" asked his mum. "It is simple to fix. I will teach her once they are married."

"Just..." Ash backed out of the kitchen. "Oh, just shut up."

Chapter Five

$\mathcal{T}$he plan was simple. Ash would meet Parvati in Soho at six-thirty, get the Koh-i-noor off this Monty fella, then head off to Dulwich Park and the fireworks at eight. And hang out with Gemma. Sorted.

This was turning out to be more fun than he'd thought.

Lucky shoved his clothes off the bed and threw herself on it. Resting her chin on a pillow, she surveyed the wardrobe scattered across the carpet. "How many T-shirts can one person need?" she asked. "And Mum told you to tidy up."

"This is tidy," Ash said. There were no clothes on the floor that didn't belong there, most of his books were up on the shelves, and the bed was made, sort of. You could even see some of the carpet. Disney wallpaper for a fourteen-year-old was social death, so it had to be covered up with posters, though poster selection was a minefield. The posters told any visitors who you were, what you were, your religious beliefs. Ash was going through a major superhero phase. Batman. The X-Men. Even a vintage Bond from the 1960s. It informed the casual observer that Ash was either a dangerous outsider with superpowers, or a total geek. It just so happened he was both.

Ash sniffed his deodorant. According to the ads, this particular brand would attract a whole planeload of European supermodels. He'd better use just a small amount.

He checked his hair in the mirror as he slid his gel-coated fingers through his thick black locks. He'd grown them out over the last few months and they were getting perilously long; the gel barely held his hair under any sort of control. "Pass us the Levi's T-shirt," he said. "The black one."

"They're all black." She picked up a random T-shirt. "What happened to all your other clothes?"

"Thought it was time for a new look. Anyway, a lot of my old stuff didn't fit any more." After his time in India, he'd come back a different shape. The old Ash had been 'cuddly'; this new Ash was as sharp as a razor.

"So you've decided to go all skintight and superhero-ish?"

"Something like that."

As Ash took off his shirt, he saw the scar — a pale white line locked in the dark skin, wedged between hard muscle at the top of his stomach. He drew his fingernail along it. That was where Savage had pushed the arrowhead in. Another Ash had died that night in the ancient capital of the demon king. Another boy had bled to death on the sand-covered flagstones before the Iron Gates. Now Ash was a dead man walking, brought back to life by Kali to be her weapon.

"Do you miss him?" he asked Lucky. "The old Ash?"

"You're still here. Same as you ever were."

Ash slid the T-shirt on. "We know that's not true."

"Where it matters, it is." She glanced at the mirror. Ash stood there, the T-shirt taut across his chest, clinging to the contours of his torso. He double-knotted his Converse All Stars. It wouldn't do to go tripping over a loose shoelace.

Ash pulled out his shirt drawer and dropped it on the floor. He stretched his arm to the back of the dresser and felt around. His fingers touched bare steel. The object was taped to the back panel of the cabinet. He ripped the tape off.

Hands tightening round the hilt, Ash pulled out his *katar*.

The Indian punch dagger was thirty centimetres long, the blade almost half the length. Its handle was shaped like an H, gripped along the short, horizontal bar, with the wide triangular blade jutting forward, so the attack was delivered via a straight punch. The tip was diamond-hard and designed for penetrating steel armour. It was like no other weapon in the world, unique to India.

Lucky drew in her breath. "I didn't know you still had it."

Ash checked the edges. Still razor-sharp. "You approve?"

"No." She sat up. "I don't want you getting involved with Parvati."

Ash took out a folded piece of leather. He'd made the scabbard himself one evening at the school workshop, doing some after-hours work to earn more credits. He slipped his belt through the straps and then put it on. The katar went into the leather sheath, nestling in his lower back.

"Ash…"

"I'm just doing her a favour, that's all." Ash put his Victorian Army greatcoat on over the katar, a knee-length number, his 'Sherlock Special'. He checked himself in the mirror. The coat hid the katar perfectly, but with a flick he could instantly grab it. Lucky peered over his shoulder.

"You'll knock 'em dead," she said before grimacing. "But not in the literal sense. OK?"

"OK."

"And Gemma will be there." Lucky sniffed the deodorant and wrinkled her nose. "Who knows, you might get your first real kiss tonight."

"I've kissed a girl before."

"Really? Who?"

There was a long pause. "Parvati."

"Parvati? As in daughter of Ravana? As in half-demon assassin?" Lucky leaned forward. "What was it like?"

"All I remember was the abject fear and the sense that I was about to suffer a slow and hideous death."

"I'm sure it'll be better next time round," she replied.

Chapter Six

An hour later, Ash got off the bus at Piccadilly Circus. Despite the cold, London was buzzing. Tonight was the fifth of November, Guy Fawkes Night. Fireworks flared into the night sky, but a dingy fog was sinking over the city, steadily smothering all light and colour.

Ash checked his mobile phone. Parvati wanted to meet at the Royal Bengal Restaurant. He went along Shaftesbury Avenue, with its theatres showing musicals and Shakespearean plays. The Lyric had a revival of *Faustus*, and a glaring red devil loomed over the passers-by, his face split by a bloody grin. Ash turned down Great Windmill Street and away from the bright lights and bustling streets into a very different part of Soho.

Soho still had an edgy, forbidden atmosphere, especially for a boy with parental locks on his computer. His parents would go mental if they knew he was wandering around here at night. In spite of the gleaming towers and flash shops, most of London still lay upon ancient streets and winding lanes, which made Soho a labyrinth of seedy, dark alleys where dimly seen figures lurked in the doorways and the encroaching fog seemed to choke all colour, fading it to grey. Ash kept his eyes down.

"Nice coat," said Parvati as Ash entered the restaurant. The place was packed with diners and smelled of spices – fried onions, cardamom and garlic. A waiter slipped past holding a sizzling balti tray. Molten butter shone on the fresh naan bread. Ash's mouth watered. "Dinner first?"

"Just tea." Parvati pointed out of the window. "Monty's flat is round the corner."

The neon lights from the bar opposite filled the front window with garish colour, and it took Ash a second to realise there was someone waiting at the table for them.

"This is Khan," said Parvati, taking a seat.

Khan stood up and reached across to greet Ash. "Namaste." His voice was a deep, rumbling growl – the sort of sound that wouldn't be out of place in a jungle. Over six feet tall, the guy had bronze skin with cropped light brown hair, and the stitches on his dark purple shirt strained against the pressure of his muscles. He met Ash's gaze with confident, amber eyes. Despite his size, he moved with feline grace.

Ash felt Khan's nails prick his skin as they shook hands. He sat down, acutely aware that everyone in the restaurant was watching him. No, they were watching Khan. The phrase 'animal magnetism' sprang to mind.

❖

Dark stripes marked Khan's arm. Ash didn't need any more clues to know what sort of *rakshasa* this guy was. "Tiger," Ash said. "Yes?"

Khan nodded. Once, and not that long ago, Ash hadn't believed in rakshasas. They were the bad guys in Indian mythology, immortal shape-changers that had fought humanity thousands of years ago over rulership of the world. The *Ramayana* was the story of that long-ago war, recounting how Prince Rama had defeated Ravana, the biggest and baddest of the rakshasas, and led humanity to victory.

Rakshasas were legends. Now here Ash was having tea with two of them.

Parvati put her hand on Khan's arm. Ash's blood boiled at the way she smiled at the tiger demon. "Khan and I go way back. He's here to help."

Khan grinned. "Sikander, wasn't it? You were leading the maharajah's infantry to the left, I was with the royal body-guard." He stretched out his arms and the grin grew even wider. "Now that was a fight. Nothing gets the blood going like an elephant charge. I don't care what the historians say – Sikander crapped his pants."

Sikander? Ash frowned. Wasn't that the Indian name for...

"You fought Alexander the Great? Seriously? What was he like?"

Khan put out his hand, holding it around shoulder height. "Shorter than you'd imagine and, on that day, in need of a change of underwear."

Ash stared at the two of them. Khan was showing off, name-dropping Alexander like that, but Ash had to admit

❖

the story was still pretty awesome. He was into history, thanks to Uncle Vik. What his uncle would have given to be here, sitting with a pair who had been part of all the history he could only read and guess about. But the two of them treated it so casually, barely acknowledging the legends they'd met. Maybe if you were a legend yourself things like fighting Alexander the Great didn't seem like such a big deal.

Parvati laid her mobile phone on the table and pointed at the map on the screen. "There's an easy way into Monty's place from the side alleyway. It's blocked off so no one goes down there."

"Any visitors we should know about?" asked Ash.

"Like Savage?" replied Parvati. "Let's ask Monty. Nicely."

"Nicely?" Ash grinned. "You're terror made flesh, Parvati."

Parvati stopped and looked at him in a particularly meaningful way. "That's an interesting phrase, Ash," she said. "Where did you hear it?"

"Dunno. Just made it up, I suppose." Ash couldn't miss the way she was looking at him now. Worried. "Why?"

Parvati shrugged. "I thought I'd heard it before. Some time ago."

A minute later they were climbing over a large rubbish bin that hid the alleyway from view. A greasy kitchen exhaust duct rattled and spat above their heads, and black plastic bin liners, stinking with rotten vegetables, lay scattered under foot. A mangy dog tore at one of the bags and sniffed at the spilled rubbish. Khan gave a throaty growl. The dog whimpered and fled.

"I don't like dogs," said Khan.

❖

"It's high up," said Parvati, ignoring him.

She was right. There was a single window facing into the alley, but it was about four metres up and semi-opaque.

Khan shrugged. "Will that be a problem?"

"No," said Ash. He stepped back and focused on the small window. Closing his eyes, he drew down within himself, feeling his mind, his senses, descending into a dark swirling maelstrom somewhere where his soul might be.

Ash shuddered and enjoyed the electric thrill as preternatural energy swelled within him. It was the rush of riding a tidal wave. No, like riding a tsunami.

Ash opened his eyes and gazed about him.

Every sense buzzed on overload. He could see the very grains of the brickwork, each stroke of the brush on the paint that covered the walls. He smelled and separated every odour, however faint: the pungent, moist cabbage leaves that covered the floor, the gurgling drains with old, sooty rainwater, the sharp, sweet stink of petrol.

He looked up at the window and merely reached for it. It wasn't much of a jump; he barely flexed his muscles, and then he flew upward. A moment later he touched down on the narrow window ledge, balancing on his toes four metres above the ground. He perched there for a moment, ear pressed against the window. Nothing.

Ash curled his fingers and drove his fist through the glass. He peered into the darkness beyond; to him it was as bright as day. A small, simple, smelly old bathroom. He climbed in.

There was a snarl from behind him and suddenly Khan was there. His nails were a few centimetres longer than before,

❖

and Ash saw the faint ripple of black-striped fur across his arms.

Parvati slipped in behind Khan, and suddenly the bathroom was awfully cramped.

"This is cosy," she said. "Shall we wait here for Monty to join us?"

Ash opened the bathroom door and entered Monty's flat.

Aged, yellowed wallpaper hung off the walls and patches of snot-green mould stained the ceiling. They went into the living room and found it covered with discarded books and tottering piles of newspapers that went back years, decades even. The furniture looked like it had been collected from skips. The table was missing one leg and rested on a pile of bricks. More books filled the shelves, stuffed in with no sense of order. Ash registered the number of titles specialising in Indian jewellery. Flies buzzed around an unfinished meal. Green mould covered the cups, and the plates were encrusted with who knew what. And his mum complained about his room being untidy. She would have a heart attack if she saw this place.

"There's no one at home," said Ash. He picked up an old bowler hat. Strange, it was the only clean thing here. A set of clothes sat, neatly folded, beneath it.

"Thanks for stating the blindingly obvious," said Parvati.

"Disgusting," said Ash. "There are mouse droppings everywhere."

Parvati turned to him, finger to her lips.

Ash listened, not sure what for — something that didn't fit, something that was wrong.

There, behind the pile of magazines. He could hear a scratching. Too steady to be an accident. The noise stopped, as though something was aware it had been heard. There was even the delicate huff of a breath being held.

Parvati's hand shot out and a second later she had a rat dangling from her grip.

A rat. Great.

Parvati took off her glasses and held the rodent tightly. It squealed as it stared into her cobra eyes. She flexed her jaw, widening it far beyond normal dimensions.

"For heaven's sake, Parvati, you need to eat it right now?" said Ash.

"Hear that?" asked Parvati. She was addressing the rat. "Looks like you're dinner." Her jaws widened and her fangs sprang out, each slick with deadly poison. Her tongue, forked, flickered out across its whiskers.

The rat scrabbled desperately but vainly. It twisted, head straining, and the tiny black eyes looked straight at Ash, imploring him for help.

"Please!" it squeaked in a tiny voice. "Don't let her eat me!"

Chapter Seven

$\mathcal{P}$arvati held the rat upside down by its tail, swinging it slowly back and forth. "I'm going to let you go. Don't even think about fleeing, or the only hole you'll be running down will be my gullet. Understand?"

It looked like the rat was trying to nod. Not easy, being upside down.

"I'm sorry, but can we have a reality check?" said Ash. "That rat. It talked."

The rat fell, and in a second it was on its feet, nose and whiskers twitching. It rubbed its eyes and Ash swore it stamped its foot. Then it shook itself like a dog coming out of a pond. But instead of water, minute hairs tumbled off its body. The pink, oily skin pulsed and bubbled as the rat spasmed. Its squeak rose to a high, sharp violin screech as it blew up like some distorted balloon. Arms stuck out of the pink, swelling flesh and irregular patches of black hair spiralled out from its deformed head. The arms lengthened and the claws twisted into hands. Within seconds the rat was gone, and a pale, naked man stood before them.

The man grinned as he covered his privates with his hands and stood at an awkward, gawky angle. A stumpy pink tail still flicked back and forth. He glanced around. "You couldn't pass me my clothes, could you?" he said. "It's just a bit draughty."

Parvati tossed him his bowler hat.

"Who are you?" asked Ash.

"The name's Monty."

Parvati's own nose wrinkled up in a look of disgust. "A common rat demon."

"Now, there's no reason to be rude, your highness." Monty shifted his shoulders, trying to strike a more proud stance, not easy while holding a bowler over his private parts. "Common. Of all the cheek."

"Let's play with it," said Khan. His nails were five-centimetre claws. He tapped them on the table, dragging little grooves through the wood.

"Easy, tiger," said Parvati. But there was a malicious edge to her voice.

Monty registered the deadly looks. He backed away, but just bumped against Ash. He sank to his knees, grabbing his hands and dropping his bowler hat. "Sir, you look like a reasonable man. Surely we can come to some arrangement?"

Khan spoke. "Whatever he says, it'll be lies. The rats are the lowest caste of rakshasa. Hardly rakshasas at all."

Ash slowly slid his hand out and wiped it on his trousers. "An arrangement?"

"Your protection, sir. In exchange for information."

"Your information had better be top quality," said Parvati. She'd revealed more of her own demon form, with green scales clustered round her throat and her cobra eyes acutely slanted, large and hypnotic. Her tongue flicked the air, tasting Monty's fear.

Monty looked around at all three of them. "What do you want to know?"

"We're looking for the Koh-i-noor. We understand you've just stolen it," said Ash.

"The Koh-i-noor? You think I'd have something like that?" He shook his head. "Way out of my league. Try Sotheby's. They've got a special department for that sort of stuff."

Khan's roar shook the windowpanes as he pounced, crossing the room in an instant. He lifted Monty up by the throat, pushing the rat demon high into the air until his head was touching the ceiling. Khan's canines were long and much thicker than Parvati's. What they lacked in venom, they made up for in sharpness. They could tear Monty open with minimal effort.

"Wrong answer," Khan snarled.

"Oh, the Koh-i-noor!" cried Monty. "I must have misheard. It's my ears; full of fur."

Khan dropped him. The rat demon lay on the floor, coughing.

Ash helped him up. "So you steal. Is that what rat demons do?"

❖

"We've all got to earn a living, put some cheese on the table, as it were," said Monty. "I do a bit of this and a bit of that. It's not like the old days, when we were top dogs."

"The Plague Years," said Parvati.

Monty sighed. "Golden days. I miss them. Demons nowadays got no sense of pride, no sense of history."

"There still a lot of them around in London?" asked Ash.

Monty snorted. "Working for those big banks in Canary Wharf."

Ash laughed. "There's profit in misery." It was the Savage family motto.

Monty put on a pair of trousers and a jacket. Then he scooped up his bowler hat and tapped it into place and sighed with satisfaction. "Now, to business."

Ash looked at the demon. This guy had stolen probably the most heavily guarded items in the entire country? He looked more like the kind of bloke you'd find on a street corner selling knock-off perfume. "How did you do it?"

"Ah, sir, we have our professional secrets."

Khan growled. Monty gulped. "Well, if you really want to know. The sewers."

"Sewers? The drainpipes? Wouldn't they have grilles and bars to prevent that sort of thing?"

"You're a very clever lad, if I may say so. That's what I've always said, brains always triumph over brawn." Monty gave Khan a look of superior disdain. "The sewer defences are designed to prevent human-sized infiltration. Why, half my family lives down there. It was just a matter of time before we worked out which set of pipes led where."

Parvati smiled, maybe with just a touch of admiration. "So you just crawled into the room?"

"I won't say it was that simple, but fundamentally, yes, that's exactly what I did. The guard went out for a minute to answer a call of nature. I clamped the diamond in my teeth, which is harder than it sounds, then dived back down the drain. Four hours it took me to get back. Almost drowned in a sea of—"

"Yes, we've heard enough," said Khan. He uncurled his claws, holding out his palm. "Give us the Koh-i-noor."

Monty looked from Khan, to Parvati, and finally to Ash. "Now let's not be hasty. Surely we can come to some arrangement?"

Parvati's eyes narrowed and a soft, dangerous hiss slipped from between her lips. She sat on the edge of the table, quite still – but in the stillness was a lethal pause. Beside her stood Khan, his predatory eyes on the rat. His claws clicked and clicked with anticipation, about to take feline-rodent relations to their usual bloody conclusion. This was a glimpse into the demon heart of Parvati, and Ash wasn't sure he liked it. His friends were dangerous people.

And what does that make me?

Monty put his hand to his throat and backed away. "A teeny-tiny arrangement?" He swallowed and sweat dripped off his long nose. "Fine. Have it your way." He went to an old cathode ray-style TV in the corner. He unscrewed the back with his nail. "You have the diamond and we're even, right?"

"We'll see," said Parvati.

The back cover fell off and Monty searched inside, coming out with a small brown cardboard box. Parvati took it off him and opened it up.

The diamond caught every speck of light and amplified it within the countless facets on its surface. According to Indian legend all diamonds had their own sort of life, and seeing the Koh-i-noor glowing within the dingy room, Ash believed it. There was power, ancient and even malevolent, within its flawless heart. Rumoured to be cursed, it was said that he who possessed it would hold all the treasures of the world, and all its miseries.

Ash turned to Monty. "Has anyone else made an offer for this?"

Monty's eyebrows rose. "What do you mean?"

Ash's voice dropped with cold anger. "Did Savage want it?"

"Easy, Ash, I'll deal with this," said Parvati.

"Oh my God." Monty backed away. "You're Ash Mistry, aren't you? The Kali-aastra?" There was true, deep fear in Monty's voice. He cringed in the corner, eyes wide and breath coming in desperate pants.

Rakshasas died, like everyone else. But unlike humans, the demons were reincarnated with their memories and powers intact. It might take a few years for them to remember everything, but they didn't fear death the way mortals did.

Yet they feared Kali, the goddess of death and destruction. She was true annihilation. The end of existence. If a demon was killed by Kali or her weapon, there was no coming back. Ever.

And Ash was exactly that, the weapon of Kali.

Monty seemed to shrink. "Yes. He did. Savage wanted it."

"We've got company," interrupted Khan. He was peering through the curtains at the main street. Ash joined him.

A large white Humvee had rolled up on to the kerb, and Ash watched as a tawny-haired woman in white stepped out. Jackie, Savage's right-hand woman. She was a jackal rakshasa and one of the two directly responsible for killing his uncle and aunt. Three men also got out of the big car, rakshasas for sure, but no one he recognised. With his enhanced senses, he knew Savage wasn't in the car.

Ash gripped the curtain. He wanted to tear it off and leap down and fight them. Kill them. The power inside of him stirred and swelled, urging him on.

"Not now, Ash," warned Parvati. "We don't want to give Savage any warning."

Ash spun round and grabbed Monty. "Where is he?"

"I don't know, honestly!"

Three points of light along Monty's neck, two on the left, one at the base of his throat. A couple on either side of his head. Activating his knowledge of the kill points, of *Marma Adi*, was getting easier and easier. Ash tightened his right fist. Glowering at the petrified rat, he whispered. "I am going to count to three. Then, if the answer isn't the one I want, I will put my knuckles through what little brain you have. One…"

"Kolkata! He's in Kolkata!" Monty's gaze widened and his tail twitched in panic. "I only spoke to him today – check the area code on the mobile phone if you don't believe me.

He told me he was sending his servants over with the cash. It's true!"

"Where in Kolkata?" asked Parvati.

"Two…"

"Somewhere out of the Savage Foundation. That's all I know, I swear!"

The doorbell below rang.

"Well?" asked Khan. "Let's kill him and be gone."

"No, you promised," muttered Monty. "Please, I won't tell them anything."

Parvati sighed. "Sorry, but we know that's not true, don't we?" She looked at Ash. "Do you want to do it or shall I?"

Kali destroyed rakshasas. It was her holy duty. It was Ash's duty to serve her. Killing this rat demon was holy work. Ash would be cleansing the world. The desire to kill was like a fever, filling his head and heart. The black, swirling darkness urged him to do it: it struggled to take control of his body, to take over and then destroy.

But what would he become if he let that happen?

"No," Ash said. He wasn't going to kill anyone, even a demon, just because it was convenient. "Leave him." It was hard to make his fingers release their grip, but he did it. Suddenly he felt exhausted, soul-weary. It had taken all his willpower to hold the darkness back, and the effort had drained him down to almost nothing. His senses dulled and he could feel the superhuman strength fading. The Kali-aastra was withdrawing its power. He turned and tapped Monty's nose to get the rat's attention. "But see those other rakshasas outside, the ones Savage sent? Well, I've met Jackie before, and she'll be disappointed you don't have the Koh-i-noor waiting for her. If I were you, I'd find a hole and bury myself deep down inside it for a year or two."

The doorbell rang again, and this time it was followed by banging. Monty chewed his lip, glancing at the door and then at them. Then he threw off his hat and wriggled. Limbs shrank and hair burst out over his skin in random patches. His nose stretched and whiskers sprouted on either side of the pink flesh. A moment later a rat stood on the dirty carpet. It stuck out its tongue and blew a faint, squeaking raspberry, then darted through a gap in the baseboard.

Khan leaped out of the bathroom window and hit the ground easily and silently. Jackie and Savage's other demons had disappeared into the building. Parvati somersaulted through the air, bouncing on the opposite wall before landing without stirring even the discarded paper. Ash slid down the drainpipe and joined them, and a few minutes later they were out on Charing Cross Road.

Parvati took Khan's arm. "We'll double back now. See if we can follow Jackie and her cronies back to wherever they're based."

"I'll come," said Ash. Seeing the jackal rakshasa in the flesh had brought it all back, all the rage and pain of what had happened in India and how she'd killed his uncle and aunt and threatened Lucky. He wanted to deal with her.

Parvati shook her head. "No. She doesn't know you're here, Ash; let's keep it that way. She could lead us to Savage, and starting a fight will accomplish nothing. This isn't just about you."

❖

Ash understood. There was Lucks, his parents. He didn't want them getting involved. Keeping them safe was what mattered.

Khan backed away, leaving them alone. Parvati patted the lump of diamond in her pocket. "We did good, Ash."

"You're going already?"

"The sooner I get the Koh-i-noor away, the better." She kissed him on the cheek lightly. It was barely a touch and over almost immediately.

It didn't feel like enough.

"Parvati…"

She smiled. "It was good seeing you again, Ash. You look after yourself."

She crossed the road to where Khan waited, and then the two of them disappeared into the London fog.

Chapter Eight

"Where on earth have you been?" asked Josh as Ash came through the park gates. "It's almost nine."

"You're lucky I'm here at all." Ash waved over his shoulder. "Errands to run." He'd planned to catch the bus back, but some accident due to the fog had the traffic at a standstill. He'd ended up walking all the way.

"Well, it's been an epic waste of time so far," muttered Akbar through the scarf that covered half his face. He stood, cold, shivering and miserable in his duffel coat. "We're only here because of you, you know that?"

An impenetrable fog now covered London, hiding everything beyond three metres away. It was like being lost in a world of ghosts.

Despite the weather, the fireworks display was going ahead. There was a whoosh in the darkness and some muffled burst from *somewhere*, but all you could see was dense mist, no colours and certainly no firework explosions.

"Is anyone else here?" Ash asked.

Josh shrugged. "This is the most unbanging Guy Fawkes Night ever."

Small groups of spectators drifted in and out of the mists. Most were families with small kids waving their sparklers, but Ash recognised a few people from school.

"What's that?" He could hear something, a distant, dull roar.

"Up ahead." Josh pointed.

Through the haze of mist and smoke moved a blurry orange glow. As Ash came towards it, flickers of raw heat cut through the icy night air. Gloomy silhouettes began to solidify around them, ghosts emerging from the mist.

Ash stopped at the rope barrier.

The bonfire raged against the smothering fog. A tower of wooden debris blazed, over fifteen metres tall, the flames intense and rising twice as high. Even at the perimeter ring, a good eleven or twelve metres from the bonfire, the heat made Ash's skin flushed and sweaty. Monstrous clouds of smoke rose into the sky and millions of tiny, glowing embers swirled and danced like hellish imps in the fire-born draughts.

But the light the bonfire cast out did not extend much further than the rope ring. Beyond, the darkness ruled, crowding around the living fire, waiting for the flames to go out so it could claim everything for itself. Oblivion.

"Did you... did you see Gemma around?" Ash said.

Josh slapped his forehead. "I knew there was something else. Yeah, she's been looking for you all evening."

"Where is she?"

"No idea. Could have gone home by now."

Great. He didn't have her mobile phone number.

There was another pointless, invisible explosion as some fireworks went off. The crowd gave an ironic, half-hearted cheer.

A cold wind rippled through and the flames swayed. The radiant heat warmed only what faced the flames; Ash's back felt the chill.

"I'm getting a burger — want one?" asked Josh.

"I'll come with you," said Ash.

Dulwich Park had a small food hall attached to it, and tonight there would be burgers, baked potatoes and drinks sold to the shivering crowd. As they made their way closer to the hall, the number of people increased. It seemed everyone was more interested in the food and drink than the fireworks display.

Ash smelled the crisp odour of burning meat and heard the sizzle of onions, his mouth watering. He weaved his way through the crowd, checking his pockets for cash.

"Hiya, Ash."

Gemma grinned at him, stamping her feet to keep some circulation going. Her hands were stuffed deep into her jeans pockets and she had pulled her bobble hat low over her eyebrows.

She was here. Ash smiled back. The world seemed a brighter, happier place.

"Hi," he said. "You look frozen."

"It's not too bad by the bonfire, but this jumper's about as thick as tissue." She gestured to the hall. "Jack's gone off to get some food."

"So, Jack's still around." Now the world seemed much darker and colder.

"We're not going out or anything," said Gemma. "But, y'know how it is..."

"No, not really."

"What's wrong?" asked Gemma. She seemed genuinely concerned. Why couldn't he have more friends like her? Instead he was hanging out with immortal assassins and demons. Maybe he needed to re-evaluate his New Year's resolutions.

Less demons.

More Gemma.

He blushed. "Er, I've been thinking I've got the wrong sort of friends."

"Tell me about it." Gemma smiled, but her teeth chattered.

Ash whipped off his coat, adjusting his T-shirt to hide the punch dagger sheathed across his back. "Put this on."

"No. You're only wearing a T-shirt. You need it more than me."

"Trust me. I don't feel the cold much."

She laughed, but accepted the coat.

"What's so funny?"

"You, Ash. I remember seeing you slogging around the sports fields on cross-country runs, looking as miserable as a human being could. Muddy up to your knees, soaking wet, in last place."

❖

"Always last. Yes, I remember those runs." Him last – Jack, as ever, first.

"But you kept on going. That was either incredibly stubborn or incredibly stupid."

"Probably equal amounts of both."

"But you stuck at it. I always thought that was great. Things never came that easy to you."

"Still don't."

Gemma's eyes narrowed. "That still true? You've changed a lot, Ash."

The way she said it made the hairs stand up on the back of his neck. Gemma spoke quietly, and her tone was edged with… what? *Interest.*

She put her hands in his. "You're right, you don't feel cold."

Gemma tightened her fingers round his. He looked into her eyes, and she didn't look away.

"Oh, Ash, I've been looking everywhere for you." Parvati was standing right next to him.

Ash couldn't believe it. "What are you doing here?"

Gemma dropped Ash's hand. "Who's this?"

Parvati ignored her. "We've got trouble."

Khan joined them. He looked Gemma up and down. "Namaste."

Parvati pulled Ash aside, but Gemma followed. Parvati spun round. "Will you go away?"

Gemma glared, but Ash spoke up. "It's OK, Gemma. I'll be back in a minute."

Parvati arched her eyebrow. It was sharp and elegant and

designed to be arched. "This is Gemma? The female you want to mate with?"

"What?" said Ash.

"What?" said Gemma.

Parvati continued. "You're not familiar with the term? Procreate? Make babies with?"

Why did the gods have it in for him? Ash turned to Gemma. "I won't be long."

"Fine. Take as long as you want," snapped Gemma before storming off.

"So that was Gemma?" asked Khan, grinning like a tiger having just spotted a limp deer. "Tasty."

"Leave her alone," said Ash. "I mean it."

Khan gave a melodramatic tremble. "I'm so scared."

How could tonight get any worse?

A high-pitched cackle rose out of the fog. It was brittle and cruel, and it descended into a hysterical laugh, echoing across the park. Children began to cry, and grown-ups stared around, bewildered and not a little frightened themselves.

That's how.

"Jackie," said Parvati. "I'm such a fool. She's tracked you."

Jackie's mad, demonic cry had haunted Ash's nights many months after returning from India. Now, hearing it again, he remembered the depth of fear he'd felt the first time he'd heard it.

"How?" Ash asked.

"Scent. She must have picked it up at Monty's." Then she looked at Ash again, frowning. "Where's your coat?"

❖

Oh my God. My coat.

Jackie was following Ash's scent.

Which was all over his favourite Sherlock Holmes coat.

Which Gemma was wearing.

Chapter Nine

"I've got to find Gemma," said Ash.

People screamed as savage snarls and howls erupted all around them. A black shadow raced through the fog, hideously large with a massive head and shoulders, charging in and out of the mist on four legs.

Ash looked at Parvati, and the old understanding was there. She nodded and disappeared into the fog. He looked around. Where was Gemma? Then he saw someone who might know.

"Jack!" He ran up to the boy, who was balancing a tray of burgers and Cokes. "Where's Gemma?"

"You've got some nerve," he snarled. "Gemma's mine and she's not interested in a freak like you." He dropped the tray and put up his fists. "Time I taught you a lesson."

"I so don't have time for this," said Ash.

The howl broke in. A giant dark shape raced towards them, its heavy paws slamming on the hard earth. Jack screamed and Ash pushed him behind him.

Kali's dark storm exploded within his soul, flooding him with supernatural energy. Ash roared and leaped.

He slammed into the beast. For a second he saw burning yellow eyes and long, crooked canines, a slavering tongue. The jaws widened.

Ash instinctively thrust his hand down the creature's throat. His fingers, locked into a spear-point, tore through the soft tissue, sliced open the lungs, and then tightened round the pulsing heart. He ripped it out before the jaws could close round his arm.

The monster was dead before it hit the ground. It crashed, rolled and came to a halt at the feet of the terrified Jack.

It was a huge hyena, more the size of a lion, with massive hunched shoulders and a misshapen head, snout fatter and shorter than a natural animal. Its pelt was bristling black and spotted and the claws long and curled. Blood spewed from its twitching jaws, washing the frozen earth.

Ash turned the pulsing sac of the monster's heart in his hand. It gave a feeble splutter as it discharged the last of its blood, then it stilled. He tossed it away.

"You were about to say something, Jack?"

Jack's legs shook as tears smeared his face. There was a wet stain running down his Levi's. "No... no... nothing."

"Good."

How many demons had Jackie brought with her? Ash remembered three others in the car, but here, lost in the fog,

❖

the sounds and cries and screams were all jumbled up and coming from everywhere. A rocket whizzed horizontally across the park, trailing bright multicoloured sparks and smoke. It vanished into the swirling grey fog and exploded somewhere among the trees.

Ash ran along the wreckage of the display frames. The large scaffolds holding hundreds of fireworks had been toppled over. The timers tripped, and dozens of Catherine wheels spun like fiery Frisbees across the ground. Missiles shot off in random directions or just exploded on their frames, setting the surrounding grass and nearby trees alight with rainbow-coloured flames.

A small kid wandered alone, separated from his parents. He still held his sparkler, waving it dumbly while tears rolled down his fat cheeks. Then the fog rolled over him and he was gone. How could it have gone so wrong so quickly?

Where was Gemma?

Ash stared at the horrified faces of the people screaming and running in blind panic. Vaporous smog lay over the chaos. Then a bellowing roar shook the fog, making it tremble and ripple outward.

Ash ran towards the source of the ripples.

A tiger was fighting a huge dire hyena. A grotesque hunch-backed jackal stalked the outer ring of the battle, and behind them the towering bonfire tottered. The wooden struts cracked and the structure swayed from side to side.

And behind the tiger stood Gemma.

She was staring around madly for an escape route, but

finding none. Behind her was the inferno, and before her were the rakshasas.

Dozens of wounds covered the tiger – *Khan* – some deep and oozing thick dark blood.

Khan saw Ash.

And so did Jackie.

The tiger charged the hyena, tearing into it. Khan forced the demon back, trying to open up a path between Ash and Gemma.

But Jackie was quicker.

She sprang a dozen metres in an instant, even as Ash sprinted towards Gemma. Gemma screamed and stumbled back, ignoring the bonfire right behind her, more terrified of the slavering jaws of the demon than the unbearable heat.

"Gemma!" Ash screamed as a barrage of rockets shot over his head.

Like a thunderstorm, the fireworks smashed into the heart of the bonfire. Ash flung his arm over his eyes as the gunpowder exploded with a blinding white flash. He staggered back, dazed, as more and more firecrackers followed the smoky trail into the giant, blazing tower.

Jackie threw Gemma to the ground and stood over the cowering girl, her face a grotesque, unnatural blend of human and beast, long slavering jaws with human lips and eyes.

Parvati ran up to Ash. Ash stepped forward, but Jackie brought her fangs close to Gemma's throat. Gemma lay still and petrified.

"The Koh-i-noor, and the girl lives," Jackie growled. Spittle dripped off her canines on to Gemma's face.

❖

They were maybe ten metres apart, though it was hard to tell with the fog and smoke. Jackie's fangs were a centimetre from Gemma's bare neck. There was no way he'd make it.

Jackie's eyes blazed and her fur shivered across her shoulders. "The diamond, boy."

They had no choice. "Give it to her, Parvati."

"No."

"Give it to her!"

Parvati stepped back. "No." Her cold gaze didn't shift from the jackal rakshasa.

Ash reached to the back of his T-shirt, moving his hand ever so slowly. It was dark, the distance long, and the katar wasn't designed for throwing, but it was the only chance he had.

"Parvati, for God's sake…"

"No!"

Jackie howled and—

Ash grabbed the katar and hurled it at the rakshasa.

Gemma screamed as Jackie sank her fangs into her neck. She beat the demon with her fists, struggling under the massive, hairy monster. The katar punched into Jackie's shoulder, and Jackie released her to howl again. She stumbled back, and Ash charged.

The rakshasa shook herself, trying to dislodge the katar wedged just below her lower neck. The blade refused to shift, so finally Jackie leaped into the fog, fangs and fur soaked with blood, her mad, howling laughter echoing in her wake, Parvati sprinted after her.

Ash fell to his knees beside Gemma.

❖

"Gemma?"

Oh God, her neck was covered in blood. He put his hands on the wound, feeling the muscles quivering and the breath hissing from her ruined throat, raising red bubbles that spluttered and popped.

"Someone get an ambulance!" he screamed. "Please!"

Gemma grabbed hold of his arm. She dug her fingers into his skin, hanging on to him as if she was sinking into a dark sea, focusing on him with frightening intensity. She tried to speak, but nothing came out.

The lights of death were spreading over her, multiplying second by second. She looked radiant, covered in gold, bright as an angel.

"Gemma, Gemma..."

Ash trembled as he began to absorb Gemma's death energies.

"No. No."

He wanted to say more, to tell her it was OK, that she had to be brave and she would come back, but the words were bitter and dead on his tongue. This was Gemma and they'd played together since nursery school. Her sister was Lucky's best friend. He'd seen her almost every day of his life, and this was about to be her last.

Each bead of sweat on her shone brighter than any diamond, her skin pale as the most perfect marble. Each breath smelled sweeter than any rose. Gemma's grip weakened. Her eyes, ever changing in colour, were wide and staring, her pupils swelling until they almost consumed her irises.

❖

Ash heard sirens in the distance.

"Just hang on, Gemma. Hang on."

Heat burst within him, straight into his heart and flooding every atom of his being. The world shook around him as waves of energy pounded him, filling him with more and more power.

This was a Great Death.

Chapter Ten

Ash replayed the last moments of Gemma's life a thousand times, a hundred thousand times over the next few days. From the moment he woke, it haunted him. A fraction quicker, a centimetre truer with his aim, and it would have all been different.

He walked down the dark, lamplit street, head down and lost in memory.

The ambulance came, too late, and then the police found Ash covered in blood with a dead girl in his arms. Jack had been hysterical, shouting about him, and there were witnesses saying Ash had been with Gemma and then there'd been some argument with another girl. All these small, random details. A punch dagger had been found, smeared with blood, and the sheath strapped to his belt fitted the blade perfectly. So the police and half the school added two and two and got five.

❖

It had been a dark, lonely night in the police station before the fog had cleared in the morning and the police found a dead hyena. The wounds on Gemma proved to be from an animal bite — an escaped animal from some zoo, the police thought — and Ash finally went home with his parents.

Their silence had been awful. Lucky had looked at him with such cold hatred and disgust that though she had not said a word, he knew exactly what she was thinking. Gemma was dead because of him.

And she was right.

If only he'd stayed on the bus instead of walking back, Jackie wouldn't have been able to follow him. If only he hadn't given Gemma his coat. If only he'd been closer he would have put the blade in Jackie's skull instead of her shoulder. If only he'd been quicker. If only he'd been faster, stronger, better.

If only...

Did Jackie bite Gemma before he'd thrown the katar, or after?

Why had Parvati said "No" when Jackie had demanded the diamond?

Why?

He stared at his left hand, at the small scar on his thumb. If it would do any good, he'd cut it off right now. But the Kali-aastra was all of him, and he was it. There was nothing heroic about what he'd become. Quite the opposite. He was a curse. Elaine had predicted this would happen. Someone had ended up dead, and he was so very sorry.

But what gripped his heart with fear was the certainty that this would never end. Who would be next? His parents? His other friends? Lucky?

❖

Gemma's death had made him more powerful, and he hated himself for it. Parvati had explained, ages ago it seemed, that the more significant the death, the more power Ash gained. He hadn't realised what she meant until Gemma's energies had filled him: a Great Death. His strength, speed, agility and senses had crept further up the scale, leaving 'human' further behind. The shock of it left him dazed, far more than he'd expected.

Had his presence accelerated Gemma's death, even? Kali was a greedy, blood-drinking goddess. Had the aastra, sensing death, drawn it out? He felt sick to his guts whenever he heard his parents talking downstairs and Lucky crying. He picked up the looks and the fear from the other kids in class. His supernaturally acute hearing gathered the whispers and the quiet mutterings as he passed. The rumours about that awful night infected all of West Dulwich High.

He missed seeing her in class. Her chair remained empty as if she'd just got up, still warm with her presence so he could fool himself, even just for a second, Gemma was still there. Instead the shadows of the trees outside passed over it as the sun, winter low, crossed the sky east to west. How he wished he could make the shadows reverse their path.

Ash stared at his shadow now as it rose up against Josh's front door. He stood there, outside his best friend's house, and raised his fist. He could hear the others inside. There was Akbar's snorting laugh, and he could smell Sean's after-shave, and that they had salt and vinegar crisps out, that there was hot chocolate brewing and their takeaway pizza had cheese, olives and anchovies on it, plus some curry powder.

❖

Josh burped after a mouthful of Sprite. Sean, Josh and Akbar. His closest, oldest friends who'd known him for years and years. Ash had been just like them, and right now that was all he wanted. To be like them again. Normal, and none of this supernatural, superhuman crap.

Dice fell on the kitchen table and pencils scratched on notepaper. Akbar said something about the sorcerer casting a firestorm spell at the manticore. The game of *Dungeons and Dragons* was in full swing. Ash knocked.

Josh's laugh carried all the way to the door until he opened it and saw Ash. Then it froze on his face as he stood there, staring at him. He opened his mouth, but it took a few attempts before words came out. "Ash?"

He's scared.

Josh's heartbeat accelerated, the rapid thumping as loud to Ash as a circus drum. Sweat formed across his forehead and upper lip, and the colour faded from his face. His breath was short, shallow and panicky; even his hand trembled on the door handle.

He's not scared, he's terrified. Of me.

Ash forced a smile, even though inside his heart was tearing in two. "It's Tuesday. 'The Catacombs of Doom', remember?"

Josh's gaze shifted down to his feet. "Oh, right. It's just… we didn't think you'd come."

"I'm here now."

There was no move to let Ash in. But Josh's heart rate was over a hundred beats per minute. He looked up at Ash, biting his lower lip. He was struggling to speak, to say something, but couldn't.

❖

Ash's gaze darkened. Josh shouldn't be treating him like this. "You going to let me in or what?"

"Or what, Ash? What are you going to do if I don't?"

"What?"

"What are you going to do?"

For a second, just a second, Ash let his anger, his rejection, show. He wanted to push past. He could do it so easily. Josh couldn't stop him, he was just a human. How dare Josh judge him, what right did he have? Didn't he know what Ash had done? Josh was pathetic. Ash raised his hand and—

Stepped back.

The look on Josh's face said it all. The fear practically dripped off him. He trembled. Ash lowered his hand, wishing he could take that last moment back. He smiled at Josh, but the smile was too harsh, too much like a grinning dead man.

"Look, Josh, there's nothing to be afraid of. You know me."

"Do I? Really?"

He couldn't believe it. Did Josh think he'd killed Gemma? How could he? "I've done nothing wrong, Josh. You have to believe me. I wouldn't hurt anyone. Christ, Josh, this is me."

"I saw you, Ash. I *saw* you." Josh winced and put his hand over his face. "I'm still not sure I believe it, but I saw what you did at the park the night Gemma died."

"And what was that?" asked Ash coldly. "You saw what, exactly?"

"I saw you push Jack out of the way and shove your arm down the throat of some insane monster. I saw you rip its heart out like you were picking apples from a tree. You moved

83

❖

so fast that you practically blurred. No one can move that fast. Not Usain Bolt pumped with rocket fuel. Nobody. It was mad, but I went over to the monster and saw it was real. Jack was screaming and crying and I didn't know what was going on, but there was some giant dead dog in the grass and beside it was its torn-out heart."

"It wasn't like—"

"I am not an idiot, Ash." Josh looked back at him, sad and lost. "Then I saw you with Gemma. With that thing with a human face and jackal's body. With a girl with scales and a forked tongue. I watched you throw the knife and watched you as Gemma died. I called the ambulance, did you know that?"

"Thanks." What else could he say? Deny it? Make his friend think he was insane to believe in monsters?

No, Josh believed. He had one standing right here in front of him.

"What are you, Ash?"

"I really don't know any more."

"I think you'd better go."

Ash looked up at his mate. "You know I wouldn't let anything happen to you. Not to you or the other guys."

"Is that what you told Gemma?"

And Josh closed the door.

Chapter Eleven

shoka gazes down the hill. A few fires still burn within the village, edging out the cold desert night. Somewhere in the darkness a bullock grunts and a baby cries.

A dozen or so squat mud-brick dwellings. A fenced-off corral for the cattle. Chickens squawking within the sheds. Fields with dried-out gullies and meagre crops. To the north squat the domed grain stores. How many such villages has he visited? How many fires has he lit? How many cries has he silenced?

Not enough. Not yet.

His band swells with each passing victory. Soon it will be an army. For Ashoka has dreams beyond village raids. This is how kingdoms begin.

He thinks about his father, a king, and his older brothers. They have grand palaces and dine off gold plates while he haunts the desert, eating with his band of brigands. His father laughed when Ashoka demanded his crown. How often was he laughed at, dismissed? Now they laugh no longer. They scream. If he cannot have their respect and love, he will have their fear.

Soon, the old palace will echo with wailing women, *he thinks.* That crown, and others, will be mine. *He wonders how the old man sleeps, knowing his son is out here, carving out a kingdom of his own.*

His men wait impatiently, like dogs eager for the hunt. They check their weapons, adjust their armour, ensuring helmets are fixed and there are no loose straps. But Ashoka expects little resistance. This will not be a battle — not against unarmed, unsuspecting villagers. This will be a slaughter.

His horse whinnies and stomps its hoof; it senses the coming bloodletting. Ashoka pats its thick neck. He himself wears a mail coat over his silk tunic and heavy cotton pantaloons. His boots, stiff leather, creak in the stirrups. A bright red sash lies across his waist, a jewelled dagger tucked into the cloth. Hanging from his saddle is his sword, a single-edged talwar with a gold-bound hilt. Which chieftain, which prince, did he slay to possess it? He cannot remember; there have been so many.

The jangle of reins and the snort of another steed snaps his attention back to his men.

A sleek mare with a high arching neck and white mane bound with silver and silk trots up beside him. The rider is clad in scales, and the sabre on her hip is sheathed in green crocodile skin. She doffs her helmet, and her emerald eyes shine in the moonlight.

"The men are ready," she says.

Ashoka observes her. She leans over the pommel, waiting in anticipation, her forked tongue flicking along her fangs. Her cobra's eyes do not lower; she defies where others would bow and kneel. Perhaps that is why she has risen so rapidly in his command. And why should she bow? Is she not royalty herself? Was not her father a great king?

86

❖

"You have done well," he says.

"My lord." She bows, almost. "I am but your servant."

"Ha! Servant? I doubt anyone could command you. You are terror made flesh, Parvati."

She smiles, a rare thing, then looks down the slope. "Why this particular village?"

"Their landlord defies me. He refuses to pay tribute and so must be punished."

"Shall I send a detachment to raid the stores?" She points towards the row of round huts some distance away. "They will be full of grain this time of year."

"No. Burn them. The message will be clear. Defy me and you will be annihilated."

"And the captives?"

"What captives?" Ashoka draws his own sword. "I want no survivors."

"Slaves could be sold, my lord."

Ashoka stands up in his stirrups and turns to his warriors. "Listen to me," he shouts. He sweeps the blade down towards the village. "You are my jackals. We feed on blood and the dead. No survivors. Kill them all!"

Howls fill the night. Then the line of horsemen descends the slope, drawing their weapons, and suddenly the night is filled with the thunder of hooves and battle cries. The moon shines on swords and spears and axes, each one sharp and notched with heavy use. Chariots — light wicker contraptions drawn by pairs of steeds — rattle and bounce over the uneven, rocky terrain. A driver weaves his team through a gap between two sandstone boulders as his passenger nocks an arrow. The cavalry formation fragments as each man races his companion, eager to be the first to kill. Ashoka whips his horse and it froths at the bit, neighing with savage delight.

❖

He grins and his heart soars, a passion too primitive for words, so he merely howls as the wind rushes in his ears.

The village stirs. Men stumble from their doors, bewildered and still half asleep. A dog races up to him, but is crushed under the hooves of his horse. The steed vaults over the low defensive wall and Ashoka catches the open-mouthed shock of a villager's face before he drives the tip of his sword into it. He twists his wrist and the sword tears free. He does not even turn to look back.

Women run out, clutching screaming children and babies in their arms. They flee into the darkness. They will not escape. With a nod, three of his horsemen break off in pursuit.

He sees Parvati leap from her steed as it takes a spear in its chest. She turns in the air and her sword flashes. A head leaps off a pair of shoulders, trailing a ribbon of blood. She has not yet touched the ground. Her eyes burn with demonic light. Men fall beneath her blade like wheat beneath a reaper's scythe. She does what she does best: end men's lives.

Ashoka drops from his horse and sweeps his weapon across a man's throat without pause. He rams his shield into the face of another as he charges into the melee.

A hammer slams into his wrist knocking his sword away. He spins and sees a huge, oak-chested man wielding a heavy wooden mattock. The man is covered in minor cuts, but swings the hammer with bone-shattering power. A soldier runs to Ashoka's defence, then collapses as a single blow flattens his skull.

Ashoka discards his shield and leaps at the villager. Both fall and scrabble in the blood-soaked dust. He digs his fingers into the man's neck, squeezing—

"Ash!"

Ash squeezes the throat of his enemy as other soldiers grab his arms to try and haul him back. *The big, fat villager's face turns red and his eyes bulge.*

"Ash!" a girl screamed as she hung on to his arm. She wept and screamed again. *Is she the man's daughter? She is nothing. She is—*

"Lucky?"

Ash dropped his grip and his dad gasped. There was a bruise over his cheek and he lay there, coughing and clutching his ribs. Had Ash punched him?

"Oh God, Dad, I'm so sorry."

His mum switched on the light. Ash's bedroom was wrecked. His books had been thrown everywhere, the chair legs were snapped, and there was a fist-sized hole in the cupboard door.

Had he done that in his sleep? Ash stumbled back on to his bed. "I'm so sorry."

But no one listened. Mum was kneeling with Lucky beside Dad as his father struggled to breathe. Purple finger marks surrounded his neck.

Ash stared at his family and met Lucky's gaze. She stared back at him with horror and disgust. Her eyes were red with tears, but her face was hard and pale. All she could do was shake her head.

He couldn't bear to look. Instead he covered his face with his hands and sank down with a groan. What was happening to him?

Chapter Twelve

"Ash?" His mum tapped his door. "There's a friend to see you."

"I don't want to see anyone."

"Ash, I think—"

"I said I don't want to see anyone!"

The door opened. He didn't need to turn to know exactly who it was. Ash remained where he was, looking at the wall, in the dark, his back to the door. "I especially don't want to see you, Parvati."

The light came on. Ash slowly swivelled round.

Parvati closed the door, sat down on the corner of his unmade bed and, taking off her glasses, looked around.

"Is that dent meant to be in the door?" she asked.

The worst of the damage had been fixed or tidied away. Ash had straightened up the shelves and, with his dad, repaired the broken table and replaced the chair. He'd talked to his parents about it and they'd put it down to the trauma of Gemma's death. His dad now wore a cravat to hide the bruises.

"What do you want?" Ash snapped.

"To see how you're doing. We've not spoken since that night your friend died."

"Since you let her die, you mean."

When Parvati didn't respond, Ash peered at her. She'd changed. Her hair was a mess – dried out, brittle and knotted – and her skin, usually smooth and clear, bore lines and a sickly yellow tinge.

"You're ill," Ash said. "I didn't know demons got ill."

She smiled weakly. "Everyone gets ill."

"And what's happened to your eyes? The whites have completely gone." The green filled her entire socket, utterly serpentine. The pupils dilated in the semi-darkness to huge black discs.

"My demon heritage grows stronger as I age. The eyes are just the beginning. Sometimes it's hard to remember that I'm human at all."

"I'm sure I don't care." Ash stood up and walked to the door. "Well, you've seen me. You can go."

"Ash..."

"She's dead because of you," he said ever so quietly. It had to be quiet because if he let out what was really inside, he'd tear down the house. "You could have saved her."

"You think Jackie would have let her go?" Parvati looked up at him. "She would have killed her whatever we did."

"Why? Because rakshasas have no honour? Because they can't be trusted?" He opened the door for her. "You should know."

Parvati stood up. "What's the point? You're just a foolish boy. You have no idea what's at stake. You think some mortal girl's important in this? Grow up, Ash."

Ash grabbed Parvati round her throat and slammed her against the wall. His fist went back, tightened so his knuckles were white and shaking with rage.

Parvati gazed back at him without emotion. But her fangs were fully extended, each one coated with her fatal venom. This close, her large, serpentine eyes dominated her face and the curving green scales shimmered. "You want to kill me, Ash? Is that it?"

Kill the rakshasa. Wasn't that his duty? Wasn't that his reason for existing?

"You are a monster," he said, looking at her as if for the first time. "How could I have been so blind?"

"You want me to say I'm sorry?" Parvati hissed. "Beg for forgiveness? Sit in the dark and feel sorry for myself? Do you know who I am?" She shoved Ash back. "I am the daughter of Ravana. I do not beg."

She looked at him, the defiance fading with a sigh. "I'm not sorry for what I did, though I am sorry your friend is dead." Parvati reached out to touch him, then stopped herself. "But do you think you're the only one who's suffered? I've lost friends, people more than friends, so many that I can't even begin to remember them all. But each one, Ash, each one left a hole here." She pointed at her heart. "That's the true curse of immortality. Each success is so fleeting you wonder why you bother, yet each failure weighs down your soul with lead. That's why rakshasas are such monsters. We must cut out that part that feels. Better to be cold, hard, become immune to pain."

Ash lowered his fist. What was he doing? In spite of Gemma, Parvati was the closest friend he had. He owed her his life. "I just wish there was something I could do," said Ash. "Gemma didn't deserve to die."

"Ash—"

Of course. It was so obvious. "I came back from the dead. Why not Gemma? There has to be a way."

Parvati's gaze darkened. "Kali brought you back. She reawakened your heart." Her words came out cold and hard. "What you're talking about is something only gods can do. And it is a decision best left to them. Who is worthy, who is not."

"Are you saying Gemma's not worthy?"

"What I'm saying is who are we to choose?"

"Gemma is worthy. She was a good person."

Parvati's response, a bitter laugh, stabbed him deep. "Oh, I did not realise you could see into people's souls and know whether they are good or evil. You *have* become powerful."

"That's not what I mean and you know it."

"Please, Ash…" It was almost a plea. "The girl you knew is gone."

Now the thought was in his head he couldn't let it go. Was there some way to fix the mistakes of the past? Rishi would have known what was possible and what was not. Get Gemma back. A vain delusion or a real hope? His head told him one thing, his heart another. Ash looked at Parvati as she inspected

❖

elves. Why wouldn't she want Gemma to return?

..e right? Did Parvati have her own agenda?

..be stupid. If you can't trust Parvati, then who can you trust?

_.._ fell back on to his bed. "Parvati, I don't know what's going on."

Parvati's fingers paused over a history book, one Ash knew well: _The Life of Ashoka_, a biography of the first emperor of India. The West might have Alexander the Great, but as far as Ash was concerned, no one came close to Ashoka, a violent brigand who'd ended up ruling one of the largest empires of the ancient world, back in the third century BC. Parvati tapped the book, her brow knotted, then picked another one off the shelf.

The _Ramayana_. What else?

She smirked. "They've given him ten heads, as usual."

It was an old children's book. The cover was torn and scribbled on, but standing in the centre was Ravana, the demon king. Parvati's dad. He was resplendent in golden armour and had, indeed, ten heads, all glaring in red-faced fury. Prince Rama, the hero, stood to the side, his skin blue, arrow nocked in his bow. The arrow had flames surrounding it.

A magic arrow to destroy the demon king. An aastra.

Ash remembered the smell of the battlefield, the tension in the bowstring as he drew the arrow back and the fury in Ravana's gaze. The memories were so fresh and so close he could almost reach out and touch them.

Parvati had talked about meeting him in previous incarnations. The thought still freaked him out. She said he was an Eternal Warrior, destined to be reborn again and again. How many people had he been? Rama? Ashoka? Who else? He'd visited museums and looked at the ancient armour and the rusting weapons in the glass cabinets, and his hands had curled, remembering how they'd once held axes and swords and spears and shields. The weight of armour, the narrow, restricted view through a helmet. He'd seen cities burn; he'd known little peace. A perpetual state of war. That was his destiny. But it had never been as vivid as the memory of Ashoka last night. He looked at the demon girl. "I need your help." He rubbed his temples. "I had a dream last night. I was the original Ashoka, the one who became emperor of India. I dreamed I was fighting and I woke up just as I was about to kill my dad."

"The past lives are taking control? Rishi warned me this might happen. The Kali-aastra, it's sustained by violence and death. It wants more power, and your rage, your guilt, will only feed it."

"How can I stop it?"

Parvati smiled softly and sat down beside him. "I wish I knew, Ash, I really do. But that was something Rishi was meant to teach you."

"Isn't there anyone else?"

Her eyelids lowered and a hiss escaped her. She frowned. "No."

She was lying, he knew it. Why? "Are you sure? Elaine said—"

"I'm sure she did, but Elaine's no Rishi. There was no one like him."

"Then what am I going to do?"

"It's my fault. I came back into your life and stirred everything up. That's why I'm here, Ash. To tell you that I'm going

❖

and I won't be coming back. The further away I am, the better for both of us."

"You're going after Savage?"

Parvati raised her hand to her chest and Ash noticed a lump, a pouch, under her tunic. "He'll come after the Koh-i-noor." She laughed. "Like a rat after cheese, my favourite type of prey."

"Savage is dangerous, Parvati."

"And so am I. Still, I won't be facing him alone."

"You've got Khan, right?"

"Yes, I have Khan. But I am also Ravana's daughter. All Savage knows ultimately came from my father. Either from the scrolls he stole from me, or from that night he resurrected Ravana. I've studied those scrolls and learned a few tricks, and they'd counter most of what Savage can throw at me."

"Like that thing you did with your eyes?" Back in Varanasi she'd almost succeeded in hypnotising him. That eerie emerald glow coming from her eyes wasn't easy to forget.

"Mesmerism. It's part of one of the sorceries, and we serpents are especially good at it."

"Maybe, but Savage is in another league, Parvati. Let me come." The thought was in his head and out of his mouth the same instant. But why not? "I can't stay here."

"Ash, they are your family. Your place is with them."

"No. Not when I'm like this. Don't you get it? I was this close to killing my own father. Bloody hell, if I'd used *Marma Adi*, he'd be dead. I can't stay around them."

"What about things like school?"

"You think I'll be missed? I reckon it'll be a lot easier for everyone if I'm gone for a few weeks. None of my friends talk to me and everyone whispers about me behind my back." There was even a display about Gemma at the school reception with a photo of her, cards and small gifts other pupils had left for her. She'd been popular. He glanced at his textbooks stacked up on the shelves over his desk. "And how can I concentrate on French verbs knowing Savage is out there? That Jackie's still around?"

"And going after Savage will help? No, it'll only make things worse. Killing Savage will not bring you peace, Ash, it'll only accelerate your descent into darkness. Don't give in to the Kali-aastra. Don't feed it with more death."

"There is no peace while Savage is alive."

"Let me deal with the Englishman," said Parvati.

"You've had two hundred years to deal with him and how far have you got? Nowhere."

Parvati bristled under the insult, but didn't rise to it. Maybe it was a bit below the belt, but Ash didn't care. He couldn't stay here where he might lose control. He'd been lucky that he'd snapped out of it before he'd done something terrible, and that his dad had come in first; he was big and could take it. What if it had been Lucky? He could have broken her neck. "I can't stay, Parvati. Not like this."

Parvati said nothing. Her lips were fixed in a thin line and her green eyes glistened. She didn't look very happy, but she nodded. "Fine. Come."

Ash stood up. Yes, this was for the best. He'd be safely away from his family and with Parvati; they'd deal with Savage.

An electric thrill ran up his spine at the thought of returning to India. He'd never been to the city of Kolkata, on the far eastern side of the subcontinent. He looked around his room. What should he pack? There was hardly anything he wanted to take.

His gaze fell on a small portrait he'd downloaded off the Web a couple of months ago. Lord Alexander Savage, wearing the uniform of the East India Company, his blue-eyed gaze cold and aloof. In his hand he held a bulbous poppy, symbol of the opium trade that had made part of the family fortune, and on a table in the background, in among the shadows, was a set of manacles. As well as trading in drugs, Savage had also been a slaver.

Drug dealer. Slave trader. Murderer and the most powerful sorcerer in the world. Ash was going to kill him.

For the first time since Gemma died, Ash smiled.

Chapter Thirteen

"You're a stupid idiot," said Lucky.

"It's got to be done, Lucks." Ash rolled up another pair of jeans and shoved them into his rucksack.

"You're going to get yourself killed."

"Being dead didn't stop me the first time."

Lucky hurled a pillow at him. "Don't joke about this, Ash!"

The pillow bounced off his head, but it was good that things were back to normal between them after the arctic coldness right after Gemma's death. That was the thing about families: no one could stay mad for long.

"If this works out, we'll be rid of Savage once and for all. I need to do this." He squeezed in a few of his T-shirts. "Gemma deserves revenge."

"Gemma's dead, Ash," Lucky said quietly. "I was at her funeral."

He hadn't been invited. Even though the police confirmed he had nothing to do with Gemma's death, he had her blood on his hands, literally. So Ash stayed away. Gemma's family had enough to deal with without him being there. "How was it?"

"How do you think? Sad."

Ash shoved some more clothes into his bag.

"Why don't you tell them the truth? Mum and Dad should know about the rakshasas."

"The truth?" said Ash. "Has knowing what's out there made it any easier for you?"

As soon as he said it, he wished he hadn't. Lucky's face drained of all colour and suddenly she looked very small, very frail and very frightened. She knew the truth better than most. Lucky had been captured by Lord Savage and held hostage by the rakshasas for days, knowing that any one of them would be happy to tear her to pieces. Lord Savage had promised her to them, and Ash remembered how Lucky had woken up screaming every night for weeks. Their mum and dad couldn't help. They said there were no such things as monsters, but they were so terribly wrong.

Ash took Lucky's hand. "I didn't know you still had those nightmares. You know I'd never let anyone hurt you."

Lucky bit her lip. "It's not the demons that frighten me."

"Oh? What then?"

She looked away from him, dropping her gaze. "It's not important."

"Tell me."

There was a deep, bone-weary sigh and then, looking anxiously at him, Lucky told him the truth. "It's you. You are in my nightmares."

"But I saved you."

"Ash, you came back from the dead. I saw what you were, how you looked. You punched straight through Mayar. You charged straight through his body. I saw you standing there, drenched in his blood, only it was your eyes…"

Ash stared at his sister. "You never said anything. Why didn't you—"

"They were so full of rage, I couldn't believe it was you. The blood was so black and slimy on you. You looked so gaunt, I could count the ribs and the bones through your skin. Ash, you have no idea what you were when you came back. Really, you don't."

More terrible than the monsters. He'd been warned that was what he might become as the Kali-aastra, but it broke something inside him to see the fear in Lucky's eyes. That horrific night had changed them both. He'd lost more than his life. Ash held his sister's hand. "I'm sorry, Lucks. I'll make it up to you."

"Then stay, Ash. Let Parvati deal with Savage."

"Parvati's my friend. I have to help her."

Lucky shook her head. "I don't like her, Ash. And I don't know if she's your friend at all."

"What d'you mean?"

"She let Gemma die. Can't you see that?"

He went to his drawer, half pulling it out before remembering his punch dagger had been confiscated by the police.

He'd get a replacement as soon as he landed in India. Suddenly he didn't want to be talking about any of this. "She explained. She couldn't risk Jackie getting the diamond."

"Would you have done the same? No, not in a million years." Lucky pulled him round so they were face to face. "When Savage wanted the Kali-aastra in exchange for me, you didn't hesitate."

"That was different." But Lucky's comment made him uncomfortable. Parvati had been willing to leave Lucky, to abandon her in Savage's fortress. Her lives had been lonely and surrounded by bloodshed. Did she have any real feelings towards anyone? How much of her was human and how much of her was demon? How could anyone be remotely normal having Ravana for a dad?

"What about Mum and Dad?" Lucky added. "They won't let you go. You're only fourteen. You can't just leave school and everything."

Ash frowned. "Parvati's taking care of that too."

"How?" Lucky's voice had more than fear in it.

He made a spiralling motion in front of his eyes. "One of her Jedi mind tricks."

"She's hypnotising them? To think what?"

"Do you remember Robert and Susan, Dad's old university friends?" Ash said. "The story is I'm too traumatised by Gemma's death to go to school, so I'm staying with them in Manchester. Just for a week or two. Until everything's sorted."

Lucky began to cry. Her little chin wrinkled up and she sat there, tears rolling down her face. "Don't go, Ash."

❖

He hugged her. "You look after Mum and Dad." Ash grabbed his rucksack. "It'll be fine. I promise."

"You can't promise those things," said Lucky.

Ash's mum squeezed him hard. "You say hello to Rob and Sue from us."

"You sure you want to take the train up, son? I could drive you." His dad checked the display on the station. The train was due in about three minutes.

Ash shook his head. "No, it'll be quicker by train. I'll be all right."

Lucky hadn't wanted to come. She said her goodbyes at home before running upstairs and crying.

Ash looked at his parents. Should he tell them the truth? Didn't they deserve to know? But then what? Even if he could persuade them to let him go, they'd spend every minute worrying.

There were only a few people at West Dulwich train station. Ash wore his winter coat and had his rucksack on. He wanted them to leave, but wanted them to stay too. When he said goodbye to them last summer, it had been different. Then, he and Lucky were staying with Uncle Vik and Aunt Anita, swapping one set of parents for another, almost. What was he getting himself into now? Hunting down demons, sorcerers and who knew what other weirdness?

The rails rattled as the train came into view. This was it.

Ash hugged his dad. "I'm going to miss you." That was all that he needed to say.

❖

"Call us when you get there, all right?" His mum wiped her face and gave him a smile. "All right?"

"I'll text. As often as possible."

Ash got on the train and waved to his mum and dad. He waved even when the doors closed and the train rolled off. He waved until he couldn't see the platform.

Then, five minutes later, he got off at the next stop, Herne Hill. The taxi was waiting. He nodded at Parvati and Khan, both in the back, then threw his rucksack in the boot. He pushed all thoughts of his parents and his sister and his home deep down and away. There would be no room for any of that from now on. From now on he was the Kali-aastra and nothing more.

It was time to kill.

Heathrow Airport was an hour's drive away. Parvati and Khan whispered to one another at the beginning, then fell into silence. Khan actually slept. Ash watched Parvati via the side mirror. She didn't look good. Her movements were sluggish and uncoordinated. Something was off – she'd looked ill in his room, but this was way worse. "What's wrong?"

She ran her tongue over her dry, cracked lips. "Just tired. It'll pass."

Ash gazed at her. What wasn't she telling him?

The taxi drove to the cargo terminal off the South Perimeter Road. Parvati handed some papers over to the guard, and a few minutes later they were in, rolling slowly along the road that ran towards the cargo bays. Sharp aircraft fumes soaked the air and washed the evening sky with bright

❖

reds and golds and oranges. The ground trembled as a British Airways jumbo jet landed on a distant runway, the engine noise, even from here, shaking the minicab.

"This is our lift," said Khan, pointing to a plane out on the tarmac. The taxi rolled up to it and they got out.

An old, four-propeller Dakota stood in front of one of the smaller hangars. A crown had been freshly painted on the side and underneath it were the words *Maharajah Air*. The passenger door opened and an Indian man stepped out. Plump and wearing a pair of aviator Ray-Bans, he adjusted his two-sizes-too-small captain's jacket as he gazed out across the tarmac. He stroked his moustache, softly twisting the tips.

"Jimmy?" said Ash.

The man smiled broadly as he jumped down the steps and wrapped his arms round Ash, lifting him off his feet. "My English friend! Such a pleasure to be seeing you again. How is your good self?"

"Been better. And you?"

Jimmy took off his Ray-Bans and looked back at the plane. "We are a three-plane company now, *sahib*."

"Yes, but only this one has wings," added Parvati as she walked past.

Jimmy had flown Ash and Parvati out to Ravana's tomb, and had been paid handsomely for it with a bag of diamonds. It seemed he'd invested well. This new plane looked in far better nick than the rattling antique they'd last been in. Ash brushed his hand against the underside of the wing. "Rivets instead of sellotape. Which is nice."

The interior was basic, but comfortable. A small

chandelier jangled above Ash and the cabin smelled of incense and warmed-up curry. Instead of standard aeroplane seats, there were a couple of sofas, an armchair and even a chaise longue, all bolted to the floor.

"Still no seat belts?" Ash asked.

"I have better." Jimmy pointed to the small shrine in the front. Streams of smoke weaved round a statue of Ganesha, the plump elephant-headed god of travel. Well, if the gods themselves were looking out for them, what could possibly go wrong? Ash just hoped Ganesha paid especially close attention to this particular plane.

Jimmy went to the bathroom at the back and banged on the door. "We have passengers. Get out!" He smiled weakly. "I am training new cabin crew."

"You've got a steward?" asked Ash. "That's..." What he wanted to say was "absolutely stupid of whichever lunatic decided to sign up with you", but for some reason it came out as "...interesting."

There was a moan from within the bathroom, then the sound of a flush. The tap ran for a long time with much sighing and sobbing. Jimmy pounded the door harder. "Hurry up! I pay you for pouring out tea, not vomit!"

The door opened and a small Indian boy wearing a dark blue jacket at least three sizes too large stumbled out. His hair was stuck across his forehead and he hung on to the door grimly. "Ash?"

"John?" Ash leaped up and grabbed John in a crushing embrace. He couldn't believe it. John had been his only friend back in Varanasi. "What are you doing here?"

John swayed even though the plane wasn't even moving. "Ujba didn't want me around. I helped you escape, remember?"

"So you work for Jimmy?"

Jimmy grunted. "An act of charity I am much regretting." He put his cap on, screwing it low over his head, and went into the cockpit. There was another guy in the co-pilot's seat and the two of them chatted their way through the pre-flight checks.

Khan looked around the floor and stretched out on a piece of carpet. He patted his rucksack into a pillow and yawned. "Wake me when you see the Ganges."

Ash glanced around himself, then took the armchair. Parvati lay down on a sofa and pulled the blanket up to her chin. She let out a long sigh and closed her eyes.

The engines rumbled and the propellers flicked round slowly, then powered up and buzzed into full life. John gulped. He covered his mouth and ran, stumbling, straight back into the bathroom.

First the cabin juddered. Then it shook violently, almost throwing Ash from his seat. The chandelier swung back and forth, jingling. Something rattled within the fuselage. Ash hoped it wasn't anything critical in the 'staying in the air and not crashing in flames' sense.

"I'd forgotten this bit," he said, clamping his fingers on to the armrests.

Chapter Fourteen

Why was it he could fall asleep on a bus, on a train and even on a bicycle, but not on a plane? Ash shifted in the armchair, the blanket tucked under his chin, and tried to balance his cheek on the pillow. Not working. The steady drone of the propellers filled the tin can of the cabin. Ash looked around. It was dark beyond the small round windows. He wondered where they were.

John lay on the floor, snoring softly. Khan was up, legs crossed and teeth sunk deep into a large piece of lamb. The juices, red and very raw, dribbled down his chin as the bones crunched. He peeled off a strip with his nail and offered it to Ash.

Ash shook his head.

Parvati slept. The chandelier chimed overhead and the few lights cast her face in a sickly yellow tone. Or maybe it wasn't the lights. Her scales were flaking off her face, and the skin was drawn and tight over her bones. Her eyelids opened, just a razor's width, and a feverish green fire burned in her gaze.

"Parvati, what's wrong?"

Parvati struggled to sit up. She straightened the blankets and Ash glimpsed the bony body beneath it. How could she have lost so much weight so quickly? When she coughed, the air rattled within her withered lungs. She sank back into her seat, too tired even to speak.

Ash saw the golden lights of death shining all over her.

"She'll be better when we get back to India."

The two of them moved to the back of the plane, away from Parvati's hearing. "What's happening to her?" asked Ash.

Khan frowned. "I thought you'd know. It's the Koh-i-noor."

"The aastra?"

"Of course. Rakshasas cannot possess the tools of the gods. They were crafted to be used against us. The Koh-i-noor robs her of her life because she was not meant to carry it. It's only because of her human heritage she's lasted this long."

"Where is it?"

"Round her neck."

"I'll get it off her, then." But as Ash stepped towards her, Khan placed his hand on his shoulder.

"No, I can't let you do that." Khan scowled. "I'm not so sure she wanted you to have it. Aren't things hard enough already with you being the Kali-aastra?"

❖

Ash didn't meet the tiger demon's gaze. "I don't know what you mean."

"Just because I'm ridiculously handsome does not make me stupid," said Khan.

Ash snorted. "Who says you're handsome?"

Khan crossed his arms. "I hear you've been having bad dreams."

"Nothing strange about that. Everyone has them from time to time."

Khan shook his head. "No. Parvati told me this might happen. It'll get worse as time progresses. The past will become more and more real until you cannot separate it from the present. What you are, Ash Mistry, will vanish under the waves of stronger, deeper souls. Especially those like Ashoka."

"Wait," said John as he joined them in one of his rare ventures beyond the bathroom. "You were Ashoka? The emperor Ashoka?"

Ash nodded.

John sat down opposite him, fascinated. "Cool."

"Wasn't as great as all that," Ash admitted.

Khan picked up a bottle of water and with a sharp swipe of his claw took off the top. He gulped it all down. "You know what his name means?"

"No. Never really thought about it."

"Without sorrow." Khan smacked his lips and tossed the bottle away. "I've met some bloodthirsty humans in my time, but Ashoka was in a class of his own."

"No. He was a great man. He was an emperor," said John. "Everyone knows that."

"Oh, I'm not denying he was great, but there's only one way to forge an empire, little man," said Khan. "And that's by killing absolutely everyone who stands in your way. Genghis Khan told me that, and he should know." Khan paused. "Or was it Napoleon? Short fellow on a horse. Wore a funny hat."

Khan was telling the truth, Ash had to admit. He had never felt such coldness and cruel ambition as when he'd dreamed he was Ashoka. He'd relished the death and the terror he'd brought to that nameless village. Revelled in it.

"How can I stop the memories from affecting me?" Ash asked.

Khan shrugged. "You can't. Kali brought you back. Did you never think there would be a price?"

Chapter Fifteen

There was nothing more surreal than arriving in a strange city, in a strange country, at three in the morning.

The streetlights glowed vague and insubstantial through the dense mist that covered Kolkata. Lone cars crept along the silent streets, and Ash looked out at the beggars and homeless families lying under thin cotton sheets on the pavement, with nothing but flattened cardboard boxes as mattresses. Mangy dogs sniffed at the rubbish piled in the alleyways, and skeletal cows roamed everywhere, nibbling at trash.

Khan snored in the back seat of their taxi. Parvati still looked terrible, bordering on hideous. She had a shawl over her head, but was more demon than human now. Her skull had mutated into a flat, serpentine wedge, and a cobra hood spread out on either side of her neck. The venomous fangs glistened and her tongue constantly flicked out, tasting the air. Scales covered her hands, and each nail was a long, slender needle.

John shifted, stuck as he was with Khan to his left and Parvati to his right. He'd decided to tag along with them after they'd landed. A life of flying didn't suit him and Jimmy hadn't been sad to see him go. His eyes stared at the unfamiliar city. "And I thought Varanasi was gloomy," he said.

"You want to go back there?"

"Not likely." He smiled at Ash. "I owe you."

It was good to have John around. When Ash and Lucky had been hunted by Savage and his demons, he had turned out to be their only friend. The boy had lived in the Lalgur as one of the many half-starved urchins that haunted every big city in India, stealing food and trinkets and tourist gear for Ujba, who was a major player in Varanasi's criminal underworld.

Ujba. Ash scowled as he remembered the crime lord. Ujba had been given the task of training Ash in *Kalari-payit*, the ancient Indian martial art. It had meant weeks of brutal beatings by Ujba's best students. Ujba believed in the school of extremely hard knocks. John had helped Ash and Lucky escape Ujba's den.

He'd also helped them get in touch with their parents. So Ash's dad had sent John money to help find his mother, who'd abandoned John in Varanasi when she hadn't been able to cope.

Ash knew John had found his mum, but wondered why he wasn't with her now. Had something gone wrong? He'd asked, but John had been evasive, moving the subject on to something else. Perhaps his mother hadn't wanted him back after all. Ash would find a better time to talk about it. Maybe his dad could send some more cash to help.

Kolkata had been the capital of British India for two centuries, and as the taxi rolled on through the city, Ash got a sense of its faded grandeur. Old, elegant Victorian buildings stood cloaked in regal squalor, their walls haphazardly repaired, windows broken or boarded up, cracks emerald-fringed and moist with mould. The taxi splashed through ocean-sized puddles, and every weed or strip of green was blooming thanks to the recent monsoon rains.

"There," said Parvati. "Stop there."

Khan yawned, displaying a fine set of canines. "Home at last."

Home? Ash got out of the front passenger seat and looked around. "Where's the hotel?"

Parvati opened the taxi door. "We're not staying at a hotel."

Why did Ash suddenly get the feeling this was going to be no fun at all?

A high wall stretched along a run-down street. Palm trees creaked along the road, which was filled with pot-holes and exposed drains. Rats, big rats, scrabbled up loose wiring that hung down from the electricity poles. They followed Parvati along the wall to a large, ivy-covered gate. The air was dense with musk and mould.

Ash read the carved sign above the gate, heart sinking even lower. "The English Cemetery?" He gazed past the rusty iron railings. The place looked like a jungle. "Don't tell me we're staying here."

❖

"OK, I won't tell you we're staying here." Parvati tossed her rucksack over the railings. The gates were held closed with a heavy chain, but there was enough slack for her to slip through. Khan growled and vaulted over the gate, clearing the uppermost spikes with a metre to spare. He looked back, grinning.

"Think there'll be snakes?" asked Ash. The grass was over two metres high.

"Plenty," said John. "But I've stayed in worse places."

"The Lalgur was better than this," said Ash.

John flinched. "I wasn't talking about the Lalgur."

"Where then?"

But John just twitched his head, evidently not wanting to talk about it, and followed Parvati through the gap.

"I know I'm going to regret this. A lot," Ash said to no one in particular, but feeling it needed to be noted, as he'd bring it up later under the heading "I told you so" when it all went wrong. He chucked his own rucksack over, grabbed the rusty railings and climbed up.

Crumbling limestone tombs and headstones lay obscured in the overflowing foliage. Creepers hung down from banyan trees and huge palm leaves littered the winding, weed-choked path.

"What is this place?" Ash asked. He'd taken out his torch and shone it on a nearby headstone. 'Sergeant Thomas Compton. Died 1802.'

"Calcutta was just a small cluster of villages until the East India Company set it out as one of their headquarters," said Parvati, using Kolkata's old English name. "It became one of their three presidencies in India. It was from here, Madras and Bombay that they ruled the country."

"And this is where they buried their dead?"

"There's a Scottish one further down the road," Parvati said. "Even in death they did not want to mix with the locals."

"Or with the Scots, obviously," said Ash.

The grass shook beside him and a sharp bark burst out as two dogs leaped on to the path. Their fur was torn and patchy, tight against their ribs. Spittle hung from their yellow teeth.

"Leave them," said Parvati. "They're harmless."

"They're rabid," said Ash, wondering if all his injections were up to date.

The dogs glowered, guarding their patch of grass, and Ash gave them a wide berth, with John keeping Ash between himself and the pair of feral beasts.

Ash was soon hopelessly lost. Parvati guided them around and around. There were mausoleums to entire families slain by disease or war, broken stone angels weeping over dead soldiers, and vast marble tombs of the great and good.

John squeezed Ash's shoulder. Small lights shone up ahead.

Slowly, figures came into view. Dressed in cast-off clothes, they sat hunched over small cooking fires and passed around tin plates of food. Crude tents assembled out of rags and plastic sheets lined the side of the path.

"Wait," said Ash. "There's something wrong."

The figures moved towards them. But some crept on all fours, their skins bristling with thick hair. Others stood straighter, but the fire shone off skin made of scales or armoured carapaces. One, a child, shook his head and snorted through tusks jutting from his lower jaw.

Rakshasas.

Ash pushed John behind him. "Get ready to run." He moved into a ready stance, weight evenly spread out on the balls of his feet, arms loose as whips.

The tree bough above him creaked and eight red eyes gazed down. A huge, eight-limbed woman slid down a silver rope of spider silk.

Parvati stopped in front of them.

"Parvati…" said Ash.

She didn't move.

Then, one after the other, the demons stepped forward. They bowed and touched Parvati's feet, a sign of deep respect. Even the spider-woman scuttled forward and crouched before the demon princess, her mandibles clicking. She looked like Makdi, the spider-woman who'd served Savage back in the Savage Fortress, but while Makdi had been arrogant and cruelly beautiful, this one was spindly and wretched.

Rakshasas were meant to be terrifying and powerful, not pitiful. This lot were a motley group, riddled with deformities, totally unlike the sleek human-animal hybrids in Savage's crew.

"Who are they?" Ash whispered to Khan.

"The lost and the damned," he growled.

A huge, grey-skinned man made his way through the crowd, each step shaking the ground and making the tall grass quiver. He was easily the most gigantic person Ash had ever seen.

❖

Big ears flapped on either side of his head, and a pair of thick tusks jutted from his upper jaw. He groaned as he bent down to the ground and put his head to Parvati's feet, the ultimate submission.

"Your royal highness," he said. "We bid you welcome."

Chapter Sixteen

"They look like they want to eat us," whispered John.

"You?" said Khan. "You're not even an appetiser."

Ash sat with them on a gravestone as Parvati consulted the big elephant rakshasa, Mahout. One of the demons passed them a bowl of rice and spicy vegetable curry, but otherwise they kept separate. Only Khan seemed relaxed, but then he always did. He sniffed at the curry.

"Could do with a bit of beef," he said. "Goat would be nice. It's been a while since I've had some goat. Or human. Nothing beats a soft bit of man flesh."

John gulped and shifted further along the fallen gravestone.

"Leave him alone," said Ash. He looked over at Parvati. A couple of lamps had been set up inside a large mausoleum. Ash noticed the old East India Company initials and a scroll with the name 'Lord Cornwall' on the mausoleum, almost obscured by the vines creeping across the roof. "This guy must have been a player. His tomb's twice the size of everyone else's."

"Old president," said Khan. "Once, all of the province of Bengal was his."

Parvati was deep in conversation, leaning over some maps with Mahout and two other rakshasas. A small silk bag lay between them – the one with the Koh-i-noor inside.

"Where did they come from?" Ash asked. "These rakshasas?"

Khan shrugged. "Not all demons followed Ravana."

"That include you?"

"Tiger rakshasas follow no one. We do what we please." Khan pointed a long nail at a group of small demons gathered round a pot. "Cockroaches. Scorpions. There," he gestured to two perched on the roof. "Crows. They're untouchables, lower caste demons. Ravana and the other royals would not have them, so they've turned to Parvati."

Ash understood. Parvati's mother had been human, so Parvati wasn't considered a true 'royal' rakshasa. It seemed that those who could find no one else to lead them had decided to follow her. India was a country built, and divided, by caste – much like the old English class system, but a thousand times more complicated and a thousand times older. There were Brahmins, the priests, at the top. Next came the warrior caste, called the Kshatriya. After that were the merchants and farmers and then the lower castes. Finally, there were the untouchables. He'd never thought the rakshasas would be similarly split.

❖

"And what are you?" said John.

"Warrior caste, of course," said Khan. "Like all other predators."

"And Parvati. She must be a Brahmin," said John. "They're the highest caste, after all."

Khan shook his head. "No, rulers come from the warrior caste. Brahmins aren't allowed to bear arms. They are usually advisers, the power behind the throne, as it were."

"So who are the Brahmins in the rakshasa world?" said Ash.

"There is, was, a race of serpents, called nagas. Ravana was descended from them, hence Parvati's cobra heritage."

"Ravana was a Brahmin?"

"Originally, yes. But Ravana, instead of following the Brahmin path, chose to become a warrior. Moving from one caste to another is exceedingly rare, but then Ravana was an exception to most rules." Khan licked his fingers clean. "The nagas were the wisest of us all, but they disappeared soon after Ravana's defeat at the hands of Rama. I've not seen one since. Probably extinct by now."

Ash looked around the group. "How many of you are there? There must have been thousands at Ravana's rebirth. What happened to them? Those that survived, that is."

Khan pointed up at the sky. "See those stars? Every one of them is a rakshasa soul."

"That's a lot."

Khan smiled and his eyes, amber as fire, shone with wicked amusement. "Afraid?"

"I'd be stupid not to be."

❖

Khan slapped Ash's back with a roar of a laugh, nearly knocking Ash over. He had to take a second to recover his breath.

"Don't worry, mortal," said Khan. "Most were killed in the great war with Rama. The sky burned with the fire of the gods. Aastras blazed down from the clouds and from the bows of Rama and his generals. Countless rakshasas were slaughtered. They won't be reincarnated in a hurry, if ever."

"But only the Kali-aastra truly destroys," said Ash. "Isn't there a chance that they may come back?"

"All at once? How? No. In a small, thin stream, perhaps. Not enough to be a threat to humanity, alas." Khan looked up at the star-filled night and sighed. "Perhaps Ravana could have done it with his sorcery, brought down all those wandering spirits. But there is no Ravana now and there never will be."

Ash looked to Parvati. She and Mahout were deep in discussion in the empty mausoleum a distance away. The rest of the motley band of rakshasas were camped around the larger tombs for shelter. There was something he needed to know and didn't want Parvati or the others hearing. "It must be nice, knowing you'll come back."

"I suppose. Never really thought about it."

"It's different for us mortals."

"You get reincarnated, don't you? Hardly different at all."

Ash frowned. "We don't remember our pasts. But there must be a way, a spell or sorcery or something that allows us to come back, the way we were?"

He couldn't shake it from his mind, the idea of bringing Gemma back somehow. But there was no point discussing it with Parvati. Khan was as old as her, he'd lived as many lives, he might know something that could help.

Khan peered at Ash, eyebrow arched suspiciously. "What did Parvati say about this?"

"She said that when we're gone, we're gone, for ever."

"Then you have my answer."

"But—"

Khan raised his hand. "Enough." He stood up. "Now, I've been cooped up in a plane for a day and would like to stretch my legs. Goodnight, Ash."

Well that conversation had been a big fat failure. Frustrated and too agitated to sleep, Ash put his bowl aside and joined Parvati.

"You're looking better," he said. Parvati wasn't back to normal, but her skin had returned to its smooth, unblemished tone and her hair, instead of looking brittle and dull, was again as sleek and black as a raven's wing. "What's going on?"

A map of the city lay spread over a sarcophagus. Mahout was busy marking the map with red dots, holding the thick marker pen with his trunk.

Parvati indicated the red dots. "Savage is in one of these places, if my information is correct."

"There must be a hundred."

"A hundred and fifty-three," said Mahout. "Libraries, military establishments, hospitals. Financial houses. A few factories. All connected with the Savage Foundation. If we look thoroughly, we'll find Savage."

❖

"You're sure you haven't missed any?" Ash asked.

"I never forget."

"How long's that going to take?"

"As long as necessary," said Parvati. "Fifteen million people live in this city, Ash. We need to be patient."

"And what about the Koh-i-noor? Where is it?" The small silk bag had disappeared.

"Under here." Parvati tapped her nails on the stone lid of the tomb.

"Wait a minute," said Ash. He looked up at the big elephant. "Do you know what type of aastra the Koh-i-noor is? Does anyone around here know?"

Mahout shook his big head, his ears flapping back and forth across his face.

"Nobody? At all?"

"Sorry, Ash," said Parvati. "Look, the Koh-i-noor is nothing but bait. Bait to get Savage. That's what you want, isn't it?"

It just didn't make sense that no one knew what the aastra could do. The Koh-i-noor was the most famous diamond in the world, and the rakshasas must have come across it in one of their past lives. "Didn't you serve with the maharajah of the Punjab? Didn't he own this?"

"No one knows how to awaken the diamond, Ash. Why can't you let it go?"

"Isn't it worth trying to find out what it does? It could help."

"What's the point? That's not important."

"Not important? Gemma died for it."

"If you want me to say I'm sorry again, then listen: I am

124

sorry," Parvati said. "But there's nothing anyone can do about her death. Don't distract yourself, and get over your guilt and failure. We all fail, but we need to move on. Forget her."

Forget her? Of all the wrong things to say, that was the most wrong. "Yes, and I know it means nothing to you, but this is *Gemma* we're talking about. She had family, she had people who loved her. She wasn't like you."

The temperature dropped about twenty degrees. Parvati threw Ash an exceedingly dirty look and marched off with Mahout right behind.

Khan let out a long puff. Ash hadn't noticed him lounging at the entrance. "Beautifully handled, Ash."

"I thought you'd gone off for a walk."

Khan grinned. "And miss all the fun? I've rarely seen Parvati this upset."

"Why's she so upset?" Ash punched the stone. "*I'm* upset. I've come all the way out here and there's something she's not telling me."

"About what?"

"The Koh-i-noor." It was an itch he couldn't reach. Why did no one know what sort of aastra it was? Why did no one want to find out? Savage was after it, so it had to be important. "I don't know what's got into Parvati."

"At some point replay that conversation in your head and you'll know. Despite being a killer, a demon princess and the heir to Ravana's throne, Parvati, you may be surprised to hear, is rather sensitive. I suppose it's her human half."

"She's four thousand years old. She's seen kingdoms come and go. Time means nothing to her."

❖

"The years pass just as slowly for us as they do for you. She's been lonely for most of those four millennia. Lonely and homeless."

"She's never had a home? Why not?"

"What palace could equal that of Lanka?" said Khan. "The courts of the Moghul emperors were no better than cow sheds compared to the kingdom of her father. Never bothered me, because I've always preferred the jungle, but I think Parvati still misses it."

"What happened to it?"

Khan shrugged. "What else? It was destroyed. If you humans are good at one thing, it's wiping out civilisations. It's amazing you've lasted this long, given your passion for genocide."

"She hated Gemma, that's for certain."

"She envied her," replied Khan. "For all the reasons you so indelicately pointed out. Family. Being missed. Being loved. No one's said that of Parvati. Her reputation prohibits that sort of thing."

"What about you? You're as old as her."

"Me? Firstly, tigers are solitary creatures. Secondly, hey, look at me." He puffed out his chest and flexed his biceps. "Do you honestly think I have problems getting company?"

Ash laughed. "You really are totally in love with yourself, aren't you."

"You'd better believe it."

"Think I should say something?" Ash asked. "To Parvati, I mean?"

"She'd do anything for you, you know that, don't you?"

126

❖

"I didn't ask her to."

"Friends shouldn't need to ask."

Ash came up and sat down beside Parvati at an overgrown, weed-filled fountain somewhere in the heart of the graveyard. Heavenly nymphs — *apsaras* — forged from bronze, held out empty jugs and cups, their empty nozzles choked with foliage and rust.

Ash smiled. Parvati did not.

Ah, not going to be as easy as all that, he thought. *This is what you call your classic 'awkward moment'.* Ash needed something to break the arctic levels of ice. Facing a demon horde or dealing with some 'fate of the world in the balance' scenario would be easier than trying to apologise to Parvati. Where to begin? With the truth.

"I'm such an idiot," he said.

"Yes. You are."

"You weren't supposed to agree so immediately."

"What was I meant to do, then?" said Parvati.

"Listen, Parvati. I'm sorry about what I said earlier. You know I didn't mean it. It's just, Gemma's dead because of me. That's not what it was meant to be like. Y'know, being a hero and everything. Heroes don't fail."

"Then you've got a lot to learn about being a hero. Heroes fail more than everyone else."

"That doesn't make sense. At all."

"You fail. You try again. And again and again. Keep on failing until you finally succeed. That's what being a hero is. But some things can't be fixed, and you need to learn to live with them and move on."

"It's Friday," said Ash suddenly. "This time last week I was standing in the canteen, sweating buckets and asking Gemma out. How can so much have changed in a week?" He shook his head. "Jeez, if I'd known what was going to happen I would never have even spoken to her, let alone asked her out to Bonfire Night."

Parvati sighed. "That's the advantage of being mortal. You only need to learn to live with the mistakes of your current life. Rakshasas remember their past lives. We're never free of our guilt."

"Things like giving Savage your father's scrolls?"

"Yes, I think that would be in the top ten of 'my bad'." Parvati shifted uncomfortably. "He'd promised to make me wholly human, something I thought I desired."

They'd talked about it once, how she'd wanted to be mortal, to feel what it was to belong and to be loved, something no rakshasa could ever have.

She smiled wryly. "That said, I remember some of the stupid things you did too."

"What? Where?"

"You really want to know?"

"Of course not, but you've started now, so how can I not know?" Ash paused. "How bad was it? The 'Oops, Captain, but I didn't see that iceberg, and are you sure we've got enough lifeboats?' sort of bad?"

Parvati gazed up at the stars. "I was serving Penthesilea, queen of the Amazons. We'd been summoned by Prince Paris to defend Troy against the Greeks."

"You fought at Troy?"

❖

"So did you. You were one of King Priam's sons — I can't recall which, he had fifty. Anyway, it looked like it was over. Achilles was dead and the Greeks were feeling pretty hopeless. One day we looked out across the city walls and the entire army was gone. All that was left was a huge wooden horse. An offering to Poseidon, god of the sea, for a safe journey home."

"I've a bad feeling about this," said Ash.

Parvati tapped her chin. "What was it that you said? Let me remember…" She snapped her fingers. "Ah yes. You said 'How pretty! Let's get it. It'll look lovely in the city square.'"

Wow. He'd fought at Troy. Cool. "We've been through a lot together," said Ash.

Parvati nodded and took his hand, squeezing it. "And we've always made it, in the end." She summoned one of the rakshasas. The demon, a small whiskered boy with twitching ears, rushed forward and touched her feet. "Now get some sleep, we've a busy time ahead. Bhavit will show you to your room."

Chapter Seventeen

The days passed with no sign of Savage. Parvati didn't only have her rakshasas out searching; there were others helping her as well — beggars, rickshaw drivers, stall keepers. The downtrodden of the city were the ignored — and therefore the best spies. Ash watched how they came up to Parvati, touched her feet, and offered her gifts. This was a side of Parvati Ash hadn't seen before. The noble. The commander. The worshipped. But in spite of all these eyes and ears looking out for him, there was nothing on Savage.

Had Monty lied? Maybe Savage was a thousand miles away in another country, making his plans while they rotted in the damp, mouldy heat of Kolkata.

But Ash did learn more about the Englishman. How he'd come with the East India Company in the late eighteenth century and how he'd robbed and murdered his way up and up the company's hierarchy until he eventually met Parvati. He'd got her father's scrolls from her, starting his career in sorcery.

Some of the rakshasas could do a little magic. Mahout, the big elephant, had two masteries, and from him and a few of the other rakshasas, Ash gained a basic understanding of the ten sorceries.

The classical elements, Earth, Air, Fire and Water, accounted for four. Mastery of Air, for example, allowed a sorcerer to fly, communicate with the birds, and, if skilful enough, even control the weather. Then there were the next four sorceries – the humours: Blood, Yellow Bile, Black Bile and Phlegm. Codified back in ancient Mesopotamia, they controlled the mind, body and emotions of all living creatures. Parvati was an expert in a few of those, hence her ability to hypnotise. The final two were Space and Time. A master of Space could teleport, which Ash thought would be pretty amazing. Never late for school ever again. No one could agree if you had to learn them in any order, but all concurred that Time was the most powerful, and the most dangerous.

"Has anyone ever mastered Time?" Ash had asked Mahout. "Actually used it?"

"How would we know?" Mahout replied. "How can you know if the past has been changed? Impossible, because we are trapped within the time stream of that changed past. Only someone outside of the stream would see the difference, be able to compare what is to what had been before the change. They would know there had been an alternative history that had happened, but had been deleted. But the wise, even if they have the power, do not meddle with Time. Even Ravana chose not to use that sorcery, although he had mastered it."

"Why didn't he go back in time and change things? Make sure he beat Rama? It would be easy."

Mahout shook his head. "You might change one event, but that would lead to a whole new series of outcomes, potentially even worse than the ones you sought to correct. Whatever you do, destiny is inescapable, young Ash. Ravana was doomed to fail. Are you not the proof of that?"

"What about Savage? What masteries does he have?"

Another argument followed. Mahout was convinced Savage had to know the humours, balancing them within himself to extend his lifespan. The spider-woman thought he had some knowledge of the elements, learned while in the Far East. But no one knew for sure — neither what he was capable of, nor where he was.

Ash joined in the search for Savage, using it as an excuse to get out of the cemetery and discover this new city. Kolkata couldn't be more different from Varanasi. Varanasi was a place of temples and steeped in deep, ancient Indian religion. The narrow streets teemed with holy men and pilgrims. Kolkata, meanwhile, was a memorial to the British Empire, the capital of the Raj until 1917. Whitewashed Anglican churches and stately, grand government buildings lined the wide boulevards.

The first stop on this tour was the Victoria Memorial with John. The memorial symbolised Britain's two-hundred-year rule over India. At dawn the vast domed roof of the

❖

memorial hall shone with a soft eggshell glow, and the gardens surrounding it filled swiftly with day-trippers and picnics and tourists and touts. Kites rose up among the trees, crowding the sky with multicoloured diamonds made of tissue paper and bamboo.

Ash took a viewpoint up on the shoulder of a huge lion statue, watching the multitude come and go, vainly hoping he would catch a glimpse of Savage. He must have been here once. This was his sort of place, a centre of power. The building looked a lot like the Capitol building in the United States: huge dome, wide wings, a colonnade and statues of the great and the good everywhere. When Ash said this out loud, John scoffed and spat some nutshells at the feet of the statue of the governor. The statues were all of Englishmen, he said. From their point of view, Indians could be neither 'great' nor 'good'.

The rest of the day was spent hopping on and off the rattling tin trams that still served as the main mode of public transport. The vehicles were invariably packed with people hanging off the railings and handles by their fingertips, scuttling on or dropping off whether the tram was moving or not. At first, Ash was amazed there weren't mangled bodies on every street, but by evening he was doing the same, swinging on to the back of any passing carriage, then leaping off as it slowed round the corners.

The next day of searching was similar: heat, astounding sights and no Savage. And so it went. Ash's days were spent exploring the city, and his nights were...

His nights were haunted by dreams. Each morning Ash

awoke exhausted. Unlike before, when the dreams had been a single memory, now they came in their broken hundreds: snatches and glimpses of his past lives, lasting a few seconds before rushing to another with no sense or order. He lived them, smelling the corpses, tasting the blood, relishing the slaughter. The dark dreams filled his sleeping hours, then fled like cowards by sunrise. He overflowed with bloodlust. Once he woke up from a dream so clear, so vivid, that he rushed out, expecting to see dead rakshasas scattered all around. He washed his hands afterwards, desperate to rid himself of the blood that was only spilled in his nightmares.

He needed help, that was for sure.

Maybe he shouldn't have come. Kolkata was Kali's city. Legend had it she had been dismembered and her toe had fallen in the river here, at a place called Kali-ghat in honour of the story. From Kali-ghat came the name Kolkata.

The worship of Kali soaked the bones of the city. Her image was everywhere, with plenty of statues and temples dedicated to her. Ash had passed by the nineteenth-century main temple of her cult, where a goat was beheaded over her shrine daily, washing the statue of Kali in blood. A century ago they'd sacrificed humans in the same spot.

So, on the fourth day in Kolkata, Ash woke in a bad mood. He slipped on his sandals as he got out of his hammock and gulped his water bottle down to empty.

"John?" he called. They'd planned to head down to Fort William today and search another cluster of red dots on Mahout's map.

"Not here," said Parvati. "I don't think he likes sleeping

134

among us rakshasas. Can't imagine why." She sat atop the mausoleum Ash used as a bedroom.

"How long have you been up there?"

She jumped down and frowned as she approached him. "You do not look well."

"Thanks," Ash replied. Parvati was different too, more demonic with her body covered in light green scales and her eyes huge, her fangs clearly visible. Maybe she was letting her hair down, in the demonic sense. "It's getting harder," he admitted. "Can't sleep at night."

"Your past lives, yes? What is it like?" Parvati shifted up close and put her hand on his.

"It's like I'm standing in the rain," he started. "A total downpour. I'm getting drenched, but each drop that hits me is another memory. There are so many I can't make sense of them. I see castles and cities that are now just dust in history. Some are my homes, places I've grown up in and fight to protect. Others I burn. Then the faces. Faces of people I've fought and defended. Of people I've tried to save and didn't. Parvati, I wish I could cut it all out of my head. I've done terrible things."

"Anyone you recognise?"

"Rishi, a couple of times. It's as though he's been after me throughout history. Him, and you."

"You see me?"

"Your age changes, but there can't be too many half-human, half-cobra girls in the world. Sometimes we're friends and sometimes... we're not." Ash sighed. "I wish Rishi was here. He'd know what to do."

Parvati sat for a long time, doing nothing but holding his hand. Then she took a deep breath, like she had made some decision. "He did. That is why he sent you to train with Ujba."

"Yeah, not one of Rishi's better ideas. I don't think I learned anything with Ujba except how to get punched. A lot, and very hard. What sort of teacher is that?"

"He taught you how to fight. That involves taking hits as well as giving them out."

"Some days I was beaten up so badly I could hardly walk. He let his cronies terrorise everyone else, he made John's life hell and he *hated* you. Ujba was nothing but a thug." He remembered those days, trapped in the stifling heat of the training hall of the Lalgur, deep underground.

"An interesting term to use for Ujba, but most correct," she said.

"I called Elaine last night," said Ash. He held out his mobile phone. "I had to. She told me Rishi had spoken to her and given her the names of people who could help me, if things got bad."

Parvati let a scowl slip, then her gaze narrowed with curiosity. "And what did she say?"

"Nothing, it went straight to voicemail. But I got a text this morning. An address. You know it?"

She looked at the screen and nodded. "It's not far from here."

"I feel like I'm losing myself. There are so many people in here —" he tapped his head — "all shouting. The dreams are so real, so violent. They're getting worse and I'm worried

I'm going to wake up one day and find out I've done something... extremely homicidal."

Parvati shivered and the scales sank under her skin. Her fangs retreated and she drew out a pair of sunglasses, returning to her human guise. She took his hand. "Let's go."

Chapter Eighteen

$\mathcal{B}$eyond the quiet seclusion of the graveyard, Kolkata was up, awake and busy. They crossed the road, filled with honking cars and even human-powered rickshaws — two-wheeled vehicles pulled along the street by a single man, no horse or bicycle. It looked like a horrible lifestyle, the men thin, their passengers heavy.

But as Ash walked along the streets, his feet seemed to find their own path. He looked up at buildings around him. A cold dread filled him, and for a moment he wondered if this was still a dream. He'd been here before once. He was sure of it.

"What is it?" Parvati asked.

"*Déjà vu*," said Ash. He stared ahead. "There's a place round that corner. Wait here."

Parvati said nothing.

Ash waved down the traffic to give him space and crossed the road, leaving Parvati behind him. He passed by a blind beggar who squatted under a torn umbrella, plastic cup in hand. Smoke drifted out of the darkness. The walls tilted and almost touched together a couple of floors up. Only a crude assembly of wooden supports kept them from collapsing. Ash ducked under them and crept down the alleyway.

"Hello?"

Whatever this place had been, now it was a crumbling shack. No door, walls lopsided, and window frames warped and covered in tangled weeds.

Ash stepped in, putting his foot on the marble threshold.

An old temple. There was a brass hook above him from which a bell would once have chimed. Plain white marble tiles, crushed and uneven, covered the floor. Litter, blown in by the wind, filled the corners, and the dust drew strange patterns upon the ground. Cobweb curtains hung off the wooden crossbeams, and Ash brushed them aside as he approached the altar and the statue upon it.

Kali stood above the cringing form of a demon, her ten arms fanned out. In one hand she carried a severed head by its long hair, its eyes half closed and tongue hanging out, limp and dumb. In the other hands were weapons ranging from spears to swords to a noose. The paint had flaked off the statue, exposing the bare stone beneath, but that only made her more terrifying, as though she were sloughing off her own skin. Murals decorated the wall behind her, but in the poor light, Ash couldn't really see what they were.

A cold wind, a whisper of breath, caressed his neck. Ash spun round.

"Parvati?"

There was no one there.

No one.

"Hello?"

Another Kali temple. But why did this one feel so different? Kolkata was an alien city. He'd never walked its streets or seen its sights 'til a few days ago. But this temple was like... coming home.

He'd trodden these tiles before. He felt familiar dips and grooves, as though his toes had once rested in them during a time past. He touched the altar and searched the stone for nicks and marks. Instinctively his nail ran into a long shallow groove, something left by a blade. There were others.

People have died here.

Kali loves death best. Wasn't he proof of that? He became more powerful the more he killed. Kali blessed him. He ran his fingertips over the scored stone, shivering as old memories swirled in the dark places of his mind, memories from a previous life, maybe, of holding down a struggling victim and drawing a blade across his throat, the blade leaving a light scratch on the stone. Even now he felt the victim squirming against the altar. Ash's hand tightened as it remembered wrapping itself round the man's hair, gripping his head steady for the knife.

A hand touched his back.

Parvati gasped as Ash spun round and stopped his punch

❖

a millimetre from her face. Ash stepped back, his heart tripping with panic. "I'm sorry, Parvati, I don't know what happened."

"It's your past lives. They're guiding you now, subconsciously." She looked worried and put her hand on his cheek. "They were afraid this would happen."

"They?"

"They as in Rishi and I." A man sat in the darkness, by the doorway. Somehow Ash had walked straight past without seeing him. He was hunched over a small plate, and he wore a loose tunic and baggy trousers, a yellow scarf dangling round his thick neck. He put the plate aside and stood up, stretching until his head almost brushed the underside of the temple ceiling. His fingers smoothed down his black moustache.

"Ujba," Ash whispered.

"I prefer *'guru'.*"

"What are you doing here?"

"Elaine sent for me. There is much more for you to learn, boy," said Ujba. "Especially now that you are the Kali-aastra."

"You?" said Parvati as she saw Ujba and her fangs lengthened on instinct.

"Only I know how to deal with the Kali-aastra," said Ujba. "You are one of us, boy."

"And what is that, exactly?" Ash said.

"A devotee of Kali." Parvati glanced around the small chamber.

"Well, forget it. I'm not training with you any more." Ash nodded to the doorway. "Let's go, Parvati."

❖

"It was Rishi's wish," said Ujba, "that if anything happened to him, I would continue your training."

That made both of them, Ash and Parvati, stop. If Rishi had wished it, how could they say no?

Parvati narrowed her eyes as she gazed suspiciously at Ujba, but her fangs retreated behind her lips. "I don't like this any more than you do, Ash, but he's right. He's a Brahmin of Kali."

"I thought Brahmins weren't allowed weapons."

"There are many things that do not apply to the worshippers of the black goddess," said Ujba. He looked at Parvati. "Leave us."

Parvati hesitated, looking not at all happy, then gave a short nod. "I'll be back at nightfall, Ash." She left.

Ash wanted to go too, to turn on his heels and follow her out. But then what? More nightmares he couldn't handle? Another attack when he was asleep? He was getting out of control.

But Ujba? Why Ujba?

"So what do you want me to do?" he said.

Ujba reached behind a column and took out a broom and tossed it to Ash. "Clean."

"Clean?" Ash answered. "How's that going to help?"

"I am your guru. You do as I tell you."

"I've come a long way from the Lalgur, Ujba." The big man was a brutal teacher, his lessons harsh. Even now Ash could remember every punch and kick he'd suffered, every bruise and cut he'd got training with Ujba. But that was then, when he'd been slow and unfit and human. Now he was the Kali-aastra.

"You think there's nothing left to teach you?" said Ujba.

"Something like that."

"Perhaps you can show me some of this extraordinary skill? I would be most pleased to watch a true master at work. Perhaps I might learn from you?"

Ash bristled. Ujba clearly didn't believe him.

"You hesitate?" said Ujba. He slapped his chest. "Do you need an opponent? Use me. Don't be afraid of hurting me. I certainly won't be afraid of hurting you. Come, then."

"I don't think—"

Ujba moved. His punch caught Ash square in the chest and launched him off his feet. Ash landed and then flung himself aside just as Ujba's foot smashed into the wall, barely missing his face. Ash swung his fist, but Ujba jabbed his fingers into Ash's armpit, and his arm went limp.

Marma Adi. He knows—

The next blow was a light tap under his ribs, but it felt like a cannonball. Ash couldn't breathe. He stumbled back, his legs wobbling, then fell.

Ujba walked over to the broom and picked it up. He returned and stood over Ash.

"Feeling will return in ten minutes." He dropped the broom on Ash. "Then you clean."

Chapter Nineteen

So Ash cleaned. He brushed the worst of the cobwebs away, swept the floor, arranged candleholders around the shrine, and put fresh garlands of marigolds round Kali's neck. Ujba watched, immobile but for the occasional twitch of the stick in his hand.

Eventually the guru clapped his hands. "Enough. Let us see what you remember. Honour Kali."

It was late morning and shafts of sunlight illuminated the temple, piercing through the cracks and holes in the roof. The day's heat, moist with the oncoming rains, weighed the air down and sweat shone upon Ash's bare torso. He took three steps back and faced the statue. He hadn't done this since he'd left the Lalgur. He put his palms together. He began his salutations to the black goddess.

The moves came slowly, old memories re-emerging under

the gaze of guru and goddess. Ash unleashed blows, sank into dives and rose up with high-arching kicks. The old strength surged through him, accelerating his moves, multiplying the power of his strikes. This was what the Kali-aastra wanted. He twisted aside from imaginary attacks and reacted with bone-shattering punches of his own. The final move was the low stance before the goddess, touching the floor before her. Honouring her.

Sweat poured off his back. Ash stood up and ran his hand through his hair, away from his eyes.

Ujba scowled. "I thought you were the Kali-aastra. The weapon of the divine."

"What? Did I make a mistake?" He knew he hadn't. "I did that perfectly."

"Perfection is the least of my expectations." Ujba stood up and slapped the wall with his palm. "The Kali-aastra should demolish walls with his kicks. He should slay armies with his bare fists. Your attacks should shake mountains."

"That's impossible."

"I demand impossible things, then." He watched Ash with his small black eyes. "Rishi was a fool."

"Don't you dare say that."

Ujba scoffed. "Did you know him? At all?"

"He saved my life and my sister's. He was one of the good guys. He rescued me from the Savage Fortress. Don't remember seeing you there."

"He should have told me about the Kali-aastra. Perhaps then he would still be alive. That's the trouble with clever men – they sometimes outwit themselves."

❖

"What do you want from me?" said Ash. "If I'm so useless?"

Ujba shrugged. "I thought I could train you, help you unlock the powers of the Kali-aastra. Teach you how to manage your past lives."

"You can do that?"

"Teach you? That depends on your willingness to learn. Your respect for your guru."

"Isn't respect earned?"

"Do you want to learn or not, boy?" Ujba looked at him with barely disguised contempt. "You have these gifts, but you squander them. Worse, you reject them. No wonder each waking moment is pain. Look in the mirror, boy. You're being eaten from within."

"The Kali-aastra gives me strength."

"It is the only thing keeping you alive. And poorly, it seems."

Ash stared hard at the dark man. Was it that bad? He touched the scar on his stomach. The nightmares, the waxing and waning of power, all because of who he was, what he was. The Kali-aastra. Could Ujba teach him to control it? If there was even a small chance, he had to take it. He couldn't carry on like this.

Reluctantly, Ash made a decision.

"Teach me, then," he said. "I want to learn."

Ujba put his hands to Ash's face and peered closely into his eyes. "You dream? Of your past incarnations?"

"Yes."

The guru nodded slowly. "You must learn when to fight

and when to yield. A warrior must combine flexibility with rigidness. You fight against the others, your past selves, instead of bending. Look for the path of least resistance and attach yourself to that."

"How will I spot it?"

"Your previous incarnations do not come at random. There is a purpose to them wanting your attention. By yielding, you make them allies. Consider them guides. At different times, as your needs change, different personalities will come to your aid. You just need to recognise them among the multitude."

"How?"

"That wisdom is not easily acquired." Ujba picked up the broom and turned it in his fingers. "You will dream tonight, most likely. Do as I say and we will talk again tomorrow. But I do have one other piece of wisdom, one which is well meant, though I know you'll ignore it."

"Tell me."

"Do not trust the rakshasa. Her kind and ours are eternal enemies. I am your guru."

Ash laughed. "Parvati? In what alternate universe would I trust you instead of her? She's always been on my side."

"As have I, boy, though you've been too blind to see."

"Ash?"

They turned and there, in the doorway, was Parvati.

"Am I early?" she asked.

Ujba addressed Ash. "Tomorrow." Then, with one last dark look at Parvati, he left.

"He so doesn't like you, does he," said Ash as he wiped the sweat off his face.

❖

"He has reason." Parvati approached the shrine. She slid her fingers over the cracked altar stone, feeling the grooves and indentations. "Let's go. This place is evil."

"That's almost funny coming from a demon."

"Didn't Ujba tell you? About who worshipped here?"

Her voice quivered as she spoke. Ash's heart skipped a beat. Parvati was frightened. He hadn't thought that possible. But that cold, dreadful breeze haunted the edges of the temple, and Ash flexed his fingers, thinking of the man, the sacrificial victim, whom he'd held against the altar once upon a time.

"Who?" he asked.

"Kali's most devoted and deadly servants." She met his gaze and there was old terror in her eyes. "The Thugs."

Chapter Twenty

"*Y*ou mean like out of *Indiana Jones and the Temple of Doom?* The Thuggee?" asked Ash. They'd gone to a café for dinner and found a quiet corner away from the small crowd of men watching and cheering the cricket game on the old crackling TV.

"I forget most of your education comes from Hollywood," said Parvati. "What do you know about them?"

Ash tried to remember the film. There was something about chilled monkey brains and Indians being badass until the white hero came along and spoiled all the fun. "They strangled people quite a lot."

"Yes. It was the old way. They killed their victims without spilling blood. Have you ever strangled a man?"

"No." But he'd come close, hadn't he? Ash blushed with

shame, thinking of how he'd almost strangled his dad when he'd dreamed of being the first Ashoka.

Parvati unwrapped her light cotton scarf and wound the ends round her fists. "It's hard work. The victim struggles, and unless you get the cloth in exactly the right place, knot under the Adam's apple, you waste a lot of energy achieving not very much."

"Sounds like you've done it."

"You think I'd need a scarf?"

No, of course not. Parvati's venom was lethal to man, demon, and probably god. One bite would do the job. Not for the first time Ash wondered exactly how many people she had killed in her long, long life.

"Do you know the legend of how the Thugs were made?" she asked.

"Not something that comes up in the National Curriculum."

"Kali was fighting a terrible demon. A demon as powerful as Ravana, and she was alone. All the other gods had fled." Parvati had a faraway look. It wasn't as though she was telling a story, something she'd read or been told by another person. It was as if she was remembering it from her past.

She continued. "So there she is, stabbing and slashing at this rakshasa. But she can't defeat him. Every drop of blood she spills, out grows another rakshasa. Soon she'll be overwhelmed."

"What does she do?"

Parvati ran her palm over her arm. "The goddess takes sweat from her body and creates two men. She rips a strip of cloth from her skirt and gives it to them. They kill each and every rakshasa." Parvati made a twisting movement with her fists. "Strangling them."

"Killing them without spilling any blood."

Parvati nodded. "The Thugs were created to be demon killers. To follow the path of Kali. Over the centuries they became greedy, petty-minded and corrupt, using their skills for highway murder and robbery. But you're missing the bigger picture."

"What's that?"

"The first men she made, they were Kali-aastras." Parvati sighed. "The Thugs believed that if they killed enough, performed the correct rituals and observed the right omens, they would gain supernatural powers. They believed that by murder they might become Kali-aastras themselves. Like the first of Kali's creations. Like you."

Kali loves death. He'd been told that, ages ago. He gained power through death, so why wouldn't the Thugs believe the same thing? Weren't they, the Thugs and him, all servants of Kali?

"I'm not a Thug," said Ash.

"But you are, Ash. Kali made you to kill demons, like the first two Thugs. You are her weapon, her right hand. The hand that slays."

"I may have these powers, but that doesn't mean I'll use them."

She smiled weakly. "I know, Ash. But the Kali-aastra might not give you a choice. The more powerful you grow, the more it will demand of you."

❖

"And Ujba? Is he a Thug?"

"In a manner of speaking. He knows all the old rituals and skills. He understands what the Kali-aastra is capable of better than anyone else. But his goals are not your goals. He worships Kali in a way that's rather antisocial."

"He's a killer?"

"He kills for what he believes in." She looked at him over her sunglasses. "And in that he's not alone, is he?"

"Then how is he going to help me?"

"By teaching you to channel your past, your other lives. Think about it." She tapped Ash's temple. "Think what knowledge lurks in there. What skills. If you could access your former selves in a controlled manner, you could use their abilities, what they know. You say Ashoka's one of your previous incarnations. Don't let him control you. *You* control him, instead. If you could use all his military wisdom and warcraft, you would be unstoppable."

Ash sank back into his chair. "It's never going to end, is it."

Parvati smiled softly, but shook her head. "Not in this lifetime, nor any other."

Chapter Twenty-one

*A*nd again they come. Ash screams as the images tumble through his mind, memories and emotions and dreams of countless people he has been since the beginning.

He is a red-robed soldier standing in a shield line as the sky darkens with arrows.

He urges his horse to a gallop as he raises his spear for the——

Hands tied, he takes steps to the scaffold. The sun shines on the headman's axe as he lifts it and the birds caw from——

More and more they assault him, and Ash feels as if he's drowning. He struggles against the endless torrent and——

Ashoka sits upon a horse, hand resting on his hilt. Beside him is a young woman in scaled armour——

He sits upon a horse, hand on his sword hilt. Beside him is Parvati.

He is with Parvati.

❖

Ash pushes the others away, letting the spirits wash over him, and he guides himself towards this one moment, this one life.

Ashoka sits upon his horse, watching another city burn. The ash, even from here, is hot and the night sky boils over with dense clouds of smoke, lit by the roaring flames of temples, of palaces, of homes and shops and people. Sparks of tinder float in the darkness like the eyes of a million demons.

The soldiers drag the slaves. Each one chained to the one in front, the lines stretching back to the horizon. Most are dumb with despair, dirty, some bloody and dressed in rags as they proceed along the road, a mute, living line of misery. Somewhere in the darkness there rises a long, wailing lamentation as the women find the corpses of their husbands and sons among the slaughtered.

The sound pleases Ashoka. It sounds like victory.

"They will call you emperor after this," says Parvati. The rakshasa princess rests upon a corpse, takes off her boot, and shakes out the dust. The man, breathing but hours ago, full of life, hope, joy and dreams, is nothing more than part of the scenery now. With a sharp tug, Parvati pulls off his turban and begins to clean her sword with the long cloth.

Ashoka looks down from his saddle. "Emperor Ashoka. I like it."

"And then what?" Blood shines upon her armour and her hair, plaited and wrapped round her head to prevent it being grabbed in battle, is speckled with gore. She wipes her face and leaves a trail of red across her pale cheeks. The green, serpentine eyes glow. "More war?"

"Do you tire of it, sweet Parvati?"

She scoffs. "Mortal, I have seen such sights that would haunt even you. This —" she sweeps her hand over the burning city — "was but an hour's work for my father."

"Your father was the lord of the demon nations. I am but a man."

❖

"A man. Cruel, vain and petty." Parvati bows mockingly. "My father would have enjoyed your company. You and he would have had a lot in common."

"More than you think." Ashoka smiles at the confusion in the demon princess's eyes. He nods to his bodyguard. "Bring him."

His men drag an old man forward and throw him to the blood-soaked ground. It is the priest. His face is bruised and his clothes torn and bloodied, and he clutches a silver box to his chest. He kneels on the ground, head bowed. "My great lord," he croaks.

Ashoka swings down from his saddle and stands in front of the man. He rests his hands upon the hilt of his sword. "Tell me, Parvati. They say your noble father was the greatest sorcerer the world has ever known."

"No other being has ever mastered the ten sorceries," says the rakshasa girl.

Ashoka snaps his fingers. "The box, old man."

"My lord, you do not understand—"

Ashoka grabs it and kicks the man back into the dirt.

The box is small, delicately engraved with ancient symbols and sigils of power. It is warm to the touch and heavier than it should be. The object within has weight.

"They say Ravana could transform himself into anything, or anyone. They say he could cross from one side of the world to the other in an eye-blink. Is what they say true, Parvati?"

"It is."

"Could he raise the dead?" challenges Ashoka.

"That no one can do."

He opens the box and takes out the object within.

Parvati gasped. "The Koh-i-noor."

❖

Ashoka grins. "The Brahma-aastra, yes. They call it the Life Giver."
He leans closer to the man. "Have you awoken it?"

"Yes, my lord."

With one hand holding the massive, glowing gem, Ashoka draws out
his sword with the other. Parvati says nothing, but her eyes narrow.

"Hold him," orders Ashoka.

The old man cries out as the guards grab him. Ashoka tightens his grip
upon his hilt and lays the blade against the man's thin body. The Koh-i-
noor pulses within Ashoka's grasp, and beams of light rise out of its faces.
The colours change and brighten and the stone begins to burn.

Ashoka grins. "Now, the test."

The blade enters the old man's chest. A thick fountain of blood bursts
from the wound, spraying the guards and Ashoka. The old man's screams
rise to a feverish pitch, and he thrashes in the grip of the guards, his
scrawny body filled with a hideous, desperate strength. But eventually he
slumps, his skin glistening with dark blood.

Ashoka draws out the sword and hands it to one of his men. He raises
the limp head by its white hair and stares at the closed eyes and the slack
jaw. More blood dribbles from the dead man's mouth and his tongue hangs
dumbly.

Ashoka holds the glowing jewel and moves it back and forth so the light
blazes upon the pale flesh.

The limbs, dead and bloodless, twitch.

Ashoka gazes intently at the dead man.

The dead man's eyes open and gaze back.

Chapter Twenty-two

"It's a Brahma-aastra," said Ash. "It's the Life Giver. It raises the dead. And you *knew*."

He still couldn't quite believe it — that Ujba had been right about Parvati, that she couldn't be trusted. His guts churned in turmoil with anger, disappointment and betrayal.

"Maybe we should discuss this privately, Ash," said Parvati.

The other rakshasas were just waking up in their soggy camp. Last night's downpour was now a fine falling mist with water dripping off the huge, shiny green leaves into dirty brown puddles. A few small campfires flickered, fed with rubbish and semi-dry twigs. The ragtag demon followers of Parvati set about cooking breakfast as they shifted through the graveyard under wet blankets and tatty old coats. Mahout glanced at Ash, a hint of sadness in his little eyes, but Ash snarled back. Mahout had known also, and hadn't told him. Had they all known about the Koh-i-noor?

"Why not here?" Ash's knuckles and finger joints clicked as he locked them into fists. "Or are you worried everyone will find out what a liar and traitor you really are?"

Parvati's fangs lengthened. Even in the gloom of dawn her eyes shone murderously bright. "Because you are my friend, Ash, I'll forgive you this once. But never presume to speak to me like that again, ever."

"You let Gemma die, and all the while we've had the power to bring her back." Ash shook his head and could barely keep the tears back. "We could bring her back, Parvati. Somehow."

"That's not possible."

"It is, I saw it happen. Ashoka took the Koh-i-noor and made a dead man live. I was there."

"And so was I, Ash. It wasn't like that."

"I saw—"

"I don't care what you think you saw."

"What about Savage? He's been after the diamond from the beginning. Maybe he knows how to use it."

Parvati looked at him as if he'd gone absolutely monkey-loony insane. Then she laughed. Once, when she laughed, it had lifted Ash's heart and there was no better sound. Now it was pitiless and mocking. "Savage? Well, why don't you ask him when you find him? I'm sure he'll be happy to help."

"That's not what I mean. There might be others who can do it. Other sorcerers – good guys like Rishi."

"There's no one like Rishi. If there was I would have found him by now."

"You don't understand," said Ash.

"No, *you* don't. Listen, Ash, I'll explain this again, slowly, so it gets into your stubborn head. The Koh-i-noor cannot raise the dead. Savage is our enemy. That's it. Just follow my orders and we'll get through this. You start having your own ideas and it'll go badly for all of us, especially you."

How could she be so arrogant? Who did she think she was? "Is that a threat, Parvati? I've just as much right—"

"Will you just shut up for once?" Parvati folded her arms. "You have to let her go, Ash. Let Gemma rest in peace."

"Why?" he asked. Simply that.

"Fate, Ash, fate." Parvati sighed. "Gemma was fated to die. Because of you."

"Lies," Ash snarled. "You're just full of them. I never knew how much of a snake you really were, even your mind's all twisted." He gazed around the gathered crowd. "All these people, they're here because they want to believe in you. But they don't know you like I do. Don't know how you'll use them, get close just so you can stab them in the back, like you did me. Like you did your own father. I thought it was because you believed in something better, but now I realise it's just your nature. To lie to those close to you. To betray the ones loyal to you. Treachery – it's all you know, isn't it?"

"Shut up, Ash, if you know what's good for you."

But he couldn't. The anger needed to get out and Ash wanted her to hurt as badly as he did. "You wonder why you have no friends. Why in over four thousand years no one's cared for you and why you've been so alone. The answer's right there. You just need to look in the mirror."

❖

Parvati hissed, her cheeks flushed, her eyes filled with anger and humiliation. Ash knew he'd just destroyed all the friendship they'd had.

The other rakshasas watched in utter silence. No one moved except Khan. Slowly he stood and slowly he stalked through the long grass, eyes never leaving Ash, until he was standing beside Parvati in a warrior stance.

Parvati glared at him, matching his rage with a dark fury of her own. "Go, before I kill you," she whispered.

Chapter Twenty-three

Ash stalked away into the darkest reaches of the cemetery, chopping and swiping at the undergrowth. He kicked a tree trunk, watching the leaves quiver and shake. He kicked it again, desperate to destroy something.

It was all wrong! He didn't understand what was happening. Gemma was dead, his friends back home were scared of him, he'd attacked his dad and now this – Parvati hated him.

He slumped down on a fallen gravestone. He didn't know what to do.

Why had she lied? Did Parvati hate Gemma that much? It didn't make sense. More likely she just didn't care, or understand. How could she? She was a demon, daughter of Ravana. What did the life of one girl mean to her? Nothing.

Parvati wanted Savage dead and that was all the Koh-i-noor was to her – bait to attract the Englishman.

❖

A chill went through him. Did Savage know how to use the Brahma-aastra? Was that why he was after it? He had mastered the seven sorceries, maybe he had the secret to this as well?

If he did, and got hold of it, then he could bring Gemma back from the dead. The Life Giver – that was what Ashoka had called the Koh-i-noor. Yet who knew what other powers it might possess? Could he risk Savage getting even a sniff of the diamond?

But Parvati wanted to kill Savage the moment he came looking for it. The world would then be rid of an extremely bad, bad guy, but he wouldn't be able to save Gemma. How could Ash allow that? Gemma hadn't deserved to die, and if there was a single chance, no matter how small, how insane, chance to have her back, he had to take it. But for that, he needed Savage alive. The English sorcerer's life and Gemma's were fatally entwined. If Savage lived, then so might Gemma. If he died, then that was it for her too.

Ash grabbed hold of a thick branch, too frustrated to do anything but try to twist and rip it off. He bent the bough as far as he could and glared at the creaking limb, determined to break it.

"What are you doing?" said John. He sat on top of one of the hundreds of tombs with a banana leaf in his hand, eating some stewed vegetables with his fingers.

Ash released the branch. "Where have you been?"

"Staying out of trouble. Unlike you." He scrunched up the leaf and tossed it. "You just seem to attract it."

Ash picked up a stick and swung it limply at the unyielding

tree. "Tell me about it. Everything's gone epically wrong. Parvati's been lying to me from the very beginning. She's so caught up in avenging herself on Savage that she doesn't care who else gets hurt."

"What happened?"

Ash told him about the dream, the Koh-i-noor and how it could bring life back to the dead. That there was a way, a real way, to save Gemma. Repeating it out loud made Parvati's betrayal all the more painful. But John didn't seem surprised.

"She's a demon — what did you expect?" he said. "You can't trust anyone."

"— What's wrong?" Ash asked. John had sounded so bitter. It wasn't like him.

John stared at him.

"Out with it, John."

John hopped down. "Forget it. I'm all right." He tapped the tree. "So what are you going to do now?"

"See Ujba, I suppose."

"He's in Kolkata?" John gaped. "What... what does he want?"

"He's not after you, if that's what you're worried about. He wants to train me. I'm meant to be over there now. Apparently he agreed to continue my training if anything happened to Rishi." He scratched his thumb. "There are more powers within the Kali-aastra. He wants me to learn them."

"But you killed Ravana," said John. "Isn't that enough?"

Ash looked up at the tree. "Apparently not."

❖

John glanced around him, agitated. Talking about Ujba had obviously scared him badly. He jumped at the sound of a bird breaking cover. Ash laughed.

"It's not funny, Ash," John said. "Don't trust Ujba. He's evil."

"Come on. I know he's hard, but Rishi thought—"

"Don't be an idiot!" John shouted. He held his fists up and gritted his teeth, almost boiling with rage. Ash had never seen him so angry. "Ujba will hurt you; it's what he does. Do you think he's forgiven you for running from him? A man like that holds grudges, believe me. I know." He said the last two words with quiet despair, shuddering as he said them.

"What happened? After we left?"

"What do you think happened?"

"My dad gave you money. To help find your mum. Didn't you—"

"Oh, a couple of hundred pounds. Thanks so much. We poor Indians are *soooo* grateful to the English sahib." John put his palms together and gave a low, mocking bow. "You come and give us your spare change, then go. Bye-bye India."

"It wasn't like that, John. You know it wasn't."

"Ujba took the money off me. He… wasn't happy about what had happened. I helped you escape, remember? He didn't like that at all." John shook his head. "He beat me. I could barely walk after he and Hakim had finished. Then he kicked me out on to the streets. No one would help me, not after Ujba spread the word. You know what it's like to be starving when all around you are restaurants? When you can smell food sizzling in the pans? I tried to steal, but that just got me beaten up again. More."

"Oh God, John, I'm so sorry. I never knew."

"Of course you didn't. All your problems were behind you."

"But you found your mum, you told me."

"I had a few friends. They helped me look. She's being taken care of now."

"Friends like Jimmy?"

John didn't meet Ash's gaze, but nodded. "He was one."

Ash took his friend's hand. "John, I can't fix what's happened. But I promise, I *promise* I'll make it up to you."

John drew his hand away. "I know you will, Ash." But he didn't sound at all happy about it.

Chapter Twenty-four

"You are late," said Ujba.

"How observant of you," said Ash.

"Then we must work twice as hard." Ujba pointed at the statue of Kali. "You know what to do. Honour the goddess."

Ash didn't move. He stared at Ujba, thinking about how he'd treated John, and he felt his fury build inside him. His hands shook until he pressed them against his legs; otherwise, he didn't know what he'd do. Smash Ujba to pieces, most likely.

"Well?" said Ujba, utterly unaware of Ash's desires.

Gold lights sprung up on Ujba's skin. Not many, not many at all. Most were dim – disabling points rather than fatal.

"You are angry. Why?" said Ujba, his back turned to Ash as he leaned over something in the corner.

Where to begin? "For a lot of things, but right here, right now? For what you did to John."

❖

Now Ujba turned round. If Ash didn't know better, he'd have said the guru looked surprised.

"John? The little thief? What exactly did I do to him?"

"Beat him, starved him. Cast him out and stole his money. The money I gave him."

Ujba stroked his moustache. "The money, yes, I took it. Why not? But those other crimes? I will tell you this. I am hard, but I am not cruel. John left the same day you went with your father. Poorer for certain, but unharmed by me or any of my house."

"But he told me—"

"The boy is a thief. He was perhaps working your Western sympathies for more rupees. He has a weak and gentle face. I've told him more than once it will make his fortune. He is easy to pity. Easy to believe."

"Why would he lie to me?"

"Why indeed? This is a good question to ask yourself."

"John is my friend," said Ash. His only friend, it seemed. "He helped me escape your prison. That's why you did those things to him."

"Prison? You mean the Lalgur? You think you were in a prison? What happened when your so-called friend helped you escape my school? Were you not captured by Savage? Were you not forced to hand over the Kali-aastra to him? Was not your sister threatened with death, to be fed to Savage's demons? Was this the help John provided?" Ujba laughed, and his amusement was brutal. "I think you could do with fewer of these types of friends."

"What, and more friends like you?"

❖

"I am your guru. That is far more important." He brushed the dust off his palms. "Now, we have work to do."

Ujba took a wooden box and brought it over. It was about the size of a shoe box, made of old, dark wood, smooth and shiny with age. Elaborate Sanskrit writing covered the lid, once inlaid with gold leaf, but the letters were too worn to be read and most of the gold was gone. The guru knelt down, silently motioning for Ash to do the same opposite him.

What was going on? John had told him that Ujba had been brutal, and Ash believed him. But as Ash searched the guru's face, he couldn't be sure. Rishi trusted Ujba; he'd made arrangements for Ash's training with him. Ujba might be evil, but he was a priest of Kali. Ash was a servant of Kali. He didn't know what to believe.

Lost in confusion, he sat down.

The smell of herbs, bitter and sweet, spilled out as Ujba gently raised the lid on the box. He took out a small silver bowl – little larger than an eggcup – a folded paper packet and a razor. He shook black powder into the bowl. "Hold out your hand."

Ash did. The razor slipped over his palm.

"Ow!" Ash shouted. He stared at the thin red line. "What'd you do that for?"

Ujba grabbed Ash's bleeding hand and let the blood drip into the bowl. He muttered prayers to himself as he swirled the mixture. Then he held it up. "Drink."

Ash sniffed the oily black liquid within and almost gagged up breakfast. The smell was sickeningly sweet, but putrid, like meat left out too long in the hot sun. "What is it?"

❖

"Soma," said Ujba. "It's to bring you closer to Kali."

"Really? One whiff of that almost killed me."

"It might. Most of the ingredients are poisonous." Ujba smirked. "But you've been dead before and that didn't stop you, did it?"

"What'll happen to me if I drink it?"

"Your senses will ascend to a higher plane. You will see Kali. You will understand what she has planned for you. If you are worthy, she will unlock further powers from the Kali-aastra. If you are unworthy, you will die."

"In which case you'd better pour it down the drain."

Ujba pushed the bowl into Ash's hand. "Drink it. It's what Kali wants. You will become a true Kali-aastra, able to use all the power of Kali. You will be purged of any... weakness."

"What sort of weakness?"

"Doubt. Fear. Compassion. You are destined to do great and terrible things, boy."

"I'll be a Thug – that's it, isn't it?"

"And so much more. Once you rid yourself of your humanity you will be unstoppable. The perfect weapon of Kali."

Ujba wanted Ash to be some remorseless killing machine. A psychopath. He looked at the guru, wondering what sort of teacher Rishi had sent him. This was the price for more power? Hadn't Parvati said something about this, ages ago, when he'd first assumed the powers of the Kali-aastra? *Power corrupts. Absolute power corrupts absolutely.* She had also said Gemma was dead because of him, and the more he embraced the powers of the Kali-aastra, the more death would surround him. Who would be next? John? Josh? His dad? Lucky? He didn't want such power if that was the price. It had to stop.

"No," he said.

Ujba's voice hardened. "Don't you want to be more powerful?"

"I... don't want to become a monster," he said. "I've had enough."

Ujba pushed the bowl against Ash's chest and Ash flicked it away. The contents splashed over the clean tiles, leaving a black, oily trail. The bowl rang as it bounced across the floor.

"This lesson is over," said Ash as he stood. For the first time in ages he felt a sense of relief. This one decision he knew was right.

Ujba glowered. "You are a fool."

Ash left.

Chapter Twenty-five

Everyone ignored Ash when he got back to the cemetery. The other rakshasas didn't even look in his direction, and there was no place by the campfire for him when they gathered round it for supper. All their backs were turned to him, and the only looks he got were scowls. John just shrugged when Ash found him and then went off to get some food from one of the street vendors, while Ash parked himself away from the main party.

Parvati had lied to him, and he didn't see how he was in the wrong. How could he ignore what he'd seen in his vision?

Still, they needed to clear the air. He didn't feel like asking any of the others where she was. But he should speak to her, apologise for the things he'd said, get on with what was important. Finding Savage.

Ash went looking for Parvati without success. She and Mahout were gone. But he did find Khan, not far away, snoozing under a crude lean-to made of palm leaves. The tiger rakshasa lay flat on his back, arms behind his head with a scarf covering his eyes. The thin, light cloth fluttered with his soft snores.

"Khan? You awake?"

Khan peeled the cloth away and blinked the sleep dust out of his eyes. "What have you done now?"

"Where's Parvati?"

"No idea." He rolled over, turning his back to Ash. "I'm busy."

"You've been sleeping all day. Get up."

With a melodramatic groan and a lot of scratching and stretching, Khan stood up. "What's the problem?"

"Parvati. You think I should say something?"

"Haven't you said enough? Still, it proves one thing. She must really, *really* like you."

"How so?"

"You're still alive. The old Parvati would have had her fangs in your neck for humiliating her in front of everyone like that. It must be hanging out with mortals — it's made her mellow."

Mellow? That wasn't a word Ash associated with Parvati. "She makes it so hard; she's become totally stuck up. Look at the way everyone bows and scrapes in front of her."

Khan gave a low whistle. "Oh, and you're not stuck up at all, Mr Ash 'Kali-aastra' Mistry? You're just as bad. And Parvati's got a lot of responsibility now that Ravana's dead."

"Meaning what? She wants to take over the demon nations?"

"Better her than Savage, don't you think?" Khan picked at a canine tooth with his long forefinger nail. "Was that why you woke me, to talk politics?"

"She knew the Koh-i-noor was a Brahma-aastra. Why didn't she tell me?"

"You want to know about the Brahma-aastra, is that it?"

"You knew too?" They'd all been keeping secrets from him. Why? It didn't matter, as long as he found out about it now. "Can it raise the dead?"

Khan leaned against a tree trunk. "It's better we start at the beginning. Let me tell you about the Koh-i-noor. I first saw it in Lanka, back when Ravana was still alive and before all that trouble with Rama. He'd got it off some prince or king, I forget who."

"But rakshasas can't use aastras."

"That didn't stop him from trying. We're talking about Ravana, the demon king. Most of the rules didn't apply to him. Remember I told you he'd once been a Brahmin? He was devoted to all the gods and he gained all his magic from them, but he became so powerful that he started to think he was better than them. He had learned all the mantras, the spells, of Brahma, the Creator, and he thought he could awaken the Koh-i-noor using one such spell."

"Did he?"

"Not as far as I know. But soon after that stories started spreading that the diamond was cursed. Following Ravana's defeat, the diamond became part of the booty handed over

173

❖

to Rama, and since then it has passed from one human king to another."

"But what about the mantras? Someone surely knew how to awaken the aastra?"

"I reckon some imperfect understanding of the awakening mantra is all that exists now. The spell was passed down from one generation to the next, copied from scroll to scroll or recited from master to student. Over the centuries errors crept in and the spell changed. Your friend, Savage, probably *thinks* he knows how to activate the Koh-i-noor, though I seriously doubt it. But what he does know will cause a huge amount of trouble."

"Trouble? How can raising the dead be trouble?"

Khan smiled, and instead of his usual self-confident arrogance this smile was softer, almost sympathetic. "The ones who come back are never the ones who left, Ash. Gemma, the girl you knew — she is gone and gone for ever. Do not be tempted by false hopes. Look at Savage, what he is, what he does, all in his quest for life beyond his natural span. His search for immortality is a fool's one. He's trying to catch a cloud. You mortals have just one life, and that is for a reason. It is that knowledge that drives you to do the things you do, both good and evil. Humans excel because they know the limits of their time here. Remember the dead, honour them, but let them be. And that pain you feel, that loss — hold on to it."

Ash shook his head. Thinking about Gemma brought the pain back: a cold blade high in his chest and ice that crushed his lungs. "I don't want to feel it."

"To feel it is human. The day that agony goes, the day you care nothing about death, that is the day you become a monster, Ash."

Rain began to fall – first a few heavy drops, then it was as if the entire sky opened up and sheets of water descended. Ash stood under the cover of a mausoleum doorway, soaked through within seconds. He waved as John appeared, carrying two wrapped packets.

"Try this," said John as he joined Ash. "Fresh and hot."

Ash opened the paper and held a samosa with his fingertips. The triangular deep-fried pastry smelled delicious. He bit into it and savoured the spiced vegetable filling. John smiled as Ash gave a thumbs up. "Thanks, John." At least he had one friend he could depend on.

"Well? How did it go with Ujba?"

Ash shrugged. "Badly. I don't know what Rishi was thinking when he agreed for me to train with him."

"That deal was made when Rishi was alive. Ujba wouldn't have dared try anything while the old *sadhu* was around."

"You think Ujba was scared of Rishi?"

"Rishi was the master of the mantras of the gods. Ujba is just a big, ugly bruiser. No contest."

"I wish Rishi *was* around right now. He'd sort it all out." Ash finished the samosa, licking the crumbs off his fingertips. "That was most excellent."

"No luck with finding Savage, then?" said John.

"We're getting nowhere with anything. We've only the word

❖

of a rat rakshasa to go on, and maybe Monty was lying."
Ash looked out across the jungle. "Savage could be anywhere.
I don't think he's even in Kolkata."

"I've an idea," said John. "I've been thinking about that
map of Parvati's."

"Yeah?"

John picked up a long, drooping palm leaf and held it
over them like an umbrella. "Come on."

The downpour was in full torrential mode as they hit the
streets, which had transformed into small rivers. Dirty tan
streams ran across the pavements, and the drainpipes, unable
to cope with the immense water flow, spouted water from
every joint. Ash could see a group of rickshaws with their
brightly polished fenders and decorated canopies parked along
the front of one of the grander hotels. The drivers sat
hunched on the wall, heads tucked into their shoulders,
sharing cigarettes. No one wanted to be out in this drenching
rain.

"A lot of bookshops here, have you noticed?" said John
in a meaningful tone, gazing into a shop window.

"Maybe Amazon doesn't deliver this far east."

"Kolkata's built on books."

Now that John mentioned it, Ash realised it was true.
There *were* a lot of bookshops. They were standing in front
of one, in fact. Ash looked up at the shop sign, written in
English and Hindi.

Education Centre.

Kolkata was a famous intellectual centre, he knew that,
with lots of big universities. And universities needed

❖

bookshops. He peered into the window himself, barely able to see the store within; the glass was semi-opaque with dust. A few books on display had gone yellow with age and sun exposure, their pages crinkled in the corners.

"Looks like it hasn't changed in two hundred years," said Ash. "I bet Savage probably shopped here for his first Hindi-English dictionary."

"Exactly," said John with a smile. He opened the door. "C'mon."

The shop smelled damp and mouldy. All this paper and all this rain wasn't a great combination. There were a few bestsellers on the table nearest the counter, all neatly wrapped in plastic to keep them pristine.

The shelves were made of dark wood and absolutely stuffed with books. A local turned a squeaking rack, inspecting political pamphlets. A student hummed and hahhed as he flicked through some heavy engineering text-book.

"What are we looking for?" asked Ash.

John went to the counter. A woman in an orange sari sat behind an old-fashioned till, a copy of some black-and-red-covered paranormal romance in her hand.

"Begging your pardon, miss, but do you have any maps? Old maps?" John asked.

"Of where?"

"Of British Calcutta."

The assistant tucked a strip of ribbon into the book before closing it. She headed for the back, John and Ash a few paces behind her.

❖

"You've lost me," said Ash.

"When was Savage first here?"

"Mid-nineteenth century. Back when the East India Company was in charge."

"Don't you get it, Ash?"

"Let's assume I have no idea what you're talking about. It'll be easier."

The assistant touched a stack of papers. "Here you are."

John began rearranging the items on the table, moving books off it so he could work through the pile of maps carefully. "Savage doesn't know modern Kolkata. Does he?"

"No, he's only recently come back to India. He's spent the last century out in the Far East."

"So doesn't it make sense he'd base himself somewhere he knew?" John was turning over the maps quicker and quicker.

"A place that existed back then?"

"Yes." John stopped at one of the maps, leaning over it to read the faint copperplate calligraphy. "We need to compare a map from the 1850s with ours. We need a map of old Calcutta, not modern Kolkata. Find out which locations appear on both."

Ash quickly unfolded the modern map they'd been using. They'd marked all the one hundred and fifty potential locations on it with red felt pen. Only half had been checked so far.

"We want this one," said John.

The map he held had been printed in 1849. Calcutta was a fraction of its present size then, but Ash recognised the snaking path of the Hooghly River, the octagonal Fort

William, the neatly arranged Botanical Gardens and the main Kali Temple. Palaces of local rulers were also outlined, as were the various military compounds that housed the East India Company's troops, there to keep an eye on their mercantile and political interests.

The maps had been drawn to different scales, and the earlier one lacked the satellite accuracy of the modern one Ash had, but by using the river, the fort and the temple as reference points, they could quickly tick off which locations were common to both. Some had already been checked, others dismissed as blatantly inappropriate for Savage, being too public and exposed. But there was one...

"The cantonment." Ash pointed to a large rectangle on the outskirts of the city. "Here."

The word 'cantonment' was still used in India for a large, enclosed compound. It usually referred to civil servant accommodations, with offices and facilities like hospitals and shops within the walls. A city within a city, originally set up by foreign armies to house their troops.

"It's isolated, large, and judging by the main building, suitably palatial," said Ash.

"Perfect for Savage, don't you think?" John couldn't help but smile.

"Totally." Ash checked his wallet. The map wasn't cheap, but he had enough. "Let's get this and take it to the others."

"Don't you think we should check the cantonment out first?" said John. "If we go in loud and noisy, Savage will just run away and we're back to the beginning. Anyway, this

❖

is only an idea. He may not be there. Let's just snoop and make sure."

What better way to make it up with Parvati than to find Savage? Ash grinned. "You've changed a lot, John."

John looked at him. "I just follow your example."

Chapter Twenty-six

The last time Ash had visited India, it had been during the height of summer. He'd spent the days dripping in sweat, living in an oven. The rivers had been dry and the landscape a sea of bone-white dust. But now — after the monsoons — the countryside overflowed with life. Tall fields of green grass swayed at the roadsides and the trees were hung with sagging vines bearing massive, polished leaves.

John and Ash sat in the back of a motor rickshaw. The three-wheeled cross between a scooter and a taxi zipped in and out of traffic, taking them away from Kolkata across the Howrah Bridge. That massive cathedral of steel, seven hundred metres long and thirty metres wide, was the main crossing over the Hooghly River. Gigantic steel arches, pummelled with fist-sized rivets, stretched across from one

❖

bank to the other. It reminded Ash that when India did something, it did it supersized.

The entire frame crawled with traffic, wheeled and on foot, motorised and bullock- or donkey-driven. It felt as if the entire city was on the move. Stall owners offering snacks and drinks and trinkets lined the railings, some perilously perched on the beams above, crying out for customers. Kids weaved between the gridlocked cars, selling newspapers and cigarettes. Ash and John's rickshaw joined this sluggish river of life and machinery until they finally broke free of the city into the surrounding countryside. Night was falling, and cloying smells rose from the blooming flowers, filling the air along with musk and whining insects.

"The cantonment, sahib," said the rickshaw driver.

The rickshaw's single bright headlamp lit a path across a thicket to a cracked, vine-covered wall. The original plaster had long since crumbled away and was covered in plant growth and moss, creating a curtain of green. Tree roots broke up the short drive to the front gates, which themselves were rusty iron and bound with ivy.

Ash jumped out and approached the gates. He pulled out a small torch and shone it through the gap in the railings. The light didn't reach far, but he could make out a row of derelict bungalows, almost lost within the overgrowth. Trees rose and spread over the central path, overwhelming it in darkness. Cicadas chirped their nightly songs from the trees and bushes.

John tugged at the gates. They were held fast by the vines. The place looked like it hadn't been used in a century. It

❖

might have once been all neat lawns and cosy verandas, but now the jungle had reclaimed it, quashing all signs of civilisation under a sea of tangled roots and leaves.

Ash looked up and down the long wall. No lights, no signs of anything or anyone.

"I don't think this is the place," he said. There was nothing here but jungle and insects.

"There could be another way in," said John. He tested one of the thick vines clinging to the wall. "We could get over easily. If you're up for it."

"Shall we go back, sahib?" The rickshaw driver was already wheeling his vehicle round.

"We've come all the way out here," said John. "We might as well take a look."

"You wait here," said Ash as he handed the driver a fistful of rupees. The man looked at them, clearly confused about why they'd want to be out here at this time of night, then shrugged, switched off his engine. He held up both hands.

"Ten minutes, no more," he said.

"Fine. Ten minutes." That should be more than enough time for a snoop around.

John put one foot up and swiftly climbed to the top of the wall. "Come on," he said.

Ash took hold of a sticky, sap-coated vine and a few moments later crossed over the wall and dropped down into the darkness within the compound.

They hid among the tall grass, watching and listening. The nearest bungalow was about fifteen metres away, now half submerged under heavy leaves and tree roots.

❖

And then Ash saw someone.

The figure was resting his hand on his chin, looking at something on the ground. All Ash could see was the moonlight shining on his curved back. Ash put his finger to his lips and waved that John should wait where he was.

In spite of the grass, Ash made no more noise than a faint breeze. He put one foot softly down in the lush, damp earth, waiting for it to absorb any sound before moving the other foot. The bamboo kept him hidden in deep shadow.

Ash blinked, drawing up his dark powers. He would use *Marma Adi* to knock the person out. All he needed was to search the golden marks on the man for something non-fatal. But he couldn't see anything on the dark figure, and certainly no golden map of death.

What was wrong?

He stepped out of the bamboo, now less than ten feet away from the man. The guy hadn't moved.

Ash paused, digging deeper into the swirling energies within the pit of his soul. Raw, intense energy surged through him, but the glimmering lights did not appear.

It didn't matter. He'd punch the guy in the back of the head. Definitely knock him out and hopefully keep brain damage to a minimum.

Ash was right behind the man. He pulled back his fist and swung.

Then he screamed and hopped back, shaking his pulsing arm. He cradled his hand, groaning as pain filled it with fire.

John ran up. "What's wrong?"

Ash kicked the unmoving man. "It's a bloody statue!"

And not just any statue, but a life-sized copy of *The Thinker* by Rodin. He should have recognised it.

Now that Ash looked around, he noticed that there were dozens of statues scattered everywhere. Some were hidden by moss or entangled by vines and ivy; others just lay fallen on the ground. It looked like someone had emptied out an art gallery or a museum and dumped the statues here.

John pulled some loose vine off a rusty statue of Shiva. The statue's face and body were pockmarked by years in the rain.

"You crying?" asked John.

"So would you if you'd just punched solid bronze." Ash carefully unflexed his fingers, hoping he hadn't broken them. More tears sprang from his eyes. It really, *really* hurt.

They walked towards the first bungalow. Creepers reached from the trees to the roof like green flags, and large moths flitted in the night sky. The mustiness of the cantonment smothered Ash.

"Creepy, aren't they," said John, poking one of the statues with a stick.

Yes, they are, Ash thought. They were from all parts of the world, some classical Greek, most Indian, some modern, many ancient. Most were copies of copies, a few sculpted with care and art, others crudely thrown together and misshapen. Ash couldn't shake the feeling that he was walking among the dead. Lifeless, empty eyes gazed at nothing, their forms frozen and slowly decaying. There were hundreds of them. It was worse than the graveyard.

The bungalow was uninhabitable. The wood was warped

❖

and rotten all the way through. The veranda seat creaked, and a couple of lizards scurried across the wicker chairs.

"Hasn't been used in decades," said Ash. He stopped at a notice board on the main street. There was a poster, yellow and streaked, advertising a hymn recital on March 13, 1941, with tea afterwards, organised by Lady Middleton. There was also a small card referring to a missing cat called Gladstone and a list of the army's cricket fixtures for the summer.

This is time travel, Ash thought. OK, not in a blue police box or through some wormhole in space, but he could feel what this place must have been like when the British had been here. They'd made the cantonment a small piece of England, with tea parties on the lawn and Sundays with the vicar. They came all the way here and brought all their Surrey entitlements with them. They'd made sure India was kept out, beyond the gates.

Now look at it. Moth-eaten furniture and rotten, crumbling bungalows, their prim English gardens turned into swampy jungle.

He and John moved further into the compound. The statues filled the paths and lurked in the lush greenery, some so covered in vines they looked like they could have been dryads, tree spirits.

Ash, hands on hips, looked up and down the crossroads. More bungalows on either side, with a parade ground ahead. "Let's look over there." If they couldn't find anything, they'd head back before their ten minutes were up and the rickshaw driver left.

The parade ground was surrounded on two sides by office buildings, with a derelict but still magnificent hall at the

❖

head, a strange hybrid of English mansion and Indian palace with domes and battlements and towers. But the jungle surrounded it, a green giant stretching out its fingers of moss and bark, its many arms hugging the broken roof. Tall mangrove trees spilled their massive roots through windows and ran like monstrous tentacles over the walls.

Ash stepped on to the open parade ground.

What's wrong with this picture?

He bent down and inspected the grass along the edge. The stalks were ragged, but when he touched them, he felt a clean diagonal tip.

"Someone's cut the grass," he said.

It could be something, or it could be nothing. He looked at the statues gathered round the perimeter of the field. One, a replica of *David*, caught his attention. It had been made well, but something wasn't right. The grass all round it had been trodden on, he realised, great areas flattened as though an army had marched over it.

But where was the army? There was nothing here but statues.

"This is pointless," said Ash. "Let's go."

"No. Let's look around a bit more. Be sure."

"You really have changed, John. You weren't like this at the Lalgur."

"It took guts to help you escape." John turned his back on him. "And for what?"

"What do you mean?"

"You really don't remember, do you?" He spoke with cold rage. "We had a deal, Ash."

❖

"But you escaped! You said you got out."

"Oh, yes. I did. I got out. I made a whole new bunch of... friends."

"Who, John?" A chill dread seeped into him.

"Friends who gave me money. Who helped me find my mother. Who still send her a thousand rupees every month."

"Tell me who these friends are."

John met his gaze. "What wouldn't you do to help your family?" He pushed Ash out of his way and retreated towards the line of statues. "I'm not sorry. I want you to know that. I'm not sorry."

Ash tensed, looking around as John disappeared into the darkness. But there was nothing. He was surrounded by lifeless stone. He glanced again at the statue of *David*.

Then, the stone grinding loudly in the still night air, *David* turned his head.

Chapter Twenty-seven

*A*nother statue, fallen down and tied to the earth by thick vines, began to struggle against its bonds. The vines snapped as it pulled free a bronze arm. Its joints creaked as it stood.

One by one, the statues moved. Slowly, as though waking from a long, deep slumber, they shook free the tangling creepers and the rust of decades from their joints. Then they began moving faster. A Chinese stone lion jumped off its pedestal; the trees trembled as it landed. A heavy foot thumped behind Ash, and he tumbled sideways as a six-armed Shiva tried to grab him. Its hands clanged together.

Ash retreated to the main street and stared as dozens of now-living statues lumbered towards him. Where had John gone? What had he done?

The trees creaked. The ground shook violently and a cloud

of leather-winged bats burst from their hidden perches within the foliage. Leaves tumbled down and the entire jungle came to life.

Ash looked up in mute horror.

Tree trunks bent, then splintered.

A groaning noise, then crashing, as the trees fell towards him.

And then something began to emerge. Something huge. As it stepped over the broken trunks, its footfalls made the ground buckle.

The statue towered over the forest, twenty-five metres tall, its grey body mottled with moss, weeds growing like veins across its stony flesh. It wore an embroidered and pitted skirt, and bracelets and necklaces were carved round its wrists and neck. The bare torso was sculpted with the lean muscles of a young man. Bats shrouded its head like a dark, chaotic halo. The head was as big as any of the bungalows. The statue raised a truck-sized fist, dust showering from its joints as it curled its huge fingers.

Ash started to run, not even conscious of having given the command to his legs. But he didn't seem to be getting any further away. The shadow of the giant figure covered him, and the sound of rumbling stone drowned out his own panting breath and pounding heartbeat. His legs seemed sluggish, each step small, insect-like compared to the immense reach of the creature behind him. Was this how he was going to die? Swatted like a fly?

The wind roared as the fist swept down and Ash hurled himself forward. The ground shattered, throwing broken paving slabs, old rocks and large chunks of soil into the air. The shock wave lifted Ash off his feet and he crashed into, and then through, the wall of one of the bungalows. Bits of plaster, wood and mouldy old thatch fell over him as he lay, coughing, head spinning, among the ruins.

Fear — empty, drowning fear — threatened to overwhelm him. The giant statue peered down through gaps in the roof; his fingers, as long and wide as building columns, ripped through the tiles and groped blindly within. Ash bit down hard to stop himself from screaming. The massive fingers broke apart the wooden frame as if it were made of balsa wood.

Run. Just get out of here. Nothing smart, nothing heroic, just run.

Ash shoved the chunks of plaster off and got up into a crouch. He felt sick, dizzy, frightened.

Outside, the feet of the hundreds of moving statues sounded like distant thunder, a constant rumbling, uneven and gross with threatening violence. The bungalow rocked on its brittle old beams.

A vast, black shadow loomed over him, blocking out all light. The timbers over his head creaked and splintered, and in a long, thunderous wave of tearing and ripping, the roof came off.

The statue peered in, searching for him, his vast head blocking out the sky. It tossed the ragged roof away and reached down with its hand. Ash heaved himself to his feet and scrambled over the broken walls and fallen struts as the statue's palm, easily three metres wide, flattened the room he'd been in, cracking through the floor and shaking the

❖

building's rotten foundations. The second hand crunched down in front of him, and he slipped over some mossy carpet to stop just before the fingers grabbed him.

The bungalow couldn't take any more. Walls tottered and fell, and Ash turned just in time to see a support beam swing down. He ducked, but not fast enough. It struck him across the back and he was sent reeling into the corner.

He tried to get up, but a wall of stone encircled him. Ash pushed as trunk-thick fingers closed round him. He tried to scrabble out of the massive hand, but was caught round the legs, waist and chest.

Ash struggled, but what could he do? His powers were useless. This thing wasn't alive, so it didn't have glowing points of weakness. The giant statue lifted him out of the bungalow. Stone monkeys leaped upon the thing's arm and scurried up to perch on its shoulder. A little more pressure and Ash would burst like a grape. The statue straightened, lifting him higher and higher until it held him before its blank eyes. This close, Ash could see the weathered, cracked skin and the centuries of moss that covered its grey flesh. He could do nothing but glare and snarl, "Well? What are you waiting for?"

He'd been stupid and it had got him killed again. But this time there would be no coming back.

But the statue only held him. Why had it gone so quiet?

"Ash Mistry?" said a voice from below — a voice Ash recognised immediately. "Is that you up there?"

Chapter Twenty-eight

Ash had dreamed of what it would be like to hear that voice again. It was rich, proud and arrogant, the voice of a man who thought he owned the world and everyone in it. Its deep, powerful timbre made him shiver with dread and anger. That voice had haunted his dreams and given birth to his darkest nightmares.

The statue lumbered side to side as it settled down into a kneeling position. Still holding Ash within its inescapable grip, it turned its hand so he was facing the gathered assembly below him. The vast crowd of statues — animal, human and monstrous — stood immobile. But there were others among this field of stone and iron, and the closest was a figure in a white suit.

Lord Alexander Savage stood there, looking up, his hands resting on his tiger-headed cane. Ash stared, slack-jawed.

❖

Savage was not how he remembered him. The last time he'd seen him, Savage had been young, beautiful and inhumanly perfect.

This man was anything but perfect. The suit hung off a skeletal frame with withered, parchment-thin skin that flapped upon the spindly limbs. Huge, dark liver spots covered the hairless scalp, and large yellow teeth dangled from shrunken gums. The lips were pale, thin and cracked. He looked ready to collapse, and leaned heavily upon the cane.

But his eyes – his eyes shone with feverish power. Black upon black, they were the eyes of night, of pure darkness.

Beside him were Jackie and John. John trembled as the rakshasa put her clawed hand on his shoulder. Just at the edge of the moonlight, half hidden in the jungle, were Savage's hyena rakshasas, cackling.

Ash looked at Savage, hate rising in his chest, churning in his guts. The distance between them wasn't great, but held as he was it might as well have been a million miles. The Englishman's smile widened.

"So glad you could accept my invitation," said Savage.

Ash tried to move a little, but the statue only tightened its grip, crushing his chest until he was gasping for breath. It lowered him until he was just off the ground, eye level with his enemy.

"You look upset, Ash," said Savage.

"And you look like the Elephant Man's less handsome older brother."

"Very amusing, boy. Is that what passes for wit in this day and age?" He tutted and shuffled closer, bringing with

194

him a putrid rotting odour. Not only did Savage look like a ten-day-old corpse, he also smelled like one. "Ravana made me young again, as you well remember, but his magic failed the moment you killed him. And here I am, back where I started, thanks to you."

Yes, it was true. Savage had been a living skeleton when Ash had first met him. "Glad I did something right," he said.

Savage didn't appear to hear. He plucked at the shirt hanging loosely over his chest. "Now only my magic, such as it is, keeps the flesh and soul together. But it's falling apart. I can feel it."

"More good news."

Savage paused and looked at him, eyes filled with hate. Then he smiled and pointed up at the giant statue with his cane. "What do you think of my Jagannath?"

"What is it?" Ash asked.

"This one I found down south, at an abandoned temple near Bangalore. The Jagannath is the god Vishnu in his aspect as lord of the world. You will not believe how much trouble I had getting him here."

"And you got him – them – all to move?"

"Yes, my *loha-mukhas*." He tapped a nearby statue. "The Jews call them golems, but they must build their creatures from scratch. My magic can transform any inanimate object into some semblance of life. It's a trick I learned in China, near Xian."

Ash slumped in the thing's grip. Ujba had told him he needed to learn all the powers of the Kali-aastra but, in his arrogance, Ash had thought he had everything he needed.

195

❖

"It took me a while to realise what had happened with the Kali-aastra," continued Savage. "It broke, didn't it? You had a part, the part that allowed you mastery over death, the ability to kill any living thing, didn't you?"

Ash said nothing.

"And when I used it, I got the part that allowed me to destroy — to smash things apart. That's how I was able to open the Iron Gates, you see. If you had tried, you would have failed. We both got what we wanted from the Kali-aastra."

Until now, thought Ash. What he would give to be able to destroy his stone trap.

"Where's the arrowhead now?" asked Ash.

Savage sighed. "Buried under a billion tons of sand out in Rajasthan. Like my dreams." His eyes flickered red for a moment before darkening to midnight. "I've been looking forward to meeting you again, Ash, and, I must admit, it turned out even better than I had hoped, thanks to your friend here."

John backed away. "I've done what you wanted. I've told you where the Koh-i-noor is and brought him here."

Savage smiled slowly. "The English Cemetery — correct?"

John gulped. "Yes. The demon princess is there, with her followers."

"Hardly a concern." The Englishman gave Jackie the slightest nod. "Yes, I should reward you."

They're going to kill him.

For a second, just a second, Ash wanted John dead. He wouldn't be here, trapped and helpless, if it wasn't for him.

Ujba had been right; John had lied to him. Even now it didn't seem possible. But, right or wrong, John had done it to help his mum. Would Ash have done any different? If Ash had thought more about John's needs, he would have helped him more to find his family. Instead he had let Savage do it. Could he really blame John?

But now Savage didn't need John any more. Even from here, Ash saw the hungry look on Jackie's face, the saliva wetting her lips. She was waiting for the order, but Ash was not about to let another friend of his be killed by the jackal rakshasa. Begging them to let John go wouldn't help; they'd take delight in killing him while Ash watched. So he needed to do the opposite. Ash needed to demand they kill him.

"The best reward is death," Ash snarled. "The traitor deserves to die."

Savage twisted the cane top, a silver tiger head with ruby eyes, revealing a few centimetres of blade. The cane was a swordstick.

"My thoughts exactly," Savage said. He drew the narrow shining steel out and touched the tip against John's heart. "I have a rule to use traitors only once. If someone is happy to betray his best friend, how on earth can I trust him?"

Sweat dripped down Ash's brow and he flicked his damp hair out of his eyes. "Think I care?"

John yelled and turned to flee but Jackie leaped in his way. He ran to the side, but she was there. In the shadows beyond her, the hyena rakshasas prowled. Their bestial amber eyes were the only light in the otherwise complete darkness, and the trees shivered with their growls.

❖

Jackie grabbed John and hurled him to the ground.

"Ash…" begged John.

"Your bed," said Ash. "Lie in it."

Savage's eyes narrowed. "You have changed, boy. There's a healthy ruthlessness there. You remind me of me when I was your age." He spun the sword in wide arcs. "It's such a shame we're on opposite sides. Ah well."

Ash grinned as Savage raised the blade. His eyes met Jackie's and the grin broadened.

The sword flashed.

Then halted. Jackie held Savage's wrist, the tip of the sword a finger's width from John's eyeball.

"Wait," Jackie said. She glanced towards Ash. "He is the Kali-aastra."

Savage frowned. Then he stepped back and laughed. He waved the sword at Ash. "Good, very good. Very, very good."

They've fallen for it.

Savage lowered the blade. "What would happen if I killed this boy? His death energy would pass into you and make you stronger, would it not? And he's a friend, someone you cared about. Lord knows, it might even be a Great Death. We can't be having that, can we?"

Ash said nothing. But inside he sighed with relief. He'd saved John. Savage couldn't kill his friend if it risked Ash becoming stronger, perhaps strong enough to break free of the loha-mukhas.

Savage turned to John. "Run, boy. Run fast and run far and do not look back."

John got up and looked at Ash. Tears ran down his cheeks

❖

and he looked dead inside. Ash wanted to tell him it was OK, that he didn't blame John. But if he admitted to caring for him, Savage might use that against him. Better John think Ash hated him. It would keep him alive longer.

Ash glared at him. "Better start now. Once I'm free, I will find you."

John fled. Ash heard his sobs well after he'd vanished into the dark.

Savage gripped Ash's face, meeting his gaze. "I so want to kill you. But I did that once already, and look what happened? You came back. You killed Lord Ravana."

"This is just revenge?"

"Hardly. This is about the Koh-i-noor. You were an unexpected bonus. I need the diamond, the Brahma-aastra. The Life Giver will repair all… this." He gestured to his hideous body.

"You know how to awaken it?"

"There is a way," said Savage.

Ash's heart leapt. Maybe they could save Gemma, like some true hero. He'd prove Parvati and Khan wrong. But before he could ask more, Savage hissed and panted, even emitting a brief, harsh scream as his body swelled and mutated. His spine stretched against the suit jacket and lumps grew on his skull. Then, chest heaving, the deformities reduced and Savage's body reverted to its normal, frail shape. He stared up at Ash. "See what you've done? I have more power than ever, but my body cannot contain it. More magic than mortal flesh can bear."

"I don't feel bad about that at all." Ash met the Englishman's gaze. "So, the Koh-i-noor will repair you. Then what?"

❖

"And like a comic villain I will tell you everything?" Savage shook his head. "No, I want you to know just enough so all that follows will be because of your failure. In our last meeting the game went to you. That was beginner's luck."

"Luck was you getting away that night."

Savage bristled, but said nothing.

"So that's it? You're going to kill me? Skewer me with your sword?"

"Just stick you like a pig? After all we've been through together?" Savage waved the slim blade. "No, I've something far better in mind."

Chapter Twenty-nine

The Jagannath twisted its wrist and pressed Ash into the ground. As it opened its fingers, he squirmed, but it pressed harder, flattening him into the earth until he felt as if he was under a steamroller. Then hard, unyielding hands gripped his arms and ankles. The Jagannath slowly released him, and two stone and marble monkeys, each the size of a man, lifted Ash and carried him through the cantonment. Branches and leaves brushed his face, and the monkeys' hold was every bit as firm as the Jagannath's. Twist as he might, Ash remained trapped in stone.

Engines revved and headlights came alive in the dark. After a few minutes a convoy of trucks emerged along the road. Savage glanced back as he stepped into the lead vehicle. "He's coming with us."

The trucks had high-sided wooden walls painted with

garish scenes and designs – panoramic mountain views, the paint smeared with oily smoke and the wood chipped. A whole field of headlights shone from the front, joined with strings of multicoloured Christmas lights that flickered on and off randomly. The line of vehicles was less a convoy and more a parade. It might seem stupid to have such distinctive vehicles, but here in India, the trucks and minivans were all the same, brightly and extravagantly painted and lit. These blended in perfectly.

The monkeys clambered into the back of the lead truck and squatted down among wooden crates and trunks, Ash suspended between them. Then the engine shifted gears noisily and spewed out a cloud of black smoke, and they were on the move, rocking from side to side as the truck bounced over the uneven ground and in and out of the pot-holes that punctured the old cantonment road. Ash winced with each jolt; it was like being on the rack, dangling by his ankles and wrists, the sockets stretched 'til they almost popped.

Where were they taking him? Ash twisted his head as they drove, but all he could see was the moonlight shimmering on the glossy black surface of the river.

The truck rumbled deeper into the countryside, past sleeping villages and the occasional herd of cattle resting by the road. Other trucks roared past with horns blaring and engines thundering. Ash glimpsed all this through the ill-fitting wooden panels on the side of his truck. He also caught a better look at the crates in the back with him. They were all large, at least two by two metres. One had its lid off and was filled with packing straw. As the truck interior was briefly

❖

illuminated by the headlights of another passing car, Ash glimpsed a stamp on the side of one box.

INDIAN RAILWAYS ROUTE 2841.

Savage was taking a train ride. But where to?

Ash didn't have time to ponder as the truck jerked and the wheels rumbled upon the echoing frame of another bridge.

The brakes shrieked and one of the crates slid forward. It slammed into the first monkey and the stone beast tottered forward as there was a sharp crack.

The corner of the crate had broken and a stone face gazed out of the straw. It turned its head, that of a snarling demon with a leonine mane, then sank back down into the straw as if hibernating. More loha-mukhas.

The rear panel crashed down and the headlights from the vehicle behind filled the truck with harsh, blinding light.

"Bring him down. Just you," said Savage.

The two monkeys moved swiftly. One released Ash's ankles while the other wrapped its arms tightly round his chest, trapping his arms within its embrace. Even with his legs now freed, Ash could do nothing. The monkey had to weigh a couple of hundred kilos. It hopped down, its stone feet clanging on steel.

The entire convoy had halted on a bridge. Ash hoped that someone might be passing, but they were in the depths of the countryside, isolated and miles from anywhere. Savage gazed out at the river roaring between the supports beneath them. The bridge was another iron monstrosity, all vaulting beams and wide spans and fist-sized rivets. The iron bore patches of orange rust and the road itself was poorly tarmacked, cracked in places so the river could be seen, the headlights catching its flashing, foaming white spray as it collided with the vast, monolithic concrete supports.

A sudden, dull crash was followed by a sharp snap as a tree trunk collided with one of the plinths and shattered into a million slivers. The river was in full spate, swollen by the monsoon rains.

"Come here, Ash, close to the edge," said Savage.

"I'm perfectly fine here."

The monkey stepped forward. Ash pushed his feet against the railings, trying to stop it from getting to the edge, but the monkey was too strong, and he cried out as his feet slipped and the ragged edge of the iron beam scraped the back of his leg, ripping open his trousers.

Jackie laughed and joined Savage. She leaned over the edge and worked a bolt back and forth, the steel grinding against its socket. She gave it a hefty kick and the side fell away. It tumbled for a sickeningly long time before it splashed into the raging waters, more than twenty-five metres below.

"A bit closer – the view is rather splendid," said Savage.

Ash dangled over the black, churning waters. The monkey still held him to its chest, its own feet just barely on the bridge, its long toes curled round the rusty iron edge.

Savage let slip a low whistle. "I wonder how many thousands of gallons are flowing under this bridge every second. Look how high the river is; you can barely see the support plinths. Do you know, I remember when the only way across this river was a spindly old rope thing, like a cat's cradle."

❖

He tapped the metal with his cane. "That was a hundred years ago. Wonder what's down there? You'd be surprised what gets washed up against the legs. Boats, cars, houses even, swept away in floods and trapped, too big to get between the foundations."

"Thank you for the history lesson, Savage. I'd like to get back in the truck now."

Savage turned to face him and smiled. "Goodbye, Ash."

Holding Ash tight, the monkey jumped.

Chapter Thirty

They tumbled over and over as they fell. Ash froze. All he could do was stare at the kaleidoscope of blurring dark strips of the iron bridge and the headlights above and below him, reflecting off the raging waters as they crashed and surged between the massive concrete legs of the bridge. The wind howled as he cartwheeled through the air, ripping the tears from his eyes and the breath from his mouth. He took a single gasp and locked shut his teeth as—

—they slammed into the river and all went black.

Ash shook himself to consciousness a second after hitting the water. Water gurgled in his mouth and he almost swallowed again as the surface, glistening with moonlight, receded away. The monsoon-swollen current ripped him and his captor along as fast as they were sinking, and a second, bone-jarring jolt punched the air from his lungs as they crashed into one of the concrete plinths that the bridge stood upon. The monkey's grip slackened, loosening its hold on his left side, and Ash heaved hard, but then the water accelerated between them and Ash was scraped along a surface, scouring the skin off his body. He bit down ferociously to hold in his scream.

How long could he hold his breath? Not long enough. Even though he was far more powerful than a normal human, he had his limits, and being submerged under a million tons of water was one of them. Savage hadn't needed to kill him up close and risk Ash returning more powerful than ever, like the last time. He was going to die down here, and this time there would be no coming back.

While the marble monkey was heavy, the river was stronger, and they turned over and over like a pebble, bashing along with the flotsam and jetsam of garbage that lay at the foot of the bridge.

I can't hold on. Fire filled Ash, and he just wanted to breathe. Blood pounded in his skull as he fought the crushing weight of the water and the stone creature's embrace. Then, in the corner of his eye, he glimpsed light shining off metal. Instinctively he threw his weight towards it, kicking madly with his freed legs, desperate to shift direction, just a few centimetres.

He hit the river bottom and rolled in the mud upon the stones, some small and others the size of boulders. He blinked the mud from his eyes and saw the metal object three metres away. It was the rusty skeleton of a motorised rickshaw, half submerged in the bank. The cloth canopy had long

❖

since disintegrated and the front wheel had sheared off. It was this, half buried in the mud, that Ash wanted.

Oh God, he had to breathe! Lungs and chest aching, he could barely think; his head felt fat and swollen in agony. His jaw throbbed as he locked it shut.

He twisted his arms and something creaked. Even with his ears filled with the raging waters, he heard, he felt, the monkey's left arm give. The impact with the plinth must have cracked the loha-mukha's arm, weakening it. Driven insane with desperation, Ash pulled and shoved, not caring if he broke his own arm, needing to get out. The stone groaned as he worked his entire torso from side to side. The monkey's arm began to give way. It was a battle now, Ash's body both his saviour and his enemy. If he could just hold his breath a few seconds longer... but the more he struggled, the more he wanted to open his mouth; instinct fought will.

The monkey's arm bent. It snapped.

Left arm free, Ash pushed and stretched towards the wheel rim jutting out of the mud. He leaned as far as he could, kicking the water with his heels to tilt him another couple of centimetres. If he could just reach it...

His first two fingers scratched the rim, and that was enough.

Ash dragged the rim closer, pulling against the muddy grip. It was about a foot in diameter, a heavy steel circular disc weighing about fifteen pounds. The edge wasn't particularly sharp, but it was all he had.

Bubbles slipped from his lips. He couldn't hold on much longer.

Ash lifted it up with his left hand and swung it as hard

as he could through the water against the monkey's right arm, aiming at the fingers.

The blow glanced off, barely chipping it.

Oh God, he couldn't do it. More bubbles burst out, and Ash's arms and legs felt heavier than the monkey now. He struggled to lift the disc.

Concentrate. Concentrate. He glared at the thick fingers that held him trapped. His own tightened round the heavy steel disc.

Ash rammed the disc against the monkey's hand. Its fingers shattered as the last of Ash's breath tore free in a burst of bubbles. He dropped the disc and pushed. He pressed his heels against the inanimate stone, heaved with his left hand, and twisted his body as far as it would go. The jagged edges of the broken limb dug into his belly, tearing deeper into his flesh the harder he struggled. Blood, black and cloudy, swelled from the tears. He didn't care.

Ash spasmed as his body began to give up. His will, his heart raged, but he wasn't strong enough.

Savage wins.

No. That could never happen.

The thought pushed him harder, beyond the madness of this fight. Beyond the dark river and the mud and the bubbles disappearing above him.

Another centimetre. That was all there was between him and Savage. It came down to a distance shorter than a fingernail. If he couldn't get that much further, Savage would have won.

Not in this universe.

❖

The monkey's fractured hand snapped, and Ash kicked free.

Thrashing upward, his neck stretched as far as it would go, Ash kicked and flailed towards the surging surface, eyes locked on the undulating patterns of moonlight above him. The current, still strong, carried him three metres downstream for every one he rose. His arms felt like lead, and each stroke took double the effort of the last. His legs barely kicked now. The surface seemed miles away.

He gave up. His arms sank to his side, slowly, and his feet dangled loose and powerless in the flowing water.

Then someone touched his shoulder. Long, stiff fingers caressed his hand and Ash snapped hold. He locked his hands round the extended limb and pulled.

He gasped and swallowed as he rose free of the water. Then he looked for his rescuer. No, not someone, he realised – the branch of a tree, leaning over the water's surface, its tips submerged. It had been the twigs he'd felt on his back.

His heart pounded with joy and fear. He'd come so close, so close. Every part of him quivered with exhaustion, but Ash heaved himself up the branch until only his legs dangled in the river. Then, clumsy as a snail, he slid along on his belly, wincing as the twigs and stubs poked him. Eventually he dropped down along the marshy edge of the river. The bridge was a quarter of a mile away and dark. Savage was gone. Shivering, aching, bleeding, puking river water, Ash waded the last few metres and crawled up the muddy bank.

C'mon, the hard bit's over.

Savage was on his way to get the Koh-i-noor. Ash had to

warn Parvati. Not only did she have no idea Savage was coming with an army of indestructible statues, but her deadly bite was useless against the loha-mukhas, and Khan's claws would snap on their impenetrable skin. If he didn't get going, Parvati and her rakshasas would be slaughtered. Ash couldn't let that happen, not when they'd parted the way they had.

I have to get back. Warn Parvati that Savage is coming with an army of stone.

But as he crawled through the long grass, Ash collapsed into the wet earth and knew no more.

Chapter Thirty-one

He looked like one of the kids that clogged the streets of Kolkata, begging at traffic lights or waiting at hotels and posh restaurants for tourists. Ash didn't care. Covered in dirt and dressed in rags, he headed back to the city by hanging on to the back of a truck as it rattled along the road with the rickshaws and bullock carts.

How long had he been unconscious? He wasn't sure. A day at least. It was evening by the time he reached the outskirts of Kolkata. He'd managed to beg some bananas and a chapatti, but still shivered with fever. His dip in the river had been almost too much. He closed his eyes.

I want to go home. There, he'd admitted it. He wanted to see his mum and dad, see Lucky. He'd thought he was tougher. He'd thought he couldn't be beaten, now that he was the Kali-aastra. Savage had shown him the error of his arrogance.

Whatever move he made, Savage countered. Last night had almost been checkmate. And next time?

But he couldn't leave Parvati. He needed to see her, know she was OK, and make everything good between them.

Thunder rumbled overhead and the clouds, black and fat, hung over the city, ready to burst. The downpour hit just as Ash turned the corner into the English Cemetery.

Something was wrong. Police vans blocked the road and there were crowds gathered at the cemetery gates. People had gathered round a massive hole in the cemetery wall. Piles of rubble lay scattered on the street, over the tombs, and in the undergrowth. Khaki-uniformed policemen held the gawkers back with their long wooden staves, and a lemonade maker had set up his stall beside the broken masonry.

Ash pulled at a man's sleeve.

"Excuse me, but what happened?"

The man scowled as he looked down at Ash, who was filthy with mud and dust and his clothing in tatters. He brushed his sleeve off, and his hand went to protect his wallet in his pocket. "Begone, boy."

"What happened?" Ash said, with more than a little firmness, a little more anger.

The man looked down again and took a step back. He touched his neck as if Ash was about to wrap his fingers round it, and swallowed. "No one knows. It happened last night. They say some beggars have been killed."

"Beggars?"

"Beggars who were using the graveyard for shelter. One of the big mausoleums has been vandalised."

❖

"Whose?"

"The old Company president. Cornish or something."

"Cornwall?"

The man nodded.

Ash ran round the back of the graveyard and sneaked over the wall. All around him were shattered gravestones, torn-up trees and demolished tombs. The mausoleum Parvati had used as her headquarters, and as the hiding place for the Koh-i-noor, was nothing but rubble. The domed roof had been smashed in. The bronze doors themselves lay twisted and buckled in the grass five metres away. The surrounding trees were snapped in half, as if something huge, unyielding and incredibly strong had just marched straight through them. The grass and earth were a mess of heavy footprints. Some were way too large and too deep for normal humans.

Savage and his loha-mukhas had struck hard.

Then, on the edge of his hearing, Ash picked up a quiet step. Someone else was hiding here. The bough of the branch above creaked with the weight of a body.

Ash jumped. Ploughing through the branches and curtain of leaves, he grabbed the scruff of a neck and pulled the figure down with him, throwing him to the ground. Then he saw the frightened face.

"John?" Ash whispered. "What are you doing here?"

"Where else could I go?" The boy stared up at him. John was scared, but his big eyes hardened with defiance. "Are you going to kill me now?"

Something black and angry stirred inside Ash as he loomed

❖

over John. He had betrayed him and given Savage the Koh-i-noor. What would Kali want? What would Ujba tell him to do? That was easy. But that wasn't going to happen.

"You put your family first. Who can blame you for that?" said Ash.

"You're not going to kill me? What about what you said at the cantonment?"

"I had to call Savage's bluff. I needed him to believe I wanted you dead to absorb your death energies. Sorry if I scared you, but it was the only plan I had." He held out his hand. "Get up, mate."

"I *am* sorry."

"So am I, John." He really was. John had been desperate, and Ash knew what that was like. There'd been a breakfast, not so long ago, where Savage had promised Ash and his sister freedom in exchange for the Kali-aastra. Ash had given it to him almost immediately when Savage threatened to kill Lucky. He'd handed over the most dangerous weapon in the world to save his sister. John's crime was no bigger than his. Ash turned back to the broken mausoleum. "Savage and his loha-mukhas?"

"Yes. I got here just before them. I thought maybe I could warn Parvati, but it all happened so fast. Savage just… appeared."

"Appeared how? In his trucks?"

"No. Just like out of a cloud of smoke. Like a magician. He had his loha-mukhas with him."

"Then what?"

"A big fight. Savage hung back and got the stone monsters

❖

to do all his dirty work. But there was more." John tapped a fallen slab. "I saw him. He waved his hand and the tombstones just flew through the air. The big doors — he wasn't even near them and they tore themselves off their hinges."

"What about Parvati? And Khan?"

"They knew they couldn't win. She went for the Koh-i-noor, but Savage practically dropped a tree on top of her." John sighed. "My fault, Ash. I told Savage everything. Where you were, and where they'd hidden the diamond. It was all over in five minutes. He used his magic. It was unbelievable. He was all over the place."

"What do you mean?"

"I mean, just 'poof'." John pointed at one corner. "One second he was there." He pointed at another. "Then in an eye-blink, over there. He had his statues doing the same. How can you beat someone like that?"

Teleporting. Savage had mastery over Space. That was a bad thing. "Do you know where Parvati is?"

"I don't know where any of them are. I've been here all day, but no one's come back." John glanced around. "What should we do? Wait here?"

"No, we need to go after Savage." He could wait for Parvati, but there was no guarantee she'd come back here; there was no reason to. Maybe she had gone to chase down Savage already.

"We've no idea where he's gone."

"Maybe, maybe not. I saw a stamp on the crates he was using to carry some of his statues. It was for the Indian

Railways and there was a number, 2841. You have any idea where that goes?"

"Easy to find out. But what difference will that make? He's got the rakshasas, the stone men, and now the Koh-i-noor," said John. "There's no way we can beat Savage."

"There's always a way."

And Ash could think of one, but he didn't like it.

Chapter Thirty-two

"I've been waiting," said Ujba.

Only the spluttering light of mismatched candles opposed the gloomy darkness of the temple. Weird shadows drifted back and forth across the uneven walls — creeping phantoms and ghosts of victims past, trapped where their lives washed the altar. The statue of Kali was glossy red. Blood dripped from her face, into her open mouth and down her bare chest.

"A sacrifice?" said Ash. "Anyone I know?"

"Just a goat," said Ujba.

"Glad you could restrain yourself."

Ujba lit another candle. "So, you've failed. Again."

"You know what happened at the cemetery?"

"Of course. I have as many spies here as I do in Varanasi."

❖

"Then why didn't you help find Savage? You could have stopped all this."

Ujba's lips turned into a fierce frown. "I offered you my help and you rejected it. Why should I offer more?"

"Is this where you say 'I told you so'? Let me save you the effort. You were right; I was a fool. I can't beat Savage, not as I am. I need more power."

"The Soma?"

"If that's what it takes."

Ash's heart trembled as he watched Ujba nod. He'd thought the guru might say something, maybe even object because he'd rejected him earlier. But the guru acted as if this was all part of his plan. Like he knew Ash was always going to take the Soma.

"This will show me how to fight? How to destroy anything?" Ash asked. If it worked, then Savage's loha-mukhas would be no threat.

"Do you know what Kali is?"

"The goddess of death and destruction. What else is there?"

"Kali means black, but the word also comes from Kala – time. Kali is the essence of time. Time is the ultimate force of destruction. Even the universe, in time, will end."

"And that helps me how?"

"Parvati spoke to you about your past lives, I assume?"

"I've even met a few."

"Once you have taken the Soma, you may step out of time yourself, according to the priests, but the effects vary."

❖

"I can time travel?" Ash said. If he could do that, then he could repair all his mistakes. He could fix everything. Just hop back and save Gemma.

"No. That is one of the sorceries, and that you will not be taught. No man should have that power. It is the path of fools. Even Ravana, though he knew how to travel back and forth through time, dared not use it. He understood that whichever path we take, it all leads to the same place."

"Then how will this Soma affect me?"

Ujba tapped his temple. "Inside here is all the wisdom, all the knowledge of all your past selves. Nothing is forgotten, as it is stored in the soul, and you, the Eternal Warrior, have only one soul. You may have been a hundred other people, a thousand, but that is just a suit of clothing upon your true self. Your *self* is unchanging. The soul remembers all those lives. If Kali is generous, and you devout, she will open the paths to all those memories and skills. If you are afraid, you will be able to draw on the courage of Rama. If you are confused, the wisdom of Ashoka. Think what it would be to know all the arts of war, every martial art, every weapon skill."

"I feel there's a massive 'but' coming."

For the first time ever, Ujba smiled. Ash couldn't believe it. It wasn't a nice smile – too wolfish to be warm – but the lips curled upward and some teeth showed, so technically, Ujba smiled. "Yes. But with so many lives, so many personalities, all advising, all demanding, all trying to control you, your own willpower will be your only defence. Let it waver, even for a moment, and your own personality will be washed away into the sea of all the others. Perhaps for ever, and who knows who may take charge."

"Oh joy."

"But the advantages outweigh the risks. Time stretches forward as well as back. You will see the threads of the future, see how one thing affects the other. Glimpses of what lies ahead. If you can understand them, you will be considered wise indeed."

See the future? Now that was something. "Then let's get this over and done with."

Ujba went to his medicine box. Over the next few minutes, in the dim candlelight, Ash watched him mix his ingredients. He ground leaves into a small silver bowl until all was a fine black powder. He worked in silence, whispering mantras as he worked. Ash tried to keep still, but he fidgeted impatiently. He just wanted the medicine and wanted to get out of there, after Savage.

Ujba stroked the razor round the rim of the bowl, making the metal hum. Then he faced Ash. "Blood," he said.

Ash held out his hand. A moment later there was a small cut and Ash let a few drops drip into the bowl. Ujba stirred as Ash tied a cloth round the thin red line.

"What exactly goes into this Soma?" asked Ash.

"Best you not know."

"And what will happen to me, when I drink this?"

"It's poisonous, so you'll probably die. At least for a while."

Ash took the bowl and sniffed the contents. Putrid didn't begin to describe it. He wasn't sure he'd be able to swallow it, and if he did, there was a good chance it would come

❖

straight back up, along with his supper of lentils, potatoes and spinach. "Don't you have something of a less... fatal full-fat flavour? Y'know, diet Soma or something?"

"You are the Kali-aastra. It will protect you. The Soma will show you Kali."

"And what if Kali doesn't like me?"

"Then she will eat your soul."

"You're so not selling this," said Ash.

"Do you want to defeat Savage or not?" asked Ujba. "Did you think it would be easy? That Kali would just give you her blessing, merely because you asked? Gods want sacrifices. They want payment, like everyone else. There is nothing for free in this world or any other." He reached over to the Soma and drew it back. "I thought we had a deal. But I understand. Next time, when you're crying over the corpse of another friend, remember I could have helped you."

Ash looked at the man, then at the bowl. He didn't want to drink it. It was more than that it would probably kill him; after this, there was no going back. He didn't know what he might become after drinking the Soma, but he had a feeling the phrase 'bloodthirsty monster' might be involved.

But then what if he did meet Savage again and it was just as big a failure as it had been the last time? Would Savage kill Parvati? How many more of his friends would die?

"Give it to me," said Ash.

Ujba smiled and held out a small brown lump. "Eat this first."

"What is it?"

"Goor. The flesh of the tiger. It's consumed by Thugs before they go on their journeys. It's good luck."

"Not for the tiger, it isn't."

"Be at ease. It's only raw sugar." Ash put the lump on his tongue and swallowed. The sweetness might help him hold down the drink.

He raised the bowl to his lips. "How long will the Soma last?"

"If the Soma works properly, it will open a door here." Ujba tapped the centre of his forehead. "The inner eye. There is no closing the door afterwards."

"And if it doesn't work properly?"

"Death, if you are lucky. Insanity if not. Perhaps your mind will crumble under the wisdom of Kali and you'll spend the rest of your life in a coma or as a drooling imbecile."

"Oh double joy."

Ash closed his eyes and gulped quickly, emptying the bowl in three swallows. The liquid burned like that one time he'd drunk some of his dad's whisky, but as he put the bowl down, he was thinking that it wasn't that bad after all.

"Bitter," he said. But that was all.

Only his mouth was dry, very dry.

Ujba leaned closer.

Ash shivered. He felt as if a cold winter wind was blowing. The freezing air cut his skin. A sharp pang gripped his stomach, twisting it and screwing it into knots. He bent over, his muscles seizing up.

Ujba began to fade. Ash reached for him, but his hand

❖

moved sluggishly. The pain was increasing, spreading out from his belly to his limbs. It was as if his blood was boiling within him.

Ash spat and stared at the bloody spittle on the tiled floor. His eyes were hot and swollen, bloody tears forming a thin film over them.

"Help me," he whispered. Another spasm shook him and he buckled under the agony. The pounding of his blood was deafening, and each heartbeat sent bone-breaking tremors through his body.

Ujba looked towards the statue. "Accept my offering, Kali."

Ash tried to breathe, but all that came out was a feeble hiss. He gazed at Ujba, his vision becoming dull. Then everything faded as his last breath escaped.

Chapter Thirty-three

$\mathcal{A}$sh walks silently towards the light flickering in the darkness. He passes vague, shadowy outlines of others, bodies that are mere cloaks for a single soul that returns again and again for battle. They touch him, phantom caresses both comforting and despairing. There ahead of him shines a figure, a being both human and something more. It is the light from this being that casts all the other shadows.

The Eternal Warrior.

He has no form: it is flesh that has form, and he has worn so many bodies over the endless eons. Ash is merely another.

Ash steps into the pool of light closest to the being. It senses him, and the flames stir and take on a vague human outline. It gazes down at him. It knows what Ash wants.

Ash looks about him. There are others there, ghosts of the past, stirring within the grey fog.

"Who are they?" Ash asks. Some are dressed in bronze armour, heavy

scarlet cloaks draped over their shoulders. Some wear jewels and silks, others rags or unfamiliar clothes. They come from all lands and all epochs. They are African, Indian, Mongolian, Caucasian, male, female, young, old. The Eternal Warrior is of all nations, all ages. One man, old and wizened, has the round, flat features of an Inuit. He meets Ash's gaze with eyes of infinite sorrow.

"They are us," says the burning soul. "Here to welcome you."

All of them? The crowd stretches to the horizon, perhaps beyond. Ash hesitates. "I... didn't know there were so many."

"Many, but one."

"No. I can't do it."

"She comes."

Ash turns and faces the pyre. The blue flames roar silently. The touch of Agni, the god of fire, does not penetrate this world.

He sees there is a body lying on the flames. "No. It can't be."

"Your old self, to be burned away," says his soul.

He watches his skin blacken and crack. He sees his hair catch light and the fat dribble off his molten flesh. Bones break out from under the crisp, brittle skin.

A figure rises up out of the fire, tall and fierce.

"You are hers now, Ash."

She stands upon his burning corpse, and she is beautiful. Her long black limbs glisten with sweat and her chest rises and sinks with panting eagerness. The flames dance around her, shades of blue turning to white, to the colour of a midnight sea, licking her legs and caressing her taut belly.

Kali.

She glares down at him, her red tongue hanging with hunger and her eyes blazing with violence. The third eye, the destroying eye, opens the merest slit and the light from it blinds Ash. The heat is unbearable and he screams.

The fire of her eyes melts him to the core, stripping off skin and muscle and bone to what is beneath it all: his soul, exposed and raw beneath the devastating gaze of the goddess.

Then the pain ends.

Ash, curled up on the barren ground, slowly opens his eyes, expecting to see himself black and charred beyond any hope of life. Instead, his fingers are clean and supple. His arms lean, dark and strong. He stands and sees himself transformed, built of fast, lethal muscle and hard, merciless edges and angles. Not the smooth curves and softness of flesh, but the keenness of a blade.

Ash bows and claps his hands together. He performs the greeting ritual of Kalari-payit. He sweeps his limbs in long, low blows and high kicks, and ends bowed before the goddess.

Kali's chest heaves with eagerness as she curls her long talons into a fist.

She shows Ash how to punch.

Kali raises her foot.

She shows Ash how to kick.

Her limbs dart, and blows and strikes come fast and furious until Kali is a hurricane of movement. Each action is of ethereal grace and beauty, fluid and elegant, like a tidal wave rolling over a mountain.

Ash follows. In her footsteps. In her shadow.

He mimics her movements, her attacks, her ferocity. Ash feels another pair of arms tear from his body. Another. Glistening with his blood, new limbs rip out of his torso, the flesh peeling away to reveal glossy, bloody bones. He stares at his hands, now claws, and runs his long tongue over his fangs. He dances in his own ashes.

He is now fully a thing of Kali.

Chapter Thirty-four

His mouth tasted of dust. Ash blinked and spat. He lay on the temple floor, the cold stone pressed against his skin. Dimly, he felt the vibrations of the city through the ground, and his ears pricked at the soft breeze moaning through the temple, the creaking of the old wood. Ash lifted himself up and settled down on his haunches. The temple was empty. Sunlight shone through the missing tiles in the roof. A large cockroach scuttled across the floor, pausing for a moment to look at him.

I'm alive. I think.

He touched his ribs, half expecting to find a second – or third – pair of arms sticking out. Nope, no new body parts. On the outside, he was still the human Ash. Good news so far. He stood up, checking that all was normal. Nothing had changed. His muscles weren't any bigger, and as he ran his tongue over his teeth, he was pleased to find he hadn't grown fangs either.

He closed his eyes, recalling the many people he'd seen in his vision. Those guys in bronze armour and red cloaks. Ash knew enough of his history to recognise the most kick-butt warriors of the world, the Spartans. If Ujba was right, he should know ancient Greek. What about counting to ten?

"Er... er."

Hello, in Greek?

"Er."

Anything, in Greek?

"Er."

So the Soma had been a big fat fail. He wasn't any different.

A flutter of cloth caught his attention. A yellow scarf hung from a low beam, pinned in place with a katar. Ash took a firm grip and worked the punch dagger back and forth until it came loose. He took the scarf and wrapped the dagger within it.

Suddenly, pain cramped his stomach, and Ash groaned as black spots danced in his eyes. He put his hand against a stone column, leaning on it as he steadied himself.

A series of cracks flowered out from his palm. Ash lifted his hand. The palm print was a centimetre deep. He followed the line of a crack down the white marble. The crack itself was only a hair's breadth in width.

Ash put his finger against the minute line. And pushed.

The marble splintered. Ash pushed harder.

The column trembled and jagged tears ruptured along its length. The roof began to creak.

❖

Ash stopped. He drew his hand back and then slammed his palm against the column. It exploded into a million white shards of marble, shooting out and riddling the wall like bullets. Ash glanced up as the ceiling bowed and the wooden beams splintered. He ran.

He was halfway down the alley before he turned and watched. The old temple groaned as the roof fell in. The wooden posts and beams within cracked and snapped; the old plaster shattered, tossing out white clouds of dust. Then the roof caved in with a dull boom.

The hazy morning sky had a hint of rose to it and there was not a single cloud. A light, chilly mist floated on the streets and down the alley. Birds chirped in the rooftops, stirred by the faint dawn light.

Ash looked around.

He felt the brittle bricks in the wall, the pattern of the grain on the door and the cracks along the metal water pipes. A car passed, and Ash's body vibrated in harmony to the chugging, spluttering engine. He heard the hissing steam coming out of the minute hole in the radiator, and felt how the bald, worn-out tyres bounced over the small stones.

He looked at the driver, smoking a cigarette and blowing the smoke out of the open window. Ash could taste the tar that coated the man's lungs from his breath.

These were all the signs of death and decay. Ash could feel the world rotting around him. And all he needed to make it collapse was to give it a little push. The wall. The door. The car. The man. He gazed at him and a sharp blossom

❖

of heat burst right in the middle of his forehead as he focused on the driver.

The driver takes a red packet of cigarettes from his shirt pocket and lights one. The man shifts gears and rolls forward, searching for a gap in the traffic. He cries out as ash from his cigarette burns his hand. He shakes it and doesn't see the yellow bus, its horn blaring a warning but the noise lost in the city's din. The man stares in horror —

Ash blinked. What had just happened? The taxi hadn't moved. He looked down the road and there was a yellow bus, but it was still half a mile away. The taxi driver wasn't even smoking.

Then the man reached into his pocket and took out a packet of cigarettes. The packet was red.

Ash's heart sped up. He knew *exactly* what was coming next. He was going to light it and drive into the middle of the road. The yellow bus got closer.

The man lit a cigarette and shifted the gears and with a shudder and a cough of smoke, his taxi rolled forward into the junction. Rickshaws and cars and bicycles wove away, but the flow did not slow. The taxi driver, holding his cigarette loosely out of his side window, glanced up and down.

Ash waited. Any second now the ash would fall and burn the driver's hand.

The driver winced and shook his hand, dropping the cigarette. The car kept moving and was now in the centre of the road.

Ash watched the bus; it wasn't far now. It was unwinding like an action replay. Each second was identical to what he'd seen in his mind only moments earlier. The future was unfolding before him.

❖

The traffic parted and the bus, battered and yellow, its racks piled high with boxes and suitcases and crates and passengers, loomed out like a whale pushing through a school of fish. The sunlight shone off the dusty front windscreen as the bus driver pushed hard on his horn.

The man, still blowing on his burned hand, did not notice.

Then the driver saw the bus. He stared in horror, then fumbled at his wheel and the gear stick. The bus began to brake and a wall of dust rose up before it.

The taxi reversed two metres and the bus thundered past, missing the car by centimetres and the passengers waved and swore at the taxi as they shot by.

Ash shook his head. He'd seen it all seconds before it actually happened.

He'd glimpsed the future.

He rubbed his forehead, half expecting to feel a third eye there, but found nothing. The Kali-aastra hummed louder than ever within every atom in his body. The Soma had done its work.

He was ready to face Savage.

Chapter Thirty-five

"You look different," said John.

John had salvaged some stuff from the cemetery, so at least Ash had a clean change of clothes: a pair of baggy trousers and a loose tunic. He'd washed off the dust and mud at a standpipe and got loaned a lump of soap for a rupee. "You mean more handsome?" Ash said.

"More something."

"I've been taking my vitamins."

"Just as long as that's all you've been taking."

Ash rolled up the katar and packed it in a rucksack with a shawl and a few other travelling bits and pieces, like a compass, torch and pair of binoculars. John had gone to the train station and found out that the 2841 train went down the western coast of India, all the way to Madras. Ash had no idea why Savage was heading south but, without Parvati

❖

around and with no better ideas, he was going to follow. He pulled the toggle of the rucksack. "You know you don't have to come. There'll be trouble."

John packed up his own meagre belongings. "I was responsible for getting you in this mess. Wouldn't be right if I didn't help fix it."

"We have a plan?"

John nodded. "Find Savage. Get the Koh-i-noor back. You do what you do best."

"And what's that?"

John waved his arms in a kung-fu-style flourish. "You know, all this."

Ash slipped the rucksack on and looked around to see if he'd forgotten anything. "How are we getting to the airport?"

"We're not. Bad news. No Jimmy," John replied. "Engine failure."

"How bad?"

"The starboard one fell off halfway across the Indian Sea. He's sailing back."

The plan was falling apart and they'd not even started. Ash had hoped to save a day at least by flying down to Madras. He'd never been that far south and had no idea what to expect. Since Madras had been another of the main headquarters of the East India Company, it no doubt was familiar territory to Savage. They couldn't risk losing him again — though hiding an army of statues, including one twenty-five metres high, wouldn't be easy. "Then what are we going to do?"

❖

John handed Ash a slip of paper. A ticket. "Take the train too. There's one at dusk."

Ash threw down his backpack. The train was delayed by three hours, so there was nothing to do but wait on the platform. The world could be in total peril and he couldn't save it because of a herd of cows on the track. Harry Potter never had these problems.

So he sat there, waiting, in the Kolkata train station, a grand imperial building that had been the pride and joy of the British Raj. The grandeur was still evident but, like so much of the city, the structure was succumbing to a sort of benign decay. Worn and crumbling, operating with ancient systems and a vast army of staff, the station had the feeling of a home. Life existed here; it was more than just a place to pass through.

Ash gazed across the tracks at a small single building called the Coolie House. A row of porters squatted in the shade, passing around a cigarette. Small children, orphans, runaways, those just lost, darted between the stacks of luggage, across the tracks, and through the stalls collecting trash – mainly empty plastic water bottles – or asking for handouts from the few Western travellers who had decided to see India by rail. A boy, younger than Lucky, balanced a battered tin tray on his head to deliver a dozen small glasses of milky tea to the khaki-uniformed staff at the signal box.

Where was Parvati? Her mobile phone was dead. It wasn't just that he missed her and was worried about her – he *depended* on her. This was her territory, and he needed her around. The encounter with the Jagannath and Savage's loha-mukhas still haunted him, reminding him that this wasn't a game. The stakes were high and he didn't know all the rules.

Simply put, he was afraid. Afraid Savage had more tricks up his sleeve. That the Soma hadn't worked properly, that he was out of his league. He'd left a message for Parvati at the cemetery, a letter tucked under the remains of the mausoleum. He had no idea if she'd ever find it, but what else could he do?

Dear Parvati,

Savage is taking his loha-mukhas on the 2841 train down to Madras, just in case you didn't know. I've no idea why he'd be going south, but I'm following with my trusty padawan, John.

I'm sorry for what I said, and even more sorry for not listening to you. You were right and I was wrong. That will have to do as an apology as I've a train to catch and the world to save. Again.

Your friend,
Ash

Not the best letter ever. He'd wanted to put in more, about the injustice of Gemma's death, about trying to do something good and be more than just an instrument of Kali, about how, in spite of all his previous lives, this hero business was still new to him, and hey, who didn't make mistakes and he'd never said he was perfect, and frankly, Parvati could have done a better job explaining things to him instead of being all superior and stuck-up, and while she was his closest friend and everything, she could be so pig-headed, and if she'd just dialled down her ego a little, she might have heard what Ash had been trying to say and they wouldn't be in this mess, which, when you really thought about it, was as much her fault as it was his, not that she'd ever admit it.

But Ash had decided not to write any of that.

When Ash had heard he'd be going on the sleeper train, he had entertained ideas of oak-panelled Pullman carriages, white-gloved attendants and small, exquisitely furnished compartments with their own porcelain washbasins. Basically the Orient Express. Instead they approached a carriage that turned out to be nothing more than a big steel crate with bars on the windows. John checked the tickets. "This is us," he said.

"You're joking. This is for cattle, not people."

"I only had enough money for third class."

Ash sighed and climbed in. The carriage comprised of open compartments along one side of a narrow corridor. Each compartment had a pair of triple-decked bunk beds facing each other. During the day, everyone sat on the lowest bunk, with the upper two folded up against the wall. The attendant came round in the evening to unfold the top bunks, with a sheet and pillow for each passenger, and then it was lights-out.

Old women in fine saris sat while moustachioed businessmen shouted into their mobile phones and mothers wrestled with screaming kids and squalling babies. One boy, forefinger firmly fixed in his left nostril, watched Ash and John settle in.

Ash peered out of the window as the train pulled out of the station. Passengers dashed across the tracks to climb in through the open doors, helped on board by the other commuters. The train ran through grand avenues of steel track lined with the pastel-coloured government buildings. It weaved through gleaming new towers and raced along through the shanty towns that encircled the city.

Then they were running smoothly on raised tracks along endless paddy fields, and Kolkata disappeared behind the wall of swaying palm trees.

That night, everyone slept except Ash. The carriage rumbled and the wheels screeched and rattled endlessly. The fans above him droned like a squadron of mosquitoes. Couldn't they afford to oil them? The noise put Ash's teeth on edge.

He thought about Ujba and what he'd said about Ash's past lives. He thought about all those people he'd seen, faces going back thousands of years from all over the world. Ashoka had been somewhere in that crowd, and Ash wanted to find him and learn more about the Koh-i-noor, especially now that Savage had it. So, with the train rattling along, the fans buzzing and the other passengers snoring, Ash closed his eyes.

He began to blank out the world around him. He let the rocking of the carriage pass through him so he felt as if he was floating, rather than resting on a shaking bunk. The noises around him faded and he lost touch with himself as he sank further inward.

He passed by grey-bearded men and women dressed in

❖

thick robes and wearing heavy jewels from ancient times. Ahead and around him there were others, some with swords or spears, some with scrolls and books or pots and quills, and he wondered what their lives had been like. Had they won their battles or lost? Parvati had told him once that the Eternal Warrior could fight for either side, for good or evil, but now as Ash looked further into his past lives he realised it wasn't so simple. You could be hero and villain, often simultaneously. He'd been Brutus, the Roman who'd murdered Julius Caesar to save the Republic, but instead only brought about the reign of the emperors. By attempting good, his legacy had been tyranny and the era of Caligula and Nero.

Ash had ridden with the Mongols, slaughtering their way from the steppes to the very heart of Europe. But from the bones they'd built the first global empire and allowed the exchange of science, technology and new ideas between the East and West. Such great evil leading to good.

What part would he play? Would he be a hero or a villain? He had no idea. But right now he needed one man, a conqueror who, more than most, had been both.

Ashoka. Where are you?

Chapter Thirty-six

shoka looks down at the bodies of his dead soldiers. He raises the burning diamond high and the beams burst from the many facets of crystal, pushing back the darkness. The pure white light shines upon pale, bloodless limbs, on blank, empty eyes, on drawn, pale lips. Their bodies are scored with wounds and their clothes rent and encrusted with dried patches of blood. Limbs have been hacked off and others crushed under the blows of maces and clubs.

"Rise, brothers, rise," he urges them, thrusting the Koh-i-noor ahead of him.

Behind him he hears the uneasy shuffling of his bodyguards, the sibilant hiss of warning from Parvati as she sees how much greater he is than her father.

"Rise!"

The diamond burns within his fist and shakes with power. A dull, deep drone vibrates from the rock and the light increases to a blinding intensity. Ashoka shields his eyes.

A harsh, desperate cry pierces the night. First one, then others. The diamond is almost unbearable now, but even as his skin burns, Ashoka holds fast.

He stares as the dead move. Groaning, they flex their limbs and drag themselves up from the bloodied earth of their graves. Then, one by one, they stand. Their eyes are dull and carry the light of Yama, and their mouths twist into savage, hungry leers. A deep, inhuman snarl rattles from the throat of the nearest and he extends his arms, reaching out for Ashoka. His guards form a wall of spears between him and the risen dead.

"No," whispers Parvati. The four blades of her urumi, her serpent sword, rattle free. She steps towards the men as they shuffle on ungainly, stiff limbs. A few, their legs broken or missing, crawl forward, clambering over each other with eager, monstrous bloodlust. One guard rams his spear through the torso of one, but the man, the creature, continues despite the injury, grabbing him and dragging him away from the line. The guard screams as they surround him, sinking their nails and teeth into his flesh. They pull and tear and devour.

More and more of his bodyguards fall beneath the relentless mass until they can take no more and flee. Ashoka remains, the diamond still glowing in his hand. Parvati strikes, her urumi flickering, slicing and ripping. But there are too many.

The living dead turn their hungry gaze towards him.

"No!" cries Ashoka.

"No," cried Ash, wiping the sweat off his face. He grabbed

his water bottle and drained it in four gulps. Water spilled over him as he tried to stop his hand from shaking.

That was horrible, a nightmare. Ashoka had used the Brahma-aastra, but something had gone seriously wrong. By trying to do good, he had only created a greater evil.

The ones who come back are never the ones who left. That's what Khan said. If Savage used the diamond the same way, he was likely to kick off a zombie apocalypse. Ash wouldn't need a punch dagger to face down the undead, he'd need a chainsaw. If this was what would happen if anyone used the diamond then Gemma was better dead and at peace.

Resurrecting Gemma. It was, always had been, a foolish hope. With that hope gone, all he had was despair. He'd go home and have to face the fact he'd failed. Josh and his other mates were afraid of him, and what about Lucky? She'd more or less said he'd become a monster.

Some hero.

He got up and walked to the end of the carriage. The door was wide open — no health and safety concerns here — and he watched the midnight landscape roll by.

The journey time was twenty-six hours, but John had told him that in India, that could mean thirty hours, or thirty-six. He'd checked the map at the station to get an idea of the route they were taking. Madras was way down south, almost at the tip of the subcontinent, a stone's throw from the island of Sri Lanka. The train followed the eastern coastline along the Bay of Bengal, and wove through mangrove swamps and jungle. Palm leaves brushed the tops of the carriages and the scent of lush vegetation, softly decaying in the damp heat, mixed with the smoky exhaust of the old diesel engine up front.

Occasionally the jungle fell away and Ash gazed out across the still sea. The sky, dazzling with diamond light, shone upon the deep blues and greens of the water, stretching all the way to the horizon. Small black silhouettes – uninhabited islands – dotted the otherwise featureless ocean.

Stations came and went. At the bigger ones, tea sellers and porters sleeping on their carts stirred into languid life from under their threadbare blankets as the train clattered in. Hawkers sold drinks, ran errands and handed snacks wrapped in palm leaves through the bars to yawning passengers.

John joined him as the night rolled on. "View's better up top," he said. He leaned out of the door, stood on tiptoe, grabbed the top of the door frame and lifted himself out in a single, nimble move, as sprightly as a monkey.

The train was picking up speed and rocking from side to side. Getting up on the roof, at night, with low branches, sounded pretty damn stupid. Ash couldn't climb like John. The boy was small and light; Ash wasn't.

John leaned over the edge, his upside-down face quizzical. "Well?" he asked.

"What if I slip?"

"Make sure you don't."

"But what if I do?"

John frowned. "Then, I think, you'll be crushed to death under the wheels? Probably."

"Sod it," said Ash. "You only live once."

243

❖

John smirked. "We both know that's not true."

Ash pulled himself up, fingers scrabbling for a second before John grabbed his arm and helped him on to the roof.

They weren't alone. A man lay asleep, his head resting on a small tucked-up package. Further down, a trio of labourers passed round a steel dish and a bottle.

"I love trains," said Ash. "The feeling that you can go on and on, the world changing all around you, but you're just sitting still."

"Sounds lazy."

"Laziness is a vastly underrated quality. I used to be an expert in lazy."

"You and your decadent Western ways." John took a packet of Indian pastries from inside his shirt. "I lifted these at the last stop. Best while they're still warm."

More samosas? Fine by him. Ash nibbled at the corner of the deep-fried meal, wanting to make it last. "Where do you think you'll go, after this is over?"

"Get my mother and move. Go somewhere nice and quiet, like Kashmir. We've relatives up there." John held his hand under the pastry, trying to catch even the smallest of crumbs as the wind blew around them. He didn't waste anything. "Kashmir's very beautiful. There are lakes of pure blue and they're as still as mirrors so the sky shines above and below. And you have beautiful boats, like floating palaces really. I had a postcard of one once. That's where I'd work."

"I'll make sure that happens. This time."

"Your father a rich man?"

❖

"No. He's an engineer. Mum's an accountant. We get by, but we're not rich."

"That what you're going to be? Follow in your dad's footsteps?"

Ash shrugged. "Never thought much about it. I really wanted to be a computer-game programmer. Trouble is, all that fantasy stuff doesn't feel quite the same now."

"Now you've seen real monsters?"

"Something like that. Found out they're not that easy to beat."

"You're lucky you have a choice."

"Yes, I suppose." Parvati and Ujba didn't seem to think so. As far as they were concerned, he was the Kali-aastra, and that was that. "You know, I always wondered why Superman even bothered being Clark Kent."

"What?"

"Think about it. Why be a normal person? All that time he's working at the *Daily Planet*, there's an earthquake happening or volcano exploding somewhere in the world and he's not there to save people. He's in the office, watching dancing cats on YouTube like everyone else."

"Is there a point to this conversation, or are you just rambling?"

"He doesn't want the responsibility. Simple as that. He doesn't need a secret identity; he could be Superman twenty-four-seven, but he isn't. He has to be Clark or he'd go mad. You understand?"

"No. Not even a tiny bit." John looked worried. "Are you all right?"

"Forget it."

The two of them sat up on the roof as the train slowed down to a small station, alone in the middle of the jungle. There was a single small building and a long crumbling platform. Huge flowers grew along the borders of the station, and the air was thick with musty pollen. A few small storerooms lined up behind the main building, such as it was, and there were several fenced-off vegetable gardens.

Ash pointed at one. "What happened there?"

The fence was broken, ripped out of the earth, and the entire vegetable patch trampled to paste. The trees beyond and the long grass had been just as thoroughly flattened.

"Elephants," said John. "Pain in the arse. Looks like a big herd got a taste of the station master's tomatoes."

"Yes, where is the station master?" There was usually a man with a lantern waving the train through, even in the smallest stations like this one.

"Ash?"

"What?"

"You're scratching your thumb."

He hadn't even noticed, but he was. He glanced at John. "I'll only be a minute."

Ash slid down the side of the carriage, using the window bars as footholds, and stepped on to the empty platform. After a few seconds John came down and joined him.

"Ash?" he asked, close behind.

Ash sniffed the air. His thumb was seriously itchy. He walked up to the flowerbed.

❖

It wasn't just the vegetables that had been trampled. Lying in amongst the broken tomatoes and clumps of coriander was a body. It had been a man – the station master, most likely – but now it was a pulped, red-and-pink smear.

John let out a small gasp as he saw the body. Ash continued searching. It took a second for his eyes to adjust to the night gloom, but then he made out a shape in the mud – a deep imprint depressed about ten centimetres into the black soil. Whatever had made it had been incredibly heavy and large.

It was a footprint, but a size bigger than any human's.

Now he'd seen one, he saw others. Some human, some animal, some who-knew-what, but all heavy and sunk deep. All heading into the jungle.

"Not elephants," he said. "Loha-mukhas."

Chapter Thirty-seven

A few minutes later, the train was gone and the two of them stood on the empty platform. The only sound was the tick-tock of the old station clock.

"What's out there?" asked Ash. As far as he could tell, there was just jungle. Why had Savage bailed out here?

"No idea. I've never been this far south."

The loha-mukhas had trampled a path through the foliage wide enough for a bus. Ash swatted at clouds of insects as they descended to feast on his blood. The high-pitched whine of mosquitoes echoed around his ears, and as they ploughed through the swampy terrain, he was soon soaked from head to toe.

"Why are they picking on me?" He slapped the back of his neck as another mosquito took a quick snack. "They're eating me alive."

"It's your bland English blood," John answered. "Ours is too spicy."

Ash splashed waist deep in the murky water. Maybe if he put his head under? He took a deep breath and was about to sink under when John gasped.

"What?"

John pointed at a knobby log floating nearby.

The log blinked.

A pair of yellow crocodile eyes gazed from just above the surface.

"What should I do?" asked Ash.

"Just punch its nose," suggested John. "Isn't that, you know, a thing you do?"

"I thought that was sharks."

The crocodile swished its tail and floated closer. Ash thought about his katar, but it was stuffed deep in his backpack. He made a fist, ready to punch.

This is going to be the stupidest thing I've ever done. And I've done plenty.

"Just think of it as a handbag waiting to happen," said John from high up in a tree.

How did he get up there? Ash wondered. The guy was half monkey. "Utterly unhelpful."

The crocodile stared at Ash, its ancient, yellow eyes seeming to look deep into him. Then the giant reptile turned, and with a slow, languid swish, disappeared into the swamp.

Ash drained his third bottle of water. He must have lost half his body weight in sweat in just the last two hours. His

❖

clothes clung to him, and the air was so thick and heavy that breathing was like pulling air through a wet flannel. The insects obviously had a taste for him and had told all their friends.

The trees were also full of monkeys. The creatures watched them from their shrouded perches. Big eyes in black furred faces, their long tails hooked round branches, some with wide-eyed babies hanging off them, others grooming each other or just sitting there, watching. The further they went, the larger their audience grew. An army of monkeys.

John peered along the trampled path. "Can you smell it?"

Mixed in with the slimy odour of rot and damp decay was a crisper, cleaner scent. The air felt fresher than it had earlier. "The sea?"

On they marched. Despite the flattened foliage, the path they were following was slow going. The terrain rolled and dipped and dived through mangrove swamps, across deep streams and ravines of broken rocks. Ash's legs and back ached and John was falling further behind.

They stopped, exhausted and hungry. Ash lay down on a slab of stone. Moss served as a thin, mushy mattress and the stone was flat. They'd rest for a while, get some strength back, then continue. He swallowed the last of the water. His super strength and stamina were fading. The trek through the jungle had taken more out of him than he'd expected. He felt – almost – human.

He slid his fingertips over the edge of the stone. "Funny, these are chisel marks." He peeled off a patch of dark moss.

The rock was scratched and grooved, but so heavily weathered the marks looked natural. Still, the dimensions of the slab were perfectly rectangular. No natural force would shape rock into a rectangle that neatly.

John inspected his own perch. "Look here." The boulder he'd been sitting on was actually three of the same slabs, stacked one upon the other.

"Paving stones," Ash said. "Big ones, and very old."

"But this only leads to the sea," said John.

Ash looked at the stones again. It was obvious they were man-made. But why, and why here? "You sure there're no cities or towns this way?"

John frowned. "Doubt it. It's all just swamp."

The monkeys chattered frantically. They jumped up and down on their branches; some hopping from slab to slab, slapping their hands on the stone and crying out.

"What do they want?" John asked.

"If I spoke monkey, I'd ask."

Warily, they continued along the smashed-up path, the swamp filled with the howling of monkeys.

They hit the cliff top an hour later at twilight. *Just in time*, thought Ash. He hadn't been keen on groping around in the swamp in the dark and walking straight down the throat of a waiting crocodile. Their company of monkeys lingered, but they kept further back, afraid to leave the safety of the trees.

An arch of grass-covered rock jutted out from the cliff. Ash peered over.

Vast house-sized boulders sat in the waters, their jagged

❖

corners rising out of the dark sea like the jaws of a leviathan as waves crashed and spewed upon them. A row of small islands stretched out towards the east. A wind was brewing on the sea, and storm clouds gathered on the horizon.

"Looks like Cornwall," Ash said. "That's an archipelago off the far western point of England. It looks as though it's stretching out to some distant island."

"Are those lights?" John pointed to one of the larger islands a mile or so away.

Ash took out his binoculars.

John was right. While Ash couldn't see any path leading up the tall cliffs of the island on this side, it was flat once you got to the top, and hidden among the palm trees were some small tents with lanterns. A wisp of smoke rose from a campfire. Figures of all shapes and sizes, some human, some not, moved around the plateau. He saw a pair of over-large stone monkeys lugging a large suitcase.

But no Jagannath. That was a relief. Ash might have knocked down a rickety temple to Kali, but he didn't feel ready to test himself against a thousand tons of solid stone. His guts tightened as he watched a white-suited figure move among the tents. Savage.

"There's a path down to the beach." John started down the slope. "Come with me."

The sea gently heaved upon the sandy beach. Once he'd climbed down, it didn't take long for Ash to spot the continuation of the stone path they'd followed all this way. Time and tide had broken it up, and the slabs tilted or sloped at

❖

odd angles, but Ash could see the path ran in a straight line into the water, disappearing into the waves after a few metres. A vast field of seaweed drifted from side to side across the shelter of rocks. Why a path into the sea?

"What's Savage doing out there? Waiting for a boat?"

"You don't have a plan?" asked John.

"Me? I'm the strong but silent type."

"You? Silent? I've never met anyone whose mouth was more disconnected from his brain."

"I'll take that as a compliment."

It was another eight hours 'til sunrise, and judging by the campfires on the island, Savage was bedding down for the night.

"We'll wait a bit," said Ash. "Give Parvati time to find us."

"You think she'll come here? How?"

Ash prodded John's forehead. "She's smart. She'll have a plan. Several, most likely." He yawned and picked a dry patch of sand. It was cool and there was something soporific about the sound of waves lapping on the beach. "I'm having a little nap. We'll take turns. Give me a couple of hours, then wake me up, OK?"

John snored softly in the grassy verge at the foot of the cliff, while Ash sat on the shore, looking out at the dim thread of grey on the eastern horizon. He'd slept fitfully, his dreams still haunted by his memories of Ashoka and the twisted revenants he'd brought to life with the Koh-i-noor. So he woke after a few hours and let John take the lion's share of rest, in spite of the bone-deep weariness that hung over him. The campfires on the far island were now just dim red glows, dying in their embers, and figures were moving about. It looked like Savage wanted an early start.

If they were going to do anything, it had to be sooner rather than later.

Savage was within easy reach. He had the Koh-i-noor.

What would Parvati do? That was the question.

Whatever needs doing.

Ash kicked John's leg.

"Whuuh?" John rubbed his knuckles in his eyes and shook the sand from his hair.

Ash flicked off his sandals. "I'm going."

"You're joking. Aren't you?"

"Nope. I'm tired of waiting."

"Do you have any idea what you're doing?"

"Do I ever?" Ash wrapped his yellow scarf round his waist and tucked the katar into it. "I'm going after Savage. He's over there."

"Then what?"

"I'll get the Koh-i-noor first and kill him second." That's what Parvati would do.

John looked at Ash. "You're really going to kill him?"

Ash nodded. He was the Kali-aastra; that was what he did, and no one deserved death more than Savage. "I've killed before. Ravana. Mayar. Even that vulture demon Jat."

"Oh, yeah, you're practically a serial killer, Ash."

"That's not funny."

"Murder *isn't* funny. You killed those others in war. I heard

254

❖

about them from your sister. You saved her life and that's why you did it. This is different. This is creeping up behind someone and slitting his throat. You're not that sort of person. I hope you're not that sort of person."

"It's what Parvati would do."

"She's a demon, Ash."

"I'm not saying it's what I want. It's just... what other choice do I have? How else am I going to stop him?"

"I'm just saying it's a bit extreme. Let's wait. If we've found this place, I bet Parvati can't be far behind."

That's what Ash wanted. He wanted Parvati to make the decision. If she told him to kill Savage, that would be different. It wouldn't be his choice. But then following orders wasn't an excuse for doing evil. "We've only got another couple of hours of darkness left. If I'm going to get over there, I need to go now."

"What about me?" said John.

"Head back to the old train station. If Parvati is on her way, she'll most likely come through there. You go and find her."

"And if I can't?"

"Then find someone else. Like the Avengers," said Ash as he waded into the sea.

Chapter Thirty-eight

He'd never swum in the dark before, and it was weird seeing the reflections of the stars and the light of the moon fragmented upon the dark waves. A strange green glow followed his limbs, fluorescent algae activated by his movements. He dipped his head under once or twice. The darkness beneath was endless. He felt like he was floating in eternity.

Was he halfway there? Maybe.

There was a thin strip of beach ahead, sheltered by the high cliffs. Ash, chin low in the bobbing waves, put a bit of effort in and headed for it.

His toes scraped the sand. Ash found his footing and waded the last few metres. He stared straight up the cliffs in front of him. They were grim and black, smeared with moss, and water trickled down crooked narrow channels, collecting in rock pools at the cliff bottom. Ash shook his arms, trying to get some life back into them. But they hung heavily from his aching shoulders. He shuffled towards the high rocky wall, desperate for a rest, but knowing that if he stopped now, he'd never get started again. Dawn was approaching fast. Now was the time for sneaking.

He looked for a way up.

"Crap." The cliffs were a lot taller than they'd looked from the shore.

Why was nothing simple any more?

No path up. No convenient rope dangling from the top. No escalator. Certainly no lift. Just clumps of weeds and grass sticking out of cracks in the rock. Dripping wet, legs worn from the swim, Ash searched the cliff for a handhold. He grabbed an exposed root, wedged his toes into a long crack and started to climb.

Ash crept up the dark cliff face like a spider, slowly, and planning each move. More than once his grip slipped and he found himself dangling fifty metres over the rock by just his fingertips. His arms burned and his shoulders ached like this was his worst PE class times a hundred, times a thousand. He was definitely low on battery power.

Bad time to have second thoughts about all this, Ash.

He needed a death – for someone nearby to die and allow him to absorb their death energies. Then he could take on anyone.

That was sick, thinking about death so casually. The real-isation made him shiver, or was it just the night sea wind?

❖

Savage was waiting at the top. His prize. He gritted his teeth and pushed on.

Game over, scumbag.

Eventually, with the eastern sky turning purple, Ash reached the top. He sat down to catch his breath and let his limbs recover. His fingers were numb from gripping the rock.

Ash drew out his katar. It settled comfortably in his grip. The katar wasn't flash; it didn't have gems or decorative carvings, it was as plain as could be.

It had one purpose, and he would use it for that: to end Savage's miserable life, once and for ever.

Ash looked along the uneven cliff path. The sky was bloody now, dawn an hour away. Lights shone among the tents. They stood arranged in neat military rows, each of unblemished white canvas, like small houses. The island wasn't big; it was almost square and relatively flat, though overgrown and dotted with palm trees. Ash spotted a few more of the flagstones, mostly covered in grass. He crept closer to the tents and crouched, barefoot and silent. He searched around, watching for anyone coming near. The darkness gathered around him. The shadows seemed thicker where he stood and the silence deeper.

The army of statues, the loha-mukhas, surrounded the edge of the camp. A pack of hyena rakshasas scouted the perimeter. One sniffed at the bush Ash hid behind, then wandered off.

Ash smiled to himself. His dip in the sea must have masked his scent.

He skirted round the edge of the encampment, heading towards the biggest tent. It was a plain thing, about five metres square and tall enough for a man to stand up in. The flaps were closed, but fluttered slightly in the wind. Up close, Ash saw the walls were embroidered with the crossed swords and poppies of the Savage coat of arms. There were two loha-mukhas standing guard outside, a six-armed Shiva made of bronze and a stone lion. Savage had to be in there.

At the back of the tent, Ash stopped and listened. Nothing. He scraped the edge of his katar into the heavy cloth, tearing a small hole. He peered in, but couldn't see anything; it was too dark. His heart went into overdrive and he wiped the sweat from his hands.

This is it.

Ash cut a line through the back wall. The cloth parted, the noise seeming as loud as a scream, but there was no response as he entered the tent.

Early morning light followed him through the tear and cast a soft glow over the sleeping figure of Savage. He lay on his back, shirt undone. Seven skulls marked his chest in a circle pattern, each one glowing softly with a pale, almost radioactive yellow. They were deep brands, and Ash, for a moment, wondered how much they had hurt. He knew they were a symbol of Savage's growing magical power, the number of sorceries he'd mastered. He'd only had five skulls when Ash had faced him in Rajasthan. Three more, and he'd be as powerful as Ravana.

Beside the bed was a small, low camp table. Savage's cane rested on it, next to a small leather satchel. Ash flicked it

❖

open. The Koh-i-noor lay inside in its silk purse. He put the satchel over his shoulder.

Ash knelt down beside the bed and pressed the razor-sharp edge of the katar against Savage's throat.

Chapter Thirty-nine

The pale, almost translucent skin of the Englishman was reflected in the mirror-like steel. A thick blue vein stood out, running from behind his jaw to somewhere under his shoulder. It would take only a little pressure to open it.

Ash tightened his grip on the hilt. His palms were slippery. He stared at the passive, sleeping face, eyes gently closed and his mouth just open.

Savage was pure evil. Ash would be doing the world a favour in killing him. It wouldn't even be hard; he was asleep and defenceless. This wasn't like fighting Ravana, or even any of the other rakshasas with their fangs and claws and totally negative attitudes. Ash had bathed in their blood, so why was his hand trembling now?

Just do it and feel guilty later.

❖

But his arm wouldn't budge. He couldn't even get himself to lean over and sort-of-cut-Savage's-throat-by-accident.

Coward!

Would Savage hesitate? Would Parvati? It wouldn't even cross their minds. Ash was the Kali-aastra. Death was his job. But still he couldn't strike.

I can't kill a defenceless man.

"Difficult, isn't it?" whispered Savage, his eyes still closed.

"Don't move."

"I am completely at your mercy."

"I could kill you right now."

"Yes, you certainly could," said Savage. "But I doubt it. Heroes don't murder people in their beds."

"Just watch me." Ash leaned over Savage, the flat of the dagger on his skin."

"You do it and your friend will remain cold and dead in her grave."

"What do you mean?"

"The Brahma-aastra, of course. The Life Giver." Savage's eyes opened slowly. "I can bring your friend back."

"Yeah, as a zombie. No thanks."

"Listen to me, Ash. Do you think I'd waste all this time, money and effort if I didn't know how to do it properly? I'm insulted you think so little of my abilities."

"How?"

"Let me get up and I'll show you."

Ash held the blade to Savage's throat. "You stay right there. Just tell me."

"Is that it? You expect me to talk?"

❖

Savage was bluffing. He wanted to drag things out, hoping one of the rakshasas or loha-mukhas outside might come in and rescue him. Enough was enough. "No, Savage, I expect you to die."

Sweat shone on Savage's wrinkled face. "Listen," he said with rare desperation. "I've read the histories of Ashoka, how he tried to use it and all he awoke were monsters, zombies as you call them, instead of living, breathing humans. Agreed?"

"The mantra, the spell, that activated the aastra was wrong" said Ash. "There's a mispronunciation in there, or some other error that's crept in over time. That mistake means that when you use the Brahma-aastra on the dead they don't come back, not as they once were."

Now Savage smiled – sly, reptilian. "But there was one person who knew the correct, flawless mantra. He learned it from Brahma himself."

"Ravana."

"Yes. Lord Ravana knew the spell perfectly. But because he was a rakshasa, he couldn't use the aastra."

"And you know it? The proper mantra?"

"I know where it is. And with your help, I could get it and save your friend. I'm the only hope she has." Savage turned slowly so they faced each other. "The Brahma-aastra is no weapon. It cannot be employed for anything but healing. Used properly, it can repair any wound, cure any sickness, raise the dead. Look at me. I'm dying, boy. The diamond is my only hope. Do you honestly think I'd use it if there was a risk of being turned into some mindless, shambling monstrosity?"

❖

"How do I know this isn't some plot to bring Ravana back? You did it before."

"You're the Kali-aastra, boy. When you killed Ravana, you killed him for good. And why would I bring him back now? I only freed him to regain my youth and learn more sorceries. I was going to destroy him myself afterwards, using Kali's arrowhead."

"You're lying."

"Who would want to live in a world ruled by Ravana? Not me. I just wish you'd waited until I'd absorbed more of his magic, at least enough to stop me looking like this."

What should he do? Savage couldn't be trusted, but everything he said made sense.

And Gemma could be brought back to life. Hope surged through him again. Think what it would be like, having her back. All the damage, all the mistakes, would be undone. He could still save her.

"I'm no super-villain, Ash," said Savage. "I'm old, weak and dying, trying to hang on to whatever life I have left. Would you deny a person, terminally ill, the chance to save himself? Of course you wouldn't. Let me prove myself. If I am telling the truth, then think of the lives we'll save, starting with your friend. If I'm lying or can't awaken the Koh-i-noor, then kill me. I won't stop you. I don't want to go on like this."

Ash lifted the dagger away. "One chance, Savage. That's all you've got."

"That's all I'll need." Savage swung his feet off the bed. He put his hand on the cane. "Shall we?"

❖

"Wait." One hand still holding the katar point in Savage's back, Ash whipped his scarf round the old man's neck, so it became a leash. "I wouldn't want you running off." He pushed Savage out of the tent.

Ash kept close behind Savage, ready to use him as a shield if anyone tried to attack him. Everywhere he looked there were loha-mukhas and rakshasas. "Tell them to back way off."

"You heard him," said Savage.

The nearest, the Shiva statue and the stone lion, obeyed, their faces blank. The monkeys and the huge *David* watched, their joints creaking as they moved their heads to follow Ash and Savage's walk into the heart of the encampment. Seagulls cried overhead and the sea rustled below, but otherwise the only sound was Ash's galloping heart.

If Savage tried to double-cross him, it would be the last thing he ever did. Ash would skewer him and pray the death energies would be great enough for him to fight his way out.

"Looks like rain," Savage said, peering at the black clouds in the distance that just hid the dawning sun. "Morning, Jackie."

Jackie stood at the open tent, mouth agog and eyes saucer-sized on seeing Ash. She lunged forward, but halted as Ash dug the katar in deep enough for Savage to cry out. "Stay where you are," Savage said.

"Let me kill him, Master," she snarled. "I want to eat his heart."

"I have other plans," replied Savage. "Ash and I are now... partners."

"But Master—"

"No, Jackie." He met her gaze, and Jackie, growling deep in her throat, stepped back.

"Shall we get down to business?" Savage said.

The wind was picking up and lightning flashed on the horizon. Savage shuffled to the edge of the cliff, Ash close behind him. The wave tops frothed as the sea, so still and silent last night, churned far beneath them.

"This will do," said Savage. Ash realised they were on a square platform. Grass covered most of it, but bare stone could still be seen where the grass had been eroded. He looked back at the beach he'd swum from. Was this still part of that road that they'd found in the jungle? Then he turned back towards the storm, still so far away. Where did the road end? Somewhere out in the middle of the sea?

Savage touched the scarf round his neck. "You can loosen this."

The nearest henchman was Jackie, and she was just a pounce away. But Ash let the cloth slip free and wrapped it round his waist as a sash.

"Thank you," said Savage. "And now, to work." He raised his cane and peered far into the distance. His lips moving silently, his cane drew symbols in the air with sharp, swift cuts.

The ground around them trembled and shifted.

"What are you doing?" asked Ash.

"Things you wouldn't believe, boy." Savage pointed out to the sea with his cane. "You've heard of Lanka, I suppose?"

❖

"Of course. Ravana's kingdom."

Savage grinned. Ash had seen that face before, frighteningly hungry and obsessed. "Out in the middle of the sea. And Rama's army, when he came for Ravana, was stuck on the land there, unable to cross."

Ash shook his head. "No. Rama's army attacked Lanka. Rama had them build a bridge stretching all the way across the sea..."

His gaze fell upon the stone slabs under his feet.

"Not a bridge, but a causeway," said Savage. "That was four thousand years ago. The sea was lower then. Now the causeway's sunk under fifteen metres of water."

The waves rose and struck the island. Out in the distance the storm grew wilder. Great blinding flashes of lightning burst across the churning clouds. The wind howled around them, making Ash stagger.

"Lanka was a series of island kingdoms," continued Savage, "sustained by Ravana's magic. When he died, they disappeared, one by one, under the waves. They're still there, but many hundreds of fathoms deep. But that's where we'll find what we're looking for."

All around them, rocks and small stones rolled and bumped into one another. The earth beneath them surged and buckled, flexing like a springboard. One after the other, the loha-mukhas each turned to face the sea, watching the storm.

"I am master of the elemental sorceries, Ash," said Savage. "Air, Water, Fire and Earth. I can make the very stones dance. And what else are these —" he spread out his hands to include the army of statues — "but stone, brought to life by me?"

Ash stared as slabs of stone rose out of the waves. Covered in seaweed and coral and dripping with barnacles, one after the other they broke the surface, creating a road across the water.

"You're raising the road to Lanka," whispered Ash.

"Yes," hissed Savage. His face was rigid with the effort. His skin peeled and flaked and his body withered and re-formed as the magic stole his life force. Ash watched as blue veins pulsed against his tissue-thin skin, and Savage bent double, as old and as frail as a skeleton. His white hair fell out in patches. "But not just the road."

By now the storm was in its full fury. Twenty-metre-high waves crashed against the rocks, followed by huge tidal waves and heralded by winds that caused the heavy statues to sway. Lightning dazzled the black sky and thunder roared like the screams of the gods.

Palace spires, ancient, twisted, black and cruel, pierced the boiling waters from below. Ash watched tall towers, stout castles and gardens made of coral rise out of the ocean depths. Water cascaded down paths and off roofs, rivers running from the heights of the palaces back into the sea.

Lanka, the capital of Ravana, rose out of the ocean.

Chapter Forty

Savage screamed, his bones stretching and melting as the magic backlash hit him. The skull brands on his chest pulsed with light. His face melted like wax under a blowtorch, obscenely running and re-forming, exposing raw muscle and bone as the body rearranged itself. Ugly blotches of pus and blood swelled under the skin and then sank away. His forehead bubbled and beads of blood dribbled from his eyes. He threw back his head and gave a hissing cry.

Ash watched with morbid fascination. This was more than just Savage's life force being robbed and fought over.

Savage groaned and stiffened. He clutched his head and pushed against the bloated lumps upon his skull. The magical energies within him twisted his limbs and marred his flesh with grotesque, cancerous growths. But Savage fought against them, and eventually he returned to his normal, though decrepit, shape.

Panting, saliva dribbling from his lips, he stared at Ash. "Now you understand why I need the Brahma-aastra. I cannot go on like this."

"I think you're mistaking me for someone who gives a damn, Savage." But briefly, Ash pitied the Englishman — and felt something akin to awe. Out where there had been nothing but sea, there now stood an island. If Savage could raise whole lands, then maybe he was telling the truth about the diamond. "I just want Gemma back, as she was."

"A promise is a promise." One of the loha-mukhas came up behind Savage and helped him slip on a fresh white linen shirt. "The secret to that lies in Lanka, upon the Black Mandala."

Mandala? Ash's dad had one at home. It was a religious painting, usually circular. Monks and other holy people used them to aid in their meditations. But he'd never heard of a black one. All the ones he'd seen blazed with colours.

"What is it?" Ash asked.

"Something Ravana created. In layman's terms, it is a scroll with the mantra of Brahma upon it. You give me an hour to study it, and I will awaken the aastra. I'll transport us to England, and you'll be holding hands with your friend before dusk."

Ash looked at the island. Water still cascaded down from the highest hills, and the entire place shimmered in the bright sunlight. The city of Ravana. He couldn't believe it. "What else is in there?"

"You tell me. You've been there before, as Rama."

Rama, the human prince who had conquered Lanka, and one of Ash's past lives. But nothing of the scene before him stirred any memories. Ash's focus was locked on to the first Ashoka. Maybe there wasn't any room for other memories right now.

"All I know are the myths," said Ash.

"Like me when I first came to India," Savage said wistfully. "Back in the eighteenth century, this country was a land of myths, as mysterious and as fantastic as that island over there. You have no idea how awe-inspiring it was to see my first elephant, to see the Himalayas. The wonder of it all."

"What happened?" The way Savage talked about India made Ash envious, almost. The marvel in Savage's voice was still there.

"I discovered many new things. I acquired great knowledge of an esoteric nature. I learned much, but understood little." Savage accepted a jacket from Jackie and adjusted a marigold in the buttonhole. "Look at Rishi. He was as powerful as I, but he restrained himself, avoided the traps I fell into. Magic's a drug: the more you use, the less effect it has, so the more you need to do even the smallest of spells. It is an endless downward spiral."

"Then why don't you stop? All the things you know, all the lives you've lived, couldn't you—"

"Use it for good? Is that what you're going to say?"

Ash blushed. It sounded so childish, but that was exactly what he meant.

271

❖

Savage put on a pair of stout boots. "Don't you think I've tried? I taught others magic, hoping to create a society of wise men, but that failed. They competed against each other for power, wealth and influence. Power corrupts."

"You had apprentices? Where are they?"

"In hell, I hope. It's as much as they deserve." Savage checked his cane, sliding out his sword and giving it a flourish in the shining sunlight before clicking it back in place. "But there is Lanka, and the day is passing. You and I, boy, are partners on a great adventure."

"That doesn't mean I trust you," said Ash.

A sly smile cracked over Savage's pale face. "Of course not."

Lanka lay before them, at the end of the wave-washed causeway. The storm had vanished as suddenly as it had arrived. Blue sky appeared through the patches of cloud, and the wind now just ruffled Ash's hair. Large waves broke on the beach, but they were half the height they'd been just five minutes ago.

Lanka glistened in the morning sun. The city looked like it had been made of coral and sculpted rock, not built, but grown. The spikes and edges of the buildings were ragged and sharp. It was a place where if you didn't watch your step, you'd be torn apart.

"Beautiful, isn't it?" said Savage.

"And dangerous," said Ash.

"Dangerous indeed." Savage's eyes, two black obsidian orbs, narrowed. "Are you afraid?"

"How can I be when you've got my back?"

Jackie growled, but Savage laughed and she backed down,

❖

her fur rippling across her shoulders. "Come, we are wasting time," said Savage.

Savage assembled his party: Jackie, of course; five of the hyena rakshasas and five loha-mukhas. A pair of stone monkeys carried a set of heavy iron-bound chests on their heads. Then came the six-armed Shiva and two winged gargoyles that looked as if they'd just come off the roof of Notre Dame Cathedral. It was like some bizarre expedition from the Victorian era, the brave white explorer and his native bearers. Ash wouldn't have been surprised if one of the trunks included a china dining set.

"We need all of that?" Ash asked.

"Lanka will be defended. Better we be cautious. I wouldn't want something unpleasant to happen to you."

"Sure you wouldn't."

The rakshasas led them down the steep path to the causeway, sniffing the route. Ash stayed close to Savage, his hand on the katar, the diamond in the satchel. The loha-mukhas trailed behind.

The road lay about half a metre above the sea. Waves splashed across the weathered and seaweed-covered stone. Strange formations of coral had attached themselves to the causeway, decorating it with multicoloured foliage. Bright greens, radiant yellows, blues and golds all shone upon and within the rectangular slabs, as if they had been draped with gems.

Ash fell into step with Jackie.

"Glad to be going home?" Ash asked.

"Lanka was the greatest city in the world, mortal. It is a holy place."

❖

"Looks like it could do with a bit of paint."

Jackie glanced at him with a look of cold fury. "You killed my only two friends."

"And you killed Gemma," Ash replied, his voice low and threatening.

"A mortal? What was she?" Jackie snorted. "Mayar was a great, great rakshasa. He wore the skins of princes and feasted on the eyes of kings. Jat was a lord of birds; we ate the dead on countless battlefields. Carrion kings we were. And you killed them both. You, a small, pathetic child."

In spite of what he was, or was becoming, he didn't want to kill anything or anyone. But this close, it was as if he could smell Gemma's blood on Jackie's claws.

Jackie put her hand on Ash's chest, her claws just scratching his tunic. Two hyena rakshasas stood just behind her, and the other three, somehow, had slipped behind Ash. He glanced at Savage, but the Englishman was not paying attention in that 'I know what's going on, but I'm pretending I haven't seen anything' sort of way.

"Classic playground ambush," Ash said. His punch dagger sat tucked in his sash. "Really, Jackie? This the best you can do?"

Jackie knew how to grin — lots of teeth and bad attitude. "What's to stop me from just taking the Koh-i-noor off you right now?"

Ash dropped his shoulder and the satchel slipped off. He caught it by the strap just before it fell into the water. "This?" He swung the satchel back and forth, higher and higher, holding the strap by a finger. "And what's to stop me letting go and sending it to the bottom of the sea?"

Savage cleared his throat. "No more dawdling. We've still some miles to go."

"It's not over between us," said Ash as Jackie joined the other demons.

Where were Parvati and Khan? Ash constantly looked back, hoping to see them on the shore, but he was too far away.

He wished they could see what he saw. A bloody huge island with palaces and everything had just risen out of the sea. Even for Parvati, that had to be something special. And it was Lanka, her home.

Ash searched the chopping waves, wondering if there might be some boat out there bringing the two rakshasas to the island.

Instead he spotted the fins.

Chapter Forty-one

Suddenly the causeway seemed terribly narrow and slippery."

"Don't fall," warned Jackie. "I want to save you for myself."

"I can swim," snapped Ash.

Jackie pointed. "Won't make any difference to them."

A few of the dagger-cruel fins darted off to the side, and Ash saw a froth of water jet out. A curving, dark grey shape glided along the surface before submerging again. A whale.

The fins dipped under after it.

The other sharks changed direction and shot towards the commotion. The water churned and turned red as more and more of the deadly sea hunters attacked the whale. The sharks piled into one another, utterly focused on feeding and ignoring anything else. They slithered over each other and fought and gouged as great chunks of pink meat were torn off and shaken loose.

Ash stepped away from the edge as the waves lapped red over his toes. Even from here he sucked in the energy from the death, but it was sickeningly tainted, savage with mindless frenzy. The images of teeth and tearing and flesh slick with blood filled his mind, choking him. He wanted to stop it, but part of him craved more. A new strength surged through him. He licked his lips.

It went on for minutes, and all of Savage's party watched with mute horror or admiration. Savage, cane tucked under his arm, put a brass spyglass to his eye.

Finally the sharks broke away from their feast. A few smaller ones lurked and dived near the kill, but the bigger ones pushed their way back into the open sea. However, one pack – there was no other word for it – swam towards the causeway. They were in formation, a tight, accelerating V with the biggest shark at the front.

They wanted dessert.

The sharks gained speed, and the waters rolled out in sharp waves. Black fins slipped parallel to the causeway, getting closer and... stopping.

"But sharks can't stop," whispered Ash. It was one of those freaky bits of useless information he knew.

Then slick, dark bodies with leathery skins and wide, long snouts clambered up on to the path ahead of them. Their beady black eyes were still fresh with desire and bloodlust, and in their grinning mouths Ash saw the serrated teeth of the ultimate predator. Their faces shrank and narrowed as their tails split

❖

into legs, melding into human limbs. Their side flippers grew longer and thicker and were soon strong human arms. They resembled humans, and would have passed easily for them from a distance, but their eyes stayed the soulless black buttons of a shark, and their teeth remained ferociously wicked.

The leader of the sharks shook off the worst of the seawater. He picked a string of red flesh from his teeth and tossed it into the sea.

Savage stood his ground, immobile, as the rakshasa approached. Whatever else Savage was, he was not a coward.

The shark-man grinned, a smirk that could have fitted Savage's head into it with space to spare.

"Looking good, Alex," said the shark-man.

"The same could be said about you, you old rascal," replied Savage. "Still chewing up Australian surfers?"

Then Savage and the shark rakshasa laughed and embraced.

After he greeted Savage and the other rakshasas, the shark-man came over to Ash. His grey skin shimmered with seawater, and Ash saw gill slits on either side of his neck. The rakshara frowned and walked round Ash, inspecting him from all angles. "Tell me, how exactly did this piece of fish bait kill our king?"

"I agree, he's not much to look at," said Savage.

"Hey!" Ash said. What did they mean, 'not much to look at'?

Half the pack remained in shark form, circling in the water. The other shark rakshasas waited ahead of the party. Of all the rakshasas Ash had seen, they were the least human, their skins thick and scaly. Two still had back fins, and all

❖

looked uncomfortable out of the water, moving unsteadily as they got used to having legs.

The lead shark-man, ignoring Ash, glanced back towards Lanka. "There are a lot of curses still in place. We've dismantled the outer ones, but beyond the walls, you'll have to tread carefully."

Savage smiled. "I would expect nothing less."

The sharks dived back into the sea, transforming before they'd even touched the water. Their fins sliced through the green waters and were soon lost among the waves.

"Let's move," said Savage.

Ash searched around him. There was sea in every direction. Even if Parvati and Khan were out there somewhere, with the loha-mukhas guarding the causeway and the sharks patrolling the ocean, the chances of them getting to Lanka without being torn limb from limb were pretty negligible.

And — *what curses?*

This was Ravana's capital. This was the heart of the demon nations. There would be treasure, for sure. Magic? Yeah, pretty damn likely. And none of it would be lying around in easy-to-access locations. The word 'deadly' sprang to mind. So did 'lethal', 'fatal' and 'extremely hazardous to your health'.

How did he keep ending up in these situations? Ash was going to have a serious talk with his career advisor when he got home.

It took almost half a day to reach Lanka. The sun passed over its zenith and began its descent over the land behind them. The causeway bore signs of extensive damage the closer they got. Great chunks had been broken off and turned to rubble.

❖

With the city walls a mile ahead, the party paused.

"Battle stations," ordered Savage. One of the loha-mukhas, a monkey, lowered the trunk it had been carrying. Savage took out a leather gun belt and a bandolier that went over his left shoulder and clipped on to the belt just over his right hip. An old German Mauser 'Broomhandle' pistol went into the holster across his belly. He jiggled the belt and bandolier, shifting his shoulders until the gear sat comfortably, and then he put on a pair of thin leather gloves, his tiger cane tucked under his arm. The leather creaked as he flexed his fingers and made a fist. Savage caught Ash watching him.

"What did you expect?" Savage asked. "A whip and fedora?"

"Why do you need them? Can't you just lightning-bolt everyone? Or just teleport us to where we need to go?"

"I could, but I prefer to save my magic for when it's truly necessary. You've seen what happens when I use it." He gestured to the satchel. "You want to save some of the power in that for Gemma, don't you?" He peered at the city walls. "And I can't teleport because I don't know where to teleport to. I've no idea of the layout. The last thing you want is to jump into a wall, half in and half out. Human and brick atoms are not very compatible."

Savage continued his preparations, checking and loading his pistol, then counting the rounds on his bandolier and spare ammo in the pouches on the belt. He double-knotted the laces of his boots and gave them a tug. "You won't believe the number of men I've seen die on a battlefield because they tripped over their laces."

Ash scratched his thumb. "It's the little things that make all the difference, right?"

Savage tapped the cane against his heel. "It's a shame we're not on the same side, boy."

"Yeah, like together we could rule the galaxy."

"So sad. In my day we would quote Shakespeare or Homer."

"I can quote Homer. I've memorised entire episodes of *The Simpsons.*"

"Master, we are ready." Jackie stood a few metres away, dressed for a fight. Her arms were protected with stiff steel plates with blades projecting from the forearms. Under her T-shirt, her body was covered in a light tawny fur, revealing her muscles across her shoulders and back. Her thick mane rippled in the wind and long fangs filled her elongated jaw. She'd taken off her shoes so her toes, long and tipped with sharp claws, clicked on the stone. Steel plates covered her thighs and shins.

The five hyena rakshasas were similarly armed, protected on the arms and legs, but not over the torso. Ash realised the armour they wore allowed them to transform safely: wearing something over the body would have either prevented it from working or been excruciatingly painful, as their animal shapes were very different from their human ones.

"Lets move," ordered Savage. The monkeys hoisted the trunk back up and the party continued towards the city, with Ash walking alongside Savage.

"What are you expecting?" asked Ash. The island ahead of them had been sunk under the seas for thousands of years. What could possibly be alive in there that required all this?

❖

"I'm expecting the worst. I always do. Helps me stay alive," said Savage.

"What are these curses that shark went on about?"

"After Ravana was killed, his brother, Vibheeshana, took the crown. He was almost as great a magician, but without the passion, without the ambition."

"What happened?"

"The rakshasas left. Soon the city was empty but for Vibheeshana and his court – noble rakshasas holding on to their faded glory. All rather sad and somewhat pathetic. Then on one fateful night there was a terrible storm. Waves, dozens of metres high, crashed on to the shore, and the land shook with violence. By the time the storm broke, Lanka had vanished."

"Just like that? It seems very... convenient."

Savage looked towards the island. "Some say it had only been sustained by Ravana's magic. With him gone, the island just collapsed. Others believe Vibheeshana himself destroyed it. Who wants to rule an empty kingdom? He was frightened that people would come and try to discover Ravana's secrets or search for treasure among the ruined palaces. So he laid curses and traps all over the island to deter the greedy, and then as a final precaution sent the entire thing to the bottom of the sea."

"Sounds like this Vibheeshana was a clever guy."

The walls of Lanka rose straight from the ocean. The causeway had been reduced to rubble for the last hundred metres, and Ash moved step by step, occasionally having to crawl over the broken slabs, slick with seaweed and covered in sharp coral and shells.

❖

He almost didn't see that the rest of the party had stopped.

"This is it," said Savage.

Pearly white walls shimmered in the sunlight. When Ash looked deeper into them, there were a myriad of other colours swirling within: reds, pinks, greens, blues and others, fractured and crystalline, sending multicoloured beams deeper into the infinite space within the stone. The twisting rose-hued stones formed strange, glorious tree-like structures along the battlements, their branches made of coral and their trunks encrusted with barnacles. The city looked like it had become overgrown, but with petrified foliage.

Ash gazed up and up. "Those walls must be fifty metres high at least." He put his hand against them. Perfectly slick; a total nightmare to climb. "You sure you don't want to teleport?"

"Please, Ash, assume I've planned for this." Savage turned and faced the sea. "I'd stand back too, if I were you."

The sea looked perfectly calm.

"Any minute now," said Savage.

"Right. Any minute."

There were a few waves.

"Impressive," said Ash. "Not."

Then the waves rose and tumbled, white foam spraying along the tops. A huge mass moved under the water, rising. Ash pressed back along the wall, fast.

Metre by metre, a vast head appeared. Seaweed hung off it like green dreadlocks and water ran from its brow. Ash groped for handholds as a three-metre wave fell over everyone on the causeway. Everyone, that is, but Savage.

Ash spat out the salty water. "So that's what you did with the Jagannath."

The giant stone creature rose until the water only came up to its waist. Up close, in the daylight, it was still utterly awe-inspiring. The head creaked as it gazed down at Savage.

"Please give me a door," said Savage. He pointed at a spot in the wall. "Just there."

A massive fist pounded the walls, over and over again. First tiny lines burst like spiders' webs over the surface. Then chips shot off in all directions, and long, splintering cracks radiated out from the pummelled surface. The sudden, sharp blows echoed well beyond the other side of the city walls. The smaller loha-mukhas buried their fingers in the broken wall and tore out great chunks of the pearly stone, hurling them into the sea. It took no more than a few minutes before a hole had been made, roughly three metres wide and two metres high. The Jagannath stopped and stood still as seagulls circled round its head.

One of the hyena rakshasas crept near. He shook his mottled black fur as he inspected the hole, wrinkled his snout, and growled. He turned to Savage. "Smells bad."

"I'm not interested in the smell."

The hyena growled once more and leaped in through the opening. His claws skittered across the rubble, and then there was silence.

A sudden, petrified howl made Ash's hair stand on end. There was a bark and snapping of jaws, followed by another noise – a faint, mournful keening, or shriek. The hyena

❖

yelped, the sound of it fading as though it had fallen down a long deep well; then nothing.

Savage peered in the hole. "Hmm," he said. "That's not a good sign."

Chapter Forty-two

"After you," said Savage.

"Now why would I want to do anything that stupid?" asked Ash.

"I thought you were a hero, Ash. Heroes go first." Savage touched the wall. "You're the Kali-aastra, destroyer of demons, remember? And this is their city."

Ash met the cold, arrogant gaze of the Englishman. In the complete blackness of Savage's eyes, there was a thin circle of deep red where the edge of the iris would have been. Subtle hues lurked within — sometimes deep, like looking into the endless night sky, other times shallow, like black paint across glass.

"Well, if you're too chicken," said Ash, "I'll take a peek."

The rubble half filled the hole the loha-mukhas had made. Light moved and played on the other side, strange shadows and colours sliding over the broken wall. Ash stepped in, breathing lightly, every muscle and nerve on hyper alert.

The hyena had disappeared.

Ash took control of his breathing, letting his supernatural abilities rise up out of the depths to stir the Kali-aastra into action.

The passage through the wall went on for hundreds of metres, even though the wall itself couldn't be more than five or six metres thick. As he crouched in the opening, the exit was just a small bead of light at the far end of the crooked tunnel. It looked like reality was being left behind.

Lights danced within the translucent stone. Some of the lights formed almost complete shapes, humanoid and not; others drifted like jellyfish.

Ash shuffled a few metres in, fingers tight round his katar. There was still no sign of the hyena rakshasa, except for a red stain within the wall that faded away the closer he got to it. The tunnel forced him into an uncomfortable crouch, moving crab-like, eyes and ears alert to any danger. He kept low to avoid the rough edges and sharp corners of the broken coral. Small spikes of stone jutted out from the walls, and water dribbled from the cracks, forming small sparkling pools.

"Ouch." Ash winced as he splashed into one. He hopped out and sat down, inspecting his sole.

A small spine of coral stuck out of the flesh. Not deep, and *he pulls the spine out easily.*

A spot of blood falls.

Coral spines grow out from the place the blood lands. They thicken

❖

every second, and from each branch more sprout, each covered with slim, needle-pointed thorns. Nails of stone mutate into knives, their edges serrated and designed for carving flesh. Within seconds the tunnel is blocked by a wall of deadly thorns, both ahead and behind him. Ash grabs hold, but more spikes erupt from the barriers, piercing his palms. Trapped, unable to go forward or back, he watches in helpless horror as long skewers rise from beneath him and sink down from above. He screams as they bury themselves in his limbs and torso. Blood sprays from his wounds, feeding more of the bloodthirsty stalks. Two narrow needles, their points glistening, push out from the walls and stretch towards his eyes...

Ash rubbed his forehead and inspected his foot and the nail of stone sticking out of it. He had been seeing the future: blood activated the trap. The hyena rakshasa must have stood on a spike or sliced a little skin on one of the edges; all easily done. And the more blood poured out, the faster the deadly stalks grew. He pulled out the small spike and wrapped his scarf round his foot. He'd have to tread carefully and stay out of the puddles.

So he moved slowly along, shuffling forward step by step and giving any edge or spine a wide berth. Sweat dripped from his forehead, fat and hot, running down his tunic and limbs as he focused on the path ahead. It didn't look like he was getting any closer to the end. How long had he been in here? Minutes? Hours?

The sweat coated his palms and soles. The dampness soaked through the scarf, and when Ash picked his foot up, he saw the faint outline of a red circle on the shining stone.

Move, Ash, move!

Forearms crossed in front, he charged ahead as twigs of

❖

sharp coral burst out of the tunnel's inner walls. He barged through the branches, shattering them before they grew too thick, but he was scored with dozens of cuts. Spear-tipped stalactites sprang out above him. One tore a patch of skin off his back, and more stalagmites shot up, catching his heels with their slim, sharp tips.

Ash roared and dived forward as the tunnel filled with hundreds of teeth, a vast serpent closing its mouth, trapping him within. The exit was right before him, a bright shining light that stood for life and freedom, but if one more hook caught him, he was dead.

Ash tumbled out as the tunnel sealed behind him. He fell flat on his face on warm, sunlit stone. His clothing hung raggedly off his scratched and bleeding body, each cut stinging. "Mega-ouch." He rolled on to his back and gazed up, happy to see the sun and the sky and the clouds. Happy to be breathing and not completely holey, like a sieve.

The spears and nails of coral scrapped against each other as they retreated into the walls. The tunnel reopened and within seconds there was no sign of the danger. It appeared temptingly safe.

He looked around. The street running along the inside of the perimeter wall was neat with wide marble paving slabs. Large bundles of green seaweed lay against the walls, with long strands criss-crossing the ground like a cat's cradle, or a web. The buildings here were just tumbledown wrecks. Weird, twisted trees of coral and limestone rose out of the ground and wrapped themselves round the ruins.

❖

But it was the shifting lights that caught Ash's attention. Shadows flickered across the ground, but there was nothing or no one to cast them. Black shapes slid in and out of the hidden corners, figures made up of the void, with no physical substance beyond the thickness of darkness.

And they whispered to Ash in languages long faded from the world, but full of urging. Cold fingers caressed him; shivers ran down into his soul.

"What do you want?" Ash asked.

Mumbling groans and pitiful moans. He felt the stone-heavy despair, the weariness.

"Well? Are you all right?" shouted Savage from the far side of the tunnel.

"I'm peachy. Come on through," said Ash. "Just don't cut yourself."

The creeping black shapes began to retreat, slowly, warily, their dark thoughts still attending him. The whispers were cruel, angry, but Ash felt their trembling fear too.

Savage Jackie, and the remaining four hyena rakshasas clambered through the tunnel, weapons drawn and eyes searching for danger. Next lumbered in the three-metre-tall statue of Shiva, then came the two stone monkeys, one carrying Savage's trunk on its head, and finally the two gargoyles.

Jackie gazed about, mouth open in awe. "It's changed so much."

Of course. This had been Jackie's home, many lifetimes ago. For the first time Ash looked at the rakshasa with some sort of understanding. Eternal exiles, that was what rakshasas were; an outcast race. Jackie tenderly put her hand on a nearby door.

"Which way to the palace?" asked Savage.

Jackie bit her lip as she checked the path. Then she pointed northward.

Savage drew his pistol. "Let's go."

Ash had never been anywhere so alien. Towers formed of pure coral rose up beside jagged spires of crystal and metal. Streets shimmered with marble, and the squares were decorated with grotesque and monstrous statues of pocked and corroded bronze. Winged fiends with serpentine tongues and leonine bodies sat perched on the rooftops, their bodies covered with multicoloured coral. Many of the buildings had been destroyed, and there was rubble and demolished remains everywhere. War had come to Lanka. Ash crossed a large crater, where the heat of some long-ago blast had turned the entire square to glass. He touched the smooth, curved pit edge.

"Aastras," said Jackie. "Rama and his army sent down fire from the skies. Lanka burned for many days."

"You started it," said Ash. "Ravana kidnapped Rama's wife."

Jackie laughed bitterly. "And you think that justified all this? The utter annihilation of a civilisation?"

They walked on, doubling back where the streets had been destroyed by fallen rubble or transformed by coral and other growth that had crept over the city during the millennia it had lain at the bottom of the ocean. The sky darkened and the clouds shifted from pink to purple.

❖

They entered a large square dominated by what looked like a giant swimming pool, easily over a hundred metres long and almost the same width. Steps led down two metres to the bottom. It was empty but for algae.

Ash noticed Jackie beside the pool, head bowed and palms pressed together. She was praying. As she finished, she met his gaze and started. There were tears in her eyes. Embarrassed, she abruptly wiped them away, then stormed off to speak with the hyena rakshasas.

A rakshasa crying? Ash hadn't thought it possible.

"The rakshasas are a warrior race," said Savage, standing beside him on the pool's edge. "They value their honour more than their lives."

"Like the Rajputs," said Ash. The Rajputs were a clan of ancient Indian warriors, and there were plenty of tales of their battles and wars. They would rather die than admit defeat.

"Yes. Very much like the Rajputs."

"Why was she crying?"

"What do you see, Ash?"

Ash looked at the pool. It was made of large square blocks of sandstone, fitted together so neatly there wasn't a gap wide enough for a slip of paper. It was clearly for water storage. "It's a tank, isn't it? This was how the city's water supply was distributed. Some tanks would be for washing and bathing, some purely for drinking."

"Very good. What else?"

Ash walked along the pool. He spotted cracks and black smudges along the stone. "There's been a fire here."

"A huge bonfire, in fact. I imagine the sky must have been filled with smoke. Or flame."

"What did they burn?"

"When the Rajputs face certain defeat, do you know what they do?"

Ash nodded. "The men put on their finest clothes and jewellery and charge the enemy. They fight until every one of them is killed. A 'death or victory' sort of thing."

"You think that heroic?"

He frowned. This sounded like a trap. "Of course."

"Do you know what happens to the women and children? The old folk left behind?"

Ash shook his head. His eyes fell on the scorch marks and an uneasy dread crept over him.

Savage walked down into the vast pit. "The Rajputs would break up their furniture, their doors, everything and anything that burned. They piled it all in here. Then they poured ghee all over it. Ghee burns hot and fast."

Ghee. The thick, high-fat butter used in all Indian cooking. And it was also used to accelerate...

"They built a funeral pyre," said Ash. "This is one giant funeral pyre, isn't it."

"The children they drugged, so they wouldn't know what was happening," said Savage. "Then, with their babies in their arms, the women leaped into the flames. The old folk followed so the conquerors would find nothing but ash."

"I... that's horrific."

"That is a warrior's honour. Jackie's people did this to themselves rather than face the humans' vengeance."

❖

Ash stepped back. He didn't believe it. He didn't want to believe it. "But Rama. Rama was a good man. He would never let such a thing happen."

Savage laughed contemptuously. "Rama, perhaps. But he had hundreds of generals under him. They in turn had thousands of soldiers beneath each of them. Men who had suffered years of war, men who'd seen their own cities and families slaughtered. Men who had nothing left in their hearts but hate and bitterness. Do you think they would be *restrained* when they conquered Lanka? That they would not take revenge?"

Ash said nothing. What could he say? Savage was right.

Savage continued, "I've seen slaughters like you couldn't imagine. There's not a war in the last two hundred years I've not been a part of. I've witnessed what man does to his fellow man, the things he'll do just because the other fellow's skin is a bit different in shade or he follows this god and not that one. If there's one thing we humans have always been good at, it's genocide."

Ash looked towards Savage. "Is that what's kept you going all these years? War?"

"You wound me, boy. Look at us. I am here to uncover the secrets of the Koh-i-noor. Secrets your friend Parvati wanted kept hidden. How is she, by the way?"

"Still desperate to kill you."

Savage sighed. "Rakshasas know how to hold on to a grudge."

"You tricked and betrayed her, Savage. You took her father's scrolls of magic from her. But I think she hates you because you once promised to make her human. She'll never forgive you for that."

"Parvati's pure poison, boy."

"No, you just don't get her." Ash knew that, trapped between two races, Parvati suffered the worst of both – the immortality of her rakshasa heritage and the human desire for companionship, for love, with the loneliness of thousands of years of seeing loved ones and people she cared about die. The world moved on, but she didn't. "Perhaps you wouldn't be so keen for immortality if you really knew what it was like. It's a curse."

"A curse? Who doesn't want to live for ever? You and I are the same, Ash. We've both cheated death once, and now we know it's possible, why settle for less? You want your friend back, and I want to see what lies ahead."

"We're not the same." The idea made him sick.

"Perhaps you are right. Once I discover how to fully awaken the Koh-i-noor, I will be able to heal any sickness, cure any disease. I will be able to resurrect the dead. Tell me, is there any parent in the world who has lost a child who would not want me to succeed?

"Now, let us consider you, Ash Mistry. Your touch brings death to the guilty and innocent alike. It is a power you barely control. You worship a goddess who revels in slaughter, and you are here for nothing more than revenge. Not to better the world, not to redress some wrong, just for revenge and to satisfy your own pride. I wield the Koh-i-noor, the bringer of life. You are the Kali-aastra, and bring only death. Am I wrong?"

❖

"That's not how it is. I'm not the bad guy here," said Ash.

Savage just smiled. But he was wrong. Wasn't he?

Chapter Forty-three

"*T*he greatest treasures will be in Ravana's palace," said Savage.

"And I suppose they'll be well guarded?" asked Ash.

"Exceedingly well guarded."

"By who? Or what?"

Savage looked up towards the buildings on the hills overlooking them. "By the most powerful spells. The most deadly traps and terrifying guards."

"What a surprise. Another suicide mission. And this is going to work because...?"

"Because this time you and I are working together."

"Yeah, I'm not quite clear how that happened." Ash still couldn't pinpoint the moment he and Savage had gone from being mortal enemies to Best Friends For ever. "You'd better be right about this," he said.

❖

"If I'm wrong, then I'm dead," said Savage. "But I'm not wrong." The streets and buildings changed. The paths were wider, the buildings grander and the atmosphere more… anxious.

The dull grey sky returned and spread a gloomy shadow over the city. The wind whispered sad and cruel things just at the edge of hearing. It whirled down the streets and moaned through broken windows and empty doorways. Shadows continued to move of their own accord, not driven by any light Ash could see. No one spoke, and Ash's nerves were as tight as violin strings. He almost wanted some attack, some action. The waiting and the searching was exhausting, never knowing if a trap or some threat might be in the next doorway or round the next corner.

Ash touched the pale, shimmering marble wall and traced his fingers over the softly undulating curves. He winced at a sudden sting and drew his hand away sharply. Four red fingerprints remained on the surface before they were sucked into the depths of the marble.

"My fingers," said Ash, holding them up. "They're bleeding. I think the wall just bit me."

"We're in Lanka, boy," replied Savage. "An impossible realm."

Jackie halted. She held her breath and stared.

Savage joined her. "At last."

A wide avenue stretched out before them. The air rippled and parted. Ash peered at it closely, but it was as if he was trying to see something on the other side of a waterfall. The air was transparent, but fractured and disruptive.

298

❖

"Ravana's palace," said Savage.

With those words, the view ahead crystallised into reality. The fragmented patterns of light, a view through a broken mirror, assembled into a single whole. Needle-like towers protected by a curtain of spikes. Walls of glass with passages of nails and spears. Long ribbons of shell along the paths, their edges as keen as razors. The stones bore tormented faces, for ever frozen in the ecstasy of torture. All Indian temples were decorated with apsaras, divine maidens of extraordinary beauty, heavenly *houris*. Here the apsaras were cruel and harpy-like, with talons and mouths filled with broken and jagged teeth, eyes glaring with fierce hatred. They clung to the columns and stalked along the upper balconies, immobile yet alert.

Icy fear stroked Ash's heart and shivered in his soul. The others clearly felt it too, and Jackie swallowed loudly.

A cloud of despair drifted from the tallest towers and spread across the city, shutting them off from any warmth or sunlight. This was a realm separate from the world of life and colour, the gloomy, dead kingdom of a race that abhorred nature: demonkind. Standing at its very heart, Ash sensed how the world recoiled from it. Every element of his body wanted to retreat.

Steps, cracked and tumbled, led up to a smashed, open gate. The rubble was oily from thousands of years of being submerged, encrusted with barnacles and littered with the flotsam of the deep ocean, with bones of ancient creatures and weapons rusted to almost nothing.

Jackie touched the ground reverently. "This is where we

❖

made our last stand." She gazed out across the city. "We'd heard rumours that Ravana was dead, but we'd sworn to defend his palace no matter what. You could see the banners of Rama's armies all the way to the city's edge. Mayar led Ravana's royal guard and I was there, by the outer courtyard. We'd all prepared for a glorious death."

"But that never happened, did it?" said Ash.

Jackie spat on the step. "No. Our new king surrendered. Vibheeshana, Ravana's own brother. He was as mighty as Ravana, but a coward. He knelt before Rama and handed over his sceptre. A rakshasa, kneeling before a mortal. Even now I feel the bile in my throat. So instead of honourable death, we became exiles. Vagabonds. Thus ended the reign of Ravana."

Ash looked about him, at this ancient battlefield where a whole race was wiped out. He almost, *almost* felt pity for the rakshasas. Here in this immense plaza, they had become a near-extinct species. In one day they had been toppled from their golden thrones to become refugees, hated and hunted by their conquerors.

Jackie looked out from a broken lump of rock. "The sky was on fire and you could hear the cries of the gods themselves. The universe trembled when Ravana died."

"I know. I was the one who killed him, twice."

"You have no idea what you did." The bitterness was still acid sharp, yet tempered with weary acceptance. The story of Ravana had finally ended in Rajasthan, and it had been Ash who'd written the last line.

Savage snapped his fingers and pointed at two of the hyena rakshasas. "Sniff it out."

❖

They nodded and swept up the steps to the vast entrance of the palace. They nuzzled along the stones and snarled at the dark, open mouth of the doorway, and then both went in.

Savage looked back at the loha-mukhas. "Come on then."

The statues remained stationary. The Shiva statue was still and the monkeys frozen with their tails high loops in the air. The gargoyles both had a foot in the air, midstep.

Savage glared and raised his cane. "I gave you an order."

They remained as still — *well, as still as statues,* he thought.

"Your spell's worn off," he said.

"No, it's been nullified," said Savage. He peered into the doorway, twisting the cane in his hands. If Ash didn't know better, he'd have thought Savage was looking a bit anxious. Maybe a little afraid.

What was in there? Something more powerful than Savage?

Ash was halfway up the steps already. Despite the dread radiating from the palace, he couldn't help himself. His curiosity was too great. How could he not want to look? Being in Ravana's palace was like being at the heart of time, at the greatest moment in humankind's existence. It was here that humanity had inherited the earth. All that had followed, the thousands of years of human civilisation, its domination, was decided on this spot. What was inside?

Ash paused, still fifteen metres from the doors. He couldn't penetrate the gloom beyond the palace opening, but he felt—

From within, one of the hyena rakshasas howled. Then there was a hiss and sudden silence.

❖

A moment later the rakshasa's head rolled out. It tripped down the steps, slowly at first, then tumbling faster as it built up speed, splashing wild patterns of blood over the marble with each bounce, until Savage stopped it with his boot.

"What a shame," he said, looking down at the dead eyes. "I rather liked him." He kicked it down the last few steps.

Ash breathed in the vanishing spirit of the rakshasa. This was death, and it was sweet. Power surged along his limbs and his heart swelled. He grinned hungrily at the perfume of spilled blood and drew the katar.

So, treading through the puddle of blood, Ash crept into Ravana's palace.

Chapter Forty-four

"Hello?" said Ash.
Hello. Hello. Hello.
"Anyone home?"
Home. Home. Home.

His voice echoed down and down into the palace. He sensed a yawning vastness before him. Cold air drifted around him and moaned in the space above him. Who knew how high the ceiling was? Columns wound their way upward, each one unique, disappearing into the infinite darkness. Some were stout, others slim, some carved with delicate designs and images, others faceless, but threaded with veins of colour in the marble.

Ash stepped further in, a chill wrapping itself over him like a cloak of ice. Goose bumps rose up over his bare skin and clouds of frosty breath spread out as if he was exhaling his soul.

Savage and Jackie came in a few paces behind. The remaining two hyena rakshasas entered last, sniffing at the bloody trail left by their dead fellow. Savage had his pistol in his left hand, his cane in his right. Jackie prowled in semi-beast form, still lumbering along on two legs, but hunched over with a huge muscular torso and thick, fur-covered arms. The click of her long toenails on the marble floor echoed through the palace.

Long spears of hazy, pearly light fell from hidden windows high in the walls. Glittering dust motes drifted in the cool wind and the slanting darkness, stirred as the trio passed by. Savage paused by Ash and silently handed him a torch. They stopped at the headless body of one of the hyenas. Blood soaked its fur and flesh, and the spine had been neatly, almost surgically, severed.

"Where's the other one?" asked Ash.

"Look," said Jackie.

Claw marks ran across the floor into a dark doorway. It looked as though something had been dragged away... something like a hyena rakshasa. The two left whined pitifully, and their tails hung low between their legs.

Voices moaned. The walls splintered like cracked ice and Ash saw swirling images forming within. The stone began to bulge and grow as faces pushed themselves against the surface. Fingers, crooked and hooked, reached out desperately; mouths widened and long, eager tongues lashed out. Ash backed away, but Savage wasn't quick enough. One bony claw locked round his arm and pulled.

Savage put the pistol against the stony limb, and the hall

thundered with bullets. They sparked as they ricocheted off the marble, and Ash ducked as one nearly clipped his ear. Savage struggled frantically, the sleeve of his jacket tearing free and the pistol clicked on empty. But he was dragged closer, more hands and talons rising from the wall, embracing him.

Ash shoved the tip of his katar into a crack and twisted it sharply. The hand holding Savage shattered as if made of ice. Ash swept his blade into a pair of long claws, focused on the minute points of weakness he could see shining upon them, and they erupted into a thousand pieces. Jackie hauled Savage away as the limbs, snarling faces and clutching fingers vanished back into the stone, denied their prize.

Savage wiped his forehead. He inspected his jacket with the sleeve dangling loose and pulled it off. "I must have words with my tailor. Such poor stitching." His voice shook, unable to hide the fear beneath the pithy remark. He shook Ash's hand. "Thank you."

I saved Savage's life, Ash realised. *I'm such an idiot.*

They descended a series of disjointed stairs. Some were wide with handrails of silver, studded with precious gems; others were of creaking rotten wood, and one was made of pale bone. Savage paused at each of them, inspecting faded symbols and writings that had been carved at various points and junctions. More than once he stopped to let the others get a few steps ahead before catching up. Eventually the party reached a narrow corridor. Unlike the rest of the palace, this one was mathematically square, the walls, floor and ceiling each of identical length. Ash pointed his torch down it and saw that each surface was covered with tiles.

❖

Savage wiped the slime off the nearest tile. "Interesting," he said. "Harappan pictograms."

Ash's blood went cold. Uncle Vik had been an expert on the ancient language of Harappa. It was the reason Savage had employed him. "Can you read it?" he asked.

"They're too badly worn away. This entire building has been submerged for thousands of years, so it's not surprising so much is damaged." He nodded to one of the hyena rakshasas. "Off you go."

The rakshasa sniffed the floor, then took a few steps. His paws brushed the algae covering the tiles.

A low, grinding noise shivered down the corridor. The long, rectangular path began to rotate. Sections twisted as if the corridor had been made up of five open boxes connected together. One box turned clockwise, the other anticlockwise, the walls becoming the floor and the ceiling becoming the walls. The hyena rakshasa tumbled sideways, around and around as the corridor turned, not fast, but unevenly. He scrambled to the second section, but failed to find his balance as the box turned in the opposite direction at a different speed. He left a trail of smeared green slime where he'd fallen and slid.

The grinding stopped and the corridor settled back into place. The floor on which the rakshasa had first stood was now the ceiling. His paw prints were up there, but then he'd slid down the side, across, back up to the ceiling, and down the floor and wall of the second section. He was covered in green, snot-like filth, but, shaking himself, otherwise unharmed.

❖

"That doesn't seem too bad," Ash said. Sure, they'd get knocked about a bit, but as death traps went, he'd faced worse at the local summer fair. He took a step and—

Savage stopped him. The Englishman was staring at the hyena.

The rakshasa barked as tufts of hair shed from him. He tried to get back to the group, but after a few wobbly steps, he slumped to the ground. His fur turned grey and his body began to decay. The fur sank away until his pelt hung on mere bones, before the skin likewise thinned and crumbled. Within seconds there was just a skeleton, and then even that cracked, eroded to dust and blew away.

"We need to get from here to the far end without touching the wrong tiles," said Savage. "Remarkably simple, if you know the right sequence of tiles."

"Do you?"

"Haven't a clue." He looked at the floor. "Fifty tiles on each face, four faces, five sections. A thousand tiles exactly, and probably only a handful safe to stand upon. And the corridor will start turning once you enter, so you must time your steps perfectly, otherwise you'll be tilted off, hit the wrong tile and disintegrate."

Ash blew out a long whistle. "I've come across this before."

Savage looked surprised. Then he smiled. "Ah, in one of your past lives, yes?"

"No. In an old *Dungeons and Dragons* scenario – 'The Clockwork Maze'. A nightmare it was, with the map constantly changing and the traps moving positions. I lost my tenth-level paladin in that adventure."

❖

Savage said nothing, but just looked at Ash as if he was a lot less than sane. A lot less. But he'd survived the maze, thanks to Josh's wizard. And, as luck would have it, they had a real live one here.

"Can't you teleport to the other side?" Ash asked. "That's how we beat the maze."

Savage frowned. "Whatever blocked my control of the loha-mukhas is also stopping me from using my mastery over Space."

So, scrap the *Dungeons and Dragons* solution. Ash smiled at the last hyena rakshasa. "Good luck."

The demon whimpered and retreated, tail well and truly between his legs.

Savage watched him, tapping his heel with his cane. Ash didn't like it. "What?"

"You've changed, Ash. You've acquired an interesting disregard towards the suffering of others. I've seen it before, mainly in psychopathic killers, but rarely in a child. I really am most impressed."

"That's not true," he snapped back. "I care about a lot of people."

"You've just seen a living, sentient creature die quite horribly. You passed a headless hyena rakshasa earlier without batting an eyelid. Are you remotely concerned? No, you joke. I wonder: why is it you're here?"

"To awaken the Koh-i-noor. To bring Gemma back."

"Really? What were your feelings towards her? Do you really care for her, or do you merely want to assuage your guilt? You can't stand that you failed, and *that's* what hurts

❖

you, not Gemma's death. You just want to make yourself feel better. You don't care about her."

"That is not true." Savage was just trying to get under his skin. But Ash glimpsed the cowering hyena and there was a sharp rush of heat, shame, in his heart. The demon was afraid, and Ash had made a joke of it. What had Ujba said? That he should purge himself of weaknesses like compassion. He glared at Savage, chilled that the Englishman might be right.

Savage smiled. "And you call me a monster."

Chapter Forty-five

Ash dried his palms on his trousers for the third time in as many minutes. He looked down the long, dark corridor and listened to the faint, melancholy whispers of the wind as it blew towards him. The torches lit the first ten metres; beyond were just glints of light on the ancient, slimy stone. He glanced over his shoulder. Savage, Jackie and the remaining hyena rakshasa watched him intently. "See you on the other side," he said and stepped on to the first tile.

So far so good. He narrowed his gaze and channelled the power of the Kali-aastra to see ahead, just a second or two into the future. Visible to no one but himself, a soft, faint trail of golden motes stretched out in front of him. The lights shone and burned out, marking the routes that would kill him. He saw shadowy images of himself, his futures, explore the way ahead. Flickering and pale, like mirages, they stepped on tiles and worked their way along the ever-changing tunnel. Some faded away, destroyed by the traps; others grew stronger, more solid the further they got, moving from one safe tile to the next. It was in their footsteps Ash followed.

As he reached the halfway point in the first section, the ground started to tremble. It shifted clockwise and the terrible groaning of stone upon stone grew louder as he jumped to the next tile, already at an angle to the horizontal. He slipped on the wet green algae, tottering on the edge of the tile before leaping to the next, focused on the square some three metres ahead.

Further away, two of his future selves stepped into the last segment. One took a wrong step and vanished.

Ash landed as the floor became the wall and he searched for the next tile; he had only a second to jump. Which tile was it? What had been the wall was now the ceiling and the golden path to it was fading, while another was glowing brighter as it became the floor. Ash jumped, bouncing off one tile and on to another. His toes just touched the edge before he stopped. The next section of corridor was turning in the opposite direction and faster. The golden paths were blinking on and off like strobes at a disco. No route was safe except for a second.

This was impossible. But he had to move; the ground was rotating. He sprang forward, ricocheted off one tile on the wall, and used it to launch himself another five metres to a bright golden landing point in the corner of a floor.

Halfway there, almost over.

Idiot. You're only halfway. It can still go wrong if you start acting cocky.

❖

Sweat dripped off him and his chest felt as if it was on fire. Every sense tingled and power surged through him. Ash catapulted forward, drawing on everything he had as all five sections of the corridor rotated, the first, third and fifth clockwise, the others anticlockwise. He was unstoppable, hitting one tile and then another, his toes barely touching the stone slabs as he chased the golden path shining brightly ahead.

Ash slammed down on the hard marble on the other side of the corridor with both feet and skidded a few metres before turning back. God, his lungs burned! He stood there, taking huge breaths, but immensely relieved. He'd done it! He'd used his inner eye, as Ujba had called it, to see the future and plan out the safest route. Back down at the far end was the bright dot of Savage's torch. Ash just needed to explain which tiles were safe.

The torch blinked off.

The air hummed and Ash stepped back as a sudden draught rose from a rent in the air – a tear in space. Ash glimpsed endless night, a fathomless darkness decorated by minute shining points. The air turned blizzard-cold, and then Savage was standing there, right in front of him. The tear vanished, leaving Jackie and the hyena rakshasa shivering where the rip had been.

"You said you couldn't use your magic," Ash snarled.

Savage shrugged. "I might have misled you a little, but I wanted to see what you were capable of. And may I say, I'm very impressed. You really are very good."

"You lied to me."

❖

"Come now, Ash. Don't tell me you aren't a little pleased with yourself for having made it? Think of my trick as empowering you to new heights."

Ash wasn't having any of it. "Let's move."

Chapter Forty-six

Down, down and down they went. Sometimes they wandered in the darkness, guided only by the beams of their torches and Jackie's memories. Other times they would enter halls lit by strange glowing ghosts, ethereal bodies that haunted the ruins. But always down.

The ceiling of the latest room curved over them, making Ash feel as if he was descending into the throat of a monster. The support beams arched like a beast's ribs. The upper ridge of keystones could have been the joints of a spine.

Broken mirror frames lined the walls. The glass lay shattered upon the floor. The light in here, rather than being reflected in the glass, rose out of it.

Ash took a few more paces in before he spotted something on the floor among the debris. He picked it up.

A pair of reading glasses. One lens was broken and flecked

with blood. The frame, thin and bent, had two large hooks behind the ears so they'd sit firmly in place no matter what happened. Ash straightened out the kink. The glasses looked familiar. He looked into the lenses.

Ash stumbles down the slope towards the Mercedes. The car lies crumpled, the tyres torn and the roof caved in. His uncle and aunt are in there.

The smell of petrol clouds the air as he approaches. Broken glass is scattered over the dusty, furrowed earth. There is a constant tapping sound. His heart quickens.

"Uncle Vik?"

Ash?

Ash runs forward and crawls into the car. He waves an object in his hand. "I found your glasses."

His uncle sits in the driver's seat. His head is distorted and blood seeps from a hole in his forehead. The tapping sound comes from the wiper hitting the bent frame of the windscreen.

Ash takes his uncle's hand. "Are you hurt?" he asks.

We're dead, Ash.

Ash looks to the rear. His aunt lies there, her neck broken. "Why?"

Because of you, Ash.

He wants to deny it, but it's true. They would be alive, but for him. "I. . . I didn't mean to."

You are the Kali-aastra. You kill everything you touch.

"No, it was an accident."

Aunt Anita sits up, and her hideously twisted neck creaks as she turns her lifeless gaze towards him. Her fingers, broken and black, touch his neck softly, but firmly.

❖

Uncle Vik faces him. He smiles and blood swells in his mouth, dripping down his upturned face. We miss you, Ash.

"*I miss you too.*"

Stay with us. That way we won't be so lonely.

"OK."

Aunt Anita's fingers tighten round Ash's neck, but he doesn't fight back. He killed them both and should be with them. He deserves this.

His breathing is hoarse and his head pounding as his air is cut off. His vision goes murky and dark. He's dimly aware of a white shadow in front of him, one of bright silver steel.

The fingers drop their grip and Ash gasps. He stares around, bewildered, as Aunt Anita screams.

Savage drags his aunt out of the car, pulling her out by her hair. She flails at him, but Savage is young, strong and utterly ruthless. He throws her to the ground and drags the blade from his cane.

"No!" *Ash cries out.*

Savage pushes the sword into Anita's heart. Blood spurts as she screams, washing his white suit in crimson. He tugs the blade free and approaches Ash's uncle.

"No!" *Ash hurls himself between Savage and Uncle Vik, but Savage knocks him aside without breaking his step.*

Uncle Vik hisses, eyes red with rage and unholy bloodlust, but Savage, gaze cold, flicks the tip of the blade across his throat. Uncle Vik covers the wound, but the blood washes through his fingers and he sinks to the ground.

Ash, knees in the dirt, stares up at the Englishman.

"You killed them," *he accuses.*

"No, Ash. You did." *Then Savage twists the glasses from Ash's grip and tosses them away.*

*

❖

Ash gasped. He gulped big, lung-swelling quantities of air as if he'd been drowning and just broken the water's surface.

"What... happened?" It had been just like he'd remembered, his uncle and aunt dead from the car crash. The stink of petrol lingered even now.

"Mastery of the Humours. A combination of Black Bile and Phlegm, which control the emotions and mind, used to manipulate your dreams," said Savage. "We're up against someone very, very good."

"And you were there too." Savage had gone into his mind. How dare he?

"I had to come in to save you." Savage brushed the dirt from his clothes. "You entered a nightmare and it almost got you. Someone looked into your heart and found what you feared most."

"Death? Being killed?"

"Hardly. No, you fear failure. You feel you should have saved your uncle and aunt, and the guilt of failure almost killed you, Ash. The same as with Gemma." Savage slipped his sword back into his cane. "You want to be this superhero who always succeeds. The sort who always does the right thing and follows the right path. I sympathise. I was just the same, once."

"You, a hero?" Ash scoffed. "That'll be the day."

He heard a deep, distant rumble, and the roof above them creaked. A light sprinkle of dust fell over him. He looked up and saw thin cracks along the stone. "How far underground are we?"

"Many fathoms," said Jackie. "Ravana's private chambers were deep under the sea, inaccessible but for this route."

❖

"What else is down here?" asked Ash.

"Let's go and find out." Savage pushed Ash, not softly, ahead. "Let's not linger here. We don't want you having another nightmare."

Chapter Forty-seven

The hall's roof rose over fifty metres above their heads, supported by a forest of columns. Broken statues lay scattered across the floor as if they'd entered the lair of Medusa. Some were stone, others bronze or strange metals that glowed with golden light, casting weird shadows across the shimmering water that rippled ankle-deep across the floor, which was itself one unimaginably huge mosaic. Ash couldn't take it all in – it was too big – but he could see what it was. A map.

Upon the map, awesome dragons flew across sapphire skies and creatures strode across mountains and shining cities, where courtiers sat among soft cushions, their attention captivated by jewel-clad dancing girls. At the summit of a snow-clad mountain, wreathed in swirling clouds, sat Ravana, lord of all. Beneath him, wrapped in chains and kneeling in humble homage, were the gods. There was war, there was love, death and birth, and the lives of maharajahs and peasants, of gods and demons. Ash followed a line of blue rivers as they crossed empires that were now less than dust.

"Ravana's kingdom," said Jackie with soft awe. "He was the first Alamgir."

Ash recognised that word from one of his books about the Moghuls, the ancient emperors of India. It meant 'universe conqueror'. But if anyone had the right to be called Alamgir, it was the demon king.

Water dripped down from the ceiling. The groaning from without was louder now, and it sounded like the sea was pounding against the building's shell. The remaining hyena rakshasa sniffed at the nearest column, then relieved himself on it.

"Are we totally lost or what?" said Ash.

"No, we're very near." Savage scrutinised his surroundings. "Though being near isn't good enough. It's the last step that's the most slippery." He checked his pistol, drawing back the slide and letting it slam sharply back in place. The abrupt metallic rap sounded like a gunshot in the vast space.

"We expecting trouble?" Ash asked.

Savage shook his head. "No. Trouble's already come."

A splash brought Ash's attention to the wavering shadows ahead. One after the other, long-dead lamps rose into the hall, casting a chaotic battle of swaying and entangled images across the columns, across the water. The flames multiplied a thousand times, a million, on every wave and droplet.

The air in front of them shimmered and the lights around

❖

it spiralled with dazzling colours. Ash shaded his eyes as a dark outline began to form within the white heart of the blaze. A gale suddenly screamed to almost ear-piercing heights, forcing them back. The wind bit Ash's bare skin so hard it burned. Then it calmed and the light died. Ash blinked the white spots out of his sight.

A man stood before them. Three metres tall and naked but for an elegant white and gold loincloth, he was young and slim, and his dark skin was covered with occult symbols. Ash realised the figure was standing on the water's surface, only his soles getting wet. The symbols slid and mutated over him, merging and rewriting themselves constantly. Upon his forehead, like a third eye, was a glowing brand. Even from this distance Ash counted nine skulls.

Nine sorceries. Savage knew only seven, and he was the greatest sorcerer in the world.

Ash had a bad feeling about this. A really bad feeling.

The man's black-on-black eyes gazed over the party.

Savage tucked his cane under his arm and bowed. "My lord Vibheeshana."

Chapter Forty-eight

The demon lord, Ravana's brother, kept his distance, but even from here Ash sensed the power surging within the immortal's spirit.

"You must turn back," he said simply.

"I served your great brother, my lord." Savage stood up now, coolly appraising the rakshasa prince.

"You serve only yourself, Savage." Vibheeshana's voice sank low and the threat within it was unmistakable. "And do not take me for a fool. I know why you are here."

"I also know of the vow you made to Rama." Savage smiled contemptuously. "The deal you made so that you could take Ravana's throne when he died."

"Deal?" asked Ash. "What deal?"

Savage continued, his eyes never leaving the demon lord's. "It's well known that Vibheeshana sided against his own kind, that he served Rama and betrayed his brother."

"My brother was on the path of destruction. If he had only listened, he would not have brought doom upon himself and his people."

"He died honourably, as a warrior should," snarled Jackie. "Not cowering behind the skirts of a mortal, begging for his life."

"You forget your place, dog," said Vibheeshana. His eyes glowed and the air hummed electric around him, momentarily wrapping him in a haze of heat and power. The water under his feet bubbled and hissed. The demon lord hadn't made a move, but those glowing brands, the cool confidence, the utter lack of fear couldn't have been a clearer warning.

Do not mess with me.

Savage, Jackie, one rather petrified hyena rakshasa and Ash. Against a demon lord. They should quit now. He could wipe the floor with them. But then Gemma would stay dead. Ash had come so far, but Vibheeshana had powers that were off the scale. Ash tried to use his *Marma Adi* to search for some weakness, but the golden spots never settled on the rakshasa; they just flickered and drifted away. It was all too unclear.

Vibheeshana shook his head. "I saved our race, our existence. Do you not understand? There were those in Rama's army who wished our total annihilation. For what Ravana had done, can you truly blame them?"

Savage straightened. "You swore to serve Rama, and in exchange he gave you the throne of Lanka."

"Even when it sank beneath the waves, I did my duty. There are treasures here that must never leave." Vibheeshana

❖

met Savage's gaze. "Treasures you cannot begin to comprehend."

"Look, sir," said Ash. "We want to awaken this." He held out the Koh-i-noor. "We just want the Black Mandala."

"Child, you have no idea what you ask."

Ash shoved the diamond back in the satchel. "It's the only way I can save my friend."

"Stand aside, lord," said Savage.

For a guy facing a demon lord who was master of nine of the sorceries, Savage seemed incredibly sure of himself. Ash hadn't moved and, he noticed, neither had Jackie.

Savage joined Ash. "You are my ace of spades, Ash."

"He's already tried to kill me with the dream," said Ash.

"No," answered Savage. "He used your own guilt against you. That's subtle, but once you know the trick, easily beaten." Fire sparked within Savage's black eyes. "Remember your oath, Lord Vibheeshana? Your oath to your master and king, Rama?"

"I remember."

"You swore to serve him *for ever.*"

The demon lord's gaze faltered. "I did."

What was going on?

Savage put his hand on Ash's shoulder. "Just ask him for the Black Mandala. He'll give it to you."

"Why would he give *me* it? I'm just..."

Ash Mistry. Yes. But you've also been Ashoka, first emperor of India. And a Trojan noble. And a Spartan warrior.

And, once, a prince of Ayodhya. Rama.

Ash looked at Vibheeshana. "Give me the Black Mandala, my lord."

❖

Vibheeshana raised his hand. "Sire, please reconsider. Come no further."

Savage pointed his cane at him. "And who's going to stop us?"

The sound of metal sliding across metal, the sound of razors caressing each other, was unmistakable. A figure stepped out from behind a nearby column, lithe, clad in green scales, and emerald-eyed. Her long black hair had been swept up and tied in a compact braid. In her hand twitched the urumi, the serpent sword. The four whip-like blades hissed with anticipation.

"I am," said Parvati.

Chapter Forty-nine

"You took your time, Ash," said Parvati, her eyes never leaving Savage's.

The hyena rakshasa cackled and Jackie dropped to all fours beside it, now more beast than woman, all except for her deformed head, a grotesque amalgam of both. Jackie and the hyena spread out to either side like stalking predators, wary, but searching for an opening in Parvati's defences.

The hyena sniffed the air. It paused, eyes widening as the hall echoed with a deep-chested growl. A huge tiger appeared from between the thickset columns, his golden eyes glistening with pending violence. Khan had joined the party.

Wow. This gathering was about to go cataclysmically bad any second now. Ash came closer to the tense trio of Parvati, Vibheeshana and Savage. He needed to calm things way, way down.

❖

"Listen, Parvati, I need Savage alive," he said. "He can help me."

"Stand aside, Ash."

"Listen! He can resurrect Gemma with the Brahma-aastra. I know he can."

Parvati showed absolutely no emotion. "There are bigger things at stake than a single girl." She raised her fist and the urumi blades began to weave in the air as though they possessed life of their own. "This has been a long time coming, Savage."

Parvati flicked the urumi and the blades whipped out, four silver tongues of lightning, any one capable of decapitating a man. Ash leaped between Parvati and Savage, his katar ready. With one hand he shoved Savage aside, and with the dagger he knocked one, then two of the blades off their path. The third shot across his leg and the fourth sliced his face, drawing a thin, stinging line across his cheek. A few centimetres lower and it would have opened his throat.

"Step aside, Ash." Parvati drew the urumi in, slowly circling to get a shot at Savage.

Ash touched his stinging cheek. "What was that?"

"A warning. There won't be another."

"You're my friend, Parvati, have you forgotten?"

"You're mine, Ash." Her steps barely stirred the water. "But if you don't get out of the way, I will kill you."

Jackie, aided by the remaining hyena rakshasa, circled Khan. Her bristles were up and stiff, and she slavered and snapped angrily at the silent, bright-eyed tiger-rakshasa.

Ash had a chance to save Gemma, and Parvati wasn't going

to let him. What did one more death mean to the demon princess? Nothing; less than nothing.

But she was his friend. Ash lowered his katar. She deserved one more chance.

"Please, Parvati. Let me save Gemma."

Parvati paused and the four steel whips fell silent beside her. Then her lips thinned with harsh conviction and she replied grimly, "No."

Fire rose in his veins and intense heat flooded his heart, accelerating it and opening floodgates of adrenaline and more. The Soma. He shivered with the growing power, the brightest pain focused in the centre of his forehead.

Golden lights spread over Parvati, lights only Ash could see. Not only did he spy the golden death points, but he glimpsed glittering lines, paths, through the space between them. They ran from her to him and back again, ever-changing patterns of attack and defence. Moves and feints exposed themselves so he could see the fight spread out before him. He watched a weaving path that would mean his death, and he watched new snaking lines shine bright, showing him how to turn defeat into lethal victory.

Ash closed his eyes. He breathed deeply, feeling the Soma possess him. Then, eyes narrowed so as not to be blinded by the bright, shining paths all around him, he surrendered himself to the dance of Kali.

Chapter Fifty

*P*arvati shot past Ash, intent on killing Savage. Ash ducked under the screaming steel whips and knocked her arm aside, spoiling the attack. She stared at him for a fraction of a second, bewildered, then retaliated with a shock wave of jabs and kicks that slid and slipped between his defences, forcing him back. The paths exploded in all directions and Ash reacted like lightning, parrying a finger strike to his throat, untangling himself from a choke hold, and launching his own counter-attacks against half a dozen bone-breaking strikes, any one of which would have crippled him.

Without the Kali-aastra, without the Soma, he would have been dead ten times over in just a few seconds. He somersaulted high over Parvati, bouncing off the nearby column to land ten metres away.

❖

Elsewhere, Savage fought Vibheeshana. Fire and shimmering walls of heat burst all around the Englishman as the demon lord threw a wave of ice daggers at him. The hall thundered with the sound of the supernatural forces the two men summoned. Walls creaked and columns buckled and shook.

Ash's body ached and he was panting already. He rested, crouching, trying to get his breath back, trying to get some cool air into his burning and bruised lungs.

She's trying to kill me.

Parvati stepped backwards on unsteady legs, sweat dripping over her pale face. She put her palm against a red swelling on her cheek.

"That... hurt." There was a hint of a cold smile as she said it. "Not bad, Ash."

Had he done that? He hadn't even realised.

"It doesn't have to be like this, Parvati."

"Then stand aside and let me kill Savage."

The air temperature dropped ten degrees and the water drained away from around Ash's ankles. He felt the air rush around him, a freezing wind that accelerated and became a scream.

Savage drew up a wall of water, first ten, then fifteen, then twenty metres high. The wave shivered and undulated, held in magical stasis as frost and then ice spread across the surface, creating a solid wall. The ice creaked and groaned. Splinters, long dagger-shaped shards of frozen water, sheared off and multiplied.

Ash dived behind a fallen column as Savage sent wave after

wave of razor-sharp spikes across the hall towards Vibheeshana. Small skin-slicing splinters, others large enough to skewer a horse, and still others the size of boulders, exploded as they smashed into the stone columns and punched craters into the mosaic, hurling up more shrapnel. The ceiling shook and quivered as the columns that supported it and the sea above began to weaken. Vibheeshana stumbled back as the minute blades cut his skin, and then he whipped his hands in front of him so the ice evaporated into a bellowing cloud of steam, filling the hall with hot mist.

Howls and roars echoed from the spreading fog as Khan and Jackie fought. The hyena rakshasa lay dead on the floor, its throat torn out, head still attached by a strip of fur.

And Ash stalked Parvati.

Chapter Fifty-one

S *he's my friend.*
    But she's a demon.
She saved my life.
But she has killed thousands.

The confusion flooded Ash's head. He couldn't think clearly. The Soma? Was it affecting him? Making him see Parvati as something that had to be destroyed?

She is good. She's just doing her duty.

And you are the Kali-aastra. Do yours. Kill the rakshasa.

The punch came out of nowhere and almost took Ash's head off. He fell head over heels and sprang up, dazed, but on automatic. A cross-arm block stopped the kick and he avoided the body slam with a sudden handspring. Still, as he shifted into a battle stance, his senses swam. The mist hid everything beyond a few metres away.

❖

"You're trying to kill me," said Ash.

Silence and fog. Parvati was an assassin, and would use both to take him out.

All around him lay rubble: huge chunks of floor smashed apart, leaving craters and fallen columns. The roof above groaned ominously as somewhere in the distance another huge column crashed down, sundered by the magic swirling between Savage and Vibheeshana. Both were using their command over the elements, Savage now brutally raising fires and winds and ripping open the stone while Vibheeshana deflected and quashed the attacks just as rapidly. The air itself hummed with electric currents, and sparks buzzed and flew across the fog. Elsewhere Khan roared and Jackie howled as they fought each other.

How did I end up on the 'bad guy' side of the fence?

Ash stepped across a wide, jagged crack in the floor. The mosaic, once filled with dark beauty, was in ruins. The small tiles had been scattered in all directions and large chunks were nothing but powder now.

There was only one way to end this. Ash wanted Gemma back, but what was the price? He peered into the haze and caught a glimpse of silvery steel and a vague figure stepping closer.

Did she want him dead? Really?

Parvati could have bitten him. Her poison guaranteed death. But she hadn't. She'd tried to disable him; that was what these attacks were.

They'd been through so much together. Fighting each other was utterly wrong.

❖

But it came down to Gemma. He knew Parvati: the only way through her was to kill her.

It was her or Gemma.

Ash thought of Gemma taking his coat. The way she smiled at him in class. They'd been friends since primary school. They'd played that stupid board game every day, all summer.

She was dead.

"Parvati, please. I just want to save my friend."

"I am sorry, Ash." The voice whispered out of the fog, from a direction unknown. "But Gemma is gone. If Savage tried, what you'd have is a monster."

"Not if he recited the proper mantra. From the Black Mandala."

Parvati laughed. The sound was cruel and sad. "The Black Mandala is the ultimate source of my father's power. Savage would want it not only to awaken the Brahma-aastra, but to learn the remaining sorceries. He'd be as great, as terrible as Ravana, the master of all reality. He's been using you, Ash. Now do you understand?"

He felt lost. "But Gemma…"

Parvati appeared. The fog rippled around her as she approached. The urumi dangled in her loose grip. "The Black Mandala should stay here." She dropped the weapon. "But the choice is yours." Parvati touched his cheek. "Let her go, Ash. For both your sakes."

"I…"

The sound of breaking stone was as loud and sharp as a cannon shot. Chunks of marble shot through the air and knocked Ash off his feet. He crashed down, shaken to his bones. Blood, hot and sticky, dribbled down his back as he tried to get up. His spine screamed and he fell back on his face.

The column above him groaned as the supports cracked, then shattered. With an awful slowness, it began to topple. Dust showered down as blue electric sparks jumped and burst across it, breaking off chunks and slivers that tumbled like the beginning of an avalanche.

Ash stared, paralysed, as the column collapsed. He struggled to his knees, but the dark mass of the falling column covered him, and all he could do was watch it accelerate towards him. He wasn't going to make it.

Parvati grabbed him and twisted hard, spinning Ash out of the path of the crumbling tower. The impact threw him off his feet and the sound almost burst his eardrums. He couldn't even hear his own screams.

Ash lay on the floor, gasping in the dust. Thin trickles of blood ran down his torso and limbs from dozens of cuts. He put a hand against his back and pulled at a blood-slicked marble shard, fighting the sickening agony as the edges cut along his spine. Then it came free and Ash gasped with relief. Slowly he got to his feet. He wasn't dead yet. Biting down on his lip, he wrenched out the splinters in his arms. Blood dripped from the gaping holes, and Ash stumbled with dizziness.

All around him columns began to bow and crack. Great tears rent the ceiling as jets of seawater poured through the fractures, each one expanding moment by moment as lumps

❖

of stone tumbled down. The hall was collapsing in on itself. Already the water was splashing round his knees.

Ash approached the fallen column, sweeping the dust from his face. "Parvati?"

Blocks the size of a car lay within a cloud of dust. The floor beneath them was cracked and thrown up like the frozen surface of a wave.

Ash spotted a glimmer of metal and picked up the urumi. Two of the blades had been sheared off and the remaining pair were pitted and scored by the stone. He dropped to his knees, gazing hopelessly at the immovable rubble. "Parvati?"

Chapter Fifty-two

Ash heard footsteps rapidly approaching him. The dust and fog parted as Vibheeshana appeared. He stared at Ash, then at the weapon in his hand. Ash dropped the urumi.

"She's trapped," he said as he tried to shift a huge boulder. She had to be trapped. The alternative was too horrible to think about. He sweated and strained, but it didn't move a millimetre. "Help me."

"Step away." Vibheeshana's skin shone with sweat and he was cut and bruised all over. He moved slowly, and his breath was ragged. Savage had hurt him badly. But he gathered himself, straightened, and pressed his fingers together, weaving and locking them in weird bone-flexing patterns. The nine skulls pulsed with a stark, golden light.

The rubble began to rise — delicately at first, so as not to cause any of it to fall on top of another piece and crush

337

❖

Parvati. Small brick-sized lumps floated away, trailing pebbles behind them. Vibheeshana closed his eyes as his lips moved with silent spells.

The larger rocks began to float impossibly and drift off.

"Come on," Ash whispered.

They would save her. Vibheeshana would lift the rubble away and they'd save her.

A giant rock rose over him. Ash blinked as grit fell into his eyes. Then, the shadow of the rock having just passed over him, it smashed to the ground.

"Vibheeshana?" Ash said. *That almost crushed him!*

Vibheeshana groaned, arching his back. He jerked again, staring wildly at Ash. His lips reddened and parted, and blood dribbled down his chin. A narrow steel sword blade tore through his chest in a sudden burst of scarlet. He went up on his toes as the blade, pushed from behind, stuck out further and further. He reached out to Ash, asking him to help, to do something. Ash took the demon lord's hands, and Vibheeshana crushed his with desperate strength. The sword began to draw itself out, sinking into the dark flesh, where the sigils thrashed and squirmed as blood covered them.

Vibheeshana collapsed, Ash holding on to him as they both sank to the ground.

"Sometimes it's worth getting your hands dirty," said Savage, stepping over the dead Vibheeshana with sword in hand. He wiped the blade clean on his sleeve, marking the white cloth with long strips of crimson, and slid it back into the cane. He smiled at Ash, a grotesque leer through blackened teeth and shrivelled gums. "Thanks for distracting him. I couldn't have done it without you."

Ash stared at the bleeding corpse. His fault. His fault. Oh God, what had he done? Vibheeshana dead and Parvati under tons of rock. He couldn't save either.

Savage must have seen the confusion and misery on his face, because he laughed. "Still such a child, aren't you? Didn't I warn you once not to get involved in grown-up plans?"

Ash spun round, but Savage raised his cane, and a rock shot out from the pile and hit Ash square in the forehead, knocking him off his feet.

Savage stood over him. Ash could make out three blurred images, melding and splitting each time he blinked. Waves of nausea rolled over him as the pain in his head swelled, overwhelming him. Savage flicked his narrow sword so the point was above Ash's shoulder. He pushed the point in.

Ash cried out as the Englishman twisted the blade. Then, with a second flick of his weapon, he cut open Ash's satchel.

The Koh-i-noor fell out. Savage put it in his jacket pocket.

"I don't need to kill you," he said. "But you'll never know why."

Then he blew some dust off his cane, rubbed the tiger head clean, and tapped it against his forehead in salute. "Goodbye, Ash Mistry. It's been a pleasure."

Savage left. His laughter echoed long after he'd gone.

Chapter Fifty-three

"*R*ama…"

Ash groaned. The pain throbbed in the centre of his skull as if someone had put a pneumatic drill in his brain. He got up and gasped as the agony multiplied. His head weighed about a million tons. He clutched it with both hands, afraid it was going to break apart.

"Rama…"

Ash opened his eyes and let his vision clear. Out of the fading blurriness he saw Vibheeshana. His fingers twitched and his mouth moved.

"Rama…" said the demon lord. "Hurry."

Ash crawled to him, ignoring the blood staining his hands and knees. He lifted the demon lord so his head rested on Ash's lap. Vibheeshana looked up at him. "My lord Rama. I tried. Forgive me."

❖

He's delirious. He thinks I'm the prince.

"What can I do?" Ash asked. "Tell me how to save you."

"Not important," said Vibheeshana. "You must stop Savage from getting the Black Mandala. Ravana wrote the secrets of all ten sorceries upon it. Savage aspires to be as great as my brother."

"But how? No human can contain all that magic. Savage would be torn apart." He could barely handle the seven sorceries he had already mastered, twisting into hideous shapes each time he cast a spell.

"That's why he wants the Brahma-aastra. It would counteract any changes, prevent the colossal energies from destroying him." Vibheeshana sighed as he sank into Ash's arms, then a humourless smile spread across his bloody lips. "But he's twice the fool. Ravana cursed the diamond. He told me that if he couldn't use its powers, then no one could."

"No…"

Ash stopped himself, and there in the flooded hall, cradling the demon lord, he knew Gemma was never coming back. That he'd failed as completely as anyone could. It wasn't fair, it wasn't fair. A sob caught in his throat and he tightened his grip on Vibheeshana, as if he could squeeze another answer, a better one, out of the dying rakshasa prince.

He could picture her in the canteen, looking at him with her hazel eyes. Her shivering in her thin jumper on Bonfire Night. Her standing in his hall.

Her smile.

All that was gone, and for ever. "It's my fault. All of it."

❖

Vibheeshana looked at Ash with immeasurable sadness and put his blood-stained hands on Ash's cheeks. "No. Never think that. Parvati told me why you were here. You wanted to save your friend."

"I should have listened to Parvati." He looked hopelessly at the mountain of rubble. She was still there, somewhere. Had he lost her too? "I should never have come."

"You came because you hoped, and few things are as powerful as hope. That is how the world changes. Now let her go. Give her, and yourself, peace."

Ash should have known Savage was lying. Deep down, didn't he know that? His own desires had blinded him. He'd only heard what he'd wanted to hear. Now the terrible truth came to him. There was one mastery Savage wanted above all others. The sorcerer had talked about fixing his past mistakes. "He wants to go back in time."

"Savage is insane; he doesn't understand," Vibheeshana whispered, his strength fading. "To change the past destroys the future. That is why Ravana never used his mastery over Time. My brother was wise enough to know that, at least."

"Where is the Black Mandala?"

Vibheeshana pointed to the opposite doorway. "Quickly now. Lanka will not last long without my magic to maintain it."

"But what about Parvati?"

The demon lord smiled. "My niece has escaped more deadly traps than this. Please, there is little time. You must stop him."

❖

Ash gritted his teeth and hissed. "Savage is a dead man."

Vibheeshana didn't reply. A last breath whispered out as the demon lord, the brother of Ravana and the last king of Lanka, died.

Chapter Fifty-four

"SAVAGE!" Ash ran through the hall. "SAVAGE!"

There was just one exit. Ash barrelled towards the crooked archway as the lintel bent and split and the roof above him cracked. Jets of seawater sprayed down. A huge crack rent the wall above him and a waterfall burst through, creating a mighty roaring wall of water twenty metres high. Foam fizzed and sprayed everywhere, soaking Ash as he raced through it. Vibheeshana's death had revived him, closing up his wounds and adding power to his rage.

"Savage!"

The corridor was lit by spluttering lamps. The floor shifted to the side and Ash grabbed hold of the wall. There was a sharp hiss and a sudden shot of water as another fracture appeared in the ceiling.

We're all going to drown.

❖

But he would kill Savage first. His uncle and aunt. Gemma and Vibheeshana, dead, all because of Savage.

And him. He'd led them down the path of destruction.

Why fight destiny? You are the Kali-aastra. You are the death-bringer.

His fingers tightened round Parvati's urumi. Unable to find his katar, he'd grabbed her weapon instead. Two blades were missing, but it was lethal enough with the remaining pair.

A light shone ahead of him – not the flickering flames of a lamp, but a bright, clear, steady glow of pale blue. Ash slowed down. He carefully wrapped the two remaining blades of the urumi into a loose loop. He didn't want the metal to scrape together and alert Savage.

The door in front of him was open just wide enough for Ash to look into the room beyond. Ravana's treasury. The light reflected off the extravagant bronze panelling, engraved with glorious scenes of beautiful nymphs and mighty demon lords. It was studded with precious gems, each one glittering. Ash, as silent and as certain as death, slipped in through the narrow gap.

The entire ceiling was made up of millions of small crystals. It was like being inside a diamond. Gold coins, jewellery and gems lay scattered across the carpeted floor. There were statues of silver with eyes of sapphire. Crowns lay gathering dust, discarded in the corners and now home to spiders. Here were Egyptian statues, Mesopotamian engravings on golden plates, and cups wrought with swirling Chinese dragons. Ash recognised some of the styles and designs. His bare toes sank into the mouldy, algae-covered carpet, which smothered whatever sound his footsteps might have made. The thunder of the collapsing hall behind him and the encroaching sea seemed dull and distant.

The glow of pale blue still came from round the corner. Ash stepped towards it and peered ahead.

The air crackled and sparks jolted out of thin vapours that seemed to be emerging from a black surface on the far wall. A vast circular scroll hung there, suspended in a frame of iron.

The Black Mandala.

It was glossy black and decorated with shimmering patterns, also in black. Concentric circles seemed to turn and spiral in and out, trapping Ash's gaze. Minute figures guarded each ring, demons and things yet more hideous, so that his eyes burned with pain looking upon them. The painting gave off a low, powerful hum, something soul-deep, and it drew Ash irresistibly towards it. He struggled to breathe, captivated as he was by the Mandala. The painting sucked in everything, an abysmal void as all-consuming as any black hole. In the patterns he saw galaxies, stars, the endless depths of the universe, as if the Mandala held it all within it. But even deeper within that infinite darkness, Ash sensed a lurking presence, something beyond the boundaries of existence.

Savage sat facing the Mandala. His back to Ash, his ankles up on his knees, he meditated in the classic yoga lotus position, his attention completely consumed by the painting. The Koh-i-noor blazed in his left palm, casting a blue light out in all directions.

Ash swayed, unable to take his eyes off the blackness. It

was as though he was tottering on the edge of a fathomless pit, some unknown power tempting him to jump. There would be no pain, because the fall would never end. He would tumble through all time, over and over. How long? It would have no meaning. Time wouldn't exist if he fell.

His heart pumped harder and harder in desperation. He grabbed hold of the table beside him and knocked over a pile of stacked jewels. Plates and bowls and countless jewels chimed and rang as the treasures fell upon each other. But the ringing noises distracted him from the hypnotic patterns on the painting. Distracted him – and Savage.

Savage was on his feet, tiger cane in one hand and the Koh-i-noor in the other. "You're becoming quite annoying, boy." Already his flesh was firm and strong, his skin smooth and unblemished.

Ash released the urumi. The two blades unravelled and lay along the floor. He flexed his wrist and the steel rattled with anticipation. Ash peered through his death senses, using *Marma Adi* to find the way to kill Savage.

But all the golden points dimmed on Savage. Rather, paths of power radiated from the Mandala, strengthening him. Through his shirt glowed the outline of a new skull, the eighth, which had begun to take shape upon his chest. Soon he'd be as powerful as Ravana ever was. And as invulnerable.

The skulls on Savage's chest burned, first a brilliant, bloody red, then brighter, turning yellow and finally blinding white. The air buzzed and the table shook. The weapons hanging from the wall clattered against each other. The hairs on the

❖

nape of Ash's neck rose, and the air around him thickened, making it hard to breathe.

The paths of power between Savage and the Mandala multiplied. The eighth skull was almost complete. Two more were appearing as faint outlines.

Then the colours of the Koh-i-noor changed. The brilliant azure light dulled and turned foul with sickly greens and vile browns, pulsing in the sorcerer's hand. The hand began to melt. The flesh bubbled as Savage's fingers fused together.

"What's happening?" Savage stared at the hand as the arm twisted, the muscles flexing unnaturally. His bones distorted under the skin, and Savage howled as his neck twisted sharply, almost turning his head backwards. His skull inflated on one side as the other sank, his cheekbones collapsing. Teeth tumbled from his slack jaw.

"Ravana cursed the diamond, Savage. You should have known better than to trust a demon king."

"No, it can't be." Crackling sparks jumped over Savage's body and his eyes filled with lightning. "This is your doing. Time to die, boy."

Chapter Fifty-five

Savage swept up the cane, and the air burst as a lightning bolt erupted from the tiger's eyes.

The urumi screamed as Ash flicked out the two blades.

Electrical sparks from Savage's magical attack shot off in all directions, shattering mirrors and punching holes in the walls and ceiling. Ash shimmered with blue light, uncontrollable energy screaming along his nerves. But he gritted his teeth, sweat evaporating off him, and stood up, his skin tingling as the sparks danced across him, leaping from his fingertips on to the rattling metal around him. The shock waves hit him again and again as the very air burned. His flesh blackened under the scorching heat and he thought he'd burst apart, but something held him, an iron core of strength that protected him from incineration.

He almost collapsed the moment the lightning ended.

❖

He groaned as the smoke rose off his skin and the stench of his own burning flesh filled his nostrils. But, slowly, strength returned, and the wounds covering him began to heal. The blistered flesh cooled and turned back into a healthy, firm brown. He stood in a smouldering crater of molten rock, but he was fine, when he should have been a pile of ash.

Vibheeshana. That was why he was alive. He'd been with the demon lord as he died and had absorbed his magical powers. And a master of nine sorceries always trumped a master of eight. Instead of being fried by the lightning, Ash had survived.

Ash gazed at the urumi. The metal had completely rusted. The hilt crumbled as he closed his fist. The carpet under his feet was burned away and smoking, and the wall had a big dent in it. The only sound was the *chink chink chink* of gold coins falling off a broken table.

"No…" Savage said.

Ash looked at the Black Mandala. It was powerless now. One tip of the urumi had ripped it in two, destroying its magic. The ragged paper flapped in the breeze.

"No…" Savage stumbled over, cradling his left arm, which now ended in a bloody stump. He moaned with impotent rage and slumped down to his knees. "It's too much…"

Savage's massive, deformed head now rested upon a stick-thin neck. The skull was so huge that the skin across it was stretched to a tearing point. The flesh, yellow, cancerous and flaky, hung upon a twisted, mutated skeleton, the legs different lengths, one with a huge foot twisted backwards. The fingers of his remaining hand had melded together as well and were more like a flipper, the nails curled and thick. Any resemblance to a human being was purely incidental.

But his eyes — his eyes shone with feverish power. Black upon black, they were the eyes of night, or pure darkness. One was swollen, a bulbous growth stricken with yellow pus that dripped from sores across his brow.

Savage's severed left hand lay near Ash's feet, its fingers still curled round the Koh-i-noor. The second blade of the serpent sword had cut his hand off his wrist.

Ash pressed his foot on to the severed appendage and the fingers opened. He took the bloody diamond and put it firmly in his waist sash. He looked down at Savage, moaning on the floor, pale and deformed.

The room shook and the walls bowed, cracks burst along them and the columns began to splinter. Ash sat down.

He'd stopped Savage. Destroyed the Black Mandala once and for all. He'd done it.

But there was no escaping. They were deep under the Indian Ocean, and water was already spilling into the room. Outside he could hear the dull roar of the sea flooding the corridors and hall. The route back to the surface would be underwater by now. What he would give to just magically appear at the shore.

Hold on…

"Get us out of here," said Ash. "Teleport us back to land."

"Do it yourself," Savage snarled back. "You've absorbed Vibheeshana's powers, haven't you?"

He could be right, but Ash had no idea how to make use of the demon lord's energies. He could end up on the moon or send different parts of his body in a dozen different directions.

"We had a deal, Savage." Million to one shot, but things were desperate. He pulled out Savage's belt and buckled it as tight as he could around the man's forearm. The blood flow from the stump lessened, then stopped. He needed Savage alive, just a bit longer.

"Look at me. One more spell and I'll explode."

Ash grinned. "Now that I'd like to see. But at least you'll die trying."

"I can't do it. I've never moved that far. And I don't know where to go. I need coordinates, a sense of the target arrival area. I need—"

"Just get up!" Ash lifted Savage up and dragged him to the door. If they could get nearer to the surface Savage might stand a better chance. Better than no chance at all.

Water flooded the corridor, and they had to fight against the rapidly swelling current. The hallway rocked and fractured, and with each shudder more water burst out from between the cracks.

The roaring sea deafened him as it was amplified by the narrow confines of the corridor. The water was waist deep by the time they got to the entrance to the hall.

The waterfall that had erupted from the wall slammed down over them as they entered. Ash disappeared under the water, but never let go of Savage. He came up coughing and spluttering, shaking the water from his ears.

❖

"Come on!" Ash shouted.

Savage struggled to escape, but he was too weak from blood loss. One foot was now so enlarged that the toes had torn through the leather boot.

Then Ash heard something above the roaring water.

Perched on one of the broken columns was a tiger, its fur gleaming and soaked. The waters swirled around it as it flicked its tail back and forth. Round its neck hung a girl in green-scaled armour. Her cobra eyes met Ash's, and there was something that looked like a smile.

Ash pointed at them. "We're bringing them with us."

Savage stared in horror. "I can't! I can barely take the two of us."

"Then let's hope you can hold your breath for a really, really long time," said Ash as he waded across to them.

Parvati and Khan leaped into the water and joined them. Parvati hugged Ash very hard like she was never going to let go. Then she peered at him and gave him a light slap.

"Ouch," said Ash. "What's that for?"

"Being suicidal," she said. She stared up at the mighty wall of water descending from on high. "You should have got out while you still could."

"Where's Jackie?"

"She fled. Should have followed her. Now it's too late. The exit corridor's collapsed. We're not leaving here, Ash. I'm sorry."

Ash dragged Savage forward. "That's why I brought him."

Parvati frowned. "What?"

"He's getting us out of here, aren't you?"

❖

Savage stared at Ash with pure, volcanic hate. He gritted his teeth so hard Ash thought they'd crack. His veins throbbed in his forehead. "I do this, I go."

Ash glared back. "Get us out, Savage."

Parvati grabbed Ash's hand. "Are you totally sure about—"

Chapter Fifty-six

Sunlight shimmered above him, fragmented upon the waves, and long beams shone down into the deep blue depths of the sea. The water surged, and Ash swam upward through it, kicking hard towards the light. Bubbles slipped out from between his lips. He fought the water, pulling himself higher.

He gasped as he broke the surface. He stared around frantically and saw Parvati burst out of the sea nearby. The sun was bright, warm and oh so welcoming. He felt like he'd been underground for ever.

Khan, back in human form, had Savage round the waist. He pointed beyond Ash's shoulder. "The shore."

They swam and spluttered the last hundred or so metres until Ash felt sand under his toes. Waves rose over his head and he was knocked over twice before he decided to just

❖

crawl back to the beach. Even on his hands and knees, he barely had enough strength to do so, and he was embarrassingly glad when Khan dragged him the last few metres and dropped him on to the sand.

Ash lay there, on his back. "I thought cats hated water."

Khan grinned, his canines still long. "Not tigers. We love it."

Parvati gazed back at the sea and raised her hand in farewell.

Ash struggled up to see what she was looking at. Great waves were pounding the cliffs and walls of Lanka as it slowly sank beneath the swell. The earth shook as the walls protecting it crumbled, gigantic slabs of pearly marble tumbling down as towers toppled into them. Palaces slipped into the foam, hills disappeared back into the depths. The Jagannath swayed as the waves crashed against it again and again. The giant statue fought back, bracing itself as the waves grew higher and more powerful. Finally one towering wall of water engulfed it. The waters frothed and great jets shot up high into the sky as the last of the towers descended into the abyss. Then the churning sea settled, finally at peace.

Lanka was gone.

Savage groaned as he rolled over. His arms and legs jutted out from his bloated body at odd angles, forming strange shapes. His eyes were almost hidden under a huge swollen brow, a cliff of bone under a cancerous strip of yellow skin. There was no way he should be alive, not like this. The Brahma-aastra had stopped the magic from destroying him, keeping him alive, but in this cursed, monstrous shape. Savage was broken in every way possible.

Parvati, Khan and Ash gathered in a loose circle round him as he lay cringing in the sand.

Savage raised his arms, crossing them in front of his face, hoping perhaps that those two bony limbs might hold off the killing blow. In spite of everything, even like this, he still wanted to live.

"Why, Savage?" Ash asked. "Is this 'living'? Are you that afraid to die?"

"You have no idea what waits for me on the other side of death." His voice, feeble and weak, was little more than a faint croak.

"So tell me."

Savage lowered his arms a fraction. "Would that make any difference?"

"You need to ask?"

Ash saw the golden map fall and spread over Savage, a dazzling constellation of lights so bright and dense it seemed as though the old man's body was a single glowing mass. He just needed to touch him, and Savage was dead.

The old man tried to wet his lips, but there was no saliva in his mouth. He closed his eyes, but not before a tear slipped out, a small, single crystal of sadness that slowly rolled down his cheek, weaving its way through the wrinkles and old scars, rising over the bony cheekbone and down the other side, hanging on his jaw before dripping off.

Ash touched the Koh-i-noor, warm against his belly. They'd said it was cursed from the very beginning. There had been

357

so much death because of Savage. If he killed him, would it be revenge for his Uncle Vik, his Aunt Anita, for Vibheeshana and Gemma? Innocent lives destroyed because they crossed paths with Savage?

Ash shuddered. They'd all crossed Ash's path too.

"Ash…" said Parvati. "I could—"

"No. He's mine." Ash raised his fist. Death would be instant and very permanent. "Goodbye, Savage."

"Goodbye, boy."

And in an explosion of light, Savage vanished.

Chapter Fifty-seven

"**H**ow could I have been so stupid?" said Ash. "He still had his magic!" They stood on the beach, staring at the empty spot where Savage had been lying just moments ago, the sand still indented with his shape.

Parvati nodded. "But that spell will have cost him. He so much as pulls a rabbit out of a hat, it'll kill him now."

"You sure?"

"No."

Could he be nearby? "Come on, let's look around. Khan, you head down the beach and I'll go that way—"

"Easy, Ash," said Parvati. "Savage isn't stupid. He'll have gone somewhere familiar to him, and I doubt it'll be within a thousand miles of here."

Ash kicked the sand. "So we've lost him again." He looked out at the now-calm sea. It was as if Lanka had never existed.

❖

"What are you going to do with that?" asked Parvati.

The Koh-i-noor. It wasn't glowing any more. It settled in his hand, cold and heavy. Just a shiny stone. "I don't know."

"Who's hungry? I smell breakfast," said Khan. He turned his head and sniffed the air. Then he pointed to the top of the cliff. A weak stream of smoke drifted like a smudge against the morning sky.

"How did you find me?" Ash asked Parvati as they clambered up the slope.

"I had a few spies in the English Cemetery even after Savage's attack. They brought me your letter. Once I knew Savage was heading down south, it was obvious he was making for Lanka."

"There was a lot more I wanted to say in that letter."

"Tell me now."

Where to begin? "I was blind, Parvati. All I could think about was fixing my mistakes and bringing Gemma back, no matter what. I almost let Savage win – I *trusted* him, how stupid was that? I almost let him gain all of Ravana's powers, just so I could cheat death."

Parvati held his hand. "I trusted Savage once, so I know how cunning he can be. He promises you things and you want to believe him. It's easy to do. But you did it for the right reasons, Ash."

That was what Vibheeshana had said, before telling Ash to let Gemma go.

"How do you do it, Parvati? Cope with losing people you care about?"

"Remember what was best about them. Take joy in having

❖

known them. Strive to be the person they wanted you to be. That's how you honour the dead."

Ash nodded. He'd try. He cleared his throat and gestured towards the ocean. "How did you get out to the island? The route was guarded by sharks and all sorts of magic."

Parvati smiled and there was devilish amusement in those big eyes of hers. "Ash, Lanka was my home. There isn't a secret passage or hidden chamber I don't know about. And my uncle was there to greet me." She sighed. "It was good to see him again."

"I'm sorry I couldn't save him."

"No, I think he deserves his rest. You destroyed the Black Mandala; no one will ever be able to learn Ravana's magic."

"And you knew I'd make it through?"

"You've taken the Soma, haven't you." She looked at him as if trying to see behind his eyes. She didn't wait for an answer. "Of course you have. How else could you have survived both Savage and Vibheeshana's magical traps? There's no stopping you now."

"You make it sound like it's a bad thing. We beat Savage, didn't we? Stopped him from getting the Mandala or the Brahma-aastra."

"At what price, Ash?" There was a long pause and her tongue flicked between her lips, her big pupils dilated. Ash heard, ever so quietly, a threatening hiss. "You are the Kali-aastra and the weapon rakshasas fear above all else. And I am a rakshasa. Where will it end between us?"

Ash wanted to laugh, but it died in his throat. He wanted to tell Parvati not to be silly, that they were friends and

❖

nothing would ever get between them, that she had nothing to fear from him. But that would all be lies. She should be afraid. The things Savage had said made Ash afraid himself. Maybe, maybe some time far away in the future, or maybe someday soon, Ash would become the monster Kali wanted him to be. A remorseless killer, more of a monster than the things he fought.

"Being a superhero's not half as much fun as I thought it would be," he said.

Parvati touched a fang with the tip of her tongue and smiled mischievously. "I'll keep an eye on you. You're not so tough."

"As if! You think you can take me on? You and whose army?"

"That army," said Parvati as they approached the top of the cliff and saw some of her rakshasa followers mingling round a campfire. "And this is just the beginning, Ash."

Mahout stood as they approached and gave Parvati a huge hug. John sat hunched over the flame, turning a small crude spit with a trio of fish skewered on it. He grinned as Ash reached the camp, then handed over the first skewer. "Consider yourself saved."

Ash sat down and peeled off the cooked meat with his fingers. The other rakshasas gathered round Parvati and Khan, leaving them alone. John gave him a skin of lukewarm water. "Well?"

"Savage got away again."

"How?"

Ash slumped down on a rock, exhausted. "Later, John."

❖

"What about the diamond?"

He patted the rock in his sash. "Safe."

"What now, Ash?"

Ash finished his meal. He watched Parvati smile and laugh with her followers. She accepted their bows and they in turn accepted her command. There was something different about Parvati now, and seeing her surrounded brought both a pang to Ash's heart and a sense of unease. But she seemed happy, and why shouldn't she be? She was with her people. There were people he wanted to see too, and he was weary.

"I'm going home," he said.

Chapter Fifty-eight

*A*shoka sits, bone-weary, upon his horse. The snow falls heavily and his eyelashes are encrusted with ice. Great white clouds billow out from his horse's nostrils as it heaves steadily through the dense, snow-filled path.

He is the Emperor Ashoka. His name means 'without sorrow'. He would laugh, but his chest aches. Without sorrow. He has much to be sorrowful about. Even now, weeks later, his dreams are haunted. Haunted by unliving creatures that snarl and claw and try to drag him into darker realms. They are the faces of friends and allies, but in their eyes blaze a hellfire, and all around them is a miasma of putrescence. They creep from each shadow, alive, yet dead. The fighting had been hard and close, but eventually the monsters had been destroyed, their bodies piled high on a pyre and their ashes scattered to the winds.

He turns as he hears the jangle of a bridle and watches dully as Parvati urges her own steed beside his. She peers up the mountain slope. "There. Look."

Through the curtain of snow, Ashoka glimpses a building, a temple. The path is guarded by ferocious statues of warriors, and the roof, a dome, is surmounted by the trident symbol of Shiva. Beyond rise the crystalline peaks of Mount Kailash, the god's home.

"I cannot go further," says Parvati.

Ashoka stops, fear cloaking him. "No, just see me to the door. I beg you."

Parvati says nothing, but stays where she is.

How can he go there? He gazes at the terrifying statues and sees in their cool gaze judgement. Judgement for the things he's done. Every night he is haunted by the spirits of the dead — and there are so many. Men, women, children. Some are covered in sword wounds, others black and still aflame, others with crushed skulls and limbs.

A priest appears through the white. He wears a thin orange cloth about his waist, but otherwise he is naked to the elements. Ashoka wears furs upon furs and is still chilled to the bone. This man's feet are bare as they step lightly through the drifts. He carries a straight bamboo staff and has a cloth bag slung over a bony shoulder.

Ashoka dismounts his horse.

Then he, an emperor, prostrates himself before a spindly old man dressed in rags.

"Rise, Ashoka," says the priest.

The emperor gazes into deep azure eyes, full of warmth and wisdom. The man's grey dreadlocks are piled high upon his head, and he touches the sandalwood beads about his neck, smiling at Ashoka. "We are pleased that you have taken the pilgrimage."

"I have much to atone for, guru."

"Call me Rishi."

Ashoka fumbles in his pocket and pulls out the diamond. Eagerly he holds it out. "A gift. Please, it is yours."

Rishi's eyes narrow as if he senses the dangers within its flawless surface. Ashoka stops breathing. What if he doesn't take it? What if he has to bear it, cursed thing that it is? How much more horror will it bring him? But Rishi nods, and then it is safe within his bag. "Come, my emperor. We have much work to do."

Emperor and holy man vanish into the swirling snow.

Ash switched on the side light in his bedroom. Four in the morning. He passed his hands through his hair. God, he was exhausted. Even when he had OK dreams like that one, the broken nights were taking their toll.

He had been back in London for three weeks now. As glad as he had been to see his parents and Lucky, the return had been difficult. His first adventure had been out in India, and that had been easy to leave behind. This time around, the horror had been on his doorstep, and the consequences and reminders of it were here as well. Some days he'd pass by her house on the way to school. He'd slow down, even stop, half expecting the door to open and see her come out, school bag over her shoulder, smiling. But the door never opened. Now he took another route to school and avoided her place entirely. He hadn't slept a full night since he'd been home.

The first day back at school had been a nightmare. If he'd thought being away a few weeks would have helped people get over Gemma's death, he was sorely mistaken. The memorial display at the school entrance hall had grown, with lots of new photos from friends joining the main school one, and the wall was covered with messages.

And they still blamed Ash. Why had he gone? Where had he gone? The rumour mill went into overtime while he was away. Some said he'd been arrested by the police, or that he was on the run for Gemma's murder, or he was in hiding to avoid reprisals. Jack had done his best to stir it all up until the whole school, even if they didn't say it to his face, thought Ash was a killer.

They had no idea, Ash thought.

Josh, Akbar and Sean were making a bit of an effort to bring him back into the fold, but even Josh, his oldest mate, had taken almost a week before he'd spoken to him. He still looked at Ash as if he didn't really know him, or trust him.

Ash got up and went to his closet. He reached up to the back and drew out an old book, *The Story of India*. He opened it and lifted out the Koh-i-noor from the cavity he'd cut through the pages.

What should he do with it? He couldn't just turn up at a police station and say he'd found one of the Crown Jewels on the street. The thing still weighed more than it should: it felt lead-hearted.

Footsteps whispered on the carpet outside.

"You might as well come in, Lucks."

Ash's sister opened the door, and then, with a quick look up and down the corridor to make sure their parents were still asleep, snuck in. She saw the diamond in his palm. "More bad dreams?"

"Ashoka's not letting me go." He held out the diamond. "It's this. He wants me to do something with it."

"Like what?"

"Maybe I should have left it in Lanka. Too late now." He closed his fingers round it and squeezed the rock, wondering if he could crush it if he wanted to. Maybe, but maybe not, and all he'd get was a shard of it stuck in his skin. He knew what had happened the last time he mishandled an aastra.

"What about Parvati? Did she have any ideas?"

Yes, what about Parvati? Things had been awkward after Lanka. Khan had stayed just long enough to gather lots of praise and then he'd left without saying goodbye. That was just the tiger's way. Ash and John had returned to Kolkata while flights were arranged, Ash to London and John to Kashmir.

Then Parvati had said goodbye, and that was it. She'd continue the hunt for Savage, and there'd been an unspoken offer for him to stay and help, but in all honesty Ash was sick of it. Nothing good had come out of anything, except maybe for Parvati. He had watched uneasily as more rakshasas gathered round her. They looked at her with an awe bordering on worship – the same way they'd once looked at her father. Ash didn't need to be reminded of that.

"We didn't talk much about the diamond," he said to Lucky now. "I think she was happy to see the back of it."

Lucky frowned. He could see she was worried. And Ash knew exactly why. He looked like death – dark-eyed, gaunt. Something was eating him up from the inside.

"What else?" asked Lucky.

"It's Gemma. What I tried to do."

"Ash..."

"Yeah, I know." Ash bounced the gem in his hand. "I

betrayed my friends and helped Savage, and all because I thought I could cheat death. If I hadn't been stopped, I would have brought Gemma back, and she'd have been a monster."

"But you were stopped."

"Only at the very end, when it was almost too late." Ash gazed into the diamond, seeing himself distorted in the crystalline faces. "I can't undo the past. I look at Savage and see what I might become. That's the path of blind obsession, and I think Ashoka's trying to show me another way, but I just don't get it."

Lucky peered around the room. "Could you talk to Dad about Ashoka? He and Uncle Vik were always crazy about history."

"And Dad chose to name me after a man who spent his career burning and slaughtering. Gee, thanks, Dad."

"That's not all Ashoka was." Lucky got up and yawned. "You know he turned his back on war. He became a pacifist, embraced religion. His name was even changed, wasn't it? To Devan something something." She took the diamond from his hand. "If you don't do something with this soon, I'm going to use it to buy a pony."

Hold on. Devan... what? Something shot through Ash, something unfamiliar but bright. Something like hope. "Lucks, you know what? You're smarter than you look." He sprang up and went to his shelves. "It's got to be here somewhere."

Lucky yawned. "That's me, Lucky, the girl genius, and don't you forget it. Goodnight."

Ash searched his books. He found one about the rulers of India. On the front was a painting of Shah Jahan, the Moghul emperor who built India's most famous monument, the Taj Mahal.

Ash flicked through the pages until he got to Ashoka. There was the meaning of the name he knew so well: without sorrow.

But as Lucky said, he also had another name, a title.

Devanampiya.

Beloved of the gods.

Devanampiya created monasteries, went on pilgrimages, studied with the Brahmins and monks of all sects. Some histories believed he converted to Buddhism, others that he became a sadhu, a holy man.

Beloved of the gods.

Ashoka's first step had been to get rid of the Koh-i-noor. Suddenly Ash knew exactly who should have it.

Chapter Fifty-nine

I am going to prison. That or the loony bin.

Shining frost covered the grave. The flowers and tributes round the headstone sparkled as if made from jewels. Ash took hold of his shovel.

His breath came in big white clouds as he dug into the frozen earth. It was early December and painfully cold. A single dark cloud covered the sky like a shroud, and flakes of snow descended lightly, drifting down in the still night.

On to Gemma's grave.

He thought of her smiling at him in the dining hall, of how her hair shone, of the kind way she treated him. She was his friend and always would be.

Ash threw great black showers of dirt, digging down and down. He worked steadily, stopping only for a drink of water

❖

and a quick look around the graveyard to make sure he was alone.

This is insane, but what else can I do?

The shovel edge cracked against wood. The sharp, abrupt sound shocked Ash to a halt. He'd broken the coffin lid.

Moonlight shone upon golden hair.

Ash chucked the shovel out and dug the rest of the dirt off the lid. He got out a screwdriver, but soon gave up trying to open the lid that way. Instead, he dug his fingernails into the side of the lid and tore it off.

Gemma lay upon the silk lining, clumps of soil on her white, lifeless skin. She held a bunch of withered flowers in her fingers.

"I'm sorry, Gemma," he said. There should be more. He should tell her how much he hated himself, how he'd failed everyone because he'd thought he was better than they were. How he'd trusted Savage. How he missed her.

Ash bent down and took her hand, noticing its coldness and the papery skin that wrinkled round her slim fingers. He cleared a few strands of hair out of her face. The brittle threads cracked.

Gemma didn't feel like a person, someone who'd once breathed and laughed. She felt utterly alien, as cold as the earth. Whatever had made her human — her life, her soul — had gone.

But in spite of the scent of decay, he could still smell her perfume. It lingered on her skin, the delicate aura of flowers and the soft hint of summer rain on the grass.

"Rishi told me we always come back," he said to her. "I

372

❖

believe him, but that doesn't make this any easier. It hurts, Gemma, and that's good. It means you took a part of me when you died. I wish I could give you more, but I hope you'll be happy with this."

Ash took out the Koh-i-noor. He put it softly among the dried rose petals that covered her chest. The diamond glinted and a faint silver hue spread over Gemma, and for a second, a mad desperate second, Ash thought she might awake. But she was dead, and the colour was just the moonlight coming out from behind a cloud.

"Goodbye, Gemma. Rest well."

Ash closed the lid, pushing it firmly back in place.

It didn't take him long to fill the grave. He worked steadily, sweating hard, but did not draw on his powers. Gemma deserved more, his human effort. He was the Kali-aastra, but he was more than that. Ashoka had gone from warrior to man of peace. *Be what you want to be; be better than you are.* That was Ashoka's message. The Kali-aastra didn't have to define Ash.

His arms ached and his back was a single mass of agony as he finally patted down the last of the soil. The snow was falling heavily now and would cover the grave soon enough, and there'd be no sign that it had been disturbed. He arranged the flowers round the headstone, and climbed over the high iron railings that surrounded West Norwood Cemetery.

Chapter Sixty

*A*sh brushed the dirt off his tracksuit as best he could and checked the time. Just gone half six. Mum and Dad would be up now. He'd sneak in, get changed, and be off to school.

He dug his hands into his pockets and lifted his hood over his head. The snow smothered the high street and a lorry was off-loading fresh bread to the local supermarket. The shops had their Christmas decorations up and there was a ten-metres-tall Christmas tree in front of the church, lights sparkling within its green needles.

Ash took a deep breath as he glanced back at the graveyard. He could barely see past the railings as the snowfall began to increase, fat flakes drifting in the still, freezing air. He couldn't see Gemma's grave.

A new start. That's what he needed. Enough saving the

world; he just needed to get back to being a fourteen-year-old. That was hard enough.

SAVING THE WORLD.

The words were on a billboard, huge and epic, spanning the entire roof of the supermarket. Ash grinned. *Yeah, let someone else do it for once.* He adjusted his hood and—

Stopped and stared at the billboard.

The left side showed a small African child, malnourished and crying and face covered in flies, lying in her mother's arms as a doctor gave her an injection. The right side was the same girl, smiling and healthy and standing in a field of wheat. Her eyes were bright and she wore a beautiful printed dress. SAVING THE WORLD. ONE CHILD AT A TIME ran over the whole image.

But what made Ash's blood freeze was the logo at the bottom corner. Poppies with a pair of crossed swords.

Savage's coat of arms.

It was nothing to worry about, surely. The Savage Foundation was a big multi-national business; sooner or later, Ash would come across it. It employed thousands around the world, people who had nothing to do with Lord Alexander Savage.

But as Ash continued home, he couldn't shake a creeping unease. Why hadn't he ever noticed the poster before? It must have been up there for days. He would have walked past it on his way to school.

Five minutes later, he turned the corner to his house. He pushed open the gate and saw a brand-new Range Rover parked in the drive.

❖

He closed the gate. The snow was confusing him and he'd gone to his neighbour's house. His dad drove a ten-year-old Ford C-Max.

Weird. This was his gate. This was his drive.

But whose car was that? His gaze fell on the licence plate.

MISTRY I.

Something caught in his throat. His dad had always wanted a personalised number plate, but Mum had always vetoed the expense. And the Range Rover was brand new. No way could they afford something like that. Some new company car scheme his dad hadn't told him about? Yes, that had to be it. Or maybe he'd been promoted. The directors all had flashy cars.

Ash unlocked the door. The kettle whistled and the radio murmured in the kitchen as his parents chatted and got breakfast ready. He kicked off his All-Stars and rushed to his room. It was already seven.

He threw his clothes on the bathroom floor and showered, then dried off.

"Ashoka! Breakfast!" shouted Mum.

Damn. She only called him that when she was angry with him. He must have left muddy tracks on the carpet.

Ash opened up his cupboard and grabbed a shirt. He shook the water off his head as he buttoned it up, only to discover the shirt didn't fit. He pulled it off. It was one of his old ones, back when he'd been big and blubbery, before his Kali-inspired diet and fitness regime. Mum must have got it mixed up. He looked for another. That was the big size too. He picked up a T-shirt, but it was his old Nike baggy shirt that he'd sent to the charity shop three months ago.

What was going on?

Ash put the T-shirt on and a spare pair of jogging bottoms, then went downstairs.

Breakfast lay on the table as usual. The newspapers and a few magazines were neatly piled in the centre. Mum had a coffee in one hand while adjusting her earrings with the other. "Wasn't sure if you were still here."

"I went out for a run." He looked at her. "When did you get the new haircut?"

Mum laughed. "You've only noticed it now? Ashoka, I've had this style for months."

Dad came in. "Has anyone seen my watch?" He ruffled Ash's hair without really looking at him. "Morning, son."

"Look on top of the fridge," said Mum.

Dad did. "Ah. Here we go." It was big, gold and shiny.

Ash's eyes narrowed. "And since when have you had a Rolex, Dad?"

Dad clipped it round his wrist and gave it a quick polish. "You know how long. And no, you cannot have one until you're eighteen. We discussed it, remember?"

Lucky came in and looked around the kitchen. "Mum, I can't find my hat anywhere."

Mum waved back towards the hall. "It's where you left it after your last lesson, with your riding boots."

"So when did you start riding lessons?" Ash asked. "Last couple of weeks?"

❖

"Since we came back from India, dur-brain."

This wasn't right. None of it. Ash stared at his family. There was something different, but what, exactly?

Then he noticed the wall behind Lucky. "Where's the photo?"

Mum poured out some tea. "Hmm?"

"The photo of Uncle Vik and Aunt Anita. It used to be right there." Instead of their old wedding photo, which had hung in that space since their deaths, there was a picture of Lucky sitting on a black and white pony, looking very pleased with herself. Ash stood up, heart racing. How could they take down the photo?

"Are you all right, Ash?"

"This isn't funny," he said. "Where is the photo?"

Dad looked at Ash, frowning. He shook his head. "You look different, Ashoka."

"Why are you calling me 'Ashoka', Dad?"

Dad looked at Mum and she shrugged. He picked up a piece of toast, though he still watched Ash with an odd expression. "We thought that's what you wanted. When you came back from India, you said you wanted us to use your proper, Indian name."

"No. No, I didn't."

Lucky rolled her eyes. "He's gone mental. I knew it would happen sooner or later."

"Where is the photo?" Ash insisted.

Dad smiled. "We've plenty of you and your uncle and aunt. We could put one of them up. You know, from your holiday."

"But they're dead, Dad." Savage had killed them. They knew that!

Dad frowned. "Who's dead?"

"Vik and Anita? No, you know they're fine," replied his mum, confused. "Are you sure you're all right? You do look a bit pale."

The world had gone mad.

Mum smiled. "Wait, I've got something to show you. You know how you're always going on about Lord Savage?" She flicked through the newspapers and took out *Time* magazine. "Here. It's their annual 'Man of the Year' issue."

Lord Alexander Savage.

He stared at Ash from the photo – young, beautiful, smiling benevolently. They'd given the cover a metallic sheen so he looked less like a human and more like a golden god. His skin was inhumanly smooth and perfect, unmarked by wrinkle or blemish. His eyes were hidden behind his shades, but the smile chilled Ash to his soul. That was a smile of a man who'd won everything.

Dad clicked his tongue. "They'll be making him Prime Minister next."

No. No. NO. Ash gripped the magazine. "This isn't right."

Dad put his hand on Ash's arm, but Ash shoved him off. He backed up against the door, staring at them. "Who are you?"

Mum looked worried. "Ashoka..."

"Stop calling me that!" Ash grabbed Lucky's arm. "What happened in India? You *know* what happened."

"Ow, Ashoka, you're hurting me!"

❖

"I said stop calling me that!"

Lucky stared at him, pale and eyes wide. Tears dripped down her cheeks and Ash's fingers sprang open. He wouldn't hurt his sister, not ever.

But was this Lucky?

"Son, you look sick," said Dad. He reached out, but Ash pushed back through the door, away from them. He stumbled into the hall and, just wearing his socks, out the door.

He had to get away.

Heart racing, he ran along the road, with no idea where he was going. He bumped into a man coming out of the newsagent, knocking the paper out of his hands.

Ash reached down instinctively to get it. "Sorry, I didn't see you..."

Prince William was on the front page of the *Independent*. Then Ash read the headline.

KING WILLIAM CELEBRATES A YEAR ON THE THRONE.

Knees in the snow, Ash stared at the newspaper, hoping against hope this was some joke. He checked the date. Today. It was today.

"My paper, please?" said the man.

Dumbly Ash handed it back and stood up. It was all different. Everything. Something had changed. Not with a bang or a thunderbolt or with storms. But something had changed, and it was all different.

Ash couldn't breathe. His chest felt like a massive weight was pressing down on it. Kids walked past him on their way to school. A dog yapped at him, but Ash, eyes blurred with tears, just stood there, utterly lost.

❖

What had happened? Last night, he'd left home after talking with Lucky, *his* Lucky. He'd gone to the graveyard and everything had been the same until he got home. His parents, his sister, were different people.

It had to be Savage. Savage had changed the past. He had mastered Time and done it, just like he said he would.

Because Savage changed the past, Ash's family had developed in different ways, their lives taking other paths. Things had happened, and hadn't happened. He blinked. His uncle and aunt were alive. They'd never had the car crash. That was a good thing, wasn't it? But what else was different that he didn't know about?

"Ash!"

He wiped his face. Who was that?

"Ash!"

A group of Dulwich High students were on the opposite side of the road. He peered through the curtain of snow, just able to make out someone waving at him. He stepped towards the person, raising his hand instinctively.

It was Josh, wrapped up for an Arctic expedition, his eyes and nose just visible between the collar of his coat and his low-drawn hat. He raised his gloved hand. "Ash!"

A boy bumped Ash's shoulder as he passed him from behind. "Sorry," said the boy, waving back to Josh. "Hey!"

The ground tilted and Ash grabbed a lamppost, his legs suddenly jelly. This boy was the same height and build as Ash, just a bit plumper, with the same hairstyle, maybe a little bit shorter. He wore a pair of Converse All-Stars and carried a backpack just like the one Ash owned. He was wearing Ash's greatcoat, his Sherlock Special. He crossed the road and joined Josh.

Ash stood in the middle of the road, looking at them. A car beeped its horn, but he didn't move. He couldn't. He was frozen in time and space.

The boy slapped Josh's well-padded shoulder. "I thought I told you, Josh. I'm not Ash Mistry..."

The boy smiled. He smiled just like Ash did. He had his smile. He had his eyes, his nose, his face.

"...I'm Ashoka."

Mike Rossiter is a film-
maker, whose work TA and
EMMY awards. He won the Golden Fleece at the Dijon
Film Festival for his documentary on the attempted
recovery of the B29 bomber from northern Greenland. In
2001 he filmed the search and recovery of the body of
Donald Campbell and his record-breaking jet boat,
Bluebird, from Coniston Water. In 2004, he filmed the
discovery of the wreck of the *Ark Royal*. He lives in
North London.

ARK ROYAL

The Life, Death and Rediscovery
of the Legendary Second World War
Aircraft Carrier

MIKE ROSSITER

CORGI BOOKS

ARK ROYAL
A CORGI BOOK : 9780552153690

Originally published in Great Britain by Bantam Press,
a division of Transworld Publishers

PRINTING HISTORY
Bantam Press edition published 2006
Corgi edition published 2007

3 5 7 9 10 8 6 4

Copyright © Mike Rossiter 2006
Map © Malcolm Swanston at Red Lion Posters Ltd 2006

The right of Mike Rossiter to be identified as the author of
this work has been asserted in accordance with sections 77
and 78 of the Copyright Designs and Patents Act 1988.

Set in 12/16pt Times by
Falcon Oast Graphic Art Ltd.

Corgi Books are published by Transworld Publishers,
61–63 Uxbridge Road, London W5 5SA,
a division of The Random House Group Ltd.

Addresses for Random House Group Ltd companies outside the UK
can be found at: www.randomhouse.co.uk
The Random House Group Ltd Reg. No. 954009.

Printed and bound in Great Britain by
Cox & Wyman Ltd, Reading, Berkshire.

The Random House Group Limited makes every effort to ensure that the
papers used in its books are made from trees that have been legally
sourced from well-managed and credibly certified forests. Our paper
procurement policy can be found at: www.randomhouse.co.uk/paper.htm.

Picture Acknowledgements

All photos are courtesy the author where not otherwise credited

IWM = Imperial War Museum, London

First Section
Engine room, installation of boilers and launch [ZCL/A015/000]: Wirral Museum, Birkenhead; Lady Maude Hoare, wife of the First Lord of the Admiralty, launches the *Ark Royal*, 13 April 1937: TopFoto.co.uk

Christmas menu and pudding stirring: courtesy Percy North; page from the *Illustrated London News*, 3 December 1938: Illustrated London News Picture Library; Chief Petty Officer R. A. W. King, champion baker: Fox Photos/Getty Images; officers' mess on board the *Ark Royal*, *Illustrated London News*, 10 August 1940: Illustrated London News Picture Library; Michael Wilding, John Clements and Michael Rennie, stars of *Ships With Wings* directed by Michael Balcon, 1942: BFI Stills

Top left, top right: courtesy Percy North; loading a bomb: IWM A3776; Fulmar landing: IWM A3836; torpedoes on deck, April 1941: IWM A3842; Swordfish on the lift to the hangar: IWM A3770; extra pilots standing by: IWM A3740; planes taking off and landing from the *Ark Royal*, taken from HMS *Sheffield*, May 1941: IWM A4042

Photos courtesy of the subjects

Second Section

Sinking of the *Admiral Graf Spee, Illustrated London News*, 6 January 1940: Illustrated London News Picture Library; centre left: courtesy Percy North; the *Strasbourg* prepares to escape, battle of Oran, 12 December 1940, film still: IWM HU63609; fire on a French warship, battle of Oran, 12 December 1940: © Hulton-Deutsch Collection/ CORBIS; top right and immediately below: courtesy Percy North; Sir James Somerville addressing the ship's company on the flight deck of the *Ark Royal* off Gibraltar, 23 October 1941: IWM A3836; concert given by a troup of Spanish dancers, 23 October 1941: IWM A5848

Captain Gunther Lutjens: Keystone/Getty Images; *Bismarck* from *Ark Royal*: courtesy John Moffat; *Bismarck* during the battle, taken from the deck of the *Prinz Eugen*: akg-images; survivors from the sinking of the *Bismarck*, 27 May 1941: mirrorpix; Junker 87: aviation-images.com

Top left and top right: TopFoto.co.uk; bottom left: IWM A6325; bottom right: popperfoto.com; last hours of the *Ark Royal*, drawing by Percy Home from *The Sphere*, 22 November 1941: Illustrated London News Picture Library

Some of the last men to leave the *Ark Royal*, as seen from on board HMS *Legion*: IWM A6315; crew members arriving in England, 25 November 1941: Keystone/Getty Images

Third Section

Ark Royal at Birkenhead: Wirral Museum

Ark Royal in Gibraltar: courtesy Percy North

Fulmar coming in to land: IWM A3637; Swordfish: courtesy Percy North

Ark Royal guns, *Illustrated London News*, 30 March 1940: Illustrated London News Picture Library

The Mediterranean November 1941

Axis or under Axis control
Neutral countries
Allied or under Allied control
Allied convoy route

Acknowledgements

Throughout the book, I hope I have mentioned everyone who was instrumental in helping me find the wreck of HMS *Ark Royal*, or in finding out more about its past. However, there are a few people whose contribution was vital. The first was Rick Davey, of C&C Technologies Inc., without whose advice and experience the project would probably never have got started. In addition, I have to thank Thomas and Jimmy Chance, the owners of C&C Technologies, who offered the use of their ship *Rig Supporter*, and its highly sophisticated equipment, without any consideration of a return for themselves or their company.

The final key contribution to the search for the *Ark Royal* was provided by Paul Allen, who offered his yacht *Octopus* and everything that was necessary to film the wreck, and to care for and entertain the *Ark Royal* crew members who came aboard. I also have to thank Bonnie Benjamin-Pharris, and Jacqui Sullivan at Vulcan Productions for putting up with me.

I would like to thank all of the former crew members of the

Ark Royal who gave freely of their time. In particular I must mention John McCrow, whose knowledge of the *Ark Royal* remains remarkably detailed after all these years, and who spent a great deal of time transferring his knowledge on to tapes and letters for my benefit. There was far too much to include all of it in this book, but I hope it will soon see the light of day.

I received a great deal of advice from Professor Andrew Lambert at King's College, whose insight often helped clarify my confusion, and from Adam Harcourt-Webster, a colleague at the BBC, whose knowledge of the history of the Second World War often astounded me. I was greatly encouraged by my agent, Luigi Bonomi, and helped considerably by Simon Thorogood, and others at Transworld.

Finally, I must thank my wife Anne, and my two sons, Alex and Max, for putting up with endless disrupted weekends and holidays while I confronted the unfamiliar prospect of writing a book. Needless to say, any errors that the patient reader might discover are solely my responsibility.

Preface

On a fine September day in 2004 I was on a fantastically well-equipped and luxurious yacht, its dark blue hull and white upper decks gleaming in the Mediterranean sun. As it moved slowly over the calm surface of the sea a pod of about ten pilot whales kept us company. The sound of their breathing as they broke the surface carried for hundreds of metres in the still air. At one point they surfaced barely a dozen metres from the yacht. But no-one on board was paying the slightest attention. Throughout the vessel, people's eyes were intently focused on a variety of screens relaying pictures from a thousand metres below the surface.

Connected by cables to the yacht was an underwater vehicle, or ROV, that was moving along slowly a few metres above the sea floor. It carried an array of powerful lights and cameras, and was making its way towards the wreck of a ship that had lain hidden since 1941, HMS *Ark Royal*, at the time one of the most modern aircraft carriers and perhaps the most famous ship in the world.

At the controls was John Moffat, an eighty-seven-year-old

Scotsman still full of mischief and energy. John was once a pilot in the Royal Navy, and he had flown an aircraft called a Swordfish, a single-engined biplane with canvas-covered wings and an open cockpit that was large enough and tough enough to carry a heavy torpedo hundreds of miles across the open sea. In May 1941 John flew one of these aircraft through an intense barrage of shells and bullets directly at the giant German battleship the *Bismarck*, one of the biggest and most powerful ships afloat. The last survivor of that historic mission, John was now staring intently at the image being sent back from the underwater vehicle's cameras as it headed for the flight deck of the *Ark Royal*. John Moffat was attempting to land on her one last time.

I had set out from Gibraltar on the *Octopus* ten days earlier, heading for the spot where I believed the wreck of the *Ark Royal* was located. The captain of the *Octopus* was eager to prove to her owner that all the new equipment that had been fitted on board the yacht was working, and would produce amazing results. A few technical difficulties with the under-water vehicle were still being worked on, but he was certain that the wreck of the *Ark Royal*, a very big ship, would produce some impressive, even awe-inspiring pictures.

That we were going to view the wreck of the *Ark Royal* was something I was fairly certain about, even though when we passed the light at the end of the breakwater at the mouth of the harbour in Gibraltar all I had was a set of images from various surveys of the sea floor, but no clear idea of what I might find once we managed to lower lights and cameras to the spot. Other, more experienced underwater surveyors and wreck hunters, had tried to find the *Ark* and failed, but I was certain that success was within our grasp.

John Moffat joined us on the ship a few days later with

some other former crew members. 'Val' Bailey used to be a pilot who flew Fairey Fulmar fighter aircraft from the deck of the *Ark Royal*. He also claimed to be the last person to be rescued from her and was certainly one of the last people actually to see the ship as she went down. Ron Skinner was a petty officer writer and had joined the *Ark* on her very first voyage from Cammell Laird, the shipbuilders. Also on board were Bill Morrison, an able seaman who had joined the *Ark* in 1940 and who worked in the hangar decks and manned the anti-aircraft guns, and John Richardson, a stoker who had worked on the flight deck as well as in the boiler room.

The *Ark Royal* herself had been a remarkable ship, a modern aircraft carrier in a navy that thought, like most navies around the world at the time, that the essential element of sea power was the giant battleship and its supporting fleet. And she had become famous very quickly. As an aircraft carrier and a modern, expensive warship, plenty of newsreels and newspaper stories had focused on her from the time she was launched. Radio documentaries were made about her; a feature film was even shot on board while she was on active service in the Mediterranean. The name *Ark Royal* had quickly assumed a celebrity no other ship possessed during the Second World War.

There have been aircraft carriers called *Ark Royal* for most of the years since the Second World War, and it was this familiarity, this name recognition, that had in part started me on my search for the wreck of the ship that made the name famous. What, after all, was the point of looking for a ship no-one had heard of? What I discovered was the complex history of a ship that mirrored that of the Royal Navy during the war with Germany and Italy before the United States fleet at Pearl Harbor was attacked by the Japanese. It was a period of the war that took the *Ark* from the North Sea to South America, back to the Arctic Circle, then to the Mediterranean, and of course into the Atlantic Ocean.

Running through the *Ark*'s story were tales of ordinary people like the former crew members who had joined us on the *Octopus*, young men, almost boys, who had been snatched up and had lived lives of quite extraordinary danger. They sailed on sunlit seas while bombs whistled through the sky, plummeting directly at their ship. Those that exploded close to the ship were hammer blows against the hull, a frightening reminder that death could be only a few minutes away. Some of them flew flimsy, inadequate aircraft against the modern fighters of the Luftwaffe, sometimes just simply failing to return from a mission or patrol, disappearing into thin air, their fate unknown. Like the Light Brigade of Tennyson's famous poem from another war, they tore 'into the valley of Death' head on against giant battleships, bullets ripping through their canvas-covered wings, shells exploding 50 feet away, tossing their aircraft sideways and filling their nostrils with the stink of high explosive.

Most of the former *Ark Royal* crew who joined us had never met each other before, but when they sat down in the dining room of the *Octopus* they began to remember stories and incidents that like the *Ark Royal* herself hadn't surfaced in over sixty years. The stories were tragic and comic in equal measure. Memories of being under attack from the air, anxious and frightened, but with nobody on the bridge of the *Ark* daring to put their steel helmets on before the captain did. And then, 'within three seconds everybody's tin hat went on'. Memories of raids on convoys, of a single shell hitting an Italian torpedo bomber boring in towards the *Ark Royal*, and the aircraft hitting the sea 200 yards from her. 'You could hear this cheer that went up all over the ship.'

The attack on the *Bismarck* is, of course, the most famous incident in which the *Ark Royal* was involved, the story that was most familiar to the crew of the *Octopus* and the engineers and operators of the ROV. Most of them were from the north of England or Scotland, some of them had in fact served at one time in the Royal Navy, and they were intrigued and fascinated by the prospect of veterans of the *Ark Royal* boarding the *Octopus*.

John Moffat had been down on a sightseeing tour to the underwater vehicle's hangar, which opened out from the side of the hull just above sea level, and he'd shown a great deal of interest in the machine. One of the pilots of the remote vehicle then hit on the idea of letting John land on the *Ark Royal* once again. The ROV was lowered into the water, and the operator in the control room slowly moved it away from the side of the *Octopus*. Then it disappeared, beginning its journey to the sea bed a thousand metres below us.

The ROV pilot sits in what is really a cockpit, a chair with controls for the vehicle on both armrests. In front of him is a screen that shows the picture being captured from the camera on the ROV overlaid with a compass bearing and depth gauge, and below that another screen shows the sonar returns. John sat down in the chair and took the controls. A million dollars' worth of equipment was suddenly in the hands of a Second World War veteran who had never handled an ROV before. But there were no mistakes. John still had a pilot's licence, and he has never stopped flying. His demeanour suddenly changed, and he seemed to be in total control, very focused and clearly understanding the 'feel' of the machine. I was looking at the young man who had flown his aircraft with steely determination through gun- and shellfire towards the *Bismarck*. He glided the ROV smoothly onto the rear of the *Ark*'s flight deck. As a cloud of sediment rose and obscured the camera, everyone who had been watching the feather-light landing on the monitors all around the yacht cheered and clapped.

John was absolutely elated. 'I don't know how I will be able to relate this,' he said, 'I really don't. But I will do my best. Oh Lord,' he added as he got up from the pilot's seat, 'it's hard to be humble.' He walked into the giant equipment hangar where a prototype submarine and an immaculate, super-fast luxury tender were stored, ready to be launched from the rear doors. He shook the *Octopus*'s captain by the hand and said, 'To think I did that after all these years. I'm the first, I'm the first!'

Suddenly, it appeared that the boundaries of time and space had been slightly altered, that the gap between the present and the past had been bridged.

1

THE SEARCH BEGINS

In recent years, many documentaries and films have been
made about one of the key naval encounters of the
Second World War: the battle in May 1941 between HMS
Hood, then the flagship of the Royal Navy, and the giant
German battleship *Bismarck*. After a brief fight, direct hits
from the *Bismarck*'s massive guns caused the *Hood* to
explode, killing most of her crew. It was a devastating
shock, to the Royal Navy, to Churchill and to the public, at
a time when British morale was very fragile.

Almost every ship of the Home Fleet was mobilized in
the effort to reverse this defeat, but it was the *Ark Royal*
which proved to be the decisive factor in the Royal
Navy's hunt to destroy the *Bismarck* and exact revenge
for the *Hood*. By sinking the *Bismarck* Britain avoided a
humiliating defeat that might have affected the whole

course of the war with Germany. For the *Ark Royal*, it meant that not only was she famous in the newspapers and in the newsreels, a fame that had been building since she was launched, but she had now taken a place in history.

The search for the wrecks of the *Bismarck* and the *Hood* have themselves been the subject of many documentaries, and both have now been located on the sea bed. Why, I wondered, had the *Ark* not received the same treatment? Some basic research quickly told me that the *Ark Royal* had herself been sunk in the Mediterranean by a submarine later that same year, in November. The crew had been saved, and an attempt had been made to tow the *Ark* to port in Gibraltar, but after several hours she had capsized and was lost. Photographs taken at the time revealed an impressive ship that towered over the smaller destroyers clustered around her. Although heeling over in the water, she looked un-damaged, and I thought immediately that the position of the wreck must be very well known, and that this splendid ship must be lying almost intact at the bottom of the ocean. It surely couldn't be any harder to locate HMS *Ark Royal* than it had been to find the *Bismarck* and the *Hood*.

A film director I greatly respect once said to me that the most important question to ask before shooting a scene, or indeed embarking on a major project, was not how it could be done but why it was being done. In my work as a producer I have made documentaries about other people's fascination with the relics and icons of history. I have spent months in northern Greenland with a group of pilots and mechanics restoring the wreck of a Second World War bomber, and weeks on Coniston Water while the body of Donald Campbell and his boat *Bluebird* were located and recovered from the lake. I think I understand people's interest in hidden objects from the past. When a ship or aeroplane that disappeared is rediscovered or brought back to the public gaze, the past is in some way being brought back to life and another chapter is added to the famous craft's story. Modern life changes quickly and profoundly. It seems to me that people's curiosity when it comes to machines like the B-29 bomber and the jet-propelled *Bluebird* is partly motivated by a realization that they represent a period in the recent past when the world was transforming. The B-29 is an iconic aeroplane because it ushered in the nuclear age; Donald Campbell was the last of the famous record breakers, and *Bluebird* seemed to mark the end of that era when British superiority was a given. Was the *Ark Royal* such a historical symbol, in a way I had yet to understand clearly? Or was there something rather more unbalanced about my interest?

As I did more research on the *Ark*, I learned that there were reasons for her fame other than the action against the *Bismarck*. The *Ark Royal* had fought in most places where the Navy had operated during the first two years of the Second World War. Perhaps most crucially she played a key role in the war in the Mediterranean – one of the bloodiest campaigns the Royal Navy has ever fought and a theatre in which Britain came perilously close to defeat, before the Japanese attack on Pearl Harbor brought the United States into the war. I was excited by the possibility of finding the *Ark Royal*, not only for the chance to see once again this imposing ship, but for the opportunity it would present to tell a different story about the Royal Navy and the early years of the Second World War.

Telling the story was one thing – I knew how to do that; finding the wreck was something else. I had never done anything like it before. Fortunately, a chance for me to find out whether locating the *Ark* was at all possible arose fairly quickly. I had to fly to Aberdeen to meet Hugh McKay, who worked for a Danish company called Kongsberg Simrad, one of the world's leading manufacturers of sonar equipment. The methods originally developed to hunt for submarines in the war had improved enormously in the years since 1945. One of the biggest driving forces had been the oil industry and its exploitation of deposits under the ocean. Equipment made by Kongsberg used sound waves to produce remarkably detailed images of objects just a few metres in size at considerable depths. McKay, a soft-spoken Scot, was one of their salesmen; he had been giving me some advice about Kongsberg's equipment and how I could use it in some projects I was developing. I decided this meeting was a perfect opportunity to raise the question of the *Ark Royal*.

Hugh sat at his desk and stared at me. I could see that I had quickened his interest. As an outsider, I am always fascinated by industries like the underwater exploration business, about which I know little; but to those working inside them the routine tasks can quickly become boring. In my experience, people are always eager to become involved in something out of the ordinary, and a search for the *Ark Royal* was definitely that.

He asked if I knew where the wreck was, and I gave him a position, in latitude and longitude, that I had found on the Internet. Hugh went out of the room and came back with a chart entitled 'Eastern Approaches to the Strait of Gibraltar'. He found the spot and looked at the depth marked on the chart. 'It's in 900 metres of water,' he said. The depth, he went on, was not a problem; it was simply a question of finding a survey ship that was in the area. It was at this point that I began to learn about the complexities of underwater surveying, and the financial implications.

Hugh explained to me that it was normal when hiring a survey vessel to pay for the ship from the time it left its home port to the time it got back. Locating a ship that was already working in the Mediterranean might save on these costs. Then he asked how accurate the position I had given him was. I confessed that I had no idea. Why should it be inaccurate? Hugh pointed out that I needed to be certain. The difference of a minute – one sixtieth of a degree – in a position of latitude or longitude can mean a distance of over a mile. 'Presumably you will want to film the wreck so you will have to locate it first, and fix its position,' he said. 'There's no alternative. You don't want to hire a ship and an underwater vehicle and then find out the position is not quite right. It would be very expensive.'

After our meeting, Hugh drove me to Aberdeen airport. He handed me my bag as I got out of the car, and over the noise of the helicopters that shuttled back and forth to the oil rigs in the North Sea we talked again about the *Ark Royal*. 'I'll make some enquiries, Mike,' he promised. 'It's a grand project, and I'm sure a lot of people will be happy to be involved. I'll speak to you in a week or so. Meanwhile, see what you can find out about the wreck's position. It's *very* important.'

My dream of discovering the wreck of the *Ark* had begun to seem possible, and back in London I immediately started to do what Hugh had suggested. As part of my research for a television series about the history of the Royal Navy, I had been picking the brains of Professor Andrew Lambert, an expert on Nelson and naval history. Shortly after my trip to Aberdeen, at one of our meetings in his King's College office tucked behind Somerset House in the Strand, Andrew gave me a pamphlet that had been published in 1942. Its title was *Ark Royal: The*

Admiralty Account of Her Achievement, and it was an illustrated history of the *Ark Royal*. Priced at ninepence, it had, so Andrew told me, sold over a quarter of a million copies. It was a classic of propaganda, so apparently balanced and even-handed in its style and approach that it was hard to believe it had been produced by the government of a country fighting for its existence. Inside the front cover was a stunning photograph of the *Ark* towering above a crowd of workers as she slid down the slipway of the Cammell Laird shipyard at Birkenhead on the south bank of the Mersey. Seeing this photograph – how huge she was! – fuelled my desire to see this great ship now lying at the bottom of the Mediterranean. The pamphlet made no attempt to cover up the ship's loss and made the efforts to save her seem heroic, with descriptions of the captain being rescued in the final moments, and the ship turning over and slowly sinking. Clearly it would not have been produced had the *Ark* not already been a household name. There was little information, however, about where the *Ark* was when she sank.

The maritime charts used by the Navy, the Merchant Marine and many weekend sailors are produced for the government by the UK Hydrographic Office in Taunton. One part of this organization, appropriately called the Wrecks Section, keeps track of all the wrecks that might be a hazard to shipping, and any other significant wrecks they are told about. I enquired if they had any information about the *Ark Royal*, and a few days later I received through the post a piece of paper, known as a 'wreck sheet', for HMS *Ark Royal*. Each wreck has a number, and this is written at the top of the page. Then the sheet gives information about the known position, whether the wreck has a distinctive sonar or radar signature, and goes on to give a brief history. The *Ark Royal* sheet gave several positions, and suggested that a salvage company based in Gibraltar had located the wreck and offered to salvage it – an offer declined by the British government. There were in fact several quite markedly different accounts of the position of the wreck, and all of them at odds with the one I had already found on the Internet.

That position had come from a draft of the *Official History of the War at Sea*, written in 1943, which reminded me that the best place to start some original research into the *Ark Royal* was the National Archives, housed in an elegant oriental-style low-rise building in Kew, on the other side of the railway tracks from the Botanical Gardens. The archives revealed that immediately after the *Ark Royal* was sunk a Board of Inquiry was convened to investigate her loss. At the height of one of the darkest and most dangerous periods of the war, three very senior naval officers, including Admiral of the Fleet Sir Charles Forbes, sailed in a destroyer to Gibraltar to take evidence and produce an initial report. Sixty years later, these documents, bound together in buff-coloured books, were brought to my desk in the reading room. Inside were foolscap sheets with original typewritten minutes, ink annotations and signatures, representing an attempt to form a narrative of the day. But the members of the Board of Inquiry did not arrive in Gibraltar with an entirely open mind. One carbon copy of a letter that was attached at the front of one of the bound documents set an ominous tone to their investigations: 'There is bound to be considerable criticism in the Services, and by the public, when it is known that this modern ship was lost in fine weather after being in tow for several hours, sunk by just one torpedo.'

The effort to make sense of the events started with evidence from Sir James Somerville, the Admiral in Charge of Force H, a flotilla of warships built around the *Ark Royal* and a battleship that was stationed in Gibraltar, and the captain of the *Ark Royal*, L. E. H. Maund. On the day she was sunk the *Ark* had apparently separated from some of the escort vessels to allow aircraft to land and take off. She was following a zigzag course slightly at variance to the rest of Force H, steering an overall course of 286 degrees (think of a compass face as a clock face: 90 degrees would be three o'clock, 180 degrees would be six o'clock, and 270 degrees would be nine o'clock). On one leg of the zigzag, at 1541 hours when her course was 290 degrees, the *Ark* was hit by a torpedo on her starboard side underneath the island – the name for the superstructure that is built to one side of the flight deck on an aircraft carrier. She was steaming at a speed of 19 knots, and the evidence from the captain and the other senior officers was that because communication with the engine room had been cut by the blast, the ship took eleven minutes to slow down and stop. I calculated that this meant the ship had travelled a distance of 3 nautical miles from the point where she was hit by the torpedo, still presumably in the same direction – that is, steaming towards a point slightly to the north of Gibraltar.

I continued to read the evidence to find out what else I could work out from it. Tugs in Gibraltar were quickly ordered to sea to help salvage the *Ark*, and according to the accounts they arrived at around 1800 hours. The pamphlet about the *Ark* that Andrew Lambert had given me claimed that she was towed at 2 knots for almost nine hours. If she was towed at this rate she must have moved another 18 nautical miles to the westward from the position where she came to a halt, and that put her in very close proximity to Gibraltar. I now in effect had three different positions: the one where she was struck by the torpedo, the position where she came to a halt, and the position where the tow was abandoned and she presumably sank. They were separated overall by some 21 nautical miles.

I turned over the pages of the inquiry minutes, stamped SECRET or even MOST SECRET, for any additional evidence that would shed light on the resting place of the wreck. There were a considerable number of attachments to various documents. There was, for example, a dead reckoning track – the record of the ship's course marked on a chart and updated at regular intervals – of the whole of the *Ark Royal*'s voyage through the western Mediterranean on what turned out to be her last operation. Also contained in the files were two drawings, one of them a blueprint of a cross-section of the ship. It showed the ship leaning at an angle of eighteen degrees in the water. The flight deck of the carrier obviously had to be unobstructed, so the funnels, the bridge and masts were located in a structure that rose from the extreme right of the *Ark*'s hull, the island. This meant that the vents from the boilers on the port or left side of the ship had to travel almost horizontally under the flight deck before turning at right angles and going vertically up through the superstructure, on the starboard side. The diagram put before the inquiry clearly showed that with an eighteen-degree list the port boiler vents would fill with water. It was assumed that this was the reason why the port boilers caught fire, and why the electrical supply to the ship, and most importantly to the ship's main pumps, failed.

A second drawing was also based on a blueprint of the hull. This time, however, it was from a sketch by the captain of a motor launch that had picked up the last men to leave the ship, who had seen the ship turn over and sink. It depicted a very large hole in the *Ark*'s side that was almost one third the length of her keel; it looked to my ignorant eyes to be large enough to defeat any damage control efforts that might have been carried out.

It was impossible to say whether it was exaggerated or not, but it was accepted as accurate by the Board of Inquiry.

One other piece of evidence intrigued and slightly alarmed me. A chief petty officer testified that only one of the tugs sent out from Gibraltar had managed to secure a tow rope to the bows of the *Ark*; the second tug, after several abortive efforts, had abandoned the task and disappeared into the night, and was not seen again till the following morning. The third had failed to find the *Ark* at all. This sounded a lot more chaotic than the published version suggested, but the Board of Inquiry still recorded the fact that the *Ark* had been towed at 2 knots for up to nine hours.

After two days in the Public Record Office I had a much better idea of the events leading up to the sinking of the *Ark Royal*, but nothing that tallied with the position I had first discovered in the *Official History* of 1943. Moreover, if the account of the Board of Inquiry was true, the *Ark* had sunk very close to Gibraltar indeed. As a further complication, the inquiry added a very bald statement at the end of its evidence saying that the *Ark* sank 22 miles due east from Europa point, the southernmost point of Gibraltar, a statement that did not seem to be backed up by any evidence at all.

I closed the last of the files and reflected on the task that lay before me. I had here minutes and memoranda from one of the blackest periods of British history, when men and women were sent out around the world far away from home to fight and to face incredible danger. The journey these senior Admiralty officers had taken to Gibraltar was itself fraught with the risk of attack from enemy bombers and U-boats. In December 1941 the outcome of the war was uncertain, and thousands of sailors' lives had been lost in the Mediterranean alone. The words they had written were here for me to read over half a century later, but I would never know what these seamen thought or felt about their own lives.

My search had resulted in a great deal more information about the circumstances of the sinking, but had created even more uncertainty with regard to the location of the wreck. The Board of Inquiry had to be the best and most accurate version of events, but discrepancies in the evidence and the bald statement of the *Ark*'s position given at the end didn't seem to tie up. The truth was that the inquiry and everybody involved in the effort to salvage the *Ark* had no real interest in where she had sunk. What was important was *why* she had sunk, and whether it could have been prevented. Did the design of similar ships need modifying, or was the sinking a result of negligence on the part of her commanding officers? These were the only questions to which the Board of Inquiry wanted answers, and in the case of the latter they concluded that there was indeed a guilty man. Captain Maund was charged with negligence at a court martial in January 1942.

A few days later, and true to his word, Hugh McKay telephoned me. He'd been talking to his contacts in the underwater survey industry and he gave me the telephone number of someone called Rick Davey, who he said would like to talk to me. The company Rick worked for, C&C Technologies, had a survey ship in the western Mediterranean. I thanked Hugh, but was mystified by his parting words: 'When you speak to him, Mike, make sure you're sitting down.'

I eagerly phoned Rick the next day to find out what he was offering. The company he represented was conducting an underwater survey for a new gas pipeline to connect Spain and Algeria, and they were using a ship called the *Rig Supporter*. There were no prizes for guessing what the ship was built for. On board the *Rig Supporter* was a unique piece of equipment which had been jointly developed by C&C Technologies and Hugh McKay's employers, Kongsberg Simrad – hence the connection. This marvellous piece of machinery was called an AUV, or Autonomous Underwater Vehicle. In other words, it was a small unmanned submarine. Several similar robots had been built for research purposes, but the one that belonged to C&C was the only one being used in commercial survey work.

There are two ways to survey the sea bed. One of them is to have a sound transmitter and receiver mounted on the hull of a boat. As the boat travels over an area of sea, sound waves pulse towards the sea floor and the echoes that bounce back are processed by computers to create very precise images of objects on the sea bed. However, there is a problem with this method: the image definition deteriorates with depth. To overcome this it's possible to use something called a sidescan sonar. A sound transmitter is lowered to the required depth and towed behind a ship, and because the sonar is closer to the target it can produce a much more accurate picture. But a much larger ship is needed to carry the cable, which can be several miles in length, and the sonar 'fish' needs to be towed at a constant speed and depth. Achieving this can be time-consuming.

The AUV on the *Rig Supporter* carried a combination of sidescan and vertical sonars, but could be set to 'fly' at a fixed depth using its own motors, independently of its support ship, eliminating at a stroke the problems of the more conventional methods of finding out what lies at the bottom of the ocean. It sounded ideal, but then I learned why Hugh had told me to sit down when speaking to Rick Davey: the ship and its AUV were currently on hire for a fee of around $120,000 a day. In a global business like the oil and gas industry such figures are not remarkable, but costs like that are impossible for documentaries, particularly when after spending all that money you still don't have a single picture to transmit. I pointed this out to Rick, but he seemed strangely unconcerned. We agreed to meet.

Rick turned out to be a calm, quietly spoken man with

a very laid-back sense of humour, which was lucky, because when we met I was very apprehensive. I knew I would never be able to raise the sort of money he was talking about from the BBC or any other TV company. However efficient the AUV was, a single day seemed inadequate to do what I thought we needed to do, and I realized we could end up having to spend over a quarter of a million pounds just to locate the wreck – more if things didn't go well. Rick still seemed unconcerned, and implied that if the *Rig Supporter* was operating in the Mediterranean, as it was, the company might make the ship available between contracts for a smaller fee, though we didn't discuss how small that might be. As he pointed out, their AUV was the only vehicle of its type in the world working commercially, and Rick thought that locating the *Ark Royal* would be a very good way to show what the AUV could do. In other words, good publicity for the company.

Inevitably we then moved on to the vexed question of just where in the expanse of the Mediterranean we were going to look for the *Ark*. I explained to Rick what I had found in the archives, and we spread out a chart to mark down the various options. My starting point was the spot where the torpedo hit the ship, and this was the most easterly point we marked. The most westerly point was the spot where I calculated the ship must have been towed to if everything that was said in the inquiry was accurate. I mentally discounted this position, because if

the ship had been towed as far as this it would ha\
visible from Gibraltar. There was no evidence that i
was, but this theoretical position did help me define the
furthest western point of the area where the ship might
be. I then plotted on the chart the positions mentioned in
the information from the Wrecks Section. Using all these
points to construct a box gave me a square that measured
16 nautical miles by 20 nautical miles.

Rick went quiet when he saw the results. We were confronted with an area as large as Greater London, and we
would be looking for an object just 244 metres long. It
was clear that to search an area this large with the AUV
would take a long time. But Rick had an alternative plan.
'We need to do a search of this area as cheaply as
possible,' he said, 'and then use the AUV to investigate
any targets we find.' In short, he wanted to go back to
more conventional ship-mounted sonar to search the
area. Rick had a survey vessel in mind, one his company
was working with, a ship called the *Odin Finder*, which
despite its name was owned by a small Italian survey
company based in Bologna. I asked how much it would
cost; Rick said he thought about $12,000 a day. He did
some more calculations and worked out that to cover the
area we had plotted on the map, a staggering 320 square
nautical miles, it might take as long as three days, with
the ship working around the clock. As Rick remarked, in
what I was to learn was a typical understatement from
him, 'We have quite a large uncertainty factor here.'

My problem now was to find $36,000. This was not going to be easy. As I mentioned, I had been developing a television series about the history of the Royal Navy for the BBC based on the underwater exploration of wrecks of ships from major battles. Some large sea battles, like the First World War battle of Jutland, had left scores of wrecks in the North Sea. They were in relatively shallow water and, although it is never an easy thing to do, it was possible for divers to locate and film them. Others, like the wrecks from the battle of Trafalgar, would be almost impossible to find, although I would have tried if someone had suggested a way. Then there were those like the *Bismarck*, in very deep water, and thus extremely difficult to film. The project was still in development stage, but I felt that mounting a search for the *Ark Royal* was worth funding. It involved a fine calculation, it was a significant sum of money, but I knew it was not a very large one in the overall budget of the sort of series I wanted to make. I also knew that success in locating the wreck of the *Ark Royal* would be a boost to getting the series made. Channel 4 had recently broadcast a programme about the *Hood* and the *Bismarck* and had achieved extremely good viewing figures. The quest to find the *Ark Royal* seemed the sort of project that might get similar audiences. As far as using licence-fee money was concerned I thought it justified because the story of the *Ark Royal* was an important part of our recent history. The wreck was part of our heritage, more important perhaps than HMS

Belfast, which was floating as a museum in the Thames. I felt no qualms on that score.

While I waited for the *Odin Finder* to finish its current contracts, Rick and I refined our plans. The water depth in the box we had drawn on the map varied between 900 and 1,300 metres. At that depth the sonar machine mounted on the hull of the *Odin Finder* would cover a swathe of sea bed about a kilometre wide, so we would have to make a series of journeys at regular intervals across the area of the box to get comprehensive coverage of the sea floor. Sound travels at about 1,500 metres a second in seawater and the sound pulse sent out from the sonar would take one and a half seconds to make its way from the boat to the sea floor and back to the boat again. This meant that the *Odin Finder* would need to travel at 3 knots to get accurate returns. We would be relying on the reflection of just one sound pulse for every square metre of sea bed, or hopefully a wreck, to tell us what we were passing over. Rick assured me that the modern sonar on board the *Odin Finder* could tell a great deal from just a few sample reflections, but I still had my doubts. Moreover, the maths confirmed that we would need to spend just over three days and nights covering the area where we calculated the *Ark Royal* lay.

We had to wait longer than I anticipated for the *Odin Finder*. That summer there were strong gales in the Mediterranean, too strong for comfortable sailing or efficient surveying. I asked Rick who paid for the time a ship spent in harbour due to bad weather. 'The company hiring the boat,' he said. 'But don't worry, on a small job like yours the chances of a big delay are slim.' This was little comfort, I thought. During this time I was continually reminded of how speculative my quest was, or just how high was our 'level of uncertainty', to quote Rick.

In the meantime I continued my research. I unearthed a series of photos taken from an aeroplane almost immediately after the *Ark Royal* had been hit by the torpedo and before the destroyer *Legion* had joined her to take off the crew. The *Ark* was already listing, and steam was pouring out of the boiler room inlets at the edges of the flight deck. Handwritten down one edge of the photographs was the time and date when they were taken, and the co-ordinates in latitude and longitude. To my horror I realized that on two of the photos separated by just a few minutes in time the position given varied by 8 nautical miles. Moreover, the co-ordinates were outside the box we had drawn on the map. Another reminder, if I needed it, of how inaccurate navigation was before the era of the satellite-based global positioning system. After looking at these photos I had no option but to tell the co-owner of the *Odin Finder*, Elisabetta Faenza, that we needed to enlarge our search area to the east. She agreed, and magnanimously did not increase the fee.

It seemed I had come a long way from my first discussions with Hugh McKay about the possibility of finding one of the major warships of the Second World War. On the face of it I had constructed a search plan, found a vessel to carry out the survey and secured some funding for it from the BBC. However, although I wouldn't admit it to anyone, the uncertainty was making me increasingly anxious, not least about my own judgement in embarking on this project.

2

BUILDING THE *ARK*

On 13 April 1937, there was an atmosphere of celebration in Cammell Laird's shipyard at Birkenhead. Hundreds of dockyard workers in clean suits, collars and ties crowded in the shadow of a ship's hull towering 30 or more metres above the slipway. In smart rows in one part of the crowd were almost a hundred sailors in blue and white uniforms. Immediately in front of the bows a raised platform had been constructed, and on it was a group of men, some in top hats and morning dress, others in uniforms of the Royal Navy. Ships traditionally are launched by women, and true to form the guest of honour on this occasion was Lady Maud Hoare, the wife of Sir Samuel Hoare, First Lord of the Admiralty in Neville Chamberlain's Tory government. And there was cause for celebration. The ship that was going to be launched was not only the result of the first big increase in the Royal Navy's budget since the end of the First World War, it was the most modern aircraft carrier ever built.

'I name this ship *Ark Royal*,' Lady Hoare announced. 'God bless her and all who sail in her!'

Lady Hoare lifted a bottle of champagne into the air, and as the crowd tensed and got ready to cheer, press men lifted their big cameras to their eyes and newsreel film started rolling. She swung the bottle on its beribboned cord towards the bows of the ship. It bounced off and swung slowly in mid-air. The crowd replaced their hats on their heads and shifted into a more relaxed pose. One of the top-hatted gentlemen on the dais retrieved the bottle and handed it back to Lady Hoare. 'Give it a good throw,' he said to her. The crowd grew expectant again, and drew breath. Once again the bottle bounced off. It was retrieved a second time, and another lady guest, smiling helpfully, leaned forward and told Lady Hoare to throw the bottle against the sharp prow of the ship. The bottle was flung again, and again it failed to break. Finally, on the fourth, rather desperate attempt the bottle smashed open, and the champagne flowed down the bows of the great ship.

At last the cheers roared out, and hundreds of flat caps flew into the air. The ship slowly gathered speed, controlled by the slow unravelling of coils of chains fastened along her length. Then the *Ark Royal*, sending sheets of spray into the air, splashed into the water.

This was a tense moment for the engineers at Cammell Laird. At a certain stage in the launch of any ship, the centre of the hull is not supported either by the water or the slipway. The longer the ship, the greater the strain on the keel, and the *Ark* was very long. For days engineers had calculated the forces that could safely be borne by the hull, and now they would discover if they had got it right. They had, and the ship slid safely out into the Mersey, barely a mile wide at this its narrowest point, and within minutes tugs had secured ropes to the stern of the carrier and were slowly easing her great bulk to the fitting-out basin.

Leonard Sweeney was a sixteen-year-old boy when the *Ark* was launched, and had just joined Cammell Laird as an engineering apprentice. A small, alert figure with a quiet sense of humour, he now lives in a peaceful suburb in Lympstone on the south coast, a world far removed from the smoke and noise of pre-war Birkenhead. The Cammell Laird shipyard stretched for acres along the banks of the Mersey, providing a living for up to twelve thousand people in the yards or the machine shops, as naval architects, electricians, crane drivers, caulkers and any number of other trades. Leonard remembers the yard 'humming with activity. There was this huge engine shop which was three-quarters of a mile long. Diesel engines were being built, turbines, propeller shafts, pumps – all sorts of engineering works were going on.' The work often proved fatal to the workers who clambered high onto the scaffolding that rose up the sides of the ship. Indeed, the yard was nicknamed 'the slaughter-house'. Leonard believes that four people lost their lives while building the *Ark*. It was a hard, noisy, smoke-filled environment. 'There was a blacksmith's shop, and there it was really stinking hot. Dust everywhere. I mean, you could hardly see from one end of the shop to the other because of the fumes.'

A large Victorian pub had been built at the main gates to the yard, and at lunchtime the entire workforce would pour out to slake its thirst. 'The arrangement was that the bartender and bar owners filled as many pint glasses as they could find with beer,' Leonard recalled. 'And these were all laid out on counters and the workmen went in, grabbed a pint of beer, started drinking it and eased their way to the rear of the pub where they paid for it. Put the money on the table and off they went. So it cleared an awful lot of pints of beer.'

The origins of the *Ark Royal* could be said to date as far back as 1923, when the Admiralty proposed to the government of the day a ten-year programme of ship-building to maintain a modern fleet. Along with eight heavy cruisers and other ships, it called for an aircraft carrier and three hundred aircraft. The programme was postponed as a result of the continuing economic crisis in the inter-war period, but the Navy did not let the plans die. Britain needed the Navy, and the Navy knew it would eventually need the ships. By 1930, various committees in the Admiralty working under the direction of the Director of Naval Construction, Sir Arthur Johns, had started to sketch some plans for a new modern aircraft carrier. The most important thing on Johns' mind was to increase the total number of aircraft that could be carried.

The Navy had six carriers in service, all of them dating from the First World War, but because of their limited capacity it was hard for them to operate effectively. These existing carriers stowed their aircraft underneath the flight deck, because the whole length of the deck needed to be kept clear for aircraft landing or taking off. If the aircraft that were landing could be brought to a halt quickly, however, then the forward part of the flight deck could be used to store aircraft, increasing the total number of aircraft that could be operated by the carrier. Arresting wires had been developed in the 1920s but hadn't been put into production, because they tended to damage the aircraft. Now the plans were dusted off to see if they could be improved. Accelerators were also investigated, to see if there was a way to catapult aircraft off the carrier without the need to use the entire flight deck for the aircraft's take-off run.

By 1933, despite the Treaty of Versailles and the creation of the League of Nations, the international situation was becoming unstable. Japan was rearming and was determined to enlarge its sphere of influence in Asia. Hitler had come to power in Germany, and the Italian government under Mussolini was threatening to expand its empire in North Africa. Prompted by these concerns, the British government decided to allocate the money required for the long-delayed naval building programme in the 1934 budget proposals, and construction of the *Ark* was finally allowed to go ahead. Sir Arthur Johns completed the drawings for the new carrier and signed them off in November 1934.

To modern eyes, these original plans seem like works of art, as unique and remarkable as ancient papyri. They are drawn to a scale of one eighth of an inch to a foot on stiff cartridge paper backed with canvas, immaculately rendered and lettered in Indian ink, and gently tinted so that various spaces and machinery can easily be identified. These plans were delivered to Cammell Laird, and the company was invited to tender for the contract to build the ship. By January 1935 estimates were being worked out on foolscap ledgers in the works offices in Birkenhead. Again using pen and ink, the detailed items needed to build a modern aircraft carrier were listed, and the costs: materials, labour and the company mark-up were calculated in the margin. For example, two spare propeller shafts would cost an estimated £6,900, and the labour charge would be £230 plus a 60 per cent mark-up; after a 10 per cent surcharge was added, the grand total was £7,990. Similar sums were done for hundreds of other items and services, right down to the expense of docking at Liverpool for trials in the Mersey.

Eventually these figures were agreed internally, and presented to the Admiralty in a formal tender document in February 1935. The total cost of the hull alone was going to be £1,496,250, and the main machinery – boilers, turbines, etc. – would cost on top of that another half a million pounds. At a total cost of over three million pounds the *Ark Royal* was not only going to be the most modern carrier, it was going to be the most expensive ship ever ordered by the Navy. The Admiralty accepted these figures quickly enough, though there was some haggling over the cost of special steel, and the contract for the hull and machinery was quickly placed in April 1935. The keel plate was laid on 16 September at an informal ceremony attended by workers, a few officials from the company and twelve-year-old Wendy Johnson, daughter of the managing director of Cammell Laird.

Although contracts had been signed, Sir Arthur Johns wanted to keep his options open about some aspects of the design. It would take time to build the hull, and there were still alternative plans for the flight deck and the ship's main armament to be considered. One thing that had been decided was how the ship was going to be powered. Six boilers would provide steam to three turbines driving three propellers. These propellers, each 16 feet (4.9 metres) in diameter and solid bronze, would turn 230 times a minute and drive the ship at 30 knots, or about 33 miles an hour.

The carrier had to be fast for several reasons. Modern aircraft were faster and heavier, and despite the arrestor wires and catapults on the *Ark*, the ship would still have to steam rapidly into the wind to provide enough wind-speed over the flight deck for planes landing or taking off. Furthermore, heading into the wind meant that the carrier would have to separate from the main fleet of ships and steam in a different direction, so speed was again essential to catch up with the fleet once flying operations were finished. The average speed at which the Royal Navy thought its fleet should be able to move was about 20 knots, so the *Ark* was expected to have an edge of another 50 per cent. Finally, speed was necessary for the *Ark* to avoid coming into contact with enemy ships. It was not designed to fight another ship, but to steam rapidly in the opposite direction as soon as the enemy was spotted. At the time the *Ark* was being built her speed compared very favourably with other warships in service, but six years later in 1940 it's unlikely she would have been able to outrun modern German or Italian battleships.

It was obvious that the main weapon of an aircraft carrier was its aircraft, not its guns. Any guns that were placed on the *Ark Royal* were going to be used solely to create an anti-aircraft barrage to protect the ship from attack. The original plans for the *Ark* put these guns low down on the side of the hull, but later Sir Arthur Johns placed them just below the flight deck, in four turrets on either side – sixteen guns altogether – where they had a clear arc of fire. The size of the guns was reduced slightly so that it would be easier for the gun crews to carry the shells. These modified plans were delivered to Cammell Laird in August 1935. As well as these main guns, there were eight machine guns placed at the front and rear of the flight deck on small decks that projected to the side, and four multiple-barrelled guns called 'pom-poms' on the flight deck to the front and rear of the funnel and the island. All of these were part of the anti-aircraft defences. With these modifications to the main gun turrets, the *Ark*'s design was more or less fixed.

There was one major constraint that the designer and the builders had to deal with, however, and that was the limit on tonnage imposed by the various naval treaties that had been signed after the First World War. These arms agreements, the Washington and London Treaties, were due to expire at the end of 1936, and the British government, partly to prevent a naval arms race it could already see developing with Japan and Italy, wanted to impose in any new treaty a limit on aircraft carriers of 22,000 tons.

Sir Arthur Johns and Cammell Laird struggled to fit their new carrier into this self-imposed limit. The amount of armour plating in the hull was reduced, and was confined to a box that enclosed the engine rooms and magazines. This still didn't bring down the weight sufficiently, and the solution eventually arrived at was to use a great deal of welding in the hull as opposed to the more normal method of riveting the plates together. It was estimated that this would save 500 tons of rivet weight in the main hull alone, equal to the weight of the main armament.

Cammell Laird had pioneered welding, and in the 1920s had built the first ship with an all-welded hull, a small coaster; this may have been one of the reasons the company was invited to tender for the *Ark Royal*. But there was a vast difference of scale between a coaster and an aircraft carrier, and Cammell Laird planned to do a lot of experimental work to test out techniques before starting construction. Ultimately about 65 per cent of the ship was welded, including bulkheads, decks, the hull plating and framing above the hangar deck, and the first 100 feet, or 30 metres, of the front of the ship. Skilled welders were not that readily available on the labour market, so the company set up a school to train more than two hundred of them.

After the launch, the *Ark Royal* spent almost another year in the fitting-out dock. Leonard Sweeney remembers the boilers and turbines being hoisted out of the engine shop and into the hull by giant cranes that ran alongside the dock. 'It was a fascinating ship,' he said. 'I think the first thing was, it was a bit awe-inspiring because of the huge flight deck. But the width was the thing. It towered over the engine shop and it looked in some cases a bit unreal. And of course the funnel was on the starboard side, and it was on the edge of the flight deck. But when you looked again it seemed to be slightly outside the edge of the deck. And it had this feeling that it could have fallen off at any minute. So it was a strange-looking ship. There wasn't much symmetry about it. The workforce at Cammell Laird had never seen anything like this before. It was a really innovative ship, and in every corner was something new. You know, hydraulic lifts and everything electrical. And inside were these vast open spaces. It was a big departure from a normal ship. A big departure.'

The most striking part of the ship was indeed the flight deck, which at 800 feet (244 metres) was much longer than the hull, by about 36 metres, with an enormous over-hang at the stern of the ship. This helped to reduce turbulence for aircraft landing on the flight deck, but the length of the hull was limited by the size of harbour entrances in Malta and Gibraltar – important harbours for the Navy in the Mediterranean. The sides of the hull rose flush to the flight deck, and at the front of the flight deck there were two accelerators that could catapult aircraft into the air.

The *Ark* towered over everything else in the shipyard because two of the decks below the flight deck were intended to carry – so it was hoped – a total of seventy-two aircraft, which represented a significant increase on existing carriers. This raised the flight deck nearly 20 metres above the water line, and caused some problems to the designers when they considered how to protect the ship against bombs. Protecting the flight deck with heavy armour plate would compromise the stability and weight of the ship, and she had been designed with an emphasis on long range and endurance, with a theoretical ability to travel over 12,000 nautical miles on one load of fuel. So the flight deck was left unprotected, and this vulnerability assumed increasing importance in the minds of those who subsequently commanded the ship.

At a meeting of the Institution of Naval Architects held in 1939, the *Ark Royal* was the subject of a paper given by Sir Stanley Goodall, the new Director of Naval Construction. It was quite clear from his tone that the *Ark* was believed to be a major advance, not only as an aircraft carrier, but in terms of the design of modern ships generally. One of the key aspects of its modernism was the decision to rely almost exclusively on electrical power. Goodall made a lengthy reference to this in his speech. '*Ark Royal* affords a particular example of the steadily increasing use of electricity in warships,' he said. 'Pumps, capstan gear, cranes, winches, gun mountings, steering gear, some engine room auxiliaries, bread baking depend upon electrical power, as well as fans, all lighting, communications and some heating. Two hundred and forty miles of cable and 620 motors are installed in the ship. The control of the whole of the ship, with a few exceptions, is centred in the main control switchboard.'

He added, 'Alternative 220 volt supplies are provided to the machines, and low-power batteries are fitted where required so that supplies to essential services may be maintained in the event of damage in action.' Sir Stanley was also proud of the standard of accommodation in the *Ark*. 'A soda fountain, canteen, bookstall and a cinema are provided. Hot and cold running water is fitted to each cabin, and cooled drinking water is supplied to various mess spaces.' In a message to the conference the then Admiral of the Fleet Lord Chatfield gave her an enormous vote of confidence when he said, 'She is a remarkable ship carrying a large number of aircraft of the size and performance we consider essential; fast both for tactical and strategical reasons, well defended against air attack, and a valuable addition to the Fleet.'

Leonard Sweeney said to me, however, that the workers at the Cammell Laird shipyard were never wholly enthusiastic about the *Ark*. When the money was allocated for the *Ark*, the naval estimates also included the funds for a new battleship, HMS *Prince of Wales*. This was the first of what was intended to be a new class of battleship, urgently needed to replace the Navy's capital ships which were now twenty and more years old. The hull of the *Prince of Wales*, a ship that at 35,000 tons was getting on for twice the weight of the *Ark Royal*, was being assembled on the slipway while the *Ark* was in the fitting-out basin. 'And here was something which was a real ship,' said Leonard. 'It had ten fourteen-inch guns.

Fourteen inches of armour plate on the sides. Five inches of armour plate on the deck. Had two aircraft which were operated by catapult. It was low in the water – in other words, it seemed to be in its element. It was a real fighting ship, and you could picture it hurling itself about in rough weather. So our hearts were really with the *Prince of Wales*. And in retrospect of course we were all, myself included, banking on the wrong ship because the *Ark Royal* was going to be the master.'

The Royal Navy had been starved of funds for over ten years, and the *Ark Royal* was an opportunity to take a great leap forward into a modern world. But one new aircraft carrier could not immediately replace the six that were currently in service, and these ships were going to have to remain with the fleet for some time. Several of them would in fact end up in action with the *Ark Royal*. All of these carriers dated from the First World War. They had been modified to some extent in 1923, but essentially they represented the very first attempts of any navy to get to grips with the invention of flight and utilize it in the fight to control the seas. The Royal Navy had been at the forefront of this revolution.

During the First World War the biggest problem confronting the Royal Navy was how to remove the threat of the German Navy, which had grown under the Kaiser to rival the British Home Fleet. It is difficult now to comprehend the size of the two fleets that opposed each other in 1914. The only major battle between them was in the North Sea, at the battle of Jutland in 1916, and this remains the largest fleet action in all history. The British Home Fleet was composed of thirty-seven battleships and over fifty destroyers, while the German High Seas Fleet was almost the same size, smaller than the British fleet by just six battleships. The battle, despite massive losses in terms of ships and men, was inconclusive, and the German fleet was able to return to port. Admiral David Beatty commanded one part of the Home Fleet, and historians still argue today about whether he or his commanding officer John Jellicoe was responsible for the tactical failures that allowed the German fleet to escape annihilation.

Whatever the truth, Beatty replaced Jellicoe as the First Sea Lord, and he quickly seized on the idea that an attack by torpedo-carrying aircraft on the German fleet while it was in harbour might be the only opportunity to defeat them. Negotiations started with the aircraft manufacturers to develop aircraft to carry out this type of attack. In the meantime, HMS *Furious*, one of three cruisers specially built to shell the German mainland from the Baltic, was converted into a seaplane carrier. This was no great loss for the Home Fleet. The ships carried enormous guns in two turrets fore and aft, but they were lightly built to go fast in the shallow waters of the Baltic, and their hulls were often damaged in rough seas. The forward gun turret of *Furious* was removed, and a hangar for the aircraft and a wooden flight deck was built that projected over the bows of the ship. Aircraft could fly off, carry out their mission and ditch beside the ship, or return to an airbase on land. Seaplanes, mounted on wheeled trolleys, could take off from the flight deck, and on their return would land on the sea and be hoisted back on board. The *Furious* became in effect the Royal Navy's first aircraft carrier, entering service in 1917.

Aviation attracted the wild and adventurous in its early years, and one flight officer on board the *Furious*, Commander Edwin Harris Dunning, thought it ought to be possible to land an aircraft on the flight deck. Aircraft landed at a relatively low speed in those days, and if the ship was steaming into the wind at full power there would be little difference in their relative speeds. Dunning approached the ship in his aircraft and side-slipped so that he was almost stationary above the flight deck. At the last minute deckhands grabbed hold of the plane and he cut the engine, settling onto the deck. Commander Dunning had made history as the first person to land an aircraft onto a moving ship. The difficulty and danger of this feat was demonstrated by Dunning's third landing, when he crashed into the sea and drowned.

He had, however, demonstrated what was possible, and a year later the rear turret on *Furious* was removed and another flight deck was added, so that now wheeled aircraft could land and take off in safety. But the funnel and bridge of the ship were kept in place, which split the flight deck in two. It was obviously preferable to have an uninterrupted flight deck stretching the length of the ship, and two further carriers, the *Argus* and *Eagle*, were ordered, both, like the *Furious* before them, based on the hulls of ships that were already being built in the ship-yards. They were completed with flight decks that ran the whole length of the ship.

On 19 July 1918, the newly modernized *Furious* went into action in an operation that would be closely imitated by the *Ark Royal* twenty-two years later. Aircraft carried on the *Furious* launched a bombing attack on German Zeppelin sheds at Tondern, a small town close to the North Sea in what is now part of Denmark. Seven Sopwith Camels carrying two 50lb bombs each managed to destroy two Zeppelins and their shed, and set fire to a second shed. Only four aircraft returned; two others crash-landed and one plane was lost, but the very first attack by aircraft from a carrier at sea was judged to be a success. The Armistice was signed before Beatty's more ambitious plan to attack the German High Seas Fleet could be carried out, but the Navy had clearly grasped with both hands the opportunities presented by aircraft.

HMS *Argus*, with its flush flight deck, was delivered shortly after the war. Having a full-length flight deck had clearly raised some problems in terms of where to put the funnels and the bridge and mast. The designers solved this problem by fitting a retractable chart room that could be raised when the flight deck was not being used, and by taking the funnel exhausts under the flight deck to the rear of the ship. The second carrier, HMS *Eagle*, delivered several years later in 1924, was built with the funnel and superstructure on the starboard, or right side, of the flight deck. Trials using model ships in wind tunnels had shown that placing the funnel in this position caused least turbulence from the hot exhaust gases for aircraft landing at the stern of the ship. This solution is the one that has been adopted by almost every other carrier in the world. A third carrier, HMS *Hermes*, which had been started at the same time as the *Eagle*, was also commissioned into service in 1923. She was a small ship of about 10,000 tons, and no other designs for such a small carrier were ever contemplated.

Finally, the Navy's carrier fleet was substantially re-inforced in 1924 when those First World War Cinderellas *Courageous* and *Glorious*, the two sister ships of HMS *Furious*, were themselves converted to carriers, and *Furious* went through a radical rebuild. *Courageous* and *Glorious* had the funnel and the superstructure, now known as the 'island', in the same position as the *Eagle* and *Hermes*. They were much bigger carriers, able to operate four squadrons of aircraft – thirty-two or thirty-six in total. They also had deck lifts, and the lower deck where the planes were stored opened on to a lower flight deck that extended over the front of the ship so that planes could land

and take off simultaneously. These carriers had many of the refinements, such as arrestor wires, that were incorporated in the *Ark Royal*, but none was as big or fast or looked so advanced and modern as the *Ark*.

There was, then, a rich experience in the Navy upon which the creators of the *Ark Royal* could draw, but the biggest influence on the newest aircraft carrier in the fleet was a wholly negative one, and that was the total removal from the Navy of the Naval Air Service. In 1918, on 1 April, the Royal Air Force was created, and at a stroke fifty-five thousand officers and men of the Royal Naval Air Service and some two and a half thousand aircraft were taken over by the new service. A protocol was worked out whereby the Navy would operate the ships but the RAF would supply the aircraft, the air crew and the mechanics to operate them. From then on there was constant conflict between the Admiralty and the new Air Ministry which started to affect the quality and numbers of aircraft that became available to the Navy.

This conflict came to a head in 1933 with the appointment of Lord Chatfield as the First Sea Lord. As Admiral in charge of the Mediterranean Fleet, Chatfield had been an enthusiastic proponent of air power. The carriers under his command, *Eagle*, *Furious* and *Glorious*, were totally integrated into the fleet, and they constantly carried out exercises during which carrier aircraft attacked surface vessels. The air crew of the Mediterranean Fleet became a highly experienced élite, and the exercises that were carried out in the late 1920s and early 1930s formed the basis of many future wartime operations. When Chatfield became First Sea Lord, he lobbied hard for an autonomous naval air force arguing that flying had become very sophisticated and maritime operations needed special skills. He drummed up the support of many senior politicians in Parliament, and Winston Churchill wrote to him saying that he 'intended to press continually in the House of Commons for the transfer of control of the Fleet Air Arm to the Admiralty'. Finally, in a last desperate bid to defeat the Air Ministry, Lord Chatfield threatened to resign as First Sea Lord if the Navy was prevented from taking control of its own aircraft. The Fleet Air Arm became once more part of the Navy from the start of 1937.

On the plans for the *Ark Royal* drawn up in 1934, before this change of control took place, there are specific references to Royal Air Force mechanics' spaces, locker rooms and so on – an indication of the extent to which the separate commands would have affected the running of the ship. It is hard to say how damaging this nineteen-year separation was to the Fleet Air Arm and the Navy. The lack of a common experience, of shared custom and practice, even the absence of a common career path, must have had an effect on the character of the Fleet Air Arm. Its effect on the Navy itself was greater. Sixty years later Fleet Air Arm veterans still talk of the difficulties they experienced on board a ship, even on those carriers that had served under Chatfield in the Mediterranean.

Swordfish pilot John Welham, a chain smoker now in his nineties with the intelligence and energy he had during the war still apparent today, told me, 'Even on the *Eagle* some of the more senior officers were definitely anti-flying. You messed up the ship, you know, so the attitude was not entirely pleasant. Some people were actively unpleasant.' Percival Bailey, or Val as he prefers to be known, was just thirteen years old when he was sent to Dartmouth, the training school for naval officers. Now in his eighties, he retains the wit and easy confidence that took him later in his career to embassy posts in Buenos Aires and Washington. According to Val, the majority of officers in the Navy held similar views to the shipyard workers of Cammell Laird. Battleships were what the Navy was about, battleships meant gunnery, and the gunnery branch dominated the Navy. 'The gunnery world thought that the aeroplane was a waste of money, that this wasn't the job,' he said. 'They didn't want carriers – they take up too much money, they have to turn into the wind and go in another direction, and they are always a bloody nuisance.'

The truth was that the Royal Navy was steeped in tradition, and that played a fundamental role in the way officers in the Navy saw themselves, and indeed in the way the Navy was viewed by the rest of the people in Britain. Val Bailey saw himself as representing something great. 'We had ruled the empire for two hundred years,' he said, 'and the Royal Navy was the world's navy in those days. I presumed everyone else in the world wanted to be a Royal Navy officer so I behaved very kindly to everyone thinking they were very unfortunate to be who they were. I was at the jubilee review, where the Home Fleet assembled, and I remember feeling this tremendous pride in the Navy. The white ensigns stretched for miles.' That emotion appealed to others who weren't necessarily going to become part of the officer class. Vic Walsh, a solid, no-nonsense chap who joined the Navy before the outbreak of war and stayed in it for thirty years, had grown up in Portsmouth. 'As a boy I remember lying in bed on a Sunday morning and hearing the sailors on their way to divisions, and you could hear their boots on the pavement, and their medals clinking. You did feel proud.' So the Navy in which the *Ark* was built to serve was one that was fairly certain of its importance in the world, and could be quite suspicious of aircraft and aircraft carriers.

When the design of the *Ark Royal* was finalized in 1934 it was expected that she would operate in the Far East, where Japanese rearmament and territorial ambitions were seen by the British government as a threat to India and imperial outposts like Singapore and Malaya. Yet almost immediately events in the Mediterranean overturned the calculations of the Admiralty. The Mediterranean Fleet was the Navy's second largest after the Home Fleet, and the maintenance of such a large force was justified on several grounds; it served to defend British interests in the Suez Canal and in the oilfields of Mesopotamia, which were of vital importance for fuelling the Navy. The Mediterranean Fleet could more easily reach Asia and the Indian Ocean if necessary, and could rapidly reinforce the Home Fleet as well.

In 1934, the Italian fascist government under Mussolini attempted to enlarge its North African empire by threatening to invade Abyssinia, or Ethiopia as it is now known, which was on the borders of the Italian colony of Somalia. An incident over a border post had occurred in December 1934, and Italy was in belligerent mood. Italian forces finally invaded in October 1935, which led to the mobilization of the Mediterranean Fleet. The League of Nations met with the intention of imposing sanctions on the Italian regime, and Britain sent the battleships *Hood* and *Rodney* to Gibraltar and *Resolution* and *Despatch* to Alexandria in Egypt.

Italian troopships were constantly passing through the Suez Canal to the exasperation of the admirals in charge of the Mediterranean Fleet, Sir William Fisher and Vice Admiral Andrew Cunningham, who wanted to blockade the canal. They had plans, should war break out, to make a sweep with strong naval forces of cruisers and destroyers up the east coast of Sicily and into the southern entrance of the Straits of Messina to bombard harbours and port installations. Indeed, France and Britain had the forces available to make sure that sanctions against Italy were enforced, but neither government had the political will to do so. Rather than adopt an aggressive policy towards Italy, the threat of war caused a re-evaluation of the Navy's position in the Mediterranean. The fleet's headquarters were in Valletta, Malta, which was only 60 miles from airbases in Sicily, so the Admiralty decided to move the fleet to Alexandria in Egypt. At the height of the international crisis air-raid precautions, including a blackout, were enforced in Valletta. So sanctions, or rather the collective will to enforce them, failed, and the Italians succeeded in their invasion. In May 1936 the Emperor of Ethiopia, Haile Selassie, was evacuated from Djibouti by HMS *Enterprise* and taken to Haifa.

In July of the same year, 1936, fascist forces in Spain under General Franco began their attempt to overthrow the Republican government. By the end of the month there were thirty-six British warships stationed in Spanish ports and in Gibraltar. This time a naval blockade was mounted, to prevent supplies from reaching either side in the civil war, but the German and Italian regimes were determined to see a fascist victory in Spain, and the Italian Navy in particular adopted an extremely aggressive policy at sea. Italian submarines torpedoed civilian ships they suspected of supplying Republican forces, and at times threatened British warships attempting to protect shipping. The Royal Navy also helped evacuate thousands of civilian refugees from the areas affected by the fighting. Val Bailey was serving as a junior officer on the old battleship HMS *Resolution* during the war and is unsure what was most disturbing, the conditions on board the ship or the impact of the conflict on civilians. 'And I was lucky enough, or unlucky enough, to be lent to a destroyer to go in and try to take off some of the Brits in Bilbao. I am seventeen years old and I'm actually seeing women tearing their clothes off to try and get a place in the boat to get away from the Spaniards. [The ship] was at war complement. It was an absolutely stinking ship. The hammocks in those ships absolutely touched each other from one end to the other. The decks were awash because the barbettes on the side weren't waterproof. The stench was not good. And I went down to report sunset to the captain who I had never met, and his cabin was enormous. I remember thinking, I'm not sure that this is absolutely right.'

Thus, when the *Ark Royal* was finally ready to be handed over to the Navy, in the four years that had elapsed between the first drawings being delivered to Cammell Laird and the completion of the carrier the world had been transformed. When the *Ark* was first thought of, the Royal Navy had little control over its aircraft and air crew; now the squadrons that would land on board would be under the control of the Navy for the first time in two decades. Far more crucially, the distant threat of conflict in the Far East had become a much more present threat of war, much closer to home. The Mediterranean was no longer a safe haven for the second largest fleet in the Navy, but a potentially hostile sea. The threat from Germany had also flourished.

Ron Skinner was one of the first crew members to board the *Ark Royal* for her trials in November 1938. A small, quiet man, he speaks forcefully, with a precise command of the English language. He fell in love with the ship at first sight. 'We went up by train from Portsmouth barracks,' he recalled. 'In those days there was a railway siding in the barracks. It took us to Birkenhead, and we marched under the tunnel into Cammell Laird's yard and there was this immense ship overhanging everything. It was quite awe-inspiring. It was absolutely wonderful inside. She was a wonderful and beautiful ship.' Royal Marine gunner Les Asher, now severely deafened as a result of his wartime service, was also part of the first steaming party. 'I got off the train at Gladstone dock and the ship was just being cleaned out. Lady cleaners were sweeping up and crockery was being unpacked in the mess. It was a brand-new ship. When I first saw the ship I was amazed. I thought, by Christopher, this is big. How are we going to find our way around this? But eventually, of course, we did.'

The *Ark Royal* was handed over to her first command-ing officer, Captain Arthur Power, on 16 November 1938. Ron Skinner remembers Captain Power, just two months later in January 1939, clearing the lower decks so that he could address the ship's crew. 'I remember to this day; it sent shivers down my spine. He said, "Is there any man here with his hand on his heart who can say that we will not be at war in six months?" He said, "It's my job to get this ship welded together as a fighting ship."'

3

'WHERE IS THE *ARK ROYAL*?'

In conversations with men who served on the *Ark Royal* during the Second World War almost inevitably at some point they will describe their fellow crew members as friendly and helpful, and call the *Ark* 'a lucky ship'. Its 'luck' quickly became part of its legend – and, as we will see, with good cause.

In 1939 there were more famous ships in the Royal Navy than the *Ark*. HMS *Hood*, the largest battleship then afloat, was known around the globe. The *Hood*, the flagship of the Royal Navy, had embarked on a world cruise in 1936, visiting the outposts of the empire, travelling down the west coast of the United States and through the Panama Canal, flying the flag and seeking to impress the world with the undimmed power of Britain's navy. But John McCrow, who joined the ship in 1939 as a newly qualified nineteen-year-old engine room artificer, or ERA, told me he had already heard that the *Ark* was known as the 'Daily Mirror Ship', because of her frequent mentions in the press. He clearly remembers watching the launch ceremony in newsreels in his local cinema in the small Scottish town of Carnoustie. He never imagined that two years later he would be walking up the *Ark*'s gangplank, the flight deck towering above him. He was particularly impressed by the experience of the crew. 'The Chief ERA had been on board since she was handed over by Cammell Laird, and knew every pipeline, every nut and bolt on the ship. I never met a better chief in the rest of my service.'

The Admiralty knew the value of publicity, but the *Ark Royal*'s fame was not sparked by anything the Navy deliberately did, although in April 1939 a film crew from Movietone News had been shown around the carrier by her captain, Arthur Power. In large part her celebrity arose from Nazi propaganda, which was to have some unintended consequences for the German Navy a little later. That she was a lucky ship, or more to the point had a lucky crew, was something that also quickly became apparent as a result of enemy action.

In 1939, on Good Friday, the Italian Army invaded Albania. The Spanish Civil War ground relentlessly on. But the main threat to peace in Europe was coming from German expansion in central Europe. Both the French and British governments had declared that they would come to the aid of Poland if Hitler moved into Polish territory. Throughout 1939 there was a sense that Europe was poised on the brink of war.

Compared with the Royal Navy the German Navy was still modestly sized, with just two battlecruisers, the *Scharnhorst* and *Gneisenau*, and a further eight cruisers, ships that were roughly the size of HMS *Belfast* (now moored on the Thames), though with larger guns. There were also thirty-one destroyers, but perhaps the most threatening to the Royal Navy was a submarine fleet of fifty-seven U-boats. Two large battleships were being built in shipyards in Kiel, the *Bismarck* and the *Tirpitz*, and when they were ready they were going to be very fast, very well-armed ships, but they were not expected to be in service until the end of 1940. The German Navy had also built three so-called 'pocket battleships', designed to sidestep the various international treaties limiting not only the size of the German fleet as a whole but that of their biggest ships. These three ships, *Graf Spee*, *Admiral Scheer* and the *Deutschland*, were small, fast ships carrying six guns that fired 28cm shells, which could cause an enormous amount of damage but weren't big enough to seriously threaten a large battleship, with its thick armour. The pocket battleships were not designed to confront other warships anyway; their main purpose was to roam the seas attacking merchant ships and poorly protected convoys. They were powered not by steam but by diesel engines, and they could travel great distances before refuelling.

As Hitler's plans to invade Poland matured during the summer of 1939, the German Navy began its preparations for war. On 23 August the pocket battleships, each accompanied by a fast supply ship, set sail, heading for positions in the world's oceans where they could threaten major trade routes. The U-boat fleet also put to sea.

It was always intended that the *Ark*, and the other carriers, would operate as part of the main battle fleet, best described as a combination of warships that could be defeated only by a similar combination of other enemy ships. It was the cornerstone of Britain's naval strategy. Historically, it was the main battle fleet that guaranteed control of the seas, and which secured Britain her resources from overseas trade and the empire. The security of these supply routes was the lifeline that afforded Britain some immunity from the depredations of war on the European land mass. And the key to the main battle fleet was the battleship – the Navy's ultimate weapon. This was not the result of some purblind conservatism in Britain's senior service; it was a generally held principle in most other navies.

It was against this backdrop that the Royal Navy eagerly embraced carriers and their aircraft, first and foremost as an aid to the battleships. The Admiralty saw that the carriers could make a vital contribution to the potency of a battle fleet. Aircraft could patrol far in 'vance of the fleet and locate enemy ships. They could attack the enemy fleet and prevent it from escaping, and once battle between the two fleets was joined they could report on the positions of elements of the enemy fleet, the movement of various ships, and, finally, direct the fire from their own battleships' big guns. In short, the carriers' aircraft were expected to control the airspace over the fleet and over a battle so that battleships could be more effective in a grand naval conflict. One thing aircraft were not expected to do was act as a substitute for the main fleet in its task of securing control of the sea. The carrier was there to support the main fleet. The *Ark Royal* would soon change that perception.

Various reports produced by the Admiralty during the 1930s estimated that in order to carry out this support task effectively at the height of a major fleet battle, as many as nine reconnaissance aircraft would need to be in the air at any one time, with six fighters to defend them. This intensity of aircraft activity would need to be maintained for many hours, if not days. One staff paper produced in 1930 called for a Fleet Air Arm totalling 405 tactical aircraft, at a time when the existing six carriers in the fleet could carry only 250 in all. It had taken almost nine years to find the money to build the *Ark Royal*; it would never be possible for the Navy to find the money for another five similar ships. To overcome this problem of resources, the Navy hoped to build aircraft that could be catapulted from other ships in the fleet, and cruisers and battleships were built with or adapted to have the ability to launch their own aircraft.

By 1939, the Admiral in Charge of Naval Aviation, Rear Admiral Reginald Henderson, a strong advocate of the Fleet Air Arm, had introduced a policy of using more than one carrier in fleet exercises, creating for the first time the possibility of integrated sea and air operations. Despite all the work of various committees and planners, however, in a moment of revealing candour the Director, Naval Air Division admitted in a memorandum dated January 1939 to Admiral Sir Charles Forbes, the Commander in Chief of the Home Fleet, 'We have no practical experience in the operation of modern aircraft with a fleet.' When war started, the *Ark Royal* was going to have to make up the rule book as it went along.

The Home Fleet of the Royal Navy, to which the *Ark Royal* was now attached, sailed to its war stations on 24 August. Under the command of Admiral Sir Charles Forbes, the fleet comprised four battleships, three battle-cruisers, two aircraft carriers, the *Ark* and *Furious*, five cruisers and three destroyer flotillas. On 3 September, the day when war with Germany was officially declared, it had just completed a sweep of the seas to the west of Britain and was returning to Scapa Flow, its base in the Orkneys. Ron Skinner was on the *Ark*, and he remembers the announcement of war made by Captain Power over the ship's public address system: 'Do you hear there? This is the captain speaking. I have just received the order to commence hostilities against

Germany.' I asked Ron if he had felt any uneasiness now that he was at war and, in a sense, on the front line. Dismissively, he replied, 'We were not surprised in the slightest, or alarmed. It was something we had been expecting.' Val Bailey remembers being more excitable, although he was in a hospital ward in Gibraltar at the time. 'Almost immediately I heard an air-raid siren. I sprang into action, and there I was, this nineteen-year-old moving quite ill people out of their beds to evacuate them to an air-raid shelter. Then a senior doctor came in and told me to mind my own bloody business.'

The war at sea started in deadly earnest within hours of the formal declaration of hostilities, and the advance manoeuvres of the German fleet paid off. A passenger ship, the SS *Athenia*, had sailed from Glasgow on the morning of 3 September bound for Montreal. A German U-boat, *U-30*, sighted the ship when it was 250 miles north-west of Ireland, and despite orders from the German Naval High Command not to sink unarmed vessels without warning the captain of the U-boat, Lieutenant Commander Lemp, fired two torpedoes at the ship. One hundred and twelve passengers, including twenty-eight American citizens, and crew of the *Athenia* were killed – the first casualties of the new war between Germany and Great Britain.

It was immediately obvious that the U-boats that had already taken up their positions around the British Isles were going to present a very serious threat. The

Admiralty put into effect a convoy system to defend merchant shipping, but there was still a large number of ships in transit to British ports, and they were perfect targets for the U-boats. In the first week of the war, 65,000 tons of merchant shipping was sunk.

Winston Churchill had been a persistent critic of the Chamberlain government and its policy of appeasement. Now, with war finally breaking out, Chamberlain, in an attempt to silence a powerful and vocal critic, brought Churchill into the War Cabinet, putting him in charge of the Navy as First Lord of the Admiralty. Churchill knew it was absolutely vital to blunt the U-boat menace. German troops were continuing their blitzkrieg in Poland, but the only direct conflict between British and German forces was at sea. If the U-boat campaign against British shipping was successful, it would cause serious damage to British morale and encourage those voices in the Cabinet who believed that the war was an avoidable mistake. There was a severe shortage of escort ships and anti-submarine warships so Churchill moved twelve destroyers from the Mediterranean Fleet to help strengthen the anti-submarine patrols. In addition, three aircraft carriers, *Courageous*, *Hermes* and *Ark Royal*, were mobilized as the nucleus of 'hunter-killer groups' to actively search for and sink the hostile U-boats. The *Ark Royal* with a group of destroyers patrolled the North Western Approaches, where the *Athenia* had been hit, and the other two groups were stationed to the south of

Ireland, the Western Approaches. Churchill likened these hunter-killer groups to a cavalry division. It was an extremely risky strategy, and a task for which the carriers had never been intended. In theory, aircraft from the carriers could search large areas of ocean, forcing the submarines to remain submerged, but in practice the carriers themselves were targets. These large, expensive ships had been placed in grave danger.

On 14 September the radio operators on the *Ark Royal* received a dramatic signal for help from a steamship, the SS *Fanad Head*. It said that the ship was being pursued by a surfaced U-boat at a position about two hundred miles away from the *Ark* near Rockall Bank. The *Ark* carried five squadrons of aircraft on board, and usually a squadron was made up of twelve aircraft. There were two squadrons of Skuas, a fighter/dive bomber, and three squadrons of Swordfish, a large, single-engine biplane used as a reconnaissance torpedo bomber. All squadron numbers in the Fleet Air Arm began with 8, followed by a 0 if the squadron was a fighter squadron and 1 if it was a torpedo reconnaissance squadron. A flight of three Skua aircraft from 803 Squadron took off, each armed with a single 100lb bomb and four small 20lb bombs under their wings. Immediately the Skuas had taken off, a flight of six Swordfish aircraft from 810 Squadron followed.

While these aircraft were taking off, another U-boat, which had remained completely undetected by the sonar of the *Ark Royal*'s destroyer escort, was lining up the carrier in its attack periscope. The captain of *U-39*, almost unable to believe his good fortune at having such an enormous target in his sights, fired two torpedoes from his forward torpedo tubes, directly at the sides of the *Ark Royal*. Fortunately, the lookouts on the *Ark* were alert. The wake of the torpedoes was spotted by Signalman Hall, who shouted the alarm. Captain Power on the bridge ordered the helm hard over, turning the bows towards the tracks to present the smallest possible target. The torpedoes missed, one of them exploding harmlessly astern. The destroyers, positioned around the *Ark* so as to screen her from exactly this sort of attack, then located the submarine on their sonar and moved in for the kill, dropping depth charges and forcing the submarine, now badly damaged, to the surface. Forty-nine of her crew were rescued before the submarine sank. The *Ark* had just claimed the first U-boat to be sunk in the war. It was an enormous boost to the morale of everybody on board. But she had been incredibly fortunate to survive this attack. Her reputation as a lucky ship grew from here.

The aircraft that had taken off to find the *Fanad Head* had spread out to search the area, and the first Skua to spot the ship was piloted by Lt Richard Thurston. The U-boat was *U-30*, the same submarine that had torpedoed the *Athenia*. Her commander, Lieutenant Commander Lemp, had fired a shot from his deck gun at the *Fanad Head*, which had come to a stop, but he had allowed its crew to take to the lifeboats and had sent a four-man party to board the cargo ship to salvage food for his submarine, and then to lay demolition charges. Lt Thurston saw the submarine on the surface and in a split second decided to drop his bombs on it; but he was so low that splinters from the explosions hit his plane, setting it on fire. He crashed into the sea. He and his observer, Petty Officer James Simpson, managed to get out of the cockpit, but only Thurston succeeded in reaching the *Fanad Head*. Exhausted, burned and almost overcome by the cold, he was pulled on board by one of the German boarding party.

The submarine, surprised and alarmed by the sudden arrival of the Skua aircraft, had crash-dived, leaving a crew member floating in the sea (he too had swum to the *Fanad Head*). The second Skua to arrive on the scene attempted to bomb what the pilot, Lt Commander Dennis Campbell, believed was the submarine just under the surface. Then he signalled to the ship's crew in the lifeboats that help was near, and returned to the *Ark*. The submarine surfaced again just as the third Skua flew low over the *Fanad Head*. The pilot, Lt Guy Griffiths, reacted instantly and he too dropped his bombs at low altitude. Their explosions ripped his rear fuselage apart, and he crashed into the sea. His observer, Petty Officer George McKay, was trapped in the aircraft as it sank, but Lt Griffiths also made it to the *Fanad Head*, which now had five German seamen from *U-30* on board and the two pilots from the crashed Skuas.

U-30 surfaced once more, and Lt Commander Lemp

told the two pilots to jump into the sea with the boarding party, because he was going to torpedo the boat. No sooner had they been dragged aboard the submarine than the first of the six Swordfish aircraft from the *Ark* were spotted. *U-30* dived again, and Lt Commander Lemp fired a torpedo at the *Fanad Head*, which broke in two and sank. One of the pilots, Michael Lawrence, had already dropped his bombs on what he believed was a submerged U-boat shortly after taking off from the *Ark*, so he could only fire his machine gun and drop a smoke float, but the other Swordfish attacked the submarine with their bombs. *U-30* was damaged, but she managed to escape, reaching Iceland a few days later where a severely wounded crew member was put ashore. Then Lt Commander Lemp took his submarine back to port in Germany. The British pilots were taken by the Gestapo and placed in a prisoner-of-war camp.

The *Ark* returned in triumph to Loch Ewe, and the story of the first German U-boat to be sunk in the war was splashed across the front pages of the Sunday papers. Churchill visited the *Ark Royal*, where the crews of all the warships that had taken part in the sinking of the *U-30* were assembled for an inspection by the First Lord of the Admiralty. It was a vindication of the ingenious policy of using carriers to hunt submarines and an extremely important boost to morale.

Churchill returned to London by train the next day, where he was met on the platform by Sir Dudley Pound, the First Sea Lord. What Pound had to tell his political master was extremely serious, and he wanted to be the first to break the news to Churchill. On 17 September the aircraft carrier HMS *Courageous*, one of the three big cruiser conversions, had been patrolling with an escort of destroyers off the south-west coast of England when a U-boat fired two torpedoes at her. They had both hit their target, and one of the Royal Navy's precious carriers and its aircraft had sunk in just fifteen minutes, taking 519 crew to their deaths. The *Ark Royal*, of course, had only narrowly avoided a similar fate. The sinking of *Courageous* spelled the end to the use of carriers against U-boats, and the hunter-killer groups were disbanded.

Before the start of the war, there had been a serious debate at senior level in the Navy about the different types of aircraft needed on a carrier, and how many squadrons of each type should be carried. At the core of this dispute the single most important question was how the fleet could defend itself against air attack. The traditional view was to rely on anti-aircraft fire. This view came under attack from Reginald Henderson, the Rear Admiral Aviation, in 1934, when he raised the question of increasing the numbers of fighter aircraft in the Fleet Air Arm. He had analysed the results of aircraft operations in the First World War and discovered that 95 per cent of aircraft shot down were the victims of aerial combat. Anti-aircraft artillery seemed largely ineffective.

The Tactical School in Portsmouth considered the question, and disagreed. Their view was that air interception was too unreliable to be a dependable defence against air attack. It was better, they argued, to rely on massed anti-aircraft batteries.

Many former Fleet Air Arm pilots have suggested to me that the problem was the dominance of the gunnery branch in the Navy, and that the believers in the battleships and their big guns were not prepared to accept that they were vulnerable to air attack. There may be some truth in this, but it is also true to say that aircraft were becoming faster, and without radar the warning time available to launch aircraft against an attacking force of bombers was inadequate. The belief that gunnery was the key to attack from the air was still firmly embedded in December 1939. The Commander in Chief of the Mediterranean Fleet, Admiral Sir Andrew Cunningham (based in Alexandria), felt able to write in a letter to Sir Dudley Pound, who had suggested that the fleet might be easy prey to enemy bombers, 'I hope your new doubts about battleships and aircraft is unduly pessimistic. As far as I know not a single hit has been made on a Navy target and surely our battleships have been constructed and reconstructed to stand up to a bomb or two. The answer is a considerable improvement in the quality and quantity of the ships' anti-aircraft fire.' Before long Admiral Cunningham would be forced to eat his words.

On 24 September, ten days after the *Ark Royal*

narrowly avoided two torpedoes, a British submarine, HMS *Spearfish*, was severely damaged by a prolonged depth charge attack by German destroyers in the Kattegat, the stretch of water between Denmark and Sweden. The submarine evaded her pursuers and surfaced, but was so damaged that she had to remain on the surface for the voyage back to port. As she made her way home, she was met first by a group of destroyers and then by the *Ark Royal*, with the battleships *Rodney* and *Nelson*, who escorted the submarine the rest of the way.

The three large ships, which together comprised an important part of the Home Fleet, were shadowed by a group of German Dornier seaplanes slowly circling at a safe distance from anti-aircraft fire. A flight of three Skuas took off from the *Ark* to intercept them, and they succeeded in shooting down one of the reconnaissance aircraft. This again was one for the record books: it was the first German aircraft to be shot down in the war, and once again the *Ark Royal* could claim the credit. However, the small force of valuable capital ships had been spotted and it was reasonable to expect that the Luftwaffe would attempt to mount an attack very shortly.

Despite the fact that the Skuas had been flown off the flight deck to shoot down the reconnaissance seaplanes, Vice Admiral Lionel Wells, the Vice Admiral Aviation, who was on board the *Ark* at the time, made no attempt to set up an air patrol of fighters to intercept any attacking bomber force. Instead, all aircraft were recalled and struck down into the hangars, where they were drained of fuel to reduce the risk of fire if the ship was hit – further evidence of the deep-seated belief that the correct defence against air attack was anti-aircraft fire.

Within the hour five Heinkel twin-engine bombers approached and were met with a barrage of anti-aircraft fire from the *Ark* and her escort. The *Ark* had been well armed to defend herself against this sort of attack. There were the sixteen 4.5-inch guns that could fire shells set to explode at a predetermined height, there were multiple cannons that fired 20mm shells at any individual aircraft making low approaches, and finally there were the machine guns mounted fore and aft to deter dive bombers. In addition to all this, of course, the destroyers and the battleships were firing their anti-aircraft guns at the approaching planes. The first four bombers took evasive action, but despite the massive ack-ack onslaught the pilot of the fifth Heinkel persisted in his attack until the *Ark* was in his bomb aimer's sights, and he released a large 1,000kg bomb. A bomb of this size would easily have penetrated the *Ark Royal*'s thinly armoured flight deck and caused mayhem inside the hangar decks, killing seamen, destroying planes and starting devastating fires.

Several of the *Ark*'s crew saw the bomb fall. Ron Skinner, who was on the bridge, recalls it well. 'All I can say at that moment is that it looked as big as a bus,' he said. 'It was heading straight for us, and I do not know how it missed.' In a classic manoeuvre, the captain ordered a hard turn to starboard and the ship heeled over. The bomb exploded with incredible force 30 metres off the port bow, producing an enormous plume of water and smoke that rose high in the air. Ron felt the ship lift out of the water, and a tremor travelled along her length. She rolled sideways, and clouds of smoke and soot were blasted out of the funnel. She seemed to hang at this acute angle for a lifetime as water from the blast cascaded onto the flight deck. Inside the ship everything toppled and crashed to the floor – books, papers, crockery, anything that wasn't secured. Then, slowly, the *Ark* righted herself.

It was another incredible near-miss, the second time in less than a fortnight that the *Ark Royal* had escaped catastrophic damage. From now on the crew were convinced that she was a lucky ship. Once again the *Ark* was in the newspapers, this time with the story of the downed German seaplane. But it was Joseph Goebbels, the Reichsminister for Propaganda and National Enlightenment, who was to set the seal on the *Ark Royal*'s celebrity status.

The pilot of the Heinkel bomber whose bomb had narrowly missed the *Ark* reported the possibility that the carrier had been severely damaged. From his point of view, and that of his crew members, it wasn't obvious that the *Ark* had managed to emerge unscathed from the plume of water. Subsequent German reconnaissance flights located two battleships but failed to find an aircraft carrier accompanying them. The propaganda machine of the Nazi government swung into action. The next day at half past five in the evening, Hamburg Radio broadcast in rather broken English: 'We have an important announcement for listeners. Where is the *Ark Royal*? She was hit in a German attack on September 26th at three p.m. Where is the *Ark Royal*? Britons, ask your Admiralty.' The claims escalated. A week later the official newspaper of the Nazi Party in Germany, the *Volkischer Beobachter*, published on its front page an illustration of the *Ark Royal*, her bows rearing out of the sea under the force of a massive explosion on her flight deck. On 26 September this same newspaper had published, under direct orders from Hitler, a story that Churchill had instructed the captain of a British submarine to torpedo the *Athenia*, hoping that it would turn the United States against Germany. The German government had its sights clearly set on Churchill and the Navy.

Churchill was extremely sensitive to the power of propaganda and took all statements made by the Nazi propaganda machine very seriously. He personally assured President Roosevelt that the claims about the *Athenia* were untrue, and told the War Cabinet at its meeting on Sunday, 1 October that the United States naval attaché in London was with the fleet and able to observe for himself that the *Ark Royal* was undamaged, moreover that the British naval attaché in Rome had paid a personal visit to the Chief of the Italian Naval Staff to reassure him that the German claims were false. The cinema newsreels, the equivalent of TV news coverage today, were also encouraged to counter the German propaganda claims.

Remarkably, Hamburg Radio and their English propaganda announcer William Joyce continued to broadcast the question 'Where is the *Ark Royal*?' The claim and counter-claim became the subject of broadcasts and newsreels around the world, and the name of the *Ark Royal* gained an international currency. It was to rebound, with double the force, against the German propagandists.

The German pocket battleship *Graf Spee* had sailed from Kiel in August, at the same time as other units of the German fleet had put to sea. With secret orders to be opened in the event of war, the *Graf Spee*'s captain Hans Langsdorff had taken up his station in the South Atlantic.

Captain Langsdorff began his war against British shipping with an attack on a liner that had sailed from the port of Pernambuco to Bahia in Brazil. The ship, the *Clement*, was stopped by the German warship, the crew was allowed to take to the boats, and then the ship was sunk by shellfire from the large 28cm main guns. The *Clement*'s crew were left in their lifeboats to make their way to the coast, but the captain and the chief engineer were taken prisoner aboard the *Graf Spee*. They were treated well, and two days later were handed over to another ship that had been stopped, a Greek freighter. They were bid a fond farewell by Captain Langsdorff and the other officers of the *Graf Spee*. The Greek ship, being neutral, was allowed to continue to its destination, St Vincent.

Captain Langsdorff was a gentleman, and he fought by the gentlemanly rules of warfare of another age. He saw his job as harassing and capturing British trade and shipping, sinking the ships but not killing sailors. He was also, however, a clever tactician, adept at turning his chivalrous instincts to his advantage. News of the *Graf Spee*'s activities in the vicinity carried by released sailors to the nearest port was useful publicity, announcing his presence in an area from which he in fact departed, leaving a false trail for his pursuers. No sooner had the officers from the *Clement* been handed over than the *Graf Spee* headed east, travelling across the South Atlantic at high speed. Within the next ten days Captain Langsdorff sank two further ships and seized two more, then doubled back on his course and headed south to rendezvous with the depot ship *Altmark* to take on fuel and fresh food.

News of the sinking of the *Clement* had reached the Admiralty shortly after it occurred, and the hunt for the raider was started. The *Ark Royal* and the battleship *Renown* were ordered into the South Atlantic. The *Ark* could carry out a search over a wide area, its aircraft able to fly over two hundred miles from the ship in all directions, but the *Graf Spee* was small and fast with a long range, and the depot ship was adept at disguising its identity as it refuelled and provisioned at various ports. Once more the *Ark Royal* found itself detached from the main fleet, searching for a lone commerce raider in the expanse of the South Atlantic – a far cry from its intended purpose of bringing an enemy battle fleet to decisive action.

After sinking a merchant ship named the *Trevanion*, the *Graf Spee* refuelled and provisioned from the *Altmark* almost in the dead centre of the South Atlantic in the last week of October 1939. Three weeks later she reappeared two thousand miles away, this time in the Indian Ocean, and sank the British tanker the *Africa Shell* off the coast of Lourenço Marques in what is now Mozambique. The crew of the tanker were again allowed to escape and make for the shore in the ship's boats. Langsdorff promptly steered a course north, deliberately passing close to a Dutch liner so that the passengers could take photos of the German warship, then headed south and once more steamed into the Atlantic.

The Royal Navy's forces were already stretched very thin. There were several carrier and battleship forces engaged in pursuit of the German raiders. As well as Force K, *Ark Royal* and *Renown*, there was *Glorious* with the battleships *Warspite* and *Malaya*; *Eagle* with two cruisers, *Gloucester* and *Cornwall*; *Hermes* in company with the French battlecruiser *Strasbourg*; *Furious* with the *Repulse*; and *Argus* with the battleship *Queen*

Elizabeth. It was remarkable testimony to the extent to which three lone raiders could tie down a large part of the Royal Navy. Apart from HMS *Eagle* in the Indian Ocean and Force K in the South Atlantic all the other task forces were in the North Atlantic. Britain also had a small detachment of four cruisers in the South Atlantic, at Port Stanley in the Falklands, under the command of Commodore Harwood: HMS *Exeter* and HMS *Cumberland* armed with 8-inch guns, and HMS *Ajax* and a New Zealand cruiser *Achilles*, both armed with 6-inch guns. Commodore Harwood believed that sooner or later the *Graf Spee* would need to take on more fuel and stores than could be carried by a single support ship, and it was likely that it would rendezvous with supply ships heading out from Montevideo or Buenos Aires. His cruisers headed north to patrol off these ports.

The *Ark Royal* and *Renown* continued to patrol in the South Atlantic, and on 1 December they headed for Cape Town to refuel. The long periods steaming at sea meant constant hard work, and wear and tear in the engine room. John Asher remembered the drudgery of the boiler rooms:

'The boiler rooms were pressurized, by fans forcing air into them from intakes under the flight deck. Airlocks were essential, for a sudden drop in pressure can cause flames from the oil sprayers to blow back into the boiler room, causing fires and serious burns to the stokers on duty.

'Each boiler has ten oil sprayers in place, and speed is

regulated by increasing or decreasing the number of sprayers operating at any time. An oil sprayer has to be frequently changed for cleaning to maintain its efficiency. Changing over oil sprayers requires thick leather gloves as all the metal parts are extremely hot. The sprayer is held in a bench vice and stripped down and all the parts are thoroughly cleaned in paraffin. It's then reassembled and made ready for use. Another stoker will be working, using a long steel poker to chip away the clinker which has built up around the edge of the combustion chamber in the boiler. It is very hard work especially when aircraft are always landing on and off, and a lot of sprayers are in use to keep up speed.

'It seems that as soon as all the combustion chambers and sprayers are cleaned, the job has to start all over again.'

As the *Ark Royal* neared the Simonstown naval base a message was received from the *Doric Star*, a British cargo vessel, saying that she was being shelled by a battleship. She gave a position that was off Walvis Bay, a port in what is now Namibia. It was 1,500 miles away, and it would take the *Ark* and *Renown* three days to reach the spot. Captain Power, of the *Ark*, decided that before he could make the run more fuel was necessary. Even if Force K went to the spot where the *Doric Star* was under attack, the *Graf Spee* would be long gone by the time they arrived. It was no way to hunt down a single ship in the expanse of the southern oceans, especially one with the speed and range of the German commerce raider.

Twenty-four hours later another distress signal was intercepted, this time from the *Tairoa*, which was sunk in a position west of the point where the *Doric Star* had been attacked. The *Graf Spee* was busy and seemed to be heading south-west. The German raider had been at sea now for over three months. Was it now time for the *Graf Spee* to meet up with other German cargo ships that were getting ready to depart from ports in South America? Vice Admiral Wells, in command of Force K, agreed with Commodore Harwood's reasoning that the most likely place for the *Graf Spee* to head for was the River Plate area between Argentina and Uruguay, with the ports of Buenos Aires and Montevideo to the north and south of the wide bay. So Force K also headed west, but on 6 December the Admiralty ordered the *Ark Royal* and *Renown* to change course and head north.

On 13 December, Commodore Harwood in the *Ajax*, with the cruisers *Exeter* and *Achilles* in formation, saw smoke on the horizon. His forces had been reduced because *Cumberland* had had to return to Port Stanley to refuel. Nevertheless, *Exeter* was sent to investigate and her captain reported, 'I think it is a pocket battleship.' After months at sea, the German battleship had finally been spotted, not by the large number of carrier and battleship task forces that had been scouring the oceans, but by a small force of ships that was significantly weaker than its quarry. Force K, with bombers, torpedo-carrying aircraft and the large guns of the *Renown*, was several days' sailing away and would not be much help to Commodore Harwood.

He decided to split his force in two, so that the captain of the *Graf Spee* would be forced to divide his fire, or ignore one of the British units, which would make it easier for them to get closer and bring the battleship in range of their smaller guns or torpedoes. The *Exeter* had bigger guns than the other two cruisers and was the first to return fire on the *Graf Spee*. Captain Langsdorff concentrated his ship's fire on *Exeter*, and the 28cm shells caused carnage. Two of her gun turrets were hit and put out of action, killing and maiming the gun crew inside. A direct hit on the *Exeter*'s bridge killed or wounded everyone except the captain, and fires broke out on the mess decks. The ship was also hit in the hull, and seawater was flowing in, causing the ship to list by seventeen degrees. *Exeter* had become a place of death and destruction, with fire, smoke and fumes filling the crew spaces, the terrible noise of exploding shells, and the firing of the one remaining turret adding to the chaos. Within an hour she had to stop firing and slow down. In the words of Captain Parry on the *Achilles*, 'My own feelings were that the enemy could do anything he wanted to. He showed no sign of being damaged. His main armament was firing accurately. The *Exeter* was out of it so he had only two small cruisers to prevent him attacking the very valuable River Plate trade.' The casualties on board *Exeter* were sixty-one dead.

With the *Exeter* crippled and no longer a threat, the *Graf Spee* did not then direct her guns against the two smaller cruisers; instead she put up a smoke screen and headed away to the west. Captain Langsdorff had quickly made a tour of his ship and decided to run for port, for the *Graf Spee* had not escaped from the battle as lightly as the British imagined. She had been hit by seventeen shells that had caused damage to the bow and killed thirty-seven German sailors. But among the senior officers on board there was some doubt as to why Langsdorff broke off the attack. Nothing vital to the ship's machinery or armament had been damaged.

Throughout the day the two cruisers *Ajax* and *Achilles* trailed the *Graf Spee*, until she reached the River Plate and anchored off Montevideo harbour. International law stated that any warships belonging to a country at war could stay in a neutral harbour for twenty-four hours without jeopardizing the host country's neutrality. If the ship stayed longer than a day it was liable to be interned, along with its crew. The British naval attaché in Montevideo, Captain Rex Miller, and an intelligence officer from the embassy sailed around the *Graf Spee* in a boat and were perplexed as to why the ship had taken refuge in the harbour. Both they and the Uruguayan authorities believed that the ship was relatively un-damaged. There was a large shell hole in the bow, but it was well above the water line, so the British ambassador requested that the Uruguayan government enforce the neutrality regulations against the *Graf Spee* – that is, order it to leave Uruguayan national waters or face internment.

However, Commodore Harwood didn't want to face the *Graf Spee* again without some reinforcements to his battered little flotilla of cruisers, and on 16 December he asked the British Embassy to do what it could to delay the departure of the German battleship. Several methods were used. A British cargo ship was instructed to leave port immediately, thus taking advantage of another convention that stated a warship from a belligerent country must not leave port within twenty-four hours of a departing merchant ship of a country involved in hostilities. The British naval attaché and the intelligence officer visited Harwood on the *Ajax*, still patrolling outside the three-mile limit. The 8-inch-gun cruiser HMS *Cumberland* had now arrived from her station in the Falklands, but this was no guarantee of overwhelming success. *Exeter* had suffered badly at the hands of the *Graf Spee*, and so too could the *Cumberland*.

As soon as the *Exeter* had first sighted the *Graf Spee* she had sent a general signal, and Force K had turned around and headed towards the impending battle. But the *Ark* and *Renown* were almost two thousand miles away at the time, and the former was also low on fuel again. Although *Renown* was better armed and more heavily protected against shellfire than the *Graf Spee*, Admiral Wells did not want to go into battle without good reserves of fuel. He made the decision to refuel at Rio de Janeiro, in Brazil. When the *Renown* and the *Ark Royal* docked at Rio the British Embassy staff in the city, eager to counter the still prevalent German propaganda about the *Ark* having been sunk by a German bomber, encouraged the local press and newsreel crews to film the ship in dock. But Rio de Janeiro was a thousand miles away, and even if Force K could make 30 knots, it would take them almost thirty-six hours to join the cruisers outside Montevideo. Captain Langsdorff must have realized this. The *Graf Spee* was loading stores quickly and had told the Uruguayan government that it would leave port the following day.

Captain Miller, the British naval attaché, then came up with a plan to throw dust in the eyes of Captain Langsdorff and the German Embassy officials in Montevideo. Fuel for the *Ark Royal* was ordered in the port of Buenos Aires in Argentina, on the other side of the River Plate. Information about this order was quickly and deliberately leaked to the press in the city, where it was immediately passed to the German Embassy in Montevideo. It naturally reached the ears of Captain Langsdorff too. Already uncertain about his course of action, the threatened presence outside the harbour of the *Ark Royal* with her companion the *Renown* tipped the balance. Langsdorff became convinced that there was no possibility of escape. In a signal to Berlin he said, 'Strategic position off Montevideo. Beside the cruisers and destroyers *Ark Royal* and *Renown*. Close blockade at night; escape into open sea and breakthrough to home waters is hopeless ... request decision on whether the ship should be scuttled in spite of insufficient depth in estuary of the Plate or whether internment is preferred.' The reply from Berlin rejected internment.

Langsdorff was correct in his assessment. There was no way out for him. However brave or skilful his crew or however fast his ship, it was inevitable he would be tailed until an overwhelming force of British ships and aircraft sank his ship and killed his men. At just after five o'clock in the evening of 17 December, the *Graf Spee* slowly steamed out of Montevideo harbour and the British cruisers altered course to meet her, no doubt with some trepidation on the part of the crew. When the *Graf Spee* was about six miles out of Montevideo she stopped her engines. Boats began to ferry the crew to a German freighter that had followed her out, and then there was a stunning explosion. In the words of Commodore Harwood, 'She was ablaze from end to end, flames reaching almost as high as the top of the control tower. A magnificent and most cheering sight.'

The German crew, in the freighter *Tacoma*, were taken to the harbour of Buenos Aires in Argentina where they remained interned for the rest of the war. Three days after the *Graf Spee* was scuttled, in his room at the Naval Arsenal in Buenos Aires Captain Langsdorff shot him-self. He understood only too well that his greatest weapon was his ability to disappear in the vastness of the southern oceans, and that once he had been found his life, and those of his crew, would be measured in days. But it was German propaganda that had made the *Ark Royal* a famous ship, and that fame had made it easier for the British Embassy in Montevideo to spread their web of deceit and misinformation, and turn the screw on Captain Langsdorff. It was the first time that ships a thousand miles away had taken part in a battle at sea.

The victory at River Plate was exceptionally welcome news for Churchill, the Admiralty and for the country as a whole. There had been a depressing series of losses at sea, caused not only by the *Graf Spee* but by the new magnetic mines U-boats were releasing around Britain. The casualties grew, and on 4 December the battleship *Nelson* had been hit and damaged. But in the three months since the start of the war the *Ark Royal* had constantly been in the newspapers and on the newsreels, and the stories had been of victories over the enemy. Only her crew knew how lucky she had been.

The *Ark Royal* and *Renown*, still hundreds of miles from the River Plate, changed course and sailed east once more, to Dakar on the African coast. After a few days' leave for the crew they put to sea again, this time bound for Portsmouth.

4

THE NORWEGIAN CAMPAIGN

By February 1940, the *Ark Royal* had returned from its lengthy voyages in the South Atlantic and was moored at the dockside in Portsmouth harbour. The almost six months that had elapsed since the start of the war with Germany had, after the initial flurry of false alarms and the panicked rush for air-raid shelters, been peaceful on the mainland. The war was not delivering the airborne destruction and chaos that had been thought inevitable, and in Britain it began to be known as the 'Bore war', or the 'funny war'.

The war at sea, however, was far from boring or funny, as the losses caused by German U-boats and pocket battleships mounted. Britain had already suffered the loss of an aircraft carrier, and a U-boat had penetrated the Home Fleet's harbour at Scapa Flow, sending the battleship *Royal Oak* to the sea bed with hundreds of her crew. There had been some victories though, and the First Lord of the Admiralty Winston Churchill had done everything in his power to make sure that these success stories were brought to the attention of the public, with triumphant headlines in the press and constant references to them in the House of Commons. The *Ark Royal*, which had brought down the first German aircraft and sunk the first U-boat, always featured heavily.

The men who were now coming aboard the *Ark Royal*, taking the place of those who had been promoted or had been transferred to other ships, knew that they were joining a ship that had started to become a legend. Robert Elkington, a signalman who had already been in the Navy for several years, joined the *Ark* from the battleship HMS *Barham*, stationed in the Mediterranean. A tall, thin man now in his eighties, with a slightly sardonic sense of humour, Robert talks slowly, perhaps as a result of the years he spent surfing the radio waves, hunting down transmissions from enemy aircraft and ships hundreds of miles away. On *Barham*, one of the elderly battleships in the Mediterranean Fleet, he listened to and copied down the coded messages of the Spanish and Italian navies, sending the results in sealed envelopes directly to the Admiralty in London. He claimed to be able to tell the nationality of a telegraphist sending Morse code from the minute variations in timing between the long and short signals that Morse comprises. As far as he is concerned, moving from an old battleship like the *Barham* to the *Ark Royal* can be summed up in one word: 'Glamour! It was sheer glamour. She had that aura. As soon as you stepped on board you knew that everybody loved the ship. Fantastic.'

From Portsmouth, the *Ark* sailed to Scapa Flow where its squadron of Skua aircraft were flown off to the naval air station at Hatston to strengthen the defences of the anchorage in the Flow. Then the *Ark* sailed south to carry out exercises with the Mediterranean Fleet.

The Skua aircraft, which had been on the *Ark* since the beginning of the war, were the most modern in the fleet. They were all metal, low-winged monoplanes with a single radial engine. The pistons were arranged in a circle around the propeller shaft, giving it a stumpy, sawn-off look at the front. The tail fin was upright, and the wings were straight and square at the ends. The Navy thought that all aircraft should carry an observer, to act as navigator, to carry out reconnaissance and to operate a rear defensive gun. As a consequence the cockpit was a lengthy structure with an upright canopy that looked more like a greenhouse than the rounded canopy of a Spitfire. The Skua was meant to be both a dive bomber and a fighter, and the general opinion of it was that it could do neither job very well. This wasn't completely true, as some of the pilots of 801 Squadron based at Hatston would prove, but the most modern fighter carried on the *Ark Royal* was certainly inferior to the best fighters in the RAF and other European air forces of the time.

The Skua had taken years to come into service and the Fleet Air Arm was paying a price for years of neglect caused by lack of funds, and the loss of control of its aircraft to the Royal Air Force. Reading some of the documents concerning the origins of the Skua now available in the National Archives, it becomes quite clear that the process by which the Navy had to acquire its aircraft from the Air Ministry was riven with distrust and incomprehension on the part of both services. The process wasn't helped by the desire on the part of the Navy to have aircraft that could be catapulted from battleships and cruisers, which meant that they had to be light in weight and fitted with floats, as well as be able to fly from aircraft carriers on a wheeled undercarriage. The Air Ministry suggested that the Navy acquire two different types of aircraft, but the Navy was unwilling to accept this for budgetary reasons. When the Air Ministry couldn't find an aircraft manufacturer to accept what was clearly an impossible design brief, the Admiralty admitted defeat and settled for an aircraft that would fly from carriers, have a considerable range and carry a crew of two. It also had to carry a 500lb bomb, as well as be able to shoot down other aircraft. At the time the Admiralty was finalizing this requirement, naval doctrine was that fighter aircraft flying from carriers would only be in combat with other carrier-based aircraft, and that their main purpose was to protect other aircraft that were acting as spotting planes during a naval battle.

So poisonous had the relationship between the Admiralty and the Air Ministry become by this point that the documents in the National Archives suggest that the final specification for the Skua was sent by the Air Ministry to its contacts in the aviation industry without the Admiralty having had an opportunity to approve it. The resulting plane was dogged by problems. When the prototype was tested, it was found that the plane had a dangerous habit of falling into an uncontrollable spin. The Air Ministry informed the Admiralty that they thought the Skua was incapable of doing its job. Blackburns, the manufacturers of the aircraft, solved the problem of the plane's stability by lengthening the fuselage, but in the Navy's eyes the plane was fatally compromised. Two other aircraft had also been placed on order: the Roc, based on the Skua airframe but with a four-gun turret mounted in the rear of the cockpit, and the Fulmar, a fighter that was earmarked to replace the Skua as the main fighter for the fleet. All these aircraft suffered massive delays in production and were extremely late in entering service.

The Admiralty were in utter despair at the state of their aircraft as war approached. One memorandum summed up the situation:

The Skua was designed four years ago by Blackburns to combine the functions of fighting and dive bombing.

This was a mistake, since the functions are incompatible, and dive bombing will not again be combined with fighting. The Roc, a two-seat fighter, and the Fulmar, a two-seat front-gun fighter, are also on order. The Fulmar is unnecessarily large since it was designed as a light bomber and was forced on us because of delays in Skua and Roc.

The Air Ministry then informed the Admiralty that the Roc was also not up to specification, and that they wanted to cancel it. This caused consternation in the Admiralty. Another internal memorandum reveals the hopelessness with which the situation was viewed:

The position from the point of view of the development of specialized aircraft is serious. No concrete advance has been made since the Nimrod and Osprey [two biplanes designed in the 1920s] started to come into service 7 years ago. If the Skuas fail and the Roc is abandoned there will be no fighter aircraft but Gladiators in the Fleet Air Arm worth mentioning until the Fulmar comes along. This may be delayed and then further deficiencies will arise.

It was out of this mess that the Skua finally entered service. Its reputation preceded it, and as an aircraft it is generally seen to be a failure, though among pilots who actually flew the Skua opinions can be more nuanced. Lt

Peter Goodfellow, who eventually became a Fulmar pilot in 808 Squadron on the *Ark Royal*, flew Skuas as part of his training and doesn't have a good word to say about them. 'The Skua was a terrible aeroplane,' he said. 'You got the feeling that if you got too slow then you were in terrible trouble because the thing would spin and spin violently. It was a pretty desperate aircraft.' On the other hand, Lt George Baldwin, who later became a squadron leader, went on to serve in the Naval Air Fighting Development Unit, and flew over ninety types of aircraft in his flying career, thinks the Skua wasn't at all bad. It was, he claims, a very easy aeroplane to deck-land, with a wonderful view. 'It was quite a modern aeroplane in many ways, but its flying controls were heavy, so to do a roll it was a good hard heave. And it was slightly under-powered. You couldn't do proper aerobatics in a Skua. It was a very good dive bomber; the dive brakes were super. You could do a seventy-degree dive with full control and it dive-bombed very accurately.'

In March 1940, George Baldwin had just finished his pilot training, and he had learned to do deck landings in the Skua on the old carrier HMS *Argus*, which then was stationed in the French port of Toulon. It wouldn't be long, however, before the deficiencies of the Skua were to be a matter of life and death for him and other air crew in the Fleet Air Arm. Britain's war with Germany was soon to become very intense.

* * *

On 7 April a German fleet set sail from harbours in northern Germany on Operation Weserübung, a lightning invasion of Denmark and Norway whose audacious aim was the capture of key points along the 1,000-mile length of the Norwegian coastline. To make sure that the invasion was perfectly co-ordinated, the forces of troop-carrying ships and escorting warships staggered their departure over two days. Those task forces heading for Narvik and Trondheim in Norway had the longest journeys to make and were the first to depart. Fourteen troop-carrying destroyers were escorted by the battleship *Scharnhorst*, with the *Gneisenau* and the heavy cruiser *Admiral Hipper* in support. Once the troops on the destroyers had been landed in Narvik, these ships would then rejoin the battlecruisers and form a major task force to defend other parts of the invasion fleet heading for more southerly ports. Another force comprising the cruiser *Admiral Hipper* and four destroyers carrying 1,700 troops was going to seize Trondheim, and again once the troops were landed the warships would re-form with *Scharnhorst* and *Gneisenau*. It was an extremely well-thought-out plan.

In command of the northbound flotilla on the *Gneisenau* was Vice Admiral Günther Lutjens, a tall man with a serious, slightly introverted character, a veteran of the German Navy from the First World War. Lutjens knew that if the Royal Navy discovered his small fleet on its long journey north to the Norwegian Arctic, he would be seriously outgunned and the invasion would fail. But various pieces of intelligence about increased activity in German ports, and information from RAF reconnaissance flights, were never correctly interpreted by the Admiralty. Lutjens had a clear run.

A further landing was planned for Bergen with the light cruisers *Konigsberg* and *Bremse*, with 1,900 troops, and landings were also to be made at the towns of Kristiansund and Arendal. The Norwegian capital Oslo was targeted by 2,000 troops in the cruiser *Blucher* and the pocket battleship *Lutzow*. These German fleet movements heralded a full-scale invasion, for once the initial assaults were completed, planned reinforcements of another 3,700 troops would arrive by cargo vessel.

Equally important to the outcome of the invasion was the part played by the Luftwaffe. Five hundred transport planes carried troops into Norway as part of a second wave of reinforcements, and within a few days a further fifty thousand troops were in place. The operation was supported by 290 bombers, 40 dive bombers and 100 fighters. It was a brilliantly executed invasion, all the disparate forces carrying out their tasks with remarkable co-ordination.

Resistance by the Norwegian forces, who were unprepared and lightly armed, was sporadic, but they still managed to cause some casualties. *Blucher* was sunk by gunfire from shore batteries at Oslo, and *Konigsberg* was hit as she approached Bergen, although the occupying troops were only temporarily delayed. The damage caused to the *Konigsberg* by the Norwegians' defensive gunfire was enough, however, to prevent her from joining up with Lutjens' fleet, and she remained in the harbour at Bergen so that the crew could carry out repairs.

The British response to the invasion of Norway was confused. News that *Scharnhorst* and *Gneisenau* had put to sea was slow to reach Admiral Sir Charles Forbes, Commander in Chief of the Home Fleet. He sailed late on 7 April but did not appreciate, and neither did the Admiralty, that the German force was part of an invasion attempt. Forbes believed that the German ships were attempting to break out into the Atlantic to attack merchant shipping, so he steamed a course to the northeast that meant he never made contact with the enemy fleet. Moreover, he did not take his aircraft carrier, HMS *Furious*, to sea with him, fearing that it would be sunk by torpedoes, just as *Courageous* had been a few months earlier. *Furious* was finally ordered to sea on 8 April by the Admiralty, but she left port without her squadron of Skua fighter aircraft.

On 9 April, Admiral Forbes's fleet was steaming north when it was attacked by a group of German bombers. *Furious* still had no fighter aircraft embarked, so the only defence available to the ships was their anti-aircraft guns, which of course, according to pre-war doctrine, were the best defence against air attack. Unfortunately this proved not to be the case, and despite some of the ships using up nearly half their ammunition stocks, bombs hit and sank the destroyer HMS *Gurkha*. Admiral Forbes had got off lightly, but he was shocked by this loss and ordered the Home Fleet to withdraw from the area controlled by German land-based aircraft. This was effectively the whole area south of Bergen, although, as the Germans strengthened their position, the reach of their aircraft spread ominously northwards up the Norwegian coastline.

The *Ark Royal*, of course, was in the Mediterranean taking part in exercises with the Mediterranean Fleet when the invasion of Norway started, and the Skua squadrons, 800 and 803, were based in Hatston in the Orkneys, defending the anchorage of the Home Fleet at Scapa Flow. One of the pilots from 800 Squadron, Lt Cdr Geoffrey Hare, had been loaned to the Royal Air Force to help with the identification of German ships. He spotted *Konigsberg* tied up at the mole in Bergen and the RAF staged an attack on the German warship with Hampden and Wellington bombers. They failed to score any direct hits on the target. When Hare returned to his squadron at Hatston, the two squadron commanders decided that the port of Bergen was within range of the Skuas, although the total journey time would be close to the limit of their endurance. There would be no spare fuel available to engage in a fight with enemy aircraft if they met any, and their navigation would need to be spot on.

On 10 April fifteen Skuas, each armed with a 500lb armour-piercing bomb, took off on the long flight over the North Sea. Approaching from the south-east at 12,000 feet, they spotted the cruiser tied up at the mole. The key to dive-bombing a ship is to attack along the length of the vessel from bow to stern. The standard way to attack was to fly over the target until it appeared at the rear of the wing, on the port side, and then, as George Baldwin described it, 'You'd roll the Skua over the vertical until you were pointing at the target. And then you'd straighten up, and to get an accurate delivery of the bomb you had to pull the nose up a little bit to allow for the fall of the bomb. Which meant you didn't actually see the target when you pressed the button to drop the bomb. It was pure judgement, or guesswork – whatever you want to call it.'

The Skua pilots had decided to split their attack, to divide any anti-aircraft fire, but their arrival took the crew of the *Konigsberg* completely by surprise. As the Skuas passed, 8,000 feet machine gunners on the *Konigsberg* did start firing, but there was no response from the other heavier anti-aircraft guns on the cruiser. The first bomb to hit the ship probably destroyed the electrical power; other bombs, most of which were on target, caused further damage, and started fires. One of the pilots who had become separated on the flight to Bergen could see when he arrived late on the scene that the *Konigsberg* was sinking by the bows with flames and a column of thick black smoke rising into the sky. The attack had been a complete success, and nearly three hours after it ended the *Konigsberg* sank.

This was the first time a major warship had been sunk by air attack, and it was an important victory for the Fleet Air Arm. Whatever doubts may have been expressed about the Skua before the aircraft entered service, it had proved extremely effective in the skies above Bergen. Admittedly one aircraft went into a spin on the way back to Hatston and crashed, but all the other aircraft returned safely, though extremely low on fuel and with some minor damage from anti-aircraft fire. It had been a successful operation carried out with great daring, stretching the performance of the crew and the Skuas to their limit. However, this victory made little difference to the overall situation that now confronted the British government. The *Ark Royal* had still not been recalled from the Mediterranean and British forces generally were in no position to take quick advantage of the loss of the *Konigsberg*, or the demoralization it had brought to the German troops in Bergen.

Shortly after the outbreak of the war, Winston Churchill, as First Lord of the Admiralty, had been arguing that Britain should cut off supplies of Swedish iron ore to Germany by invading the Norwegian port of Narvik, through which the iron ore was exported. Plans were worked up for the Navy to transport troops across the North Sea and disembark them at Narvik, although the Army had no experience of or equipment for the extreme conditions of an Arctic winter. Troops were mobilized and ships were continually being loaded for an invasion that was constantly being postponed. The indecision of the Chamberlain government was mirrored by their French counterparts, who as allies in the war against Germany quite naturally insisted on being consulted about the invasion of a neutral country.

The German invasion had now made these concerns about access to Swedish iron ore completely irrelevant. There were much bigger issues at stake now, both strategic and political. Britain and France had been at war with Germany for seven months, and if they proved incapable of preventing Hitler from taking over two more neutral countries, there would naturally be enormous pressure on the Allies, both internationally and domestically, to seek a rapprochement with Nazi Germany. The more pressing strategic issue was the enormous advantage possession of the Norwegian harbours gave to the German Navy and its U-boat fleet. At a stroke Germany had outflanked Britain and made it much harder for the U-boat menace to be contained. The need to land troops in Norway and deny Hitler a total victory was more urgent than ever, but the conditions in which the Navy had to do this had been transformed.

As Admiral Forbes had already realized, the Navy was now highly vulnerable to German bombers based in Norway. British troops had been landed at Narvik on

14 April but had been unable to move forward to confront the German troops based in the town because of deep snow. Other landings by small contingents of British troops had taken place in Trondheim fjord, in preparation for a concerted assault from the sea on the town of Trondheim itself. The Luftwaffe, however, had occupied the airfields near Trondheim and Admiral Forbes realized that they presented a serious threat to any British landings, so on the night of 16 April he sent the cruiser HMS *Suffolk* to bombard Sola airfield.

The next day *Suffolk* was heavily bombed by the Luftwaffe for over six hours. In all there were thirty-three separate attacks, by a combination of high-level bombers and dive-bombing Stukas. One large 1,000lb bomb put the *Suffolk*'s rear gun turrets out of action and caused the rear of the ship to start taking in water. Even when the *Suffolk* came within range of the Skuas based at Hatston the attacks continued. She managed to struggle back to port in Scapa Flow, dangerously low in the water, her decks awash and her crew desperately fighting to keep the ship afloat. The rudder controls were destroyed and her hull was riddled with holes made by bomb splinters. Admiral Forbes now knew that any ships trying to land troops in Trondheim would be overwhelmed by the large number of bombers the Luftwaffe could put into the sky. The plans to seize Trondheim were abandoned, which left the small forces that had been landed to the north and south of Trondheim under attack. They slowly retreated to take up defensive positions at the towns of Namsos and Andelsnes.

If any progress was going to be made in Norway by British troops, the air support to the fleet and to the troops already on the ground needed to be strengthened. The Skuas based at Hatston had been at the limit of their range when they bombed the *Konigsberg*; only carrier-based aircraft could offer support to the troops further away at Narvik and Trondheim, men dreadfully exposed to bombing and strafing by the Luftwaffe. The situation was desperate, so the *Ark Royal* and the *Glorious* were finally ordered to steam out of the Mediterranean to form a carrier task force whose orders were to 'protect naval ships and convoys, to give cover to the troops at the landing places and to attack the German-occupied airbases in Norway'.

The *Ark Royal* was at Scapa Flow on 23 April, taking on stores and landing new pilots in Skuas and Rocs. The Roc, of course, was the version of the Skua which the Air Ministry had so urgently wanted to cancel at the last minute. George Baldwin was one of the air crew who flew onto the *Ark Royal* as she steamed north-east to meet up with Admiral Forbes's Home Fleet. The *Ark* arrived in Norwegian waters on 26 April, and it wasn't long before George was flying into combat for the first time. He discovered he had the naturally aggressive instincts of a fighter pilot. 'My first operational flight was on 27 April,' he said. 'I was sent up as number two to another Skua flown by a very senior pilot because I had no experience. We were flying at 8,000 feet, which was the standard way in, and we had only just got about 20 miles inland on the patrol line, which was above the German line at Andelsnes, when I saw a Heinkel bomber below me at about 2,000 feet. So I dived, did the attack I'd been taught to do, filled it full of lead, killed both the rear gunners, and then I was too close so I did the classic fighter school breakaway. I was only nineteen.'

The carrier task group stayed well away from the coast, sometimes by as much as 120 miles, hoping to avoid attacks from bombers based on the mainland. The *Ark Royal* wasn't fitted with radar so the only warning the ship's crew received of an impending attack by approaching enemy bombers was if they had been sighted by the defensive screen of destroyers. This left almost no time to launch a section of fighters before the bombers were above the *Ark*. Some of the escorting cruisers, like the *Sheffield* and *Curlew*, however, had been fitted with radar and could spot aircraft approaching up to 50 miles away.

Signalman Robert Elkington remembers that the air group on the *Ark Royal* was quick to understand how they could benefit from radar-equipped ships. The *Ark*'s air signal officer was Lt Commander Charles Coke, an observer in the Fleet Air Arm, and he and Elkington occupied a small office under the bridge on the *Ark Royal* where signals were received from the radar operators on the *Sheffield*. The ability to identify enemy aircraft 50 miles away allowed the *Ark* to launch her aircraft with enough time for them to reach altitude and intercept the bombers, though even with this advance warning the *Ark*'s pilots found themselves at a disadvantage because of the lack of power of the Skuas and Rocs. It was a rudimentary ad hoc arrangement, limited by the fact that in order to preserve radio silence the messages between the *Ark* and the *Sheffield* were passed either by flag signal or Aldis lamp.

On 28 April a series of attacks rained down on the *Ark* by Junkers 88 and Heinkel 111 bombers flying out of German bases on the Norwegian mainland. George Baldwin had been assigned to a Roc, and he attempted to pursue one of the bombers at low level. 'It was absolutely fucking useless,' he recalled. 'The Roc was a Skua with no front guns and a turret in the back. We chased the Heinkel at nought feet across the sea – it had just dropped a load of bombs; luckily they missed the *Ark Royal*. We chased him across the sea flat out and our full speed was exactly the same as his. And every time we managed to get close and the air gunner turned the turret, the drag on the four guns made us lose 20 knots of speed immediately.'

There was a massive Luftwaffe presence in Norway, and it soon became apparent that the carrier task force was not going to defeat it. The battle in Norway had been lost. The War Cabinet in London decided to move the troops out of Trondheim, and the role of the carrier group was now to cover the withdrawal.

On 1 May, the Luftwaffe made a concerted effort to sink the *Ark Royal*. The assault was heralded at eight o'clock in the morning by a surprise attack from a Ju88 bomber that arrived totally unnoticed and dropped its load of bombs, which fortunately for those on board missed the *Ark* by about 40 metres. This was followed by another attack in the afternoon by five high-level bombers all of whose bombs missed, then very shortly after that another unseen aircraft dropped a stick of bombs that fell in a straight line in the sea, miraculously just missing the bows of the carrier but so close that the whole of the forward flight deck was covered in spray. So far the *Ark*'s famous luck was holding out.

Three hours later another formation arrived, this time a combination of dive bombers and high-level bombers. The anti-aircraft guns began to fire a barrage, particularly against the dive bombers which were potentially the more dangerous. Les Asher, the Royal Marine gunner in the rear starboard 4.5-inch anti-aircraft gun, remembers that on hearing the order 'Barrage to commence, commence, commence!' everyone 'went hell for leather. And the back of the 4.5-inch turret is open so there was always somebody looking outside to see what was happening. And all the information on the range and the fuse setting was done automatically. You lifted the shell up, put it on the tray, pushed it into a bracket and the range was set automatically, by information that came from the transmitting station that took their information from the range finder. It's rather surprising when the guns are firing. You get a really dry mouth. It's not fear, it's apprehension. There's so much going on you just get on with your job, and then you're glad when it's over. But when the guns are firing and the pom-poms start, there is always a lot of noise going on. And that, of course, is where I first lost my hearing.' The noise of that gunfire and the deep explosions of the bombs filled the air, and could be felt inside the hangars and engine rooms. Columns of water exploded all around the carriers and their escorts.

Ron Jordan, one of the armourers for 800 Squadron, vividly remembers those days the *Ark Royal* spent off Norway. 'Can you ever forget it?' he said. 'As the raids started the bugle sounded on the Tannoy and the fireproof curtains in the hangars would come down. And we could hear the 4.5's firing. Then of course the pom-poms started and we knew that we were warming up a bit. And then we hear one or two bangs, and shrapnel rattling against the sides. Just living there and waiting. I came to the conclusion that if we got hit we'd get killed, with all the petrol and explosives that were on board. One bomb in the hangar and I think we'd have gone. At times we thought, is it ever going to stop? Is it going to end?'

These sentiments were shared by Admiral Forbes. He believed that to keep the carriers on station off the coast of Norway was running an unacceptable risk. The army was evacuating from Namsos and the effort to get all the troops off would be finished by 3 May. The carriers were ordered back to Scapa Flow, to refuel and rearm, and to allow the crews to obtain some rest.

At Scapa, Captain Arthur Power, who had commanded the *Ark Royal* for all of her service life, and had prepared her crew for war, left the ship for promotion, and a post in the Admiralty. His replacement was Captain Cedric 'Hooky' Holland, who had spent the previous two years as the Naval Attaché in the British Embassy in Paris. Captain Holland would renew his acquaintance with the French Navy sooner than he expected, but his first, immediate concern was the continuing debacle in Norway.

The only British presence left in Norway now was the two small contingents outside Narvik, the most remote and northerly town on the coast. These troops became the focus of a renewed effort to salvage something, at whatever cost, from the failure of Norway. The British government and Winston Churchill had never been able to shake off their fixation with Narvik and its supposed importance to iron ore supplies to German industry and armaments. As a result, the troops in Narvik, rather than being recalled, were, under Churchill's aggressive prompting, brought up to a strength of 30,000 men. But Narvik was about to become a sideshow to the dramatic events unfolding in the rest of Europe.

The military catastrophe of the Norwegian campaign was a political disaster for the Chamberlain government in the UK. In a debate in the House of Commons on 7 and 8 May it became apparent how isolated Chamberlain was. Clement Attlee, leader of the Labour Party, put it most succinctly: 'Norway followed Czechoslovakia and Poland. Everywhere the story is "too late".' On 9 May, Chamberlain accepted that he should resign. The only question was, who should take his place? The next day, Winston Churchill was summoned to see the King and was asked to form a government. On that same day, the German Army, a massive military juggernaut that had paralysed the political leadership of Europe for years, invaded Luxembourg, the Netherlands and Belgium, and marched towards Paris.

With France, Britain's only ally, falling apart under the German blitzkrieg, Narvik was an irrelevant sideshow. More than that, it was a black hole that would have absorbed ships, resources and men's lives. It was now vital to recover as much equipment and as many troops as possible from Norway to help assist in the defence of France. On 24 May the War Cabinet gave the order to evacuate Narvik once and for all – but not before it had been captured from the German Army and made un-usable as a port. As Ron Skinner remarked to me, 'I think Narvik was the only place where the evacuation had been planned before it had been captured!' Narvik was finally taken from the small German garrison in the town on

28 May, and after a brief assessment that confirmed it was no longer of any use as a port, preparations were made to abandon northern Norway.

The *Ark Royal*, the *Furious* and the *Glorious* were sent north of the Arctic Circle to provide air cover to the British troops in Narvik, and to escort the convoy returning to England. A squadron of Hurricane fighters had been transported to Norway by the carrier HMS *Glorious* to help defend the Allied troops against attacks from the Luftwaffe. Their commander, Squadron Leader Cross, did not want to abandon these valuable machines in Norway and thought that it was worth making an attempt to land them onto one of the carriers on station off the coast. The flight deck of the *Ark Royal* was 100 feet (30 metres) longer than that of the *Glorious*, which was an extremely important consideration to pilots who had never landed on a flight deck before, but the deck lifts on the *Ark* were too narrow to carry the Hurricanes with their full wing span, and the flight deck would quickly become congested. Cross decided it was better to use the *Glorious*, and the squadron of Hurricanes successfully landed on her flight deck – a remarkable achievement given the absence of an arrestor hook on the fighters.

The *Glorious* then left the *Ark Royal* and the convoy she was escorting and steamed back to Scapa Flow on her own. Officially the reason for this dangerous course of action was that she was running low on fuel, but the reality was that the senior command on the ship had collapsed. The captain had become mentally unstable and had removed the Commander Air from his position, and wanted to return to the UK as quickly as possible to institute a court martial against him. Such a move was the height of irresponsibility, and there has never been an explanation of why the captain of the *Glorious* was given permission by the senior officer of the task force, Admiral Wells on *Ark Royal*, to abandon the mission of escorting the convoy. It was to prove a fatal mistake.

At the beginning of the Allied troops' final assault on Narvik, the battleships *Scharnhorst* and *Gneisenau* had sailed from Kiel in Germany and headed north, to take the pressure off the German troops by bombarding the Allied positions. When these ships were underway, Admiral Marschall, the commander of this task force of German warships, was told that there were reconnaissance reports of large numbers of British troop carriers and warships heading west. Admiral Marschall was ignorant of the British retreat from Narvik, but he decided in any case that these ships were a more interesting target than the proposed attack on Narvik and changed course to search for them.

On 8 June, a lookout on the *Scharnhorst* saw smoke on the horizon. They had failed to intercept the British troop convoy. They had spotted, instead, the aircraft carrier *Glorious*, with an escort of just two destroyers. The *Glorious* had launched no reconnaissance patrols that morning and there were no Swordfish ready to be armed and flown off to attack the German warships, which were spotted by lookouts on board *Glorious* before they opened fire. Desperate efforts were made to put some Swordfish in the air armed with torpedoes, and three aircraft were brought up from the hangar deck and ranged at the end of the flight deck, but it was far too late. *Scharnhorst* opened fire with her 11-inch guns at 1632, shortly after tea time. Before the Swordfish engines could be started they were blown to pieces by the shells that ripped into the flight deck and exploded in the hangars. *Glorious*'s deck was not armoured, and the ship had almost no protection against the big guns of the German battleships. Explosion after explosion wreaked death and destruction throughout the carrier, and at 1740 the order to abandon ship was given.

The bridge had received one of the first incoming shells from the *Scharnhorst*, cutting off a radio signal that was in reality far too late to save the *Glorious* and her crew. A fragment of this desperate plea for help was received on the *Ark Royal* by Robert Elkington, who was in the communications room, earphones on, probing the ether for an unguarded signal, the rapid dots and dashes of a signalman's Morse key that might reveal the presence of an enemy aeroplane or a lurking submarine. 'Suddenly there was this burst of noise, "2PB" in Morse,' he recalled. 'Well, I knew what that meant – two pocket battleships – but that was all there was. It didn't last long enough for me to get a fix. I took the signals pad to the petty officer in charge, but there was no position, nothing.'

The *Glorious*'s two escorting destroyers, *Acasta* and *Ardent*, were also sunk by the *Scharnhorst* and *Gneisenau*, but not before they had steamed directly at the far more powerful battleships with guns blazing, *Acasta* managing to hit and damage the *Scharnhorst* with a torpedo. But it was all far too late to save the *Glorious*. Another carrier had been lost, and 1,519 sailors and airmen were dead or missing. The brave attack of the destroyers did, however, force Admiral Marschall to abandon his original mission to search for the troop convoys, and instead he headed east for shelter and repairs in Trondheim Fjord.

On 11 June, during a raid on Trondheim, the RAF spotted the presence of the German warships. The Admiralty came up with a plan for Skuas from the *Ark Royal* to mount a dive-bomber attack on the *Scharnhorst*, so the *Ark* was sent to avenge the loss of *Glorious*.

Skuas from the *Ark Royal* had carried out any number of missions over Norway during the evacuation from Trondheim and Narvik. Pilots from 800 and 803 Squadrons had shot down attacking bombers and broken up air attacks, but everybody knew that the Skuas were not capable of taking on German fighters. In the hands of determined and capable pilots, however, Skuas could get away from the fast, manoeuvrable and heavily armed Messerschmitt 109 fighters. George Baldwin described an incident to me when he had succeeded in doing just that. 'My squadron arrived over Bergen at 8,000 feet and started their dive bombing,' he said, 'and two Messerschmitt 109s arrived and shot four of them down. I decided to fly into the coast at nought feet, and it was only after I climbed up to height and dropped my bomb that they spotted me. This 109 was chasing me, and I thought two things: he won't like low flying at full speed, and he won't like flying over the open ocean. Most fighter pilots don't. I flew right down and my air gunner was saying he's getting closer and closer, so I flew at nought feet, absolutely nought feet, straight at the rocks in the island which lies just off the harbour, and turned, Jesus Christ as hard as I could, round the rocks and stayed very low and out to the open ocean, and he just gave up. So I knew about being chased by Messerschmitts.' Despite this escape, George had no illusions about the chances of survival in a fight. 'You really had no chance against them. They were infinitely more manoeuvrable, they had a better front armament, they were faster, they had been trained to shoot things down, and they were dying to shoot us down. Absolutely committed.'

What everybody hoped for with an attack on the *Scharnhorst* was a repeat of the brilliantly successful sinking of the *Konigsberg*. However, the *Scharnhorst* was a much bigger and more heavily armoured warship, and conditions were vastly different from just two months earlier. It was much later in the year for a start, and there was continual daylight; the weather was better, and visibility was greater. Furthermore, Trondheim had been occupied by the Wehrmacht for some time and the anchorage was well defended against air attack. A Luftwaffe airbase was located close to Trondheim, at Vaernes.

Fifteen Skuas were to take part in the attack on the *Scharnhorst*, nine from 803 Squadron and six from 800. Ron Jordan, the armourer from 800 Squadron, knew that something was up when they were ordered to load the Skuas with 500lb armour-piercing bombs – not a normal load for a combat air patrol or an attack on shore installations. 'To get two squadrons ranged together, we knew that it was exceptional,' he said. 'You see, we normally ranged three aircraft at a time on the flight deck. And of course with the 500lb armour-piercing bombs, you only use that against a warship. There was a feeling that it was going to be a very stiff job.'

At midnight on 13 June, the Skuas took off from the flight deck of the *Ark Royal*, formed up and headed towards Trondheim. A diversionary raid by the RAF on Vaernes was scheduled to take place at the same time, but they arrived early, and there was no common radio frequency between the RAF and the *Ark*. When the Skuas arrived over the target they were met with an enormous barrage of anti-aircraft fire, and the air crew discovered that rather than prevent the squadrons of Messerschmitt 109 and 110 fighters from taking off, the RAF raid had instead alerted them in advance so that they were already in the air, ready to pounce on the Skuas. The Skua crews attempted to carry out their attack, diving along the length of the ship from alternate ends to try to confuse the anti-aircraft fire, but it was a failure. Just one bomb hit the *Scharnhorst*, and it bounced off the thick armour plating. Eight of the Skuas were shot down by German fighters.

Ron Skinner remembers the increasing despondency as the *Ark*'s crew waited for the aircraft to return and land. 'We waited until the planes, if they were still flying, would have run out of fuel. I think we slowly realized that sixteen of our air crew were not going to return. It was a great blow, I think particularly for those involved in the flying operations. It affected us for days. We called it Black Thursday.' Some of the bodies of the air crew are buried in a cemetery near Trondheim, and Ron has just recently been there to put flowers on the graves of people he still remembers as nineteen- and twenty-year-old men. Ron Jordan recalled, 'In the mess we auctioned items from the people who had got killed for the relatives and wives. We all had a bit of a prayer and a get-together. It was very depressing. I'd never seen that before of course, but they said that was normal practice after an action.'

This last, almost suicidal mission ended the Norwegian campaign. The *Ark Royal* had survived a very intensive two months of war, acting not as an aircraft carrier in a major 'big fleet' action, but standing off the coast of a remote land war, providing reconnaissance and air cover for troops, and acting as a long-range bomber force. It was a role the Navy and RAF never thought would be necessary. The experience had welded the crew together, and they had shown that they were efficient and effective. Despite the *Ark Royal*'s lack of radar, some rudimentary form of fighter control had successfully been implemented. The loss of the air crew over Trondheim had been a tragic and unnecessary end to this short struggle. Hindsight, of course, is a remarkable thing, but if the *Ark Royal* and the other carriers had been better equipped, had they had more modern planes and had they been used correctly from the start, the war in Norway might not have been such an abject defeat for Britain.

Still, the incompetence and failures that bedevilled the British response to the German invasion of Norway paled almost into insignificance compared to the catastrophe in Europe that overwhelmed Britain in June 1940.

5

DEATH TO THE FRENCH

On the same day that Winston Churchill became Prime Minister, 10 May, the fascist government of Italy under Mussolini joined the war against Britain and France. Things were going very badly for the two allies. British and French armies had failed to hold the German advance in France, and with the growing prospect of military defeat a political crisis enveloped the French government. On 14 June the German Army marched into Paris; two days later Paul Reynaud, the French Prime Minister, resigned, handing power over to Marshal Henri Pétain. On 22 June Pétain, whose government had moved from Paris to Tours, then from Tours to Bordeaux, sought an armistice with Germany. From that date France was split into two: the northern half of the country, including the whole of the Atlantic coastal area, was under German occupation, and the southern part was under the control of the Vichy government, an administration nominally independent from, but an ally of, the German government.

HMS *Ark Royal* had returned to Scapa Flow after the heavy losses over Trondheim. She then sailed for Gibraltar with HMS *Hood*, the largest ship in the Navy, an elegant and fast battleship, 'the pride of the fleet'. With three destroyers for an anti-submarine escort, the two large ships arrived in Gibraltar on 23 June.

The events of the last two months had thrown British strategy in the Mediterranean into absolute chaos. It was the end point of a process that had started in 1935 with the Italian invasion of Abyssinia and the attempted imposition on the Italian government of League of Nations sanctions, which Britain and France had undertaken to enforce. This international crisis, of course, had prompted the move of the headquarters of the British Mediterranean Fleet from the island of Malta to Alexandria in Egypt – much further away from Italian airbases in Sicily and the main Italian port of Taranto. In the years since then, in an attempt to create a modern navy that could enforce Italian interests in the Mediterranean and Africa, Mussolini had poured money into building new battleships and submarines – an expansion that was naturally viewed as a threat by both Britain and France, who agreed that in the event of a conflict with Italy, Britain would assume responsibility for the eastern Mediterranean while the French Navy would seek to control the western basin from its base in the port of Mirs el Kebir at Oran in Algeria.

The collapse of France raised crucial questions about this strategy, and they were discussed at a series of crisis meetings in the Admiralty and in the War Cabinet. Should Britain pursue an active war against Italy? Germany and Italy had helped install the Franco regime in Spain; would Franco remain neutral or throw in his lot with the fascist axis? Was Gibraltar capable of being defended? The chiefs of staff took the view that neither Malta nor Gibraltar was capable of being defended, and Sir Dudley Pound, the First Sea Lord, contemplated abandoning the Mediterranean.

Churchill refused to consider this course of action. From his point of view there were very great issues at stake. A withdrawal from the Mediterranean would weaken British ability to defend the Suez Canal and ensure continued access to the Middle East oilfields. Also of prime importance was the way such an abandonment of the Mediterranean would be interpreted, not only by Britain's enemies but in the neutral countries of the area, such as Turkey, Greece and Spain, that might yet be won over to a coalition against Germany. Withdrawal would also have ramifications on opinion in the United States, where there was a great deal of discussion about the wisdom of backing Britain, a country that, it was believed, would inevitably be forced to seek terms with

Germany. Churchill was convinced that after the defeat in Norway and the occupation of France it was absolutely necessary to demonstrate that Britain had made a break with the policies of negotiation, even though in the Cabinet there were still senior figures like Lord Halifax, the Foreign Secretary, who thought it wiser to maintain a dialogue with Italy and Germany. To win the day, Churchill needed to provide concrete proof of his determination, to Parliament and to the population of Britain.

The Mediterranean, then, was not going to be abandoned, and with this decision the *Ark Royal*'s fate was sealed. She would form the nucleus of a force based in Gibraltar to be known as Force H, and the Admiralty appointed Admiral James Somerville to lead it.

Somerville was, on the face of it, a strange choice. From a solid and respectable family, part of the Somerset squirearchy, James Somerville had gone to Dartmouth Naval College in 1897 at the age of fifteen. He saw action in the Dardanelles in the First World War, and developed an interest in radio telegraphy and signals. By 1936 he had been appointed Rear Admiral (Destroyers) in the Mediterranean Fleet, and during the Spanish Civil War he had several brushes with the Italian Navy, whose submarines often targeted British ships. His active career had, however, been cut short in 1939 when he was diagnosed with tuberculosis and placed on the Retired List. When war started, he was called back to the Admiralty, to the Signals Division, and became responsible for the development of shipborne radar. His return to active service was made permanent when he became assistant to Admiral Bertram Ramsay, who was in charge of the evacuation of the British Expeditionary Force from Dunkirk. Somerville was an intelligent and witty man with a strong independent streak in him. He was not afraid to speak his mind. In 1939 he gave a talk for the BBC Home Service about the Royal Navy, and this was the first of regular broadcasts over the next few years about the conduct of the war and the *Ark Royal*.

Somerville's orders for Force H were, initially, short and to the point. In order to guarantee the Royal Navy's position in the Mediterranean, the priority task was to prevent the French Mediterranean Fleet anchored in Oran harbour, and in the naval port of Mirs el Kebir a few miles along the coast, from falling into the hands of Germany or Italy. If necessary, the French ships would be sunk. During his journey down to Gibraltar, Somerville received several messages from the Admiralty refining the plans for Operation Catapult, as it was now called. On 30 June the Admiralty signalled, 'As we desire to prevent ships getting into German or Italian hands, with as little trouble and bloodshed as possible, it is under consideration to give [the French] these alternatives:

1. To steam their ships to a British port.
2. To sink their ships.
3. Have their ships destroyed by gunfire.

Your plan should be based on giving them the three alternatives. You will be informed as soon as possible which alternative HMG [His Majesty's government] decides to give them.' There were also indications that the role of Force H was going to be wider. Somerville intercepted an Admiralty signal to Admiral Sir Dudley North, the Commanding Officer of North Atlantic Station in Gibraltar, asking for his opinion about what Force H could do to neutralize any bombardment of Gibraltar if Spain became hostile. Somerville's comment was, 'I was somewhat surprised at receiving this message, since I understood . . . that Gibraltar as a naval base would be completely untenable.'

Somerville arrived in Gibraltar in the early evening, and held a meeting with all the senior naval figures and the Commanding Officers of Force H. The French ships that most worried the Admiralty were the two modern battleships *Dunkerque* and *Strasbourg*, and another older battleship, the *Bretagne*. They would seriously affect the balance of power in the Mediterranean if they fell under the control of the Axis navies. The captain of the *Ark Royal*, Captain Cedric Holland, had been the naval attaché in the British Embassy in Paris shortly before the war and had a very good knowledge of the policies and personalities of the current French government, and more importantly the French Navy. He, like Somerville, North and the other officers present, was strongly opposed to the use of force. Their proposal was that there should be a show of force, if necessary, and that the French ships should only be sunk after they had been evacuated. There was a serious worry that shelling the ships in Oran and Mirs el Kebir could only be achieved with a great loss of life. It was the view of almost everyone at the meeting in Gibraltar, and also in the Admiralty in London, that the French admirals would be bound to see that they had no alternative but to give in to British demands.

The date set for Operation Catapult was 3 July, and Somerville proposed that Captain Holland should go to Mirs el Kebir as an emissary to Admiral Gensoul, the French commander in chief. Captain Holland arrived off Mirs el Kebir in the destroyer *Foxhound* early in the morning of 2 July and he was allowed to enter the harbour. A little later Force H, which was now a significant fleet with not only *Ark Royal* but the battleships *Valiant*, *Resolution* and *Nelson*, and the flagship *Hood*, two cruisers and eleven destroyers, arrived to take up position outside the harbour at Oran. A reconnaissance aircraft had flown off from the *Ark Royal*, and it reported that the French battleships and cruisers were raising steam and taking down their canvas deck awnings, indicating that they might be preparing to put to sea. At one o'clock that afternoon, Swordfish aircraft flew off from the *Ark Royal* with an escort of Skua fighters and laid magnetic mines in the mouth of the harbour, putting further pressure on the French admiral.

What the Admiralty, Somerville and Captain Holland had failed to foresee was that the French Naval High Command saw no reason to hand over its ships to Britain. The general opinion was that Britain was not going to be able to hold out for much longer without following the French down the path of negotiating with Germany. Moreover, the French equivalent to a First Sea Lord, Admiral Darlan, had accepted a post in the Vichy government of Marshal Pétain, and Admiral Gensoul saw Darlan as his legitimate superior officer and the Vichy regime as the legitimate French government. In addition to that, the terms of the armistice between France and Germany had been drafted with some sensitivity towards the French Navy. Hitler had no desire to drive the French admirals into the arms of the British and had agreed that the French fleet should remain under French control. Darlan had sent secret signals to Gensoul and French admirals in other ports in the French colonies instructing them to sail to neutral ports in the United States if there were any moves by Germany or Italy to take possession of French warships. As far as Gensoul was concerned the British had no cause for alarm, and there was no excuse for the Royal Navy to blockade his ports and mine the entrances to his harbour. These feelings were vigorously made known to Captain Holland when, finally, after several ultimatums, Gensoul agreed to meet him.

The terms of the agreement between France and

Germany were known to the British government, but as far as Churchill and the First Sea Lord Sir Dudley Pound were concerned the word of Hitler was worth nothing. That fact had been amply proved by the fate of Czechoslovakia, Poland, Belgium, Norway, and now France itself. As for the signals from Darlan to Gensoul, the Admiralty was worried that the Germans had obtained the ciphers to the French naval codes, and that the authenticity of messages from Darlan could not be trusted.

In the afternoon of 3 July, the Admiralty received reports that other French warships were heading to Mirs el Kebir to relieve Gensoul. They signalled to Somerville – 'Settle matters quickly or you will have reinforcements to deal with' – and Somerville had no alternative but to signal to Gensoul that if the terms of the British ultimatum were not agreed to, Force H would open fire at 1730. Now Captain Holland, still in heated discussions with Gensoul, sent a message to Somerville on the *Hood* saying that the crews of the French ships were being reduced and that the ships would proceed to Martinique or the USA. It was a last desperate effort by the captain of the *Ark Royal* to prevent an attack on the French fleet, but it was too little and too late. The officers who had so vehemently opposed the use of force against the French, and who had believed utterly that it would not be necessary, had been driven by the determination of Churchill and the Admiralty, and the complacency of French admirals, to a course of action they abhorred.

Holland was allowed to leave Mirs el Kebir in the motor boat in which he had arrived. He was picked up by HMS *Forester* at about a quarter past seven in the evening. Twenty minutes after he left Mirs el Kebir harbour, Force H opened fire. The massive guns of the *Hood* and the *Valiant, Nelson* and *Resolution* erupted with yellow gun flashes and thick smoke, and shells whistled through the air to land in the harbour.

Val Bailey was a lieutenant on the destroyer *Active*, and had had a ringside seat all day. *Active* had been patrolling outside the boom that controlled the entrance to Mirs el Kebir, keeping watch on the movements of the ships inside the harbour. 'I had had absolutely no idea what was going to happen,' he said, 'and as we scuttled back to the fleet the guns started firing and went whistling over our heads. I'd never seen big guns firing before, and suddenly there I was in the middle of a big ship action. It was startling, I can tell you.' When the guns started firing, *Active* lost no time in getting back to the main body of Force H, but shells from the French shore batteries and the battleships in the harbour were finding the range of the British warships. The French used coloured dye in their shells to help identify each ship's fall of shot, and Bailey was covered in pink water from one very near miss.

Three minutes after Force H started firing, a huge explosion took place in the harbour and an enormous column of smoke billowed into the air, rising for several hundred feet. This was the battleship *Bretagne* blowing up, taking the lives of over 900 French sailors with her. A shell had penetrated her decks and exploded in a magazine. She capsized slowly.

Two Swordfish had taken off from the *Ark* and were circling over the French ships, carrying out their classical role of spotting the fall of shot, but with three battleships firing into such a closely confined area it was impossible to tell whose shells were falling where. Clouds of thick oily smoke from fires and explosions blanketed the harbour, and at 1812 Somerville ceased firing, just seventeen minutes after the onslaught had begun. The damage to the French ships was catastrophic. Shells had not only hit the *Bretagne* and destroyed her, but the *Dunkerque* and the *Provence* were also badly damaged. The former was holed, and had been slowly beached on the mainland near the village of St Andre; the latter had been set on fire, and with flames and smoke pouring out from a massive shell hole on her superstructure she too was slowly driven ashore to stop her from sinking.

However, the most modern and powerful battleship in Mirs el Kebir, the *Strasbourg*, had managed to cast her moorings and was heading for the entrance to the harbour when the first incoming shells detonated. One of them hit one of her escorting destroyers, which completely lost her stern, but *Strasbourg* continued through the harbour bar, with some other destroyers, and escaped into the

Mediterranean. At high speed they headed east, towards the *Ark Royal*.

The *Ark Royal* had taken very little part in the destruction of the French ships in Mirs el Kebir harbour, but her flight deck had seen an enormous amount of activity throughout the day. Two Swordfish aircraft had flown off the *Ark* at five o'clock that morning on a dawn patrol, and then, as the darkness lifted, had acted as an anti-submarine air patrol. Within the next hour and a half six more Swordfish flew off to search for Italian or French warships that might be at sea in the area, as well as three Skuas to act as a fighter escort for Force H and another Swordfish to reconnoitre Mirs el Kebir and Oran harbours, and to provide assistance for *Foxhound*, the destroyer carrying Captain Holland to his meetings with Admiral Gensoul. As the day wore on these aircraft landed on to refuel and were replaced by others. Some twenty aircraft were landing and taking off at roughly two-hour intervals. In addition to these regular aircraft movements, plans had been made to bomb the heavy ships in Mirs el Kebir, and the submarines and smaller craft in Oran harbour. A torpedo attack on the battleships in Mirs el Kebir had also been prepared. And of course both harbour mouths were mined by two flights of Swordfish aircraft.

Several aircraft were lost during the day as the flying programme became disrupted and they ran out of fuel. The original plan to bomb the battleships in Mirs el Kebir had been scheduled to take place at five thirty in the afternoon, but it was postponed because of Somerville's desire to see a resolution to the conflict without firing on the French fleet. As a consequence, the bombed-up Swordfish were ranged at the end of the flight deck for over an hour while aircraft returning from patrols landed on. Eventually, six Swordfish, heavily laden with four 250lb armour-piercing bombs and a further eight 20lb anti-personnel bombs, rolled along the flight deck and heaved into the air. As they circled the carrier and formed up, three Skuas were flown off to act as a fighter escort. Then they set course for the harbour at Mirs el Kebir, but it was too late: the *Strasbourg* had already cleared the bar.

The *Strasbourg* now became the main target, and the Swordfish and escorting Skuas on their way to the harbour at Mirs el Kebir were radioed with instructions to divert from their bombing attack and head for the French battleship. She and her escort were soon spotted by a Swordfish reconnaissance plane and their course, which was directly towards the carrier, was reported urgently to the *Ark*. She immediately went to full speed and steered a course in the opposite direction, but the *Strasbourg* and her destroyers were intent on reaching the safety of a French port and continued to head north-east with HMS *Hood* in pursuit.

Within minutes of the six Swordfish and three Skuas taking off from the *Ark*, the Skuas had seen five French fighters attacking the spotting Swordfish flying near the starboard quarter of the carrier. The Skuas drove them off, but one Skua, flown by Petty Officer Airman Riddler, spun into the sea. The plane and its crew were never recovered so it was impossible to say whether the Skua had been shot down or whether Riddler and his air gunner had been the victim of the Skua's tendency to dive into an irrecoverable spin. So it was only two Skuas that flew with the Swordfish towards the *Strasbourg*. At 12,000 feet another group of French fighters attempted to attack the Swordfish, and the Skuas once more took on a superior force. The nine French fighters and the two Skuas went into a dogfight, and two of the French fighters were hit and dived away. During this fight both the Skuas had problems with their forward firing guns jamming. Three more French fighters appeared, but again the Skuas intercepted them, allowing the Swordfish to make their bombing attack on the *Strasbourg*, which they did by approaching from the north and diving at the battleship from a height of 4,000 feet. By this time the *Strasbourg* was firing its heavy anti-aircraft guns at the planes. There were no hits observed on the *Strasbourg*, although a 250lb bomb would have only slightly damaged an armoured battleship. The flight returned to the carrier, but two of the Swordfish had to ditch in the sea on the way back when they ran out of fuel. The two Skuas then encountered a French flying boat, and Sub Lt Brokensha made an attack and put one of its engines out of action.

It had been a long and stressful mission, with three aircraft lost and two crew members dead, but the *Strasbourg* steamed on untouched. Her escape had taken Somerville totally unawares. He had failed to foresee that the French ships would attempt to leave harbour while under fire from his battleships and make a dash for safety. He admitted to his wife later that his personal antipathy to the whole operation, certainly to the use of force against the French, had affected his judgement. 'To you I don't mind confessing I was half-hearted,' he said, 'and you can't win an action that way.'

The raid on the *Strasbourg* led by the *Ark Royal* was not, however, the last attempt to sink the French battleship that night. Before the Swordfish and Skuas had returned from their bombing attack, another six Swordfish aircraft from 818 Squadron had been armed with torpedoes. With the light fading, at ten minutes to eight they took off to launch a torpedo attack on the French warship.

The Swordfish aircraft that flew off into the dusk looked completely anachronistic, with two sets of wings supported by struts and wire, an open cockpit, huge wheels on struts that didn't retract, and a skin that was largely canvas. The whole affair was pulled through the air by one large radial engine that appeared to be stuck on the nose of the fuselage. The Swordfish looked like a relic from the First World War. It was in fact designed in the early 1930s, and had first entered service in 1936. It had a very slow speed, and could land and take off quite easily from the deck of the carrier. Its large wing area enabled it to carry heavy loads, and it was extremely stable, which was an advantage when dropping torpedoes. Almost every pilot who flew it regarded it as a safe, reliable aircraft. It was easy to repair, and could take enormous damage and stay flying. It did have some disadvantages, though. The engine was started with a flywheel, mounted behind the engine. Two ground crew would have to turn a crank and get the flywheel spinning as fast as possible, then the pilot would engage a clutch, the primed engine would turn over and fire, and the propeller would become a lethal disc just feet away from the two ground crew. It was not an easy thing to do in safety on a pitching deck.

It took a variety of qualities to be a Swordfish pilot. Patience and stoicism were virtues on long, slow patrols over the empty ocean in an open cockpit, hoping that the observer in the rear could correctly calculate the return course back to the carrier. Courage was also necessary. A torpedo was essentially aimed at a ship by pointing the Swordfish at it and flying low and steadily towards the target while gunfire was pouring towards you. The pilots of six of these aircraft were now going to do exactly that as they headed towards the *Strasbourg*.

Screened by six destroyers, the *Strasbourg* was heading towards Toulon at a speed of about 26 knots. By the time the Swordfish had made visual contact with the battleship the sun was low on the horizon, and the Swordfish made their initial approach from the west, out of the setting sun. The crew of the ship were at action stations, and when the pilots of the Swordfish approached to identify the ship they immediately put up a heavy anti-aircraft barrage. The agreed plan of attack was to fly into a position so that the aircraft were ahead of the *Strasbourg* and its destroyer screen, and on their starboard side, so that the battleship was silhouetted against the afterglow of the setting sun in the west. Splitting into two flights of three, the pilots flew at 50 feet above the sea in a wide sweep across the course of the French ship and its escort. Thirty minutes after their first sighting, the Swordfish pilots were in a position to start their attack.

Dropping to a height of 20 feet, the two groups headed between two of the escorting destroyers at the starboard quarter of the ship. The general principle was to judge the speed of their target by the size of the bow wave, and to set the sights to make allowances for that speed when launching the torpedo. Flying very low above the sea, the pilots set their sights for speeds of between 22 and 30 knots. As they flew between the two escorting destroyers they were fired on by both ships, but were not hit. The two section leaders started the attack together, their sections following them in line astern, planes in each section launching simultaneously. The conditions were now so gloomy that the attack went ahead unseen by the lookouts on the *Strasbourg*, and very little anti-aircraft fire was directed at the Swordfish from the battleship. It was also too dark to see any hits, although the estimate of the pilots was that one or two may have been obtained. In fact none was. The attempt to stop the *Strasbourg* had failed again.

It had been an extremely long day, with the first aircraft launched at 0500 hours and the last Swordfish landing back on the carrier at 2310. Throughout that time the *Ark*'s aircraft had played an extremely important role in the attack on the French fleet, and this was the first time that the *Ark* had attempted an attack on a warship steaming at speed. But the *Strasbourg* had escaped.

Somerville had, of course, objected in the strongest possible terms against opening fire on the French fleet. In that letter to his wife he expressed his anger. 'The thought of slaughtering our former allies was repugnant,' he wrote; 'we all felt thoroughly dirty and ashamed that the first time we should have been in action was an affair like this'. And it was not only the morality of his actions that concerned Somerville. The action had released the French from their armistice agreements, and Somerville was concerned that they would now be an active enemy in the Mediterranean, making his task to secure the western Mediterranean more difficult. He saw no reason why he should go out of his way to make another enemy when the Italians already had superior air and naval forces in the area. Moreover, the attitude of the Spanish

The massive bows of the *Ark Royal* dwarf the crowd gathered to see the launch in 1937.

Top: The boilers and the steam turbines were all manually controlled by the engine room staff.

Middle: Two of the *Ark's* six boilers are hoisted on board in the fitting-out basin.

Bottom: Lady Maude Hoare swings the champagne bottle against the bow. It broke after four attempts.

The *Ark Royal* was the longest ship to be launched on Merseyside.

Conditions on the *Ark* were better than most other warships. Even in wartime the Christmas menu promised turkey, and oranges, figs, nuts and dates. Captain Holland helps mix the plum duff (*top left*). Chief Petty Officer King shows off his skills, and the officers' mess tablecloths.

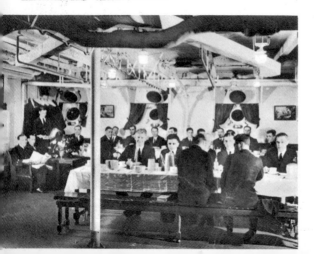

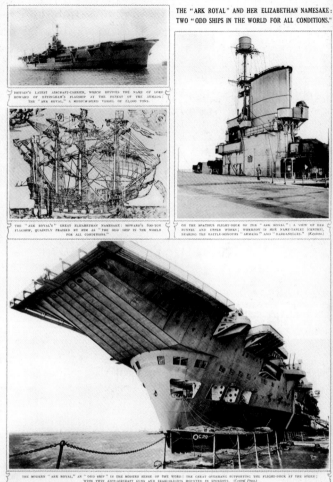

THE "ARK ROYAL" AND HER ELIZABETHAN NAMESAKE: TWO "ODD SHIPS IN THE WORLD FOR ALL CONDITIONS."

BRITAIN'S LATEST AIRCRAFT-CARRIER, WHICH REVIVES THE NAME OF LORD HOWARD OF EFFINGHAM'S FLAGSHIP AT THE DEFEAT OF THE ARMADA: THE "ARK ROYAL," A MEDIUM-SIZED VESSEL OF 22,000 TONS.

THE "ARK ROYAL'S" GREAT ELIZABETHAN NAMESAKE: HOWARD'S 800-TON FLAGSHIP, QUAINTLY PRAISED BY HIM AS "THE ODD SHIP IN THE WORLD FOR ALL CONDITIONS."

ON THE SPACIOUS FLIGHT-DECK OF THE "ARK ROYAL": A VIEW OF HER FUNNEL AND UPPER WORKS; WHEREON IS HER NAME-TABLET (CENTRE), BEARING THE BATTLE-HONOURS "ARMADA" AND "DARDANELLES." (Keystone)

THE MODERN "ARK ROYAL," AN "ODD SHIP" IN THE MODERN SENSE OF THE WORD: THE GREAT OVERHANG SUPPORTING THE FLIGHT-DECK AT THE STERN; WITH TWIN ANTI-AIRCRAFT GUNS AND SEARCHLIGHTS MOUNTED IN SPONSONS. (Central Press.)

The Navy's latest aircraft-carrier revives a name of great renown, no less than that of Howard's flagship at the defeat of the Armada, with the result that [...] architecture displays [...] n-honour, the "Dar-[...] urchased during con-[...] ppy inspiration, given [...] raft-carrier. The old [...] emi-cannon. Howard

wrote of her to Burghley, when he heard the Armada was about to sail "And I pray you tell her Majesty from me that her money was well given for the *Ark Raleigh* [she had originally belonged to Sir Walter Raleigh and was purchased for £5000], for I think her the odd ship in the world for all conditions." As regards the modern "Ark Royal," we regret that it was erroneously stated in our last issue that she is the world's largest aircraft-carrier. There are, indeed, several larger carriers, both in our own and foreign navies, notably the U.S.S. "Lexington" and "Saratoga," and the Japanese "Akagi."

The *Ark* was always a celebrated ship. The *Illustrated London News* ran a photo spread on the *Ark* when she was handed over at the end of 1938. Actors Michael Wilding, John Clements and Michael Rennie starred in a feature film shot on the *Ark* in 1940.

Above: A Blackburn Skua, ready for take-off. Designed as a fighter and dive bomber, it was slow and underpowered.

Left: A 500lb bomb is hoisted onto the flight deck ready for loading onto a Skua.

Right: A Fairey Fulmar fighter lands on, its arrestor hook down. This four-gun fighter replaced the Skua, but was still slower than enemy fighters.

Left: Torpedoes in their trolleys are lined up on the flight deck – the *Ark's* most effective weapon against ships.

Right: A Swordfish biplane and a Skua wait to be launched by the *Ark*'s catapults.

Left: A Swordfish with its wings folded is taken down on the lift to the hangars below.

Air crew had their own ready rooms, and aircraft would be flying on and off the *Ark* throughout the hours of daylight.

Clockwise from left: John Moffat as a young sub-lieutenant. Ron Skinner looks pensively out to sea. John Richardson on the *Ark* in Gibraltar. Bill Morrison as a young rating.

Below: Val Bailey looks out of the cockpit of his Fulmar.

government could become more hostile, and Gibraltar was impossible to defend against a determined air attack. Force H was still untrained, and the destroyers based in Gibraltar had limited range. The main enemy was Italy, and so far Force H had not fired a shot in anger at them.

The French fleet affair was not yet over. The following day, 4 July, the *Ark Royal* readied an attacking force of Swordfish and Skuas armed with semi armour-piercing bombs in order to carry out a dive-bombing attack on the beached *Dunkerque*. Force H ran into thick fog, however, and by 0600 hours the *Ark* decided to abandon the attack because of the danger to planes from anti-aircraft fire if they made their attack in broad daylight. Force H returned to Gibraltar. Somerville received orders to make sure that the *Dunkerque* was out of action by means of a further bombardment of the harbour. He was convinced that this would lead to even more casualties, particularly among the civilian population in the small villages north of where the *Dunkerque* lay. He asked for permission to attack the ship with torpedoes and bombs from the air, and this wish was granted.

Force H set out again, and on 6 July were once more to the west of Mirs el Kebir. Permission to use the Swordfish aircraft in a torpedo attack was received by Somerville at three that morning, so there was little time to plan the operation and prepare the aircraft. At 0520 the armed Swordfish were flown off the *Ark Royal* with an escort of Skua aircraft.

The attack was to be made by a first wave of six aircraft, and then two more waves of three aircraft each. The attack was complicated by the position of the *Dunkerque* because she was beached so close to the shore, near a battery of anti-aircraft guns, making a beam attack very hazardous. It was hoped that the aircraft could approach out of the rising sun to achieve an element of surprise. This was successfully completed by the first wave, which flew along the coast at about 7,000 feet, and as the sun rose above the horizon the flight leader, Lt Compton, led the aircraft in a shallow dive over the breakwater. They dropped all their torpedoes without any opposition. The flight claimed five out of the six torpedoes were successful in hitting the ship.

The next waves were not so lucky. The defences had been warned, and the air crew of the three Swordfish came under heavy anti-aircraft fire from the batteries. They had to take violent avoiding action, the black bursts of exploding shells as close as 80 yards. Captain Newson, the pilot of the lead Swordfish, reported that the sound of the explosions could be distinctly heard, and the concussion felt. They attacked the ship from the same direction as the previous flight, heading over the breakwater and launching their torpedoes at the starboard side of the *Dunkerque*. Captain Newson's air gunner fired at a group of sailors running to man a machine gun on the mole. As the three Swordfish made their getaway, behind the headland at Mirs el Kebir point, they saw a large explosion, and they assumed that one of the magazines had exploded. In fact a lighter had been moored next to the *Dunkerque* to offload ammunition, and it was this that had exploded, though it caused considerable damage to the hull of the battleship. The final wave took a different approach, attacking the port side by flying over land and coming in over the town of Mirs el Kebir. They too were fired on by the anti-aircraft guns, and scored a direct hit on a tug that completely disintegrated but they caused no other damage.

While making their getaway, the pilot of one of the Swordfish, Sub Lt Pearson, saw splashes on the sea in front of him and he realized that they were caused by machine-gun fire from above. The observer, Lt Prendergast, then saw a fighter breaking away, and almost immediately saw another fighter approaching out of the sun. Pearson turned very hard to the right, narrowly avoiding a burst of machine-gun fire, then doing the same to escape a third burst of fire from the French fighter. The fighter returned for a third attack from astern, and Pearson made a 180-degree dog-leg turn and dived beneath the fighter. The Swordfish was hit this time: a hole appeared in the port side of the engine cowling, the rear gun, torpedo release gear and radio were smashed, the tail controls and the right aileron were damaged, and several ribs in the lower right wing were destroyed. Despite this the Swordfish stayed aloft and the dogfight continued, Sub Lt Pearson extracting every advantage he could from his plane's low speed and manoeuvrability by flying along 100 feet above the sea. A third French fighter moved into the attack, and Pearson again executed a hard right turn, this time getting the fighter in his sights and firing off about fifty rounds with his front-mounted machine gun. The French fighters then abandoned the chase and Pearson returned to the *Ark Royal*.

The attack on the French fleet had been a bloody one, with a death toll of over two thousand and several warships completely disabled. The *Ark Royal*'s aircraft, the Skua fighters and the Swordfish torpedo bombers, had constantly been in the air and had shown how quickly they could make a variety of attacks. Somerville was grateful for their presence. Attacking the *Dunkerque* with torpedoes rather than using the *Hood* and the other battleships to shell her had saved a lot of civilian lives, and the pilots had shown that they were capable of making a successful attack in a well-defended harbour, and taking on land-based fighter aircraft. The attack on the *Strasbourg*, however, had not been decisive. The torpedoes, with their Duplex warheads, were prone to failure, and their target, unlike the stationary *Dunkerque*, had been steaming along at 30 knots – a very different proposition.

For Somerville, however, this was a minor issue. He had made his objection to this unilateral declaration of war against the French quite obvious, not only to his fellow admirals but to Sir Dudley Pound and the Prime Minister. It didn't go down well with them. Churchill spoke in the House of Commons a few days later to answer his critics and justify his actions against the French fleet. He made it plain that in his view the operation had been a success. It had demonstrated to the world that Britain, under his command, was prepared to be ruthless and to take whatever action was necessary to fight the war in which it was engaged. In a way the shelling of the French fleet had been Churchill's personal declaration of war, a signal that there would be no going back. The first shots in Britain's war against Germany and Italy, the fascist axis of Europe, had been fired in the Mediterranean, albeit against the French, and Force H and the *Ark Royal* were in the front line.

6

THE *ODIN FINDER*

My plan to search for the *Ark Royal*, which was meant to be the focus of a story about the Royal Navy in general and what I was increasingly thinking of as the battle of the Mediterranean in particular, had so far gone very well, but it was not without its difficulties.

I had worked out the logical place to search for the *Ark Royal*, and in collaboration with Rick Davey of C&C Technologies, the Louisiana-based surveying company, I had calculated how to do it, but it took another six months before I was able to put any of these ideas into effect. We had decided to survey the sea floor in the part of the Mediterranean where the *Ark Royal* sank using a hull-mounted sonar device on a boat called the *Odin Finder*. Rick had been working with the company that owned the boat, and it seemed the most economical way to search a large area. The plan was to make use of the *Odin Finder* in the few days available between major surveying contracts. The months went by, however, and that summer there were gales in the Mediterranean that reached speeds of over 70 knots, making survey work impossible. I waited and waited. The pipeline survey the *Odin Finder* was carrying out dragged on and on. Finally, one morning in July, Elisabetta Faenza, a director of the company GAS that owned the boat, telephoned me. The *Odin Finder* would be putting into Almeria on the southern coast of Spain in a week's time, and would be ready to take me out to sea. I couldn't have been happier.

As I boarded my plane at Heathrow I was relieved that at last I was going to see some concrete action after all the research, planning and telephoning that had gone on over the past few months. It was now over half a year since I had first discussed searching for the *Ark Royal* with Hugh McKay, the salesman at Kongsberg Simrad in Aberdeen. I had raised some money for this search on the understanding that it would be the centrepiece of a television series about the history of the Royal Navy. Even with these funds we would be dependent on companies like GAS and C&C Technologies providing time and equipment at well below their commercial rates. But finding enough money to produce the whole series had not been going very well. Documentaries can be quite expensive to make, particularly if they involve filming underwater, and it was vital to raise more cash from foreign broadcasters. For the BBC, that meant the Discovery Channel in the United States, and not surprisingly they questioned why a US audience would be interested in British history. The upshot was that the BBC couldn't afford to make a series about the Royal Navy because it was too British. There was little I could do about this, but I was banking on the fact that success in finding the *Ark Royal* would put fresh life into the TV series. There was a lot resting on this trip.

In retrospect, even at this early stage I should have considered whether it was wise to continue the search, but I had already invested too much of my time and energy. What had started out as a slightly romantic dream of finding the wreck of a very famous ship had become something too tangible to walk away from. At the start of my research, with the sixty-year-old documents recording the sinking, I had become doubtful about the prospects of success. The process of looking closely at all the findings of the Board of Inquiry and working out how the search would be accomplished had, however, restored my confidence. The evidence I had gathered, including the various contradictory positions I had seen written down the edge of some aerial photographs taken at the time, had to be viewed in perspective. Their accuracy, I reminded myself, was important only to me. It had not been important to the pilots and seamen at the time, for whom errors of a few miles could easily be corrected. Navigation sixty years ago was a question of using a compass, a chart and an assessment of wind and currents. For hundreds of years ships had navigated thousands of miles across the oceans; pilots and observers of the Fleet Air Arm patrolled over the sea for hundreds of miles and managed to locate their aircraft carrier again even though it might have moved 70 or 80 miles from the point where they took off. Occasionally pilots did get lost, but it was rare – testimony to the fact that their navigation skills were very good.

The *Ark Royal* had been torpedoed, and it was close to Gibraltar when it happened – there could be no doubt about that. We had worked out a number of different possible positions for the wreck's location, but I had my own hunch where we were going to find it. I felt sure it was going to lie on a line that connected the position where the torpedo struck the *Ark* to the furthest point to which the *Ark* could have been towed. Rick Davey and the people at GAS had looked over my evidence and seemed satisfied with my analysis. It was not therefore something I could easily abandon.

I arrived late in Almeria and went to meet the technicians from GAS who would do the survey. They were still in their hotel, because the *Odin Finder* had suffered another delay and was not due to arrive in port until the following day. It was the very first time I had met any of the people who were going to carry out the search. The chief surveyor, Massimo Magagnoli, was in his forties, with dark curly hair and a flamboyant, confident air about him. Elisabetta Faenza, the co-owner of GAS, had also come to Almeria and she was charming and elegant, although I got the impression that she did not often go to sea. Perhaps she felt it wiser to be on hand because of the unorthodox nature of the survey, and the customer. Over dinner I got on well with Massimo, Elisabetta and the three other young technicians, Alessandro, Sergio and Giorgio, and I realized that they had a long acquaintance, and clearly would work well together. It was reassuring. Massimo had worked out that we could travel at a rate of about 4 knots over the search area and that this would take about fifty hours, allowing us time to investigate any targets that we found. It would take a day to travel to the search area and then return, so we should be able to do everything we wanted in the three days we had agreed. I mentioned my concern about the accuracy of the sonar signals in the depth of water we would be working in, partly to show that I was not completely ignorant, but Alessandro had no doubts that the sonar on the *Odin Finder* could locate the wreck. 'It's a big wreck,' he reassured me. 'If it is there, we will find it.'

I hadn't realized that part of our search area was in Spanish waters and Elisabetta had had to obtain a licence to carry out the survey. She had said that the survey was for experimental purposes. The area was part of a busy shipping lane, and was also used as a submarine exercise area. The Spanish maritime authorities had suggested that an alternative area be used for the 'test', but had not insisted. So everything was in order, and all we needed now was the boat.

The next day, as promised, the *Odin Finder* cruised slowly into the port of Almeria. The area of the town closest to the old port is dominated by a covered elevated conveyor that once carried minerals and ore to the ships in harbour. But most of that industry has finished and the port is now mainly devoted to ferries taking passengers to North Africa and other destinations along the Mediterranean coast. The *Odin Finder* had a lonely berth on the far side of the harbour, but she was easy to spot. At 600 tons and about 50 metres in length she was much smaller than a car ferry, and had a distinctive 'A' frame winch on the rear deck. Fuel and fresh food were being loaded when we got to her, garbage was being thrown into containers on the quayside, and the captain was talking to port agents. Massimo took me to the canteen for a glass of wine and a plate of pasta, negotiating the narrow stairs and passageways of a working boat.

It was summer, and because of the busy ferry traffic out of the port of Almeria we could not get a pilot to take us out until seven that evening. But on time, with the pilot on board, we finally headed out past the lighthouse at the end of the mole. As I felt the bows lift to meet the swell of the open sea my heart filled with a sense of relief and anticipation. I was at last, after many months of waiting, starting the search for the wreck of the *Ark Royal*.

Before we had finalized our search area, Rick Davey had asked some of the surveyors in his company, C&C Technologies, to make an assessment of the operation. Their view was that at best it had a fifty-fifty chance of success. I thought that was too pessimistic. I had sat at the desk in the Public Record Office and read and touched again the documents and drawings that had been produced sixty years ago. I believed that they held the key to finding the *Ark*. I was sure my calculations would prove correct, and I anticipated success. The line along which I believed the *Ark* lay crossed two of our planned survey lines, and I looked forward to locating the wreck on one of these survey lines by the end of the first day. We were due to start our first line of search, which would be the southernmost edge of our box, at about seven the next morning.

We headed west out of Almeria. Darkness fell, until the only things visible were the lights of ships on the horizon and the beams of distant lighthouses. Content that my search would soon be over, I went to my bunk and fell asleep.

The next morning I awoke to find that the noise of the engines was muted, and the boat was pitching and rolling. My view of the sky through the porthole was obscured every so often by white-capped waves surging past. I made my way to the bridge and discovered from the first officer that a storm had blown up in the night and we were sheltering near the coast, off Malaga. We could not conduct a survey in these conditions. In answer to my question of when the wind and the rough seas would ease, he shrugged. 'A few hours, maybe more.'

Finally, after several excruciating hours, we picked up speed. The weather was abating and there was the prospect that by the time we got to the search area it would be calmer. Over lunch, Massimo said that on our present course it would be quicker to start our search on the eastern edge of the survey area, head south, then run our first line on the southern side. Then we could go back to our original plan, gradually working north. Eager to make a start, I agreed. The eastern edge of our box was determined by the recorded position of the torpedo impact. I believed it was highly unlikely that we would find the wreck there, but who knew?

When a vessel is working on a survey, the ship is not really controlled from the bridge. The captain is responsible for maintaining a course and speed, and for the safety of the ship, but the ship is really directed by the survey team below decks. Because a survey ship has to follow a predetermined course and speed it has a right of way, and special lights and flags are hoisted at the mast-head to warn other ships to alter course.

The survey team works in what is known as the lab. It isn't a laboratory at all, of course; it's a large room that can accommodate technicians, surveyors and represent-atives of companies hiring the boat. Around the room at various work stations are a variety of computer screens which are duplicates of the radar and Decca navigator screens on the bridge, but they also display, in various ways, visual interpretations of the sonar echoes returning from the sea floor. These echoes can be represented in a colour display as a plan or sideways view, each image gradually moving across the screen every second or so as the returns are processed. In the lab of most survey ships there is nothing to indicate that you are on a boat. On the *Odin Finder* there was one small window at the rear of the room that looked out over the rear deck. For the next two days, there would be two technicians on duty here day and night as we carried out our hunt. This was the nerve centre of the boat, and it was here that the first evidence of the wreck would be seen.

As soon as the *Odin Finder* entered our box of co-ordinates and turned south on the first leg, the big sonar machine in the hull switched on. From that point on I could not stay away from the lab. I forgot that this search might go on for two days and nights and that, although the survey technicians would be working in shifts, I had no-one to relieve me. But I could not bear the possibility that I would miss that revelatory moment of finding the *Ark*.

Within an hour the *Odin Finder* had suddenly slowed and gone off track. The images on the screen no longer depicted a steady increase in area. Instantly, Massimo was on the telephone to the bridge. I could not understand the Italian conversation, so I went out of the door onto the rear deck. A large bulk carrier with four giant cranes rising high above its deck was steaming past within a quarter of a mile of us, a big bow wave indicating its speed. It had paid scant attention to the signals at our masthead. I looked around and went up to the bridge. The radar there showed a lot of ships all around us, their projected courses criss-crossing our own. In the excitement of the search I had momentarily forgotten that we were crossing one of the busiest shipping lanes in the world. We were trying to cross the nautical equivalent of the M25. The captain had now taken over from the first officer on the bridge. He looked at the large ship passing close to us and shook his head. 'We cannot raise anyone on the bridge,' he said. 'Never mind. In half an hour we turn, head west and stick to the pattern. There should be no problems.'

Andrea Pupa, the captain of the *Odin Finder*, was a tall, quietly spoken, urbane man in his late forties who had been too busy while we were in Almeria to do anything but shake my hand. Now he turned and asked me if I was comfortable, and if I had slept well. We talked, and he was clearly curious about what I was trying to do. I filled him in on some of the background. 'But tell me, why do you think you can find this wreck?' he asked. He pulled the chart of the area out of a drawer and spread it on the table. 'Show me.'

I explained to him what I knew, and as I went through the story he drew little crosses on the chart, repeating what I had done a few months ago. Then he roughly drew a box around them. 'Mike, you know that the chances are slim,' he said. I explained that there were some discrepancies but that in a sense they had to cancel each other out. We knew the *Ark Royal* had sunk. We had drawn our search area large enough to accommodate any errors. Where else could the wreck be?

He pulled a fax out of a drawer that had been sent to him from C&C Technologies. It was the analysis that had been done for Rick Davey, which I had already seen. Andrea had highlighted the assessment that there was only a fifty-fifty chance of success. 'You know, I must say I agree with this,' he said. 'In my experience things are never where you think they are at sea. All these things happened sixty years ago.' I explained to him that I had seen the assessment and pointed out what I really felt about the Board of Inquiry, that it contained fresh evidence from eye witnesses. He looked sceptical. 'You know, people in circumstances like a boat sinking, like any accident, they never remember very much.'

Then he asked an extremely difficult question: 'Do you know what you will do if you don't find it?'

I was silent. This was a question I had lived with for some time, but for which I had no answer. All I could say was, 'I have gone over all of these positions. I think we have made a lot of allowances for errors.'

Andrea was quiet for a moment. He was a sensitive

man, and he realized he was touching a very delicate nerve.

'OK, very good. You know, Mike, we will do whatever we can to help you. If you have any problems, ask me.'

I believed him. The bread and butter work of underwater surveying can be extremely monotonous. Most of the people in the industry are intelligent and well educated and welcome the opportunity to search for something like the *Ark Royal*. It engages their intellectual curiosity in a way their daily work does not. Andrea's offer was heartfelt, I was sure.

But he had raised an issue that was very sensitive, and which I, for whatever reason, had refused to acknowledge. What I was trying to do was a huge gamble. I knew nothing about this business. I barely understood the technology, and others who had tried to locate the *Ark Royal* had failed in the past. There was no reason why I should succeed. I had been given enough money to pay for the *Odin Finder* for just three days. I had warned people that if three days was not enough I would probably ask for another day's surveying, but it had been made plain to me that this was not going to be popular. In the months since the idea of making the series about the history of the Royal Navy had first been proposed, it had proved expensive and difficult to fund. If I returned to London empty-handed having spent so much of the licence fee payers' money, I could not expect much mercy.

I went back to the control room. We had returned to

our southerly track and had nearly reached the point where we were going to turn west and survey our first line along the southern edge of our search area. We had passed over the point where the *Ark* had been torpedoed and, as I'd expected, nothing had been picked out by our sonar. The captain's question had triggered a level of anxiety in me that nobody seemed to share. As the hours of searching passed, the excitement and tension grew. Sergio and Alessandro, the technicians on watch, were talking animatedly, occasionally glancing at the screens to make sure that we were on course, at the right speed, and that the sonar was working properly.

The *Odin Finder* travelled west, into the sunset silhouetting not the Rock of Gibraltar but Ceuta on the North African coast, the westerly current growing stronger as we approached the Straits. Then, at the end of that survey line, we turned and headed east, on our second line, and I stayed glued to the sonar screens. I was behaving irrationally, unable to tear myself away from the lab and its hypnotic screens in case I missed some discovery, not trusting the technicians on duty, whoever they were. Eventually, Massimo persuaded me to go to my bunk and sleep.

The next day I woke extremely early. Today we should be covering lines four and five, the area where I was convinced we would find the wreck of the *Ark Royal*. The weather was fairly calm but grey, a close mist hanging on the sea, obscuring the horizon. I went on deck. A school of pilot whales was slipping in and out of the waves just off the port side, dark grey and glistening, keeping pace with the boat then vanishing and reappearing a few hundred metres away. I went into the survey room, which was now becoming fetid with cigarette smoke and the smell of people who had stayed awake through the early hours. The two technicians on duty were playing rock music and talking animatedly. I looked at the screens. We were on our third line across the search area and nothing had so far been seen. Despite the fact that everything was being recorded by the computers I assiduously marked the stages of our survey on my own chart of the area. The next line of our survey would cross one of the lines I had plotted from the torpedo's impact to the point where, according to the Board of Inquiry, the tow had been abandoned. Over the next twelve hours we should be passing over a cluster of positions, one of which had to be the final resting place of the *Ark*.

I had a late breakfast in the canteen, walked around the deck, and on to the bridge. The *Odin Finder* was heading into the morning sun which was slowly burning off the haze over the sea. A small boat, workmanlike with its blue hull, white superstructure and orange day-glo patches, sailed sedately where sixty years ago great battleships, destroyers and the *Ark Royal* herself had sped out to war. I thought of the comments of Admiral Somerville, who remarked several times on the very difficult conditions the Straits of Gibraltar presented to his sonar operators hunting for enemy submarines. Huge differences in temperature and salinity caused by a mixture of Mediterranean and Atlantic waters created enormous blind spots, while often whales, rather than submarines, had been the recipients of depth charges dropped by patrolling Swordfish aircraft. Our sonar was far more sophisticated, or at least I hoped it was, and the pod of pilot whales whose fins could still occasionally be seen breaking the surface was safe now from sudden death.

All was quiet on the bridge, apart from the animated conversation between Elisabetta and the captain. Every so often Andrea would scan the horizon, check the screen that showed our position and the course of other ships moving around us, then resume the conversation that seemed to have no beginning and no end. He had a coffee brought up from the galley for me.

I felt slightly uneasy whenever I was out of the lab, but I knew that this was irrational. I couldn't understand why the technicians showed only a cursory interest in the screens that charted the progress of the survey, but I knew they would realize very quickly if there was any sign of anything out of the ordinary, even though in the event they would continue the line until the end. Most likely we would finish our survey of the whole area before returning to any target that seemed to require further investigation.

I returned to the survey room. We were about to start

line four of our survey, and Sergio told me that nothing had been recorded on line three. This wasn't quite true. He showed me indications of two or three depressions in the sea floor, but in his view they were purely geological. I was surprised. When I had started discussing our survey with Rick Davey, we had both assumed that there would be several targets we might need to investigate further with the AUV that C&C Technologies had developed.

Still, I felt certain that the crucial area of our search was now approaching, the northern part of our search box. However irrational it was, at this point in the survey nothing could take me away from the computer screens. The *Odin Finder* proceeded slowly along the allotted course, the sonar returns appearing on the screens with metronomic regularity. Line four eventually finished. Nothing.

We turned into line five and slowly headed towards Gibraltar. Halfway along we started to see a sudden change in the sonar returns, the colour of the graph-like pattern on the screen changing from green to yellow, then a bright red. Yes! But Massimo, after glancing at the screen, returned to his conversation. Almost in disbelief at his indifference, I asked what he thought it could be. He looked again. 'It's very high,' he said. 'Almost 50 metres.'

'Is it the *Ark*?' I asked eagerly.

'I think it's a hill.'

As the returns continued, his analysis was confirmed.

The object was 60 metres high and almost 300 metres in width. It was nothing like the *Ark*.

Eventually line five finished too and we returned for line six. The journey along this line became almost unbearable for me. The fate of the whole enterprise rested on what we would find over the next few hours. But apart from more returns from the hill we had located on the previous line, again we saw nothing.

As we neared the end of line six, I went out on deck. This trip over a balmy Mediterranean had lost its charm. The sun was silhouetting the Rock of Gibraltar, and once again the pod of pilot whales was keeping the ship company. I was exhausted, from tension and lack of sleep. The rear deck was noisy with the clang of chains against the 'A' frame and the pounding of the diesels, and there was no escaping the fumes from the engine room uptakes. I waited for the ship to turn, then went into the survey room again. This was the last chance. The next four hours had to bring success.

My tension produced a chilling effect in the survey room. The sociable conversation between the team members ebbed away as we slowly proceeded east. Massimo disappeared halfway through the line, but I paid little attention. Minor changes in the sea bed would raise my hopes, only to see them dashed as they became another part of the sea bed's undulations. As we neared the end of line seven, and the most northerly part of our search area, I experienced a sudden onset of extreme depression. Before we got to the end I knew I had failed.

I sat in the lab not knowing what to do. I had made some miscalculation but did not know what it was. There were disjointed discussions going on behind me, and I felt the ship turn. The phone in the survey room rang and Giorgio handed it to me. It was the captain.

'Mike, can you come to the bridge?'

I knew what he was going to say. I had come to the end of the period we had contracted for, and Andrea obviously wanted to discuss the logistics of our arrival back in port.

I went up to the bridge. Massimo was already there, and it was clear that he and Andrea had already been talking to each other. This must have been the reason he had left the survey room earlier. They had several charts spread out on the table in the bridge.

'So, nothing, eh?' Andrea said.

'Massimo,' I said, 'are you sure the equipment is working OK?'

He looked at me and smiled, although in retrospect he could have been forgiven for being angry. 'That's what everyone says, Mike. Listen, last year we searched in the Adriatic for a Jaguar aircraft that had crashed in the sea. The air force guy was certain he knew where it was. The pilot had got out, they had a GPS position, and they knew exactly where the plane crashed. But we did not find it, and they blamed our equipment. But we found it quite a way away. And here you have no GPS, and it is sixty years ago.'

'Mike, why are you looking here?' Andrea asked.

I knew the assessment from C&C Technologies was at the back of the captain's mind. I went over the story once again, from the torpedo to the eye-witness report of the sinking, marking the points on the chart.

'But what about the sinking? How did it happen?'

I recounted what I had read in the evidence. The ship had capsized sufficiently for the hole in her side to be identified, suggesting to me that the *Ark* had turned completely over. Andrea then said that the *Ark* could have drifted for some time, just below the surface. 'What goes on below the surface is strange,' he said. 'Ships don't necessarily sink straight away. She may have just hung in the water and drifted for some time.' He looked at the chart. 'The question is, where?'

'It is unfortunately a very big sea,' said Massimo.

'This is where the currents go,' Andrea continued, pointing at the chart, 'so if she was sinking slowly and drifting, that means we should look in deeper water. That is what I would do. But it is your search. We can give you another day, but you must decide what to do with it.'

'We will finish the eastern line,' Massimo added, 'then in one hour you must decide what to do. Where shall we go – north, east, west or south?'

I was stunned. Andrea and Massimo had decided that they wanted to find the *Ark* if they could, to the extent that the *Odin Finder* was mine for another twenty-four hours. No mention had been made of an additional fee, so Elisabetta must have agreed to the extension, although she was nowhere to be seen.

I went down to the lab and pored over my own charts. The meeting had banished my sense of isolation, and I felt a wave of gratitude for their support, though I had no idea what to do. Andrea's advice was probably sound, but I had little to go on. Massimo had retrieved a chart of the surface currents in the Mediterranean. We knew from our search that currents changed throughout the day, becoming faster as the day wore on. But Andrea believed that the *Ark* had drifted below the surface and we knew nothing about the behaviour of the sea at depth.

Massimo entered the survey room. The time to make a decision was approaching, and nobody was going to make it for me. I looked again at the chart, drew a deep breath and said, 'We'll go this way.' I drew two lines that extended the search area by another 32 square miles. After a brief conversation with the bridge the *Odin Finder* changed course, and the deed was done.

Elisabetta, Andrea and Massimo had thrown me a lifeline – or had they merely extended the agony? I thought there was a lot of sense in what Andrea had said, and certainly he and the survey crew had more experience than I. But if the *Ark* had drifted for some time below the surface, she could have ended up fifty or more miles away, in any direction. For the next few hours I paced backwards and forwards on the rear deck, staring at the darkening sea and the pinpoints of light on the southern coast of Spain. A small voice in my head persistently told me that I had taken the wrong decision, that I was headed in the wrong direction, that if there were any errors then they were in the recorded position of the *Ark* when she was torpedoed, and that she had headed further north than I had calculated.

I went to the galley for a meal and a glass of wine. Massimo and Andrea were there, and I joined them. Their obvious commitment to the success of this search had removed any reservations I had about revealing my doubts, and I told them that I was anxious that we were heading in the wrong direction. Andrea was emphatic: if the currents and the sea bed were to be taken into consideration, then it didn't matter where the *Ark* had been torpedoed; we were searching in the direction she *had* to take. Of course, he added, if we were out by 50 miles then we were lost.

Later that night, at about 2 a.m., I went to the darkened survey room. We had covered another line and drawn another blank. Every second the screens depicted another line of sonar echoes, getting slightly bluer as the depth increased. I stayed for an hour, but then the fatigue of the past few days really hit me. I was convinced now that I had failed, and that tomorrow I would need to think about where I went from here. I did not know how I was going to explain my failure. It seemed obvious that with nothing to show for the amount of money that had been spent the series on the history of the Navy was never going to see the light of day. Yet, depressing as this was, I knew that my failure to find the *Ark Royal* would have far more serious personal consequences. I had done all that I could to work out the area we had so fruitlessly searched. If I had made an egregious mistake then I could perhaps better come to terms with my defeat, but I could not see where I had gone wrong. Yet I had failed, and I knew that nobody would be more critical of that than I. I knew that when I got back to the UK I would feel seriously demoralized. Then again, I have always been blessed with a somewhat fatalistic temperament.

Once more I retired to my cabin. I was so exhausted that despite the heat I went straight to sleep. At eight o'clock in the morning I woke up, showered, and went to the lab.

Massimo was there. 'Mike, we have a contact,' he said.

'What do you mean?'

'We saw something about two hours ago. There is something there.'

'Why didn't you wake me?' I spluttered. I couldn't believe they had let me sleep.

'It was on the edge of the track. We will finish this line in half an hour and then we will go back. Then we can be certain. But look at this.'

I looked at the picture Massimo brought up on the screen from two hours ago. Sure enough, right on the edge of the swathe of our sonar beam a sudden blip of red showed in the blue. It lasted for two pulses, then it was gone. I reminded myself that we had been fooled like this before, by holes and the edges of sea mounts in other parts of the search area. I stared at the screen. Could I dare to raise my hopes this time? Massimo turned the screen back to real time. He had a very good idea of what was going on in my mind.

'Mike, go and have breakfast,' he said. 'In two hours we will have a better view.'

He was right. There was only one way to do this and that was the methodical, professional way in which the crew of the *Odin Finder* normally worked. If it was there, we would find it. Excitement wouldn't change anything.

I went for coffee and some fresh pastries, and after that for a walk on deck. The sky was grey, a mist hanging over the sea, a pale yellow sun threatening to burn through in an hour or so. I steeled myself to stay calm, to be prepared for a false alarm, and went to the lab.

The ship was on the next track, heading in the opposite direction. As we approached the point where we had seen the anomaly we now had an overlap, and there was the hard red blip again, slap bang in the middle of the swathe of sonar pulses. Massimo was intent now. 'It's 20 metres high,' he said.

'Is it a rock?' I asked.

He twiddled a few knobs and changed to a different representation on the screen. 'I think it is man-made.'

Then it was gone again. 'We will finish this line,' he said, 'then come back and take another angle.'

'Do you have the time?' I asked.

He grinned. '*Certo*. Of course.'

Two hours later, we were looking at the anomaly again. The EM 3000 sonar mounted on the *Odin Finder* was not the most up-to-date piece of equipment, but the computers on board could still extract a lot of information from the reflected sound beams, and Massimo interpreted it for me. 'It is 20 metres high and maybe 200 metres long. I think it is the right size.' Those were the dimensions of a wreck the size of the *Ark Royal*, resting on its keel. Massimo was certainly treating the signals as though this were a significant object.

I looked at the screen, though it was hard for me to understand what he was investigating. The objects seemed relatively insignificant in the kilometre swathe of sonar signals. It was only the sudden change in height above the sea floor that indicated something was there. And there was another puzzling thing about the contact. There were in fact two targets, the large one and a smaller one, separated by almost a kilometre. Massimo's analysis was that both targets were reflecting as though they were metallic and man-made, with sharp, definite edges. It *was* a significant object, the first one we had found in over three days of endlessly probing the sea floor with our sonar beams.

The *Odin Finder* had done its job, and the crew made

preparations for the trip back to Almeria. All the technicians crowded into the survey room, and there was a sense of achievement and satisfaction that they had done the job. Elisabetta also came down and congratulated me. 'Mike, well done, you have found it. I am so pleased for you,' she said. I thanked her, profoundly, and I went off and thanked Andrea as well.

But as we headed back to Almeria and the results of the survey were downloaded and printed off in the various forms underwater surveyors use (I still have a chart of 289 square nautical miles of the Mediterranean sea floor contoured in rich blues and magentas), I realized that there was much still to do. All we had found was a target that needed further investigation. I was slowly appreciating that I was working in a profoundly abstract world. The object of my search was deep on the ocean floor, so deep that I would most likely never be able to see it with my own eyes, certainly never touch it. Furthermore, I had no idea what it looked like. We had ascertained the shape and position of this target with at best a hundred individual sonar echoes, but when I looked at the hard copy coming out of the chart printer that was located in the lower decks of the *Odin Finder* it was just a black and white pattern that looked like the interference on a television screen. Lines running across the frame correlated with dates and times and the position in degrees, minutes and seconds, and there in the middle were two solid black square shapes, one larger than the other.

It was not a great deal to show for our efforts, or, I thought, to assuage the almost crushing sense of defeat I had experienced just hours earlier. I had my doubts about whether it was enough to persuade the powers-that-be in the BBC to go ahead with more investigation. I had a target, but was it really the *Ark Royal*?

7

THE MEDITERRANEAN WAR BEGINS

Force H under Admiral Somerville had carried out their attack on the French fleet and had permanently disabled the battleships *Dunkerque* and *Bretagne*, but the *Strasbourg*, the most modern battleship in the fleet, had escaped and had managed to seek sanctuary precisely where the Admiralty did not want her, in the French home port of Toulon.

Somerville now had to consider how Force H could replace the French fleet as the gatekeepers of the western Mediterranean. It was unclear in July 1940 just how aggressive an enemy the French would be. There was no doubt, however, that the fascist government of Italy would seek to increase its influence in the area. Somerville had already experienced the combative attitude of the Italian Navy during the Spanish Civil War, when he had been in command of the Destroyer Flotilla of the Mediterranean Fleet.

Italian forces in the western Mediterranean were numerically far superior to anything Somerville could command. Their warships were all modern or modernized, fast and well armed, with several bases and full repair facilities in important ports like Taranto and Genoa. They could shift their forces fairly easily from the eastern to the western Mediterranean, and they had a string of agents in sympathetic or neutral countries bordering the sea who constantly monitored the movements of the British fleet. After the *Hood* was withdrawn from Force H to the Home Fleet, on the fourth of August, all that Somerville could command was his usual flagship the *Renown*, modernized but slow when compared to the modern Italian battleships, the *Ark Royal*, a radar-equipped cruiser like *Sheffield* and a flotilla of destroyers. In addition, the Italian Air Force had bases that stretched from the north of Italy to Sicily and Sardinia, and could assemble concentrations of both high-level and torpedo bombers with fighter protection throughout the central Mediterranean. In Norway, *Ark Royal*'s aircraft and the Royal Navy generally had experienced the dangers of operating against an enemy that could call on modern land-based bombers and fighters. They had never fought against the Italian Air Force, but the *Ark Royal*'s air crew were still flying the Skua fighter bombers that had proved so vulnerable to the Messerschmitts over Trondheim harbour in May.

One of the problems the *Ark* faced was that its deck lifts were narrow and could only accommodate aircraft built with folding wings. In July, Captain Holland had asked the Admiralty for work to be done to widen the lifts so that RAF planes like the Hurricane could be used, but the *Ark* had been designed with the flight deck as the main strength deck, and any modifications would need a major refit in a shipyard. The *Ark* could not be spared for this length of time. So Somerville had to rely on the three squadrons of Swordfish reconnaissance torpedo bombers and the two squadrons of Skua fighter bombers the *Ark* normally carried. They were Force H's aggressive force against the Italian Navy, and other targets, and its defensive shield against submarines and attack from the air.

Knowledge of how they would survive in this new and hostile environment arrived quickly. Churchill and the Admiralty wanted to take advantage of any surprise British aggression against the French fleet might have caused, and ordered a strike against the mainland of Italy. Three days after Force H returned to Gibraltar from the second attack on the *Dunkerque* it sailed once again, this time to attack the Italian base at Cagliari in Sardinia. Somerville had been urged by the Admiralty to take the *Hood*, *Valiant* and *Resolution*, the battleships still under his command, to bombard the port and the Naval Air Station at Elmas in Sardinia. Somerville demurred, believing that the bombardment would force the ships to steam too close to the Italian bases, leaving them vulnerable to mining and submarine attack. Instead, he planned to launch an air attack with Swordfish bombers.

On 8 July, Force H sailed from Gibraltar. It was a significant force, comprising the *Hood*, the *Valiant* and the *Resolution* as well as the *Ark* and the cruisers *Arethusa*, *Faulkner* and *Delhi*. Eight hours later three waves of Italian bombers flew over the fleet and started their bombing run. The struggle between the Royal Navy and the Italian Air Force, which had been anticipated for several years, had finally arrived. The hostile aircraft were not detected by the cruisers' radar and the first wave of aircraft were seen only a few seconds before their bombs fell. They exploded with loud cracks and the accompanying spouts of water but did not cause any damage. A second wave of aircraft was then observed by radar, and by 1750 hours the anti-aircraft guns of the fleet were blazing. A third wave also managed to approach without being detected, but were fired on before they could release their bombs.

Forty aircraft attacked Force H, dropping over a hundred bombs, which Somerville thought were 500lb high-explosives. Had they hit a ship they would have caused some damage but would not have managed to sink it. They could, however, have caused chaos on the *Ark Royal* if one had penetrated the flight deck. The *Ark*'s Skuas were in the air during the attacks and their pilots claimed that two enemy aircraft had been shot down and two damaged by anti-aircraft fire, although they thought that the anti-aircraft fire was generally not that accurate. It was Somerville's opinion, and presumably of those on the *Ark* who had experience of the Norwegian campaign, that the accuracy of the high-level bombing was close to that of the Luftwaffe.

The Norwegian experience was still very much on the Navy's mind, and Somerville was very unhappy about the situation that was developing in the Mediterranean. In his Report of Proceedings, he wrote quite clearly: 'As a result of this, our first contact with the Italian Air Force, it appeared to me that the prospects of the *Ark Royal* escaping damage whilst operating within 100 miles of the coast the following morning were small. I therefore decided the Force should withdraw to the west and proceed at its highest speed in order to increase the range from Sardinian aerodromes.' Somerville had retreated. The Italian Air Force had caused no damage to the British fleet, but had won a victory nevertheless.

To compound Somerville's failure, on 11 July two destroyers attacked an Italian submarine on the surface. While one of the destroyers was attempting to ram the submarine, the other was torpedoed, and it later sank. In the ensuing hunt for the submarine, Italian aircraft scored some near-misses on the destroyer *Foxhound*. It was a chastening experience for Somerville, and it showed quite clearly that the Italian Navy and Air Force were not going to let the Royal Navy do what it wanted in the Mediterranean.

In a letter to the First Sea Lord, Somerville set out his fears. 'Calling off the attack on Cagliari was a most distasteful decision to make,' he wrote, 'but I felt it was most improbable you would want *Ark Royal* put out of action in view of our limited objective.' It was clear that the lack of warning of air attack from radar was a major problem. *Valiant*, one of the battleships in Force H which had radar, was able to report the presence of aircraft, but it was impossible for the operators to tell which were hostile and which were the defending Skuas. 'The Skuas failed to locate any enemy aircraft until late in the afternoon,' Somerville continued, 'when they shot one down. The first bombing attack at 1630 was unobserved until the bombs fell.' Then, commenting on the destroyers' failure to sink the submarine (their depth charges were set to safe), he wrote, 'This shows how essential it is for the units of this force to be properly worked up. Until they are I can have no confidence that they are ready to do their stuff.'

Over the next two weeks Somerville did start to work them up. Ships in harbour were given daily exercises in communication, height finding, target spotting and other air defence procedures. Practice gun firing with live rounds, of both main armament and anti-aircraft guns, was also carried out at sea to the east of Gibraltar.

It was not long before Force H again had to put to sea

and face the Italian Air Force. Malta had been abandoned as a naval base in 1936 during the crisis over the Italian invasion of Abyssinia, but the decision to attempt to maintain British control of the Mediterranean meant that the island now had to be defended, and more fighter aircraft were needed to ward off attacks by Italian bombers over Malta's towns and harbours. Operation Hurry was the plan conceived to achieve this – the delivery of Hurricane aircraft from the UK to Malta. No-one knew at the time how massive these operations would become; several hundred aircraft would eventually be taken to the island. Malta became the base from which all offensive operations against the Italians, and the Germans in North Africa, were mounted. The maintenance of this island in a hostile sea was to absorb an enormous amount of the *Ark*'s war effort.

The plan was that the old First World War aircraft carrier the *Argus* would sail from England with twelve Hurricane aircraft on deck, escorted by four destroyers. On reaching Gibraltar, the *Argus* and the destroyers would form up with Force H and sail for Malta. When the *Argus* had reached a safe distance from the island the Hurricanes would fly off the flight deck to Malta. It was thought that the RAF pilots could not fly and navigate at the same time, particularly over the sea, so they were to be led to their destination by two Navy Skua aircraft.

The mission to bomb Cagliari was now to be incorporated into this overall operation, with the intention of preventing the use of the airfield by the Italian Air Force and misleading them about the true purpose of Force H's departure from Gibraltar. Somerville assumed that the Italians had spies in the Spanish town of Algeciras, constantly monitoring British ships arriving and departing from Gibraltar. In order to mislead these watchers, Force H often left Gibraltar and headed west, steaming into the Atlantic for several hours before changing course and passing east into the Mediterranean through the Straits under the cover of night.

As they made their way eastwards, the *Ark Royal* and Force H were on alert for the expected presence of the Italian Air Force. At eight in the morning of 1 August, one day into the mission, a section of three Skuas took off from the *Ark* to intercept Italian aircraft that were shadowing the fleet.

Robert Elkington, the telegraphist, put his experience in the Mediterranean before the war to good use. 'One of my duties was direction finding, and the Italians used a frequency very close to that of our aircraft. I heard this peculiar un-English Morse – I swung my compass coil and got him nice and true and clean. I kept reporting it, and the Communications Officer plotted a rough position and fighters were sent and before long we got "Tally ho" on the radio. It was a three-engine Cant and it was immediately shot down of course. From then on, almost as soon as we left Gib, a search would be on all the time by radio or radar, for Italian reconnaissance planes.'

Later in the day, the anti-aircraft gun crews went to action stations and six more Skuas took off to form a defensive air patrol over the fleet. Sure enough, thirty minutes later the first wave of Italian aircraft was seen approaching. The ack-ack started, but despite the training Somerville had given the gun crews over the last two weeks it still appeared to be inaccurate. However, it was more concentrated and made a more effective barrage, and when a second wave of nine bombers attacked from a different angle the fleet was able to make a rapid change of course and continue firing at both waves of bombers. One of them was hit, and most of the bombs fell short.

About eighty bombs were dropped by the Italian aircraft, but Somerville was of the opinion that the attack was much less determined than the previous one in July. Whether this was due to more effective anti-aircraft fire or the fact that the *Ark*'s pilots were in the air waiting for the bombers was hard to say. One of the Italian bombers was shot down by a Skua, of 803 Squadron, and no more attacks from the Italian Air Force took place that day.

The *Ark Royal* and the *Hood*, with a cruiser and a group of destroyers, then separated and set off for the position where the Swordfish would fly off to attack the aerodrome at Cagliari, leaving the main fleet with *Argus* and its Hurricanes to continue eastwards. At two thirty in the morning of 2 August, a group of Swordfish, nine carrying bombs and three armed with mines for the harbour, flew off the deck of the *Ark Royal*. One aircraft crashed into the sea, and its crew were lost; the rest headed off into a westerly wind that threatened to slow them down and delay their arrival over the target.

This attack was a crucial event for the *Ark Royal* and its air crew, and indeed for Admiral Somerville. He was in charge of a still untrained fleet operating against a still untested enemy with the awareness that he was responsible for the *Ark Royal*, an extremely valuable ship he could not afford to lose. He had abandoned this mission the previous month because he had judged that it was not worth the risk to the carrier. That risk had not really diminished, and in a letter to his wife he revealed his very human anxieties about the operation:

At 2.30 a.m. in the pitch dark on Friday as we were mucking about only 100 miles or so off the Itie coast I thought of all the possibilities – destroyers, MTBs [motor torpedo boats], submarines, cruisers, bombing attacks at daylight, etc. – and began to feel that it was all a bit sticky and the temperature of my feet dropped appreciably.

And then in the pitch dark I saw a small shadow separate itself from the great shadow of the *Ark*. The first Swordfish taking off. And then I thought of those incredibly gallant chaps taking off in the pitch dark to fly 140 miles to a place they've never seen, to be shot up by A/A guns and dazzled by searchlights and then, mark you, to fly over the sea and find that tiny floating aero-drome with the knowledge that if they don't find it they're done. Well, that shook me up and I realized how small my personal difficulties were compared to theirs.

It was daylight when the Swordfish reached their tar-get. They were met with heavy anti-aircraft fire, and one of the aircraft was badly damaged and had no choice but to land on the enemy airstrip. But the two hangars were hit and in flames, four aircraft were blown up, and several buildings were destroyed or badly damaged. In addition, three mines were dropped in the harbour at Cagliari. The *Ark*, meanwhile, had changed course to meet up with the remainder of the fleet after the Hurricanes and their Skua guides had flown off the *Argus*, and by eight in the morning the Swordfish had returned to the *Ark* and both groups of ships had re-formed into one fleet.

Throughout the day the *Ark*'s Swordfish and Skua squadrons maintained patrols as part of the anti-submarine screen, and as fighter cover for the fleet. At midday, a reconnaissance aircraft was located by the radar set on the *Valiant*; a Skua intercepted it and shot it down. By the afternoon of 4 August all the ships of Force H were back in Gibraltar. There had been some casualties among the Swordfish squadrons on the *Ark* but the operation was a great success. A squadron of Hurricane aircraft had reinforced Malta, an Italian aerodrome had been bombed, and an attack on the fleet by Italian bombers had been repulsed by a combination of anti-aircraft fire and the *Ark Royal*'s fighters. Operations were possible against the Italian mainland, and the Italian Air Force was not as deadly as Somerville had feared. The planning and the training he had introduced as a matter of urgency had apparently paid off, and Force H had begun to establish itself in the Mediterranean.

Admiral Somerville left Gibraltar on the *Hood* on 4 August bound for Scapa Flow, and then went by train to London. He had been called to a meeting at the Admiralty to discuss the next major operation the *Ark Royal* was going to carry out, Operation HATS, or 'Hands Across the Sea', which was designed to reinforce the Royal Navy's Mediterranean Fleet under Admiral Cunningham in Alexandria. A modern aircraft carrier, *Illustrious*, and the battleship *Valiant* with two cruisers and some destroyers were to be escorted from Gibraltar to Malta, where guns were going to be unloaded from the *Valiant*; from there the ships, to be known as Force F, would make for Alexandria, the main British base in Egypt. This fleet of warships could travel fast enough through the Mediterranean to avoid attacks from submarines, and both *Illustrious* and *Ark Royal* would be able to launch enough fighters to repel any attack from the air.

The operation was complicated, however, by the desire of Churchill and the War Cabinet to use the opportunity to transport tanks to Alexandria to reinforce the British

Army under General Wavell. Wavell was planning to launch an offensive against the Italian Army in Tripoli and needed to build up his forces. Somerville objected to the inclusion of heavy tank-carrying ships on the grounds that the transports would inevitably slow the fleet down and make it more vulnerable. Most of the reinforcements for Alexandria and the British Army in Egypt went via the Cape Route, although this added weeks to their journey time, but in Somerville's view this was by far the safest route. Admiral Cunningham had also sent a written memo to Sir Dudley Pound, the First Sea Lord, backing up Somerville, and their combined objections carried the day. Churchill, however, thought that they and the Admiralty were being far too cautious. He was to return to the question later.

Somerville travelled back to Gibraltar in HMS *Renown*, the ship that was to remain his flagship for some time, and he was accompanied on this journey by the *Illustrious* and the other ships that were going to reinforce the fleet in the eastern Mediterranean. On 30 August they set out from Gibraltar. *Illustrious*, unlike the *Ark Royal*, carried her own radar, and three other ships, the cruisers *Coventry* and *Sheffield* and the battleship *Valiant*, were similarly equipped. With four radar sets at his disposal Somerville would be able to steer the fighters on to approaching bomber formations, and at the same time keep an eye out for other incoming enemy aircraft.

On the second day out of Gibraltar radar detected a

shadower, and the standing patrol of three Skua aircraft was directed towards it by radio. After a 55-mile chase, Lt Spurway, the leader of the Skua section, fired a burst of machine-gun fire into the Cant floatplane, which caught fire and started to break up. Two of the crew managed to bale out. Four hours later the radar operators detected another Italian reconnaissance aircraft, and the standing air patrol of three Skuas was again successfully directed to shoot it down.

Diversionary attacks on the aerodrome and seaplane base at Cagliari were planned again, but this time there were to be two of them on two separate days. The first attack on Elmas aerodrome took off at five minutes past three in the morning of 1 September. Nine Swordfish aircraft armed with four 250lb bombs formed up over a floating flare dropped in the sea ten miles from the *Ark*. Their attack was made at six in the morning. When they dived to their bombing height of 3,000 feet they were fired at by anti-aircraft guns, but they succeeded in dropping their bombs and starting several fires and were able to rendezvous with the *Ark Royal* by eight o'clock. The second attack took place the next night, although this time the target was obscured by low cloud and fog. The Swordfish dropped several flares but could not identify any targets. They fired at some searchlights, but jettisoned their bombs into the sea before returning to the *Ark*.

Somerville reported that the force had remained in

effective bombing range of Italian airbases for at least forty-eight hours. The crew had been at Action Stations for long periods of time. Heavy air attack had been anticipated, and indeed hoped for, because he was confident that with the number of fighters available to him and the number of anti-aircraft guns mounted on the ships he would be able to deliver a blow to the Italian Air Force which might have a telling and lasting effect. Somerville thought that the absence of any aggressive move by the Italians against the fleet could be accounted for by the quick destruction of reconnaissance aircraft on the first day, and the first attack on the aerodrome at Elmas, as well as nervousness on the part of the Italians at the concentration of fighters the carriers could launch.

The *Ark Royal* and its air crew had proved their worth to Somerville. In little more than eight weeks since retreating in the face of an overwhelming air offensive, Force H supplied Malta with a badly needed squadron of Hurricane fighters having escorted a fleet of reinforcements through one half of the Mediterranean. Aircraft from the *Ark Royal* had carried out two attacks on Italian airbases and had accounted for several Italian bombers and reconnaissance aircraft with the loss of only one of their own aircraft. The *Ark* and Somerville could be justifiably proud of their achievements.

It wouldn't last.

The *Ark Royal* was detached from Force H and went to West Africa to assist in the attempt to persuade the

French African colonies to switch their allegiance from the Vichy government to the Free French Forces under General de Gaulle. When this mission ended in failure, the *Ark* sailed north to Liverpool, where she spent some time in dock for a refit. Apart from repairs to parts of the main machinery, she was fitted with a new flight deck barrier that would help to speed up the process of aircraft landing.

Many new members of the ship's crew joined her at this time, and one of the squadrons of Skua fighter aircraft was replaced with a squadron of Fairey Fulmars, a fighter that was a variant of the Fairey Battle bomber. The plane had failed as a bomber in the RAF, being slow and unable to carry a significant bomb load. It was, however, faster than the Skua, and it carried more guns. As far as the Fleet Air Arm was concerned it was a stopgap machine over which they had little choice. As far as the pilots were concerned, the plane had strengths and weaknesses. Val Bailey, who had by this time managed to transfer to the Fleet Air Arm and was undergoing flying training, thought that the Fulmar was a marked improvement on the Skua. It had eight guns, just like the Hurricane, it was a solid, safe plane to deck-land, and it was very comfortable, like flying an armchair. But it just wasn't fast enough. The Swordfish squadrons were also new to the *Ark* and comprised newly trained air crew, many of whom were from the Volunteer Reserve, or hostilities-only servicemen who had joined the Navy because of the war and were not career naval officers.

Liverpool was under constant attack from the Luftwaffe during the time the *Ark Royal* was in Liverpool docks. Many of the crew believed that the *Ark* was as important a target as the city, so it was a disturbing time for all of them. They had endured air attacks in Norway and in the Mediterranean, but it was shocking to realize that Britain was also being bombed nightly, and that their relatives and sweethearts were also facing danger. The realities of the total war in which the British people were engaged were extremely harsh.

On 3 November the *Ark Royal* sailed from Liverpool and arrived in Gibraltar three days later. Almost immediately, on the seventh, she sailed with Force H on another mission to Malta, Operation Coat. This time the reinforcements were troops and warships for the Mediterranean Fleet. A total of 2,150 troops were embarked on the battleships *Berwick* and *Barham*, the cruiser *Glasgow* and six destroyers.

Force H had changed slightly by the time of the *Ark*'s return. The *Ark* was still under the command of Captain Cedric Holland, but the Vice Admiral (Aviation), Admiral Wells, who had been a flag officer on the *Ark*, had gone and not been replaced, so Somerville could exercise slightly more direct control over her. The cruiser HMS *Sheffield* had also joined Force H, and she had experience of working with the *Ark* as her radar direction ship during the Norwegian campaign. This collaboration was to be

German claims that they had sunk the *Ark* in 1939 were a godsend to the British Ministry of Information. The claims were graphically illustrated in the *Nazi Volkischer Beobachter* and broadcast by German radio, giving the *Ark* international renown.

The *Ark* was everywhere.
The German pocket battleship
Admiral Graf Spee explodes off
Montevideo harbour (*right*). A stick
of bombs narrowly misses the
Ark off Norway (*below, left*). The
air crew were not so lucky. Many
were lost, and some are buried
near Trondheim (*below, right*).

Bottom: The Strasbourg (*inset*)
tries to escape. French sailors
struggle to rescue their shipmates
at Mirs el Kebir.

THE ILLUSTRATED LONDON NEWS

SATURDAY, JANUARY 6, 1940.

A COLUMN OF SMOKE SHOOTING HUNDREDS OF FEET INTO THE AIR PROCLAIMS THE IGNOMINIOUS END OF THE "ADMIRAL GRAF SPEE": AN AMAZING AERIAL PHOTOGRAPH UNIQUE IN NAVAL HISTORY.

Above: Italian bombs again just miss the *Ark*, and explosions obscure the *Ark* in the Mediterranean (*inset*).

Right and below: Rear Admiral Somerville congratulates the crew after another successful convoy, and Spanish dancers entertain them in Gibraltar. The censor pencils out the warships in the background.

Admiral Günther Lutjens (*right*) had commanded several successful naval operations, and he was rewarded with command of the *Bismarck*, the most modern and powerful battleship afloat. Its enormous firepower – it is pictured here firing at night (*below*) – was a match for any British warship. But when the *Bismarck* was spotted and photographed by one of the *Ark's* Swordfish (*bottom*) Admiral Lutjens and most of his crew had only a few more hours to live.

OPPOSITE PAGE:
Desperate oil-covered survivors from the *Bismarck* struggle for life in the icy Atlantic (*top*). Just one week earlier, German Stuka dive bombers had failed to halt the *Ark* in the Mediterranean.

The *Ark* listed heavily almost immediately. Most of the crew abandoned ship directly onto the decks of HMS *Legion*. Black smoke poured out of the funnels as the engine room crew struggled to relight the boilers. The popular version of events described in the illustration proved to be highly misleading.

The Ark Royal sank within 25 miles of Gibraltar.

"*She toppled over like a tired child Her stern reared up for a moment & then gently she sank beneath the waves*" *14 hours after being struck*

"*A powerful little tug appeared on the scene & proceeded to take the Ark Royal in tow — a period of 12 hours*."

"*Gradually the became less p. "Steam & smok evidence tha Ark Royal wa to help hersel harbou.*

"The Ark Royal was listing
alarmingly to starboard"

"I could see men
sliding down ropes to
the Destroyer's deck"

"Others leaped into the sea
from a height of 70 feet.
Carley floats were bobbing
about the carrier's hull.

Destroyer takes off
greater part of ship's
company.

Below: This dramatic photo shows the first crew members climbing down to the deck of the *Legion*. Ron Skinner in a white cap stands by a railing and watches the destroyer approach. To the left, further along the hull, Val Bailey and Percy Gick have started to lower a boat. All of the crew except one made it back to the UK (*left*).

developed further over the next few months, and the relationship between the radar operators on *Sheffield* and the signals department and fighter direction officer on the *Ark* was to become an extremely proficient one. The disadvantages were that not only were the pilots on the *Ark* 'pretty green', as Somerville wrote to his wife, but the crews of many of the other ships had not had experience of working together and fighting off air attacks.

They were in action almost straight away. On the first day out of Gibraltar, at six o'clock in the evening, south of Sardinia, three Fulmar aircraft from 808 Squadron were preparing to land on the *Ark* when a Savoia Marchetti 79, a three-engine bomber, was identified by the *Sheffield*'s radar. The Fulmars were directed by radio telegraphy, Morse code, from the signallers on the carrier. The Italian aircraft was sighted by the leader of the Fulmars at 3,000 feet and they climbed to 6,000 feet where they themselves were spotted by the gunner of the Savoia Marchetti, whose pilot immediately dived at full speed down to sea level. The Fulmars chased the Italian bomber but they took some time to get within range because they had a relatively narrow margin of speed, and they were slowed by the drag from their landing hooks, which had already been lowered. When they reached sea level, the three Fulmars attacked the bomber from the rear in succession. The Italian aircraft crashed into the sea.

Yet another raid on Cagliari was planned to act as a

diversion from the main force of ships. Nine Swordfish aircraft took off in the dark at 0430, their exhausts emitting blue flames and sparks in the dark. They formed up on a flame float dropped in the sea near the *Ark* and then headed for Elmas aerodrome. The Swordfish were armed with 250lb bombs, some fitted with delayed-action fuses, incendiary bombs and small high-explosive bombs. On their way to the target the planes passed through thick cloud, but all managed to arrive at roughly the same time, dropping their bombs from a height of 3,000 feet and causing some heavy fires to start. There was little enemy gunfire and all the planes and their crews were able to return to the *Ark Royal*, landing at 0745.

Two hours later, the combat air patrol of three Fulmars was again directed by radar to intercept another Italian spy plane, this time a Cant seaplane, that appeared at 0950. The three Fulmars were 5,000 feet above the Cant and dived to overtake it, using clouds as cover. They attacked in a V formation to the side of the aircraft, and then made another attack from the rear. The seaplane burst into flames and crashed.

It was a more serious situation two hours later on the same day when twenty-five Italian bombers attacked Force H and the troop-carrying warships. The formation of bombers approached at a height of 13,000 feet and were located by the radar on the *Sheffield* when they were 50 miles away and on a course towards the fleet. The three Fulmars on patrol were told to climb to 15,000 feet and the pilots saw the approaching bombers when they were 5 miles away from the Fulmars and about 10 miles away from the *Ark Royal*. The bombers were flying in a wide circle, so the Fulmars attacked the leader from the beam, their eight machine guns firing simultaneously, then breaking off and firing at any other bomber that appeared in their sights. This made no impression on the bombers, which continued their steady approach until they were in position to drop their bombs. They fell across the fleet in a straight line. There were explosions on both sides of the battleship *Barham* carrying its 700 soldiers, then on either side of the *Ark Royal*. Miraculously they all missed.

Three Skuas had also been flown off the *Ark* to assist the Fulmars, and they flew into a position to attack some of the rear sections of the bomber group. Lt Spurway, the leader of the section, said that all guns on the Skuas were fired until they stopped working. In all, over four thousand bullets were sent into the formation of bombers, but again this did not disrupt the attack. Lt Spurway commented bitterly, 'Our aircraft were at a great disadvantage as the speed of the enemy in formation was slightly higher than the top speed of the Skua. This lack of performance in our aircraft made it extremely hard to carry out effective attacks.' Somerville agreed with Lt Spurway's remarks, and added some worrying words of his own to the Report of Proceedings, the weekly report he was obliged to send to the Admiralty. He remarked that the fighters had seemed unable to break up the bomber attack, moreover that the anti-aircraft fire was again inaccurate, bursting too low. He went on to say that many of the pilots had very little experience, and the form of attack, from the beam, was probably not well judged. Furthermore, the observers in the new Fulmars wanted a gun, which of course they'd had in their previous aircraft, the Swordfish and the Skua, mounted in the rear cockpits. Trials were taking place with a sawn-off Lewis gun, reported Somerville.

The *Ark Royal* and Force H returned to Gibraltar on 11 November. Four days later the *Ark* again set sail, this time on Operation White, to cover the old aircraft carrier *Argus* which was ferrying twelve Hurricane fighters to reinforce the defences of Malta. But the winds started to increase in speed and the sea started to get rougher, so many of the flying operations were cancelled, though a section of fighters was kept at readiness in case any hostile aircraft were detected by radar.

Admiral Somerville then received reports that some Italian warships were in the area south of Naples. Assuming that the Italians knew of the current operation of Force H, and that the Italian Navy might try to intervene, Somerville wanted to launch the Hurricane aircraft as far to the west as possible. The winds were still from the west, and the pilots of the Hurricanes and the captain of the *Argus* calculated that the aircraft could be flown off from a position about longitude 6 degrees east, which gave a flying distance of 400 miles to Malta. This was a long way for a single-engine fighter to fly over a featureless sea, but the Hurricanes were to fly off in two flights of six, each accompanied by a Skua aircraft. To ensure that they were successfully guided to their destination the two flights would also be met by a Sunderland flying boat and a Martin bomber from Malta, with experienced navigators on board. The Hurricanes would carry sufficient fuel to give them a range of 520 miles, and they had the added advantage of a tailwind behind them.

While the Hurricanes took off from the *Argus*, at first light, aircraft from the *Ark Royal* provided fighter cover, and sent reconnaissance patrols to the east. All the aircraft were successfully launched from the *Argus* by eight in the morning. From that point the operation started to unravel. The Martin bomber never succeeded in meeting up with its flight of Hurricanes, and only four Hurricanes and one Skua managed to reach Malta. The rest either couldn't find Malta or ran out of fuel because of an unexpected headwind. Somerville was particularly angry to discover that the observer of the second Skua, whose flight failed to find Malta at all, was a sub-lieutenant in the Royal Navy Reserve who was on his very first operational flight. Operation White was a tragic failure.

The next mission Force H took part in raised even more doubts about the experience of the pilots who had left Liverpool on board the *Ark Royal*, and gave Churchill the opportunity to attack Somerville, about whose instincts he had harboured severe doubts ever since the assault on the French fleet at Oran. The mission's aim was to reinforce the British Army and other forces in Egypt with another convoy to Malta and Alexandria. This time it was a combination of Operations HATS and Hurry, and it had an extra sense of urgency because of the invasion of Greece and the decision to move some of the British Eighth Army to support the Greek government.

The convoy was going to be made up of three mechanized transport freighters, the *New Zealand Star*, the *Clan Forbes* and the *Clan Fraser*, carrying a cargo of tanks and armoured equipment, and a contingent of Royal Air Force personnel who were needed in Alexandria. The vessels carrying the armoured equipment would sail from Britain and would not call at Gibraltar; instead, their escort of corvettes and destroyers would join them as they passed Europa point, the southernmost tip of Gibraltar. The RAF personnel arrived in Gibraltar in a transport ship, the *Franconia*, and were transferred to the cruisers *Manchester* and *Southampton* for passage through the Mediterranean. Force H would meanwhile sail to the north of the cruiser and motor transport ship convoy, providing air cover and surface protection from attacks by the Italian Air Force and Navy. At a point roughly south-east of Sardinia, Force H would meet a fleet from Malta comprising the battleships *Ramillies* and *Berwick* and some cruisers, who would then continue to protect the convoy on its journey to Alexandria.

Somerville was concerned about the distinct possibility that the convoy would be intercepted by the Italian Navy. An attack on the Italian fleet in its harbour at Taranto by Swordfish aircraft flying from HMS *Illustrious* had been a blow to the Italian forces in the Mediterranean, severely damaging as it did three of their battleships. The rest of the fleet was moved from Taranto and directed to ports in Naples and La Spezia. However, British intelligence had lost track of the rest of the battleships. Somerville believed that the obvious strategy for the Italian Navy was to reinforce the western part of the Mediterranean and force a fight with the slow convoy. He stressed to the Admiralty that in his view the Italians could concentrate three battleships and several cruisers in the period between Force H leaving Gibraltar and the time when they were accompanying the convoy on its journey south of Sardinia.

On 26 November, Force H set off from Gibraltar, and by the end of the day had located the convoy and taken up position sailing on a course parallel to them at a distance of twenty-five miles to the north. The next day, the *Ark Royal* flew off nine Swordfish aircraft to act as long-range surveillance for the convoy, covering an area 100 miles to the north and west of the convoy and Force H. At the same time, anti-submarine patrols were launched, and so was a standing patrol of fighters. In addition, a squadron of Swordfish had been armed the night before with torpedoes and were standing by in case there was any contact with a force of Italian warships.

At ten in the morning, the patrolling Swordfish saw that the situation Somerville had been most concerned about had in fact occurred. Sixty miles to the north-west of the *Ark Royal* and Force H was a substantial fleet of Italian warships comprising two battleships and a destroyer escort; 10 miles away was a further force of three cruisers and destroyers. They were steaming directly for the convoy.

Somerville told the *Ark Royal* to launch a strike force of Swordfish torpedo bombers, and at the same time ordered Force H, now comprising his flagship *Renown* and her escorts, to make full speed to meet up with the *Berwick* and *Ramillies*, which were approaching from Malta. They met up just before noon, and the combined force altered course to confront the Italian fleet, although various reports from the patrolling Swordfish left Somerville in some doubt as to how big the enemy fleet was and what ships were in it. Moreover, it is quite likely that the Italian battle fleet changed course to the east when they realized they had been observed by recon-naissance aircraft, because they were sailing to the east, away from the convoy, by a quarter past eleven.

The first strike force of Swordfish was flown off the *Ark* at 1130 hours. The air crew were the most experienced available, what Captain Holland of the *Ark* later described as 'our first team', but out of nine aircraft only five had ever previously dropped a torpedo in action. Some had had perhaps two practice drops, some as many as eight. The Swordfish approached the battleships from the west, out of the sun, at an altitude of about 6,000 feet. They dived over the destroyer screen and went low to make their attack. There was no attempt to split up the flight so that torpedoes could be launched from different positions, to split the anti-aircraft defences and make it difficult for the target ship to manoeuvre and comb the tracks of the torpedoes. All the pilots launched at the same point, to the front of the leading battleship on the starboard side, except for the leader, Lt Commander Mervyn Johnstone, who launched his torpedo at the rear of the two battleships. The battleships and the destroyers were firing a lot of anti-aircraft fire at the planes and it was, according to Johnstone, heavy and accurate fire, causing damage to three of the aircraft.

Two torpedoes were seen to explode in the sea, but one explosion with a lot of brown smoke was observed on the far side of the leading ship. A considerable amount of AA fire continued to be directed at the planes as they made their escape, twisting and turning, keeping as low as possible, and as Johnstone said, 'it is very difficult in an attack of this sort to get any idea of what is going on until you get a report from everyone in the squadron. It is extremely difficult to observe anything on a low-level attack. You are never on a steady course for more than about five seconds. It is very difficult when you are manoeuvring to get out of gunfire to look around and see what is going on.' It wasn't until the flight of Swordfish had landed back on the *Ark Royal*, almost an hour after the start of the attack on the Italian fleet, that the air crew formed the conclusion that one of the Italian battleships might have been damaged.

In the meantime there had been an exchange of shells between the Italian cruisers and Force H, and one of the patrolling Swordfish observers reported that an Italian cruiser had come to a standstill, a fire burning in the rear turret. The pilot, Sub Lt Henry Mays, said, 'I noticed she was burning furiously aft, and after having looked at my silhouettes and another careful look at this ship I decided she was of the San Giorgio class. I stayed over her for nearly half an hour and then returned to the *Ark Royal*. This cruiser had been stationary for the whole of the time I had been shadowing her and she opened fire with short-range armament on one occasion.'

Somerville's main forces were struggling to maintain speed to overtake the Italian ships, who were now clearly returning to the Italian mainland as fast as they could, and Somerville was also getting dangerously close to the enemy coast, which was now just 30 miles away. He decided at this point that the protection of the convoy was the more important task and broke off the pursuit of the Italian ships, although in fact neither *Renown*, *Ramillies* nor the convoy's escorting cruisers were capable of making enough speed to intercept the Italian ships. On receiving the report of the burning Italian cruiser,

Somerville instead ordered the *Ark Royal* to make an air attack and attempt to sink her.

When Captain Holland had been told that the first strike force had probably hit one of the Italian battleships, he had ordered a second Swordfish strike force into the air with orders to locate a damaged battleship, or, if this proved impractical, to attack any other target. The leader, Lt Commander James Stewart Moore, approached the retreating Italian ships on a course of 30 degrees. He realized that in order to attack the battleships he would have to pass close to the cruisers before reaching the main target, thus allowing the crew of the battleships ample warning of their approach. The alternative was to fly around the fleet and attempt to approach the battleships from ahead, but this would take some time. As Moore was considering his options he saw Italian fighters manoeuvring over Sardinia, and he reasoned that he would have to get the attack over with quickly or accept the risk of seeing it disintegrate under enemy fighter attack. Another consideration that weighed on his mind, he reported, 'was the very untrained personnel in the striking force. It seemed that if I gave them a difficult target I would probably have no hits at all, whilst the rear cruiser, quite unscreened, seemed much more promising. I decided to attack the single cruiser.'

Moore led his nine Swordfish into the attack at 1320, and his torpedo and that of his wingman dropped almost simultaneously. They then turned and zigzagged to avoid anti-aircraft fire. The cruiser started to turn into the torpedoes, and as she did so Moore saw a mound of water about 30 feet long and as high as her forward deck appear under the bridge. The ship continued her turn and was then attacked by another sub flight, but the cruiser continued on her way, completing a circle and rejoining her companion ships. The last group of Swordfish attacked not the last cruiser but the leading one, and no hits were observed.

While this attack was going on the *Ark* had launched a force of seven Skua aircraft with orders from Somerville to locate the burning cruiser and attack it with 500lb bombs. They took off at 1500 hours. They could not find any trace of a damaged cruiser, but their leader, Lt Richard Smeeton, saw three cruisers of the Condottiere class steaming north in close formation at about 25 knots. He climbed to 8,000 feet so that he could begin his attack out of the sun. He led his flight into a bombing run on the last ship of the line, and all the aircraft except one released on target at about 900 feet, but no definite hits were seen. They were completely unopposed, having achieved outright surprise, but as they made their getaway they received some heavy anti-aircraft fire.

Meanwhile, the Italian Air Force had very belatedly flown to the assistance of the Italian ships, and at 1635 fifteen bombers concentrated their attack on the *Ark Royal*, getting within range despite the patrols of Fulmars and Skuas. Around thirty bombs fell close to the *Ark*, but she emerged through the clouds of smoke and spray unscathed, with all her guns firing. That was the last effort by the Italians to attack the convoy, and it achieved its aim of transporting the armour and personnel to Alexandria.

However, twenty-five British aircraft had attacked the Italian fleet on three separate occasions throughout the day and had achieved precisely nothing. Taking into account the failure to obtain any hits when the *Ark*'s Swordfish had tried to stop the *Strasbourg* escaping, the success against shipping at sea by carrier-borne aircraft was far less than pre-war exercises had forecast.

As John Moffat, a Volunteer Reserve Swordfish pilot, described it, the training he had received was rigorous. It included judgement of the speed and course of a ship from observation of its bow wave and wake, and he had practised dropping dummy torpedoes in the Clyde against moving ships, every drop recorded by a camera mounted on his aeroplane's wing. But it was hard enough to judge speed, distance and height during an exercise; it was another question altogether to do it when the ship you were attacking was firing every gun it could bear at you in a desperate effort to shoot down your aircraft and kill you. Some of the attacks carried out by the *Ark*'s air crew were relatively unopposed, but many had been met with heavy gunfire.

Part of the problem may have been the fuse fitted to the warhead of the torpedoes carried on the *Ark*. A normal old-fashioned contact fuse relied on an impact with the target to detonate the explosive in the warhead. In order for this to work the torpedo had to hit the target fair and square, on the side of the hull, the place where most modern warships had their thickest armour and were often invulnerable to the small warhead of the 18-inch torpedoes carried by the Swordfish. To overcome this, a fuse known as the Duplex fuse had been developed that was triggered by the influence of the magnetic field of a ship. The theory was that a torpedo with a Duplex fuse could be set to run deeper so that it would explode directly underneath a ship, causing greater damage. There was a great deal of scepticism about the reliability of these new fuses, particularly on the part of the Swordfish crew, but their orders were to continue to fit them.

There were other problems too, such as the lack of communication and poor reporting, that needed addressing. It seemed clear as well that initial planning of the attack was not very thorough, and that little attention was paid to tactics to divide the enemy fire.

Admiral Somerville and Captain Holland of the *Ark Royal* had little time to address these failings when they returned to Gibraltar. The escape of the Italian fleet had been immediately noticed by the Admiralty, and before Somerville could make a proper report of the incident he was told that a Board of Inquiry had been set up and Admiral of the Fleet the Earl of Cork and Orrery was arriving in Gibraltar to conduct it. Somerville now had two Boards of Inquiry to deal with, one investigating the failure of Operation White, which had seen the loss of over two thirds of those Hurricanes flown off to reinforce Malta, and now a far more serious inquiry into his handling of Operation Collar.

The second Board of Inquiry was in a sense pre-ordained. It had been ordered by Winston Churchill, who had of course objected to Somerville's quite outspoken opposition to the attack on the French at Mirs el Kebir. Churchill's view that Somerville was lacking in the fighting spirit needed to win the war had not been diminished by his constant unwillingness to take further action against French shipping. He had as well been outspoken in his defence of Admiral North, in charge of the North Atlantic Station in Gibraltar, who had been unjustly blamed and forcibly retired for failing to stop French warships leaving the Mediterranean. He had also, of course, vigorously stated his opinion that the HATS convoy would be running an unacceptable risk if it tried to escort cargo vessels carrying tank reinforcements. Churchill wanted to remove him, and Somerville's failure to intercept the Italian fleet was his chance.

But Somerville was saved, essentially for three reasons. The first was that he was unambitious, and saw his current position as a postscript to a career that had effectively ended when he was invalided out of the Navy in 1938. This was why he was prepared to be outspoken

– a trait he himself realized sometimes made him difficult to deal with. In this particular instance he had absolutely no qualms about criticizing the Admiralty and its peremptory decision to hold an inquiry. Secondly, Somerville was a well-known figure, a broadcaster and the Admiral in Charge of Force H and the *Ark Royal*, which also had a high public profile. He would not go quietly, a fact he made very clear; his sacking would create political problems for the government and the Admiralty. Somerville was saved as well by the fact that many of his fellow admirals, including those in charge of the inquiry, believed that it was unjustified. They would go ahead with the inquiry but make sure it was favourable to Somerville. In a letter to Somerville, the chairman of the Board of Inquiry said, 'These people impatient for results exist both in and out of the Admy and in high quarters (I speak from personal experience) and no doubt have raised their voices on this occasion, and the most expeditious way of silencing them has in this case been adopted. As a result I do not think you need anticipate hearing anything further. This is as far as I can judge and sincerely hope.'

And so it turned out, although Somerville remained angry at the slur on him and the men under his command. He thought it an underhanded way to save him. Somerville had written lengthy letters to the Admiralty, pointing out that he had been faced with a dilemma during Operation Collar. If he had abandoned the merchant ships to pursue the Italian fleet they would have been left defenceless against air attack and other units of the Italian fleet. Moreover, there was a serious possibility that the *Ark*'s safety would have been jeopardized. The Admiralty prevaricated on the question of what he should have done, refusing to address the point. Even after the subject was closed, Somerville continued to raise this question, pressing the Admiralty for clarity before every operation in the Mediterranean.

When the inquiry was completed, Somerville paid a visit to the *Ark Royal*. A series of training exercises had been initiated on board the carrier, and Somerville was able to take part in some of them – torpedo exercises, practice dive-bombing flights, and exercises in fighter interception and combat. It was clear that he intended his visit to help remedy some of the deficiencies brought to light during the attack on the Italian fleet. He talked to the air gunners and emphasized the importance of regular communication with the carrier, and other aircraft. As he toured the ship, he gave encouragement and praise as well as gently highlighting the need to maintain a high level of efficiency.

Somerville's nephew Mark was a lieutenant observer in Fulmars in 808 Squadron, flying with Lt Commander Tillard, the squadron's commanding officer, who had been responsible for shooting down several Italian aircraft. Mark Somerville penned a letter to his uncle that was full of praise for the tour. 'The general view about the visit is that the ship is now operating under a Flag Officer who not only understands the general aspects of Naval Aviation but who has also taken the trouble to investigate the practical and personal side of it,' he wrote. The visit certainly did an enormous amount to boost morale on the *Ark* after the critical interrogation by the Board of Inquiry. Somerville could not resist another jibe at the Admiralty in his Report of Proceedings for the period. Remarking on his visit, he wrote, 'I am convinced that when opportunity serves, it is most desirable that Senior Officers should take part in such practices that they may acquire a full appreciation of the problems which face the FAA pilots and observers.'

Somerville's criticism of many of the tasks Force H was asked to carry out was based partly on a lack of clarity about the purpose of Force H, and also on Somerville's assessment of the strategic situation in the Mediterranean. Force H was originally set up to control the western exit to the Mediterranean, and to carry out offensive operations against the coast of Italy. Subsequently, to these were added the passage of reinforcements to the eastern Mediterranean; control of all major units of the French fleet; the tracking down of raiders in the Atlantic; preparations for the defence of Gibraltar should the Spanish enter the war on the Axis side; the capture of the Azores, to pre-empt a German seizure; and possible forays into the Indian Ocean in the event of war with Japan. It was a lengthy list, and as

Somerville was always keen to point out there were no substitutes for either the *Renown* or the *Ark Royal*. So weak were his forces that the destroyer flotilla in Gibraltar could not find the ships to mount anti-submarine patrols of the Straits and provide an effective destroyer screen for Force H on its forays into the Mediterranean.

Somerville's assessment was that he simply did not have the resources constantly to monitor French shipping in the Mediterranean, as he was asked to do; he certainly could not afford to create a situation that might turn the Vichy government into an active enemy. Gibraltar was far too vulnerable to air attacks from the French bases in North Africa, and he would never be able to deal with a combined French–Italian fleet. His attitude towards seeking a conflict with the Italian fleet was also governed by his view of the balance of forces in the Mediterranean. The task of destroying the Italian fleet was secondary to the need to maintain the RAF and the military in Egypt, and now also in Greece. The Admiralty never in his view gave enough weight to the fact that the Italian Navy, as well as being numerically superior, had the advantage of air support from a shore-based air force. The Italian air and naval forces had been poorly co-ordinated during Operation Collar, but they might get it right next time. Somerville argued that for forthcoming operations in the Mediterranean Force H should be enlarged, if not by additional cruisers, then by another battleship. The Navy was, however, being stretched by the war in the Atlantic as well as in the Mediterranean. It was unlikely that Force H would receive significant reinforcements in the short term.

Indeed, the fact that the *Ark Royal* was stationed at Gibraltar, the gateway between the Mediterranean and the Atlantic, meant she was now in a perfect position to fight on both fronts. Rather than Force H being reinforced and strengthened for the tasks of supporting the military offensive in the Mediterranean, it now found itself being called upon to reinforce the Home Fleet in the Atlantic. Already feeling extreme pressure from the Italian forces in the Mediterranean, the demands placed on Force H were threatening to push them to breaking point. Events over the next few weeks would only increase this. The Luftwaffe were about to join the war in the Mediterranean with dramatic effect. The role of the *Ark Royal* would become increasingly significant in shaping the ensuing conflict.

As Christmas and the New Year approached, events were to take an even more desperate turn, and the demands on Somerville, Force H and the *Ark Royal* would be even more acute. To understand why, it is necessary to look at events in the eastern Mediterranean at the end of 1940.

8

SHOWING THE FLAG

HMS *Illustrious* was one of the most modern carriers in the fleet, built after the *Ark* and designed specifically for combat in areas like the Mediterranean, where air attack from shore-based aircraft was to be expected. As a defence against bombs the *Illustrious* had been constructed with an armoured flight deck, and because this affected her weight distribution, the ship and all the carriers that were built to the same design sat lower in the water than the *Ark*, and therefore had just one hangar deck, which limited the number of aircraft that could be carried. The trade-off was thought to be necessary, and certainly the *Illustrious* and its new Fulmar fighter aircraft operated aggressively in the eastern Mediterranean, supporting supply convoys to North African ports and to Greece.

The commanding officer of the Mediterranean Fleet, Admiral Andrew Cunningham, was less concerned about the threat from the Italian Air Force than that posed by the Italian Navy. It was a significant force, with several modern battleships and cruisers and a large number of destroyers and submarines. This fleet was based in the port of Taranto in Puglia, inside the 'heel' of Italy, and its presence was a constant anxiety to Cunningham. The Italian fleet had so far avoided a direct confrontation with the Royal Navy, and if Cunningham could eliminate them and reduce the threat they posed to his ships and convoys, then several of his battleships could be freed for duty in the Atlantic. The question was, how to do this if the Italian Navy wanted to avoid a major fleet action?

Taranto's location, deep in the Gulf of Taranto surrounded on three sides by the Italian mainland, made an attack from the sea impossibly risky for Cunningham. However, as a consequence of the Italian invasion of Abyssinia in 1936 and the possibility that Britain would be at war with Italy in an attempt to enforce League of Nations sanctions, the Royal Navy had worked out a plan to attack the Italian fleet in Taranto, not with surface ships but with torpedo-carrying aircraft. The captain of the *Illustrious*, Denis Boyd, and the ship's flag officer Rear Admiral Lumley Lyster had been a part of the planning staff back in 1938 and knew a great deal about the plan. It was a simple matter for them to dust it off and rework it for the present situation.

Taranto had two natural harbours, a small inner one that was accessed by means of a short canal from a much larger one that was shielded from the sea by two large moles. The bigger warships of the Italian fleet moored in this harbour, while the smaller destroyers and cruisers docked in the inner harbour. The final plan presented to Cunningham by Captain Boyd and Rear Admiral Lyster called for the *Illustrious* and the smaller HMS *Eagle* to steam to a position in the Ionian Sea about 170 miles from Taranto, and then to launch twenty-four Swordfish armed with torpedoes and bombs to make a night attack on the fleet. The main targets would be the battleships in the outer harbour, but bombs would also be dropped on the destroyers and a seaplane base in the inner harbour. It was an audacious and very risky plan. The port of Taranto was well protected by anti-aircraft fire, the ships were protected by torpedo nets, and there were fighter aircraft based at airfields a short distance from the port. But the attacking force would have the advantage of surprise, and the cover of darkness.

Shortly before the scheduled day for the raid there was a fire in the hangar of the *Eagle*, so only the *Illustrious* could take part in the attack. Some Swordfish from the *Eagle* were taken on board *Illustrious*, and on 11 November twenty-one Swordfish aircraft took off from the flight deck of HMS *Illustrious* on this extremely hazardous mission. Three of the Italian battleships moored in the harbour were sunk, and three cruisers and two destroyers were badly damaged. In addition, the Swordfish managed to destroy the seaplane base on the shores of the inner harbour, and the port's oil storage tanks were left blazing. Only two of the aircraft were shot down. It was a remarkably successful attack and, as we have seen, it forced the Italian Navy to remove the rest of its fleet to the port of Naples. Admiral Cunningham's problem had been solved. Moreover, having lost three battleships while in the safety of one of their most important harbours, the Italian Navy had suffered a massive blow to its morale.

Yet the enormous strategic advantage that the raid on Taranto gave to the Royal Navy in the Mediterranean was relatively short-lived. In January 1941 units of the German Army landed in North Africa to reinforce the Italian Army, and a large element of the Luftwaffe, the Tenth Air Corps, or Fliegerkorps X, was moved from Poland to Sicily. This small, self-contained air force specialized in anti-shipping attacks and mine-laying and boasted 150 Heinkel 111 and Junkers 88 bombers alongside an equal number of Stuka dive bombers. There were also fifty Messerschmitt 109 fighters and several squadrons of the long-range twin-engine fighter, the Me110. Their presence was as threatening to the Allied war effort in the Mediterranean as the build-up of the Afrika Korps under General Rommel in North Africa. Fliegerkorps X was a well-integrated force that had already proved, in Norway, that it could wreak devastation on warships. Indeed, within a few months the German Army would be rolling the British Army before them in Greece and North Africa, and Rommel and his Afrika Korps would be holding daggers to the throats of British troops around the Nile, Alexandria and the Suez Canal.

The withdrawal of the Italian fleet from Taranto was quickly seized upon by the Admiralty as a perfect opportunity to pass another convoy from Gibraltar to Alexandria with reinforcements for the Eighth Army. The plan was to take 4,000 tons of ammunition, 3,000 tons of seed potatoes and a squadron of Hawker Hurricanes to Malta, with another ship continuing to Alexandria. The convoy's journey down from the UK was disrupted by the presence of the *Admiral Hipper*, a German cruiser, in the Bay of Biscay, which forced the *Ark Royal* to put to sea on Christmas Day and almost caused a mutiny among the crew (as we shall see in the next chapter). The *Ark* escorted the convoy to Gibraltar, but it was not until 6 January that the convoy headed east towards Malta and the Sicilian channel.

This stage of the journey was marked by an attack by ten Italian bombers, which were driven off. The fleet had adopted a tactic of firing its anti-aircraft guns in a co-ordinated barrage, a system where shells were fired at set heights, forcing attacking aircraft to fly through a wall of explosions. The Fulmar aircraft from the *Ark* also took off to break up the attack, and Lt Commander Tillard, the commanding officer of 808 Squadron, shot down two of the Savoia Marchetti bombers. On the evening of 9 January, the *Ark* and Force H left the convoy having, in the words of Admiral Somerville in a letter to his wife, 'seen them to the front door of the next parish'.

It was at this point that the complicated manoeuvres to cover the safe delivery of the ships to Alexandria started to go wrong. *Illustrious*, with her escort of battleships *Warspite* and *Valiant*, was waiting to meet the convoy after it had passed through the Sicilian channel by the island of Pantelleria. They had taken up a position further to the west than normal, and on the morning of 10 January *Illustrious* was steaming to the north-west of Malta. The weather was fair, and visibility was excellent. Sailing this close to Sicily was extremely risky, and both Captain Boyd and Rear Admiral Lyster had pointed out to Admiral Cunningham that *Illustrious* could provide air cover for the convoy from a much safer position, further away from the Italian airbases on Sicily. Cunningham, who was never as intelligent about the use and vulnerability of his carriers as Somerville was when it came to the *Ark*, had overridden their objections, saying that the presence of the carrier had an excellent effect on the morale of the fleet.

Shortly after midday, two Italian torpedo bombers flew low over the sea towards the *Valiant*, dropping two torpedoes that fell behind the warship as she steamed east. Then the radar on the *Illustrious* detected two large formations of aircraft approaching from the north. As they got nearer they were identified as German aircraft, a combination of twin-engine Junkers 88 medium bombers and the notorious Junkers 87 or Stukas, the single-engine dive bombers with a highly distinctive V-shaped crank in their wings whose banshee-like screams had come to symbolize the terror of the German blitzkrieg on Poland and France.

Admiral Cunningham recorded in his diary that 'a very heavy, determined and skilful dive-bombing attack developed on the fleet, mainly directed on *Illustrious*, and lasting for some ten minutes'. The pilots of the Stuka squadrons had spent many hours practising their dive-bombing technique on targets drawn on the runway of their base in Sicily which reproduced the shape of the *Illustrious*'s flight deck. She was quickly hit by six large 1,000kg bombs, dropped on the flight deck by Stukas whose pilots flew so low over the ship that they were often level with the compass platform on the carrier's island. The handful of Fulmar fighters on the *Illustrious* were simply overwhelmed by the numbers of German aircraft, and the carrier's armoured flight deck offered little defence against such large armour-piercing bombs. Both deck lifts were hit, and fires started in the hangar deck, killing many of the air crew who had taken part in the attack on Taranto just two months earlier. The steering gear was damaged too, and the ship steamed in circles for some time before the damage control parties managed to free the rudder again. All the time the attacks continued. The fountains of water from near-misses sometimes completely obscured the carrier.

Illustrious eventually managed to steam to Malta and put into the dockyard in Valletta for emergency repairs. The Luftwaffe did not stop, however. The next day, 11 January, a wave of Stukas attacked the cruisers *Southampton* and *Gloucester*, destroying the former and badly damaging the latter. Attack after attack also rained down on the *Illustrious* while she was in dock, but after several weeks she was patched up sufficiently to steam to Alexandria and head, via the Suez Canal, for an American shipyard to be rebuilt. She had not been sunk, but she was lost completely to Cunningham and the British war effort in the Mediterranean.

Any advantage Britain had achieved in the Mediterranean as a result of Taranto had now been completely wiped out by the Luftwaffe. There was no question of any more convoys being sent through the Mediterranean, and as Cunningham said, 'the fleet itself would operate by day within the range of the dive bombers only at considerable risk. In the absence of a modern aircraft carrier it therefore became necessary to abandon any idea of offensive operations against the enemy's coast.' This, of course, had an immediate effect on the *Ark Royal* and her crew. The Admiralty had been planning to replace her with the *Illustrious*'s sister ship

Indomitable, but now *Indomitable* had to replace *Illustrious* herself in the eastern Mediterranean, as soon as it became possible to get her there, and the *Ark* would have to stay in Gibraltar. A badly needed refit for the ship and home leave for the crew were now indefinitely postponed.

But there were bigger problems now facing Cunningham in the aftermath of the loss of the *Illustrious* than lack of home leave for a ship's crew. The Luftwaffe's onslaught led to a serious loss of prestige for the Royal Navy, and it wasn't clear how that would affect the two most important neutral countries at either end of the Mediterranean, Spain and Turkey. Their attitude to Britain and the Axis powers was crucial to Britain's ability to continue the war in North Africa and the Mediterranean. The *Ark Royal* and Force H now had the task of demonstrating to Spain that Britain was still a potent force to be reckoned with. This was a really pressing issue, because there were rumours that the Spanish were considering their position about the British presence on the Rock of Gibraltar, and a summit meeting between Mussolini and General Franco was due to take place in February. The question of Spanish assistance to Italy was certain to be discussed between the two dictators.

Admiral Cunningham was also eager to see an attack on northern Italy, because it would dissuade the Italian fleet from returning to Taranto now that the threat from *Illustrious* had been removed; it should also make the

Italian Air Force shift some of its squadrons to the north. In the event the Admiralty proposed a two-pronged attack: the bombardment by the warships of Force H of Genoa and, along the way, an attack on the Tirso Dam in Sardinia by Swordfish aircraft. The dam had been built in front of Lake Tirso and was responsible for supplying a third of the island's electricity. The Admiralty supplied an intelligence assessment, which said that the dam was only three feet thick at the top and could easily be breached by a torpedo.

Somerville discussed this operation with his senior officers and the captain of the *Ark Royal*, most of whom opposed the plans. It was not hard to see why. The mission to bombard Genoa would take the *Ark Royal* and Force H past Sardinia, very close to the Italian mainland and well within range of the Italian Air Force; moreover, the attack on the Tirso Dam would alert the Italian defences at an early stage in the operation. *Illustrious* had been lost because the risk from shore-based aircraft had been ignored. It seemed foolish to do the same thing with the *Ark*, especially as she was now the only lifeline to Malta. As for the attack on the dam itself, launching torpedoes required that the Swordfish fly low and steady for some time, and if the raid was to be successful all the aircraft would have to fly predictably on a line down the lake towards the dam. They would make a perfect target for anti-aircraft guns whose crews would have the benefit of a lengthy arc of fire from dry land. The

Admiralty had suggested, however, that the defences of the dam were light, and that the aircraft would have the benefit of surprise.

Somerville had, of course, often objected to missions that in his opinion jeopardized the safety of the *Ark Royal* and its air crew. There was no question that these two operations, Result and Picket, were extremely risky, but he knew that the arguments for the combined operations were, in the circumstances, fairly compelling. For a start, he was extremely conscious of the vulnerability of his base at Gibraltar and knew that a change in the Spanish policy of neutrality would lead to its evacuation. He also knew that Cunningham in the eastern Mediterranean needed help to take the pressure off his depleted forces.

Result and Picket were given the go-ahead, and on Saturday, 1 February, the *Ark Royal*, with *Renown*, *Malaya* – a battleship sent as reinforcement by Cunningham to Somerville at the end of 1940 – *Sheffield* and a screen of destroyers, was steaming at high speed towards Sardinia where, very early the following Sunday, a group of Swordfish aircraft would fly off to attack the dam.

The weather worsened. By 0200 hours, as the *Ark Royal* approached the take-off position 60 miles off the coast of Sardinia, there was a 37-knot wind blowing from the west. The Swordfish would be flying into this wind when they returned from the raid, and the *Ark* would have to remain in the same position to give them any chance of making it back safely. This would not only delay the attack on Genoa, it would also increase the risk to the whole force if the *Ark Royal* was spotted by enemy reconnaissance aircraft while loitering in the flying-off position. But there was no alternative, and the Swordfish aircraft were brought up on the hangar lifts, their torpedoes mounted, and they were ranged at the end of the flight deck.

The *Ark* pitched in the rough sea amid sudden squalls of rain, and in the dark of early morning the deck was extremely hazardous. In such high winds and with a heaving ship there was always the danger of a collision between aircraft, or an accident involving ground crew. The mechanic turning the handle to start the engine was only ever a few feet away from sudden death. The flight deck was slippery with oil and moisture, and the powerful wash from the spinning propellers combined with the gale-force wind threatened to blow the mechanics and aircraft handlers off their feet. Albert Arnell was an aeroplane rigger on the Swordfish aircraft, and he gave me this graphic description of his job when a squadron was being launched: 'When it came to take-off time we would get the order to start engines as the ship was turning into wind. If you're on the chocks at the back then it's a hell of a wind. You can't look into it and open your mouth because if you do it will blow your cheeks right out here. You're lying on the deck holding onto two chocks and they're flying off in front of you. It comes to your turn and you hang on for grim death. If there's a white line painted on the deck you hang onto it if you can. If you keep low you will go under the propellers so it's a matter of keeping your nerve. It's quite something to see a plane launched. It disappears over the bows, and you're on the flight deck and you look at everybody's neck going up about another six inches to see if it's gone off all right.'

Despite the conditions, by six o'clock eight Swordfish aircraft had taken to the air and were on their way to the Sardinian coast. The weather was too rough to launch the Skua fighters, so a patrol of Fulmar aircraft was kept in the air from seven in the morning. The Swordfish formed up in sections on their way to the coast, where the weather was dark and it was raining hard. Seven of the pilots turned out to sea to wait for light, but the eighth, flown by an inexperienced crew, entered cloud at about 5,000 feet and was unable to see land. The cloud thickness varied between 5,000 and 9,000 feet, and this pilot never managed to locate the target.

Before long, the seven other Swordfish flew inland to the Tirso Dam, and the first to attack made an approach along the length of the lake. It immediately came under heavy fire from anti-aircraft batteries set up on either side of a bridge crossing the foot of Lake Tirso. It abandoned its attack, turned and tried another approach, but again was met by very heavy ack-ack. The pilot reckoned he would never get through such a thick barrage, so he abandoned the attack and jettisoned his torpedo.

The rest of the strike force, now down to six aircraft, made individual approaches. Two aircraft, the first flown by Lt Godfrey Fausset, the pilot who had led the attack on the Italian cruisers at Spartivento, avoided the anti-aircraft batteries at the foot of the lake and turned to make their run towards the dam. They were also met with heavy ack-ack but managed to drop their torpedoes before taking violent evasive action to avoid getting hit. As a result they were unable to see whether they had hit the dam or not. The third Swordfish to attack flew at extremely low level all the way in from the coast, following the river that fed the lake. Flying at 50 feet the whole way, the pilot, Sub Lt Charlier, took the crews of the anti-aircraft batteries totally by surprise, made his drop and was only fired at when he was making his getaway. As the Commander (Air) on *Ark Royal* remarked, his method showed thought and initiative. It was unfortunately to no avail. Only one other torpedo was launched at the dam, by Sub Lt Ken Pattison, who lost his leader in the clouds, dived and found himself almost above the target. Too high, he turned, and again under a heavy barrage launched his torpedo at a height of 150 feet travelling at 145 knots.

The dam remained intact.

Seven Swordfish returned to the *Ark* – the eighth was shot down, its crew taken prisoner – and had landed on by 0905 hours. The weather was getting even worse, so the *Ark* signalled to Somerville that it would probably be impossible to carry out the second part of the mission. The present wind and sea conditions meant that aircraft could not be flown off in the dark, and the low cloud that was forecast would make an attack difficult. If there was any further increase in the wind, it would be impossible to carry out deck landings. At ten past seven that evening it was still blowing a gale and the attack on Genoa was abandoned. The *Ark* and Force H returned to Gibraltar.

On the way they carried out a series of training exercises that covered the spectrum of operations the *Ark* had to deal with. Four Skuas practised dive-bombing attacks on the other ships in Force H, Swordfish crews practised torpedo attacks on the escort destroyers, and another Skua dived at the *Ark* for an hour for a gunnery training class. The lessons of the failed attack on the Italian fleet had been taken to heart and every opportunity was being taken to hone the skill of the air crews, which were now often joining the ship with little experience.

It seemed to Somerville and the captain of the *Ark Royal* that the Italian forces had been forewarned about the attack on the dam. The information from the Admiralty that the dam was lightly defended had certainly proved wrong. Somerville believed there had been a serious breach of security. In the circumstances, the *Ark* had been lucky to lose only one Swordfish and crew. From this point on, to prevent information being leaked in the run-up to sensitive operations, the *Ark* and the other ships in Force H were kept at one hour's notice for steaming, preventing the crews from taking shore leave.

The most important part of the mission, the attack on Genoa, might have been cancelled because of poor flying conditions, but the reasons for carrying it out – the need to influence both the Spanish government and the Italian Navy – had not gone away. A week later the *Ark Royal* and Force H was again steaming to the east in order to carry out the bombardment. This attack on the Italian mainland still posed enormous risks to the *Ark* and Force H, and the anti-submarine and fighter patrols were instructed to avoid being seen by merchant ships and radio warning of their course so that Force H could take avoiding action.

Aircraft from the *Ark Royal* were detailed to mine the entrance to the harbour of La Spezia and bomb an oil refinery at Livorno. At five in the morning on Sunday, 9 February, fourteen Swordfish flew off carrying four 250lb bombs each, followed by four aircraft carrying magnetic mines. John Moffat of 808 Squadron was one of the pilots in that mine-laying force. Their main aim was to achieve surprise by making a very quiet low-level approach over the town of Spezia itself. With engines throttled back, flying into the prevailing wind, the Swordfish were virtually silent. The town already had some of its lights on; Moffat's observer remarked that the people must be going to Mass. All four aircraft dropped their mines. Meanwhile, eleven of the fourteen Swordfish that had the Azienda oil refinery at Livorno as their target succeeded in making a rendezvous over the town and dropped their bombs, causing a large explosion. Two of the three aircraft that had lost the target made their way to Pisa where they bombed the marshalling yards. Unlike the previous operation, the raiders from the *Ark Royal* had achieved almost complete surprise; the anti-aircraft fire only started once the raid was underway. One Swordfish was shot down and the crew were taken prisoner, but by a quarter to nine in the morning all the other aircraft had landed back on the *Ark*'s flight deck.

The bombardment of Genoa was carried out by the big guns of the *Renown* and the *Malaya*, and they opened fire at a quarter past seven. Somerville, on the *Renown*, was uncomfortable about the whole operation. He knew it was inevitable that civilians would be killed, and in a letter to his wife he wrote, 'War is lousy. For half an hour we blazed away and I had to think of Senglea, Valletta, London and Bristol to harden my heart.' The bombardment was devastatingly effective. Salvoes from the *Renown* ripped up the railway track at the marshalling yards and damaged factories on both sides of the River Polecevera. A shell in the vicinity of the power station caused a large explosion in an oil tank. The dry docks and warehouses were also hit, but one of the observers from the spotting Swordfish remarked once he had landed back on the *Ark*

Royal that he'd seen whole rows of houses knocked down like a pack of cards by a single shell.

Their job done, Force H left the scene and by half past nine had rejoined the *Ark Royal*. Now was the most dangerous part of the operation. The Italian defences had been well and truly notified of the presence of the *Ark Royal* and Force H, and it would require eight hours' steaming before the ships were out of range of the Italian Air Force. The small fleet was quickly located by reconnaissance aircraft, and two shadowing aircraft were shot down by the *Ark*'s combat air patrol. Just over an hour later the first attack was made. Two bombers targeted the *Ark*, but their aim was off. With remarkable luck, Force H was covered by a deep haze that effectively obscured the ships from aircraft above. For several hours the ships sailed on, and Ron Skinner remembers that the noise of bombers circling overhead created enormous tension on board the *Ark*, where the crew stood at action stations expecting the enemy aircraft at any minute to burst through the clouds. But they never did, and the *Ark Royal* returned safely to Gibraltar.

Somerville was astounded that so remarkably audacious an operation had achieved such complete surprise, particularly in light of the previous adventure on the Tirso Dam. The raid received considerable publicity in Britain and was an enormous boost to the government after the loss of the *Illustrious*. The war in North Africa was not going well, and the losses in the North Atlantic to the German U-boat campaign were mounting. Once more the *Ark Royal* and Force H had pulled off another coup and given the country some very welcome good news. Moreover, the talks between Mussolini and Franco did not result in any change in Spanish policy towards Britain and Gibraltar.

It had been a turbulent few weeks during which the Royal Navy's power in the Mediterranean had waxed and waned, but after the successful attack on Genoa confidence aboard the *Ark Royal* was again at a high. But harder challenges lay ahead.

9

OPERATION TIGER

It is hard to appreciate today the extent to which the size of the Royal Navy was reduced during the decades before the start of the Second World War. The global obligations and ambitions of the Royal Navy at the height of the British Empire's power were by 1939 impossible to sustain. War quickly started to expose the cracks in the façade. Churchill's decision to wage war against Italy and to seek to maintain control of the Mediterranean despite French capitulation was stretching the Royal Navy to the limit. The *Ark Royal* found itself at the heart of the unfolding events, moving rapidly from theatre to theatre, strengthening weaknesses in the fleet wherever they occurred.

The Commander in Chief of the Kriegsmarine (the German Navy), Admiral Erich Raeder, had spent a considerable time in the 1920s analysing German naval doctrine and strategy during the First World War. He had come to the conclusion that the most effective part of the German naval offensive was not the giant battle in the North Sea between the German High Seas Fleet and the British Grand Fleet, but the efforts of the commerce raiders that roamed the South Atlantic and the Pacific, attacking merchant shipping and tying down large numbers of British warships. Raeder had pursued this policy in the current conflict, and it had proved to be just as effective. The *Graf Spee* had not sunk a large amount of commercial tonnage, but it had forced the Royal Navy to send the *Ark Royal* and *Renown* to the South Atlantic, and other task groups of carriers and battleships to other oceans. Once there they spent weeks fruitlessly scouring the area for the German pocket battleships.

The French defeat in 1940 had allowed the Kriegsmarine access to the Atlantic ports on the French coast, and this gave Raeder's strategy a new lease of life. That year had in fact proved to be one of the most tumultuous in history, the German blitzkrieg overwhelming all opposition throughout Europe. The *Ark Royal* had been extremely active throughout the year, in Norway and in the Mediterranean, and by the end of the year she was tied up in harbour in Gibraltar.

Christmas Day 1940 started like any other on the *Ark Royal*. Engine room artificer John McCrow described the atmosphere at six o'clock in the morning in the ERAs' mess: 'It is early morning and the mess decks are still dimly lit with the shaded blue night-time lighting. Rows of oatmeal-coloured canvas hammocks are gently swaying with the motion of the ship. There is a soft creaking sound coming from the ropes securing the hammocks to the rails fixed to the deck head above. From the scuttles in the metal ducting of the ventilation system comes the swishing sound of the air passing through. Someone murmurs in his sleep and there is an occasional snore. These are the sort of noises of the night. At six o'clock, halfway through the morning watch, the stillness is shattered by the loudspeakers blasting our reveille. The main lighting comes on and a voice shouts, "Wakey wakey, rise and shine, you've had your time, now I'll have mine. Lift up and stow!"'

You could normally tell the day of the week on the *Ark* by the lunchtime menu. 'Sunday was the crème de la crème day, always tomato soup, roast beef, Yorkshire pudding, roast potatoes, and custard with tinned sliced peaches. There was a soup served every day. On Thursday it was mulligatawny, and then I think Irish stew was the main dish on a Tuesday. The amount of bones always outweighed the meat. On a Friday we usually had fish for the main course. The plate of lovely golden battered fish and chips was not all that it seemed. When cutting through the batter a piece of salted cod with a black skin would be revealed.' But on Christmas Day

1940 the crew were looking forward to a day of rest and a slap-up Christmas dinner. The menu had already been printed and it promised giblet soup, a proper roast turkey and chipolatas, Brussels sprouts and roast potatoes. The captain, 'Hooky' Holland, had been photographed stirring the Christmas pudding mix in enormous basins, and after dinner a women's concert party was scheduled to come on board to entertain the crew in the hangar decks.

By one thirty in the afternoon the Christmas dinner had been eaten, and on the various mess decks illicitly saved bottles of the daily rum ration were being passed around. 'It was about two o'clock in the afternoon, when we were thinking about the afternoon show, when over the Tannoy came, "Red watch below!" So we said to ourselves, "They're joking," but it was repeated. "At the double!" Nobody moved. Then the senior chief engineers got going, and then the chief stokers are coming out – their mess was further along from us. But no-one on the stokers' mess deck would move. They were not going down below; they were having their Christmas Day. And the senior engineer came along and he was up on one of the mess deck tables shouting a few rude words, and they were shouting them back at him. Eventually they managed to get the stokers down below. But it took two and a half hours before we were underway.'

The *Admiral Hipper* was threatening a convoy 700 miles east of Cape Finisterre; she was a sister ship of the

Prinz Eugen, a heavy cruiser armed with 8-inch guns. Hit by shells from the warship that was escorting the convoy, HMS *Berwick*, the *Hipper* retreated and put into Brest harbour for repairs. By the time the *Ark* arrived on the scene the convoy had scattered, and the carrier spent three days locating and shepherding the merchant ships back on to their course, under the protection of another escort ship. A further three days later the *Ark* was back in port in Gibraltar.

Raeder had proved his point. It was clear that access to the French Atlantic ports was of enormous benefit to the Kriegsmarine, and that the rapid deployment of two commerce raiders could bring the *Ark Royal* out of the Mediterranean. For the Royal Navy, this was a grave situation. German armed forces were starting to threaten British positions in the eastern Mediterranean. The Luftwaffe had attacked the *Illustrious*, Malta itself was under continual air attack, and there was a build-up of German armed forces preparing to come to the assistance of the Italian Army in Greece. The Royal Navy was being stretched by the need to fight from Alexandria in the east through the entire Mediterranean, into the Atlantic and up to the north of the Arctic Circle off Norway.

In February 1941 Admiral Somerville signalled to the Admiralty his proposal for a series of operations in the western Mediterranean to threaten enemy positions on the Italian coast and relieve pressure on the fleet in the east. The Admiralty replied that he was not to do so, as

Force H was going to be deployed on the protection of trade routes in the Atlantic.

There was a pressing reason for the Admiralty's message to Somerville. On 5 February those veterans of the Norwegian invasion of 1940, the German battleships *Scharnhorst* and *Gneisenau* under the command of Vice Admiral Günther Lutjens, had slipped into the Atlantic and were heading for the convoy routes. Their campaign was proving highly successful. Working in collaboration with a fleet of U-boats, the *Scharnhorst* and *Gneisenau* accounted for over twenty-six cargo ships either sunk or captured, and the torpedoing, by a U-boat, of the battleship *Malaya*. Now every convoy had to have a battleship escort, with its own anti-submarine escort. The *Ark Royal*, with Force H, was detached from the Mediterranean once again to patrol the Atlantic in search of German surface raiders.

Ark Royal and Force H put out from Gibraltar on 8 March and headed west towards the Canary Islands. Their orders were to relieve the *Malaya* from escort duty of a convoy and allow the damaged battleship to proceed to port in the United States for repairs. It was near the Canaries that the *Scharnhorst* and *Gneisenau* had been operating, and liaising with the U-boat flotilla. The *Ark* tried to keep a force of Swordfish torpedo bombers ranged on the flight deck in permanent readiness in case of an encounter, and during the first few days of their patrol the Swordfish were kept on the flight deck overnight, but the wet weather affected the aircraft. Night-time rain put the radios on the Swordfish out of action, and damp affected the engines. After that the aircraft were moved down to the hangar decks.

On 10 March, Force H made contact with the convoy. *Malaya* departed and the *Ark Royal* increased its readiness for action. The Skua squadron on board was kept armed with 500lb semi armour-piercing bombs, despite the fact that these had proved ineffective against the heavy armour of the *Scharnhorst* during the last attack against it in Trondheim Fjord. For the next seven days the *Ark* had the responsibility of escorting the convoy on its course across the Atlantic. An intensive flying programme was carried out. Three-quarters of an hour before sunrise an anti-submarine patrol of three Swordfish armed with depth charges was flown off. After patrolling around the convoy, they took up a position 15 miles ahead. A relief patrol of anti-submarine Swordfish also armed with depth charges was kept ranged on deck at readiness, the pilots' observers and telegraphist air gunners waiting in the squadron ready rooms. In the afternoon all-round searches were carried out by nine aircraft, patrolling as far ahead as 120 miles, and during this time a torpedo armed force was kept at readiness throughout the day, as were relief shadowing aircraft should a surface raider be spotted.

Such operations took their toll on both aircraft and men. Sub Lt John Moffat remembers the excruciating routine. The crew would come out onto the flight deck and climb into the cockpit up the small metal steps inset into the Swordfish fuselage, taking care not to put a flying boot through the canvas covering. The engine was started by two flight mechanics inserting a huge starting handle in the side of the cowling and, when everything was ready, turning it as fast as they could. This rotated a flywheel in the engine, and when it was at sufficient speed they would yell and the pilot would press the ignition switch, firing up the radial engine. John would sometimes mistime the ignition switch, and 'they would have to start all over again. There would be curses and God knows what else – which I was not meant to hear of course.' Then the Swordfish, at full throttle, would roll down the flight deck, lift off and head out over the sea on patrols that according to John 'were excruciatingly boring, lasting for three hours or more, over the broad expanse of empty ocean'. The pilots on these patrols would fly over 100 miles away from the *Ark* in a set pattern over the sea, then they would return to the carrier that would in the meantime have moved to a new position. Navigation was by dead reckoning most of the time, the observer hoping to keep an accurate plot of the aircraft's course, with any variations in wind direction and speed accurately recorded.

It was intensely monotonous, lonely and dangerous, and there were casualties. On 15 March a Swordfish failed to return to the carrier from a long-range patrol.

There was no signal, although radio silence was the norm so it was unlikely any distress message would have been sent. A Swordfish and three crew members had just silently disappeared. The pilot could have taken the wrong course and run out of petrol, or crashed because of mechanical failure. John Moffat recalled, 'I parcelled up his clothes and belongings, addressed them to his family and handed it in for posting when we got back to Gib. And then you put it out of your mind. There but for the grace of God.'

On the twelfth day of the mission the *Ark Royal* sighted HMS *Kenya*, the cruiser detailed to take over the protection of the convoy. The *Ark* then concentrated on a search for German supply ships that might lead Force H to the *Scharnhorst*. Six Swordfish aircraft and three Fulmars were flown off and three supply ships were finally spotted, the *Bianca*, the *San Casimiro* and the *Polykarp*. Swordfish were sent off to shadow each of them in the hope that eventually they would liaise with the German warships. However, it soon became obvious that the crews had been given orders: on being spotted they should abandon their ship and scuttle it. The pilots' instructions were to prevent this, if necessary by opening fire with their forward-mounted machine guns.

John Moffat was sent to shadow the *San Casimiro*, and when he arrived he found that the crew were preparing to lower the ship's boats prior to scuttling her. He flew at the ship and fired at the lifeboats, but the forward machine gun was designed to fire through the propeller, and the interrupter mechanism that prevented the bullets from damaging the propeller blades made the rate of fire extremely slow. John believes he could have fired faster with a revolver. While he was trying to damage the ship's boat on one side, the boats on the other side were being lowered, and the crew set fire to the ship before abandoning it.

Another patrol, trailing the *Polykarp*, was having more success. Five Swordfish and three Fulmars had been flown off the *Ark* at four in the afternoon in the belief that the Fulmars with their greater speed would take less time to establish contact than the Swordfish. One of the Fulmars was piloted by Lt Commander Tillard, and his observer was Lt Mark Somerville, Admiral Somerville's nephew. As they searched for the *Polykarp*, they saw below them two German warships steering north. They had spotted the *Scharnhorst* and the *Gneisenau*. Unfortunately their radio chose this vital moment to break down; they could do nothing else but fly at maximum speed back to the *Ark Royal* with the news of their sighting. They landed at half past six.

Captain Holland considered his options. He had seven Swordfish aircraft on patrol, and ten left on board. He immediately had one Swordfish prepared to head to the last reported position of the *Scharnhorst* and *Gneisenau*, which because of the radio failure on the Fulmar was now an hour old. The nine remaining Swordfish were armed with torpedoes and were ready on the flight deck at 1845. In the meantime the captain was calculating ranges and flying times, for the enemy battleships were some 140 miles away and dusk was falling. It would be impossible for the Swordfish to make contact with the two German warships before nightfall. Lt Commander Tillard and Lt Somerville argued that as they had first spotted the *Scharnhorst* and *Gneisenau*, they should take out a Fulmar and search again, which they did, but after an hour on patrol with the light fading they gave up and returned to the *Ark*, landing on at night. The next morning a thick fog lay over the sea to a height of 3,000 feet. Contact with the *Scharnhorst* and its sister ship had been lost completely.

That day, a Swordfish was catapulted off the flight deck on an anti-submarine patrol. The catapults or accelerators were trolleys mounted on the forward part of the flight deck which were fastened to the fuselage of the aircraft being accelerated. When the order to launch was given, the aircraft's engine would be running at full speed and a hydraulic piston under the flight deck would propel the trolley forward, releasing the aircraft at the end of its run. This time, however, the Swordfish did not release from the trolley, and the fuselage broke up. The front part, including the cockpit with the crew and the depth charges under the wing, hurtled into the sea. The crew were seen swimming away, but the great bows of the *Ark* ploughed over the aircraft. The depth charges sank to their predetermined depth and then exploded. Robert Elkington was in his mess at the time, level with the water line in the bows. 'It was an enormous crash,' he recalled, 'and I was sitting with my back to the side of the ship. I was thrown onto the floor as if a horse had kicked me in the back, and I thought my back was broken.' The impact of the explosions under the hull caused the ship to whip into the air, and on the *Ark*'s eventual return to Gibraltar several splits in the hull had to be repaired with concrete.

Despite the accident, efforts to search for the *Scharnhorst* and *Gneisenau* continued, but Lutjens evaded them and headed safely for Brest, the French port on the Atlantic coast. He had had a very successful and bloody cruise.

The *Ark* had been in the Atlantic almost without a break since early February, when she finally docked in Gibraltar on the first of April. Admiral Raeder's strategy was really paying off. The continuous air patrols, totalling on some days as many as thirty-seven flights, had taken its toll on the men and machines. In the two weeks from 10 March the number of serviceable Swordfish on the *Ark* dropped from a total of twenty-seven to fifteen. Meanwhile, back in the Mediterranean things were also rapidly deteriorating for Britain.

Rommel had opened an offensive in North Africa and was advancing towards Egypt. The German Army, which had been concentrating in Albania, invaded Greece on 6 April and began to drive back the Greek and British armies. By the end of the month it was clear that Greece was lost. Troops and artillery taken from General Wavell's Army of the Nile had been unable to stop the German 12th Army from overrunning the entire country. Those men would now need to be evacuated. In North Africa, the British Army, weakened by the loss of the men and materiel sent to Greece, was now unable to withstand the Afrika Korps' attacks. Cyrenaica, with the exception of Tobruk, was once more in enemy hands.

Wavell had reported to the War Cabinet in London that a German Panzer division had been identified in North Africa. He told them that he urgently needed tank reinforcements to deal with this threat. Even before the evacuation of Greece had been completed, a convoy of five mechanized transport ships left England for Egypt carrying the new tanks that would bolster Wavell's forces. Since the Luftwaffe's entry into the war in the Mediterranean most supplies to the British Army of the Nile had travelled the long route around the Cape of Good Hope. The Admiralty was again extremely reluctant to attempt to run a convoy through the Mediterranean, but Churchill was impatient with these anxieties. 'The fate of the war in the Middle East, the loss of the Suez Canal, the frustration or confusion of the enormous forces we have built up in Egypt . . . all may turn on a few hundred armoured vehicles,' he said.

He would brook no opposition, and ordered the convoy to go by the shortest route.

Operation Tiger was the result, which would, if successful, deliver 307 tanks to Alexandria and 43 Hurricane fighter aircraft, in crates, to be assembled by the RAF in Egypt. HMS *Breconshire*, the special supply ship, would transport fuel and munitions to Malta, and the battleship *Queen Elizabeth* and two cruisers would also travel the length of the Mediterranean under the protection of Force H to reinforce Cunningham's fleet in the eastern Mediterranean. On 5 May the *Ark Royal* sailed west to meet this convoy. Somerville called these transport ships 'ships that passed in the night', because they never stopped at Gibraltar, passing instead under cover of darkness through the Straits with Force H.

There had been some changes in the *Ark Royal*. Captain Holland's health had been deteriorating in the year that he had commanded the carrier, and he left the ship to recuperate, and then became a staff officer in Gibraltar. The new commander was Captain Loben Maund, fresh from a post in Combined Operations, where he had been responsible, among other things, for working up plans to invade the Italian island of Pantelleria. His knowledge of the strategic situation in the Mediterranean was now going to be severely tested.

The *Ark Royal*'s squadrons of Skuas had now been fully replaced by Fulmar fighters, and there were two squadrons of these planes on board, 803 and 807, though out of the nominal number of twenty-four aircraft only twelve were serviceable and fit to fly. If the Luftwaffe attacked the convoy their tactics would be similar to those deployed on *Illustrious*, whose Fulmars were swamped by a far greater number of Stuka dive bombers and Messerschmitt fighters. There was almost no chance that the small number of Fulmars on the *Ark* could stand up to a Luftwaffe onslaught.

It was impossible to know whether the complicated manoeuvres carried out by Force H and the components of the convoys ever fooled the Italian spies in Algeciras, although they may have assumed that the Navy would never, now, dare attempt to pass another convoy down the length of the Mediterranean. Admiral Cunningham's fleet in the eastern Mediterranean was heavily engaged in the evacuation of the British Army from Greece, and his sailors were paying the price for pre-war decisions that left the fleet bereft of fighter protection. On 8 May, in the waters off Greece, two destroyers, *Diamond* and *Wryneck*, came to the assistance of a troop ship that had been bombed and was struggling to reach safety. Between them they took off seven hundred troops and headed at top speed for Crete. They were, however, still in range of the German Stukas, and both destroyers were bombed and sunk. Just one officer, forty-one ratings and eight soldiers survived the deadly attack.

Almost simultaneously, at the other end of the Mediterranean, Force H and the Tiger convoy was spotted by an Italian reconnaissance aircraft. They were three days out from Gibraltar and they had so far evaded detection, but it couldn't last. The presence of this enormously tempting target, a convoy of five large transports with a maximum speed of 14 knots with the *Ark Royal*, the *Renown* and other major warships for company, caused a rapid mobilization of the Italian and German air forces.

At 1345 on 8 May eight aircraft were sighted approaching very low on the starboard bow of the *Ark Royal*. 'They were wicked-looking brutes,' Somerville recorded, and they were also dangerous: Italian S79 torpedo bombers whose pilots had a reputation among the sailors on the *Ark* for pressing home an attack despite a barrage of anti-aircraft fire. One bomber was shot down and crashed into the sea in an eruption of water and wreckage, but the others continued doggedly on their course through gunfire from machine guns and rapid-firing cannon, heading for the two big ships. They dropped their torpedoes inside the destroyer screen designed to protect the *Ark* and the *Renown*. Each aircraft launched two torpedoes simultaneously, and the *Ark Royal* took immediate evasive action to comb the tracks, two torpedoes passing down the port side and the other two avoided on the starboard bow. Admiral Somerville saw one of the torpedoes heading straight for *Renown*, his flagship. 'Now we're for it, I thought, but would you believe it, the damn thing had finished its run

and I watched it sinking about 10 yards from the ship.'
Two more of the torpedo bombers were hit by the hail of
close-range weapon fire as they flew low over their
targets, and crashed into the sea.

The torpedo bombers had been accompanied by a
squadron of CR42 fighters, and their formation had been
spotted by *Sheffield*'s radar ten minutes before they
were seen from the *Renown*. The two Fulmars that were
already in the air, flown by Lt Commander Tillard and Lt
Hay, saw the fighters climbing to attack them. Outnumbered three to one, both pilots dived to make a
head-on attack, passing directly through the enemy's
formation. The Fulmar flown by Tillard with his observer
Mark Somerville went into a steep dive and was last seen
trying to level out at 500 feet. Lt Hay, in the second
Fulmar, started to follow him down but was attacked
during the dive by two CR42 fighters; to evade them he
turned into clouds and then dived down towards the fleet,
where he was fired on by the destroyer in the anti-
submarine screen. Fortunately, it scored no hits.

A section of three more Fulmars, which had taken off
from the *Ark Royal* when the enemy formation was
identified, also saw a group of six CR42 fighters coming
up to attack them, and they dived into a head-on attack.
A confusing mêlée ensued during which Lt Taylour shot
off the wing tip of one Italian fighter but was himself shot
up by an attacker closing in behind him. His Fulmar was
hit, and his observer, Petty Officer Howard, was badly

wounded. The other two Fulmars, flown by Petty Officer Dubber and Lt Guthrie, were both badly damaged in the dogfight, but Guthrie, after pulling out of a steep spin at a very low altitude, found one of the Italian 579s in his sights and attacked it twice before his guns failed.

These four shot-up Fulmars – Tillard's plane had disappeared – now circled the *Ark*, waiting to land, which they managed at 1437 hours. The torpedo attack and the battle in the air had lasted just one hour. The guns were now silent, the ready-use lockers in the 4.5-inch gun turrets and the magazines of the rapid-firing cannons restocked and ready for the next attack. The excitement and the adrenalin rush of action, the chaotic noise of every gun in the fleet hammering away, was gone, to be replaced by a quietness that could barely be heard through the ringing in the ears of the gunners. Everyone was keyed up, waiting for the next attack. In the hangar decks, the warning bells on the lifts were sounding as planes were brought down from the flight deck, the fireproof curtains were raised and the fitters and armourers frantically tried to repair the aircraft. An already pathetically inadequate number of fighters on the *Ark* had just been reduced from twelve to seven, an observer was in the sick bay being operated on, and the commanding officer of 808 Squadron, who had been on the *Ark* since November 1940 with several kills to his credit, was dead, as was his observer, Lt Mark Somerville.

It had been a brutal sixty minutes, and another attack

could occur at any minute. The *Ark Royal* worked hard to keep four Fulmars in the air as a permanent combat air patrol, aircraft landing and refuelling every hour to make sure that they would always have enough endurance to take on the enemy.

The next phase in the air battle for Operation Tiger started at 1510 when *Sheffield*'s radar spotted a reconnaissance aircraft circling the fleet. Two Fulmars were directed by radio to intercept and shoot it down. At the same time, these two Fulmars and the other section of two making up the permanent patrol spotted an Italian S79 bomber. They all converged on it, shooting enough bullets into it to break it up in the air. As the Fulmars returned to the fleet one of them had to ditch in the sea, its engine pouring out white fumes. The crew were rescued by a destroyer, but the aircraft sank quickly.

At a few minutes after four that afternoon, *Sheffield*'s radar plotter reported several formations of aircraft approaching from various points of the compass, and two of them appeared to be large. Having seen off two waves of attack, the prospect of another must have filled the crew with dread. Their situation was desperate. Only a handful of fighters were available and every pilot had seen combat at least once already that day. All available aircraft were flown off, instructed to climb to 8,000 feet and circle at 5 miles' distance. Three Fulmars from 808 Squadron were sent to intercept the formations, but one was forced to return to the carrier when the pilot was unable to retract his undercarriage. The other two Fulmars, flown by Lt Kindersley and Lt Hay, in the air for the second time that day, continued with the attack. Hay shot at a CR42 from behind, causing it to turn away, then took on three S79 bombers in a head-on attack, disrupting their formation and causing them to jettison their bombs and seek shelter in cloud. Meanwhile, Lt Kindersley was manoeuvring to attack a group of bombers when he was ambushed by four CR42 fighters; he decided to fly into the fleet's anti-aircraft barrage, where the enemy fighters refused to follow. After this attack was broken up the two Fulmars were then directed by the air control officer on the *Ark* to intercept another aircraft that had appeared on *Sheffield*'s radar. The aircraft was another S79 bomber, and Lt Hay shot it down in flames. The third Fulmar in the air was flown by Petty Officer Johnson, who avoided three Italian fighters attempting to fire on him from the rear and then saw an S79 bomber which he chased and eventually caught, firing all of his remaining ammunition into it. By then he was 30 miles from the fleet and had to be directed home. He landed at almost five o'clock in the afternoon.

While Hay and Johnson were making their attacks, three S79 bombers penetrated the anti-aircraft barrages and headed for the *Ark Royal*, coming out of the sun, which was now low in the west, clearly hoping to drop their bombs down the centre line of the ship – the ideal approach for an air attack. The *Ark* manoeuvred rapidly to port and opened up with all of her guns. She had been designed and built with a multi-barrelled pom-pom platform on the port side, but they had been in such short supply that even now, this far into the war, the pom-poms had not been fitted. John McCrow in the engine room heard the crack of the big guns and then the machine-gun fire opening up and knew that the ship was in immediate danger. 'I used to curse the bastards who had not given us that pom-pom when I felt the ship heeling over and everything opening up,' he said. One bomber did not survive the bullets and the high explosive the *Ark*'s gunners blasted up into the sky; it turned away and jettisoned its bombs in a desperate attempt to gain some height, but crashed into the sea. The machine gunners and all the flight deck crew, crouched in the walkways at the edge of the flight deck, saw the two other bombers boring on towards them, turning to follow the *Ark* and releasing their bombs. They exploded close to the bows on the starboard side, just ahead of the ship. The *Ark* had escaped again.

At 1720, four aircraft from 807 Squadron took to the air, flown by Lt Cdr Douglas, Petty Officer Leggett, Lt Gardner and Lt Firth. As they climbed to reach another enemy formation Gardner heard a sudden bang. His port wing dipped, and he realized that the panel covering his four machine guns in the port wing had been ripped off in the slipstream. He requested permission to land on the carrier again, but then saw that the *Ark* was firing at another group of approaching bombers. This was not a good time to try to land on, so he climbed and attacked one of them, getting in several bursts before losing his target in cloud. When Gardner gave up the chase and left the cloud he was fired at by the escort ships, so he too sought the shelter of the clouds and waited for the firing to stop before landing on the *Ark* to have his wing panels replaced. The other three pilots also attacked the Italian bombers, firing at and chasing them for some distance, constantly hampered in their pursuit by the low speed of their Fulmar fighters. They too eventually lost their prey in the clouds. They continued to maintain a patrol, occasionally being fired on by their own ships.

Throughout the day, Force H and the transports carrying the tanks and Hurricanes for Egypt had been steaming ever closer to Sicily, and at 1918 hours the radar operators on *Sheffield* picked up echoes that they interpreted as large formations of aircraft approaching from Sicily, 42 miles away. The information was immediately passed to the *Ark Royal*. It was yet another massive incoming attack, and this time it could easily be the Luftwaffe from its airfields in Sicily. The news was received with trepidation, for the reason why some of the Sea Lords in the Admiralty, and Somerville and Cunningham, had argued against trying to pass a convoy of vital reinforcements through the Mediterranean was now materializing. It was the Luftwaffe, whose deadly dive bombers had crippled *Illustrious* and were now sinking British warships rescuing the British Army from Greece.

The Commander Air on the *Ark*, Commander Henry Traill, and the captain rapidly assessed the situation. There were three Fulmars in the air, which would need refuelling in another forty-five minutes, and they had already been in combat so had used up a lot of their ammunition. There were a further four Fulmars on the *Ark Royal* that could make it into the air again, making a grand total of seven aircraft with which to defend the fleet and the convoy on which, according to Churchill, the fate of the British Army in North Africa depended. It was a daunting task. I once asked Val Bailey, who had flown a Fulmar in 808 Squadron on the *Ark Royal*, whether he had ever been frightened. 'We were young and we were fighter pilots,' he replied. 'We had the invincible belief of the young in our own immortality. And anyway, you just had to get on with it. You certainly weren't going to hang about and wait to get bombed – the bloody gunnery people couldn't hit anything. No, you got worried, because there were a lot of things to worry about and go wrong, and because you had so much to do, but you didn't get frightened. Although there was every reason to do so.'

The pilots still in the air on that evening of 8 May were joined by the other four aircraft. Lt Gardner's Fulmar had been repaired and he took off again for his fourth fighter patrol. Petty Officer Dubber, Lt Taylour and Sub Lt

Walker followed him off the *Ark Royal*'s flight deck, their Merlin engines hauling the heavy aircraft slowly into the air. Those seven pilots with their observers in the rear cockpits were all that now stood between the *Ark Royal*, Force H and the approaching German dive bombers. They went into the fight extremely aggressively, despite the overwhelming numbers of enemy aircraft that confronted them.

The German aircraft had split up into different sections, and the fighter direction officer on the *Ark* thought they were preparing to make a concerted attack from three directions so that the *Ark* would always be presenting a perfect target to at least one section of dive bombers. The three fighters already on patrol at 8,000 feet were directed by the *Ark* to fly to the north of the fleet, where the radar operators on *Sheffield* had identified a number of aircraft circling above some stratus cloud. As they approached they saw that they were a group of fifteen Stuka dive bombers under the protection of six Messerschmitt Me110s, twin-engined long-range fighters. Lt Commander Douglas turned into the Me110s and fired at two in turn, seeing the second one he had hit go down into cloud. The rear gunners of both Messerschmitts returned fire, and Douglas's Fulmar was hit in the leading edge of both wings, and his hydraulic system was damaged. Petty Officer Leggett, Douglas's wingman, dived straight on to the circling Stukas, but one of the German fighters attempted to intercept him. Leggett turned inside the Messerchmitt and fired a burst of machine-gun fire into the cockpit, putting the rear gunner out of action; the German aircraft seemed to stall and turn, and it dived into cloud with a trail of white smoke behind it. Lt Firth was met by two of the German fighters climbing towards him and he made a head-on approach, firing into the leading aircraft. This one also turned away and dived into cloud with smoke pouring from one engine. The second Messerschmitt was also fired on by Leggett, and this too manoeuvred away from the attack into cloud.

These three pilots had, in an incredibly brave and aggressive approach, driven off six Messerschmitt fighters, probably damaging at least three. The three Fulmar pilots continued to search for them under the cloud but could not locate them. They were soon running short of fuel and ammunition and had to return to the *Ark*.

The four pilots who had taken off from the *Ark Royal* had now climbed to 9,000 feet and saw that as well as the six escorting Messerschmitts there was a group of sixteen Stukas and another group of twelve. Lt Taylour dived into the latter to break it up, carrying out several attacks and pursuing the Stukas into cloud for about 30 miles. His plane was hit and the starboard undercarriage leg dropped down, forcing him to return to the *Ark*. Petty Officer Dubber, who was Lt Taylour's wingman, made a head-on attack, then turned and started firing from the rear quarter. One of the escorting fighters then attempted

The underwater photograph clearly shows the inverted fairleads and the projecting bracket for the navigating light, also visible in the photograph of the *Ark* being fitted out.

Left: The very first sonar trace of the *Ark* obtained by the *Odin Finder* was only understandable by experts.

Below: The AUV on the *Rig Supporter* obtained more information, (*bottom*), but even this needed interpretation.

Left: The *Octopus*, one of the largest yachts in the world, took the search for the *Ark* to its conclusion.

Right: Val Bailey, Bill Morrison, John Moffat, John Richardson and Ron Skinner look at the *Ark's* blueprints on board the *Octopus*.

Below: The Octorov, purpose-built with special lights and cameras, is launched from its hangar on the *Octopus*.

The giant anchors are revealed in the ROV spotlights.

The trail of wreckage contains lockers, with cups and teapots still unbroken, and even small batteries are highlighted by the lights on the ROV (*below*).

This black and white photograph (*centre*) shows the bows of the *Ark* being painted in Alexandria. The 36-inch searchlight (*top right*) is also revealed, and the depth markings are still there on the hull (*bottom right*).

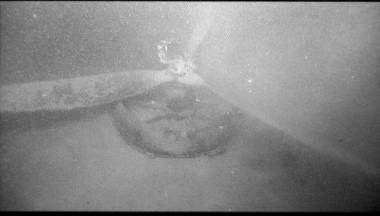

The Fairey Swordfish (*top*) were the workhorses of the *Ark Royal*. Very little remains on the bottom of the sea, but propellers (*middle*) and engines (*bottom*) can still be picked out.

The all-metal Fulmar fighter survives slightly better (*middle*), but it's impossible to know if this was one flown by Val Bailey (*top*).

Bill Morrison, Ron Skinner, John Moffat, Val Bailey and John Richardson at the end of their exploration of the wreck (*bottom*).

The 4.5-inch anti-aircraft guns could elevate almost vertically. Here (*below*), the rear turret manned by Les Asher is adorned by a Rock Fish, caught in the lights from the ROV.

Above: The camera zooms into the interior of the turret, catching the light reflected from the optical gunsight.

to protect the dive bombers and made a stern attack on Dubber's Fulmar, which he evaded by diving into cloud.

Lt Gardner had split off from Lt Taylour's section and aggressively attacked the other section of sixteen Stukas, pouring a burst of gunfire into the nearest one which turned over and dived into the sea. He then hurtled his plane through the formation of Stukas, firing at close range at several others. His own aircraft was hit, bullets smashing the windscreen and punching holes in the engine's radiator, but he managed to break up the formation and several of the Stukas started to jettison their bombs. Gardner's aircraft was badly damaged and he had to return to the *Ark*, but his number two, Lt Firth, continued to attack a formation of three Messerschmitt 110s, which scattered into cloud. Searching for more targets, Firth then flew on and attacked a formation of Stukas before becoming embroiled in a dogfight with an Me110 which broke off the action. Firth again launched his fighter at the Stukas, pursuing a straggler into cloud with smoke pouring from it. Firth's air gunner, Leading Airman Shave, saw at least one Stuka go down in flames.

By 2139, all of the Fulmars had landed back on the *Ark Royal*. Not one Stuka had succeeded in making an attack on the fleet, despite their overwhelming superiority. Yet the day wasn't over. A separate attack had started at half past eight that night. Having sneaked in under the radar while everyone was focused on the attack from the German dive bombers, three low-level torpedo bombers flew at the *Renown* and the *Ark Royal*. One broke away after anti-aircraft fire started to hit it, and bits of its fuselage were seen flying off, but the other two launched their torpedoes. *Ark Royal* for the second time that day made a sharp turn to port and the torpedoes passed 50 metres away on the starboard side.

This was the final attack of a day that had seen the *Ark Royal* and Force H facing an onslaught of over fifty aircraft in total, defended by a maximum of twelve serviceable Fulmars out of two squadrons on board. The Fulmar, it should be remembered, had been an aircraft accepted into service by the Navy as a stopgap. It was heavy, barely faster than the bombers its pilots were attempting to shoot down, and less manoeuvrable than both Italian and German fighters. There was a sense of puzzlement on board the *Ark Royal* that the German dive bombers hadn't pursued their attack with more determination. There was a theory that the German pilots had mistaken the Fulmars for the more effective Hurricane fighters. Yet they had faced Fulmar aircraft when they successfully dive-bombed *Illustrious*, so this seems unlikely. The German attack was made late in the day, as it was growing dark, and the vigour and aggression of the Fulmar pilots might have proved a nasty surprise. Several of the Stuka formations were broken up, so the German pilots might have become unhappy about continuing their attack, which was clearly going to be aggressively opposed, in the dwindling light. Whatever the reason, the actions of the pilots, air gunners and observers of 807 and 808 Squadrons had saved an extremely vital convoy.

Several days later Admiral Somerville was told that Winston Churchill had been extremely nervous about Operation Tiger and was very pleased that it had got through. The events of 8 May make it clear that he was quite right to be anxious. The report of Captain Maund stated, 'The immunity of the convoy and fleet from damage due to air attack on this day is largely attributable to the work of this small force of fighters, made possible only by the exceptional efforts of the personnel of the flight deck and hangars.' The fighter direction had been extremely efficient in directing what few aircraft were in the air to their targets. It was just a pity that the fleet's anti-aircraft guns were not so well directed: many of the *Ark*'s pilots found themselves avoiding friendly fire. The only tragedy of the day had been the loss of Lt Commander Tillard and Lt Somerville, Admiral Somerville's nephew. They never returned to the *Ark* and their plane was never found.

Two days later, the group of destroyers that had escorted the transport ships through the Skerki Channel to Malta were returning west when they were attacked by four bombers flying low and using broken cloud as cover. None of the ships had radar or any air defence. Four sticks of bombs were dropped, and the *Faulkner* was severely damaged by a cluster of four or five near-misses very close to the stern. Her speed was cut in half, but she managed to limp back to meet Force H, and eventually reached Gibraltar. It was a salutary reminder that the threat from the air never went away.

The success of Operation Tiger was an enormous boost to morale. The *Ark Royal* and Force H had shown that the presence of the combined air forces of Italy and Germany did not mean that the Mediterranean was a no-go area, though it had been an extremely close-run thing. The *Ark* had become a highly efficient warship, and in combination with the *Sheffield* she was now adept at maximizing the limited air resources available to her.

The *Ark Royal* and its aircraft had succeeded in doing something that it was never intended to do, and which pre-war naval strategists had not thought possible. It had contested control of a sea that ought to have been dominated by the superior land-based aircraft of the enemy.

Shortly after returning to Gibraltar the *Ark* was steaming east again, this time in company with the carrier HMS *Furious* carrying a deck cargo of Hurricane aircraft that were to be flown off to reinforce Malta. It was just another reminder of how important the *Ark* was to Britain's war effort in the Mediterranean.

Later that month she would also prove her value in the war in the Atlantic, becoming the nemesis of a German admiral whose path had crossed the *Ark*'s several times before.

10

THE *BISMARCK* INCIDENT

On 21 May 1941, the *Ark Royal* was steaming into the wind near Cape Bon, on the coast of Tunisia, the western point of the Sicilian channel. It was first light, and the air still had a night-time chill to it. Flight deck crews were busily readying two Fulmar aircraft for take-off. Behind them, clustered at the rear of the flight deck, were twenty-one Hurricane aircraft fitted with long-range fuel tanks. Their pilots were making final checks on their course and working out their fuel consumption before walking out to their planes, eager to take off and get to Malta without being seen by an Italian or German reconnaissance aircraft. There was a sense of urgency in the air, for the *Ark Royal* and *Furious* were close to Sicily. With the Hurricane aircraft on the flight deck they could not launch Swordfish for anti-submarine patrols, and they were defenceless if they were attacked from the air.

The two Fulmars took off, followed by the Hurricanes, but the pilot of one of the Fulmars could not retract its undercarriage so he circled back towards the *Ark Royal*. The Hurricane pilots didn't understand what was happening and, following orders to the letter, stuck to him like glue. Communication was impossible because of radio silence, so the crew of the Fulmar, aware that the Hurricanes were eating into their fuel while they circled the carrier, headed for Malta. They knew that the excessive drag from their undercarriage, dangling in the slipstream, would shorten their range, making it impossible for them to reach their destination, but they decided that their first priority was to lead the Hurricanes to Malta, whatever their own fate. It was an act of extraordinary courage. They took the Hurricanes within easy reach of the island before ditching in the sea. Five other Fulmars and forty-seven Hurricanes arrived successfully in Malta. The mission was a success due largely to their sacrifice. Two days later, the *Ark Royal* was back in Gibraltar.

Far to the north, while the engines of the Fulmars and Hurricanes were running up on the flight deck of the *Ark*, two German warships steamed through the waters of the Skagerrak between Denmark and Norway, heading north. The *Bismarck* and the *Prinz Eugen* were beginning Operation Rhine, the latest sally into the North Atlantic as part of Admiral Raeder's strategy against the Royal Navy. Yet there was a significant difference in the threat posed by this operation. The *Bismarck*, a ship launched in August 1939, was one of the most modern battleships afloat, and one of the most powerful.

She had been laid down in the shipyard of Blohm and Voss in Hamburg in 1936. She was named after the great Prussian general and the first Chancellor of Germany, the creator of the modern state of Germany. That his name should be chosen was an indicator of the national pride that had been invested in this great modern warship. The launching ceremony drew deliberately on this tradition: the ship was launched by Bismarck's granddaughter, and the guest of honour was Hitler himself, whose ambition far exceeded the wildest dreams of the Prussian generals.

There was no other ship at sea that could match the *Bismarck*. Her main armament was eight large guns that could fire shells 38cm in diameter, each weighing almost 800kg. These giant shells could be hurled through the air over a distance of 36 kilometres. In addition, the *Bismarck* carried twelve smaller 15cm-calibre guns that were equal in firepower to a British cruiser. There were also a large number of anti-aircraft guns of different calibres. She was the largest ship afloat because she was so heavily armoured. Of her maximum weight of over 50,000 tons fully loaded, over a third comprised armour protection. At her water line there was almost 39cm of plating, and her designers were confident that she could resist any projectile fired at her from any distance. Even with this enormous weight, the *Bismarck* was almost as fast as any of the modern battleships in the Royal Navy. And it wasn't just the size and armament of the *Bismarck* that made her such a formidable ship. The Kriegsmarine had developed two systems of firing control that were extremely accurate, as the conflict between the *Exeter* and the *Graf Spee* in 1939 had demonstrated. The primary method and the most modern was Seetakt, a form of radar that could locate targets in poor visibility and provide accurate ranges and bearings for the gun directors. There was also a visual range-finding mechanism that was precise and very easy to use, which was important amid the chaos and confusion of a battle.

When they sailed through the waters between Denmark and Norway, the *Bismarck* and the *Prinz Eugen* were the most modern and most powerful naval task force afloat. The Royal Navy had never had to face *Bismarck*'s like before. Under the command of Admiral Lutjens, the hero of the Norwegian invasion in 1940 and the latest successful convoy raiding operation by the *Scharnhorst* earlier that year, they were about to continue a strategy that had so far proved extremely successful in the war against Britain.

The fact that one or two warships could absorb the efforts of a large part of the Royal Navy was, of course, an important part of Raeder's strategy. It was his view that any naval operation had to be seen in relation to its effect on other theatres of the war. Against an enemy that was overstretched, a battleship putting to sea could tie down a significant portion of the enemy's fleet. Raeder calculated that the presence of these two battleships in the Atlantic – the *Bismarck* capable of defeating any other warship that might be escorting a merchant convoy, leaving the *Prinz Eugen* free to sink the civilian ships without any hindrance – would have the maximum impact on Britain's war effort at a time when Germany was putting more and more resources into the Mediterranean war. The situation for Britain was growing increasingly difficult, and the Royal Navy's grip on the Mediterranean was becoming weaker.

The Afrika Korps under the command of General Rommel had overwhelmed the British Eighth Army in the Western Desert and advanced to the borders of Egypt. The Royal Navy had had to evacuate some fifty thousand troops from Greece, twenty thousand of whom had been landed in Crete, joining an existing force of another ten thousand. Churchill insisted that Crete must remain in British hands, although General Wavell in Cairo and the New Zealander General Freyberg on the island itself were sceptical that the forces on Crete, mostly disorganized evacuees from Greece, would be able to withstand a German invasion should it come. Admiral Cunningham, the Commander in Chief of the Mediterranean Fleet, had already protested to Churchill about the increasing number of vital tasks his dwindling number of ships had to carry out. His constant complaint was his inability to do anything in the face of overwhelming German air superiority. Churchill had written to Cunningham at the end of April, barely able to disguise his exasperation, though he had at least a little good news: the two battleships *Nelson* and *Rodney* were being taken away from the Home Fleet in the Atlantic and sent to reinforce Cunningham's ships in the Mediterranean.

In your last para you wonder how I could have suggested that *Nelson* and *Rodney* should be spared from the Atlantic to join the Mediterranean Fleet. I thought they were especially suitable because of their deck armour and the apprehension entertained of dive-bomber attack. Whether or not they could be spared depended on the situation in the Atlantic. About this I will now inform you. I have been for a long time in correspondence with President Roosevelt. He has now begun to take over a great part of the patrolling west of the 26th meridian West ... The easement and advantage of it to the Admiralty is enormous and of course it may easily produce even more decisive events; therefore you do not need at this moment to be unduly concerned about the Atlantic, and can devote your resources to cutting off enemy communication with Africa ...

Then, on 20 May, Germany launched an airborne assault on the island of Crete. Thousands of paratroopers dropped from the skies, their transport planes protected by squadrons of fighters and dive bombers. At the same time German troop ships landed reinforcements on the north of the island, who captured the airfield. It was while the British Army and Navy were engaged in a desperate and bloody battle for the control of Crete that the *Bismarck* weighed anchor and slid out of the fjord at Bergen. The next few days were to become some of the blackest moments of Britain's war against Germany.

Admiral Lutjens wanted to take advantage of fog and low cloud to make his break-out into the Atlantic undetected. The Admiralty had, however, become aware that the *Bismarck* was on the move. A reconnaissance Spitfire had photographed her at anchor in the fjord near Bergen; a second reconnaissance flight revealed that she had departed, and it was now a question for the Admiralty of guessing which route into the Atlantic Lutjens had chosen. The task of intercepting the German warships was given to Admiral Sir John Tovey, Commander in Chief of the Home Fleet, who considered that Lutjens had two options open to him.

The first was an attempted pass either to the south or to the north of the Faeroe Islands. The southerly route was not ideal for the German ships because it was within range of RAF aircraft in northern Scotland, so the northerly route, between the Faeroes and Iceland, seemed the most logical. It was the widest gap between Greenland and Britain, and it was the most difficult to cover with reconnaissance aircraft. Tovey stationed three light cruisers in this area, and they were supported by *King George V*, a modern, recently commissioned battleship, and the aircraft carrier *Victorious*. In company with these ships was *Repulse*, an old battlecruiser that had been on her way to shipyards in Boston for a refit before being dragooned back into the Home Fleet as reinforcement. Lutjens could also choose a route between Iceland and Greenland. The presence of pack ice made these waters quite narrow, but Lutjens may well have calculated that there was a better chance of poor visibility, giving him extra cover. This was the route he had used successfully when commanding *Scharnhorst* and *Gneisenau* earlier in the year, and Tovey calculated, quite correctly as it turned out, that Lutjens would rely on it again. It was here that he intended to set his trap. Tovey ordered two cruisers, *Suffolk* and *Norfolk*, to patrol these narrow straits, with the *Hood* and the *Prince of Wales*, Britain's most modern battleship, in a position further south. The *Prince of Wales* had only recently been handed over to the Royal Navy by Cammell Laird; dockyard workers were still on board and the ship's crew were still learning how to handle the ship. None of these ships was a match for the *Bismarck*, but Tovey positioned his two forces so that they could quickly reinforce each other once the German battleship had been spotted.

Admiral Lutjens steered for the Denmark Strait, and he was lucky: the weather conditions were overcast, with rain, and there was moderate to poor visibility, as low at times as 200 metres. As the *Bismarck* headed south-west, close to the edge of the pack ice fringing the coast of Greenland, she entered a patch of clear weather. The two British cruisers *Norfolk* and *Suffolk* were patrolling this area, but were still enveloped in a belt of fog clinging to the coast of Iceland and extending some way out into the channel. *Suffolk*, moving slowly ahead, suddenly emerged out of the fog bank into bright sunshine, and barely 6 miles away were the two German warships. Captain Ellis immediately ordered his ship back into the fog and sent a message that she was in contact with *Bismarck*. The message was not received by the Admiralty or by Admiral Tovey, but it was received by Admiral Somerville in Gibraltar, and he put Force H on orders to be prepared to put to sea in two hours. *Suffolk* was equipped with radar, so she continued to track the course of the *Bismarck* while remaining hidden in the fog.

Bismarck had not seen the *Suffolk* and was not aware that she had been sighted, but an hour later the second cruiser *Norfolk* left the fog bank and found herself very close to the German battleship. This time the lookouts saw the British cruiser and the *Bismarck* opened fire with her main armament, using them for the first time in anger. Huge gouts of water burst all around the *Norfolk* as she headed back at full speed into the fog, and a second signal was sent to the Admiralty. This time the message was picked up by both the *Hood*, which with the *Prince of Wales* was 300 miles to the south, and the *King George V*, covering the Iceland–Faeroes gap 600 miles away. Both groups of warships headed at full speed towards the enemy. The fight between the British Home Fleet and the most powerful ship of the German Navy had begun.

In the Denmark Strait, Admiral Lutjens was still steaming in a south-westerly direction, aware that he must have been reported by the cruiser that he had fired on but unaware that Admiral Holland's force, the *Hood* and the *Prince of Wales*, was approaching on a course to intercept him. At a quarter past five in the morning of Saturday, 24 May, a hydrophone operator in the *Prinz Eugen* heard what he thought were the propeller noises of ships approaching from the south-east. Half an hour later, lookouts on the *Prince of Wales* sighted the German war-ships. Admiral Holland knew that he was heading towards the *Bismarck* and the *Prinz Eugen*, but Lutjens was unclear about the type of ships that were clearly steaming towards him. He was under orders not to engage in battle with British warships unless it was an unavoidable consequence of an attack on a merchant convoy. But it was clear that he was being pursued, and he knew he might not have any choice in the matter. The *Prinz Eugen* signalled, mistakenly, that the two approaching British warships were cruisers, so Lutjens assumed that they were reinforcements for the cruisers that were already shadowing them. Anyway, there was little Lutjens could do in the circumstances. His choice of route to the Atlantic, along the southern edge of the Greenland pack ice, limited his ability to manoeuvre, so he continued his course towards the approaching *Hood* and *Prince of Wales*.

At seven minutes to six Lutjens realized that he was confronted with much more serious opposition when the *Hood* and the *Prince of Wales* opened fire with their main guns. They were two of the most powerful ships in the Royal Navy and their combined firepower might well have been enough to overwhelm the *Bismarck*, but the effect of their initial onslaught was weakened by poor identification and lack of communication. Holland, on the *Hood*, had given the order to open fire at the leading German ship believing it to be the *Bismarck*, but it was in fact the *Prinz Eugen*. The gunnery officer on the *Prince of Wales* had correctly identified both ships but no message was sent to correct the *Hood*'s mistake. Consequently the British gunnery was not focused, the *Prince of Wales* alone firing at the *Bismarck* while the *Hood* continued to direct her fire at the *Prinz Eugen*.

There was confusion on the German ships as well. Admiral Lutjens remained in some doubt about what to do. His orders were not to engage in battle with superior forces and he was not at first inclined to return the fire. But Captain Ernst Lindemann of the *Bismarck* argued that the situation they now found themselves in must counter any other orders. He was not prepared to stand idly by while his ship was shot from under him. The order was given to open fire, and both ships concentrated on the *Hood*. The German gunnery was accurate, and Admiral Holland's flagship received some direct hits. The shellfire from the *Prince of Wales* was also starting to find its target, and the *Bismarck* received a direct hit of its own from one of the huge 14-inch shells. It entered on the starboard bow above the water line and ruptured an oil tank.

Meanwhile, a fire had broken out on the *Hood*, caused by a direct hit from the *Bismarck*. Then, at six o'clock, the battle all of seven minutes old, the *Hood* was hit again by a salvo from the *Bismarck*. A mountain of flame and a yellowish white fireball burst up between her masts and she split apart in a massive explosion. White stars, probably molten pieces of metal, shot out from the black smoke that followed the flame, and huge fragments, one of which looked like a main turret, whirled through the air like toys. Wreckage of every description littered the water around the *Hood*, one especially conspicuous piece remaining on fire for a long time and giving off clouds of dense black smoke. The *Hood*, the pride of the Royal Navy, a 48,000-ton warship, had disappeared in seconds in a catastrophic explosion.

There are few eye-witness accounts of events on the *Hood* during the battle. So sudden and catastrophic was her demise that out of the total crew of 1,500, only three sailors survived. One of them, Ted Briggs, was on the compass platform, and he described his last sight of Admiral Holland sitting slumped in his chair, staring into space as the forward part of the ship toppled into the ocean. The vast majority of the crew at their action stations, locked in the magazines and engine spaces, had no chance of escape.

The loss of the *Hood* had an impact far greater than the loss of just one ship, tragic though the enormous loss of life was. The Royal Navy could not afford to lose a single battleship of course, but the *Hood* was far more than just another capital ship. She was no longer the most powerful or most modern battleship in the Royal Navy, but she was certainly the most well known and admired. She had for so many years been seen as the flagship of the Royal Navy. During the 1930s on a world tour, visiting the outposts of empire, showing the flag in the Dominions and in America, at countless Navy Days she had epitomized the power of the Royal Navy and the might of the British Empire. Now she was gone, blown apart after a few minutes of battle. Ron Skinner remarked to me that at the beginning of the war she was considered a very safe posting, and that everyone in his cadet class had been envious of those who had gone to the *Hood*. 'You lucky blighters! When it was announced over the Tannoy on the *Ark*, it was a real shock, a great blow.'

The battle was not yet over, however. With the *Hood*

now sunk, both German battleships turned their fire on to the *Prince of Wales*, and within three minutes of the *Hood* exploding the *Prince of Wales* suffered a serious hit on the bridge which killed everybody there except the captain and a signal petty officer. Another shell hit the forward fire control centre, a third shell hit the aircraft crane, and a fourth smashed into the hull below the water line but, with extraordinary luck, failed to explode. The *Prince of Wales* was also suffering some serious mechanical problems, the result of her being pressed into service on the hunt for the *Bismarck* before she had been properly worked up. One of the main turrets could no longer turn properly, and it was impossible for the ship to fire a full salvo. Captain Leach immediately ordered his ship to turn away and escape any more punishing hits under cover of a smokescreen.

It was a remarkable victory for the two German warships. In just a few minutes they had sunk one of the Royal Navy's most famous warships and seen off the challenge of a second. Captain Lindemann knew that he could pursue the *Prince of Wales* and finish her off, compounding the defeat for the Royal Navy, but Lutjens overruled him, arguing that the original mission of the German task force had to take precedence. So the two ships continued on their course into the Atlantic, followed now, at a distance, by the two shadowing cruisers *Norfolk* and *Suffolk*, and a damaged *Prince of Wales*.

* * *

This first successful if unplanned action by the *Bismarck* potentially had a far greater strategic impact than the purely tactical advantage foreseen by Raeder. Churchill had been growing increasingly gloomy since the spring of 1940: first Norway and Dunkirk, then the London Blitz, North Africa, Greece and Crete. When news of the loss of the *Hood* reached him at Chequers on the morning of 24 May he was cast into a black depression. It was, in his own words, 'a bitter disappointment and grief to me'. There was no question that the loss of the *Hood* would be a serious blow to public morale; it would also seriously affect opinion in the United States, now seen by Churchill as the only possible source of assistance in a dire situation. His pleas to Roosevelt had become increasingly desperate in recent weeks, emphasizing the serious situation in the Atlantic and urging the United States to enter the war.

Three days earlier Churchill had telegrammed to Roosevelt, 'I hope you will forgive me if I say that there is anxiety here. We are at a climacteric of the war, when enormous crystallizations are in suspense, but imminent . . . You will see from my cancelled message to Wilkie how grievous I feel it that the United States should build 3 to 4 million tons of shipping and watch their equivalent being sunk beforehand.' When Churchill heard that the *Bismarck* was being pursued by the *Hood*, he had sent a further telegram to Roosevelt, saying, 'Should we fail to catch them going out your navy should surely be able to mark them down for us. Give us the news and we will finish the job.' The events of a few hours later proved that that was an empty boast. Ever since the destruction of Oran, Churchill had striven to demonstrate to the world, but more importantly to the United States, that Britain was worth supporting and capable of fighting back. That view would not survive long if there were major defeats in the Atlantic at the hands of the Kriegsmarine.

The *Prince of Wales* and the two cruisers *Norfolk* and *Suffolk* were still shadowing the *Bismarck* but were not prepared to enter into an outright battle with her. The only hope, it seemed, of stopping and sinking the *Bismarck* lay with the other task force of the Home Fleet, which had been guarding the southern route into the Atlantic, the gap between Iceland and the Faeroes. Admiral Tovey, with *King George V*, *Repulse* and *Victorious*, was 600 miles away when news of the first contact with the *Bismarck* had been received, and he doubted he would be able to successfully intercept her before she avoided pursuit and disappeared into the Atlantic. He had to slow her down, so he ordered *Victorious* to mount a torpedo strike on the *Bismarck* with her squadron of Swordfish aircraft.

The *Victorious* had originally been on her way to Gibraltar to help the *Ark Royal* and Force H deliver a consignment of Hurricanes to Malta. She was then going to make a high-speed dash through the narrow channel between North Africa and Sicily and head for Alexandria to reinforce Admiral Cunningham's Mediterranean Fleet. Now, diverted at the start of her journey into the effort to stop the *Bismarck*, she carried only one Swordfish squadron, whose leader, Lt Commander Eugene Esmonde, was an experienced Fleet Air Arm pilot, a survivor of the sinking of HMS *Courageous* in 1939. The rest of the pilots on board, however, were very inexperienced, many of them having made their first landing on the deck of a carrier just a few days before.

They took off in a heavy sea and bad weather with low cloud and poor visibility. After a flight of almost two hours they finally caught sight of the German warship. They made their attack from the east, with the *Bismarck* silhouetted against the setting sun, except for one pilot, Lt Percy Gick, who decided to attack from the west. Coming unobtrusively out of the sun while the anti-aircraft fire of the *Bismarck* was directed against the main group of Swordfish, Lt Gick managed to get close enough to score a hit, causing a massive column of black smoke to rise from the side of the battleship. The warhead exploded against the thick side armour of the *Bismarck*, the concussion killing a crew member. It exacerbated the damage done by the shells of the *Prince of Wales*, but it was not serious enough to slow her down sufficiently for Admiral Tovey to gain on her.

The situation, for the British forces, then worsened considerably. The *Prinz Eugen* had already managed to separate from the *Bismarck* under cover of a sudden foray against the *Prince of Wales* by Lutjens' flagship, but the two cruisers *Suffolk* and *Norfolk* had managed to continue shadowing the *Bismarck* by radar ever since their first contact off Greenland. Then, while the two British cruisers were on one path of their zigzag anti-submarine course, the *Bismarck* made a sudden turn to the west and continued in a large circle on to an easterly course, passing behind them. They lost radar contact, and the *Bismarck* was now heading for St Nazaire, clear of any pursuit. Confusion spread through the Admiralty and the ships under Admiral Tovey's command. It seemed that the Royal Navy had totally failed.

As dawn broke on the morning of 25 May, not only had contact with the enemy been lost, but there was little possibility of finding her again. Visibility was worsening and there was a gale blowing. Aircraft from *Victorious* were flown off to search for the German battleship but found nothing.

Just before dusk on the 25th, Admiral Lutjens, not realizing that he had thrown off his pursuers, sent a lengthy signal to his HQ in Berlin detailing his plans. This signal was picked up by tracking stations in the UK, and it was possible to work out a rough location for the battleship, and for the Admiralty to confirm that the *Bismarck* was in fact heading for the French coast. Admiral Tovey's forces, however, had been directed north by the Admiralty who believed that the German ships were heading back to Norway; he was now too far away to intercept the *Bismarck* before she could reach the protection of Luftwaffe bombers based in France. Moreover, Tovey's flagship, the *King George V*, was running low on fuel and unless the enemy's speed was reduced he would have to abandon the chase at midnight and leave *Rodney*, a First World War battlecruiser, as the sole British warship in pursuit of the mighty *Bismarck*. The situation for the British was bleak. There was now only one hope left: aircraft from the *Ark Royal* must attack the *Bismarck* and slow her down.

At eleven o'clock Force H received orders to assume that the enemy had turned towards the French harbour of Brest, and to head north to mount an aerial search for the *Bismarck*. Somerville made plans with Captain Maund on the *Ark Royal* to be ready to fly off a reconnaissance patrol by seven o'clock the next morning, to search an area of 140 miles by about 90.

Even if *Bismarck* was located, the chances of a successful strike against her were not good, as the aircraft from *Victorious* had proved: despite a successful hit, the *Bismarck* was unharmed. And the *Ark*'s air crew did not have an impressive record when it came to torpedo attacks against ships at sea. Somerville had instigated a rigorous programme of training in Force H, but certainly the senior officers would still remember the poor showing six months earlier when Italian warships had escaped unscathed from a Swordfish attack at Spartivento.

Somerville had nearly been court-martialled as a result of that failure. In addition, the weather was worsening all the time. During the night the headwinds became so bad that it looked as though the *Ark Royal* in company with Somerville's flagship *Renown* would not be able to reach the search area until nine in the morning. The *Bismarck* appeared to be slipping out of the grasp of the Royal Navy.

The crew of the *Ark Royal* had been kept informed of the unfolding events of the past few days. As they headed into the Atlantic, John Moffat recalls, there was an announcement by Captain Maund over the Tannoy: 'We are heading north and we are trying to intercept the battleship *Bismarck*, which has come out from Norway and is now in the Atlantic. We are trying to find her, because at the moment her position is unknown.'

There had been a certain rivalry between the air crew of the *Ark* and the *Illustrious* after the attack on the Italian fleet at Taranto, and the Swordfish pilots of the *Ark* now thought they could redress the balance: 'It was a chance to show what we could do.'

At dawn the *Ark Royal* was struggling through mountainous seas, and the flight deck was see-sawing up and down by over 16 metres. No aircraft had ever been flown from the deck of a carrier in such weather. When the first Swordfish were brought up on the lift to the flight deck for the first patrol extra men were needed to hold them down. The flight deck was 63 feet (19 metres) above sea level, but waves were breaking over the forward edge. The whole ship was covered in spray. Ron Skinner remembers the scene: 'The first reconnaissance aircraft took off at around eight o'clock. The first one missed a wave by inches as it broke over the flight deck. The water coming over the bows reached back to the bridge. It was a sight that none of us would forget.' Ten aircraft in total were launched in the search for the *Bismarck*. They were brought to the centre line, their engines roaring at full power, and as the deck officer's flag dropped they would roll forward, either struggling uphill or heading downhill directly at the sea, depending on the attitude of the ship at the time. As the aircraft passed the bridge the observer read the latest instructions about windspeed and direction scribbled on a blackboard, and it was then off into the storm, heading for the search area.

With her aircraft successfully launched, the *Ark* was herself off on a new course, 50 miles to the north, where the Swordfish that had just taken off would have to try and find the German battleship. About two hours later a signal was intercepted in the *Ark* from a Coastal Command Catalina saying that the *Bismarck* had been spotted, close to the area that was being searched by the aircraft. Within twenty minutes the nearest Swordfish had also located the *Bismarck*, and the signal was sent to the *Ark Royal*: '*Bismarck* in sight'. Ten minutes later another Swordfish in the search pattern had moved to the position given by the first aircraft. Both had visual contact. With two aircraft from the *Ark Royal* now shadowing the *Bismarck*, Tovey's hopes rose from the depths of despair, but it was absolutely vital contact was not lost again. Two other Swordfish fitted with long-range petrol tanks were launched, to relieve the first shadowers.

When he arrived on the scene, Midshipman Ian MacWilliam, an observer in one of those Swordfish, was not certain whether he had spotted the *Bismarck* or the *Prinz Eugen*. The anti-aircraft fire was accurate and it was hard for the trailing Swordfish to stay in one place and make sure of its target. As MacWilliam's aircraft approached from the rear of the ship to take a photo he saw the flash of a broadside, and his pilot turned steeply away and zigzagged; the shells burst 50 yards behind them, and more ack-ack followed, at four salvos a minute. The bursts were well bunched, MacWilliam observed coolly. Captain Maund and his senior officers on the *Ark* were, however, convinced that they had found the *Bismarck*.

When the searching Swordfish came in to land, the stern of the ship was rising and falling through 19 metres. The *Ark* was so unstable that the flight deck officer, Commander Stringer, had to be secured with a lifeline so that he could remain upright. He waved the aircraft away as many as three times before he thought it was safe for them to attempt a landing, although one aircraft was lost when the stern rose suddenly and hit the Swordfish from underneath as she touched down. With the other Swordfish in a circuit all waiting to land before they ran out of fuel, the crashed aircraft was dragged to the stern and heaved overboard.

Admiral Tovey's Home Fleet ships were still over 130 miles away, and at her current speed the *Bismarck*, shadowed or not, would outrun them. She had to be stopped or slowed down enough for the fleet to reach her, and the only weapons available to accomplish that were the Swordfish's torpedoes. In the hangar decks the aircraft were overhauled and refuelled by the riggers and mechanics, and torpedoes in their trolleys were moved forward to the lifts. They would be loaded onto the aircraft once they were lined up on the flight deck. By two o'clock in the afternoon fourteen aircraft were ready to launch an attack, ranged at the rear of the flight deck. At 1445 the first plane took off. They formed up in their attack groups and headed for the position of the *Bismarck*.

Unknown to anybody on the *Ark Royal*, the cruiser *Sheffield*, the *Ark*'s constant companion in Force H, had been sent by Somerville to shadow the *Bismarck*, to make certain that this time the battleship did not escape. The cruiser was in a direct line between the *Bismarck* and the *Ark Royal*, and unfortunately she was the first ship the air crew in the Swordfish came upon. In low cloud and driving rain they turned to attack the *Sheffield*. Eleven of the fourteen aircraft dropped their torpedoes before they realized their mistake. The torpedoes had been fitted with Duplex fuses, designed to make the warhead explode not only on direct impact but also under the influence of a ship's magnetic field. In theory this meant that the torpedo could be set to run deep and explode directly under the hull of a ship, avoiding the belt of armour plating along the water line. In practice, the fuses were extremely unreliable, and they either exploded on impact with the water or failed to detonate at all. It was only this plus the drastic manoeuvres of the *Sheffield* that avoided a catastrophe. It was an inauspicious start to a mission on which so much depended.

The Swordfish returned to the *Ark Royal*. The leader of the attack, Lt Commander Coode, insisted that impact fuses be fitted on the next batch of warheads, and these were set to run at a shallow setting of 10 feet. Fifteen aircraft were armed and refuelled – all the serviceable Swordfish on the *Ark*. It was going to be a massed attack, with flights of three aircraft attacking simultaneously from all quarters, which would make it impossible for the *Bismarck* to manoeuvre and comb the torpedo tracks. It was hoped it would also confuse and break up the anti-aircraft fire.

The weather got worse as the day wore on, and there was cloud as low as 600 feet with banks of driving rain. The sea remained as rough as ever, and the pilots again had to deal with a flight deck pitching through 50 feet. 'We took off in the gloom of the evening,' John Moffat recalled, 'in poor visibility, and the motion of the flight deck got worse as the ship headed into gale-force winds.' He climbed to 6,000 feet but didn't notice the cold because the adrenalin was pumping through him. 'We were leading with the CO, Lt Cdr Coode, who was an impressive figure, a man we looked up to. We were shown the direction to the *Bismarck* by the *Sheffield* and then we entered cloud and started to ice up. The Swordfish got very unstable.'

As they flew away in line astern from the *Sheffield*, which had signalled by Aldis lamp the distance (12 miles) and bearing to the *Bismarck*, they must all have been aware of what they were about to face. Everyone knew that the *Bismarck* bristled with guns. There had been plenty of information at the briefing about her twelve 15mm-calibre guns on twin mountings, sixteen 105mm guns on twin high-angle mountings and fifty 37mm and 20mm rapid-firing guns that were mounted all around the ship. The pilots returning from shadowing the battleship had already spoken of the preparedness and accuracy of the *Bismarck*'s anti-aircraft fire. A remarkable performance would be required from pilots who had already spent several hours in the air in extremely arduous flying conditions.

As they neared the *Bismarck* they flew into a massive cloud whose base was 700 feet above the ocean and which towered to a height of 10,000 feet. As the force climbed through it, ice forming on the wings, they became separated. The leader of the first flight, Coode, descended at a point where he calculated they would be able to attack downwind from astern of the ship, but on breaking the cloud cover they discovered the *Bismarck* was 4 miles away. The ship immediately opened fire, and the barrage was intense. Coode said it began five seconds after they had emerged from the cloud and started their dive. Large bursts came up very close, including one very near-miss underneath his plane, and Coode had the strong impression that each gun mounting had its own radar control. He described the ack-ack as reddish-coloured tracer going past at about one shell a second. John Moffat in Swordfish 5C, the third aircraft in the first flight, thought it was like flying into hail. In the open cockpit of the Swordfish the noise and blast of exploding shells could be directly felt by the pilots and the observers. The smell of cordite was strong. Some bursts, Moffat and his observer Sub Lt 'Dusty' Miller reported, occurred behind them but they were always close. At one point two shells burst together 30 metres to starboard and below, the blasts of which battered the plane and turned it off its course.

After they had dived below 1,000 feet the heavy shell-fire seemed to abate. A series of double flashes were seen from amidships but the rate of fire appeared to be slower and the flashes were vivid orange with little smoke. Moffat dived as low as he could, and when he was 2,000 yards from the target the rapid-firing guns started up, orange tracer coming up at him in a dead straight line. Another pilot reported that the gun flashes from the ship appeared vivid yellow tinged with green, with cordite smoke brownish and small in quantity. Then, as the planes got closer, smaller red tracer appeared. Lt Beale, the pilot of a Swordfish in the second flight who was an experienced veteran of many of the *Ark*'s operations, said that the fire was more intense than anything he had experienced before, including the attack on Oran, the Sardinian engagement and the attack on the Tirso Dam.

Moffat got his first glimpse of the *Bismarck* as he turned into the attack on the port quarter. 'With the CO on the left we headed in at 50 feet. I liked to stay as low as possible because I thought I was more difficult to hit that way. As we came in my observer, "Dusty" Miller, kept saying, "Not yet, not yet." I thought, "My Christ, what is he talking about?" I turned around and there he was, leant right out of the cockpit holding the voice pipe, judging when to drop the torpedo. You can't guarantee that it will drop or run, and in heavy seas you have to drop into the trough of a wave or it will porpoise on the crest and run wild. I thought, "For God's sake get a move on or we'll be right on it." Then he said, "Let her go." And then, "We've got a runner." After dropping we made a flat turn to get away, flat so as not to expose the underside of the aircraft and present a bigger target, and boy did I want to get away from there.'

The intention was that the attacks by the various flights

from all sides should take place almost simultaneously, but the weather conditions and the problems of icing when flying through the cloud meant that inevitably the fifteen aircraft couldn't stay in close contact. As it was, four Swordfish initially attacked from the port side, another two attacked from the starboard side, five more attacked from the port side, and finally, another four aircraft – two of which were slightly isolated and were the focus of a great deal of concentrated anti-aircraft fire – attacked again from the starboard side. Remarkably, only one Swordfish was seriously damaged during the attack, both the pilot and telegraphist air gunner sustaining wounds. The aircraft was hit 175 times, and one of its struts supporting the upper and lower wing was severed. Nevertheless the pilot, Sub Lt Swanton, managed to fly it back to the *Ark* and make a successful landing.

On the *Bismarck*, the impact of the attack was profound. A gunnery officer on the ship thought that the Swordfish pilots had been ordered, 'Get hits or don't come back!' 'The heeling of the ship first one way and then another told me that we were trying to evade torpedoes,' he recalled. 'The rudder indicator never came to rest and the speed indicator revealed a significant loss of speed. The men in the control platforms in the engine rooms had to keep their wits about them. "All ahead full!" "All stop!" "All back full!" were the ever-changing orders with which Lindemann sought to escape the torpedoes. We had been under attack for perhaps fifteen minutes when I heard that sickening sound. Two torpedoes exploded in quick succession, but somewhere forward of where I was. Good fortune in misfortune, I thought . . . The attack must have been almost over when it came, an explosion aft. My heart sank. I glanced at the rudder indicator. It showed "left 12 degrees". It did not change.'

The *Bismarck* had been hit in the port steering compartment. Only three hits were observed by the attacking Swordfish and none was expected to have caused any damage, but this effort by forty-three young airmen who had somehow managed to find the courage to attack this heavily armoured ship, and in some cases loiter in the vicinity for some time to make an assessment of the attack, had actually succeeded in damaging the *Bismarck* to the extent that she was reduced to being the helpless prey of the pursuing fleet of battleships.

The *Bismarck* had turned to port – it isn't known whether or not this was done in an attempt to avoid the torpedo that caused the deadly damage – and a torpedo had hit the most vulnerable part of the ship. The long stern had been designed to reduce the drag of the ship through the water, and it was not sufficiently strengthened like the rest of the hull. The explosion had weakened the welded seams and the hull had collapsed on the rudders, jamming them forever in their turn to port. The *Bismarck* was now disabled, unable to steer, and was starting to head back into the Atlantic, towards Admiral Tovey.

Ironically, Admiral Lutjens, who had avoided contact with the *Ark Royal* throughout the war, first as the successful leader of the German task force in Norway then in command of the *Scharnhorst* and the *Gneisenau* throughout their successful raiding in the Atlantic, had finally been brought down by its Swordfish aircraft.

The returning Swordfish crews, landing on a wildly pitching deck, did not report any serious damage to the *Bismarck*. It was the *Sheffield*, still trailing the battleship, and a circling Swordfish that noticed her moving in a circle, no longer heading south-east towards the French coast. The course of the *Bismarck* was erratic as Captain Lindemann tried to steer the ship using alternate power on the propellers, but with the rudders jammed permanently, forcing the ship's bows to port, nothing could be done. The crew of the *Bismarck* were doomed, and they had hours to contemplate their end, like men in a condemned cell. At 2140 hours Admiral Lutjens radioed to the Kriegsmarine Group West in Paris. 'Ship unable to manoeuvre. We will fight to the end. Long live the Führer.'

On the *Ark Royal* the next morning, the crews of the remaining twelve Swordfish prepared for another strike. The wind was now so fast, over 50 knots, that the Swordfish were armed with torpedoes and their engines started while the ship steamed away from the wind. Extra men were ordered onto the flight deck to hold the aircraft steady. When all the aircraft were ready with their engines running, the *Ark* prepared to make a turn into the wind. 'Going on to full speed we put the rudder hard over,' Captain Maund recalled. 'The old ship, always a delight to handle at speed, swung round like a top, but even so she took several heavy rolls before she got round and two of the aircraft slipped as much as 8 feet sideways. It was an exciting moment with the crews holding on and the propellers heaving round. But once round speed had to be reduced to 6 knots and the Swordfish with their torpedoes took off one after the other in rapid succession.'

In the meantime, the battleships *King George V* and *Rodney* had at last come within range of the *Bismarck*. Their first salvo was fired at 0842 hours. The shells from their big guns caused serious damage to the front of the *Bismarck* and her two forward main turrets. She was travelling at slow speed in an attempt to maintain some sort of course, but she was essentially unmanoeuvrable. Shortly after receiving these first hits from the British guns, the *Bismarck* could no longer reply to the fire and she became a floating butcher's block. Heavy shell after heavy shell landed on her, causing total mayhem inside the hull. The bodies of the dead and dying lay piled up in every space, and the living scrambled through blood and smoke searching for non-existent shelter. The British ships continued to fire on the battleship for almost half an hour after her guns had been silenced, but eventually Admiral Tovey, with his flagship *King George V* low on fuel, realized that shells would not sink the *Bismarck* and ordered the *Dorsetshire*, a cruiser that had joined the ships from the Home Fleet, to torpedo her. The final act of the crew members still alive on the *Bismarck* was to set scuttling charges, and they and the *Dorsetshire*'s torpedoes finally sent what had now become a giant metal coffin to the bottom of the Atlantic.

The Swordfish from the *Ark Royal* had arrived while the shelling was still continuing, and they stayed to the end, until the last survivors of the 2,400 men who had been on the *Bismarck* were struggling in the water. Admiral Tovey did not respond to the pilots' signals requesting instructions, and they finally returned to the *Ark Royal*. Before they landed on, a German four-engined Focke Wulf bomber appeared in the sky and dropped a stick of bombs that landed in the sea to the starboard side. The battle had moved inside the range of the Luftwaffe based in France, so the *Bismarck* had been hit and crippled at the very last possible moment.

At a meeting of the War Cabinet in London on the morning of 27 May, while shells were still exploding on the *Bismarck*, Churchill told his colleagues that all chances of winning the battle in Crete had disappeared and that Britain should face the prospect that most of its forces would be lost. It was almost impossibly bad news to announce; Churchill had wanted to tell the House of Commons that afternoon that hard fighting was still continuing. Parliament met that day in Church House, opposite Westminster Abbey, because the Houses of Parliament had been bombed earlier in the year. It was an extraordinarily tense session, but during it Churchill was handed a note, and he was able to announce to the House that the *Bismarck* had been sunk. The news broke the sombre spell and prompted wild cheering.

But John Moffat does not remember the flights he made over the *Bismarck* with any sense of elation. Speaking to me in his comfortable home in the peaceful rolling hills of Dunkeld in Scotland, he said, 'The worst part of the war, the thing that always crosses my mind when it shouldn't, is my second trip over the *Bismarck*. She was smoking like fury, and just as I approached, the ship turned on its side. I flew across and there were all these bods in the water, hundreds of them; there were heads in the water. It was a terrible thing, a terrible sight really. That haunts me, the hopelessness of life. When we all got back we had a drink, and nobody said great or anything. That was why we had a drink, because we all thought, "There but for the grace of God."'

11

THE *RIG SUPPORTER*

In October 2002 I was squeezed into a Gibraltar taxi, its windows misting up and the heating full on, with Rick Davey from C&C Technologies, cameraman Richard Rankin and a sound recordist. The rain was lashing down and the streetlights were still on, although at five o'clock in the morning the sky was beginning to lighten through the low scudding clouds. We had left our hotel, driven past the old offices where the *Gibraltar Times* printed the first news of Nelson's victory at Trafalgar, and were heading for the harbour.

When we arrived at the dockside we loaded our bags and aluminium equipment boxes onto the oily deck of a harbour tender. The pilot, unshaven and with a cigarette dangling from his mouth, untied the ropes holding us to the jetty and gunned the motor. We were heading out to board the *Rig Supporter*, the boat that carried C&C's unique surveying tool – the autonomous underwater vehicle. It was the opportunity to use the AUV in the search for the *Ark Royal* that had first made me contact Rick. Now, finally, it was waiting for me and I could discover precisely what had been located on the sea bed by the *Odin Finder* five months earlier.

As we cleared the outer mole the sea got rougher, and further out it was covered in white caps whipped up by a strong westerly wind. Our boat started pitching and rolling as we made a wide sweeping circle around a big grey and white vessel that was slowly moving through the water.

'That's the *Rig Supporter*,' said Rick.

It was a big ship, about three times the size of the *Odin Finder*, with a high prow, capable of crossing the Atlantic or dealing with a storm in the North Sea. Above the stern was a helicopter landing pad.

'How are we going to get on board?' I asked.

'I'm not sure,' Rick replied.

The *Rig Supporter* had been working in the Mediterranean for weeks, and the survey crew and the technicians who ran the AUV were very keen to get home, which for most of them was back in Louisiana. They wanted to spend as little time as possible on this extra job that they had not bargained for. Furthermore, the fee I had negotiated would barely cover their fuel costs, so the project manager on board had been unwilling to spend time and money on entering harbour. I thought that transferring passengers and gear in this way was taking a risk, but short of abandoning the trip there was little I could do.

As we approached the ship it towered above us. I had half expected a companionway or a set of stairs to be lowered, but all I could see was a rope ladder hanging down the swaying side of the ship. Our boat matched the *Rig Supporter*'s speed and pulled alongside. A rope was lowered to winch up the equipment boxes, but we would have to grab the ladder and climb up to the deck above. Our boat was pitching to a height of 5 or 6 feet; if anyone missed their footing they would be crushed between the *Rig Supporter* and our boat. The sound recordist had gone extremely pale. He turned to me and said, 'Mike, I can't swim.' Being able to swim would not prevent anyone from getting killed in that dangerous gap, but I knew that now was not the time to point this out. I should not have put him in this situation at all; legally speaking I should have aborted the whole thing. But I had gone too far now to turn back. What he needed was some re-assurance, some action on my part that showed he was being considered, otherwise I would never persuade him to make a leap for the rope ladder. Any hesitation on his part out of fear would be fatal.

'Rick,' I shouted, 'we need some life vests. Can they throw some down to us?'

Rick knew that what we were doing was silly, so he

shouted up to the deckhands. Within a few minutes I was helping put one on the sound recordist. As the deck of our boat rose up he grasped the rope ladder and his feet found the bottom rung. He pulled himself up and was hauled by his lifejacket harness onto the deck of the *Rig Supporter*. We all followed safely, and within a few minutes the *Rig Supporter* had picked up speed and was heading to the wreck site, buffeted by crosswinds and an angry sea.

Once on board the ship I could appreciate why the *Rig Supporter* was so large. The survey room, or lab, was extremely spacious, with an array of screens that emphasized the enormous computer capacity the ship carried. She was designed to be self-sufficient, accommodating the AUV and its support staff as well as a large surveying party anywhere in the world.

The sonar survey from the *Odin Finder* had provided very little information about the size or condition of the target, so Rick had asked me to bring along as much background material about the *Ark* as I could. I had full-size reproductions of the large-scale blueprints of the *Ark Royal* from the Maritime Museum. I also had some enlarged black and white photos of the *Ark* on the slipway at Birkenhead, and a variety of views of the ship to help us identify anything we might capture an image of. As I spread these out on the chart table I was joined by Zak Rivers, the surveying party chief, and Phil Devall, the chief technician for the AUV. Zak was young and stocky with a goatee beard, while Phil was thin with a slightly startled air about him. Gradually the other computer programmers and the technicians gathered around.

They knew very little of what I was proposing to do. As I described the brief history of the *Ark Royal* and passed around photos of the ship almost hidden by gouts of water thrown into the air by exploding bombs, I could hear muttered comments and the odd 'wow'. I explained how I had gone back to the Board of Inquiry records and drawn up the search area, and finally how we had located this target outside it. Before I had finished talking a couple of the technicians had left the small group and were examining the blueprints, taking measurements and looking at the black and white image produced by the sonar on board the *Odin Finder*. Their curiosity had been fired. They too were becoming engrossed in the challenge of finding this wreck.

There were a few things I didn't dwell on in detail. One was that in the months since the discovery of what could be the wreck of the *Ark* by the *Odin Finder* it had proved almost impossible to get offers of co-production money for a series on the history of the Royal Navy. It was too British. This to me was a reason why the British Broadcasting Corporation, which was after all financed by British licence payers, should make it, but in every conversation I had with senior management at the BBC I could tell my arguments were falling on deaf ears. Originally I had proposed a search for the *Ark Royal* because I thought that the discovery and footage of such a historic ship could form the centrepiece of a series about the Royal Navy, and give the programmes a much higher profile when they were broadcast. Now it was beginning to look as though there was not enough money to produce the series I wanted to make, certainly nowhere near enough to film the *Ark Royal*, if that is what we had found.

I was lucky in one respect, however: I was being allowed to use the AUV and the *Rig Supporter* for almost nothing, so whatever the fate of the series I could take a few more steps in the right direction and hopefully determine whether or not I had found the *Ark Royal*. There was a distinct possibility I hadn't.

When I'd returned to London I'd had very little to show for my four-day trip and the thousands of dollars paid to the *Odin Finder* except an accurate position for what I was assured was a substantial metallic object that roughly fitted the known dimensions of the *Ark*. On paper they looked like two dark squares about 1cm by 1cm on a background of black and white dots like the interference on an old TV screen. When Rick Davey and I worked out how we were going to search for the wreck, we assumed we might have several targets that would require investigation. However, I was very conscious of a lack of time and money and it was convenient to assume that what I had found was indeed what I was searching for. It was the closest target to my original search area. But then, if the *Ark* had drifted from the point where it had capsized, as the captain of the *Odin Finder* had suggested, it could have drifted quite a way, and what we had found might be the wreck of a totally different ship.

One way of calculating the probability of locating a different wreck in that area was to give the Wrecks Section of the UK Hydrographic Office a set of co-ordinates and ask them to check if they had any relevant information. I did this, and after a few days their reply arrived. To my utter dismay I saw that in the early 1960s a bulk carrier registered in Liberia had been reported missing not far from the position of the target I had located. Had I found the wreck of a cargo ship? This possibility was too awful to contemplate. To have wasted so much time and effort, not to say money . . . There was, of course, only one way to find out, and that was what we were about to do.

Rick had told me a great deal about the AUV, but I had never set eyes on it. It was housed in a container that everybody on board referred to as 'the van', set onto the rear deck of the ship, underneath the helicopter landing pad. As I walked into the container I caught my first sight of the AUV. Under the harsh neon lights was an object like a fat torpedo, coloured bright orange, with a multi-bladed propeller and four fins at the rear, which was the narrowest part of it. It looked about 2 metres in length and over a metre in diameter. Panels on its side were being opened, and technicians wearing goggles and masks were plunging their hands inside it, as though they were operating on some strange animal. It was a remarkable piece of machinery, and was, according to Rick, the very first one of its type to be working commercially. The key to its success was its batteries which used a fuel based on aluminium and oxygen. These could drive it at a speed of over 3 knots for up to fifty hours. While it was doing this a variety of sonar sensors would be probing the sea floor and sending information back to the ship with its massive computers. There were also computers on board the AUV that could steer it on a predetermined course to an accuracy of 1 metre.

The company that owned the AUV, C&C Technologies, was owned by two brothers, Thomas and Jimmy Chance, whose father had made a lot of money from an oilfield services company in the 1960s. The Chance brothers had decided that new technology could transform the oil industry. The AUV was the result. The development costs had been very high, explained Rick, and although it was proving to be very successful it was still a long way from making a profit. Knowing how little I was paying for the privilege of using the AUV, I reflected that trying to hunt down the *Ark Royal* was not going to transform their finances in the slightest.

Back in the lab, Zak and his team had already drawn up a tentative search pattern around the target. The best way to visualize the AUV and the way it works is to think of a radio-controlled model aeroplane, except that the AUV would be flying through water, not air, and would be controlled by high-frequency sound waves, not radio signals. The AUV had cost $10 million to build so nobody wanted to be reckless with it. To avoid dangers such as a collision with a loose piece of wreckage, or getting tangled up in some old fishing nets that had fouled the wreck, Zak worked out a complicated pattern for surveying the wreck. The AUV was going to pass over the wreck at a height above the sea bed that would give the AUV about 20 metres' clearance. These distances were based on the assumption that it was the *Ark* down there, measured from the sets of blueprints I had brought on board. After two or three high-level passes the AUV would fly a star-shaped pattern over the wreck at a variety of heights and distances from it. In all we would be covering an area of about 1 square nautical mile. The end result would be that we would have a variety of different images which the computers on board would be able to combine into a three-dimensional image.

The process of preparing the computer program started. Once the loading of the information from the mother ship's computers to the AUV's was finished, the delicate and dangerous job of fuelling the AUV was started. Within a few hours of the *Rig Supporter* arriving above the wreck site the AUV was ready to launch.

The rear doors of the van opened very slowly, framing the sea and reflecting golden highlights from the late evening sun – a surreal contrast with the harsh industrial lighting of the AUV's container. The whole ship vibrated as the bow and stern thrusters fought against the wind and the current to keep the ship on a precise position. The AUV slowly slid out of its cradle then dropped into the sea. Bobbing on the choppy waves, its strobe light flashing, it looked suddenly small and fragile. Then it was gone. It would take about an hour to descend to depth, and for the technicians to test that everything was working before starting its mission.

I waited in the lab for the first signals to come back. There was a considerable amount of uncertainty and anxiety among the people gathered there. Most equipment used underwater is purpose-built, and is extremely complicated. The AUV was a unique machine and had travelled many thousands of kilometres underwater, but it was still in a sense experimental. Its very sophisticated electronics and computers were expected to work at extreme pressures immersed in salt water, and then to communicate an enormous amount of information via sound signals through water whose nature, in terms of temperature and salinity, was changing all the time. In these circumstances there is a lot that can go wrong, and the possibility of a breakdown or other form of failure is always present in the technicians' minds.

Naturally it was present in mine too, but I did not bear the responsibility for the effectiveness of the AUV. I was much more worried about what we were going to discover when the AUV reached its working depth. What would we see on our computer screens when the first signals were sent back from the object over 1,000 metres below us? Far more experienced people than I had set out to find wrecks and failed, and in a few hours I could be in for a horrible shock. The *Odin Finder* had found two targets separated by almost a kilometre and neither of them exactly matched the dimensions of the *Ark Royal*. Many famous wrecks have been found in pieces, of course. The *Titanic* lies in two large pieces, but the ship was subjected to considerable stress at the time because the rear part of the hull was raised high above the water when she was sinking. HMS *Hood* also lies in pieces, but she suffered an enormous explosion, and the *Bismarck* was not only the recipient of an enormous bombardment, she also fell several hundred metres down the side of a trench before hitting the sea bed. Many other ships have suffered severe damage to their hulls but remain intact in their final resting place. The eye-witness evidence I had read suggested that the *Ark* had simply turned over and slipped beneath the waves in one piece. There was in fact considerable room for error about what exactly we were sending the AUV down to investigate.

However, Rick Davey, who had directed me to the *Odin Finder* and had put the *Rig Supporter* more or less at my disposal, knew about most of these uncertainties and remained perfectly calm. As far as he was concerned what we were doing was the logical next step in our search.

The lab had filled with people. At each of the screens someone was monitoring the progress of the AUV on its pre-planned route, or checking the sonar imaging systems it was carrying; others just waited to see the first image appear on the screen. Slowly we followed the path of the AUV as it approached the first leg of the search pattern. Small objects were being picked up by the sonar, but it was impossible at this height and angle to tell what they were. As the AUV approached the precise position where we were expecting to find something, there was a perceptible stillness in the lab. All eyes were on the screens. It was a very tense moment. A thousand metres below us a small machine was blindly propelling itself through a pitch-black ocean and, I hoped, slowly approaching an object a thousand times its own size that had remained hidden for over sixty years.

On a large flat screen in the lab a shape appeared. There were murmurs from people crowded behind me. Zak said, 'We have a target.' It looked nothing like the *Ark Royal* or an aircraft carrier, but as the images cascaded down the screen, Zak added, 'This is big.' There was a perceptible sense of relief, and people started jostling to get a better view. But to my eyes it was hard to see what we had found. It was very high off the sea bed, about 20 metres, and had disappeared again fairly quickly. There was nothing else to see.

'Oh, hey, look at this,' Zak said suddenly.

There were excited sounds from other people in the

room. On the screen was something that filled the whole edge of the swathe of sound the AUV was sending out into the darkness; clearly it was echoing back from something very big. It continued as the AUV travelled on its course, and then disappeared again.

'What is it?' I asked.

'There's no doubt it's a very big vessel,' said Rick. 'We'll wait for the AUV to come back on its return course, and then we'll start to get a bigger picture.'

On the next run Zak was the first to read out the dimensions. 'It's nearly 200 metres long, and it's looking about 18 metres high at this point.' He looked very pleased, and very certain that we had found what we were looking for.

Over the next few hours the AUV passed back and forth over the wreck and gradually a black and white image was created, looking like an X-ray, with dark shadows and greyer tones. It was hard to read the images sometimes, but Rick and the other people in the lab had a clearer understanding of what they were looking at. Looking at a sonar image is like looking at a black and white negative, the dark shapes not real but rather the shadows of shapes. Although in the world of sonar signals and computer-generated images it is sometimes better to have a very loose concept of what is real, with the aid of the computers on board, it was possible to obtain very accurate measurements of the objects that were being detected. There was a strange pyramid-shaped object on the sea bed that was over 20 metres in height. Then, almost 700 metres away, was a large shape that was clearly a long square object, which the AUV had travelled parallel to on its first run. It was this object that was going to be the *Ark Royal*, if that is what we had found.

As the AUV passed over the wreck at different heights and directions, people gazed for a long time at the screens then moved over to the long table at the back of the lab to look at the large photos of the ship and pore over the blueprints in the hope that some shape, some silhouette would trigger a moment of recognition. Again I was reminded of how remote this whole process was, how we were attempting to visualize an object over a thousand metres away, in pitch dark, in a place where we could never go, using not light but sound, to be transformed into images. It was frustrating, but also intriguing, because these images demanded so much more from our imagination.

Zak pointed to one part of the screen. 'What's that?' he said.

I looked. There were two short parallel lines sticking out of the side of the wreck, and then another pair.

'Are they guns?' he asked.

He measured the distance between them and I laid a ruler over the blueprints. Yes, they were two anti-aircraft gun turrets. The distance between them exactly matched the blueprints. At last, here was some proof! Twenty minutes later we spotted the faint square image of the safety netting that was also clearly visible in a photograph of the *Ark*. It was outlined around what was now clearly the huge overhang of the flight deck at the stern of the ship.

I was overjoyed. For the moment I was not concerned with the strange object to the south. I knew that we had found the *Ark Royal*, and it was in one piece! But it was hard to see whether the wreck was lying on its keel or was upside down. Two strong reflections ran the length of the wreck and they were impossible to identify. Zak suggested they were the bilge keels, strips of metal that run the length of the hull on a round-bottomed ship to help with stability, but on measuring them they seemed too long. Then a shape was identified that looked as though it was one of the propellers. This did seem to be in the right place, tucked some way under the stern of the flight deck. Were we looking at an upturned ship? It was hard to say.

Then Phil Devall said something that really startled me: 'This is the *Ark Royal*, for sure. Look, Mike, that's an aeroplane. It's one of the planes on the deck when she was hit.'

I looked closely at the image on the screen. It was tiny, but the cross shape was extremely suggestive of an aeroplane.

'But how can it be an aeroplane?' I said. 'She capsized a long way from here. The planes on her flight deck would have fallen off soon after she was hit.'

I went back to the photos on the table. One of them was of the *Ark* taken from the destroyer *Legion* as she approached the carrier to evacuate the crew. A flight of Swordfish had been landing on when she was torpedoed, and six aircraft were parked up on the forward section of the flight deck ready to be taken down on the forward deck lift. One of them, presumably the last plane to have landed on before the torpedo hit, still had its wings extended. But I was sure Phil was mistaken, and thought nothing more of it. I was still convinced that the *Ark Royal* had capsized more or less in the position I had worked out from all the evidence from the Board of Inquiry and that it had drifted some way as it slowly sank. Any aircraft on the flight deck would have slid off where the *Ark* capsized.

The AUV completed its predetermined course and was brought back to the surface. I went up to the stern to watch it being recovered. In the middle of the night I saw its small strobe light blinking on and off. It had done a very good job in a very short space of time, and it had a great deal more information stored in its computers to be downloaded once it was back on board. Searchlights on the bridge lit up the sea around it, and the surface of the water boiled as shoals of fish flocked to the light. A grapnel gun was fired, and the AUV was hauled back on a cable and hoisted up onto its cradle in the van.

Mission accomplished, we headed back to Gibraltar. Everybody had agreed that we were not going to get off the boat in the same way we had got on it, and we steamed slowly past the mole into the harbour. Nearly sixty-one years earlier the two tugs *Thames* and *St Day* had headed out past this same mole, accompanied by several motor launches, to come to the aid of the crippled *Ark*. Now at last we knew where she had finally come to rest. I felt an enormous wave of relief that the initial contact made by the *Odin Finder* had proved to be the *Ark*. As I stood on the dockside and looked at the *Rig Supporter*, I also felt amazed that I had been able to get this far. I owed a great deal to the goodwill of people like Rick Davey, Elisabetta Faenza and the Chance brothers, but I was also proud that I had pulled it off through my own determination and persuasion. It was the sort of moment when I felt like punching the air and shouting 'Yes!' at the top of my voice. But I didn't.

In the lab of the *Rig Supporter* the combined sonar images had been printed onto long strips of very fine photographic paper, reproducing in a single line all the different passes that had been made over the wreck by the AUV. In some places the image was severely distorted by the height of the AUV, but in others the image was instantly recognizable. They showed in remarkable detail the railing around the flight deck, the gun mountings and other identifiable pieces of equipment. It was without doubt the *Ark Royal*. I pressed Rick on camera to say as much, but he was wise and cautious enough to avoid an absolutely categorical statement. Like Andrea

Pupa, the captain of the *Odin Finder*, he knew that nothing was certain under the sea. We would only know for sure that it was the *Ark Royal* when we had pictures of the name on the side of the hull.

Rick and I and the camera crew went to our hotel, and then went into Gibraltar. In a small, densely flowered cemetery we looked at the memorial to the dead of Trafalgar, the words from Lord Collingwood's dispatch chiselled into the stone, still legible under the moss and lichen: 'The ever to be lamented death of Vice-Admiral Lord Viscount Nelson, Duke of Bronte, the Commander in Chief, who fell in the action of the 21st, in the arms of Victory . . .' This memorial had been here when the *Ark Royal*, a ship Nelson would never have recognized, sailed out to bomb Italy, or to hunt down the *Bismarck*; when Swordfish flew past to land on the temporary landing strip at the old racecourse. The tradition was continued when a memorial to Admiral Cunningham, the man who had directed the naval conflict in the Mediterranean, was placed next to Nelson's in Trafalgar Square.

The cemetery was a sunlit, tranquil refuge after the dry, air-conditioned atmosphere and harsh industrial lighting of the *Rig Supporter*. There is nowhere quiet on a ship, especially a warship – the noise of machinery, the ceaseless thud of the waves as a ship travels across the ocean – and I wondered whether men from the *Ark Royal* and Force H ever sought some peace here. More likely the constant violence and threat of death would drive you into the noisiest bar you could find.

Later that night Rick and I looked over the printout of the sonar images with a magnifying glass. There was a shape that did look as though it could be an aeroplane. Close to it, lying flat on the sea bed, was a square piece of debris with a regular square pattern on it. But I was still unwilling to admit that we had found an aircraft. I believed the sequence of events was that the *Ark* had been torpedoed and had started to list to starboard. At some point in the night when she was being towed the list got worse and the aircraft on her flight deck slid off into the water. Later, after fire broke out in the boiler room, the tow was abandoned, the *Ark* settled even further in the water, and eventually she capsized and disappeared from view. However, she didn't sink immediately, but slowly drifted below the surface before hitting the bottom. Our initial assessment of the sonar images was that the ship was intact and that any aircraft on board would still be in her hangar decks. There was therefore no reason to find aircraft, particularly any with extended wings, on the sea bed around the main hull.

The prospect of finding an old Swordfish was exciting, though. There are very few of these old biplanes left. Perhaps the only one still flying is housed on the Fleet Air Arm base at Yeovilton. Rick and I decided that we would ask C&C Technologies in Louisiana to produce some computer enhancements of various sections of the wreck and the debris field, including the aeroplane-like shape.

A few days later, after I had returned to London, Rick emailed an image to me of this piece of the debris trail, enormously enlarged by C&C's computers. As soon as I opened it, it was clear that I was looking at a Swordfish aircraft, its wings extended. The aeroplane was lying upside down with its undercarriage in the air. It looked as though it was still in perfect condition. The square object we had spotted close to it had been labelled by Rick 'unknown debris'. I looked at it for some time, and then it struck me. I printed off the picture, and unrolled the blueprints. I measured the wing span of the Swordfish. Then I measured the sides of the square object. They were both about 10 metres. I looked again at the blueprints. The square object was the exact shape and dimensions of a deck lift from the *Ark Royal*, and the regular square pattern was the bracing on the underside.

If my interpretation of these images was correct then I had to completely abandon my previous explanation of why the *Ark Royal* was so far from the position where I believed I would find her. There was only one explanation for a Swordfish and a deck lift to be so close together in the wreckage trail of the *Ark Royal*: everything had happened in roughly the same place. The *Ark* had sunk in the spot where she had started to list and where she had also capsized. What naturally followed from that conclusion was that the story told to the Board of Inquiry about the *Ark* sinking and the efforts to salvage the vessel was inaccurate. That was the reason why all my investigations for the search we had conducted on the *Odin Finder* had not produced a result.

At that point I decided that once again I would go back to the files in the National Archives and see if there was anything in them I had missed or failed to interpret properly. However, that was for another day. For now, I had absolute proof that we had found the wreck of HMS *Ark Royal*, and I had an absolutely stunning and uniquely accurate sonar survey of the whole of the wreck site and the debris field. Moreover, in front of me was an image that was absolutely fascinating: the last Swordfish to land on the flight deck of the *Ark Royal*. Now, surely, there would be no problem in raising the money to get cameras down to film the wreck. We would at last be able to see that enormous shape once more. Those giant bows that towered over the dockyard workers at Cammell Laird were there, waiting to become part of our life again.

But there was still a mystery. In all of its passes around the wreck, the AUV had failed to get a coherent image of the massive shape 700 metres to the south of the main hull. It might be part of the main wreck, or perhaps the wreck of another ship altogether. At every step in this search I had remained unsatisfied. Every stage of the investigation seemed to raise new questions I was desperate to answer.

There was only one way to lay the speculation to rest,

and that was to mount another expedition. So I had yet another search in front of me, this time for a survey ship and a remote vehicle that could descend a kilometre into the ocean with a set of lights and a camera so that I could finally film the *Ark Royal*. Once again I had absolutely no idea how difficult that task was going to be.

12

TARGET *ARK*

When in the early summer of 1941 the *Ark Royal* entered Gibraltar harbour she was fêted as the hero of the hour, the ship that had saved the reputation of the Navy and the fortunes of Britain. It was particularly good news because at the time there was very little for Britain to celebrate in the Mediterranean. At the start of the war recommendations had been put to the War Cabinet that the Mediterranean should be abandoned because it would be militarily impossible to maintain a naval presence there. The Cabinet, in particular Winston Churchill, had roundly rejected that advice, but it now looked as though Britain was powerless to prevent total defeat in that theatre.

The German Army had stormed through Greece and captured the island of Crete. The Mediterranean Fleet based in Alexandria had lost a vast number of ships to the Luftwaffe: three cruisers, six destroyers and forty-four transports and fleet auxiliaries were lost, and two battleships, an aircraft carrier, six cruisers and seven destroyers were badly damaged. Rommel, Commander in Chief of the Afrika Korps, was gearing up to make a further advance towards Alexandria, the main base of the British Army in North Africa, whose very existence was now under serious threat. The one remaining stronghold in the Mediterranean was Malta. Everything rested on protecting the island. The ability of the submarines and bombers based there to cut the central Mediterranean supply route to Rommel's army was crucial to British plans. But Malta itself was under siege, savagely bombed on a daily basis and facing the threat of invasion. The island's survival hung on the ability of Force H and the *Ark Royal* to keep her supplied with food and weapons.

Admiral Somerville summed up the situation in his preamble to orders to the ships for Operation Substance on 20 July: 'For over a year Malta has held out most gallantly against all assaults of the enemy. Until Crete fell we were able to supply Malta from both ends of the Mediterranean, but since the evacuation of Crete the situation has changed. For the present Malta can only be supplied from the west and this is the task with which we have been entrusted.' Then he ended his message with this uncharacteristic exhortation: 'The convoy must go through!'

Operation Substance was another attempt to escort cargo ships through the Mediterranean, not this time to Alexandria at the eastern end, but to Malta itself. Before this operation started the *Ark* had carried out a number of single missions to transport Hurricane aircraft far enough down the Mediterranean so that they could fly off to Malta. The Hurricanes were transported from the UK, usually in crates by one or other of the aircraft carriers *Furious* and *Argus*. They would be assembled en route, and on reaching Gibraltar two or three squadrons of completed Hurricanes would be taken on board the *Ark* and stored on the flight deck. Then a high-speed run by the *Ark* in company with the other carrier would see both ships and their escort of destroyers within 300 miles of Malta while dawn was breaking. With the Hurricanes on the flight deck it was impossible to launch any other aircraft, so the two carriers were particularly vulnerable. There would be an anxious hour or so while the Hurricanes took off and an extremely nervous lookout was kept for Italian reconnaissance aircraft. The Hurricane pilots had a long distance to fly over the sea before coming into range of Malta, and they had to fly a course that would take them as close as possible to North Africa to avoid the Luftwaffe on Sicily. Sometimes two Fulmars guided the Hurricanes, but in later operations a pair of Blenheim bombers would fly from Gibraltar and rendezvous with the carriers at their flying-off point; they would then steer a course for Malta, the Hurricane pilots obediently following. In this way, in the month of June alone 145 Hurricanes were delivered to the beleaguered island. Operation Substance followed this up with seven merchantmen carrying 5,500 men and nearly 50,000 tons of stores. Somerville was optimistic that there was a 'fair chance' of a proportion of the convoy actually reaching its destination, though he knew it would be a dangerous voyage.

On 21 July the *Ark Royal* left Gibraltar, but by nine o'clock that morning the troopship *Leinster* had run aground. Somerville pressed on, and as expected, on the third day of the convoy the first onslaught from the Italian Air Force took place. The Italians had refined their technique over the months of war in the Mediterranean and had become increasingly effective. Attacks from high-level bombers and low-level torpedo bombers were now synchronized, making it harder for the anti-aircraft barrages to be co-ordinated. This tactic also stretched the air defence capabilities of the Fulmar fighters the *Ark Royal* could put into the air. The Fulmars had never been particularly well suited to their job. They were slow, and took ages to climb to a height where they could take on high-level bombers. They were not very manoeuverable either, and Fulmar pilots didn't want to become engaged in a fight with the bombers' fighter escorts. There would be a permanent fighter CAP, or combat air patrol, of a section of three Fulmars from day three of an operation, when an attack could be expected. As soon as enemy aircraft were picked up by radar as many Fulmars as were available would be sent into the air by the *Ark* and directed to meet the bombers, and an attempt would be made to shoot down and break up the formation to force the enemy to abandon their attack before they were above the fleet. The torpedo bombers, however, would make a low-level approach, staying below the radar, hoping to come upon the fleet unseen until the last minute.

At 0910 on 23 July, six torpedo planes and eight high-level bombers attacked the convoy and its escorts. They were extremely successful: torpedoes hit the destroyer *Fearless* and the cruiser *Manchester*. Thirty-five members of the crew of *Fearless* were killed, fires were started on board, and both engines were put out of action. Somerville ordered the ship to be sunk after the remainder of the crew had been taken on board another destroyer, the *Forester*. The *Manchester* was less critically damaged, but she had 750 troops on board so Somerville ordered her to return to Gibraltar immediately.

Later that day, in the afternoon, another attack group of torpedo bombers was picked up on the radar at a distance of 43 miles coming in from the north-west. They were five torpedo bombers, and they were sighted fifteen minutes later on the port quarter, but a section of Fulmars pounced on them and two of the bombers were shot down; the remaining three gave up and turned away. Nonetheless, the determination of the Italian attack was becoming apparent.

As the convoy approached the Sicilian channel, Force H turned west, leaving the merchantmen to make the dangerous voyage through the narrows to Malta with an escort of destroyers and the cruisers *Hermione* and *Edinburgh*. Aircraft from Malta also arrived to escort the convoy, but they failed to prevent a high-level bombing attack which damaged the destroyer *Firedrake*. The convoy was attacked for a fourth time at three o'clock in the morning by a squadron of fast torpedo boats that had set out from the island of Pantelleria, but only one ship, the *Sydney Star*, was damaged and that was by friendly fire from one of the destroyers. The convoy and its escort finally arrived in Valletta harbour on the afternoon of 24 July. The supplies had got through, but at considerable cost.

Force H continued to suffer attacks from the air as it tried to escort the damaged *Manchester* back to Gibraltar. They also had to wait to escort the cruisers and destroyers tasked with bringing empty merchant ships from Malta to Gibraltar on 24 and 25 July. On the 25th in particular a large group of Italian bombers tried to attack the fleet, but they were beaten off by Fulmars from the *Ark*. In Somerville's words, the Fulmars 'attacked with great dash and bombs could be seen being jettisoned far away. Three high-level bombers were shot down for certain.' But the *Ark* lost six Fulmars, and the crew of only four of them were recovered.

Sub Lt Alan Goodfellow, a Fulmar pilot, was on the

Ark during Operation Substance. He had been in the air when the second wave of torpedo bombers attacked the fleet on 23 July, and had shot down one bomber and its seaplane guide, a Cant 506B, a large three-engined floatplane. Goodfellow now lives in a small village in Norfolk and clearly remembers the fighting he took part in over the Mediterranean in the summer of 1941. It was a constant struggle to keep aircraft and pilots in the air. 'We were so short of oxygen that our instructions were not to use it at all except when we were in combat,' he said. 'And we were patrolling at 18,000 feet. Two hours at 18,000 without oxygen was pushing it a bit. And we certainly lost one crew that I know of through lack of oxygen. We were desperately short of ammunition. You know, everything was in short supply in that time. Their tactics, generally speaking, they came in with one wave at somewhere around 12,000, something like that, with bombs, and they would try to co-ordinate that with another wave coming in at low level with torpedoes. So you caught them up at about 12,000, and those that had been scrambled from deck would catch up with anything coming in lower down.' As well as the nervous strain on the pilots, there was enormous stress on their physical endurance as well. 'I did six patrols from the 23rd to the 25th, so in three days six patrols at two hours plus each patrol.'

There had been a newsreel crew on board the *Ark Royal* during Operation Substance, and over the next few months in cinemas throughout Britain audiences learned that 'the convoy did get through'. It certainly did, but the Italian torpedo bombers had shown that they were now a force to be reckoned with, as Goodfellow confirmed. 'As far as I recall we must have been patrolling up at 18,000 or thereabouts and were vectored on to these 79s coming in. We finished up literally at sea level. The Italians were very hot on their low-level flying. In fact, these SM79s with three engines, they flew so low that you could actually see three slipstreams on the water, rippling the water underneath. They were literally down at sea level. And of course to attack them it was more difficult. I think the Fulmar had a 50-knot advantage in speed, that's all.'

Another relief convoy to Malta was planned for September, and the importance of this convoy succeeding meant that a considerable amount of preparation went into it. There were no illusions about the necessity of getting it through: Rommel's supply line was being hit, badly, and it was holding up his advance on Egypt and the British headquarters in Alexandria. But neither were there any illusions about the difficulty of doing so: the Luftwaffe controlled the skies over Malta, and the sea around it, and they were trying to squeeze the island to death. If the Germans succeeded in cutting Malta's life-line from Gibraltar, Britain would lose the war in North Africa and the Middle East, and perhaps the war in Europe. Somerville asked for a big effort from the RAF in the Mediterranean, calling on them to keep up attacks on Italian airbases prior to the convoy entering the Mediterranean. Force H itself was heavily reinforced with the addition of two battleships, *Prince of Wales* and *Rodney*, and four cruisers. Submarines from Alexandria and Malta were stationed off Sardinia, Sicily and southern Italy to intercept the Italian fleet if it should put to sea. However, the main threat to the convoy, the Italian and German air forces, would have to be dealt with, as always, by the Fulmars from the *Ark Royal*.

On 24 September, the convoy of nine merchant ships laden with food, ammunition and 2,500 troops passed through the Straits of Gibraltar to meet up with the *Ark Royal* and the rest of Force H on the morning of the next day. Their journey was uneventful until day three of the operation, 27 September, when as expected the convoy came under air attack. Somerville knew that the enemy would try their hardest to stop this convoy. There was such a high level of anxiety that on the 26th the Swordfish aircraft in the hangars had had their tanks drained as a precaution against fire. By midday on the 27th there were sixteen Fulmars in the air awaiting an attack from the Italian Air Force. Almost an hour later, three Fulmars were directed to the north of the fleet, where they encountered twelve torpedo bombers; another nine Fulmars were sent to assist them. The dogfight spiralled down until both the bombers and the Fulmars were fighting at sea level. The Fulmars were able to shoot down one of the bombers, which crashed into the sea, and to damage another three of the bombers, forcing them to abandon their attack, but six torpedoes were dropped, although the fleet managed to avoid all of them. One Fulmar was shot down by friendly fire from the *Rodney*, and the crew were lost.

A second attack developed at 1327 hours with a group of BR20 three-engine torpedo bombers carrying two torpedoes each making an attack from the west. The Fulmars again dived on them and one was shot down, but they pressed on, and in the mêlée of low-flying aircraft and the *Ark* and the battleships taking avoiding action, a torpedo hit the *Nelson*, Somerville's flagship, in the bows. The battleship slowed and turned to leave the convoy, but soon after that a signal was received from an RAF reconnaissance patrol that the Italian fleet had put to sea and was heading south to intercept the convoy, so the *Nelson* turned and rejoined Force H. Two Swordfish were sent off from the *Ark* to locate and follow the Italian fleet, and twelve more were loaded with torpedoes. Because there were still Fulmars in the air that needed to land, the reconnaissance Swordfish were not launched until 1448. One of them was attacked by some CR42 fighters on its way to search for the enemy fleet and had to return to the *Ark*, but the other continued to the last known position. Despite spending over five hours in the air it failed to locate any of the Italian warships, because unknown to the Swordfish crew the Italian fleet had reversed its course.

Alan Goodfellow was one of the Fulmar pilots in the air; he had shot down the BR20, after a long chase. He had to wait for the Swordfish to take off before he could land back on the *Ark*, despite being very low on fuel. 'We were flying for two hours twenty-five, which is a lot, and a lot of that was at full throttle,' he recalled. 'The other two of the section landed on with literally a gallon of petrol left in the tank, but I didn't make it. No. I was on the approach with flaps down at about 150 feet and the engine cut dead. And within a very short space of time I was in the water. I managed it all right, and was picked up by the *Priun*, a Polish destroyer. When you are in the water and the bows of a destroyer are approaching she looks absolutely huge. She came by at about 3 knots and we scrambled up the nets she had let down the side. Then they put us in the ward room with a bottle of Haig, on water for a few hours.'

After the attack the *Nelson* managed to steam to Gibraltar, but she was too badly damaged to be repaired in the dockyard there and had to return to the UK. It was another victory for the Italian torpedo bombers, but the Fulmars from the *Ark* had shot down five Italian aircraft, and another three had been destroyed by anti-aircraft fire. Moreover, the most important objective had been achieved: the convoy of food and ammunition succeeded in reaching the grand harbour in Malta.

The island was an incessant thorn in the side of Rommel. His supplies, particularly of petrol, were being reduced by as much as a third because of the constant attacks on his supply convoys from Italy by submarines and bombers based on Malta. His planned assault on the British Army in Egypt had been postponed twice, and could not be delayed much longer. Hitler made a decision to send a flotilla of U-boats into the Mediterranean, much against Admiral Raeder's wishes.

On 13 November, *U-81*, captained by Friedrich Guggenberger, was cruising off the coast of Spain, waiting. The day before he had received an intelligence report over the radio that Force H was expected to return to Gibraltar after delivering yet another convoy to Malta. It was not entirely correct: the *Ark*'s latest mission had not been to escort a convoy; instead she had made a high-speed dash to deliver more Hurricane fighters to Malta. The journey to the point where the Hurricanes could take off and reach Malta had to be carried out at high speed under the cover of darkness, but bad weather had intervened, delaying the aircraft that were meant to meet the *Ark* and guide the Hurricanes to the small island 300 miles away. Cruising at high speed on a zigzag course to evade submarines, everyone on board the *Ark*, permanently at their action stations, spent anxious hours waiting for enemy bombers to strike. When the last Hurricane finally flew off, Force H thankfully headed for home. Two days later, they were nearing Gibraltar.

Admiral Somerville had been warned some days earlier that German U-boats had been sighted south of

Malaga. Force H normally approached Gibraltar to the north of the Spanish island of Alboran where it had long been assumed that German spies reported details of their course. This information would be immediately passed to the U-boats which threatened the safety of Somerville's ships, so he tried to fool the spies by steering to the south of Alboran, then ordering a rapid change of course to the north at the last minute. At half past eight on the morning of 13 November he sent a message to all the ships in the fleet warning them of the danger of enemy submarines. Swordfish aircraft from the *Ark* began flying at first light, two patrolling a wide arc about 3 kilometres ahead of the destroyer screen, with another six aircraft on long-range patrol.

Seven hours later, at half past three, the square signal light on the bridge above the flight deck changed from red to green and the last of a squadron of Swordfish aircraft lifted into the air, their single radial engines at full throttle, sending out deep, reverberating bass notes. Shortly after that, with a thud and squeal of tyres on the deck, the first of the six Swordfish that had been circling hooked onto the arrestor wire stretched across the deck. It taxied forward so that the ground crew could fold its wings ready to be taken down to the hangars. In quick succession, the other five Swordfish landed.

The first two pilots to land were Percy Gick and Eugene Esmonde. They went down to the officers' mess where others were reading, playing cards or, like Val

Bailey, playing backgammon. Percy Gick's telegraphist air gunner, Les Sayer, went to the ratings' mess, where he got a cup of tea, then, exhausted from the noise and wind of several hours spent in an open cockpit, fell asleep. The *Ark* was nearing Gibraltar, and the crews were no longer at action stations, so for the ordinary seamen on board like engine room artificer John McCrow and marine Cyril Asher it was time for a change of watch. They too went to their various messes for tea. All over the ship that afternoon, a third of the crew were being served bread and jam and a mug of tea or cocoa.

It had been a long time since the crew had had any home leave. They needed a rest, and the *Ark* needed a refit. The ship's sides were showing the streaked and damaged paintwork from countless near-misses and the blast of the anti-aircraft guns. Throughout the mess decks cockroaches were becoming unbearable, and rats were beginning to nest in any crevice they could find. In an hour or so the crew would be in Gibraltar and the rumour was that home leave and a major refit in an American port was on the cards, although many crew members recalled the last time they'd heard 'it's home for Christmas'. Instead they had put to sea from Gibraltar, on Christmas Day no less, in a fruitless search for the German battleship *Admiral Hipper*.

At twenty minutes to four, the sonar operator of HMS *Legion*, one of Force H's escort destroyers, reported hearing something on the anti-submarine sonar, but he could not identify the noise. They were close to another destroyer and the officer of the watch thought they were hearing the sound of its propeller. One minute later, at 1541 hours, the 230kg warhead of a German torpedo exploded against the hull of the *Ark Royal*. The position was reported as 36.03° North and 04.40° West. On the *Ark* there had been no warning of an impending attack. The ship was lifted violently by the explosion, and the aircraft on the deck were thrown several feet into the air. In the mess decks below, crockery went flying.

Seaman John Elias was on the lower deck of the *Argus*, watching the *Ark*. 'I saw this fountain of water shoot up from the side of the *Ark*,' he said, 'a huge amount of spray was thrown up on the starboard side, and it seemed to me that there were two explosions. She took on a list almost immediately – within thirty seconds I would say.' Captain Maund, on the flight deck when the explosion happened, saw brown smoke billowing out of the hatch of the bomb lift, which brought bombs from the magazine deep inside the hull up to the flight deck. He rushed to the bridge to find that the telegraph system to the engine rooms was not working. When the ship was finally brought to a stop it had already shipped a lot of water and was listing heavily. The torpedo had struck the middle of the ship, tearing a hole in the starboard side and opening up the boiler rooms to the sea.

There was pandemonium on the *Ark*. Marine Cyril Asher recalled, 'There was a huge crash and the lights went out. The klaxon went off and we rushed back to the guns for action stations. There was a heavy list to starboard, and we found we were looking down at the sea from the turret.' The unthinkable had happened. 'In convoy at night you would see ships being attacked and on fire. The first thing you would be aware of would be either a flash or an explosion, and you rush to action stations. You were always afraid of it happening to you, and you would think, "Thank God it wasn't me." '

Those closest to the explosion, in the engine spaces below the water line, were the most vulnerable. Senior stoker Pocock was on duty in the starboard boiler room, on the side of the ship that had been hit by the torpedo. 'The lights went out and the place filled with fumes,' he said. 'We were thrown off our balance, and water came up a few seconds after the explosion. We evacuated straight away. We went back with a light after two or three minutes and the place was half full of oil and water. Then there was a signal to abandon ship so we went up to the lower hangar deck. By the time we left the water was 10 feet above the floor plates.' Able Seaman Peter Downing, nineteen at the time, was monitoring the power supply in the main switchboard room, which directed electrical power throughout the ship. After the explosion fuel oil started to fill the compartment, and he escaped up a ladder. Next to the switchboard room was the ship's main telephone exchange where another nineteen-year-old, Able Seaman Tarbet, was on watch. 'I felt a big

explosion underneath me,' he said. 'The lights went out
and I heard the sound of glass breaking. Fumes filled the
space, and on evacuating oil poured into the space from
the door. The fumes seemed to be burning our lungs and
I felt sure that we could not last very much longer with
it. I thought our last days had come.'

The last days had certainly come for one man. Able
Seaman Mitchell was a sailor who had already seen
active service during the First World War. He was one of
the oldest ratings on the *Ark*, a fatherly figure to many
of the younger ratings, and respected by his senior
officers. He had just entered the lower steering room
compartment when the torpedo struck. Lieutenant Baker
later reported that he saw 'oil and water gushing out of
the lower steering room compartment. I considered that
nothing could be done but close the watertight hatch.'
Able Seaman Mitchell was never seen again.

The torpedo had hit between the bomb store and the
fuel bunkers, almost directly under the bridge.
Compartments on either side of the explosion started to
flood with seawater immediately, but the torrent of fuel
and fumes that hit the electricity switch room and the
telephone exchange was just as damaging. Electrical
power failed in the rear half of the ship, and it was impossible for the captain and senior officers on the bridge
to communicate with the engine room or other parts of the
vessel. The order 'action stations' was given on the public
address system but was never heard; instructions had to

be passed around the ship verbally, by runners using bosun's whistles. The *Ark Royal*, one of Britain's most modern ships, had been knocked back to the age of sail.

John McCrow recalled the confusion. 'I was having tea in the artificers' mess when the explosion happened. I mean, we were used to them, but there had been no call to action stations. Then the ship heeled over, and we expected it to come back up, but it didn't, and someone shouted, "Good God, we've been torpedoed!" Then the Tannoy gave a sort of rattle. I heard someone say "Abandon ship!" Then, "No, it's action stations!"' John struggled up the steeply sloping decks through closed-down hatches and ladders to his action stations on the flight deck.

Captain Maund and his senior officers had set up a temporary command centre at the base of the super-structure. By the time John reached them the *Ark* had heeled over even more. On everyone's mind, including that of the captain, was the fate of *Courageous* and *Glorious*, the other carriers that had sunk earlier in the war, taking half their crews to their deaths. Captain Maund turned to John McCrow and said, 'ERA, there's nothing you can do here. It's abandon ship!'

Messengers piped the order throughout the ship, and the crew assembled on the port side of the lower hangar deck and the flight deck. Ropes were flung down the side, and a destroyer, HMS *Legion*, slowly approached. Crowds of sailors lined the open galleries on the lower decks while others clambered over the edge of the flight deck that was now steeply inclined to starboard. Steam was pouring out of the boiler room ventilation shafts as men went hand over hand down the ropes onto the deck of the *Legion*.

Two of the remaining pilots in the wardroom, Percy Gick and Val Bailey, who thought they were in a slightly different league from ordinary sailors, came up with their own very individual solution, as Bailey explained. 'Percy said to me, "If we're sinking, we should lower a boat." So we went along to the port side to where the lifeboats were. There was no panic. We stopped in the stores to get some caps and waterproofs, and tried to lower a boat. But of course there was no electricity, and everything on the *Ark* was driven by electricity. So we got some hacksaws and managed after a while to swing the davits out and then lowered the boat by hand. We were just about to cast off when the captain shouted down to us and said, "What are you doing?" "As you can see, sir, we've lowered a boat." "Don't be so bloody stupid. Get back on board." So we climbed back.'

By now, thirty minutes after the torpedo had hit, Captain Maund and chief engineer Tony Oliver had received some preliminary damage reports. The *Ark*, although listing badly, had apparently stabilized in the water. The watertight bulkheads were holding, and Gibraltar was close. Admiral Somerville, Captain Maund and the senior officers knew what was at stake. The

German Navy would achieve a major propaganda coup by destroying the ship that had triumphed over the *Bismarck*. But the loss of the *Ark* would be far more serious than that. Without her, Force H was finished, leaving Malta exposed and the whole of Britain's war in the Mediterranean theatre in peril. Leaving the destroyers to defend the *Ark* against further attack, Somerville steamed at full speed in his flagship HMS *Malaya* to Gibraltar. There he immediately ordered a massive salvage operation to rescue the *Ark*. Tugs and a small fleet of other vessels put to sea to tow the *Ark* back to Gibraltar for repairs. The *Ark* must be saved!

But a serious flaw in the design of the *Ark* now became apparent to the damage control party left on board. There was no emergency source of electricity. All of the ship's power was provided by the main turbines, driven by steam from the boilers. Now the boilers were shut down, and most of the engineering staff had abandoned ship. John McCrow, now on the deck of the *Legion*, heard a loudspeaker announcement ordering all engine room personnel back on board. He made the difficult climb back up one of the ropes to the deck of the *Ark*, and almost immediately became aware of the scale of the task. 'We had very large 125-ton pumps in the hull that could shift enormous quantities of water,' he said, 'but these were useless without power. The starboard boiler room was flooded, and so was the centre one, but the two boilers in the port boiler room had escaped flooding and could be used. But we needed electricity to pump water into them, because the feed tank had been allowed to empty.'

At 1730, less than half an hour later, another escort destroyer, HMS *Laforey*, came alongside to supply water to the boilers, and to run a cable onto the *Ark Royal* so that power could be supplied to some portable pumps. Water was by this time seeping into the Marines' mess deck and the starboard engine room. Val Bailey was pressed into action. 'The ship could do nothing without electricity; we needed electricity to start our own boilers. Then a chap came on board from a destroyer with two great electric cables, but our torpedo officer [on every ship electrical power was the responsibility of the torpedo officer] was still on the *Legion*, so we stumbled about trying to work out where to connect it. We spent some time desperately struggling to get some portable pumps from the *Laforey* down into the lower decks of the *Ark* but it was hellish difficult with the lack of light and the steep angle to the doors and so on. Then I was detailed to go down to investigate the depth of water. I got a torch. It was pitch black and very eerie going below; the ship was heeling over, and it was totally quiet. The odd creak and so on. It was pretty alarming, and then after a few decks I just stepped into the water. So I went back and made my report.'

Swordfish from Gibraltar had by this time flown out to the *Ark* to supplement the anti-submarine patrols of the destroyers. They circled the *Ark*, and the photographs they took show a thick black slick of oil stretching out from the starboard side and five Swordfish still clinging perilously to the sloping flight deck, with one of the deck lifts halted in its ascent. The *Ark Royal* that had only recently sailed at nearly 35 miles an hour across the South Atlantic and the Arctic Ocean and driven its bows deep into massive waves in pursuit of the *Bismarck* was now lifeless in the Mediterranean's currents like so much driftwood.

At eight o'clock in the evening the *Thames*, one of the tugs from Gibraltar, reached the *Ark* and managed to secure a tow rope. But the big emergency pumps in the bilges were needed to reverse the list, and without power from the engines that was impossible. It was all very well to attempt a tow, but the men in the engine room were the only people who could save the ship.

John McCrow, Tony Oliver and their fellow engineers were struggling to restore some order. All they had were torches and battery-powered emergency lighting as they squeezed through watertight hatches and clambered down narrow ladders to reach the port boiler room. There was no ventilation in the engine and boiler rooms, and there was the constant threat that the ship would suddenly capsize, taking them to their deaths. The emergency supply from the *Laforey* was enough to power a pump to fill the boiler with water and fire up the oil burners. With two burners running it would take about forty minutes to raise enough steam to power a generator, and by nine o'clock they had enough steam pressure to provide power for the portable pumps. The engine control room had been flooded as well, and John and the other engineers struggled to rig alternative controls for the port boilers and the engine room. Two hours later they had one of the large pumps in the rear part of the ship working, the lights were restored, and the big ventilation fans to the boiler room were slowly rotating.

The second tug to arrive failed to get a tow rope onto the bows of the ship and then disappeared into the darkness – an unbelievable piece of incompetence at such a time. But all on board now believed that the situation had been completely reversed, and that they were proceeding at about 3 miles an hour towards Gibraltar. Admiral Somerville received a signal from the captain of the *Laforey* saying that the *Ark* 'has her own steam and power, flooding is apparently under control and no more tugs are required until off harbour'. As Somerville later remarked in a letter to his wife, 'they were too optimistic'.

Val Bailey had by this time been ordered to go forward to join the tow rope party in the bows. 'And so we sat there. Every so often you could hear these horrible noises of things crashing about inside the ship – not very pleasant at all. It seemed to me that the list was slowly getting worse.' John McCrow was still working in the port engine room, and he too knew that the fight to save the *Ark* was far from over. 'We were not making enough impact on the flooding,' he said. 'The water pressure in the flooded central boiler room was buckling the port boiler room bulkhead, and some of the watertight doors were leaking. Then a decision was made to try to raise enough steam to drive the port propeller, and that proved our undoing. For the short time that the port shaft was turning it was instrumental in creating additional stresses on the already stressed bulkheads of the ship. Compartments hitherto untouched were beginning to flood as the lower joints were leaking under the pressure of water.'

There is a very strong current in the Straits of Gibraltar at night, and the single tug that had managed to get a tow rope onto the *Ark* couldn't make any headway against it. Despite the optimistic signals that were being sent to Gibraltar, the captain and the chief engineer realized that without more power the *Ark* would never make it back to port. She was drifting helplessly in the fast current. To raise sufficient steam to power the port propeller meant that more oil burners in the boilers had to be lit. But, as Val Bailey suspected, the water level had gradually been rising inside the ship and it had flooded the vents from the boilers, blocking the exhaust of the hot gases. At two o'clock in the morning John McCrow noticed that the trunking that fed all the exhaust gases into the funnel was glowing cherry red, and that the boiler was on fire.

Smoke started to fill the boiler room and engine

spaces. The fumes became overpowering. Moving about the ship, which was leaning heavily in the water, was taxing the strength of the crew; opening air lock doors was getting more difficult because the ship was listing so much. It could take almost ten minutes to go from the engine room to the boiler room. The only means of escape on the port side was a small hatch leading into the auxiliary hydraulic room. Two engineers collapsed in the heat, and another needed artificial respiration. They had struggled for hours to save the ship, but now they realized that she was lost. 'My last recollection before leaving the boiler room,' John told me, 'was the arrival of senior engineer Clark. His boiler suit no longer white, sweat pouring down his smoke-blackened face, staring up at the pressure gauge on number two boiler, he told me to return to the machinery control room as the boilers could no longer be steamed. I clambered up the ladders in the air intake duct to get out, and all the lights went out again. The ship was heeling over as we clambered frantically up and along the steeply sloping hangar deck. It was dark when I got my turn to slide down the rope into one of the launches.'

By four o'clock in the morning the *Ark* was listing at thirty-five degrees, and ropes attached to the *Laforey* began to snap as the ship heeled over even more. The order to abandon ship was given again. Val Bailey and the rest of the crew in the bows never heard the order, and stayed in their places until the *Ark*'s flight deck was almost vertical. 'A motor launch came past with someone shouting, "*Ark Royal* ahoy! Anyone on the *Ark Royal*?" We then just walked down the side of the ship into the water, and we swam off a little way and were finally picked up by a motor launch. I think I was the last one off the *Ark Royal*.'

A gunner, Christian Herring, was the only person who clearly described the *Ark* as she sank. He had been thrown into the water as he tried to remove a tow rope from HMS *Laforey*. He swam for half an hour before he was picked up by a motor launch. After that he heard the noise of explosions as bulkheads collapsed and gave way. 'She first rolled right over on her beam ends so that half the flight deck was visible. She appeared to pause there for perhaps three minutes. She then rolled right over, and it appeared to me that a third of her length had been torn out. There was a great deal of noise and escaping air, and then I thought she had broken in two, and the two pieces were torn away from each other. The after part sank first, followed by the visible piece of the stem, and she went down from that position in two minutes.'

Since the Nazis had first claimed to have sunk the *Ark Royal*, she had steamed a distance equivalent to almost six times around the Earth, and her crew had lost count of the torpedoes and bombs they had narrowly avoided. She was a lucky ship, and for most of the crew a happy one. Under her various captains, and particularly under the direction of Admiral Somerville, the *Ark* had confounded those who had said she was a waste of money. In just five days in May 1941 she reinforced Britain's vital outpost in the Mediterranean and then destroyed Germany's biggest threat in the Atlantic. Ultimately her luck ran out under an increasingly determined and powerful onslaught by the German armed forces, but in two years of war the *Ark Royal* had played a crucial role, buoying up Britain at a time when defeat seemed inevitable. Only the *Ark* could have done it; now there was nothing to replace her.

The crew members who had abandoned ship shortly after the torpedo hit were taken straight to Gibraltar by HMS *Legion*. When they woke up the next morning they fully expected to see the *Ark* berthed at the mole in Gibraltar harbour. They were to be utterly disappointed. Both they and Britain had lost a famous ship; but they had lost a home as well.

On 19 January 1942 an application for trial by court martial of Captain Maund was heard. The charges were that he had failed to take proper steps to ensure the safety of His Majesty's Ship *Ark Royal* after that ship had been damaged by explosions, and that he had failed to ensure that His Majesty's Ship *Ark Royal* was in a sufficient state of readiness to deal with possible damage while engaged in operations of war in dangerous waters. The thrust of the indictment was that the engine and boiler room crews and repair parties had been brought up prematurely from below. It was this that had led to the loss of all steam and electrical power in the crucial hours after the torpedo hit. This was undoubtedly true, but Admiral Somerville, in a letter to his wife written shortly after the Board of Inquiry was held in Gibraltar, understood the harshness of this judgement and why Maund had ordered that the ship be evacuated: 'When you see that enormous great flying deck canted over at an angle of 20 degrees, you certainly get the impression that the ship must be going right over, and with over 1,700 people on board and the difficulty getting on deck in a carrier, I for one don't blame him for this decision.'

It seems to have been assumed without question by the court that the *Ark* could have been saved. But one important piece of evidence was never mentioned in the court martial's summing up. Lieutenant St John Hewitt Heather, the captain of Motor Launch 137 which had rescued Val Bailey and Gunner Herring, claimed that as the *Ark* capsized he saw the hole in her side. It stretched from the funnel casing to the stern for about 130 feet, and was about 30 feet wide between the centre line of the ship and the starboard bilge keel – a hole so large that it was remarkable the *Ark* stayed afloat for as long as she did. Equally remarkable were the casualty figures, as Ron Skinner reminded me sixty-three years later when we saw the wreck for the first time. 'Seventeen hundred men were saved and only one man died,' he said. 'I think the *Ark* was a lucky ship to the end.'

13

THE JOURNEY BACK

By the start of 2004 my quest to film the *Ark Royal* had hit a complete dead end. A year earlier the *Sun*, the *Daily Mail* and others had published stories about the discovery of the wreck of the *Ark Royal*. The *Mail on Sunday* had devoted two whole pages to it, and others had published pictures of some of the sonar images we had obtained from the *Rig Supporter*. I was surprised by the interest that these mainstream papers had shown, but since this flurry of publicity the year had ground on frustratingly, with meeting after meeting during which I tried to hammer out a plan and, more importantly, find the money to get cameras down to the wreck.

Underwater filming is now a commonplace event, but it still requires complicated and special equipment to do it properly. I needed to hire a ship big enough to house crew, technicians and a large, remotely controlled under-water vehicle, a robot commonly called an ROV, with its supporting cables on the rear deck. The ship would need to be able to launch and control the ROV in a choppy sea, and to be fitted with equipment so that it could keep an accurate position above the wreck, despite winds and currents. Most likely the ship would need to travel to the wreck site from a port in the North Sea, a journey of several days, before any videoing of the *Ark* could even start. Although I had become so obsessed with this project that it had assumed an importance way above the documentary I wanted to make, I still wanted the images of the wreck we might eventually capture to be broadcast on television. This meant I needed the ROV to carry the best possible cameras, and lights that could penetrate the darkness with a brightness and intensity that could approximate to daylight. Commercially available ROVs are not normally fitted with such high-powered lights and high-definition cameras. They were available, but scarce and very expensive to hire; moreover, an expert would be needed to fit them to the ROV. They were also prone to failure.

Suitable ships with such equipment earn their bread and butter by carrying out essential maintenance work on offshore oil rigs and pipelines, or by helping to build new ones. The owners of those ships need to keep them working, or at least free, for their big customers, the oil companies. I looked at various ships and talked to various companies. I had a couple of meetings with James Cameron, the director of *Titanic*, who was extremely interested, motivated like me by the fascination of what might lie thousands of metres below the sea as much as by a personal interest in any film or documentary he might be able to make about the *Ark Royal*. Finally I managed to organize a meeting in a conference room in White City with a group of managers from Thales, a large engineering multinational, and some executives and accountants from the BBC.

One of Thales' operating divisions specialized in underwater engineering and surveying, and I had approached them to see if they would be prepared to hire out one of their ships to the BBC. After several telephone conversations I realized that some of Thales' senior managers were excited by the prospect of being the first to film the *Ark Royal* and had decided to subsidize their side of the operation, to a certain extent at least. By this time the BBC was thinking about broadcasting the first filming of the wreck as a live event. It meant that more money might be available, but of course it also raised the costs and would force Thales to commit to a specific date to make their ship available.

The meeting went ahead, but before it was over I knew that our demands would make the venture impossible not only for Thales but for any company with the equipment and expertise we needed. As one of Thales' representatives said to me later, 'We would be happy to do it, but we have to be able to choose the time. If a big oil company suddenly wants us to go and investigate a problem with a pipeline or an oil rig, we just couldn't refuse on the grounds that we were doing something for television. We would be the laughing stock of the industry.' And without the live broadcast there would be less money from the BBC. However we cut it, even with the considerable assistance from Thales, there was always a funding gap. It was never going to work. I waited a few days to see if Thales would increase the amount of money they were prepared to spend, but I knew they wouldn't. I was the only person in the BBC aware of the difficulties of what we wanted to do, of how expensive delays caused by bad weather and equipment failure can be. Thales, however, understood such things only too well and knew exactly where to draw the line.

Defeat has an intensely corrosive effect on one's morale, so corrosive in fact that it is hard to judge how deeply one has been affected. It had certainly affected me very deeply, to the extent that a year later on an Airbus on the final approach to the airport at Nice I was almost certain that my trip was going to be a waste of time. I was on my way to a meeting on one of the largest private yachts in the world. It was my last throw of the dice.

About six weeks earlier I had received a very brief and, on the face of it, absurd email. It stated baldly that the sender was the captain of a yacht in the Mediterranean equipped with an underwater camera; could he be of any help with the *Ark Royal*? My instant response was to assume that the sender was a well-meaning eccentric, but he was well meaning at least, and he deserved a reply. I pointed out that the *Ark* was at a depth of 1,000 metres and it would need a very sophisticated underwater camera to take pictures of it. I thought I would hear nothing further, but the answer I received to that email made me think again. It was clear that the captain of the yacht was well aware of the problems associated with underwater exploration and did have the ability to send an ROV to depths of 1,000 metres or more. That still wasn't something I immediately associated with a yacht. The emails and then phone conversations continued.

I was met at the gate in Nice airport by the captain of the yacht, the man I had first thought of as a well-meaning eccentric. Despite his forty-odd years, Richard Bridge did everything with what I have always assumed to be a quintessentially English middle-class, boyish enthusiasm. His energy and humour were a tonic after the long months of frustration I had had to put up with at the BBC. I learned later that he had once been a senior officer on the *QE2*, and had then captained an old sailing ship taking handicapped children on recreational cruises. It was his present job, however, that was the reason for our meeting. He was the captain of the *Octopus*, a yacht that had been built for Paul Allen, one of the richest men in the world who owed his fortune to his one-time partnership with Bill Gates of Microsoft. Allen had subsequently diversified into a variety of other industries.

I had very briefly met Paul Allen before. He owned a football team in Seattle, the Seattle Seahawks, and had wanted to demolish their giant domed stadium, the Kingdome, and replace it with something more modern. I made a documentary about the demolition, which was going to be done quickly and dramatically with explosives. Just before the tense countdown started, Allen quietly paid a visit to the explosives engineers and shook everybody's hand. It seemed a nice, personal touch. He had arrived at the demolition site, I recalled, in an anonymous people carrier, but there was nothing anonymous about his yacht, which I saw as soon as we entered the port in Antibes.

The *Octopus* was at that time the largest private yacht in the world. As I walked along the dockside it looked bigger than the *Rig Supporter*. And its size wasn't the most impressive thing about the *Octopus*. The most remarkable thing about this motor yacht was the elegance of her hull and the deep gloss of her paintwork. Everything was clean and sparkling; anchors and hawse pipes gleamed in stainless steel or chrome. This impression was reinforced as I walked onto the mahogany decks, as pristine-looking as virgin snow. Richard Bridge showed me round, and it was beautiful. Passageways and staterooms were lit with concealed, atmospheric lighting, and everywhere there were thick carpets and furniture decorated in subtle hues of aquamarine and taupe. In some parts of the ship, in the cinema for example, where each seat was furnished with its own cashmere throw, it was impossible to believe that we were afloat.

I was not there to admire the work of the interior designers, however, and Richard was keen to show me the hangar from which the ROV would be launched, and its control room. Outside the guest areas the ship was just as spick and span, fresh from the showroom, but it had been built with equipment similar to a commercial survey vessel. The remote vehicle was not in the hangar that day: it was back with the manufacturers being modified and equipped with high-definition cameras and a battery of high-intensity lights all of which would be able to function a kilometre below the water line. The *Octopus* had also been built with the ability to manoeuvre so that it could maintain station above the sea bed to an accuracy of a few metres, even when the winds and sea were running fairly roughly. I had no doubt that the *Octopus* could do the job; the question for me was whether I wanted them to do it.

Richard and I went for a meal in Antibes, and then we returned to the yacht, where we were scheduled to have a conference telephone call with some representatives of one of Paul Allen's companies in Seattle. Since my first contact with Richard the project had grown. As well as filming the wreck I was going to arrange for several veterans from the *Ark Royal* to come on the cruise; a cameraman and sound recordist would accompany us to shoot footage of their reactions when they saw the wreck. The budget was expanding, and more and more people in Seattle were having a say in the management of the expedition. I jokingly said during the telephone conversation that despite the enormous information gathered during the survey with the AUV it was possible to misread sonar images; I might have located the wreckage of a Liberian-registered bulk carrier instead. When one of them then raised the question of whether the wreck really existed in the place where I claimed it was, I lost my temper and threatened to withdraw from the project immediately. In an embarrassed silence I left the captain's office and went to my cabin.

Like the rest of the guest quarters on the *Octopus* it was discreetly luxurious. I felt ashamed, for I knew what had really caused me to lose my temper. My obsession with the *Ark Royal* had grown as the difficulties of finding the wreck and raising the money to film it had multiplied. The harder it had become, so my sense of ownership had strengthened; I now found myself reluctant to concede control to anyone else. The logic of my position was, however, inescapable: if I wanted to realize my dream of seeing the wreck of the *Ark Royal*, I would have to share my knowledge of the wreck's location plus all the survey data that I had accumulated with the people who worked for Paul Allen. If I left the next day, and flew back to London without agreeing to work with the owner of the *Octopus* and his company I might never have another opportunity to view the *Ark Royal*. There was really no choice for me, though emotionally I knew I would always feel angry about any loss of control.

The next morning I reassured Richard that I was not going to take my bat away, and we tentatively set a date for the expedition to start in the middle of September. The ROV for the *Octopus* was still being modified by its manufacturers. Richard and the person who was directly responsible for it, Mark Quenneville, wanted it to be fitted with some moveable arms that could change the angle of the lights during its voyage underwater. Everything had to be designed and manufactured from scratch, and it was unlikely that it would all be tested by September. On the other hand, the weather in the Mediterranean could be severe in the late autumn and winter. It is an enclosed sea, and winter storms can create very choppy seas; conditions in, say, November might be too rough to launch the ROV. Nobody wanted to delay now that we had agreed to go ahead, and I soon realized I was not dealing any more with a defensive bureaucracy but the first-rate crew of a well-equipped ship with a well-heeled owner. They wanted things to happen, and to happen now.

On 23 September 2004, the *Octopus* slowly moved away from the dock at Gibraltar. Richard was on one wing of the bridge, looking down at the quayside as he slowly moved a small throttle lever that fed power to the bow thrusters. I still could not get used to the sight of seeing these big vessels being manoeuvred with little joysticks, as though the officer of the watch were playing a computer game. The *Octopus* slid smoothly out of the harbour and we headed for the position of the wreck of HMS *Ark Royal*. The ROV, with Mark Quenneville and Jackie Sullivan, had arrived from Seattle and was installed in its garage on the lower deck. We had two days to do a test dive and make sure that the ROV was working properly. The *Octopus* had also taken on board four ROV pilots with a great deal of experience, and we would be able to keep the ROV underwater and working round the clock if we needed to.

The weather threatened to become windy during the night, but we hoped that by the next morning it would ease off and we would be able to launch. The *Octopus* had one disadvantage that a commercial vessel didn't suffer from: the ROV was launched from a garage low down on the water line at the side of the vessel, so if the sea was too rough the ROV garage could flood, and the ROV itself would be driven against the sides of the ship. I imagined that for the designers of the world's biggest luxury yacht, building an A frame and a winch at the stern had been a step too far.

The next day the *Octopus* was about 500 metres from the centre of the wreck site, and at very slow speed, with the ship's echo sounder switched on, we headed towards it. With the sea floor a thousand metres below us the echo sounder was unlikely to show anything, but there was just a chance. The one piece of equipment that was lacking on the *Octopus* was something called HiPap, which stood for high precision acoustic positioning, a system that would have enabled the *Octopus* to locate the ROV in relation to her own position and steer it very accurately to the wreck using the survey data from the *Rig Supporter*. Instead we were going to have to steer the ROV towards the wreck using the ROV's very short-range sonar and some dead reckoning.

First, however, we had to get the ROV launched. Mark Quenneville had arrived on the *Octopus* with the ROV just two days earlier, and the complicated electronics and hydraulics that would enable us to guide and control it a thousand metres below the sea were proving more complicated than anybody had expected. The *Octopus* loitered off Gibraltar while Mark and the chief engineer toiled in the ROV hangar to make sure that the swinging arm, the array of lights and the various controls for the camera were all working properly. Our expected launch time of 10.30 a.m. was moved, then moved again, until twelve hours later the ROV was finally hoisted out of the hangar and lowered carefully into the sea. This is a delicate operation. An ROV pilot stands in the hangar with a mobile control console hanging from his neck, ready to instantly power the ROV away from the ship's side as soon as it is in the sea. Any delay or hesitation will increase the chances of a collision between the ship and the ROV causing who knows what damage to the robot and its electronics. Thankfully, the manoeuvre was completed successfully. The ROV descended to 500 metres and everything seemed to be working. At last we were in good shape, and the next day, at 8 a.m., we would be back on site ready to make the dive.

The following morning the wind had picked up again; there was a heavy swell with white caps on the waves. Moreover, in the ROV hangar two of the six HMI lights had failed and would take time to fix. We waited once more for the technicians to solve the problem. When they were finished the wind was still blowing at 25 knots, and it continued into the night.

At midnight it eased off, and we quickly decided to try and dive to the wreck. The ROV pilots gathered in the huge guest dining room that I had had converted into a control room. The captain had put a large screen at one end and we could talk directly to the ROV pilots three decks down in the ROV garage. To help us identify any pieces of the wreck we might find and guide the ROV around them, I had placed large photographs of the *Ark Royal* on the walls, and spread out on the enormous dining-room tables were copies of the engineering drawings of the *Ark* with the data from the survey we had carried out on the *Rig Supporter*.

The sonar survey became the focus of urgent attention. We gathered around the printed charts and I was anxious to point out to the ROV pilots the questions I wanted to find answers to. What position was the ship lying in? Would we be able to identify anything of the superstructure, or was the ship lying upside down? Was the massive shape 700 metres to the south of the main hull another ship? Would we be able to identify the torpedo damage on the bottom of the *Ark*'s hull? Could we find and film an intact Swordfish? The ROV pilots weren't so interested in these questions, which would all be answered eventually; they wanted to work out what pieces of wreckage might snag the ROV and its umbilical cable, trapping hundreds of thousands of pounds' worth of equipment on the sea floor before the expedition had even started.

At just a few minutes before one o'clock in the morning the garage door in the side of the *Octopus*'s hull opened once more and the ROV was lowered into the sea. Almost immediately it was snatched by a current that was speeding past, and slammed into the side of the ship. It was the same current I had seen at night in the *Odin Finder* – water funnelling through the Straits of Gibraltar into the Mediterranean. The motors of the ROV were not powerful enough to fight it, and it would be fatal to launch the ROV in these conditions. It was quickly recovered and once more checked for any damage. We had been at sea for two days and still we hadn't managed to get anywhere near the wreck. I went back to my cabin exhausted and dispirited.

The next day at 9 a.m. the ROV went seamlessly into

the water. The sea was a flat calm, a hazy mist hovering over it that was rapidly being burned off by the morning sun. It was a perfect day, and as the ROV descended deep into the sea the pilots reported that everything was working perfectly. At last things seemed to be moving in our direction.

The *Octopus* was stationed 500 metres from the southerly point of the main target, and to the west; the ROV, once it was a few metres above the sea floor, would move forward slowly until the wreck came into view. It inched forward excruciatingly. A tense atmosphere developed on the bridge for we were now so close to our target, but the forward-looking sonar on the ROV revealed nothing. By midday we were barely a hundred metres away from where the wreck of the *Ark* should be. The *Octopus*'s first officer looked at me and said, 'We should be seeing something soon, whatever it is.' Then, making a reference to my earlier joke about a Liberian bulk carrier, he added, 'Even if it's only the word Monrovia.' It was an attempt to break the tension, but I found it in extremely poor taste. I was sure that we were heading towards the wreck of the *Ark Royal*, though I still retained a germ of doubt. Like Rick Davey, I knew that you could only be absolutely certain you had found a ship when you could see the name on the side.

Slowly the ROV advanced. All we could see in front of it was the empty sea bed, and of course the deep waters of the Mediterranean, which became impenetrable a few metres in front of the beam of light from our HMIs. Then something grey and angular appeared, at the same time as the ROV pilot said, 'Something big on the sonar.'

We had arrived. Slowly moving across the television screens suspended from the ceiling of the bridge was the edge of a deck and what looked like a broken headlight. Looking at objects far below the surface of the sea is disorienting. The direction of the light from the ROV can produce strange shadows, and sediment over the years falls like drifting snow, covering and obscuring familiar features. There is also a disconcerting loss of perspective that makes it hard to judge the size of objects caught in the glare of the lights. As the ROV slowly approached I stared, puzzled for some time as to what we were looking at. It hit me suddenly that we had come stern on to the wreck and we were looking at the rear end of the flight deck, the giant overhang that was one of the *Ark*'s most prominent features. We were looking from not very far away at the safety net around the flight deck, the stern light and the Admiral's light, all of which were mounted on the stern. It was the *Ark Royal*. Definitely. There was absolutely no question about it. At last, after a search of two and a half years, I was looking at her wreck. I told Richard that we were looking at the broken stern light of the *Ark Royal*. There was no whoop of joy, no cheering or high fives, but throughout the ship there was an absolutely palpable collective sigh as the suppressed tension of the last two days was released.

I left the bridge and went down to the control centre we had set up in the dining room. On the way there I looked in on the cinema, where the large screen was showing the images from the ROV. A few people were sitting there wrapped up in throws, and one of them murmured to me, 'Awesome.' Projected onto a big screen in the darkness of a cinema it did look truly impressive. It was the best place on the *Octopus* to appreciate the scale of the wreck, but I wanted to follow the course of the ROV, and made my way to the room where Richard was poring over the plans.

The ROV was moving slowly along the starboard side of the *Ark Royal* at a level just below the flight deck. The big 4.5-inch anti-aircraft guns in their twin turrets were appearing, bathed in the light of the HMIs, and the camera operator on the ROV was slowly zooming into an optical sight above the barrel. Then we saw the water depth marks painted on the side of the hull, which enabled us to fix our position on the wreck. The rear section had hit the sea bed stern first and had sunk in the mud to a considerable depth. The rudder and three bronze propellers, 16 feet in diameter, were hidden from view, and so was the ship's name on the side of the hull. But as we moved forward the height increased until the sea bed was almost at the level of the original water line. This part of the wreck was on an even keel, so I thought it would be interesting to find out why the AUV survey we had conducted from the *Rig Supporter* had led us to believe – although Rick Davey later modified this view – that the flight deck had separated from the hull. For the moment, though, I was just happy to watch the pictures of the *Ark Royal* as the ROV was piloted gingerly along her starboard side.

Forward of the hull, where the funnel and the bridge used to be, there was a complete break in the structure, with nothing recognizable beyond torn plating and twisted and buckled decks. There was no obvious sign of any hole caused by the torpedo explosion: it was either below the level of the mud, or had been ripped away as the forward part of the hull had disintegrated. The evidence from the captain of the motor launch, who had submitted a drawing of an enormous hole to the Board of Inquiry, would remain uncorroborated.

It was now almost two in the morning, and I was extremely tired, even though I felt quietly euphoric, more relaxed now than I had been for a long time. I don't think I have ever worked for so long, and sometimes with such lack of hope, to fulfil such a focused ambition. But I was now looking at the wreck of the *Ark Royal*. At last I had got there. I had succeeded when everyone else had been prepared to write the idea off because I had refused to abandon a project that had seemed doomed to failure. One of the stewardesses on the *Octopus* brought me a huge coffee, what she called a 'cuppacino', and a cognac. Yes, I was, for the first time in months, happy.

The next day, after the dive had lasted for almost six

hours, we pulled the ROV out of the water and returned to Gibraltar to pick up four of the *Ark* veterans who were flying out to board the *Octopus*. The weather at Gibraltar was bad, and their flight was diverted to Malaga. Late that night, 26 September, we tied up at Malaga and finally four men, all in their eighties, arrived on the *Octopus*: John Moffat, the Swordfish pilot who had taken part in the attack on the *Bismarck*, who had travelled all the way from Dunkeld in Scotland; Ron Skinner, Leading Writer for the Commander (Air), who had journeyed from a small village in the Cotswolds; and Bill Morrison (able seaman) and John Richardson (stoker), who had travelled from Nottingham and Newcastle respectively. All were extremely tired, but not too tired to be amazed by their surroundings as they bedded down for the night on the largest luxury yacht in the world, guests of Paul Allen.

The weather was sunny and the sea calm as everybody gathered in the dining room the next day. We had the rest of the wreck site to explore, but while the ROV was again being prepared we replayed the previous day's voyage along the starboard side of the hull to the former members of the *Ark*'s crew. Bill Morrison was eloquent about the effort required to load the clips of 2lb cartridges into the pom-pom anti-aircraft guns, and everybody recalled that it was the noise of these guns opening up that heralded a close attack on the *Ark*. But by and large they were still tired and content to watch the hypnotic images from the bottom of the sea flow across the screen.

For the second dive we planned to head south from the stern to investigate the enormous structure 700 metres away, and the large number of pieces of wreckage that lay in between. I wanted to search for the Swordfish aircraft, the image of which we had enhanced from the AUV's sonar survey. It was fairly isolated but close to what I had identified from the sonar picture as an upturned flight deck lift, and in order to navigate to it we would need to take a fix from the large section to the south. I must say I regarded this Swordfish as the ultimate target of our search. Those antiquated-looking biplanes had proved to be Admiral Lutjens' and the *Bismarck*'s nemesis, snatching victory for Britain from the jaws of a humiliating defeat. It was these aircraft that had underpinned the *Ark Royal*'s legendary status. First, however, we had to find the large section to the south, which I was now fairly convinced was the bow section. At one time, on the *Rig Supporter*, we had guessed that the large object might be the stern, but we had seen just twenty-four hours ago that the stern was still firmly attached to the main hull.

Over lunch, Ron Skinner reminded us of the time when the 'silly little admiral', in his words, sent a flight of fifteen Skuas to bomb the *Scharnhorst* in Trondheim Fjord, and only seven had come back. 'It was my job to write their names on the board when they took off, and write them down when they had landed,' he said. 'Sixteen names were missing.'

By late afternoon the ROV was poised above the sea, ready for another dive. The weather was still fine, the sea calm, and the ROV descended to the main body of the wreck before heading south. An hour later it was travelling just above the sea bed at a fast walking pace. Pieces of debris and machinery would appear in the lights, but they were hard to identify. Even the former crew members of the *Ark* were puzzled by some of them. Then, a few hundred yards from the bow section, the ROV's sonar began to detect a substantial set of targets. Before long its lights were reflecting off gleaming metal. Lying in front of the ROV were the shapes of several aircraft, the shiny aluminium of their bodies showing through the corroded and flaking paintwork. 'They're Fulmars,' said John Moffat. 'Look, there's the tail wheel, and that's a folded wing section.'

He was right. We were looking at pieces of the slow, underpowered RAF reject that had flown through the sky over the Mediterranean sixty years ago, whose pilots, despite being hugely outnumbered, had broken up attack after attack by Italian bombers and German Stukas. These Fulmars had not been on the flight deck on the day the *Ark* was torpedoed, they were in the hangar; they had their undercarriages down and their wings folded back. I remembered Val Bailey, a former Fulmar pilot who was due to helicopter onto the *Octopus* in two days' time, telling me that as he sat in the bows of the sinking *Ark* tending the tow ropes and drinking wine he had liberated from the mess, he heard rumblings and crashing noises from aircraft in the hangar decks breaking free and plunging down the deck. The Fairey Fulmars, all of them in pieces with parts of wings missing and tail sections snapped off, must have tumbled out of the *Ark* as the ship split in two. At the court martial of Captain Maund, one of the witnesses, Gunner Herring, had described seeing the lifts jammed with aircraft as the ship capsized.

The ROV continued slowly into the wreckage, the camera lens zooming in to look at the gun ports on the wing and manoeuvring gently to peer into the cockpit, the remains of the control column and instruments still visible. It was a remarkable sight, and as the ROV slowly pirouetted around the aircraft the banter between the ROV pilots, the camera operator, Richard and me in the control room ceased. We were observing something quite unique and unexpected. The wreckage of these aircraft from the hangars of the *Ark Royal* spoke eloquently of the massive destruction that had occurred in the ship in her last minutes, as this 800-foot-long, 22,000-ton carrier had rolled over and broken open. Any remarks from us seemed completely unnecessary.

Continuing the journey south, we approached the massive target we believed marked the southern end of the wreckage area. It was so high that the sidescan sonar on the AUV had not been able to obtain a clear image.

Our first contact with it was a strange piece of debris that took some time to identify; it was the huge curved forward edge of the flight deck that had become separated. A few metres further on we saw the grey plates of the ship's side. The ROV slowly rose in the water, first 10, then 20 metres, and there, etched sharply against the darkness in our bank of lights, was the ship's keel, stretching into the gloom, with a massive kink and fracture 12 metres from the stem. The whole of the bow section was lying upside down, the giant anchors still suspended from the hawse pipes, the tow ropes that had proved useless still tied around the bollards on the gallery deck.

That evening over dinner Ron Skinner reminded everybody that John Moffat was one of the pilots who had attacked the *Bismarck*, and that according to a recent analysis of the squadron's records it was his torpedo that might have crippled the battleship. John quickly took up the story, pointing out that the classic way to avoid a torpedo was to turn the ship's head into the direction of the attack, but that the *Bismarck* had turned the wrong way, probably to avoid a separate flight of Swordfish. His description of the way the *Ark*'s flight deck pitched up and down in the storm was graphically illustrated with a twisting dinner plate; he said that no other plane would have been able to carry out that mission in those conditions. Ron believed that the *Bismarck* had to be sunk, but John was adamant: the sight of the doomed German sailors struggling hopelessly in the water was indelibly etched in his mind, and pity overrode any other emotions.

For the next dive we planned to investigate the port side of the main wreck, and it was during the briefing in the morning with the ROV pilots to plan a route round the site that Dougie, one of the pilots, suggested that now would be a good time to give John the controls. Later that day John went down to the hangar to get a good look at the ROV and to see it launched. Then he went off to the control room, from where he deftly manoeuvred the ROV onto the *Ark*'s flight deck. It was an emotional moment for him.

We did not have unlimited time, however, and both Richard and I wanted to capture as much footage of the wreck as we could. Whenever the ROV was launched we would keep it submerged for as long as it was working, but there were always adjustments and minor repairs to be made, particularly to the lights and the moving arm that carried the directional spotlight. Richard and I would sit in the control room until 4 a.m., kept awake by cups of strong coffee from one or other of the hostesses on the boat.

The opportunity to investigate the main hull and the bow section was absolutely incredible and I would have been happy to spend days looking at every inch, but there was one target out of all of those revealed by the sonar survey from the AUV that intrigued me: the image of what I was sure was a Swordfish aeroplane lying upside down on the sea floor, its wings spread. It certainly appeared to have the same wingspan as a Swordfish, and the clinching detail, for me, was what appeared to be the sonar reflection of the landing gear with its triangular struts. There were five Swordfish on the flight deck when the *Ark Royal* was torpedoed, and it appeared from the photographs taken at the time that four of these had had their wings folded back. The fifth, which had just landed, still had extended wings. I believed that we had a sonar image of this very same aircraft, and I thought that this was convincing evidence that the *Ark Royal* had not drifted for miles after it had capsized, as we had first thought on the *Odin Finder*, but had capsized and sunk more or less where we had found the wreck. Of course the wings and fuselage of a Swordfish, a biplane designed in the 1930s, were covered in fabric. The only metal parts of the airframe were the struts between the two wings, the ribs and framework of the fuselage and wings, and the area of the fuselage surrounding the single radial engine. It seemed unlikely that after six decades at the bottom of the sea a canvas-covered aeroplane would be in good enough shape to produce such a clearly defined sonar image, but that is what we had. If by some astonishing chance of chemistry the canvas covering of the Swordfish had been preserved, it would be a remarkable discovery – an almost intact Swordfish from the flight deck of the *Ark Royal* lying a kilometre beneath the sea.

The Swordfish, if that was what it was, lay close to the bow section, so after another survey of this section of the *Ark Royal*, for the benefit of Val Bailey who had recently arrived on board, the ROV headed on a north-easterly course to locate this mysterious object. As it moved slowly forwards there was no indication on the sonar that anything lay in front of it. We saw nothing but sea bed. Then, caught in the spotlight, the deck lift appeared, lying, as I'd suspected, upside down. We had gone past the Swordfish. The ROV turned and slowly headed back at a slight angle, and there, sticking up, was the wheel strut of a Swordfish. We had found it! But it was not what I had expected. It was a ghost of a Swordfish, upside down to be sure, but the undercarriage was tilted at a drunken angle. Both wings had collapsed onto each other and were lying, denuded of canvas covering, extended out from the fuselage which had itself collapsed in a pile of fragments. It seemed as fragile as paper after it has been consumed by fire. An object lesson in the interpretation of sonar images – or perhaps in the interpretation of dreams. John Moffat gazed at the images, astounded.

Over the next three days and nights we covered everything that had been identified in the sonar survey by the AUV on the *Rig Supporter*. By examining the wreck and every piece of debris we could find, and constantly referring to the copies of the original blueprints, we believed we had a good idea of the layout of the wreck site.

The wreck of the *Ark Royal* was in two main parts. The bow section, the large object to the south of the main wreck, was lying upside down and had broken off cleanly from the main hull about 20 metres back from the stem. To the north of this was a very large piece of twisted and tangled wreckage approximately 30 metres long and 10 metres high. This was the funnel and the bridge, with sections of the flight deck and side plating attached to it. Then there was the 'Fulmar field', as we called it, a surreal area of aircraft wreckage that reflected our light whenever we approached. This part of the debris field can only have been created when the ship broke apart. To the north of that lay the main hull. There was a severe tear in the side of the hull, level with the rear pom-pom on the starboard side, clearly indicating where the funnel and bridge had separated. The port side of this piece of the wreck was intact for a greater length, but the guns and their sponsons were far more damaged than the ones on the starboard side. It seemed likely that it was the port side that had first hit the sea bed.

What we found appeared to confirm the evidence of Gunner Herring. This young rating had been pulled overboard by a tow rope at four in the morning on 14 November, the day the *Ark Royal* sank. Fortunately he was picked up by a motor launch, and he observed the ship sinking two hours later. His account clearly states that the *Ark* stayed motionless on her beam ends then slowly capsized, and as she turned completely upside down she appeared to break in two; the stern sank first, followed by the bow. The *Ark* had capsized and sunk almost exactly where we had found the wreck, swept a short way to the east by the strong diurnal current streaming through the Straits of Gibraltar.

As we headed back to Gibraltar, I spoke with the former crew members of the *Ark Royal*, eager to hear their feelings. Naturally everybody said that they felt privileged to be on board and to be a part of such an experience, though John Moffat said that he had thought hard about it. Had many of the men on the *Ark* died that day he would have refused to take part; as it was, he was glad he was there. He went on to say that looking at the wreck had solved something that had been nagging him for years, and that was the question of whether the *Ark Royal* could have been saved. I had heard a variation on this view from others, notably George Baldwin, the pilot from 803 Squadron who flew Skuas from the *Ark* during operations over Norway. He said that the general view of the loss of the *Ark* in some squadrons was that it was another screw-up by the fishheads – the somewhat derogatory term used to refer to sailors in the Fleet Air Arm. John now said that as far as he was concerned the *Ark* could never have been saved; the doubt had been removed from his mind. For everyone, despite the war, despite the fear that they experienced, seeing the ship again had reminded them of friendship and solidarity. It was a happy ship, and a lucky one.

Ron Skinner was the most profoundly affected. After pointing out to me that the *Ark* had sunk with the loss of just one life, Able Seaman Mitchell's, and that 1,600 had survived – proof that the *Ark*'s luck held even after the attack by the U-boat – he was moved to tears. 'I'm just a silly old man,' he said, 'but the *Ark* was my home for three years, and those years were an important part of my life. Looking at the wreck brings it all back.'

That evening we held a party for everybody on the *Octopus*. Ron had written a poem, and it was read out.

> Was it a dream or did I see
> A vision here beneath the sea?
> A scattered frame, a shattered shell,
> The detritus from dates in hell,
> A war-torn body, sorely pressed,
> In silent grandeur, now at rest.

There was a silence in the room for some time afterwards.

14

THE *ARK* LIVES ON

The *Ark Royal*'s story continued both in public and behind closed doors long after she disappeared beneath the sea on the morning of 14 November 1941.

The Board of Inquiry that was hurriedly called to investigate why the *Ark Royal* was lost found enough evidence to charge her commanding officer, Captain Maund, with negligence. The court martial, the trial that followed from this, was held in England in February 1942. The prosecution was aggressive, challenging young ratings about their actions when they abandoned compartments flooding with water and fuel oil, and questioning the reliability of eye witnesses who described the final movements of the *Ark* as she sank. The court martial heard evidence that the explosion of the torpedo had destroyed the communication system on board the *Ark*. Many witnesses described confusing orders being passed along verbally or by bosun's whistle, as we have seen. Captain Maund was found guilty on two counts: first, he was held to be negligent for failing to ensure that properly constituted damage control parties had remained on board after the rest of the crew had been evacuated; secondly, it was found that the ship was not in a sufficient state of readiness to deal with possible damage.

It was a harsh decision, and the members of the court martial knew it. Almost immediately they started back-tracking from their judgement. That February, after the court martial was over, they wrote a memorandum to the Admiralty, explaining their decision. They recognized, the memorandum said, that they were 'expecting a very high standard of conduct of a Captain of one of his majesty's ships ... there is a very thin boundary line between an error of judgement and negligence'. Furthermore, they stated that in finding Captain Maund guilty the court had considered it necessary 'to discuss whether he was not paying too much attention to the safety of his ship's company rather than to the saving of the ship'.

Captain Maund's career didn't suffer too severely because of the guilty verdict. He was not given command of another aircraft carrier, or any other big warship, but he was given a shore-based job in charge of Fleet Air Arm bases in the Middle East. In reality, after the loss of the *Ark* there were more Fleet Air Arm aircraft on land than at sea in the Mediterranean. Six months later, in the summer of 1942, he became head of the Directorate of Combined Operations in the Middle East. He took part in the preparations for the Allied landings in North Africa and Italy, and was given the acting rank of Rear Admiral.

The Admiralty was well aware that the loss of the *Ark Royal* could not be laid too closely at the door of the captain. They had set up a body called the Bucknill Committee early on in the war to investigate what lessons could be learned from the loss of important ships in wartime. Their report on the *Ark Royal* highlighted one of her major design faults, which was the complete lack of alternative sources of electricity. Once the boilers had shut down there were no emergency generators to provide lighting, power the main pumps, or prime the main boilers again. The committee also recommended improvements to the internal bulkheads, to prevent rapid flooding of the boiler and engine rooms, and modifications to the plans of future carriers to prevent the exhaust uptakes becoming flooded if, like the *Ark*, they took an extreme list.

Over sixty years after Captain Maund was found guilty and the Bucknill Committee reported its findings, had the fact that we on the *Octopus* had found the wreck of the *Ark* and recorded it on hours of high-definition tape clarified any of the events of the night of 13–14

November 1941? It is a legitimate question that can be asked of most underwater investigations, so it is worth asking here. To answer it, it's necessary to reprise a little of what we know.

After completing the filming we were in a position to put together a very detailed map of the entire wreck site. The main part of the hull lies on a north–south axis, its front part broken off and missing, as is the funnel, the island and the whole forward part of the starboard side. The *Ark* is lying right side up, although she is deeply embedded in the mud, particularly at the stern where the heavy propellers and rudder are located (they are not visible). Seven hundred metres to the south of this is the huge bow section, lying upside down, the keel jutting up 25 metres above the sea floor. Just to the north of this lies the upturned deck lift, and the wreckage of a Swordfish aeroplane which must have fallen from the flight deck when the ship heeled over. Then, 60 metres further to the north-west is the cluster of wrecked Fulmar fighter aircraft that could only have spilled from the forward upper hangar, where they were normally kept, when the hull split in two. A hundred metres north of these wrecked aircraft are the remains of the superstructure, the island and the funnel.

This clear separation of the bow section, the main hull and the island structure into three distinct parts fully supports the evidence of Gunner Christian Herring, one of the last people to see the *Ark* sink. 'She first rolled right over on her beam ends so that half the flight deck was visible,' he testified at the court martial. 'She appeared to pause there for perhaps three minutes. She then rolled right over, and it appeared to me that a third of her length had been torn out. There was a great deal of noise and escaping air, and then I thought she had broken in two, and the two pieces were torn away from each other. The after part sank first, followed by the visible piece of the stem [the bow], and she went down from that position in about two minutes.' This description fits so closely with what we mapped on the sea floor that it is safe to say that the site of the wreck is where the *Ark Royal* finally capsized and sank – a position that is a considerable way from where she was first hit by the torpedo from *U-81*.

Add to this knowledge some extra details from the archives (mostly ignored by the court martial) and information from John McCrow, one of the *Ark*'s engineers who risked his life in the engine room as the ship slowly flooded, and it is possible to explain why the *Ark* came to rest so far from the point where she was struck, and why she had moved no closer to Gibraltar, despite enormous efforts over fourteen hours.

The *Ark* had been severely damaged by the torpedo, and the ship started listing very heavily to starboard. Initial attempts to control the flooding were hampered by loss of electricity, and the loss of communication. However, after a few hours the port boiler was relit, electrical power was once more available, the pumps began their work, the list was reduced and the ship was stabilized. On the face of it, the *Ark* had been saved. The only task left was to tow her to safety in Gibraltar.

She was, however, in the grip of a strong current, and would only be able to get to Gibraltar under her own power. The decision to get the port propeller turning again to fight the current sealed the *Ark*'s fate. The propeller turned for twenty minutes, but the increased strain on the hull opened up further leaks. The air pressure in the boiler room wasn't high enough to sustain increased power and the oil burners flashed back into the boiler room, putting it out of action once more. The pumps stopped working and the *Ark* began to list even further to starboard, until slowly she turned completely over and sank.

If this was the course of events that 13–14 November night, and I believe it was, then the *Ark Royal*'s loss seems to be the fault of no one person in particular, certainly not the captain.

The fact that the *Ark Royal* had been sunk did little to reduce her fame. That same month, November, a feature film called *Ships with Wings* was showing in cinemas throughout Britain. The dramatic sequences of Skuas taking off and landing, and mechanics urgently loading torpedoes and handling aircraft in the hangar decks, had been filmed when the *Ark* was on active service in the

Mediterranean. Proof that she had gained true celebrity status was provided by the fact that HMS *Ark Royal* received bigger billing than any of the stars of the film. Of course, many people saw the film before they knew that the *Ark Royal* was lost. Val Bailey told me that a relative of his left the cinema after seeing the film, and then saw a newspaper placard saying '*Ark Royal* Sunk'.

The film had been produced by Ealing Studios. It was an unhappy mixture of light comedy and almost documentary realism, and at first there were doubts about whether the film should be aired at all. It was shown to Churchill, who thought it made the Fleet Air Arm look ridiculous, but Pound, the First Sea Lord, disagreed with him, and the film was eventually released. Ron Skinner told me that in his view it was the worst film ever made, but it was very popular at the box office. Because of the initial doubts about the film, Michael Balcon, the proprietor of Ealing Studios, commissioned a survey of audience opinion and the impact it was having on public morale. The report was sent to Balcon, then forwarded to Admiral John Godfrey, the Director of Naval Intelligence. It said that the film was popular and well received, and mentioned that the sentimental appeal of the *Ark Royal* was a particular asset of the film.

This report may have encouraged the Navy to continue the exploitation of the *Ark Royal*'s popular appeal and produce, in the summer of 1942, the pamphlet *Ark Royal: The Admiralty Account of Her Achievement*. It sold remarkably well. It was the first of a short series of pamphlets the Admiralty authorized about the Navy during the war, and the only one about a single warship. Finally, the *Ark*'s illustrious name was given to a new, larger, more modern carrier that was launched in 1947, and with a few breaks there has been a carrier called the *Ark Royal* in the Navy ever since, although whether this will be the case in the future seems unlikely.

She deserved her fame, for she was truly a ship that changed the course of history. The crucial engagements and convoys in which she was involved were executed by ordinary human beings, young men in their teens or early twenties who didn't think at the time of the importance of what they did, or its historical significance. These members of the *Ark Royal*'s crew were underpaid clerks in the City, apprentices, Barnardo's boys or young graduates from Dartmouth. Whatever their position, airmen, gunners or engineers, they all faced enormous danger at a time when the world was in utter chaos.

For me, the enduring aspect of my search for the *Ark Royal* will not be the image of the bow appearing out of the depths, stunning and impressive as it was, but the memories of the former crew members I met and talked to. They lived through the most extraordinary times and experienced the most harrowing events, but they came through it with their humanity intact, and their sense of humour undimmed. They, and the many crew members sadly no longer alive, are what made the *Ark Royal* the most famous ship in the world.

INDEX

SINK THE BELGRANO
By Mike Rossiter

The sinking of the Belgrano was one of the most iconic moments of the Falklands war. For many it signalled Britain's entry into the war and has been seen as a politically motivated decision deliberately designed to take Britain irrevocably into conflict. Now Mike Rossiter – with unprecedented access to servicemen on both sides of the fight; sailors from the Belgrano and HMS Conqueror – gives us a dramatic and definitive retelling of the events that foreshadowed and followed on from this flash point of modern war.

With all of the pace and tension of a thriller Mike Rossiter takes us inside the battle for the South Atlantic and shows us the human drama behind the famous Sun headline 'Gotcha!'. We track the collision course between the British submarine *Conqueror* and the Argentine warship *Belgrano* – as the two sides, and everyone aboard head towards that dramatic moment just outside the exclusion zone set up the British around the Falkland Isles. We see the behind-the-scenes debates, discussions and powerbroking that led to the decision to fire the three torpedoes. And, for the first time, hear from the sailors from both sides – and their personal testimony of the hunt for the attack on the *Belgrano*, and from the Argentine side the experience of being under attack and the sinking that left 340 members of her crew dead.

9780593058428

NOW AVAILABLE FROM BANTAM PRESS

BANTAM PRESS

THE FIRST HEROES
The Raid that turned the tide after Pearl Harbor
By Craig Nelson

18 April 1942. Sixteen planes take off from a US Navy carrier in the mid-Pacific. A squadron of young, barely trained flyers under a famous daredevil, Jimmy Doolittle, they are America's first retaliation towards Japan since Pearl Harbor. Their mission: to bomb Japan's five main cities including Tokyo. Critically compromised by the discovery of the US fleet by Japanese spies, they are not expected to come back.

Having successfully delivered their bombs, most of the squadron run out of fuel and are forced to crash land in Japan, China and the Soviet Union. The stories of their journeys home are as heroic as that of the raid itself. Incredibly of the 80 flyers who took part 90% eventually returned alive to the US. *The First Heroes* tells the extraordinary story of the daring raid and shows for the first time the real story of what was to be the turning point in the war against Japan.

'The story of the Doolittle Raid lifts off the page, as rich and engrossing as any legend, and Craig Nelson proceeds to bring to vivid life the dramatic story behing the story. This is an astounding feat. Nelson is an amazing storyteller'
Doug Stanton, author of *In Harm's Way*

'In this passionate and intimate history, Craig Nelson reminds us that America's first response to Pearl Harbor was neither tepid nor undramatic, but rather one of warfare's boldest chapters of righteous revenge'
Hampton Sides, author of *Ghost Soldiers*

9780552771719

CORGI BOOKS

IN HARM'S WAY
By Doug Stanton

'A thoroughly researched, powerfully written account of a
nightmare at sea, one of the most poignant tragedies and injustices
of World War II'
Mark Bowden, author of *Black Hawk Down*

On 30 July 1945 the USS *Indianapolis* was steaming through the
South Pacific, on her way home having delivered the bomb that was
to decimate Hiroshima seven days later, when she was torpedoed by
a Japanese submarine. Of a crew of 1196 men an estimated 300
were killed upon impact; the remaining 900 sailors went into the
sea. Undetected for five days, they struggled to stay alive, fighting
off sharks, hypothermia and dementia. By the time rescue arrived,
only 317 men were left alive.

Interweaving the stories of some of these survivors, Doug Stanton
brings this incredible human drama to life in a narrative that is at
once immediate and timeless. The definitive account of a
near-forgotten chapter in the history of the last war, *In Harm's Way*
is destined to become a classic.

'Superb . . . it's the stuff about the men in the sea that'll make
you weep. Four days without water, being picked off one by one
by sharks . . . and no-one in the world even realising they are
missing. Gripping'
FHM

'The best thing we've read in years . . . their entire ordeal, from the
initial fireball to the 1968 suicide of the captain is spelt out here in
vivid, horrific detail. Brilliant stuff'
Later

9780553813609

BANTAM BOOKS

VULCAN 607
The Epic Story of the Most Remarkale British Air Attack since WWII
By Rowland White

'I more than enjoyed it, it could have been written specially for me'
Jeremy Clarkson

It was to be one of the most ambitious operations since 617 Squadron bounced their revolutionary bombs into the dams of the Ruhr Valley in 1943 . . .

April 1982. Argentine forces had invaded the Falkland Islands. Britain needed an answer. And fast.

The idea was simple: to destroy the vital landing strip at Port Stanley. The reality was more complicated. The only aircraft that could possibly do the job was three months from being scrapped, and the distance it had to travel was four thousand miles beyond its maximum range. It would take fifteen Victor tankers and seventeen separate in-flight refuellings to get one Avro Vulcan B2 over the target, and give its crew any chance of coming back alive.

Yet less than a month later, a formation of elderly British jets launched from a remote island airbase to carry out the longest-range air attack in history. At its head was a single aircraft, six men, and twenty-one thousand-pound bombs, facing the hornet's nest of modern weaponry defending the Argentine forces on the Falkland Islands. There would be no second chances . . .

'Exciting and breathtakingly pacy . . . This is exactly how modern history should be written'   Andy McNab

'Gripping, endlessly fascinating detail. I read the book in one sitting: it is an utterly compelling war story, brilliantly written'
Simon Winchester

'A masterwork of narrative history. Brilliantly described, the story of an impossible British mission is a compelling one; it's telling long overdue'   Clive Cussler

9780552152297

CORGI BOOKS

WITNESS TO WAR; DIARIES OF THE SECOND WORLD WAR IN EUROPE
Everyday accounts by the men, women and children who lived through it
Richard J. Aldrich

From the moments of unbearable tension as Europe waited for the coming conflict in 1938 to its tragic dying embers in 1945, the Second World War changed millions of peoples' lives. It was the greatest tidal wave of destruction and displacement the world had ever seen. For ordinary men and women, it was a cataclysm they could have never before imagined. Here is their extraordinary collective testimony, an alternative history of a world in motion.

Most of these diaries involved a degree of danger and secrecy. In occupied Europe a captured diary could betray friends and relatives to the enemy. Some were downright illegal, such as those kept by soldiers on the front line. Here, rare material from figures such as Joseph Goebbels, Jean-Paul Sartre, Evelyn Waugh and Noël Coward has been unearthed along with the insights of those close to Winston Churchill and Adolf Hitler.

Witness to War is the innermost thoughts of people from every walk of life. Their daily terrors, their fears and feelings, scribbled down and secreted away, are revealed for the first time. Previously undiscovered diaries have been brought to light to reveal an eye-opening, immediate and intimate glimpse of a different kind of war.

'Stands head and shoulders above all the other [WWII] books flooding out to meet the 60th anniversary. [Aldrich] gives an excellent picture of a world in agony'
Spectator (Books of the Year)

9780552151085

CORGI BOOKS

THE LAST MISSION
The Secret History of the Second World War's Final Battle
By Jim Smith and Malcolm McConnell

14 August 1945. As Japan's Emperor Hirohito recorded his message of surrender, rebel troops commanded by elite officers from the War Ministry burst into the imperial palace. Their intention was to stage a coup, destroy the recording and issue forged orders for Japan to continue the war. Had they succeded there would have been massive *kamikaze* attacks on allied forces, possibly provoking America to drop a third atomic bomb . . .

But on that fateful night, in the skies approaching Tokyo, a stream of B-29B 'Superfortress' bombers were heading towards Japan's last functioning oil refinery. Fearing that they could be carrying another atom bomb, Japanese air defences ordered a total blackout of the city and the imperial palace. In the hours of chaos that followed, the rebels were foiled and soldiers loyal to the emperor wrested back control. At midday on 15 August 1945, the imperial message of surrender was broadcast. The war was finally over.

The result of more than twenty years research by Jim Smith, who took part in that final air raid, *The Last Mission* is a gripping work of speculative investigation into one of the least known yet profoundly significant episodes of the Second World War.

'Skillfully weaving personal and archival history, *The Last Mission* gives us a haunting glimpse of just how close we came to the brink of waging a final desperate war on Japanese soil'
Hampton Sides, author of *Ghost Soldiers*

'Fascinating . . . a breathtaking blend of memoir, investigative research and imagination'
Iris Chang, author of *The Rape of Nanking*

9780553816105

BANTAM BOOKS